THE
WAKING
FIRE

Clay lunged, putting every ounce of strength and speed into his legs, ignoring the flare of agony from already strained muscles. He nearly did it, his hand brushing through Keyvine's braided hair as the King of Blades and Whores twisted aside with less than an inch to spare. Something flashed in the gloom and Clay felt the cold chill of a very sharp blade against his neck. He froze, standing with his arm still clutching at thin air whilst Keyvine stood with his bared sword-cane protruding through the bars, poised to sever Clay's jugular with the smallest flick.

BY ANTHONY RYAN

Raven's Shadow
Blood Song
Tower Lord
Queen of Fire

Draconis Memoria
The Waking Fire
The Legion of Flame

THE
WAKING FIRE

THE DRACONIS MEMORIA: BOOK ONE

ANTHONY RYAN

www.orbitbooks.net

ORBIT

First published in Great Britain in 2016 by Orbit
This paperback edition published in 2017 by Orbit

1 3 5 7 9 10 8 6 4 2

A CIP catalogue record for this book
is available from the British Library.

ISBN 978-0-356-50636-4

Printed and bound by CPI Group (UK) Ltd, Croydon CR0 4YY

Papers used by Orbit are from well-managed forests
and other responsible sources.

MIX
Paper from
responsible sources
FSC® C104740

Orbit
An imprint of
Little, Brown Book Group
Carmelite House
50 Victoria Embankment
London EC4Y 0DZ

An Hachette UK Company
www.hachette.co.uk

www.orbitbooks.net

For Paul,
because sometimes the only reward for fighting
the good fight is in knowing you did it.

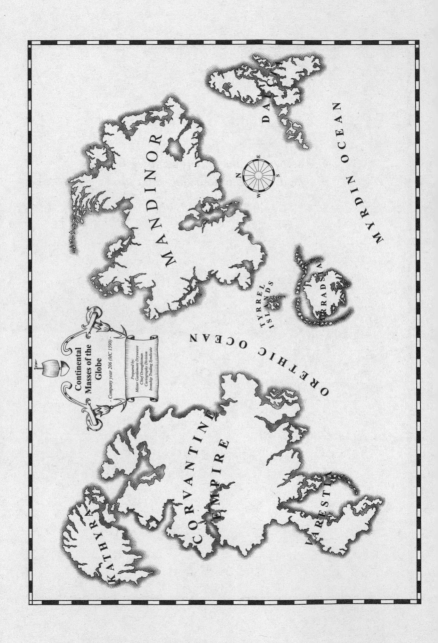

DA...

MANDINOR

MYRDIN OCEAN

N
W   E
S

TYRREL ISLANDS

...RADS...A

ORETHIC OCEAN

Continental
Masses of the
Globe

— *Company year 206 (AC 1500)* —

Prepared by:
Mister Guildamere Dryweave
Chief Draughtsman
Cartographic Division
Irmalop Trading Syndicate

KATHYRA

CORVANTINE EMPIRE

KARESTI...

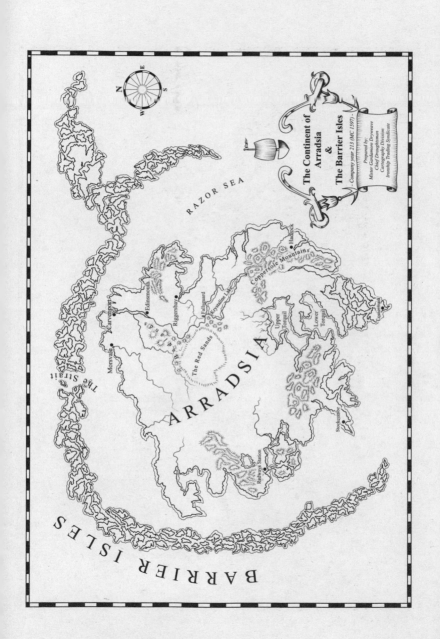

The Continent of
Arradsia
&
The Barrier Isles

Company year 213 (MC 1597)

Prepared by:
Mister Gosdamore Dryweave
Chief Draughtsman
Cartography Division
Ironship Trading Syndicate

RAZOR SEA

Hadlock

Coppersole Mountains

Edinsmouth

Riggersbye

Fallguard

Coppaline Lake

Carvenport

Upper Torquil

Lower Torquil

The Red Sands

Morsvale

The Strait

Redsaye Station

Stockcombe

ARRADSIA

BARRIER ISLES

PROLOGUE

REPORT TO: BOARD OF DIRECTORS
IRONSHIP TRADING SYNDICATE
HOME OFFICE
FEROS HOLDINGS

Report by: *Lodima Bondersil – Acting Director, Carvenport Division, Arradsian Continental Holdings*

Date: *Settemer 29, 1578 (Day 166 of Company Year 194 by the Corporate Calendar)*

Subject: *Events surrounding the demise of Mr Havelic Dunmorn, Director Carvenport Division, Arradsian Continental Holdings*

Esteemed Sirs and Ladies,

By the time this report reaches your hands you will, no doubt, have received word via the Blue-trance of the demise of my immediate superior, Mr Havelic Dunmorn, and an initial estimate of the associated deaths and considerable material destruction accompanying that tragic event. I have compiled this written account in the hope and expectation it will obviate any asinine and ill-informed rumours spread by competitors or Syndicate employees (see addendum for a list of recommended dismissals and contract terminations). It is my intention to provide a clear and unbiased account of events so as to better inform the deliberations of the Board and any subsequent directives they may see fit to issue.

The incident in question took place in and around the Harvesting and Dockside quarters of Carvenport on Settemer 26. The Board will recall Mr Dunmorn's Blue-trance communication on 12 Dimester which described the successful capture of a wild Black by the Chainmasters Independent Contractor Company, following a lengthy expedition to the south-western regions of the Arradsian Interior. I also refer the Board to the previous ten quarterly written reports from this Division concerning the increasing attrition rate amongst pen-bred stock, with Blacks proving the most short-lived of all breeds. I am sure the Board requires no reminder of the ever-decreasing potency of product harvested from inbred and youthful stock. Therefore, the capture of a live and healthy wild Black (the first such capture in more than a dozen years) was greeted with considerable excitement throughout the ranks of Syndicate employees, in that it offered the prospect of thickened blood lines and quality product for years to come. Unfortunately such expectations were soon revealed as premature.

The Black, a full-grown male of some sixteen feet in length, proved extremely difficult to handle, perennially unsettled and prone to dangerous lunges even when sedated and its jaws firmly muzzled. Several harvesters were injured in wrangling the beast and one maimed when it contrived to crush him against the walls of its pen after feigning somnolence for several hours. The cunning of the various breeds inhabiting these lands has oft been remarked upon by harvesters and naturalists alike, but I must confess to a considerable personal discomfort at the vicious calculation displayed by this particular animal, traits so far unseen in all my years on this continent.

In addition to its frequent violence the Black also refused to mate with any pen-bred female, reacting with either indifference or aggression whenever one was placed in its proximity. Added to this was the extreme reluctance on the part of the female Blacks to remain anywhere near their wild cousin, all becoming excessively agitated and vocal at the mere sight of him. So after four months, with no prospect of a successful mating and costs of feeding and caring for the specimen increasing, Mr Dunmorn ordered the beast be harvested. I have attached minutes of my discussion with Mr Dunmorn which are fulsome in their description of my opinion on the matter and require no repetition here.

Mr Dunmorn determined to make a celebration of the harvesting, a sop to local morale which has suffered recently due to the dip in markets and consequent reduction in contract terms. It was decreed, therefore, that the harvesting would take place on the same day as the Blood-lot, not often regarded as a day of merriment elsewhere but in these far-removed lands has become something of an annual festival. The prospect of a child finding themselves elevated to a life of prosperity by mere chance holds considerable resonance for those who often find their own ambitions curbed by the reality of individual ability.

To add to the festivities, Mr Dunmore intended to retain one fiftieth of the harvested product for distribution to the populace by means of a raffle. Given the current market price for undiluted Black, I am certain the Board will recognise the popularity of this contrivance, the principal reason why the area surrounding the harvesting vat was so crowded at the decisive moment.

PERSONAL NARRATIVE

I remain hopeful of the Board's understanding in reporting my failure to establish the precise chain of events leading to the ultimate calamity, a task that remains unfulfilled despite my exhaustive efforts. Many first-hand witnesses are now sadly consigned to the grave and those remaining amongst the living are often unreasoned to the point of lunacy. Exposure to undiluted product can have unpredictable consequences. As for my own account, I was not present for either the Blood-lot or the harvesting, having opted to remain at the Academy to address a large glut of unresolved correspondence.

At approximately twenty minutes past the fourteenth hour I was drawn from my labours by the tumult of screams from beyond the window. On going to investigate I was struck by the sight of numerous townsfolk running through the streets with considerable, nay panicked alacrity, many a shocked, pale or weeping face amongst the throng. Spying one of my students amidst the mob I opened the window and called her name. A bright and resourceful child, as my girls invariably are, she managed to extricate herself from the rush by means of clambering up the academy railings, clinging on as she made her report: 'It's loose, Madame! The Black is loose in the town! Many are dead!'

I must confess to a shameful loss of decision at this point, for which I naturally crave the Board's pardon. However, I trust you will recognise that this particular circumstance had never, at any point, occurred during the entirety of my three decades on this continent. After an inexcusable delay of several seconds I was finally of sufficient mind to formulate a question for my student. 'How?'

At this point the girl's countenance took on an uncharacteristic confusion and it was a full half-minute before she spoke again, her words halting and imprecise. 'The Blood-lot . . . There was a woman . . . A woman with a child . . .'

'It is customary for parents and children to gather at the Blood-lot,' I told her, not without some impatience. 'Clarify your report!'

'She . . .' My student's face then took on an expression of equal parts wonder and horror. 'She jumped.'

'Jumped?'

'Yes, Madame. With the child . . . She gathered up the child and . . . jumped.'

'Jumped where?'

'Into the vat, Madame. Just as the harvester tapped the Black . . . She jumped into the vat.'

From the blank mystification on my student's face, and the copious scorching and bloodstains besmirching her dress, I divined she would be unable to furnish further useful intelligence. Having ordered her to proceed to the dormitory and see to the security of the younger students, I recovered a full set of vials from my office safe and made haste towards the Harvesting quarter. I will not burden the Board with a full description of the destruction I witnessed during the journey, nor what I found on reaching the site of the Black's harvesting, or pause to enumerate the number of corpses, but suffice to say I saw enough to confirm the veracity of my student's account.

The vat itself was completely shattered, the solid oak planking blown to splinters and scattered in a wide radius, as was the beast's blood. It lay in thick pools on the cobbled street, or spattered onto surrounding houses where all windows had been flung open to witness Mr Dunmorn's spectacle. Those spectators not killed outright by ingestion were stumbling about or flailing on the ground, either in madness or agony. Being resistant to the blood's effects I was able to approach the remnants of the vat, observing the body of a woman half-submerged where the blood lay thickest. Her age and identity were unguessable as her skin had been blackened and charred from direct contact with the product, but from her slender proportions I judged her as young. The only sign of the Black was the shattered remnants of its chains. As for the child my student spoke of, I saw no trace at all.

A flurry of rifle-shots drew my attention towards the dockside, easily viewed from my present vantage point via the path of destruction carved through successive rows of housing. Amidst the sound of gun-fire a distinctive roaring could also be discerned. At this point I felt it opportune to imbibe a goodly portion of Green which facilitated a rapid approach to the docks whereupon I first spied the unleashed beast. It had smashed its way to the wharf, trailing blood from the tap in its neck with every step but, despite its loss, continued to wreak havoc with furious energy. I watched as it dashed the Harbour-Master's house to pieces with successive swipes of its tail before turning its attention to the vessels moored alongside the quay. A number were in the process of drawing off, the crews working with feverish industry to seek the sanctuary of the open sea, but a half-dozen evidently lacked the hands or decisiveness to effect escape.

The Black leapt atop a sturdy coastal steamer, the IRV *Equitable Share*, submerging it by virtue of its weight alone, unmuzzled jaws snapping at the flailing crewmen in the water. Turning its attentions to a neighbouring freighter, a Briteshore Minerals vessel of some two hundred tons displacement, it set about wrecking the wheel-house and stacks, all the time gaping its mouth as it sought vainly to bring forth its fire. I must pause at this point to emphasise the wise foresight of the harvesters who first took charge of the beast in severing its naphtha-ducts. Had they not the consequences are frankly too appalling to contemplate.

At this point I saw the Black rear in shock as a rifle round struck its flank, voicing a great roar of fury before launching itself at the next vessel on the quay, the cauterised stumps of its wings twitching as it instinctively sought the air. I soon identi-fied the source of the rifle-shot, spying a figure atop one of the taller, as yet undamaged, cranes crowding the wharf. Thanks to the effects of the recently imbibed Green I scaled the crane's scaffold in a matter of seconds, finding a man perched on the armature and taking careful aim at the Black with a longrifle. He fired and I saw the Black rear again, before bounding onward, landing on the broad deck of the IRV *Drakespite*, a Blue-hunter recently returned from the southern seas. The crew had unwisely chosen to contest the beast's assault, assailing it with various fire-arms, none of sufficient calibre to inflict more than a minor wound.

The rifleman swore in copious and uncouth terms as he reloaded his weapon, falling silent as I strode along the armature to his side. 'Y'pardon, ma'am,' he said in the accent of the Old Colonials, his origins also plain in the dark hue of his complexion. Having scant time to deliver a lecture on propriety, I took note of his worn but hardy clothing before settling my gaze on his longrifle: a Vactor-Massin .6 single-shot breech-loader favoured by the more successful Contractor Companies.

'Personal weapons are required to be lodged with the Protectorate on entry to Carvenport, sir,' I said.

The marksman gave the barest grin in response before nodding at the still-rampaging beast. 'Reckon I'll earn myself a pardon when I put him down, ma'am. If only he'd cease his fury long enough for a skull shot.'

I watched as the Black's tail swept the last remaining crew from the deck of the *Drakespite* whereupon it threw its head back to voice a victory roar, the blood continuing to flow from the steel spile in its neck. 'A good sight more lively than it should be,' the Contractor opined, taking aim once more then biting down on a curse as the beast bounded on. 'All that blood leaked away.'

'Your name, sir?' I enquired.

'Torcreek, ma'am. Braddon Torcreek, fifth-share hand to the Longrifles Independent.'

I took the vials of Red and Black from my supply and drank it all before taking another deep draught of Green. 'I'll hold him for you, Mr Torcreek,' I said. 'See if we can't earn you that pardon.'

With that I leapt over the marksman and sprinted the length of the armature, launching myself at a tilted mast arising from the deck of a listing freighter, one of the older ships which continue to retain sails as insurance against engine failure. The distance was perhaps thirty feet or more, well within reach of a Blood-blessed sated by Green. I caught hold of the rigging and used the resultant centrifugal forces to propel me in pursuit of the Black, a basic manoeuvre I had been teaching my girls for the better part of two decades. Arcing towards the Black at considerable velocity I called upon my reserves of Red to assail it from the rear. Naturally its hide was scorched but largely undamaged by the resulting blast of heat, but like all its kind, it proved incapable of ignoring a challenge.

It had landed atop another freighter, the crew displaying considerably less aggression than that of the *Drakespite* in the rapidity with which they hurled themselves from her rails, my Red-lit fires no doubt adding impetus to their flight. The Black whirled amidst the flaming tangle of rigging and timber, mouth gaping to cough its fiery response then howling in frustration as the flames failed to gout. I landed hard on the deck barely twenty feet from him, the glut of Green preventing a disabling injury, and stared into his eyes in direct challenge, a thing no male could ever tolerate for long. It roared again and charged, claws tearing the deck into splinters and tail coiling for a strike, whereupon it froze into absolute immobility as I called on the Black I had ingested bare moments before.

That it was a fearsomely strong beast was self-evident, but before now I had not truly appreciated the power of this animal. It strained against my Black-born grip with all its might, draining my reserves of ingested product with such speed I must confess to a sudden sheen of sweat on my brow and a growing impatience for Mr Torcreek to make good his boast. Strange then, that it is at this juncture that I must describe another sensation, a certain insight beyond the general alarm and urgency of the situation. For, as I maintained my vigil upon the beast's eyes, I discerned something beyond its animal craving for flesh and triumph: a deep and consuming terror, and not of me. I realised in that instant the Black had not been seeking revenge for its capture and torment, nor for the insertion of a steel tap into its flesh. It had been trying to get away, seeking escape from something far worse than these small, two-legged pests. It was as my mind tracked over the course of the beast's flight, from the shattered vat with its mysterious corpse through the close-packed streets to the docks, that Mr Torcreek proved himself no braggart.

The rifle bullet made a faint whine as it streaked overhead to smack precisely into the centre of the Black's sloping forehead. It gave a single spasmodic jerk, its long body undulating from head to tail, then collapsed onto the part-destroyed deck with a choking gargle.

CONCLUSION

The Board will find a full list of casualties and tally of damage in Addendum II, together with a cost estimate for repairs. As stated above, the compilation of an exact and incontrovertible account proves impossible; however, certain facts can be established beyond any reasonable contradiction.

Firstly, a woman of unknown identity, accompanied by a small child of undetermined gender, did indeed climb onto the platform alongside Mr Dunmorn as he was concluding a rather lengthy discourse on the merits of company loyalty. In all truth, Mr Dunmorn was not widely regarded as the most compelling orator which may account for the inattention of much of the crowd at the critical moment. Despite this, I have collated statements from six individual witnesses, all of good character and reliable judgement, attesting that the unidentified woman stepped out of the line of parents and children awaiting the Blood-lot and made an unhurried passage onto the platform, unnoticed by either Mr Dunmorn or the team of harvesters making ready to apply the spile to the Black's neck. The woman is described as young but I have made no progress in obtaining a more detailed description. One of the male witnesses did testify to a certain conventional attractiveness in her form and bearing but viewed her at too great a distance to provide details of hair colour or complexion. Descriptions of the child are equally vague but its height would indicate an age of eight years, the correct age for presentation at the Blood-lot.

It seems that it was barely seconds subsequent to Mr Dunmorn's order to commence harvesting that the woman gathered up her child and leapt into the vat. It is at this point that most accounts, perhaps understandably, become somewhat confused. However, my correlation of various testimonials has unearthed some key points of agreement. It seems clear that the vat shattered from within, killing poor Mr Dunmorn and the harvesters in the process. Also, the Black was not responsible for this particular piece of destruction, being secured by chains to the harvesting rig when it occurred. Following the destruction of the vat and the resultant dispersal of so much product, a general panic seized the crowd but three witnesses retained sufficient presence of mind to attest that the Black's chains were nowhere in sight as the product rained down, after which it began its desperate flight from the scene.

My conclusion is alarming but inescapable; the Black was set free by the agency of a Blood-blessed, upon whose shoulders the deaths of Mr Dunmore and so many others can now be placed. The list of suspects wishing harm to Syndicate interests on this continent is long, the Corvantine Empire being worthy of perhaps greatest attention. But I find it difficult to comprehend what advantage even they could gain from this incident. Also, what connection this hidden agent has with the unknown woman, or her purpose, remains singularly mysterious. As reported above, the woman's body was recovered, albeit in an unrecognisable condition, but the child she bore into the vat was not found at her side. Several children did perish in this incident, mainly those gathered for the Blood-lot, but all have been claimed by grieving relatives. Who this child was, or where he or she may have gone, remains perhaps the most troublesome mystery to emerge from this entire episode.

I assure the Board that my efforts to resolve these questions are not exhausted and I will continue to expend all necessary energy to provide the requisite answers.

In lieu of the arrival of Mr Dunmorn's replacement, I remain, Sirs and Ladies, your most loyal employee and Shareholder,

Lodima Bondersil
Acting Director – Carvenport Division
Arradsian Continental Holdings

I

The Red Sands

What do we mean when we use the term 'product,' that otherwise innocuous word that has become so burdened with significance over the course of the preceding century and the advent of the Corporate Age? Most readers, I'm sure, would reply with just one word, 'Blood.' Or, if they were of a more verbose inclination, they might expand their definition thusly: 'Drake Blood.' This is basically correct but has a tendency to mask the truly vast complexity of the subject addressed within the pages of this modest tome. For, as even the most superstitious Dalcian savage or illiterate Island brute can attest, there is no one type of product. I will spare you, dear reader, a fulsome technical description of each variant, and the increasing list of derivatives reaped from the carcasses of the Arradsian drake. Instead, I feel it would be more apposite, and perhaps amusing, to simply repeat a mantra taught to students at the Ironship Academy of Female Education, amongst whom I am proud to count myself:

> *Blue for the mind.*
> *Green for the body.*
> *Red for the fire.*
> *Black for the push.*

From *A Lay-person's Guide to Plasmology* by Miss Amorea Findlestack. Ironship Press – Company Year 195 (1579 by the Mandinorian Calendar).

CHAPTER 1

Lizanne

Mr Redsel found her at the prow just past sunset. It had become her habit to linger here most evenings when weather permitted, taking in the spectacle of the stars and the moons, enjoying the seaward breeze on her skin and the constant rhythmic splash of the *Mutual Advantage*'s twin paddles. Their cadence had slowed tonight, the captain reducing speed as they drew near to the Barrier Isles with all their hidden dangers. Come the morning the churning currents of the Strait would surround them and the paddles would turn at full speed, but for now a sedate pace and strict observance of charts and compass were needed.

She didn't turn at Mr Redsel's approach, though his footfalls were audible above the paddles. Instead she kept her gaze upon the risen moons, Serphia and Morvia, thinking it a pity their larger sister was not visible tonight. She always enjoyed the sight of Nelphia's myriad valleys and mountains, largely free of craters unlike her pocked and scarred siblings. *Benefits of a recently active surface*, according to her father. *But still a dead world.*

'Miss Lethridge,' Mr Redsel said, coming to a halt behind her. She didn't turn but knew he would be maintaining a gap of due propriety. Her cautious observance throughout the voyage had left her in little doubt that he was far too practised to risk any clumsiness at so crucial a juncture. 'I find you lost in the whispers of night, it seems.'

Marsal, she mused inwardly. *Opening with a quotation. Somewhat trite but obscure enough to convey the impression of a scholarly past.*

'Mr Redsel,' she replied, allowing a little warmth to colour her tone. 'Am I to take it the cards did not favour you?'

The other passengers spent the evenings engaged in various amusements, chiefly consisting of cards and amateurish peckings at the aged pianola in their plush but modestly dimensioned lounge. They were mostly content to leave her be, beyond an occasional insistence on petty conversation. Shareholder status had its advantages and none possessed sufficient standing, or gall, to impose their presence to any tedious degree. Mr Redsel, however, had been more attentive than most, though before tonight he had yet to make the approach she knew was inevitable from the moment he came aboard in Feros.

'Mourning Jacks was never my game,' he replied. 'Miss Montis took me for a full ten scrips before I had the good sense to excuse myself.'

She allowed the silence to linger before turning to face him, hoping reluctance might entice a more revealing approach. Mr Redsel, however, displayed a creditable discipline in remaining silent, though his decision to reach into his jacket for a cigarillo case betrayed a slight impatience.

'Thank you,' she said as he proffered the open case, extracting one of the thin, leaf-wrapped delights. 'Dalcian, no less,' she added, playing the cigarillo along her top lip to capture the aroma.

'I find everything else is a poor substitute,' he said, striking a match and leaning closer. Smoke billowed as she put the cigarillo to her lips and sucked the flame onto the leaf. An amateur might have taken the opportunity to let the proximity endure, perhaps even steal a kiss, but Mr Redsel knew better.

'One should indulge one's passions, where possible,' he said stepping back and lighting his own cigarillo before flicking the dying match away into the gloom beyond the rail. 'Don't you think?'

She shrugged and tightened her shawl about her shoulders. 'I had a teacher once who was fond of equating indulgence with weakness. "Remember, girls, the path to the Shareholder's office lies not in play, but diligence."' It was a truthful anecdote and she smiled at the memory, Madame Bondersil's frequently stern face looming in her memory. *It will be good to see you again, Madame,* she thought, glancing out at the two moons shimmering on the blackening waves. *Should I survive the night.*

'It seems you were an observant pupil,' Mr Redsel said. Her words gave tacit permission for his gaze to play over her bodice where the gleam of a Shareholder's pin could be seen through the thin silk of the shawl. 'A full Shareholder at such a young age. Few of us could ever hope to rise so high so quickly.'

'Diligence matched with plain luck is a potent brew,' she replied, taking another shallow draw on her cigarillo and tasting nothing more than finest Dalcian leaf. *At least he's no poisoner.* 'In any case, I would have thought you would shun such aspirations. You are an Independent are you not?'

'Indeed, at present a syndicate of one.' He gave a self-deprecating bow. 'My previous contract being fulfilled, I thought it opportune to invest some profits in finally exploring the land from which all wealth flows and makes us its slaves.'

Another quote, Bidrosin this time, delivered with a sardonic lilt to convey his lack of sympathy with so notorious a Corvantine radical. 'So, you've never seen Arradsia?' she asked.

'A singular omission I am about to correct. Whilst you, I discern, are more than familiar with the continent.'

'I was born in Feros but schooled in Carvenport, and had occasion to see some of the Interior before the Board called me to the Home Office.'

'Then you must be my guide.' He smiled, leaning on the rail. 'For I'm told there will be an alignment in but a few short months, and Arradsia is said to offer the finest view.'

'You are an astronomer then, sir?' She put a slight note of doubtful mockery in her tone, moving to stand alongside him.

'Merely a seeker of spectacle,' he said, raising his gaze to the moons. 'To see three moons in the sky, and the planets beyond, all arranged in perfect order for but the briefest instant. That will be a sight to cherish through the years.'

Where did they find you? she wondered, her gaze tracking over his profile. Rugged but not weathered, handsome but not effete, clever but not arrogant. *I might almost think they bred you just for this.*

'There's an observatory in Carvenport,' she said. 'Well equipped with all manner of optical instruments. I'm sure I can arrange an introduction.'

'You are very kind.' He paused, forming his brow into a faintly reluctant frown. 'I am bound to ask, Miss Lethridge, for curiosity was ever my worst vice, you are truly the granddaughter of Darus Lethridge, are you not?'

Clever, she thought. *Risking offence to gain intimacy by raising so sensitive a topic. Let us see how he responds to a little set-back.* She sighed, forming a brief jet of smoke before the breeze carried it away. 'And another admirer of the great man reveals himself,' she said, moving back from the rail and turning to go. 'I never knew him, sir, he died before I was born. Therefore I can furnish no anecdotes and bid you good night.'

'It is not anecdotes I seek,' he said, voice carefully modulated to a tone of gentle solicitation, moving to stand in her way, though once again maintaining the correct distance. 'And I apologise for any unintended insult. You see I find myself in need of an opinion on a recent purchase.'

She crossed her arms, cigarillo poised before her lips as she raised a quizzical eyebrow. 'Purchase?'

'Yes. Some mechanical drawings the vendor assured me were set down by your grandfather's own hand. However, I must confess to certain doubts.'

She found herself gratified by his puzzlement as she voiced a laugh, shaking her head. 'A syndicate of one. This is your business, sir? The purchase of drawings?'

'Purchase and sale,' he said. 'And not just drawings but all manner of genuine arts and antiquities. The salient word being "genuine."'

'And you imagine I may be able to provenance these drawings for you, with my expert familial eye.'

'I thought perhaps you would know his line, his script . . .' He trailed off with a sheepish grimace. 'A foolish notion, I see that now. Please forgive the intrusion and any offence I may have caused.' He inclined his head in respectful contrition and turned to leave. She let him cover a good dozen feet before delivering the expected question.

'What is it? What device?'

He paused in midstride, turning back with an impressively crafted frown of surprise. 'Why, the only one that truly matters,' he said, gesturing at the slowly turning paddles and the twin stacks above the wheel-house from which spent steam rose into the night sky.

'The thermoplasmic engine,' she murmured, a genuine curiosity stirring in her breast. *To what lengths have they gone to craft this trap?* 'The great knicky-knack itself,' she added in a louder tone. 'Which version?'

'The very first,' he told her. 'If genuine. I should be happy to show them to you tomorrow . . .'

'Oh no.' She strode to his side, looping her arm through his and impelling him towards the passenger quarters. 'Curiosity is also my worst vice, and once stirred one not to be denied.'

Indulgence? she asked herself a few hours later as Mr Redsel lay in apparently sated slumber at her side. Her eyes tracked over his torso, lingering on the hard muscle of his belly sheened in sweat from their recent exertions. She had found him as well practised in the carnal arts as everything else, another fulfilled expectation. *I doubt Madame would have approved of this particular tactical choice.*

The notion brought a faint grin to her lips as she slipped from the bed. She paused to retrieve her discarded bodice from the floor before going to the dresser where Mr Redsel had arrayed the drawings for her perusal on entering the cabin. His rather involved and inventive description of their origins had been interrupted by her kiss. She had enjoyed his surprise, as she had enjoyed what came next. For a time she had kept a lover in Feros, a suitably discreet Ironship Protectorate officer with a wife far away across the ocean and a consequent disinterest in any protracted emotional entanglements. But Commander Pinefeld had been sent to a distant post some months ago, so perhaps there had been an element of indulgence to this episode, although it had served to dispel any small doubts she might harbour about his true purpose in seeking her out.

She had seen it as he approached his climax, face poised above hers, his objective made plain in the unblinking stare he fixed on her eyes. She had returned his gaze, legs and arms clutching him tighter as he thrust at an increasing tempo, making the appropriate noises at the appropriate moment, allowing him the temporary delusion of success in forging the required bond. She felt she owed him something. He had, after all, been *very* practised.

The light of the two moons streamed through the open port-hole, providing enough illumination for an adequate perusal of the drawings. There were three of them, the paper faded to a light brown and the edges a little frayed, but the precisely inked dimensions of the world's greatest single invention remained clear. The words 'Plasmic Locomotive Drive' were inscribed at the top of the first drawing in a spidery, almost feverish script, conveying a sense of excitement at a recently captured idea. The date 36/04/177 was scrawled with a similarly energetic hand in the bottom-right corner. The imprecision of the text, however, was in stark contrast to the depiction of the device itself. Every tube, spigot and valve had been rendered in exquisite detail, the shadows hatched with an exactitude that could only derive from the hand of a highly skilled draughtsman.

She turned her gaze on the next drawing, finding it similarly accomplished, though the device now bore its modern title of 'Thermoplasmic Locomotive Engine' and featured several additions and refinements to the original design. This one was dated 12/05/177 and its neighbour, an equally impressive depiction of the machine's final incarnation, bore the date 26/07/177. *Two days before the patent was issued,* she recalled, her gaze fixing in turn on the same point on each drawing, the top right corner where a small monogram had been etched in the same unmistakable hand: DL.

'So, what do you think?'

She turned from the dresser finding Mr Redsel sitting upright and fully awake. A dim glow filled the cabin as he reached for the oil-lamp fixed into the wall above the bed. He wore the fond expression of a man embarking on an intimate adventure, the face of the newly enraptured. *So perfect,* she thought again, not without a note of regret.

'I'm afraid, sir,' she said, lifting her bodice and extracting the single vial of product hidden amidst its lacework, 'we have other matters to discuss.'

She detected a soft metallic snick and his hand emerged from the bed-sheets clutching a small revolver. She recognised the make as he trained it on her forehead: a Tulsome .21 six-chamber, known commonly as the gambler's salt-shaker for the multiple cylinder barrel's resemblance to a condiment holder and its widespread adoption by the professional card-playing fraternity. Small of calibre but unfailingly reliable and deadly when employed with expert aim.

Her reaction to the appearance of the pistol amounted to a slightly raised eyebrow whilst her thumb simultaneously removed the glass stopper from the vial as she raised it to her lips. It was her emergency vial, a blend from one of the more secret corners of the Ironship laboratory. Effective blending of different product types was an art beyond most harvesters, facilitated only by the most patient and exacting manipulation of product at the molecular level and the careful application of various synthetic binding agents. Such precision required the most powerful magnascopes, another invention for which the world owed a debt to her family.

'Don't!' he warned, rising from the bed, both hands on the pistol now, the six barrels steady and a stern resolve to his voice and gaze. 'I've no wish to . . .'

She drank the vial and he squeezed the trigger a split-second later, the revolver issuing the dry click of a hammer finding an empty chamber. He sprang from the bed after only the barest hesitation, reversing his grip on the revolver and drawing it back to aim a blow at her temple. The contents of the vial left a bitter and complex sting on her tongue before burning its way through her system in a familiar rush of sensation. Seventy percent Green, twenty percent Black and ten percent Red. She summoned the Green and her arm came up in a blur, hand catching his wrist an inch short of her temple, the grip tight but not enough to mark his flesh nor crush his bones. Any suspicious bruising might arouse questions later.

She summoned the Black as he drew his free arm back for a punch, a death-blow judging from the configuration of his knuckles. He shuddered as she unleashed the Black and froze him in place, jaw clenched as he made a vain effort to fight her grip, his tongue forming either curses or pleas behind clamped teeth. She pushed him back a few feet, still maintaining her grip, keeping him suspended above the bed. The Black was diminishing fast and she had only moments.

'Who is your contact in Carvenport?' she asked, loosening her grip just enough to free his mouth.

'You . . .' he choked, gulping breath, '. . . are making . . . a mistake.'

'On the contrary, sir,' she replied, going to the dresser and reaching for the small leather satchel concealed behind it. She undid the straps and revealed the row of four vials inside. 'It was your mistake not to hide these with sufficient rigour. It took barely moments to discover them when I searched your cabin yesterday, and only a few moments more to find your salt-shaker.' She angled her head in critical examination, using the Black to turn his naked form about. *No trace of the Sign. Not even on the soles of his feet.*

'You're not Cadre,' she said. 'A hireling. The Corvantine Empire sent an unregistered Blood-blessed after me. The Emperor's agents are not usually so injudicious. I must confess, sir, to a certain sense of personal insult. What is your usual prey, I wonder? Wealthy widows and empty-headed heiresses?'

'I was . . . not sent to . . . kill you.'

'Of that I have no doubt, Mr Redsel. After our shared, and no doubt continued intimacy in Carvenport, you would have provided your employers with enough intelligence to justify your fee a dozen times over.'

His features betrayed a certain resignation then, and she felt a flicker of admiration for his evident resolve to beg no more. Instead he asked a question, 'How . . . did I reveal . . . myself?'

'I liked you too much.' She forced the admiration down, tightening her grip once more. 'Hireling or not, you and I share a profession and I have no great desire to see you suffer. So I will ask again and strongly advise you to answer: who is your contact in Carvenport?'

Much of his face was frozen now and only his lips could convey any emotion as they formed the reply around a snarl, 'They were to . . . find me . . . I was given . . . no name.'

'Recognition code.'

'Truelove.'

Despite the circumstances she couldn't contain a snort of amusement. 'How very apposite.' She could feel the Black ebbing now, the fiery burn intensifying as it dwindled in her bloodstream. 'Oh, and if it matters,' she said, nodding at the drawings. 'They're fake. My grandfather only ever used the Mandinorian Calendar. Besides which his hands were crippled by arthritis for the latter half of his life, something he concealed due to pride and vanity.'

His lips morphed into something that might have been a smile, or another snarl, just as she stopped his heart with the last of the Black. He jerked in mid air before collapsing onto the bed, finely honed body limp and void of life.

The First Mate came to her at breakfast, formal and respectful as he conveyed the sad news of Mr Redsel's passing. 'How terrible!' she exclaimed, putting aside her toast and reaching for a restorative sip of tea. 'A seizure of the heart, you say?'

'According to the ship's doctor, miss. Unusual in a man of his age but, apparently, not unprecedented.' A crew member had seen them conversing at the prow and the First Mate was obliged to ask a few questions. As expected he proved a less-than-rigorous investigator; once she professed her ignorance of Mr Redsel's unfortunate and untimely passing no Syndicate employee of any intelligence would press a Shareholder for additional information.

After the officer had taken his leave she continued to breakfast, though her appetite was soon soured by an outbreak of hysterics at a near by table as news of Mr Redsel's demise spread. Mrs Jackmore, a buxom woman of perhaps forty years' age, convulsed in abject misery as her white-faced husband, a Regional Manager of notably more advanced years, looked on in frozen silence. Mrs Jackmore's maid eventually hustled her from the dining room, her cries continuing unabated. The other passengers strove to conceal embarrassment or amusement as Mr Jackmore completed his meal, chomping his way through bacon, eggs and no less than two rounds of toast with stoic determination.

Couldn't resist some additional practice, eh? she asked the spectre of Mr Redsel as she rose from the table, leaving her breakfast unfinished. *I did wonder if I'd have cause to rue my action. Now I believe it can safely be filed under Necessary Regrets.*

She went to her cabin to retrieve the drawings then made her way to the prow once more. The tempo of the paddles had tripled now they were in the Strait proper, the Blood-blessed in the engine room no doubt having drunk and expended at least two full vials of Red to power the engines to maximum speed. This was her third trip through the Strait and each time she had been discomforted by the sight of the waters; the general absence of waves seemed strange so far from land and the constant swirl and eddy of the currents held a sense of the uncanny. It seemed to her a visual echo of whatever great force of nature had torn so great a channel through the Barrier Isles some two centuries before.

She held up the drawings for a final inspection. It seemed a shame, they being so well crafted. But Mr Redsel may have left traces in his efforts to build an identity and, forgeries or not, the rumour of the drawings' mere existence would invariably attract best-avoided attention. She could have left them in his cabin but that would have raised further questions regarding their remarkably coincidental presence on the same vessel carrying the granddaughter of their apparent author. She lit a match and held it to the corner of each drawing, letting the flame consume two-thirds of their mass before gifting them to the sea.

I didn't tell you the forger's gravest error, did I, Mr Redsel? she asked, watching the blackened embers fall into the ship's wake to be carried into the churning foam beneath the paddles. *Although he could never have known it. You see it was my father who designed the great knicky-knack when he was barely fifteen years of age, only to see it stolen by my grandfather. My father is the author of this wondrous age, a man of singular genius and vision who can barely afford ink for his blueprints.*

She allowed her thoughts to touch briefly on the last meeting with her father. It had been the day before she took ship in Feros and she found him in his workshop surrounded by various novelties, hands slick with grease and spectacles perched on his nose. It had ever been a source of wonder to her how his spectacles managed to stay on so precarious a perch; he moved with such restless energy it seemed impossible, and yet in all her years she had never once seen them come adrift. She was fond of the memory, regardless of the words that passed between them. *You work for a pack of thieves,* he had said, barely glancing up from his tinkering. *They stole your birthright.*

Really, Father? she had responded. *I always thought Grandfather got there first.*

Over the succeeding weeks she had become increasingly uncomfortable with the hurt she had seen cloud his face at that moment. It summoned another memory, the day of the Blood-lot when the harvester's pipette left a small bead of product on her hand but, unlike the other children sniffling or bawling around her, produced no instant burn or blackened scab. She had never seen him sad before and wondered why he didn't smile as she held up her hand, unmarked but for the patch of milk-white skin on her palm. *Look Father, it didn't hurt. Look, look!*

Pushing the memory away she turned her attention to the sea once more. The Strait narrowed to the south and she could see the small green specks of the Barrier Isles cresting the horizon, meaning Carvenport now lay less than two days' distant. *Carvenport,* she thought, a wry smile coming to her lips. *Where I shall find Truelove.*

CHAPTER 2

Clay

Cralmoor's fist slammed into Clay's side with enough force to make him stagger, grunting in frustration as the bigger man dodged his sluggish counter-jab and delivered a straight-line kick at his chest. Clay managed to block the kick with crossed forearms but the force of it sent him backpedaling into the crowd. For a few moments the world became a jostling fury of jeers, insults, booze-laden spit and more than a few punches. He had to fight his way clear, fists and elbows snapping aside the drunken faces before he made it back into the chalk-ringed circle where Cralmoor waited. The Islander stood with his hands on his hips, tattoo-covered chest barely swelling and bright wall of teeth revealed by a knowing grin. *Street-scrapper don't make a fighter, lad,* the grin said. *Swimming in deep waters now.*

Clay kept his own answering grin from his lips, worried it might reveal a suspicious confidence, and launched into a series of well-practised moves. Tratter called it the Markeva Combination, a sequence of kicks and punches laid down by the ancient and most celebrated practitioner of the Dalcian martial arts. It had taken a month to learn the sequence, Clay sweating through the moves under Tratter's expert and unforgiving eye until he pronounced him as ready as he would ever be. 'Do it right, y'might actually come outta this with some credit,' the old trainer had said with an approving wink.

'I'm paying you to help me win this thing,' Clay had replied. The memory of the old man's prolonged laughter came back to him now as Cralmoor blocked every blow with fluid ease and delivered a short jab to Clay's right eye whereupon he blinked a few times before falling over. He was dimly aware of the bell sounding just before he hit the floor, and the feel of Derk's arms clamped across his chest as he was dragged to the stool, bare heels scraping sand from the floor. He returned to full awareness when Derk emptied half the water-bucket over his head.

'I believe we have arrived at the appropriate moment,' Derk said, reaching into the bag holding their two canteens, one with a plain cap, the other marked with a scratched cross.

Clay shook his head, liquid flying from his shaved scalp. 'One more round.'

'You don't have another round in you.'

'Too soon,' Clay insisted, wincing as Derk pressed a cloth against the open cut below his eye. 'Only the third bell. Keyvine'll know. Shit, Keyvine's mother would know.'

He saw Derk's involuntary glance at the raised platform at the rear of the cavernous drinking den. It was Fight Night every Venasday in the Colonials Rest and its owner never missed a bout. Keyvine sat alone on the platform, a small lamp and a bottle of wine on the table at his side. A slim, unmoving silhouette lit only by the gleam of the silver drake's head that topped the cane resting on his knees. *Not a guard nor a weapon within arm's reach*, Clay thought, a long-gestated jealousy building inside. *But still the King of Blades and Whores.*

The jealousy proved useful, stoking his anger and muting his pain. He gulped water from the white-capped bottle and got to his feet a good few beats before the bell sounded. *Fuck Markeva,* he thought, raising his fists as Cralmoor strolled towards him. *And fuck Tratter too.*

There were rules to this game, no biting, gouging or ball-stomping, but otherwise the participants were free to inflict whatever carnage they could on one another without benefit of weapons. However, Clay had always had a facility for turning words into weapons and knew how deeply they could cut, or at least distract.

'I get a go on your wife when I win, right?' he asked Cralmoor in a conversational tone, dodging another jab at his eye by the barest inch. 'Or is it your husband?'

'Got both,' the Islander replied in a cheerful tone, blocking a left hook and delivering another painful dig into Clay's ribs. 'Doubt you could take either.' He stepped outside the arc of Clay's upper-cut and slapped the arm aside before lashing out with another kick, a round-house to the head, blocked more through luck than design. 'No offence.'

'Right, I forgot,' Clay said in mock realisation, delivering another fruitless three-punch combination at Cralmoor's head. 'Your spirits make you stick your cock in anything with a pulse.' He grinned at the sudden darkness to the Islander's expression. Mention of the spirits from a non-believing mouth was always certain to rile them up something fierce.

'Careful, boy,' Cralmoor warned, his stance becoming tighter, gaze more focused. 'Been easy on you so far. Mr Keyvine owes a debt to Braddon.'

Clay's own temper began to quicken, an inevitable reaction to hearing mention of his uncle. 'Yeah? The spirits make you bare your ass to him too . . . ?'

Cralmoor crouched and charged, too fast to dodge, driving his shoulder into Clay's midriff as his arms reached around to vice him around the waist. Clay hammered at the bigger man's head and back in the brief few seconds before he was lifted off his feet and borne to the floor. All the wind came out of him as the Islander's crushing weight bore down, his forehead slamming once into Clay's nose before he drew back, rearing up with fists raised to pummel, apparently oblivious to his mistake.

This was what Clay knew, not the ring or the long-practised moves. This was now a gutter fight, and who knew the gutter better than he?

He twisted beneath the Islander, swinging his right leg around to hook Cralmoor under the left armpit, jerking with enough force to push him onto his side. Clay moved with a feral speed, scrambling atop Cralmoor and slapping an open hand against his ear, a blow he knew always worked well as a stunner. Cralmoor gave an involuntary shout, eyes bunching as he fought the sudden blast of pain in his ear, buying the two seconds needed for Clay to pin him, both knees on his shoulders. His punches rained down in a frenzy, leather-bound knuckles flaring with agony as the Islander's head jerked under the impact, a cheek-bone giving way with a loud crack.

Clay left off when his arms started to ache, clamping a hand under Cralmoor's chin and drawing back for a final blow. *Who needs the other canteen . . .*

Cralmoor's kick slammed into the back of his head, birthing a sudden blaze of sparkling stars. By the time they faded he was on his back once more, the Islander's knee pressing on his neck as he stared down with a grim and murderous glint in his eye. When the bell sounded he kept on, bearing down with greater force. He left off only when another sound cut through the din: a thin rhythmic tinkle of metal on glass.

Clay rasped air into his lungs as Cralmoor rose from him, turning to Keyvine's shadowed platform. The King of Blades and Whores was tapping the silver drake's head of his cane against his wine bottle with a steady but insistent cadence. Cralmoor took a deep breath and gave Clay a final glance, bloody and distorted face full of dire promise, before stalking back to his stool. The tapping ceased when he sat down.

Derk was obliged to half carry Clay to his own stool and hold him upright as he put the canteen to his lips, the one with the cross scratched onto the cap. 'Now?' he asked with a half-grin. Clay grabbed the canteen with both hands and gulped down the contents. The product was heavily and inexpertly diluted but still left a tell-tale burn on his tongue followed by the buzzing sensation that accompanied the ingestion of Black, like hornets crafting a hive in his chest.

Although all Blood-blessed could make use of the gifts resulting from ingestion of the four different colours of product, their proficiency with each varied considerably. Most were best suited to Green, the enhanced strength and speed it afforded making them highly prized as elite labourers or stevedores. Some excelled with Red, usually finding lucrative employment in the engine rooms of select corporate ships as the flames they conjured ignited the product in their blood-burning engines. A few were sufficiently skilled in the mysteries of the Blue-trance to earn lifetime contracts in company headquarters, conveying messages all over the world in minutes rather than months. But fewer still shared Clay's aptitude for harnessing the power afforded by the Black, the ability the ever-superstitious Dalcians referred to as 'the unseen hand.' It remained a singularly frustrating gift since Black was by far the most expensive colour and not easily sourced for a man of his station, if indeed he could be said to hold any station. The canteen had been laced with barely a thimbleful, and that the result of two full months thieving profits. Watching Cralmoor prowling the edge of the circle, gaze bright with lethal intent and muscles at full flex, Clay wondered for the first time if it would be enough.

Cralmoor came on at the first peal of the bell, the crowd's baying roused to an even greater pitch by the prospect of death, a rare but appreciated treat for those who flocked to these unsanctioned fights. Clay covered up, letting the first blow land and using a fraction of the Black to soften it, stopping the fist just as it made contact with his flesh. He gave a convincing yell of pain and spun away, Cralmoor's second blow whispering past his ear. The Islander growled in fury and dropped into another charge, Clay allowing him to connect but deflecting enough force to keep them both upright. They grappled, spinning like crazed dancers about the ring, Cralmoor cursing him all the while in some tribal Island tongue. He drove repeated blows into Clay's gut, the Black diminishing with every blow. A few more moments and it would all be gone.

Clay broke the clinch, drawing back and feinting at Cralmoor's head with a straight left, ducking under the counter and fixing his gaze on the Islander's right foot. It was only a nudge, easily mistaken for a slip, but just enough to destroy his balance and drop his guard for the briefest instant. Clay put all the remaining Black into the blow, focusing on the point where his fist met Cralmoor's jaw, feeling it shatter as flesh met flesh. The Islander spun, mouth spraying blood across the crowd. They fell into rigid silence as he staggered, eyes unfocused and steps faltering but still somehow upright.

'Shit,' Clay muttered before leaping onto Cralmoor's back and wrapping his legs about his torso. The weight was enough to finally bring him down though he continued to struggle, elbows flailing and head jerking as his fighter's instinct sought to continue the battle. It took a while, maybe three full minutes of punching and slamming his head into the boards, but finally Lemul Cralmoor, Champion of the Chalk Ring and most feared prize-fighter in Carvenport, lay unconscious on the floor of the Colonials Rest. The crowd booed themselves hoarse.

'Three thousand, six hundred and eighty-two in Ironship scrip,' Derk said, rolling the bundle of notes into a neat cylinder. 'Plus another four hundred in exchange notes and sundry valuables.'

Clay grinned then hissed as Joya pushed the needle into the edge of his cut once more. 'And the price for three tickets to Feros?' he asked.

'Fifteen hundred. A price arrived at through extensive negotiation, I assure you.' Derk leaned back from the cash-laden table, finely sculpted face more reflective than joyful. 'We did it. After all these years of toil we're finally on our way.'

'I'll believe that when we step onto the Feros docks,' Joya said, snipping off the suture and wiping the crusted blood from Clay's face. 'And not before.'

She held out a cup as he sat up on the bed. 'Green?' he asked, sniffing the faintly acidic contents.

'Six drops. All we have left.'

He shook his head and put the cup aside. 'Best save it.'

'You need to heal.'

'I'm not so bad,' he groaned, rising from the bed and feeling every one of Cralmoor's punches. 'You said it yourself, we're not clear yet. Find ourselves in a tight spot twixt here and the docks we'll be happy for a few drops of Green.'

'I could venture forth and buy us some,' Derk offered. 'Half a dozen dealers within a stone's throw.'

'No.' Clay moved to the window. It was firmly boarded to conceal the glow of their lamp but Derk had drilled a small peep-hole as a sensible precaution. Clay peered down at the maze of alley and street below, seeing and hearing nothing of note. The Blinds were as they should be in the small hours, caught in the brief truce before the dock-side horns started pealing and the daily war began in earnest. Whores, thieves, dealers, cardsharps and a dozen other ancient professions all rousing themselves from the previous night's indulgence to do it all over again, wondering, or perhaps hoping, today would see their final battle.

'No,' he told Derk again. 'We're invisible for the next two days. Give Keyvine any reminders we exist and maybe that sharp mind of his starts to pondering. And that ain't good for us.'

They had hidden themselves in the steeple of the old Seer's Church on Spigotter's Row. It was their best-kept secret and most-cherished hideout, to be used only in emergencies. The place had a clutch of lurid stories attached to it, most concerning the ghost of the Pale-Eyed Preacher said to haunt the place. Century-old legend had the Preacher murdering a dozen or so whores down in the basement. He'd cut them up to make dolls of their corpses, his reasons still mysterious and the subject of myriad perverted theories. Clay had his doubts the Preacher had ever really existed but some of the older Blinds-folk still swore to the truth of the whole thing. In any case, a long-standing ghost story proved a useful device for keeping unwanted visitors at bay; even the most desperate gutter-sleeping drunk wouldn't go near the church. The stairs were seemingly half-rotted but Clay and Derk had done some repairs over the years, nothing that would show but adding sufficient fortitude to enable a speedy climb to the top, provided you knew where to place your feet. They kept the steeple stocked with a small amount of scrip and sundry supplies, but otherwise stayed away so as not to become overly associated with the place. As for the Pale-Eyed Preacher, Clay had never seen hide nor hair of the crazy old bastard.

'You got a ship all picked out for us?' Joya asked Derk, slim fingers playing over the coins on the table. Clay had noticed before how her hands got restless when she was nervous.

'Indeed I do, darling sis,' her brother replied, consigning their winnings to a nondescript satchel, padded so it wouldn't jingle. 'The ECT *Endeavour* sails in two days.'

'An Eastern Conglom ship?' Clay asked, not turning from the window.

'Thought it best to steer clear of Ironship vessels. Too well-regulated for our purposes, don't you think?'

'Not a blood-burner then?' Joya enquired, a little disappointed. Clay knew that travelling the ocean on a Red-fuelled ship had been her ambition since childhood, one they shared along with getting as far gone from this shit-pit as possible.

'Sadly no,' Derk replied. 'We'll have to accustom ourselves to the aroma of coal smoke. Still, she's fleet enough. Six weeks to Feros with fair weather, according to the bosun. A fine and pragmatic fellow who will see us to a suitably secluded berth for due consideration.'

'You mean we have to stay belowdecks the whole way?' she said. 'Thought I'd at least get to see some of the Isles.'

'Be plenty to see in Feros,' Clay told her. He was about to move from the peep-hole when something caught his eye in the street below, a shadow cast by the two moons. It moved with caution, as did most who ventured forth in the Blinds after dark, but had a mite too much girth for real stealth. Clay kept his gaze fixed on the street as he held up a hand to Derk, palm out and fingers spread. There was a scrape of chairs and shifted brick before Derk joined him at the window, handing him one of the two aged but serviceable revolvers from the cache in the wall.

'How many?' he whispered.

'Just the one, and I think I recognise the bulk.' He watched the shadow emerge from the corner of Spigotter's and Lacemaid, a pale round face revealed clearly in the moonlight. 'Speeler, all alone.'

'What could cause him to risk the streets at such an hour with no protection?' Derk wondered softly. 'Uncharacteristic, wouldn't you say?'

Clay kept his gaze focused on Speeler's flabby face, seeing a certain desperate tension to it as he stared up at the steeple. 'Either of you tell him about this place?' Clay asked.

'Didn't even tell Joya about it until yesterday,' Derk said as his sister murmured a faint negative. 'Speeler's a resourceful fellow, though. I dare say discovering our little hidey-hole is well within his capabilities.'

Clay watched Speeler hesitate for a second then start towards the church in a determined waddle. 'Seems intent on making a house call, anyways.' He moved towards the staircase then paused to regard the cup of Green next to the bed, his many aches now flaring due to an increase in heart rate. *No use drawing a fire-arm if you can't hold it steady,* he thought, downing the mixture of water and Green in a single gulp. The reaction was instantaneous, a fiery warmth in the belly that spread out to the extremities, banishing all aches in the process. For Blessed and non-Blessed alike Green was the greatest tonic and curative, but only the Blessed enjoyed the enhancing effects it gave to the body. His vision grew sharper as he approached the stairs, hearing more acute and body seeming to thrum with added strength.

'Keep back,' he told Derk. 'Best if he only gets eyes on one of us.'

He stepped out onto the upper landing, keeping close to the wall and peering cautiously down. Speeler stood framed by the ragged square of the descending staircase, gazing up with the same desperate entreaty on his face. The greeting he offered carried to the top of the steeple, urgency and reluctance audible in the rasp of it. 'Clay, need words.'

Clay said nothing, moving with revolver in hand as he climbed down to the halfway point where the stairs apparently disappeared. In fact he and Derk had crafted a hidden step into the wall which could be slid out when necessary. He rested his arms on the worm-rotted banister, pistol dangling as he stared down at Speeler. He could see no obvious threat; the man's hands were empty though Clay knew he carried a small but deadly two-shot pistol in one of the numerous pockets of his heavy green-leather overcoat. Clay would have preferred to let the silence string out, forcing Speeler to spill his purpose in discomfort, but the effects of the Green were temporary. If he needed to act he would have to find out quickly.

'Don't remember issuing no invites, Speeler,' he said.

'And I apologise for the intrusion.' A brief flash of yellowed teeth revealed by a nervous smile. Despite the gloom Clay could see the sweat gleaming on Speeler's brow.

'So throw down your scrip,' Clay told him with an impatient flick of the revolver. He had known Speeler since childhood, an older boy who lived outside their pack but could be relied on to move their more expensive loot and supply the occasional drop or two of product. It had been Speeler who sold him the thimbleful of Black, asking no questions as was customary though it was safe odds he had guessed the purpose. And now here he was, somewhere he shouldn't be and more scared than Clay could remember seeing him.

'Come to cash in my scrip, in fact, Clay,' Speeler said. 'There's a debt twixt us. Need you to settle it, tonight.'

That he owed Speeler was true enough. It had been an ugly set-to with a dock-side crew a couple of years previously. They were all Dalcians, sailors kicked off their ships for sundry violations of company law and left with no means of living besides thievery. Desperation, combined with a tradition that prized male

aggression above all things, made confrontation with more established crews inevitable. They had ambushed Clay and Derk when
they were concluding a deal with Speeler amidst the convoluted
mass of chimney and tile where the Blinds bordered Artisan's
Row. The fat man had only two minders with him and the
Dalcians numbered ten, leaping across the roof-tops with all the
surety and speed of men accustomed to high places. It could have
gone badly but, for all their athleticism and skill with a cleaver,
the Dalcians enjoyed no immunity to bullets. Clay and Derk shot
down two and Speeler's minders another three. All but one had
fled, the biggest and therefore probably the leader, coming on
with all speed despite the blood flowing from the wound in his
gut. Clay had put his last round in the Dalcian as he got within
ten feet but it barely slowed him, leaping high with his cleaver
poised for a skull-splitting blow, then falling dead when Speeler
put two shots clean through his head.

'Tonight's inconvenient,' Clay said, disliking the necessity for
reluctance. In a society such as theirs an unsettled debt was a
considerable burden to carry, even for a man due to make his
way across the ocean in two days.

'Don't get done tonight then I will,' Speeler replied. 'Shipment
of Green and Red coming in. Corvantine stock, hence the need
for discretion and protection. Gave a commitment to the sellers,
but I'm a day late in assembling the necessary funds and they
ain't the most understanding folk.'

Corvantine stock, Clay mused. *Which means pirates. No wonder
he's nervous.* 'Where's your regular boys?' he asked.

'They'll be there, but given the awkwardness of the situation
thought I might need a little extra insurance.' He reached into
his overcoat, keeping his movements slow, and extracted a single
glass vial. 'Green.' He made an expert underarm throw, Clay
catching the vial as it came level with his chest. He removed the
vial's stopper for a sniff, nostrils flaring at the sharpness of the
scent. This was the best stuff he'd smelled in a long time.

'It's potent,' Speeler warned. 'Low dilution. Might want to hold off awhile, wait till you need it. Thought maybe you could keep over-watch. Things go bad you drink this and get me clear.'

'How much we talking?'

'Ten casks of Green, three Red.'

'My share?'

'Five percent. Once it's all sold on, o' course.'

'Ten. And I'll take it in product, equal parts Green and Red.'

'You owe me, Clay,' Speeler grated, genuine anger momentarily overriding his fear.

'If I didn't I'd already have said no. You threw down your scrip, now here's mine. Pick it up or be on your way.'

He held out the vial, ready to drop it, watching Speeler wrestle with the dilemma, his hands fidgeting and balding pate shinier than ever. *Whoever these pirates are, they got him scared enough to forego some profit.* The notion set him to wondering if he shouldn't raise his percentage to fifteen when Speeler huffed a groan and nodded.

'Bewler's Wharf,' he said. 'Two hours.'

'I'll be there.'

Clay turned to ascend the stairs, pausing when Speeler said something else, soft but sincere. 'Wouldn't have come lest my life was in the balance. You know that right?'

'Surely do,' Clay assured him with a small grin before pocketing the vial and turning back to the stairs.

Bewler's Wharf lay at the western extremity of the docks, a run-down and best-avoided stretch of quay afforded a faint sheen of respectability by the occasional berthing of an Alebond Commodities ship. However, by far the majority of vessels to call here were Independents, freelance Blue-hunters or tramp coal-burners for the most part and, every once in a while, a sleek but otherwise nondescript freighter of Corvantine design. Clay had seen her before, each time flying a different company flag and sporting a different name on her hull. But, like most in his profession Clay knew her true name well enough: *Windqueen*. Legend

THE WAKING FIRE · 39

had it she had been the pride of the Corvantine Imperial Merchant Service before falling afoul of pirates in the seas off Varestia, a region known as the Red Tides since the empire lost control of the peninsula nearly a century ago. What passed for government in Varestia had little inclination to strict observance of Company Law, meaning most pirate ships could come and go as they pleased and their crews were often drawn from the peninsula, olive-skinned folk of notoriously taciturn but quick-tempered nature.

Clay sat atop the roof of the Mariner's Rest, a tall if poorly maintained inn providing a clear view of the wharf, particularly the twenty square yards of cobbled quayside where business of this nature would most likely be conducted. The pirates were already in attendance, a half-dozen men and three women in seafarer's garb of dark cotton and sturdy boots. They were lined up in front of a tarp-covered wagon and Clay judged them a professional bunch from their spacing and the men on each flank sporting repeating carbines. The others all stood in silent vigilance, bristling with pistols and blades of varying sizes. He assumed the woman standing in the centre of their line to be the captain, or at least a senior mate trusted to conclude this transaction. She wasn't overly tall or physically imposing but had the quiet air of authority that came from command, her confidence no doubt enhanced by the brace of throwing knives about her waist and the shotgun strapped across her back.

He had come alone despite Derk's protestations. 'Are we not partners?' he had asked, his hurt tone only half-faked.

'Speeler's too scared for my liking,' Clay said, pulling his pistol's holster over his shoulder and strapping it tight. 'I may need to run, which case you won't be able to keep up. 'Sides' – he nodded at the bag containing their loot before casting a meaningful glance at Joya – 'someone's gotta watch our valuables.'

'If he's so scared you shouldn't go,' Joya said. 'Doesn't smell right, Clay.'

'It's the Blinds,' he said. 'Nothing smells right. Things'll smell sweeter in Feros, especially with a stash of quality product to sell.'

He had chosen a circuitous path, around the main Protectorate patrol routes and clear of the more territorial packs. On reaching the roof-top of the Mariner's Rest he sank onto his belly and crawled to the vantage point, wary of any betraying shadow from the two moons. Long experience had instilled in him a keen sense of punctuality and he got there early enough to witness the pirates arrive with their booty.

It was another quarter hour before Speeler turned up. He had four minders with him tonight, his regular companions Jesh and Mingus plus another two of similarly broad proportions. Clay watched them approach the pirates, the minders' eyes roving the shadowed quayside all the while. They halted a dozen feet from the woman, who duly inclined her head at Speeler's faintly heard greeting. She stood in cross-armed silence as Speeler kept talking, plump hands moving in placating gestures. He went on for a good few minutes before falling silent, clasping his hands together in tense expectation.

The woman stared at him for a long while then shrugged and turned to issue a curt order to her subordinates. A pair of burly pirates trundled the wagon forward, pulling back the tarp to reveal the casks beneath. The woman held out a hand to Speeler, inviting his inspection. The fat man made it brief, removing the stopper from two of the casks for a brief sniff of the contents before pronouncing himself satisfied and gesturing for Mingus to come forward. The minder slowly extracted a bulging wallet from his jacket and handed it to the woman. A suitably varied mix of corporate scrip and exchange notes, no doubt.

Clay saw it as the woman counted the notes. The effects of the few drops of Green had faded but the residue left an unnatural keenness to his sight, keen enough to see the surreptitious flicker of movement as one of Speeler's new minders reached into his jacket and came out with a revolver. It was a short-barrelled, black-enamel .35 Dessinger, standard issue to all Ironship Protectorate Covert Officers, meaning this night had just taken a decided turn for the worse.

It was all too quick for him to intervene, or even voice a warning shout. The Protectorate man aimed his revolver at the back of Speeler's head and pulled the trigger, blowing much of his face onto the pirate woman. The other minder was already firing, one shot each for Mingus and Jesh before they could even get a hand to their weapons. Clay scrambled back from the edge of the roof, fumbling for his vial of Green and expecting an eruption of gun-fire as the pirates sought to secure their wares and fight their way to the *Windqueen*. Instead, the outburst of violence was followed by a silence sufficiently unexpected to make him pause.

He raised himself up to risk a brief glance at the wharf, seeing the pirate woman wiping Speeler's gore from her face with evident annoyance but no sign of impending retribution. Also, her ship-mates were still standing in the same formation, none having drawn a blade or aimed a weapon. *Set-up,* Clay realised, watching the woman exchange a terse greeting with the man who had shot Speeler. *Walked into a trap with two Protectorate men at his back.* His gaze returned to the product-laden wagon. *A well-baited trap to be sure. Hard to resist, for him . . . or me.*

The suspicion grew as he scooted back, a growing under-standing of his predicament building to a certainty. *Sought me out and cashed in his scrip to get me here. Can't be a coincidence.* His thoughts flew quickly to Joya and Derk waiting at the church, unaware of the unfolding danger. He turned about, sitting up and throwing his head back to imbibe all the Green in a single swallow, his only hope of reaching them in time.

'That would be unwise, young man.'

She stood atop the inn's chimney, a woman of perhaps fifty with grey-streaked hair tied back in a tight bun, her slim form clad in black from head to toe. The expression with which she regarded him was severe, judgemental even, but also touched with a certain sympathy. *Got all the way up there without me hearing a thing,* Clay thought, the vial still poised at his lips. *Ironship Blood-blessed. And she'll have more than Green in her veins.*

It was hopeless, he knew it, he had no hope of matching her, even if he had all the product in that wagon at his disposal. But Joya and Derk were waiting, trusting him to return as they had for the last ten years. So far he'd never disappointed them.

'Don't!' the woman commanded as he tipped back the vial. The effect was as immediate as it was unexpected, the familiar tongue-burn drowned out by something far more acrid, something that tasted foul but flooded his belly with all the speed of the best product, sapping his strength in an instant of nausea. *Tainted,* he realised as the woman leapt down from the chimney, arms outstretched. *Tainted blood . . .*

He felt the woman's fingers brush his own, failing to get purchase as he tumbled from the roof, the nausea raging like fire in his gut. Then there was just the endless fall into the black.

CHAPTER 3

Hilemore

'Second Lieutenant Corrick Hilemore, reporting for duty and bearing dispatches, sir!'

Captain Trumane regarded his new officer with impassive grey eyes for several seconds, ignoring the documents held out for inspection. His gaze finally settled on the left epaulette of Hilemore's uniform, recently augmented with a single star of gold braid. 'Loose threads, Lieutenant,' he observed in a tone of predatory satisfaction, rich in the cultured tones of the North Mandinorian managerial class. 'Do you consider it appropriate to report to me in such a slovenly condition?'

'My apologies, sir. I received notice of my promotion only this morning, along with my orders. It appears I was less than diligent in amending my uniform.'

'Indeed you were. I shall forego a formal reprimand on this occasion but I will deduct a fine of five scrips from your sea pay.' Captain Trumane cocked his head ever so slightly, visibly scrutinising Hilemore's face for any sign of anger or dissatisfaction.

'Very good, sir,' Hilemore said in as neutral a tone as possible. He had met several officers like Trumane over the years and learned the folly of rising to their petty taunts. He did, however, permit himself an inner sigh of surprised exasperation at finding one of his type in command of an Ironship war vessel; martinets rarely rose high in the Maritime Protectorate; the rigours of life at sea and the demands of battle had a tendency to weed out the weak of character.

Trumane blinked and finally leaned forward in his seat to

take the documents from Hilemore's grasp. He gave no order to stand at ease so Hilemore was obliged to remain at rigid attention whilst his orders were scrutinised. The larger of the two envelopes bore a double seal, one in red wax and another in black indicating the contents were both strictly secret and required urgent attention. The smaller envelope contained Hilemore's particulars and confirmation of appointment as Second Mate to the Ironship Protectorate Vessel *Viable Opportunity*. He was surprised, therefore, when Captain Trumane opened the smaller envelope first.

'Hilemore,' he murmured after perusing the three-page letter. 'Would you be any relation to the Astrage Vale Hilemores, by any chance?'

'My cousin owns that estate, sir.'

'Hmm, your people are horse-breeders aren't they? Or some form of livestock trade, I can't remember.' He went on without waiting for an answer, 'These orders indicate your age as twenty-eight. Is that correct?'

'Yes, sir.'

'You are young to hold such a rank. Though you certainly appear older. Life at sea is rarely conducive to a youthful complexion.' He read further before issuing a soft laugh. 'Ah, promoted due to distinguished service during the recent Dalcian Emergency. Nothing like a good slaughter to reveal hidden talents. Tell me, how many of those slant-eyed swine did you get?'

Hilemore's memory abruptly clouded with the confusion and fury of that final battle with the Sovereignist fleet, their gunboats exploding one by one to the cheers of Protectorate sailors. The sea was calm that day but churned white and red by the thrashing of shipless Dalcians. *Riflemen to the rail,* came the captain's order. *An extra tot of grog for the first man to bag a dozen.*

'I didn't keep count, sir,' Hilemore told Trumane.

'Pity. Sorry to have missed it I must say. Refitting the *Viable* has occupied me for an inordinate length of time.' Trumane took his time reading the rest of Hilemore's orders. 'Appointment as Second Mate, eh? Your predecessor didn't leave much of an example to live up to, thirty years in the service and never got his own command. Would have cashiered the bugger for drunkenness if he hadn't been so close to his pension. You are familiar with the allotted duties of a Second Mate, I assume?'

'Yes, sir.'

'Which are?'

'Keeping of the payroll, oversight of ensigns, command of the ship's riflemen and boarding parties.'

'You have forgotten one particular duty, Mr Hilemore. Clearly you have never served aboard a blood-burner before.'

Hilemore managed not to flush in embarrassment. 'Of course, sir. My mistake. I am also responsible for the security and discipline of the ship's Blood-blessed.'

'Yes.' There was a faintly amused lilt to Trumane's voice as he tossed Hilemore's orders aside and reached for the second envelope. 'A task not to be envied on this ship. I'm afraid our Blood-blessed has a little too much in common with your predecessor, habits developed before my appointment I should add. He'll need taking in hand.'

'I'll see to it, sir.'

'Very well.' The captain reached for the envelope with the black seal and tore it open, Hilemore noting an anticipatory smile flicker on his lips as he read the contents.

'Report to Lieutenant Lemhill, the First Officer,' he said, glancing up from the orders. 'You'll find him on the bridge. The ship is to prepare to leave port immediately.'

Lieutenant Lemhill proved to be much more typical of a veteran officer than his captain. A stocky South Mandinorian with weathered features, his dark skin was marked by a pale crescent-shaped scar on his cheek. He was also at least ten years older than Trumane with a notably less cultured accent.

'Another northerner,' he said, scanning Hilemore's orders

briefly. 'The Maritime officer class has been going to shit ever since it started filling up with you pasty sods.' Lemhill's shrewd eyes examined Hilemore's face closely for a long moment, narrowing a little in recognition. 'Had a captain once,' he said. 'Name of Racksmith. An officer of great renown. Guessing you've heard of him.'

Hilemore gave a tight, controlled smile. There were times when bearing a close resemblance to a famous grandfather could be a singular trial. 'All my life, sir.'

Lemhill grunted, folding Hilemore's orders and consigning them to the pocket of his tunic. 'Broke your grandfather's heart when your mother married some managerial fop, I must say.'

It was a calculated insult. Lemhill, like Trumane, clearly had ways of testing the temper of new officers. 'My father,' Hilemore replied, 'was a fraud, an adulterer, an inveterate gambler and a drunkard. But, I must insist, sir, he was no fop.'

Lemhill's eyes betrayed a slight glimmer of amusement before he turned and barked over his shoulder. 'Mr Talmant!'

Next to the wheel a skinny youth in the ill-fitting uniform of a first-year ensign spun on his heels and snapped to attention. 'Aye, sir!'

'Enter Mr Hilemore's name in the ship's books, appointment as Second Mate confirmed and accepted. Date and time for my signature.'

'If I may, sir,' Hilemore said. 'Message from Captain Trumane, the ship will prepare to leave port.'

Lemhill's face betrayed only the faintest flicker of irritation. 'Our course?'

'As yet undetermined, sir. I arrived bearing dispatches from the Sea Board. Black seal.'

The First Officer issued a low, rumbling sigh as he turned away. 'Mr Talmant, when you're done with the books show Mr Hilemore to his quarters. Best if you acquaint him with Mr Tottleborn on the way.'

'Aye, sir.'

'Don't take too long getting settled, Lieutenant,' Lemhill told Hilemore, unhooking a chain holding two keys from his belt. 'I'm giving you the first watch.'

Midnight to seven o'clock. Traditionally it was an ensign's shift but Hilemore had been the new officer on enough ships by now to expect it, at least for the first few weeks. 'Thank you, sir,' he said, taking the keys. One was small, the kind typically used for cabinets or drawers, the other much larger with a complex series of teeth running along its sides.

'My pleasure, Mr Hilemore.' Lemhill turned and reached for the lanyard above the wheel, pulling it five times, the ship's steam-powered Klaxon blasting with every pull. *Five blasts,* Hilemore thought. *The signal for an imminent war cruise.*

Officially the *Viable Opportunity* belonged to the Sea Wolf class of fast cruisers, a line only recently discontinued in favour of the more heavily armed Eagle class. She was of typically sleek proportions with a low profile and the side-paddles in curving armoured casemates. However, as Hilemore followed the ensign from the bridge to the crew quarters, his practised eye picked out certain distinguishing modifications. The *Viable*'s stacks were positioned at a slightly more acute angle than her sister ships' and he saw an empty space where the forward secondary battery should have been. Also, the armour plating that normally clad the rails fore and aft of the paddles had been removed.

'The recent refit was extensive?' he asked Ensign Talmant.

'Indeed, sir,' the boy replied, casting an earnest smile at Hilemore over his shoulder. 'Eight weeks in dry-dock. New engines installed and a great deal of weight stripped out. All done under Captain Trumane's supervision. It seems she may now be the fastest cruiser in the fleet, sea trials permitting.'

'Your first ship, Mr Talmant?'

'Yes, sir. I was very lucky in the appointment. Fully expected to land in a coastal police boat, truth be told.'

Hilemore's mind immediately returned to the black-sealed envelope and the five blasts Lemhill had sounded. He couldn't help but wonder how lucky Mr Talmant would feel when their mission was revealed.

The ensign led him through a door into the mid-deck quarters where officers of the third tier in the ship's hierarchy made their home. 'Your cabin is at the port end, sir,' Talmant told him. 'This, however, is Mr Tottleborn's.' He stopped at a door halfway along the passage and raised a hand to knock, Hilemore noting a certain hesitation as he did so.

'Something wrong, Ensign?' Hilemore asked as the boy fidgeted.

'No, sir.' Talmant straightened his back and delivered three quick raps to the door. They waited for some seconds, hearing no stirrings from the cabin beyond. Talmant swallowed an embarrassed cough and tried again. This time the response was immediate, the words slurred and slightly muffled.

'Fucking fuck off! I'm ill!'

'Is it locked?' Hilemore asked Talmant, who tried the handle and nodded. 'Stand aside.'

'Sir, he's the . . .'

'I know what he is. Stand aside.'

The lock was sturdy but gave way at the second kick, Hilemore advancing into the cabin towards the unshaven sallow-faced man cowering amidst the blankets on his bunk. 'Second Lieutenant Corrick Hilemore,' he introduced himself, grabbing the man by his silk pyjamas and hauling him out of bed. The man whimpered as Hilemore forced him against the bulkhead, wincing at the outrush of gin-infused breath and the sickly odour of unwashed flesh.

'As of today I am Second Mate aboard this ship,' Hilemore informed the pyjama-clad man, 'and you are in my charge. Henceforth, when an officer of this vessel knocks on your door you will answer it with all alacrity. Whatever privilege my predecessor allowed you to imagine you enjoy is not my concern. You are a contract employee of the Ironship Maritime Protectorate, nothing more. I trust this is understood?'

'You can't hit me,' Tottleborn whined, shrinking back. 'I have an irregular heart beat and may die.' A small glimmer of defiance crept into his gaze. 'Then who will power the ship?'

Hilemore considered these words for a moment then jabbed his fore-knuckles into Tottleborn's rib-cage. 'There are some,' he said, releasing the man and letting him slide down the bulkhead to lie clutching his side, red-faced and gasping, 'who consider the Blood-blessed to hold some mystical, elevated status amongst the great mass of humanity. I'm told in the less civilised corners of the globe there are those who worship your kind with all the fervour the Church of the Seer afford the scriptures. A not unreasonable philosophy given your rarity. Why not see some divine favour in the fact that only one in every thousand of us is chosen to enjoy the gift contained in the blood of drakes?'

He crouched, leaning close to Tottleborn and speaking very clearly. 'I trust I have made my lack of sympathy with such attitudes plain, Mr Tottleborn. From now on, as dictated by Protectorate Regulations, the keys to the product cabinet and the liquor store will be held by me alone. You will fulfil every clause in your contract. I trust this is understood?'

He rose, staring down at the Blood-blessed until he gave a short nod. 'Very well.' He cast a disgusted glance around the cabin, taking in the sight of a score or more empty bottles amidst scattered papers and crushed cigarillo butts. 'Clean yourself up then restore these quarters to some semblance of decency. After that report to me in the engine room. We sail within the hour.'

Chief Engineer Bozware was only distinguishable as a North Mandinorian by virtue of his name and accent, his skin being so entirely covered in an amalgam of grease and soot as to make judging his ethnicity impossible. He waved impatiently as Hilemore stood at the hatchway, having followed custom and requested permission to enter. Hilemore and the Chief Engineer were technically of equal rank which required the observance of certain formalities.

'Just come and go as you please,' Bozware told Hilemore. 'Trust you'll have the good sense not to touch anything.'

'I wouldn't dare, Chief.' Hilemore's gaze tracked over Bozware's domain, finding that whatever his disregard for personal cleanliness it didn't extend to his engines. Most of the Chief's dozen-strong crew of sub-engineers were busy polishing every lever and bolt whilst two shovelled coal into the fire-box of the bulky auxiliary power plant squatting on the lower deck. Hilemore's gaze followed the steel rod rising from the top of the engine to the complex series of levers above, his attention inevitably drawn to the smaller and decidedly more elegant device resting in a cradle at the axis between the drive-shafts of the ship's two side-wheels. He had seen thermoplasmic engines before, mainly in diagrams, and had always been struck by their ingenious yet simple design. Looking closer at this one, however, he found it to be different, featuring some additional pipes and dials. Also, he saw a shiny new brass plate affixed to the water reservoir.

'Is that . . . ?' he began, turning to Bozware.

'A Mark Six,' he confirmed, a note of pride in his voice. 'First one to be fitted to any Protectorate vessel. New condensers and combustion chamber, co-designed by our very own captain and installed under his supervision. Overall efficiency increase of twenty-five percent, though I'm confident I can get her up to thirty before we're done.'

Twenty-five percent. Hilemore did some quick mental arithmetic. 'That would mean a top speed of . . .' He trailed off into a laugh, shaking his head.

'Thirty knots in fair weather,' Bozware finished, then gave a meaningful glance at the empty hatchway. 'Depending on the diligence of our Contractor, of course.'

'He'll be along,' Hilemore assured him. 'And I should appreciate it if you would report any future tardiness to me.'

'Glad to.'

The bridge communicator above Bozware's head emitted a sudden and insistent trill, the pointer moving to the red portion of the dial: start auxiliary engine. 'Best be about it,' Bozware said, moving the communicator's handle back and forth to acknowledge the order. He paused to glance at something beyond Hilemore's shoulder. 'Glad you could join us, Mr Tottleborn.'

Hilemore turned to see the Blood-blessed emerging from the hatchway, eyes red but considerably more alert than earlier. He had shaved before leaving his cabin and run a comb through his hair. As befitted his station he wore civilian clothes, a well-tailored waistcoat and shirt, though Hilemore frowned at finding his collar undone.

'Gets hot in here,' Tottleborn muttered, moving past him to climb the iron steps to his allotted station at the platform where the thermoplasmic engine awaited his attention.

'Be a good half-hour before we clear the harbour,' Bozware advised Hilemore. 'Safe to assume the captain will want to go to full steam once we're in open water.'

'I'll be back directly.' Hilemore moved to the hatch. 'One vial will suffice?'

'Best make it two. He's been waiting quite some time to see his pride and joy take flight.'

Coal smoke was already rising from the *Viable*'s stacks when Hilemore emerged onto the upper deck. Sailors were casting off the ties and from the stern came the rattle of heavy chains as the ship's anchor was hauled up. The paddles began turning as he climbed the gangway to the bridge, the ship's bow slowly drifting away from the quayside. Hilemore paused for a final look at Feros, his home for six dreary months. Ever since receiving Lewella's letter his mood had been dark, his days spent at the Sea Board in a grind of administration and inspections. Feros was a place of fine architecture, ancient culture and countless places where tourist or sailor alike could find all manner of gratifying entertainments. Hilemore had shunned it all, clinging to the daily schedule with monastic devotion, hoping to lose himself in labour, seeking distraction amongst endless reams of paper or hours spent drilling cadets on the parade-ground. Anything to prevent a bout of indulgent introspection, or a masochistic re-reading of her letter. *It is with the heaviest of hearts that I write these words, my dearest Corrick. Please do not hate me . . .*

'Is it your habit to dawdle before reporting to the bridge, Mr Hilemore?'

He turned, finding Captain Trumane standing at the hatchway, a certain amused satisfaction in his gaze. *A man engaged in a constant search for the weaknesses of others,* Hilemore decided. *Perhaps the means by which he maintains faith in his own superiority.*

'Chief Engineer Bozware's compliments, sir,' he said, this time opting not to offer an apology lest it become a habit. 'Mr Tottleborn is at his station and Mr Bozware suggests two vials.'

He saw a momentary indecision on Trumane's face, no doubt considering if insisting on some expression of contrition would appear undignified in front of a fully manned bridge. In the event his better judgement prevailed, though his voice retained a certain tightness as he replied, 'No, three vials if you please.'

Trumane's gaze went to the long shape of the *Consolidation*, now tracking across the *Viable*'s shifting bow. She was an undeniably impressive sight, a tri-wheel heavy cruiser with an additional paddle at the stern, bristling with batteries fore and aft, her decks crowded with sailors seeing to the endless chores arising from maintenance of such a large vessel. In addition to being the largest warship at berth in Feros harbour the *Consolidation* was also flagship of the Protectorate's South Seas Fleet and home to Vice-Commodore Semnale Norworth, Fleet Commander and the most renowned Protectorate officer of modern times. Hilemore could see no sign of the Commodore on the *Consolidation*'s bridge; in fact the *Viable*'s departure seemed to arouse little reaction from the other ships in the harbour, there being none of the usual polite signals of good luck or catcalls from idle deck-hands.

'We will be engaging the primary engine the instant we clear the harbour mole,' Trumane said, eyes still fixed on the indifferent bulk of the *Consolidation*. 'Tell Chief Bozware to spare nothing and make sure that sot Tottleborn doesn't nod off.'

'Aye, sir.'

'There will be a conference in my cabin at twenty-two hundred hours. Please endeavour not to be late. I strongly suggest you spend the intervening time drilling your riflemen.' The captain turned away, not bothering to return Hilemore's salute. 'Mr Lemhill, attend closely to your stop-watch, if you please. I shall require the most accurate measurements.'

The heavy, multi-toothed key turned easily in the lock, the safe's thick iron door swinging open to reveal its contents. The safe sat in the ship's armoury, requiring Hilemore to formally seek admission from the Master-at-Arms. He had concealed his surprise at finding the man to be an Islander, complete with an impressive stature and cruciform pattern of tattoos that tracked across his brow and along the length of his nose.

'Steelfine, sir!' The Master snapped to attention and delivered an impeccable salute. At six-foot-two Hilemore was accustomed to a certain height advantage in most meetings but on this occasion was obliged to look up to meet Steelfine's gaze.

Hilemore produced the key which the Master-at-Arms scrutinised for a moment before turning to the armoury. 'I will, of course, require you to witness this, Mr Steelfine,' Hilemore told him as the Islander's powerful hands worked keys in the three separate locks on the armoury door.

'Certainly, sir.'

'When I'm done in the engine room I intend to inspect the ship's riflemen. Please have them mustered on the fore-deck in full battle order.'

'Got fighting ahead of us, sir?' There was a definite note of anticipation in Steelfine's question, indicating that, regardless of his current status, his tribal origins hadn't been completely forgotten.

Hilemore glanced up at the Islander as he crouched in front of the safe. Senior non-commissioned officers were allowed a certain leeway, but there were limits. 'Our mission remains confidential until the captain chooses to disclose it.'

Steelfine straightened, face impassive once more. 'Of course, sir.'

Hilemore's gaze lingered on the product in the safe, arrayed in four shelves according to variant and contained in hardened leather flasks rather than glass so they wouldn't break in a heavy sea. The supply of Red was twice as much as had been available on his previous voyage aboard a blood-burner. But the stocks of other variants seemed thin, barely half of what he would have expected. 'When was this last replenished?' he asked Steelfine.

'Yesterday, sir. Noticed the shortfall, naturally. Green especially. Quartermaster says supply is thin all over and gets thinner by the year.'

Whilst the price gets ever fatter, Hilemore thought. 'It would be best if the crew remained untroubled by this,' he said. 'Doesn't help morale if they're given cause to grumble about a lack of Green aboard.'

'Indeed, sir. Mr Lemhill said the same thing.'

He returned to the engine room, where the series of levers that powered the drive-shafts rose and fell in a blur, giving rise to a rattling cacophony and thickening heat. Chief Bozware regarded the three vials of Red in Hilemore's hands with a grimace. 'Thought he might wait a while before testing her to her limits.'

'Problem, Chief?' Hilemore enquired.

Bozware replied with a grin, though it seemed a little forced. 'Best get him ready.' He nodded at the Blood-blessed. Tottleborn had seated himself on a folding chair next to the combustion chamber, apparently occupying himself with a pocket-sized periodical of vulgar content if the cover was anything to go by. *Kidnapped by Sovereignists!* the title exclaimed above a drawing of a milky-skinned and sparsely clad North Mandinorian woman recoiling in horror from a gang of leering Dalcians of bestial appearance. Tottleborn rose as Hilemore approached, offering no greeting save a churlish scowl.

'I trust your wits are fully recovered,' Hilemore said, handing him the first vial.

'Doesn't require wit,' Tottleborn replied, removing the stopper from the vial and emptying the contents into the induction port. 'A dog could do it if dogs received the Blessing.'

'But sadly, they do not.'

Tottleborn frowned at the pair of remaining vials. 'Three?'

'Captain's orders. Does it present a difficulty?'

Tottleborn shrugged and took the vials, quickly adding the contents of the second to the engine's blood reservoir and unstoppering the third. 'Not for me. Just never burned three at once before. I'm guessing this beast will really shift if the captain's new toy works as expected.'

'She may well be the fastest vessel afloat anywhere in the world.'

Tottleborn emptied all but a few drops from the third flask and stepped back. 'Does that mean I get a bonus?'

'I shouldn't have thought so.'

The bridge communicator issued another trilling alarm, quickly acknowledged by Chief Bozware. 'We're in open waters!' he reported, hands cupped around his mouth and voice barely audible over the tumult of the auxiliary engine. 'Time to light her up!'

Tottleborn raised the third vial to his lips and drank the remaining drops of Red. He stood for a moment, Hilemore reading the desire for retribution in the glower he turned on him. He met the Blood-blessed's gaze squarely, saying nothing.

'Best stand back if you don't want a scorching,' Tottleborn advised in a mutter, turning to the engine.

Hilemore took a generous backward step and watched as the Blood-blessed focused his gaze on the small open port in the side of the combustion chamber. For a second the air between

Tottleborn and the engine shimmered with heat, then the port snapped shut in automatic response to the rising temperature, the Red inside the chamber flaring into a briefly glimpsed inferno of near-blinding intensity. The pointer on the temperature dial immediately swung to the maximum position and the water reservoir began to emit a loud rumbling as its contents were fed into the chamber.

The tumult dimmed as Bozware took the auxiliary engine off-line, the numerous levers above slowing to a halt. Hilemore had always found true fascination in the workings of the thermoplasmic engine, but the comparative quietude of its operation remained perhaps its most unnerving aspect. No more than a combination of rushing water, hissing steam and turning gears, all suppressed to a low murmur. Despite that the energy being unleashed within this machine far outstripped any other device crafted by human hands.

'Sufficient power to take this ship two hundred miles,' Tottleborn commented as the primary engine's gears were engaged and the drive-shafts started to turn, slowly at first but soon revolving so fast they blurred. 'All derived from a measure of product that wouldn't even fill half an ale glass.'

And one that will only burn when set alight by one such as you, Hilemore added inwardly. 'Truly a miracle of our modern age, sir,' he told the Blood-blessed.

'A miracle that might be worth a celebration?'

'The liquor cabinet will remain locked for the time being. However, if you are in need of distraction, I will commence a daily exercise drill for the crew tomorrow. You are welcome to join.'

Tottleborn gave a heavy sigh and returned to his seat, opening his vulgar periodical once more. 'Thank you, but I have always preferred a more literary form of distraction.'

'Thirty-two knots!' Captain Trumane's fists thumped the chart table, his face flush with triumph. 'Even the great Commodore himself can't argue with that. You have the official record drawn up I assume, Mr Lemhill?'

'Aye, sir.' The First Mate nodded. 'Signed and witnessed, complete with diagrams as ordered.'

'Excellent. Mr Hilemore, please ensure the man Tottleborn is fully cognisant with the report. He will convey the contents in full during the next scheduled Blue-trance communication. When is that, incidentally?'

'Three days' time, sir. There is provision within the schedule for an early emergency communication. Though the window is very narrow, only sixty seconds per day and our Blue stocks are not copious.'

'No, let's allow the Commodore to stew over the results for a while,' Trumane said, then added in a mutter, 'Would have liked to see the puffed-up arse's face when he read it, though.'

'So it's official,' Lemhill said. 'We are now the fastest vessel on the seas.'

'Indeed we are,' agreed Trumane. 'And it appears the Sea Board has found suitable prey for their swiftest hunter.' He unfurled a chart on the table, Hilemore instantly recognising the north Arradsian coast and the dense, arcing cluster of fractured land-masses that comprised the Barrier Isles. 'Our course, gentlemen.' Trumane's finger traced the freshly drawn pencil line from Feros to a point some sixty miles east of the Strait.

'Tell me,' he said. 'Have you ever heard of the dread pirate vessel *Windqueen*?'

CHAPTER 4

Lizanne

It's different. Lizanne had taken her customary place at the prow
as the *Mutual Advantage* cleared the massive edifice of the outer
mole. Although nearly a century old the mole remained one of
the largest structures in the world, a seventy-foot-high wall of
granite that shielded Carvenport from the tides that had made
the first attempts at colonisation so difficult. At each two- or
three-moon tide the great copper doors would be lowered across
the harbour entrance to prevent the sea flooding the docks and
much of the town beyond. Lizanne's first experience of a three-
moon tide had left a sobering impression. The sight of the ocean
rising to within a yard of the top of the mole was an unnerving
reminder that, however permanent their presence on this continent might seem, civilisation could still be washed from these
shores in an instant.

She was joined at the prow by a throng of passengers, all
chattering in excitement as they passed beneath the huge green-
streaked wings of the raised doors and the full sweep of
Carvenport stood revealed. The city remained a remarkable testament to the colonial aspirations of the defunct Mandinorian
Empire, the product of a time before much of the world chose to
dispense with such fictions as monarchy or politics. Now, thanks
to this age where the rational pursuit of profit trumped archaic
attachments to flags and borders, Carvenport had blossomed into
a fully modern port that could rival even the great conurbations
of the northern continents.

Cranes and warehouses crowded the shore of the bowl-shaped

inlet where the port made its home, and beyond them the permanently smoke-shrouded vats and water-towers of the breeding pens. Farther in, close-packed slums were separated from more privileged neighbourhoods by tree-lined avenues that seemed to have gained some width in the intervening years. The buildings of the corporate quarter were taller now, all sharing a similar architectural style of low-angled roofs and high but narrow windows. Near by she heard one of the passengers waxing at length about the influence of a renowned but continually inebriated architect who had sought his fortune south of the Strait a decade before. Apparently he had designed over twenty buildings for three separate companies, earning considerable advances in the process which still weren't enough to settle his mountainous debts. Rumour had it he had slunk away on a north-bound steamer with a valise full of cash leaving his contracts unfulfilled, although his clients had clearly made considerable use of his designs. To Lizanne's eyes it seemed the talented drunk had left an impressive legacy.

Confidence, she decided, her eyes alighting on an abstract stained-glass window rising almost the complete height of a building flying the Briteshore Minerals flag. *That's what's different. Not just the size of it.* Carvenport was always rich, now it seemed to know what wealth meant in this world.

She arranged with the purser to have her luggage conveyed to the Academy and proceeded down the gangplank to the wharf. She skirted the milling gaggle of passengers seeking greeters or transport and made for the row of horse-drawn cabs at the junction of Queen's Row, the main thoroughfare into the heart of the city.

'Ironship House, miss?' the driver asked with a respectful nod at her Shareholder's pin.

'No, the Academy if you please. And I would prefer the more direct route.' She handed him five copper scrips to underline her meaning and climbed into the cab. The driver set off with a whistle at his horse, obediently making for the narrower streets bordering Bewler's Wharf. Lizanne noted some form of commotion taking place as they passed the wharf, a tall uniformed Inspector from the Protectorate Constabulary remonstrating loudly with a blocky man in cheap clothing whom she nevertheless immediately recognised as a Covert operative. The blocky man stood impassive and unresponsive as the Inspector railed at him, finger jabbing for emphasis. Beyond them, Lizanne could see steam billowing as an Independent freighter of Corvantine design churned her paddles to draw away from the quay. She could also see three lumpen white sheets lying on the cobbles, tell-tale splashes of red discolouring the cotton.

'Trouble here last night?' she asked the driver.

'Wouldn't know, miss,' he said. 'But this close to the Blinds, not a night goes by without some drama.'

The Blinds. She occupied herself with viewing the shabby, labyrinthine spectacle of Carvenport's largest slum as it passed by on her right. Her student days had seen numerous excursions here; Madame Bondersil had ever been assiduous in teaching her girls the twin values of disguise and a well-concealed weapon. *Over-reliance on your ingrained gifts can be deadly,* one of her favourite mantras. *Never forget, product is always finite.*

Lizanne caught a brief glimpse of the famous haunted church before they turned off into Artisan's Row. It seemed to have suffered a recent calamity, the steeple blackened to scorched ruin. *The Pale-Eyed Preacher strikes again,* she thought with a small grin, knowing full well such a myth would already be raging through every grimy alley and wine-shop. For all the poverty and violence she had witnessed here, she still retained a perverse fondness for the Blinds. Its outward appearance of chaos in fact concealed a place of rigid order, an established hierarchy enforcing rules with all the efficiency and ruthlessness of the Protectorate. Lizanne liked order; it was predictable whereas so much of her working life was not.

The cab proceeded along Artisan's Row with all its cacophonous workshops then into the neat lawns of Baldon Park where she abruptly decided to walk the rest of the way. She paid the driver the full fare and strolled towards the Academy amidst an occasional flurry of cherry blossoms. The park had been something of a refuge during her student days, a place for solitary reading beneath the trees and perhaps a small flirtation with one of the more interesting young men with sufficient nerve to approach her. She recalled her first serious dalliance had begun here. He had been a kind if overly serious type, as fond of books as she was, though his father, a Senior Manager at Ironship House, had eventually forced him into a junior accountancy position in Feros. It had been a slight thing, really, as short-lived and pleasing as these swirling blossoms in fact, but she had never entertained any delusions as to a shared future. Academy girls didn't marry, it was well known. He had ventured the possibility only once, after an exciting if inexpert interlude one Truminsday evening. They lay together amidst the trees bordering the park's lake, and she felt him tense as she regarded the dimming sky with a certain serene detachment. She knew he was about to say something final, something that would bring an end to these pleasant distractions. It was a little saddening but also inevitable. Madame Bondersil was always very frank about such matters.

'The Academy,' he had said, a slight stammer betraying his own awareness of the finality of the moment. But youth was ever the repository of hope. 'You don't have to . . . I mean to say, you could always leave.'

'Yes,' she had replied, getting to her feet. He rose with her and she shook the leaves from her hair before adjusting her uniform into a resemblance of acceptability. She caressed his face for a moment, smiling and planting a fond kiss on his lips. 'I could.'

She had walked away, feeling his eyes on her and not looking back. She didn't return to the park for several months and eventually discreet enquiries revealed his subsequent employment and marriage in Feros. It was odd that she had never encountered him there, telling herself it was due to her frequent absences or unfamiliarity with the more routine aspects of Syndicate business.

But there was a lingering guilty suspicion that she must have seen him, another anonymous face she had failed to recognise amongst the ranks of desk-bound number tickers.

Unlike the rest of the city the Academy seemed largely unchanged: a simple unadorned three-storey rectangular building with whitewashed walls surrounded by tall, wickedly spiked railings. The wrought-iron letters above the gate read: 'Ironship Syndicate Academy for Female Education,' a title that had always struck her as simultaneously dishonest and entirely factual. The guards at the gate stood aside with respectful touches to their caps as she approached, making no effort to enquire as to her business or confirm her identity. Clearly she was expected.

It being mid morn all the girls were at class and she made an uninterrupted progress through courtyard and corridor until she came to the winding staircase at the rear of the building. The other stairwells in the Academy led to the lecture halls and dormitories on the upper floors; this one however had but one destination. She paused at the foot of the stairs, awash in the memory of all the times she had stood here, the first looming by far the largest. She had been eight years old and recently arrived from Feros, shuffling and snuffling in solitary misery, unable to place her foot on the first step for fear of the great and terrible monster that waited above. A hand rested softly on her shoulder and she looked up to find a slim dark-haired woman regarding her with a raised eyebrow. She seemed to be of an age with Lizanne's Aunt Pendilla, which made her ancient in a child's eyes but she knew now she couldn't have been more than forty at the time.

'They told you she beats all the new girls, didn't they?' the woman asked, to which Lizanne gave a damp-eyed nod.

'Well.' The woman crouched to take her hand, the warmth of the contact somehow banishing Lizanne's fear and she followed without hesitation as the woman led her up the stairs. 'She's a bit of an ogre, it's true. But I think I may be able to talk her out of it. Just this once.'

Lizanne smiled at the memory as she climbed, remembering being guided to the office where the woman had taken a seat behind a large desk. Lizanne sat in an empty chair in front of the desk, legs dangling over the edge. 'I am Madame Lodima Bondersil,' the dark-haired woman said. 'Principal of this Academy. You are Lizanne Lethridge, my newest student.'

They had talked only briefly, Madame Bondersil explaining the Academy's rules and the correct conduct expected of a student. But in those few moments Lizanne's loneliness and homesickness faded to just a dull ache, one that would disappear completely over the coming weeks. Madame spoke with a surety and precision that dispelled childhood insecurity and in all the years that followed Lizanne never doubted for an instant that this was a place of safety and welcome. Even now the Academy felt like her only true home.

She found Madame engaged in the Blue-trance, sitting behind her desk in statue-like stillness, eyes open but unfocused, the pupils turned up and half-concealed. 'I'll fetch some tea,' Madame's secretary whispered, slipping from the room. Her caution was habitual rather than necessary. They could both have sung the Syndicate Anthem at the top of their lungs and Madame would not have stirred an inch. The Blue-trance was absolute and inviolate.

Lizanne took the seat in front of the desk, marvelling at how small it seemed now, before settling her gaze on Madame's face. *A few more lines,* she decided. *And she's thinner.* The innate strength was still there, however, in the straight-backed posture, impeccably neat hair and the plain dress of dark blue cotton adorned only by her Shareholder's pin. Lizanne smiled and allowed her gaze to wander, settling, as it often had, on the framed sketch hanging on the wall to the left. Besides the obligatory painting of the *Adventurous* on the opposite wall, the sketch was the only piece of art in the room. It had been rendered with great skill, so precisely in fact it first appeared to be a photostat and only on closer inspection were the pencil lines revealed. It depicted a dark-haired, oval-faced girl who seemed to be no older than sixteen, although Lizanne knew she had been nineteen when the drawing was made. She looked out from the frame with a half smile and a keen glint in her eye, the expression of a curious and confident young woman. *Too curious,* Lizanne decided, although she had never in fact met this girl. *And far too confident.*

'You remind me of her, sometimes.'

Lizanne's gaze snapped to Madame Bondersil, now fully returned from the trance and regarding her with an expectant expression. *She always was a stickler for formality.* Lizanne got to her feet and gave a precise curtsy. 'Madame. Miss Lizanne Lethridge of the Exceptional Initiatives Division reporting on the instructions of the Board, as per your request.'

'Welcome, Miss Lethridge. Please accept my congratulations on your recent elevation.'

'Thank you, Madame. It was as welcome as it was unexpected.'

'I doubt that. Would you care to enlighten me as to the circumstances of your promotion? A successful and profitable excursion to dangerous and exotic climes, no doubt.'

'I am employed as an experimental plasmologist, Madame. As you know. I have had no occasion to leave Feros in the past seven years nor would I be at leave to discuss such an excursion had it ever taken place.'

Madame Bondersil's mouth gave the barest twitch as she inclined her head. 'It's very good to see you again, Lizanne. Ah, tea, what perfect timing. We'll take it on the veranda.'

The veranda offered a fine view of Carvenport all the way down to the harbour, with the breeding pens forming a central point of focus. It was clearly a birthing day judging by the thickening pall of smoke rising above the vats. Lizanne averted her gaze, preferring to watch the ships in harbour. In all her years here she had only toured the pens once and had found that single visit more than sufficient. A strong stomach was a requirement of her occupation, but even she had limits. It had been the birthing more than anything else that unsettled her. The nesting drakes would breathe fire on their eggs, the waking fire, the harvesters called it. The eggs would blacken at first, then a glow would appear inside as the gases contained within took light before exploding. When the smoke cleared the harvesters would immediately scoop up the small squawking infant before their mother could begin to lick away the soot. Hardened as she was by both education and profession, Lizanne still found the screams of both mother and infant capable of sending an icy spike through her heart.

'How do you like the tea?' Madame Bondersil asked, sipping from her own cup.

'Pleasing,' Lizanne said. 'If a little unusual. A slight floral aftertaste, I find.'

'Indeed. They call it Green Pearl, the only variety ever successfully grown on Arradsian soil. Of course the Syndicate was quick to purchase the patent and ensure only the most limited supply is harvested. Can you imagine what a collapse of tea imports would do to local profits?'

'A sobering thought indeed, Madame.'

'Your journey was appropriately comfortable, I trust.'

'For the most part. I am afraid I must report a . . . regrettable necessity.' She related a carefully edited version of events surrounding the demise of the unfortunate Mr Redsel. From Madame's occasional raised eyebrow she deduced a certain awareness of the obfuscation but thankfully was spared any embarrassing questions.

'The body?' Madame asked instead when Lizanne had finished.

'Consigned to the sea the very next day. It doesn't do to keep a corpse aboard ship for any length of time. Mrs Jackmore made quite a scene, I must say.'

'And you're certain he wasn't Cadre?'

If he had been it may well have been my body they tossed over the side. 'As certain as I can be.'

'All very troubling but, sadly, not unexpected. It seems the

Corvantines have either divined our intent or are perilously close to doing so.'

'In which case, Madame, they have the advantage over me.'

'The Board told you nothing about your mission on my advice. If this Mr Redsel had succeeded our efforts would already be undone. Although, the fact that he knew your true status does cast your further involvement in some doubt.'

'I'm not sure he did fully appreciate my abilities, or know of my specialism. I believe he had been expecting a less worldly or formidable target. The Corvantines undoubtedly know of my promotion and family history. It could be they learned of my impending return to Carvenport and saw an opportunity to monitor our communications.'

'All excessively coincidental for my liking. Though they were lax in choosing an Independent for this mission. Another sign of the malaise infecting their empire. It's like a sick old dog that refuses to die. Always they strive to take back what they lost to us. You would imagine that after a century of decline they would have the decency to follow the example of the old Mandinorian royal idiots and exchange their land and privileges for company shares. But no, they cling on to ancient monarchical fantasies, revelling in their pantomime of aristocracy as if it still means anything in an age such as this.'

'Do you have any notion of who his contact might be? This Truelove?'

Madame Bondersil gave the smallest of wry laughs. 'The Imperial Cadre currently operates a dozen agents in this port, that we know of. It would be a sound wager that Truelove will be amongst the dozen or more we know nothing about.'

'Redsel presented himself as a dealer in antiquities. An avenue of inquiry perhaps?'

Madame Bondersil thought for a moment, lips pursed in apparent consternation. 'Perhaps,' she conceded. 'But also another unpleasant coincidence.'

'Madame?'

The older woman merely blinked before getting to her feet. 'Come, I have something to show you.'

They took a Syndicate carriage to Artisan's Row, pulling up outside a small but familiar workshop nestled between a foundry on one side and a gunsmith's on the other. The faded and flaking sign above the door read 'Tollermine and Son – Bespoke Technologists for Over Sixty Years.' Madame told the driver to wait and proceeded inside without pausing to ring the bell suspended beneath an equally faded sign reading 'Secure Premises – Entry by Appointment Only.'

They found no-one to greet them in the shop's front office, a cramped space of many shelves and drawers overflowing with various mechanical trinkets, apparently stored without reference to function or size. They were obliged to pause before the door at the rear of the office whilst a small optical device above the lintel swivelled first towards Lizanne then to Madame Bondersil. The door opened a second later, Lizanne smiling at the familiar aroma that wafted forth. Oil, pipe-smoke and a dozen unnamable chemicals combined into a mixture which somehow carried a sense of cosy welcome. She had always loved her visits here.

The door swung wide to reveal a dumpy man of middling years in a knee-length leather apron and an oversized revolver in his hand. 'Sorry,' he said, waving the pistol. 'Can't be too careful.'

Lizanne laughed and rushed forward to greet him with a tight hug, uncaring of the grease on his apron, planting a kiss on his bald pate as he only stood as high as her chest. 'Hello, Jermayah!'

'Mr Tollermine to you,' he gruffed, though she noted he paused long enough to return the hug before moving away. 'Guessing you want me to show her?' he asked Madame.

'Indeed, Mr Tollermine,' she replied. 'The associated documents too.'

'Come on then.' He beckoned to them with the revolver, stomping off into the workshop's cavernous interior which stood in stark contrast to the cramped outer edifice. Lizanne felt oddly gratified by the fact that the space didn't appear to have shrunk in her absence. As a child it had seemed a cave of treasures, making her laugh as she scampered from one mysterious mechanical wonder to another. The Syndicate operated its own repair shops and manufactories but there were times when Exceptional Initiatives had need of more novel devices, to be crafted and maintained beyond the sight of competitors or Imperial agents. During her tenure at the Academy, only Lizanne had been given the privilege of coming here once every week to be educated in the basics of engineering and the more obscure aspects of chemistry. She had been quick to ask why, of course, being of a somewhat aggravatingly keen mind even at a young age. Jermayah had just shrugged and said, 'Can't steal this stuff if you don't know what it is.'

He led them through the rows of mechanicals, some familiar but others of such esoteric design as to baffle even Lizanne's educated eye. She drew up short, however, at the sight of a squat, four-wheeled carriage with a bulbous collection of pipe-work and valves fitted between the driver's seat and the front axle. 'You're still working on it?' she asked Jermayah with a faintly incredulous laugh.

His expression darkened into a scowl as he glanced over his shoulder. 'Nearly done,' he muttered.

'It was nearly done seven years ago,' Lizanne said, as unable to resist taunting him as ever.

'Change the world it will,' came the growling response. 'Plasmothermic-driven carriages are the future.'

'Does the main reservoir still melt every time you activate the flow?'

'No,' came the sullen and defensive reply before he added in a softer tone, 'Engine's still too heavy. Won't move more than a few yards before the drive-shaft seizes.'

'If only you would allow me to share your designs with my father . . .'

'Miss Lethridge!' Madame Bondersil cut in sharply. 'I trust you require no reminder that Mr Tollermine is under exclusive lifetime contract to the Ironship Trading Syndicate, as indeed are you. Whilst your esteemed father has, in the most intemperate terms, rebuffed every contractual approach made by our company.'

'Quite so, Madame.' Lizanne concealed a smile as they came to the solid oaken work-bench where Jermayah spent the bulk of his time. It was usually piled high with tools and various components but today stood empty but for a leather document case and a polished wooden box perhaps ten inches square.

'You were expecting our visit, I see,' Madame Bondersil observed.

'Knew this one was back today.' Jermayah jerked his head at Lizanne as he approached the box, resting a hand on the lid. 'Guessing her mission wasn't 'specially difficult.'

'A moment, please,' Madame said as Jermayah began to lift the lid. She turned to Lizanne, gesturing at the box. 'Tell me what you see.'

Lizanne moved to the box as Jermayah stood back, her practised gaze drinking in every detail in a few seconds. It had been fashioned from redwood, one of the darker varieties, varnished and clearly old. *Fine work,* she decided, noting the near-invisible joins at the corners. *None of Mr Redsel's fakery here.* Her gaze narrowed a little as it traced over the lid and the intricate gold inlaid letters, an archaic flowing script in a language not spoken in any company holding.

'Corvantine,' she told Madame. 'Late Third Imperium. Most likely crafted in the port of Valazin at least a century and a half ago.'

'And the letters?'

'Eutherian, the language only spoken by the elite, or the highly educated.' Lizanne took a moment to formulate a reasonable translation whereupon her gaze snapped to Madame's, finding it met with calm resolve. Lizanne's mind immediately returned to the sketch in her office: Madame's most favoured pupil lost nearly two decades ago in pursuit of the impossible. 'Have you brought me here to chase legends, Madame?'

Madame Bondersil gave one of her rare smiles, not just a faint flicker of amusement this time, but an expression of genuine and warm appreciation. 'I brought you here,' she said, 'so that we might secure the future of our company by making the greatest discovery since civilised people first stepped onto these shores. Open the box, Lizanne.'

She sighed in strained amusement as she lifted the lid and revealed what lay inside. *Empty. Of course.* 'I must say this makes for a poor clue,' she said.

'Look closer,' Madame insisted.

Lizanne did as she was bid, peering at the unvarnished interior of the box, seeing only aged wood for the most part although she did detect some faint marks on the base, jagged circles intersected by narrow lines. 'Gears?' she asked Jermayah, who nodded.

'Shadows of gears,' he said. 'Someone left the lid open long enough for the sun to leave us an impression.' He undid the binds on the leather document case and extracted a drawing. It had been set down on thin paper and covered near a quarter of the work-bench when unfolded.

'Your work, I assume?' Lizanne asked, eyes tracking over the precise lines and cogs, each numbered and described in Jermayah's neat script. The mechanics were mostly lost on her. She knew a great deal but the workings of this device were best left to the technologist's eye. The words, however, were a different matter. 'Serphia,' she murmured, reading the note next to one of the smaller cogs before moving on to its slightly larger neighbour. 'Morvia.' It took a moment before she found their sister, though it was only partially complete, just twenty degrees of a circle larger still than the other two. 'Nelphia.'

She moved back from the bench, frowning as she turned to Jermayah. 'The three moons. How can you be sure?'

'Simple arithmetic. The diameter of this one,' he pointed to Nelphia's cog, 'is larger than this one,' he tapped Morvia, 'by a factor of 1.214. Which in turn is larger than the diameter of Serphia by a factor of 1.448. An exact correlation to the values of their respective orbits.'

'An orrery,' Lizanne realised.

'Quite so,' Madame Bondersil said. 'Though the Corvantines call it a solargraph. A device for precisely measuring the varied orbits of the bodies swirling about our sun, once contained within a box marked with the words "The Path to the White Drake." I assume you see the import of this?'

Lizanne gently closed the lid and traced her fingers over the letters. 'I'm afraid your translation is a little too literal, Madame. The inscription is in fact a quotation from one of the classics of Corvantine literature, a partly comic tome entitled *The Many Misadventures of Silona Akiv Cevokas*. Cevokas is widely believed to have been inspired by a Corvantine scholar from the Third Imperium, possessed of all manner of wild notions who bankrupted himself with successive expeditions to various corners of the globe until, perhaps inevitably, he was drawn to Arradsia and the fabled, always elusive White Drake. The final chapter sees him succumbing to madness somewhere in the southern highlands, all his companions having died or abandoned him during the journey. He resolves to carve an entire mountain into his own White so it can carry him home. The final paragraph sees him happily chiselling away whilst a White creeps up behind him, though by then he's too mad to notice.'

'And the inscription?' Madame asked.

'"'Ware the path of the White Drake,"' Lizanne replied. 'Though it's missing the final line: "for madness is its only reward." Still a popular saying in some Corvantine circles, mostly heard when one is considering a risky business venture.'

She turned to Jermayah. 'I assume you've attempted to recreate it?'

He shook his head. 'There's no point. Too many parts missing.'

'May I enquire where this box came from?' she asked Madame.

'Morsvale,' she replied.

The only sizable Corvantine enclave on Arradsia, Lizanne thought, her mind quickly formulating the likely purpose of her mission. 'Where you will require me to go in search of the missing contents.'

'Indeed.' Madame spoke in a flat tone, free from any suggestion of flexibility. Whilst Lizanne's contract allowed some leeway in accepting commissions from senior executives, there were those she couldn't refuse.

'Well,' she said, 'it's preferable to the alternative. For a moment I harboured the terrible suspicion you were about to order me on some mad Interior excursion.'

'No, that aspect of the mission will be left to more appropriate hands.'

'You intend to send an expedition even though the clue promised by this box has not yet been found?'

'Time is our enemy, Lizanne. Your recent encounter aboard ship underlines the urgency very clearly.'

'And where are they to go? We have no confirmation this thing exists . . .'

'That, as you know, is not true.'

Lizanne suppressed an exasperated sigh. 'She died, Madame. I know it pains you to think it, but Ethelynne Drystone perished with the Wittler Expedition.'

'They found no body . . .'

'And only the scattered bones of the others, and no trace of the White skeleton she spoke of.'

Madame paused, glancing at Jermayah. 'Could you leave us a moment please, Mr Tollermine.'

'Stop by again before you leave,' the technologist told Lizanne before disappearing into the shadowed depths of his workshop. 'Got new toys for you.'

Madame waited until Jermayah's footsteps had faded before speaking again. 'You never read my full report on the Wittler Expedition, did you?'

'It remains sealed by the Board.'

'They didn't just find a skeleton. Ethelynne recovered an egg. I saw it clearly through the trance.'

The egg of a White Drake. Undoubtedly the most valuable object in the world, should it actually exist. 'The trance can be confusing,' she said. 'A lesson you taught me long ago. The trance touches our dreams, our hearts. Sometimes it shows us lies we wish to be true.'

'You think I wanted her to find that thing?' Madame spoke quietly but with a heat Lizanne had rarely heard. 'You think I wanted to see her like that, feel her fear, her desperation? She found an egg. The others died, killing each other thanks to some maddening infection released when their harvester powdered one of the White's bones. But Ethelynne lived, and she took that egg with her.'

'The location of which you expect to be revealed by a Corvantine novelty fashioned more than a hundred years ago?'

'If it leads us to the nesting grounds of the White Drake, it may well lead us to Ethelynne. She was always a very curious soul and, even if the Whites all perished long ago, there is a chance she would seek their place of origin.'

A girl of nineteen, lost and alone in a continent of jungle and desert liberally seeded with wild drakes and Spoiled tribes for nigh-on thirty years. Blood-blessed or not, the odds of her survival seemed astronomical, and yet Madame would not let go her hope. 'The Red Sands,' she told Lizanne. 'We have contracted a company to journey there and retrieve what evidence remains of the Wittler Expedition. By the time they have done so it is my hope your investigations in Morsvale will have revealed further intelligence to aid their hunt. The box was sold at auction six months ago, purchased by one of our agents, who has not been in contact for the past seven weeks. We have to assume the Cadre knows we are in possession of it. Documents relating to its prior ownership indicate it was owned by one Burgrave Leonis Akiv Artonin, a minor aristocrat with scholarly leanings. He will be your starting point.'

'I assume it is your intention to accompany the expedition and have me relate this intelligence to you via the trance.'

'No.' Madame stood a little straighter, a small twitch of annoyance passing across her face. 'That was my original intent, however the Board were swift in forbidding it. Another Blood-blessed will travel with the expedition. You will communicate your findings to them.'

'Given your well-justified concerns about the security of this enterprise it will need to be an unregistered agent, someone as yet unknown to the Cadre and therefore capable of trancing without fear of interception. Employing such a person would be a serious breach of corporate law, not to say extremely hard to find.'

'Since when is the tedium of corporate law of such concern to you, Lizanne?' Madame Bondersil gave another smile, this one much more in character due to its facility for conveying a sense of greatly superior knowledge. 'And as to the difficulties of recruitment, I'm happy to report that we found a suitable candidate only last night.'

CHAPTER 5

Clay

He dreamed about the time he'd first found Derk and Joya, two scared kids huddled together amidst the stink and dross of Staker's Alley. Clay had dropped into the alley from the roof-top, panting a little and clutching a bag of freshly stolen preserves, six full jars of pickled herring and two of plum jam. It was raining that day, as it usually did in late Vorellum. Clay liked the rain; it frustrated any pursuers and made them more likely to give up. The store-keeper had chased him for two streets, blowing hard on his whistle to draw the Protectorate, but the sharp urgent blasts tailed off when he saw Clay scale a wall and skip across the roof-tops into the Blinds. He hadn't even needed to swallow the drop of Green in his flask.

It was the girl's eyes that made him pause, so bright in the shadows. Not fearful either, just wide and curious. Her brother was older and smarter, hissing at her to look away. 'We didn't see you,' he promised Clay as he stepped closer. Whilst it was the girl's eyes that drew his gaze it was the boy's voice that made him linger. Cultured vowels free of any trace of the Blinds. The kind of voice Clay heard on his infrequent forays into Carvenport's more salubrious districts.

'You shouldn't be here,' he had said.

The boy tensed, shuffling forward so his sister was partly shielded, staring up with wary defiance. 'And where, sir, should we be, pray tell?'

The sheer incongruity of it all drew a laugh from Clay, one which faded when he saw the hollowness of the girl's cheeks below her too-bright eyes. 'Anywhere but here,' he said, crouching to open the bag. He drew out one of the herring jars and held it out to the boy, who stopped himself snatching it immediately, wariness mingling with hope.

'We have no money,' he said.

'I believe you.' Clay pushed the jar at him and the boy took it, quickly passing it to his sister.

'You read, right?' Clay asked the boy. 'Way you talk and all. Gotta know how to read.'

The boy's head moved in a jerking nod. 'I can read.'

Clay smiled. 'I can't. But I'm a fast learner.' He frowned at a sudden tinkling, looking up to see the girl tapping a pin against the glass jar. It was small and silver, one end shaped into a drake's head, moving with an oddly familiar rhythm. Slow, steady but insistent, growing in volume until it seemed the girl was striking a hammer against a bell. He gave a shout of alarm as the jar came apart in her hand, cutting her flesh, red flashing amidst the explosion of fish and vinegar . . .

He came awake with a gasp, seeing only striped shadows and moonlight on bare stone. His mind raced through recent memory seeking answers. *Speeler dying at the wharf . . . The woman, the Ironship Blood-blessed standing atop the chimney . . . Then the fall.* After that nothing, just the dream and the sharp, rhythmic tapping which, he realised, still hadn't stopped. But the sound had changed, no longer the tinkle of metal on glass, now it was metal on metal.

His eyes found the source quickly, making him growl in confusion. Moonlight streamed through a narrow slit in the wall above Clay's bunk, the drake's head catching it with every tap of its snout against the bars, not a pin now though. Now it was the ornate silver head of a walking cane. Clay suppressed a groan of realisation and swung his legs off the bunk, sitting up to regard the shadowy figure on the other side of the bars.

The tapping stopped and the figure moved to a stool, sitting down just beyond arm's reach of the bars. He rested a hand on his cane, long-nailed fingers flexing, and sat in silence for some time. He hadn't removed his broad-brimmed hat so his face was just a blank void, unseen lips forming a softly spoken question. 'Do you know why you are here?'

Clay resisted the impulse to rub at his aching back. He didn't appear to have suffered any broken bones but from the feel of it he hadn't had a soft landing either. 'Yes, Keyvine,' he replied, eyes scanning the cell for any loose object. A nail, a splinter. Anything that might serve as a weapon. His gaze found a waste bucket next to the bunk, but it was secured to the wall on a short chain. 'I know why I'm here.'

'Really?' Like most people Clay had rarely heard Keyvine's voice, just a snatched word or two over the years. It had always seemed accentless, not cultured like Derk's, more deliberately anonymous, free of anything that might betray an origin or prior allegiance. It was also dry of any emotion, every word spoken without inflection. Now, however, Clay detected a certain amused lilt to it. 'Enlighten me.'

'You're about to tell me Cralmoor was like a son to you,' Clay said, abandoning his search for a weapon as the cell was clearly too well kept. 'Now he can't talk right, thanks to me.'

'He'll be talking soon enough. Hefty dose of Green to take care of any infecting humours and an expensive surgeon saw to that. Cralmoor is a valued employee, deserving of my largess. He is not my son. I didn't take your transgression personally, Mr Torcreek. I wanted you to know that. However, the nature of our business leaves no room for compromise.'

Clay ground his teeth together, knowing the question was tantamount to begging but he had to know. 'Derk and Joya?'

'Ah, yes. The sibling outcasts from the managerial class. I always admired your protective attitude to them, though I'm sure the relationship had mutual benefits.'

They're my friends. He didn't say it. The sentiment would mean nothing to Keyvine. 'Kept tabs on us, huh?'

'Should a king not know his kingdom? Have a care for all his subjects? I've had my kingly eye on you for quite some time. I did briefly consider taking you into my court, but it soon became apparent you had developed far too much ambition. In time you would have been the Zorrin to my Mayberus.'

Clay dimly recalled the reference, a play Derk had quoted from time to time. Mayberus had been some Corvantine emperor from long ago, betrayed by his adopted son Zorrin, an orphan from the peasant caste. *A cautionary tale,* Derk called it. *Those who would rule should not get too close to the ruled.*

'You were right,' he told Keyvine, the old jealousy flaring once more though it was soon replaced with something else, guilt and shame burning worse than envy ever had. 'It was my scheme,' he said. 'They didn't want to . . .'

'But you made them. How noble. But the transgression is too great, Mr Torcreek. You knew that, and so did they. You all knew the price should you fail to make the boat to Feros. Which brings us to my original question: do you know why you are here?'

Clay glanced around the cell and the space beyond the bars: a short corridor leading to a solid door, braced in iron. It was all too orderly and well-built a place to be one of Keyvine's dens. 'This is a Protectorate cell,' he said. 'Guess they got to me before you could. But you knew who to bribe to get in here.'

Keyvine got to his feet and came close to the bars, making Clay tense in anticipation though he strove to maintain the same slumped posture. *Well within reach. I'll need to be quick.*

'Oh no,' said the King of Blades and Whores. 'You are here because your uncle begged for your life.'

'My uncle,' Clay said, 'wouldn't piss on my burning corpse.'

'It seems he finds some value in you. There's a long-standing debt twixt us, you see. A debt I've been keen to repay for quite some time. So when your sad little scheme came to light I must say I seized on the opportunity and let him know of your imminent fate. He did seem reluctant to intervene at first but he became markedly more interested once I mentioned your true nature. It was clumsy and obvious of you to try using Black in one of my fights. Do you imagine I don't know the signs? Quite a secret to keep for such a long time, from family as well as company interests. Luckily your uncle's contacts in the Protectorate were able to contrive a suitably enticing trap, with my help, of course.'

Keyvine leaned his head closer to the bars and Clay caught the gleam of his eye in the shadow beneath the hat, unblinking and steady. 'Judging by your age I'd guess you owe your unregistered status to the day the Black got loose. Lot of confusion that day, easy to miss another screaming child amidst the chaos. Did it kill your parents?'

Just my mother. Clay closed his eyes against the memory. *Ma standing with her hand on his shoulder as he waited his turn for the Blood-lot. 'Be brave, Claydon. It'll be just a little burn, that's all.' Then everything was screams and flames and blood . . . Ma lying amidst the blood, eyes open and a ragged red gap where her belly should be. Around him people screamed and writhed as the drake blood rained down in a fine mist. Not him though; on him the red vapour left just small specks of white on his skin. He ran. Ran and ran, all the way to his uncle's house, and that proved only a temporary refuge.*

'If my uncle saved me it's for a reason,' he told Keyvine, staring into the one gleaming eye.

'Yes. I expect your unregistered status may have something to do with it. It's why poor old Speeler had to die, you see? A secret loses value with every memory that carries it.'

'How'd you get him to sell me out?'

'Speeler had a long-term male companion. Charming fellow but with expensive tastes, hence Speeler's tireless work ethic. A few cuts to the right places and he was more than co—'

Clay lunged, putting every ounce of strength and speed into his legs, ignoring the flare of agony from already strained muscles. He nearly did it, his hand brushing through Keyvine's braided hair as the King of Blades and Whores twisted aside with less than an inch to spare. Something flashed in the gloom and Clay felt the cold chill of a very sharp blade against his neck. He froze, standing with his arm still clutching at thin air whilst Keyvine stood with his bared sword-cane protruding through the bars, poised to sever Clay's jugular with the smallest flick.

'What are you?' Keyvine asked, voice soft, almost contemplative and free of anger. 'Without product in your veins, what are you? Just another piss-alley thief, albeit with an important uncle.'

Clay suppressed a grunt as the sword-cane pressed deeper, feeling the sting of the cut and a small drop of blood trickle down his neck. 'They burned, Clay,' Keyvine told him. 'The boy and his sister. More precisely, I burned them in that rotting old church. If you stop by there again one day maybe you'll see them haunting away with the Pale-Eyed Preacher.'

He angled his head so the moonlight from the single window caught his face. Clay had only seen it once before, just a glimpse one night at the Colonials Rest, a flash of something from a nightmare. The burn covered half his face, the flesh mottled and puckered from throat to forehead, the pigment dimmed by the gloom but Clay knew it to be a motley collage of red and pink. Drake's Kiss, it was called, the burn that could only result from drake fire.

'I know fire,' Keyvine went on. 'I even like fire. You could say I was born in it and in doing so learned the greatest of lessons: there is no pain that cannot be endured and survived, no obstacle that cannot be overcome. All that is required is the will to succeed, a will that allows for no distractions. You should think on that when you're off contracting with your uncle. Find me when you return, for I sense a new debt between you and me and I so detest an unbalanced scale.'

He was woken by the sound of a key working the lock on the heavy iron door. He didn't rise from the bunk, turning onto his side and blinking his bleary eyes until they found focus on the brickwork. The voice that greeted him was familiar and expected, also deep with impatient resentment. 'On your feet.'

Clay waited a good while before rolling onto his back, gazing up at the flaking plaster on the ceiling. His sleep had been fitful, richly populated by Derk's and Joya's faces, laughing sometimes, mocking at others. But mostly just burned and dead. And Keyvine. Keyvine had been there too.

'I said, get up!' the voice said with growling deliberation. 'Lest you're keen to spend the next year in here before the Protectorate decides whether to kill you or cut you open.'

Clay groaned and sat up. It was daylight now, somewhere past mid morn judging by the angle of the shadows. A tall man stood on the other side of the bars. He wore the green-leather duster and wide-brimmed hat typical of the Contractor fraternity, his hair hanging in thick braids down to his shoulders. It had been nearly two years since their last meeting but Clay still felt the same jarring disorientation when looking at his face. There were a few more lines on the forehead and the stubble on his chin was mostly grey, but the resemblance remained. *They could have been twins.*

'You gonna stare at me all day, boy?' the man demanded. 'Off your backside, we got work.'

'Since when d'you have work for me?' Clay asked.

The man angled his head, eyes narrowing with the same angry judgement he had exhibited all those years ago when Clay shambled into his home with a recently emptied pistol in hand. 'Since it turned out you were actually useful,' the man said, stepping back to jerk his head at a second man standing near the open door. Clay's pulse quickened as he recognised him as the un-uniformed Protectorate type who had shot Speeler.

'Killing the fat man was unnecessary,' Clay said as the blocky man turned a key in the lock and slid the gate open. 'And since when did the Protectorate work for pirates?'

'Shut your mouth, boy!' the tall man snapped, though his gaze was fixed on the Protectorate official. Clay noted his hand now rested on his belt, just a few inches from the butt of his six-shooter.

Doesn't know if either of us are likely to make it out of here alive, Clay realised, although the Protectorate man stood beside the bars in impassive immobility.

'Wasting time, Claydon,' the tall man said, voice hard with the urgent need to leave.

Clay sighed and got slowly to his feet. 'Always good to see you, Uncle Braddon.'

They emerged from a nondescript house on Healman's Way, a quiet road south-west of the docks mostly populated by the middle-management class. Glancing up Clay saw nothing to distinguish the house from its neighbours, same company emblem carved above the lintel, same drab curtains behind the windows. However, on closer inspection his practised eye could see the clues plain enough: a narrow gap in the brickwork on the upper storey just wide enough for a rifle, and another on the right at street level.

Expect they'll have to close this up now, he thought, suspecting they were the first two non-employees to leave the place alive.

'Enough dawdling,' his uncle snapped. He gestured to the street where a young woman waited astride a horse, clutching the reins of two more, their saddles empty. Braddon strode to the larger of the two horses, hauling himself into the saddle with unconscious ease. 'Know how to ride, I hope.'

'Well enough,' Clay lied. He took a look at the young woman as he approached the other horse. She wore a broad-brimmed hat much the same as his uncle's, though her long blonde hair was unbraided and cascaded down her back in a straight golden stream. But it was her face that soon captured his full attention. *Islander,* he realised, eyes roving the mask of tattoos that covered her skin from forehead to neck, the intricate pattern of red and green continuing on beneath the dark cotton of her shirt.

'This is Silverpin,' his uncle said, nodding at the woman. 'Bladehand to the Longrifles. You don't want to stare too long. She may take it personal.'

The woman, however, returned Clay's scrutiny with placid acceptance as his gaze lingered. He had never seen an Islander without an extensive array of designs inked into their flesh, but never one so entirely covered. 'Morning, miss,' he said, touching a finger to his forehead. She gave no response save a slight incline of her head, though he fancied her mouth curled just a little.

'Silverpin can't talk,' Braddon said, eyebrows raised in amusement as Clay made a faltering attempt to mount his horse 'Left foot in the left stirrup, unless you're planning to ride him backwards.'

They rode in silence for some time, Clay trailing along as his uncle and the woman followed Healman's south, soon passing out of middle-management country and into the tall buildings of Company Square. Clay was not overly familiar with this district, it being far too well patrolled for his purposes; a uniformed Protectorate guard stood on every corner with a repeating carbine on his shoulder. They skirted the neat lawns surrounding Ironship House, at six storeys the tallest building in the city, one storey higher than the South Seas Maritime office opposite. The buildings shared a similar design, all tall narrow windows and straight walls rising from a broad base, but whoever had built Ironship House had been at pains to ensure it outshone the others, both in its size and the opulence of its stained-glass windows and the numerous corporate flags flying from the forest of poles on the roof. Upon viewing the building any newly arrived visitor would be left in no doubt as to which company truly held power over this port.

Clay found his gaze drawn back to Silverpin as they proceeded into Carter's Walk, the broad thoroughfare that separated the white-marble mansions of the senior manager's district on the left from the closer-packed terraces of Scullion Town on the right. Her hair wasn't unusual for an Islander, especially one who hailed from the north-eastern chains. Under the ink they tended be of fair complexion, not dissimilar in fact from the New Colonials of northern Mandinor although they couldn't have been farther apart in temperament and custom. However, they also tended to be taller than Silverpin, and a little broader whereas she was all long-limbed litheness. His gaze settled on her hips, moving in perfect concord with her horse, a curved knife at the small of her back in a leather sheath, angled for a quick draw. *Bladehand,* his uncle had called her, an uncommon title he had heard a few times in relation to the Contractors who ventured into the Interior in search of fresh stock and undiluted product. *What use are blades in an age of guns?* he wondered.

As if sensing his thoughts Silverpin turned in her saddle, meeting his gaze. The placid acceptance from before was gone now, replaced by a disconcerting directness. Her eyes were a pale, icy blue, another trait common to Islanders, and he found himself squirming a little under their blatant inquisition.

'I have,' he began, turning to his uncle and finding he had to cough a little as Silverpin kept staring. 'I have business of my own. Before I do any bidding of yours.'

'Keyvine's lot will cut your throat the second you step into the Blinds,' Braddon said, not bothering to turn around. 'Best you forget any foolish notions.'

Clay's mind was quick to summon the dream from the night before. *Flames engulfing the steeple. Derk and Joya, laughing as they burned and, standing immobile amidst the inferno, a figure who at first appeared to be the Pale-Eyed Preacher, grinning madly and covered in whore's blood, but soon shifted into Keyvine, ruined features twisted into a delighted smile.* 'Foolish or not,' Clay said, aware of his thickening voice. 'I got a debt in need of settling.'

Braddon brought his horse to an abrupt halt, turning it about so he came face-to-face with his nephew. His expression was angry but also faintly weary, the face of a tutor forced into lessons with a dull and ungrateful pupil. 'Take a look,' he said, jerking his head at the surrounding street. 'What d'you see?'

Clay sighed but did as he was told, glancing around at the people passing by. Well-dressed women strolled together in pairs or trios, chattering the inane gossip of the idle rich whilst those paid to service their needs scurried to and fro on various errands, laden with groceries or pushing squalling infants in prams. Here and there a city employee swept the paving or collected litter from the gutters. It was a far remove from the familiar chaos of the Blinds but nothing he hadn't seen before.

'Nothing,' he told his uncle. 'Just rich folks and their servants.'

'Really?' Braddon turned to Silverpin with a questioning glance. She paused to scan the street for a moment, pale blue eyes narrowing slightly, then raised four fingers.

'I only count three,' Braddon said, turning back to Clay. 'But she's always had the better eye. See that lady with the little dog over by the bench?' Clay duly looked, seeing only a well-attired young woman in a dress of white and black, laughing as she tossed treats to a yapping terrier of minuscule proportions. He had taken her for either the young wife of a senior manager or an elder daughter, spoiled and filling her useless day fawning over a pet.

'So?' he asked.

'The shoes, boy. Heels just flat enough for running, and her handbag's just the right size for a brace of vials. She's Academy trained. The street-sweeper's got a carbine in his broom holder and the lad hawking news-sheets has a salt-shaker strapped to his ankle. Can't see the fourth myself but I'd lay odds they'll be on a roof-top with a longrifle. We didn't choose this route, boy, and if you have any thought our backers will allow you out of my sight till we're on our way, forget it. You're bought and paid for and it's me who did the paying so wipe that fucking scowl off your face.'

'I want Keyvine,' Clay stated, fighting his rage. 'I'm guessing you got a contract needs what I can do. You want my services then give me a day to settle with Keyvine. That's my price.'

'My business with Keyvine is settled, and I don't need it unsettled right now. What's between you and him is no concern of mine. When we fulfil this contract I expect to be gone from these shores in short order and you'll find yourself with enough Ironship scrip to buy the whole Blinds if you like. Buy it and burn it to ash for all I care. But in the meantime, you are now the Blood-blessed liaison to the Longrifles Independent Contractor Company and, unless you want a bullet through the brain, you'll act like it.'

They passed into Colonial Town a few streets on, the last remnant of the original South Mandinorian settlement that had grown here some two centuries ago. The houses were all two-storey dwellings with low, sloping roofs and many verandas, the streets just as well-kept as in Manager Country but much more lively. There was a market in every square and a tavern on almost every corner. Everything was drenched in the music that floated out of the taverns or rose from street-corner trios. Fiddle, flute, drum and pianola mingled a hundred different tunes into what should have been a discordant mess but somehow worked as a harmonious accompaniment to the ceaseless bustle. It was all a great contrast to the Blinds where music was rarely heard in daylight and skin colour varied as much as fortune. Here almost every face was as dark as his own, and yet, although he had been born here Clay had never felt at home amongst these people.

Orphans have no home anywhere, he recalled. It was something Joya had said one damp night as they huddled together on a roof-top, her gaze fixed on Manager Country, the marble mansions gleaming under the two moons and seeming very far away. Derk rarely talked of their lives before the Blinds but Joya felt no reluctance in relating tales of their fine house and toy-filled rooms, all lost the day their father had been carted off by the Protectorate and the company bailiff handed their mother a writ of seizure. Their father's crime had never been fully revealed to Clay and he suspected they barely understood it themselves, but it had been sufficiently grave to see him on a prison ship back to Feros and his family destitute. If they were ignorant of their father's eventual fate they were all too aware of their mother's and staunchly refused to discuss it. Clay had always respected their reticence though it wasn't hard to reckon it out. A woman of no means with no skills, shunned by the managerial class and cast out to fend for herself would have had few options. Whatever her struggles, however, it hadn't been enough to save her children from eking a living scrounging scraps in Staker's Alley.

We'll get it all back, Clay had assured Joya that night, putting an arm around her slim shoulders. *All the toys you could ever want.*

He came back to the present when his uncle's boots stamped onto the ground. They had stopped at an impressively proportioned house on the northern fringes of Colonial Town, just a short walk from the outer wall in fact. It was much as Clay remembered, standing two storeys high like the others but with an extensive cluster of attic windows sprouting from the roof. The addition of a decent-sized stable showed this to have been a building of some importance at one point, home to a Mandinorian Imperial Consul perhaps, in the days when such things held any meaning.

Two women waited to greet Braddon as he climbed the short steps to the main door, one tall with a purple scarf on her head, the other shorter and considerably younger. Clay found the youngster capturing most of his attention, mainly due to the pair of revolvers on her hips and the half-scowl with which she greeted him. He turned as Silverpin tapped him on the shoulder, climbing down from the saddle and gesturing for him to follow.

'Claydon,' the taller woman said, greeting him with a smile warmer than he deserved. Whatever passed between him and his uncle, she wasn't part of it and, for the brief time he allowed her, she had treated him like her own. 'Knew you'd grow up prettier than your uncle. Guess you favour your mother's side.'

'Only in looks,' Braddon grunted.

'Auntie Fredabel.' Clay greeted the elder woman with a respectful nod, before turning to the girl. 'Cousin Lori.'

She tilted her head, scowl still in place and a pout forming on her lips. 'Pa says you're now a thief and a disgrace to the family,' she said, looking him up and down. 'Guessing he was right.'

'Enough of that!' her mother snapped and the girl took a wary step back, head lowered though her eyes flashed at Clay with undimmed resentment.

'They here?' Braddon asked his wife.

She nodded. 'In the Map Room.'

'The company?'

'I cleared the house when our visitors got here, sent them over to the Skinners Rest with enough of an advance to keep them there all night. They've been asking questions, though. Skaggerhill especially.'

'Only to be expected.' Braddon nodded at Silverpin. 'Take Loriabeth to the Skinners. Make sure she sticks to the sparkle water. Claydon, time to meet your new employers.'

'Thought that was you.'

His uncle grunted a laugh, stepping into the house and gesturing for him to follow. 'You ain't that lucky, boy.'

Inside, the house was spacious with polished wooden floors and sturdy beams of thick oak, though the furnishings spoke of an upturn in fortunes since his time under this roof. The lobby through which his uncle led him featured several couches and a large gleaming table of imported oak. The walls were liberally decorated in a mix of sketches, photostats and bleached drake skulls of varying dimensions. Clay knew most to be Greens but there were a few Reds amongst them and, hanging from the wall next to the staircase at the rear of the lobby, a skull so large and jagged it could only be a Black. Clay paused for a closer look, eyes tracking over the many teeth to the gaping nostrils and eye-sockets until he found a single ragged hole in the centre of the beast's forehead.

'Is this . . . ?' he began, causing Braddon to linger on the stairs.

'That's him,' he said. 'Harvesters made a gift of him a couple of years back, part-payment for a hefty consignment of Green and Red. Finest shot I ever took.'

Clay found himself unable to look away from the skull's empty eyes, imagining what they must have seen that day. *You killed my mother,* he told it. *Did you even know?*

'Claydon,' his uncle said, voice softer than usual. 'Best not keep them waiting.'

Clay followed him to the upper floor and along a long corridor to a closed door where Braddon paused, hand on the handle 'I ain't gonna pretend there's any regard twixt us, boy,' he said, speaking softly and meeting Clay's gaze with a new intensity. 'But you've still got Torcreek blood in those veins so listen well. You want to make it out of this room alive, you choose your words carefully. You may think the Blinds is full of the most dangerous folks you're like to meet, but you never met folks like this before. Whatever they may appear to be, remember that next to them, Keyvine's a child.'

He opened the door and stepped inside, holding it open for Clay to follow. The room was large with bookshelves lining the walls and a map table in the centre where a continental chart lay, three corners weighted with heavy leather-bound tomes and one, he saw, with a revolver. Two women stood at the table regarding him in expressionless scrutiny. The one on the right was young, a little older than he but with a weight and intelligence to her gaze that spoke of considerable experience. She had the fine bones and pale skin of the North Mandinorian managerial class though her dress seemed plain for one of her station. She stood at apparent ease but Clay could see the part-concealed readiness in her stance, something he knew would be lost on less-attuned eyes.

He turned his gaze to the woman on the left, unsurprised at finding her the same grey-haired Blood-blessed he had seen the night before atop the Mariner's Rest. Her all-black attire had since been exchanged for a grey dress just as plain as that of her companion. Although their features displayed no familial simi- larity their shared bearing spoke of a deep and long-standing association.

'Thank you, Captain,' the older woman said to his uncle in a strident and precise tone.

Braddon gave Clay a final glance, grave with warning, before leaving the room, the door closing softly behind him.

'You are Claydon Torcreek,' the older woman stated.

Clay said nothing, merely returning her gaze as the woman continued without undue pause, apparently unconcerned at his lack of manners. 'I am Madame Lodima Bondersil, Principal of the Ironship Academy of Female Education. This young lady is my former student and current subordinate, Miss Lizanne Lethridge, Executive Operative of the Exceptional Initiatives Division.'

The younger woman inclined her head with a small smile. 'It is my pleasure to meet you, Mr Torcreek.'

Despite his determination to maintain a rigid composure Clay couldn't prevent the sudden upturn in his heart-beat, or the first trickle of sweat down his back. *The Academy*, he thought as the truth of his uncle's warning struck home with full force. *Two Ironship Blood-blessed in the same room.* He had never heard the words 'Exceptional Initiatives Division' before but it didn't require any great intelligence to discern their meaning. Whatever he had stepped into went far beyond the Protectorate and any back-alley deals they might make with Keyvine or the crew of the *Windqueen*.

He managed not to cough before speaking, though his voice was more strained than he would have liked. 'My uncle says you have work for me.'

CHAPTER 6

Lizanne

'I've been calling it the Spider,' Jermayah said. 'Guessing I'll have to come up with something more technical for the patent.'

Lizanne eyed the spindly device lying on the bench with equal parts curiosity and apprehension. It certainly did have something of the arachnid about it, though with four legs instead of eight. 'What exactly does it do?'

Jermayah's grin indicated that her fondness for taunting him was fully reciprocated. 'Put it on and I'll show you. Left forearm.'

She undid her cuff and rolled up her sleeve, managing not to betray any hesitation as she lifted the device. Jermayah's mechanical passions may have been principally concerned with locomotion but much of what he fashioned here was highly lethal. The device had two straps that fastened over her forearm and four copper tubes fixed together that fitted snugly just below the elbow. From each tube a narrow rubber hose led to one of four disc-shaped buttons resting in Lizanne's palm. What concerned her most, however, was the stubby cylinder protruding at a right angle from the rear of the device. It had a syringe-esque quality she found distinctly off-putting.

She raised an eyebrow at Jermayah. 'Well?'

'Press a button,' he replied, a bland smile on his lips.

She stiffened her resolve and pressed the button aligned with her index finger, being immediately rewarded with a sharp pain as the syringe-like appendage drove a needle into her flesh. She gritted her teeth, finding the needle's sting harsh but manageable. 'A self-torture device,' she said. 'How ingenious.'

'It's empty,' he said, nodding at the four tubes. 'But load it with product and you can inject it direct into the bloodstream. Each button delivers a different variant, and you can also combine them provided you've loaded it with the correct dilutions.'

Lizanne raised her arm, turning it to examine the device more closely. Its dimensions were discreet enough for it to be worn beneath the sleeve of her blouse without attracting attention. Also, during a covert mission the ability to ingest product without the need to pause and drink a vial would be a distinct tactical advantage, one the Cadre were unlikely to enjoy. 'The dosage?' she asked.

'Variable according to how long you depress the button. Three seconds for a full vial. I suggest you do some experimenting before you set off.'

'I shall.' She favoured him with a warm smile. 'Thank you very much, Mr Tollermine. This will do very well.'

'We're not done yet.' He pulled a hinged wooden box across the bench towards him, opening it to reveal a pistol of some kind. It was about the same dimensions as the Dessinger she knew so well but with distinctive modifications. An additional barrel had been affixed atop the original and a bulbous copper egg extended from behind the cylinder in place of the hammer.

'Feel the weight,' Jermayah said, stepping back. Lizanne hefted the revolver, her expert gaze quickly discerning that the weapon's calibre had been reduced to .25, enabling the cylinder to hold eight bullets instead of the usual six. Also, she noted that the secondary barrel extended over the frame to stop a quarter-inch short of the rear sight.

'Called it the Whisper,' Jermayah said, tapping the copper egg behind the cylinder. 'Compressed air. No bang-bangs, though just as much punch as black powder at short range. The egg and the cylinder are one unit and can be replaced for a quick reload.'

'And this?' Lizanne's finger traced over the additional barrel.

'That's not so quiet.' He jerked his head over his shoulder, moving away into the gloomy recesses of the workshop. 'Easier to demonstrate than to explain.'

Shiny Man was greatly altered but still recognisable. He had been fashioned from whatever scraps of metal Jermayah had lying around. The multiple holes punched into his composite skin were repaired continually so that he existed in a state of constant flux. However, the basic form remained: an uncannily lifelike sculpture of a charging man caught in midstride at the end of Jermayah's twenty-foot-long firing range. Lizanne had lost count of how many times she had shot him during her student days and was gratified to find her aim as true as ever.

She found Jermayah's chosen name for the weapon to be slightly exaggerated. The pistol made a sharp huffing sound when fired, louder than a whisper but still preferable to the blast of a standard revolver. However, the accuracy and power were impressive, her first shots slotting neatly into the gap between Shiny Man's eyes with a satisfying double clunk as the bullet penetrated both front and rear of his metallic skull.

'Very nice,' she approved, snapping off two more shots into Shiny Man's chest.

'Now for the main show.' Jermayah held up a bullet of unusual design. The ball was a lead hollow-point but the hole had been sealed in wax. Instead of a brass shell it sat in a half-sphere fashioned from glass. Lizanne's eyes quickly recognised the viscous substance inside.

'Red,' she said.

'Yes, named it the Redball.' He handed her the bullet. 'Drop it into the top barrel. Don't worry, it won't break and there's a magnet to keep it in place.'

She did as he said, the bullet sliding the length of the barrel until it came to rest against the rear sight with the glass casing exposed to the air. 'Here.' He held up a vial containing a drop of Red. 'When you're ready,' he said when she had imbibed the drop, taking a few backward steps and gesturing at Shiny Man. 'Best if you use a double-handed grip.'

It was only a small amount of Red, just enough for a narrow blast of heat at a very small target. She gripped the Whisper with both hands, lining up on the centre of Shiny Man's chest then focusing on the bead of Red she could see glimmering in the cartridge just beyond the rear sight. She summoned the product and released it in a single split-second surge, being instantly rewarded by a bright flare of unleashed energy in the cartridge followed by a gout of orange flame from the barrel. It seemed as if the pistol and Shiny Man were momentarily joined by a line of fire as the bullet streaked towards his chest, penetrating the outer shell before exploding. A ball of fire expanded in an instant, so bright Lizanne had to look away. When she looked back she found Shiny Man a smoking ruin, copper and tin melting together to drip onto the workshop floor.

'Aw,' she groaned, pouting at Jermayah in accusation.

'Time I retired him anyways,' he replied with a shrug.

She spent an hour practising with the Whisper, getting used to its slight recoil, but didn't fire any more Redballs. 'Limited supply, I'm afraid,' Jermayah told her, handing over the ammunition, a box of fifty .25 bullets and a smaller one with only six Redballs. 'Price of product being what it is, the Division wouldn't authorise any more. Tried arguing the point but the local Agent-in-Charge started going on about relative risk factors. Can't abide all that stuff.'

How heartening to know the benefits of my survival can be quantified on a balance sheet, Lizanne thought, nevertheless accepting the ammunition with a grateful smile. 'Where would I be without you?'

Her appointment with Madame Bondersil was several hours away so she indulged herself by staying awhile to help Jermayah tinker with his thermoplasmic carriage. 'Did you see your father in Feros?' he asked, handing her a spanner.

'Yes,' she replied, using the spanner to loosen a bolt on the engine mounting. 'I saw him.'

Some element of bitterness must have coloured her tone for

he sighed. 'He's a brilliant man,' he said. 'Perhaps the finest technologist of this age. You should respect him more.'

'A brilliant man, indeed,' she grunted, giving the bolt a hard
shove. 'Living in marginal poverty whilst he tinkers with his toys
and nurses his endless grudge against my employers.'

'Not to sound disloyal to the Syndicate, but they did steal your
inheritance, did they not? Your grandfather's invention changed
the whole world in the space of a generation, and yet your family
have never received a copper scrip for it.'

Lizanne groaned with the effort of working the bolt free,
exhaling in relief as it clattered to the workshop floor. 'He didn't,'
she said.

'Who didn't?'

'My grandfather didn't invent the thermoplasmic engine. My
father did, when he was only fourteen years old.'

Lizanne rose from the carriage, massaging the ache in the small
of her back. 'It's all there in the Ironship archives, Jermayah.
Shareholder status allows one to peruse the records at leisure and
it was a small matter to access the vault where they keep the confidential legal documents. Thanks to Grandfather's lengthy dispute
with the Syndicate their lawyers had compiled a full and accurate
account of how the thermoplasmic engine came into being. It seems
Grandfather had been working on a form of locomotive device
based on combustible product, but it was primitive and impractical.
My father's design, by contrast, was revolutionary and capable of
immediate application. Also, apparently, too profitable to remain
in the hands of a child. Grandfather persuaded his son to keep quiet
and ensured it was his name on the patents. A fact Ironship threatened to make public as the legal case escalated. It's often thought
that Darus Lethridge committed suicide due to his mountainous
debts, and the unbearable prospect of watching the syndicate he
hated profit from his invention. It transpires that he simply didn't
want the world to know just how much of a fraud he was.'

'You should make the facts known,' Jermayah said. 'Your father
should be credited, and compensated.'

'He won't hear of it. Such a thing would tarnish his father's legend. Besides, I find myself content to allow the Lethridge name to fade from public consciousness. Notoriety doesn't really fit with this occupation.'

He hesitated for a second, his face sombre. 'Miss Lizanne, this mission . . .'

'I don't get to choose.' She stepped close to plant a kiss on his bald head. 'And with your marvellous knicky-knacks to help me, how could I fail?'

CHAPTER 7

Clay

'Oh, we do indeed have work for you,' the older woman told Clay, gesturing to the map. 'Work of a most fruitful and interesting nature. If you could turn your close attention to this chart, I will be happy to explain in full.'

Clay moved closer to the table, eyes lingering on the revolver securing the corner. He stiffened a little as Miss Lethridge moved to his side, tracking his gaze and speaking softly, 'It's fully loaded, in case you were wondering.'

Cats toying with a mouse, he thought, dragging his eyes from the revolver to the map. He knew the shape of the Arradsian coast-line well enough, having stolen a few antique maps over the years, though their accuracy varied widely with age. This one was newly drawn, the thick waxed paper clean and free of fold marks, the curving lines of the coast and the rivers set down with the true precision of a professional map-maker and the whole thing overlaid by a grid of faint dots.

'The continent of Arradsia,' Madame Bondersil said. 'This is a small-scale re-creation combining the most accurate maps ever produced by Ironship cartographers.' Her finger tapped the black dot with the word 'Carvenport' inscribed above it, then tracked south along the Greenchurn River through dense jungles until it came to rest on a vast area of blankness stretching towards the southern plains.

'Despite two centuries of colonisation,' she said, 'there are still whole swathes of this land that remain unknown to civilised eyes.' Her finger underlined the inscription curving through the blankness. 'The Red Sands. You've heard of this place, no doubt, Mr Torcreek?'

'It's a desert,' he said. 'A wasteland with no drakes. Even the headhunters don't go there.'

'Ah, but surely you know the story of the one intrepid band who did?'

He frowned, wondering why they had gone to such lengths to ask him about a tale often told by drunks who claimed former allegiance to various Contractor Companies. 'The Wittler Expedition. It's a story. Not sure I ever believed it.'

'It's true enough, I assure you. Though over the years the factual details have been greatly confused in the public mind. Tell me, which version have you heard?'

'Wittler was a Contractor, like my uncle. Captain of the Sandpipers . . .'

'Sandrunners,' Madame Bondersil corrected. 'Please go on.'

'He and his company went looking for the White Drake and never came back. Some say the Spoiled got them all, others that they found the White and it ate them.'

'And in any of these stories was the name Ethelynne Drystone ever mentioned?'

Clay searched his memory. 'Story goes there was a Blood-blessed with them, an Academy girl. If so, I guess she died with the others.'

'No, Mr Torcreek,' Madame Bondersil told him with a sad smile. 'She most assuredly did not. I assume you require no extensive lecture on the need for discretion in this matter. Nor must I emphasise the consequences should our confidence in you prove misplaced.'

Clay's eyes snapped involuntarily to the revolver. *Fully loaded, but they don't need it. I reach for it and they know they're wasting their time. Cats with a mouse.* 'Guess you don't,' he muttered, returning his gaze to the map.

'Excellent. The Sandrunners did indeed meet an untimely end on the Red Sands but Ethelynne Drystone was not amongst them. To my certain knowledge she escaped their fate having secured possession of an egg, a White egg. I trust the significance of this is not lost on you?'

A White egg. He found himself searching the woman's face for some sign of trickery, finding only a placid certainty. 'Whites are a myth,' he said. 'Never seen, never harvested. Just tall tales from the old days.'

'The first settlers did indeed talk of encounters with Whites, but even then they were exceptionally rare and reports of their existence taken as the delusions of those who had lost their minds amidst the many horrors to be found in the Interior. As it transpires, thanks to Miss Drystone, we know they were far from a delusion and somewhere out there' – her hand played over the Red Sands once more – 'lies the evidence to prove it.'

In spite of his tension Clay couldn't suppress a laugh, though it emerged as more of a groan. 'And you ladies have some notion I might know where to find it?'

'Oh, goodness no!' Madame Bondersil exchanged an amused glance with her subordinate, who held a hand to her mouth to suppress a chuckle. 'Your esteemed uncle will do the finding, with Miss Lethridge's assistance, whilst you, Mr Torcreek, will be the conduit for that assistance.'

'The Blue-trance,' he realised aloud, his puzzlement deepening further. 'There's at least half a hundred Blood-blessed in this port, and most of them in Ironship employ.'

'Actually, there are currently thirty-five Blood-blessed resident in Carvenport, and their names are properly recorded in the Joint Company Register as per Special Edict of the Global Trade Council. Every one except you, young sir. Your value to us lies in your anonymity. Our competitors have no knowledge of your status and therefore no opportunity to intercept any communications you might make.'

'The Blue-trance.' He shook his head, a sense of entrapment adding to his already heightened unease. 'I've never done it. Never even tasted Blue. The price was always too high. Besides, who would I trance-talk with?'

'Even better.' Madame Bondersil reached into her sleeve to extract a vial, holding it out to him. The colour of the vial's contents was paler than the other product variants he knew and there was something odd about the way it caught the light. The gleam was duller than it should be, muted somehow, as if a portion of the light had been captured in the product. 'Blue,' she said. 'Fresh from the laboratory. The dilution is a relatively new formula, allowing for more control during the trance. It can become a little confusing in there at times.'

He stared at the vial, hands frozen at his sides. After a second he glanced at Miss Lethridge, who favoured him with an oddly warm smile. 'Thought there had to be some kind of . . . bond twixt the drinkers. That's how you talk through the trance, make the connection.'

'Absolutely correct, Mr Torcreek,' Madame Bondersil complimented him. 'The most clarity is achieved between Blood-blessed who have an emotional connection, the deeper the better. However, not all bonds need be affectionate, or even particularly close to be effective. In fact, considering the line of work you are now embarking upon you may want to exercise considerable circumspection in forming close relationships. To survive as a covert Blood-blessed often requires that you shun the affections of others. A truism you may well come to appreciate with terrible clarity.'

She extended her arm further, raising an insistent eyebrow. 'Shall we begin?'

He forced himself to remain immobile and summoned the nerve to meet her gaze. 'We ain't yet discussed the terms of my contract.'

Miss Lethridge gave another small chuckle. 'Isn't continued life and well-being payment enough?'

He didn't look at her, keeping his gaze on Madame Bondersil and finding to his surprise he had stopped sweating. *A White egg. Every company in the world would drain their vaults just to bid on it.* 'No,' he said. 'Not nearly enough.'

Madame Bondersil lowered her arm and the two women

exchanged another glance. 'What do you want?' Miss Lethridge asked, not without a note of impatience.

'One hundred thousand in Ironship scrip,' he said, still addressing Madame Bondersil. 'My name kept off the register for the rest of my life, and . . .' He smiled for the first time since entering the room. 'Keyvine.'

'And who might he be?' Miss Lethridge enquired.

'The current King of Blades and Whores,' Madame Bondersil informed her. 'And author of Mr Torcreek's recent misfortunes.' She paused to issue a thin sigh. 'I'm afraid Mr Keyvine negotiated with us in good faith. Acting against him now would undermine our relations with his inevitable successor.'

'Not my problem. Anyways, you don't need to do any acting, just give me tonight and a decent supply of product. It'll be done by morning and you'll be assured of my loyalty during this whole crazy enterprise.'

'Unacceptable.' Madame Bondersil's face took on a stern resolve, all trace of her previous affability vanishing to reveal a far-more-unnerving visage. 'Who do you imagine I am to be bartered with like some Blinds whore? Your life was preserved for a purpose, preserved by my agency I might add, otherwise your fall from that roof would certainly have been fatal. Your debt to Mr Keyvine is your own business. Your debt to us, however, will be paid in full. We have done murder to secure your services and will not baulk at another should your truculence prove any more aggravating.' She extended the vial of Blue once again, her gaze locked on his. 'I trust this is understood.'

On the edge of his vision he noted the corner of the map was now curled and he heard Miss Lethridge take a deliberate step back, presumably to avoid besmirching her dress.

Sweating once more, he raised his hand and opened his palm.

'A hundred thousand scrip and omission from the register,' Madame Bondersil said, dropping the vial into his hand. 'These terms are, however, perfectly acceptable.'

His aunt led him to one of the attic rooms when they were done with him, his head all fuzzy with the after-effects of the Blue-trance. 'Join us for supper when you're ready,' she said. 'Got pork and black-bean stew. Fried taters too.'

He replied with a tired nod, sinking onto the bed. It had been freshly made up, the sheets clean and crisp, and a jug of water sat in a bowl on a near by table. Fredabel lingered at the door for a moment, regarding him with a tight smile.

'You shouldn't mind Braddon too much,' she said. 'He had to beg, y'see. For Keyvine to give you up. Begging don't sit right with a man like him.'

Don't sit right with anyone, he thought, but said, 'Thank you, Auntie. For your . . . kind welcome.'

'Family welcomes family, Claydon. Or at least they should.' She smiled again and left him alone.

He lay back on the bed with a groan. Use of Blue, it transpired, was more taxing than Black or Red. His memory of the trance was dim, like a half-forgotten dream though Miss Lethridge had assured him it would become clearer with practice. For now, however, he remembered only a swirl of images amidst a discordant cacophony of mangled sound. It reminded him of a painting he had once stolen from a mansion in Manager Country: *The Great Storm*, according to the title on the small brass plate affixed to the frame. It showed a convoy of warships, all sailing vessels from some bygone age, rendered near invisible by a raging tempest that covered most of the canvas, the clouds roiling in shades of black and grey, turned yellow in one place by a flash of lightning. The Blue-trance had been like stepping into that painting the instant he drank the vial, except the clouds and the lightning were all fashioned from memories, and not all were welcome.

Derk and Joya were the first to come bubbling out of the morass, his last memory of them, just last night back in the steeple. Derk annoyed at being left behind, Joya worried, their faces smeared and stretched until they began to transform into something else. Clay had started to rage when Keyvine's face appeared, pulse pounding and the trance turning red with it.

Calm. Miss Lethridge's voice in his mind. *Focus.*

On what? he asked, rage lurching anew as Keyvine favoured him with a conspiratorial wink.

These are your memories, she told him. *Find a better one.*

His mind raced with feverish energy, fighting panic as he sought to summon some vestige of peace from his mind. *The ball-room,* he decided as Keyvine began to laugh. *Of course.*

It had been a year ago, their biggest ever score before the fight with Cralmoor. The mansion belonged to the most senior Briteshore Minerals official in Carvenport, an irascible man with a habit of firing his servants for the smallest misdeeds. It had been a former servant who got them in, a maid with a grievance and the good foresight to make some impressions of the house keys before her dismissal. The Briteshore official and his family were away, leaving the place in the care of an aged butler who was a little too fond of helping himself to the wine-cellar and an arthritic housekeeper who rarely bothered herself with the upper floors after dark. Gaining access had been a simple matter, a sip of Green then a rapid scaling of the creeper-covered rear wall to the second floor where the maid's keys gave him access to the windows. He fixed a rope for Joya and Derk to climb up after, their spoils being too numerous and weighty for just him. They went from room to room, Derk's practised eye choosing the most valuable and least cumbersome items, sacks a-bulge with loot by the time they got to the ball-room.

Joya laughing, he thought, focusing on the image. She had dropped her loot with a clatter, stepping onto the ornately tiled dance floor, arms wide as she gazed up at the chandeliers. None were lit but still they sparkled in the meagre light. She spun and spun across the floor, lithe form moving with unconscious grace, laughing all the while despite their hissed warnings.

Beautiful, Miss Lethridge commented, the image dimming with her intrusion. His momentary resentment faded when he realised Keyvine's burnt mask had now faded into the general morass. *Did she get you caught?*

No, he replied. *The housekeeper started yelling up the stairs and we ran. Didn't make as much profit as expected though.*

He remembered berating Joya for her foolishness though he saw now it had been a forced tirade, the image of her dancing more precious than any of the shiny things they had stolen that night. *The only time I ever saw her truly happy. Something I'll never see again.*

Mr Keyvine will surely be here when you return, Miss Lethridge said, sensing the dark turn in his thoughts. *Think of it as an added incentive. Now, to business.*

It had seemed to take hours though she told him time could lose its meaning in the trance, a minute could seem like a day and a few moments might cover the span of an hour in the waking world. She had him concentrate on her thoughts instead of his and he found himself wondering at the orderliness of her mind. Instead of his roiling storm, her trance was more like a series of tightly controlled whirlwinds, some light and rich in colour, others dark and shot through with an inner vein of red fire.

Tornadoes are plentiful on the plains of eastern Mandinor come the summer, she said. *I borrowed the image, crafted it to fit my purpose. You would do well to find a pattern of your own, some means of imposing order on all this mess.*

She showed him the basics of sharing information via the trance. He soon found it was more complicated than a simple exchange of words. *Words change with repetition,* she warned. *Intelligence is only valuable when unsullied by interpretation. Your understanding of a document will vary widely from an educated reading.*

Guess they don't teach charm in the Academy, he returned, his storm taking on a sullen cast.

Pay attention! She drew one of the whirlwinds closer, not as dark as some and with only a faint inner glow. It convulsed as it neared him, the whirling clouds slowing and coalescing into an image, some kind of mechanical diagram. *This is a design I obtained during a recent sea voyage. A forgery as it happens but it'll suffice for teaching purposes. Look closely, absorb the image. When we wake from the trance I'll expect you to draw it.*

His drawing had been crude and barely legible to his own eyes, although Miss Lethridge and Madame Bondersil seemed unperturbed. 'Better than expected,' was the older woman's only comment whilst Miss Lethridge gave a small shrug of agreement.

'Sleep well,' she advised Clay as he stood blinking in confusion. 'We only have one more day before your uncle's expedition sets off. Be in this room bright and early tomorrow, Mr Torcreek. Any tardiness and Madame will deduct five percent from your fee.'

Sleep contrived to elude him despite his fatigue and the lingering fogginess in his head. He lay on the bed eyes closed, hearing the dim murmur of conversation downstairs as his uncle and aunt shared their stew, and all the while the image of Joya dancing played itself over and over in his mind. *Mr Keyvine will most likely be here when you return.* Miss Lethridge was right, he knew that. *Keyvine will keep, but will I?*

He had never ventured into the Interior, his trips beyond the city wall having been infrequent forays to meet various criminal associates away from the vigilant gaze of the Protectorate. All he knew of the wider continent on which he lived had been gleaned from stories told by one-time Contractors and headhunters, none of which painted a pleasant picture. The Interior was a place of jungle, desert and tall mountains populated by wild drakes and savage tribes of mis-shapen Spoiled. If one didn't get him the other surely would and he doubted Keyvine would ever even hear the news.

For a moment it was as if the trance had returned, his mind clouding with the mingled vision of Joya's dance and Keyvine's smiling, flame-ruined face beyond the bars. 'I do so detest an unbalanced debt,' Clay whispered aloud, opening his eyes.

He waited until the sound of conversation faded, listening for the fall of feet on the staircase. 'Please, Freda, enough,' he heard his uncle say as they climbed the steps. 'I said I'd talk to him in the morning . . .' Then the soft closing of a door and silence.

Life as a thief held many lessons on the virtues of patience and it was a full hour before Clay stirred from the bed, leaving his shoes where they were and moving to the window, feet soft and slow on the floor-boards. The window proved to be unlocked and the roof outside thankfully free of any nesting parakeets that might squawk an alarm. He inched his way out, flattening himself onto the roof and letting gravity carry him over the tiles to the edge. He caught hold of it and dropped to the first-storey roof below, feet finding the apex with practised ease. From there it was a short balancing act and a leap to the ground where he rolled to absorb the impact before sprinting off into the gloomy streets ahead.

No weapon and no money, he thought. *Not to say no shoes.* It was hardly the best condition in which to approach the most well-defended building in the Blinds. He was considering which of his hidden caches would be the best choice when Silverpin dropped from a roof-top to land directly in front of him.

He skidded in alarm, bare feet sliding over the cobbles before giving way to deposit him on his rump. Silverpin was already looming above him and he shrank back, arms raised instinctively and eyes alive for the gleam of her curved knife. But instead of a blade her hand grasped a green-leather satchel, whatever was inside giving it a rounded appearance. She met his gaze and he was surprised to find no mockery in her smile, just sympathy. She dumped the satchel between his legs then walked away.

Clay watched her unhurried progress towards his uncle's house, seeing her disappear inside without a backward glance, then turned his attention to the satchel. His hands faltered as they moved to the buckles and he found to his annoyance they were shaking. He flexed his fingers and tried again, unfastening the straps with quick angry snaps of his wrists. He knew what he would find, he knew what gift Silverpin had given him but still he had to look.

Keyvine's ruined face stared up at him from the satchel, half-closed eyes dry and catching only the smallest gleam from the street-lights. There were new scars in the flesh, he saw, dried blood flaking on the mottled skin. *He put up a fight. Didn't help . . . What is she?*

Clay got to his feet, hefting the satchel. He stood there for a time, lost in indecision. Somewhere music was playing, a lone fiddler casting a mournful tune into the night air accompanied by the faint howl of a lonely dog. The road to the Blinds was open and the throne of the King of Blades and Whores sat empty. It was a silly notion, he knew. The two ladies would find him in no small amount of time and exact a severe punishment before forcing him on their mad search for the fabled White. Or they might decide he simply wasn't worth the trouble and cut their losses. Besides, Derk and Joya were gone and the only home that awaited him was a haunted church with a burnt steeple.

One hundred thousand in Ironship scrip, he thought, slowly walking back to his uncle's house. *Should've asked for two.*

CHAPTER 8

Lizanne

She spent her final day in Carvenport practising with the Spider in the Academy gymnasium and several hours in Madame's office refreshing her Corvantine. They sat beside the fire-place conversing in Varsal, the most common tongue spoken in the empire.

'Still sounding too stuck-up,' Madame judged, her own accent a perfect re-creation of one brought up in the slums of Corvus. 'Most Corvantine servants are illiterate, don't forget. Burgrave Artonin will expect a maid to possess vowels of a more clipped nature if you're going to secure a place in his household.'

'I shan't, Madame. We are certain he was the box's most recent owner?'

'As certain as we can be. Should it prove otherwise you will endeavour to glean what you can from the home of our apparently compromised informant.'

Madame leaned back in her green-leather armchair, switching back to Mandinorian. 'Your training with our new Contractor is complete?'

'As complete as possible in the time available.' Something in her voice must have betrayed a certain discomfort for Madame felt the need to press her further.

'Mr Torcreek is proving unsatisfactory?'

Lizanne thought back over her Blue-trance sessions with the younger Torcreek. At first glance the vista of his thoughts as presented by the trance appeared little more than a swirling mess, a forbidding, mostly formless tempest shot through with lightning flashes of rage and recently birthed grief. But here and there she caught glimpses of small, tightly controlled balls of memory shining bright amidst all the darkness. It would have been an easy matter to tear into these memories and discover his secrets. Given his general lack of control he probably wouldn't have noticed the intrusion, and secrets were her business after all. But something gave her pause. It wasn't that her hours tutoring him had left her with any great regard for Claydon Torcreek, but these small islands of nurtured and cherished memory spoke of a more complex man than the self-serving Blinds thug he appeared. Also, given the danger they were sending him into perhaps he deserved at least a modicum of privacy.

'Mr Torcreek is possessed of a perennially criminal mind-set,' she told Madame, deciding a strictly professional assessment was warranted. 'His loyalty should be regarded as neither deep nor lasting.'

'You are aware his erstwhile enemy has met a singularly sticky end, I assume?'

Lizanne nodded. Keyvine's head had been discovered in a pig-pen near the south wall the morning after their first meeting with the younger Torcreek, a barely recognisable half-eaten monstrosity. According to lurid rumours emanating from the Blinds, the rest of him had been found sitting alone at a table in a seedy tavern, a half-drunk bottle of wine at his side and his sword-cane on the table snapped in two.

'He wasn't responsible,' she informed Madame. 'Though the Blue-trance indicates an awareness of who was. I didn't consider further investigation appropriate.'

'I concur, as long as no connection is made to our endeavour. Wouldn't do to have Mr Keyvine's former associates sniffing around this matter.'

'I'm sure the Protectorate has suitably discouraging methods should that happen.'

'They do, but I would prefer as few complications as possible. Any direct action in the Blinds is likely to stir up a riot and provide all sorts of opportunities for Cadre operatives. Something best avoided with the mysterious Truelove still eluding us. Be sure to keep a close watch on Torcreek's thoughts during trance communications and report any troubling developments to me.'

'Of course, Madame, as far as the exigencies of my mission allow.'

Madame Bondersil voiced a very small sigh. 'I am aware, Lizanne, of the risks I am asking you to undertake. Rest assured I would not be asking if the matter was not so absolutely vital.'

'I keep abreast of the price index, as befits any responsible Shareholder. The Syndicate is looking at a three percent drop in profits by the end of the year. Finding the White will reverse the current trend.'

'There is more at stake than company profits,' Madame insisted, her expression suddenly grave. She rose from the armchair and went to her desk, beckoning Lizanne to her side. She opened a drawer to extract a file, tied with a black ribbon with a Board seal on the cover. Madame spread the file's contents out on the desk. Lizanne's tacit occupation of experimental plasmologist required a basic familiarity with product-quality graphs so she had little trouble interpreting the contents of each page.

'Predicted potency reduction,' she said, eyes moving from one graph to another.

'Quite so.' Madame's finger tapped the first page, the line on the graph indicating a definite downward curve over the coming decade. 'By the end of the decade the potency of Red will have diminished by half. The projections are even worse for the other variants. Added to that' – she extracted a final page from the file and handed it to Lizanne for inspection – 'there are the output projections.'

Lizanne read the page several times, her frown deepening. 'This can't be right. Every other report I have read indicates a slight decline in production, the effects of which will be obviated by more sophisticated plasmology.'

'The Board has sealed this report, for obvious reasons. I'm

afraid its conclusions are all too accurate. Within twenty years the output of product from all Arradsian holdings, including the other corporations, will have declined to less than fifteen percent of current levels. I don't have to explain the ramifications for the global economy should that occur.'

'The breeding pens could be expanded, more expeditions sent to the Interior . . .'

'Already begun, and the Contractor Companies return with fewer specimens and less wild-harvested product each season. The drakes born to the pens are sickly and small and the product they produce of diminishing potency. Added to that, their life expectancy is reduced with every generation. Thanks to their irksome trait of dropping dead if they are removed from the Arradsian continent, there is also no prospect of establishing breeding populations elsewhere. It seems in the space of two centuries we have contrived to bleed this continent white.'

White, Lizanne repeated inwardly, hearing the emphasis Madame placed on the word. *Everything comes back to the White.* 'We don't know what White blood does,' she said. 'Your own report of Miss Drystone's experiences indicates it may hold more danger than profit.'

'Every variant holds danger, but also power that can be harnessed if properly respected. The White promises more than all the others combined.'

The hold of the Independent coastal steamer *Islander* made a stark contrast to the salubrious accommodation Lizanne had enjoyed aboard the *Mutual Advantage.* She was obliged to sleep on a low bunk equipped with a mattress so thin it barely deserved the name. She had been led here in the small hours of the morning by the ship's bosun, ostensibly a long-serving merchant sailor of typically grizzled appearance but in reality an Exceptional Initiatives operative specialising in the insertion of covert agents into Corvantine territory.

'We'll be obliged to anchor outside Morsvale harbour till dawn,' he advised. 'They won't open the doors before then, and every vessel is subject to inspection.'

'That won't be a problem,' she assured him, placing her oilskin pack on the bunk and managing not to wrinkle her nose at the smell.

'They tell you the success rate?' he asked and she discerned a certain tiredness in his eyes, the same fatigue she had often seen in Protectorate officers with multiple battle ribbons on their uniforms.

'They did,' she said. *Twenty percent.* The statistic was sobering but not unduly off-putting. Long odds were something she had habituated herself to over the years.

'They don't trade captured agents in Arradsia,' the bosun went on. 'Not like up north. They catch you in Morsvale they'll wring what they can out of you then dump your corpse in the pens as drake food. The Arradsian Cadre plays a game without rules.'

'How long have you been in this role?' she asked.

'Twelve years now.' He displayed a wall of discoloured teeth in a forced smile. 'And every day brings a new opportunity to better serve the Syndicate.'

She turned to the bunk and opened her bag. 'I assume I won't be disturbed.'

'The captain declared the hold off-limits for three days. Told the crew there was an acid spill.'

'He's aware I'm aboard?'

The bosun shook his head. 'Special cargo. That's all he knows and he's paid enough not to ask questions.'

'Excellent. Our journey time?'

'Two days, barring bad weather and Corvantine patrol boats.'

'Is that likely?'

'Happens now and then. Was a time they were easily bribed, not so much these days. Seems the new emperor's been busy purging his army and navy of lazy and corrupt officers. The new breed are a sight more diligent.'

She extracted the Spider from the bag along with a brace of

vials and laid them on the bunk. 'I can't afford a single compromise. If it seems we are about to be intercepted, come and fetch me. I'll take care of it.'

She saw how his eyes lingered on the vials and realised he hadn't been told he would be transporting a Blood-blessed. 'I don't know what you're after in Morsvale,' he said after a moment. 'And, of course, I don't want to know. But if the Cadre catches a Division Blood-blessed on their own ground, getting fed to the drakes will be the least of your worries.'

He handed her a large canteen of water and tapped his boot against a wooden crate. 'Preserved herring and pickles, in case you get hungry.' He gave her a final glance before leaving, his expression conveying a firm conviction he was taking a young woman to certain doom. He stomped off into the gloom and she heard him climb the ladder before a heavy clunk told of the hold's hatchway being locked firmly in place.

Twelve years, she thought, removing her jacket and lying down on the bunk. *I'll have Division transfer him when I return.*

Lizanne must have fallen into a half slumber at some point for she jerked upright with the Whisper in hand at the sound of the *Islander*'s steam-whistle. The hold was mostly pitch-dark but for a narrow beam of moonlight streaming through a port-hole near the ceiling. Hearing the slowing of the engine through the bulkhead, Lizanne got to her feet and strapped on the Spider. Each vial was now fully charged and she pressed the button aligned with her middle finger, sending a small charge of Green into her veins, the gloom abating and her muscles thrumming with the effects of the product. The port-hole was out of reach of any walkway so she was obliged to leap from crate to crate, building up enough momentum to grab onto an iron beam in the ceiling, hanging suspended as she peered through the port-hole. At first she could see nothing but the sea, the waters calm beneath a mostly cloudless sky. Then she saw it, a greenish-white wake perhaps a quarter-mile distant and above it a dark silhouette, tall enough to blot out the horizon from one end of the port-hole to the other.

Warship, she realised. *Too large for a patrol boat.* She watched the massive vessel track across the *Islander*'s starboard side. From the number of guns and the three stacks rising above the curve of the paddles she judged her to be one of the Imperium class of Corvantine heavy cruisers. It was unusual to see anything larger than a frigate in Arradsian coastal waters; both the Imperial Admiralty and the Ironship Sea Board tended to keep their primary units close to home. She glanced at the stars and roughly calculated the ship's course as parallel to their own, towards Morsvale. *Ran the Strait in darkness,* she deduced. *The Protectorate pickets must have seen her though.*

The effects of the Green began to ebb as the Corvantine vessel slipped out of sight and she used the dregs to return to her bunk. On removing the Spider she inspected the small red circle left by the syringe, one of several now clustered in much the same spot to give her the appearance of an opium fiend. *A useful cover story, should I need it.*

She lay down on the bunk once more, Spider and Whisper both resting on her chest. She was making a mental note to relay her sighting of the warship to Madame in the first scheduled trance communication when sleep finally overtook her.

The wall that shielded Morsvale from the tides was not truly a wall, more an artificial peninsula divided in two by the great door providing access to the docks. The edifice appeared to have been created by the simple, but no doubt enormously laborious, means of dumping huge stone blocks into the harbour until a barrier of sufficient size had been created, large enough in fact for houses to have been constructed atop it. Lizanne gazed up at the tall, close-packed tenements in frank amazement, barely crediting the fact that people would choose to live in such proximity to the unpredictable sea. They were dimly illuminated by flickering candlelight from the small but

numerous windows, washing lines arcing between each structure like a spider-web.

'Land is at a premium in Corvantine holdings,' the bosun
explained. 'Comes from choosing to build a colony so close to a
swamp. But all the best anchorages were taken by the time the
empire took an interest in the continent.'

As the *Islander* drew closer Lizanne detected a pungent aroma
arising from the surrounding waters, thickening into a nausea-
inducing stench as they neared the wall itself. 'Poorest folk in the
city live here,' the bosun said, nodding at the effluent bobbing in
the gentle swell below the rail. 'No sewers to speak of so they just
cast their filth out the window and let the sea take care of it.'

Lizanne concealed a shudder of revulsion at her impending
task and tightened the straps fixing the oilskin pack onto her
back. It was another of Jermayah's designs, featuring an ingenious
double-flap and fabric treated with a special coating which kept
the contents dry despite continual immersion. The bulk of it also
helped with her buoyancy; it wouldn't do to spend any time on
the surface when the door opened. She wore only a tight-fitting
one-piece garment of black cotton, light enough not to become
so sodden it might weigh her down on exiting the water.

The *Islander*'s whistle sounded two short blasts and her paddles
stopped then gave a half-dozen reverse turns to bring her to a
dead stop. 'Not too late,' the bosun said as the anchor plunged
into the water. 'You can still abort.'

Lizanne glanced over at the shadowy bulk of the Corvantine
cruiser sitting at anchor just a few hundred yards short of the
harbour door. Naturally, an Imperial warship took precedence
over commercial traffic. She could make out the name painted
on her hull in elaborate Eutherian script: *Regal*. The cruiser was
an even more impressive sight at close range, dwarfing all the
other vessels awaiting the opening of the door.

Even though Lizanne still entertained reservations about the
merits of this mission, the arrival in Morsvale of a ship capable
of tipping the regional maritime balance in favour of the empire

demanded investigation. 'Thank you,' she told the bosun. 'That won't be necessary.'

'The *Islander* will return in exactly twenty-three days,' he said. 'She will remain for one tide only. Extraction before or after that date will have to be undertaken entirely on your own initiative.'

'I understand.' She rolled up her sleeve to check the straps on the Spider and nodded briskly at the stern. 'Shall we?'

'Going to be perishing cold,' he warned as they came to the anchor chain.

'I expect so.' She hopped nimbly onto the rail and took a firm hold of the anchor chain, wrapping her arms and legs about the iron links.

'Gave up saying good luck years ago.' She looked up to see his tired, hollow-eyed face poised above the rail, a very small, sad smile on his lips. 'But . . . Well, you know.'

She replied only with a grim smile of her own then loosened her grip on the chain, sliding down into the chill embrace of the stinking water below.

It had become apparent early in Lizanne's schooldays that she enjoyed an equal facility with all four variants of product, an unusual trait that ensured she was soon marked out as a potential Division operative. This was the reason for her weekly visits to Jermayah's workshop and why Madame would often favour her with a private lesson in the more nuanced uses to which product could be applied. Most of these lessons had been welcome as they invariably involved a fair amount of athletic activity, something Lizanne always enjoyed. However, she had soon come to dread one particular exercise: the proper employment of Red in an inclement environment.

Madame Bondersil would fill a bath with several buckets of ice water then order Lizanne to imbibe a small amount of Red before lying in the tub. She would then stand by with a stop-watch as Lizanne tried desperately not to exhaust the Red in a single convulsive burst. The first few attempts had seen her melt all the ice, though luckily Madame ensured there was insufficient product in her system to boil the water. Over time, however, she had learned to control the release of Red, disciplining her mind and body so that it seeped away in a continual, gradual flow, warming the surrounding water sufficiently for her to remain submerged for an extended period. Her record at the Academy had been forty-eight minutes. Tonight she would need to exceed an hour.

She pressed the requisite button on the Spider halfway down the anchor chain, injecting a quarter of a vial before slipping into the water. The chill gripped her like a vice for a split-second before she summoned the Red, the numbing cold banished in an instant. She held on to the chain, head tilted back so her nose and mouth could still draw air as she fought down a reflexive retch. The Red could keep her warm but could do nothing about the stench.

The next phase of her insertion was fairly straightforward. She would await the sunrise whereupon the harbour door would open and the assembled ships begin to make their way inside. The bosun advised the *Islander* would most likely be fourth in line to gain access. When she began to move Lizanne would follow her in, injecting Green and diving below the surface to avoid the gaze of well-armed guards manning the turrets on either side of the entrance. Straightforward, but the wait was tedious and the *Regal* sat at anchor only a short distance away.

Impetuosity, she recalled Madame saying several years ago, shaking her head in stern admonition. *It will be the death of you, young lady.* Lizanne allowed herself a grin before injecting a quarter vial of Green and slipping below the surface.

She had to dive deep to clear the cloud of effluent, finding the water below clear and surprisingly rich in sea life. One of the more appreciated effects of Green was a prolongation of respiration, allowing a Blood-blessed to remain underwater for three times the normal duration. The enhanced vision also made for an interesting aquatic experience. Schools of mackerel darted from her path, swarming and breaking apart in a fascinating dance. She caught a glimpse of a ray of some kind shaking loose a cloud of sand before flying off into the gloom, long tail whipping. The surrounding sea-bed was littered with various detritus from the tenements and, she noticed, more than a few human skulls grinning up at her from the sand. It seemed the wall-dwellers used the sea to dispose of more than just effluent.

It took perhaps three minutes before the jagged bulk of the *Regal*'s paddles came into view, the stilled blades jutting below the putrid fog. Lizanne made for the stern, hoping to find the anchor chain. She would climb a short way up and listen for any voices on the deck. If the way proved clear a closer inspection might be warranted. As she swam she was given pause by the cleanliness of the cruiser's hull, mostly free of crustaceans or the myriad scars that signified an extended time at sea. *She's newly scraped,* Lizanne realised, her interest deepening as she neared the stern. There was something odd about the shape of the hull here, a bulbous protrusion extending towards the rudder of a kind she had never seen before. Swimming closer she saw that the protrusion narrowed towards its end then blossomed into what appeared to be a massive metal flower.

She slowed and drifted closer. The odd extrusion was about three yards across and appeared to be fashioned from steel, the three petals of the flower arranged about a central cone. She noticed the flower itself was not part of the protrusion in the hull, separated from it by a half-inch gap. But it appeared new, the metal showing no signs of corrosion. *Father would know in an instant what this is,* she thought, berating herself for not inheriting the family facility for things mechanical. *Or if he didn't, Jermayah surely would.*

Her head clouded with images of the many blueprints and devices glimpsed in her father's workshop, seeking something that might compare to this bizarre discovery. It came to her as she felt the effects of both the Green and Red start to ebb, her vision dimming and a chilly hand caressing her flesh. *The fan,* she remembered. *Father's desk fan.* Summer months in Feros could be oppressive, the air heavy with a clammy, strength-sapping heat. Never one to appreciate the loss of a day's work her father had built a small fan, driven by a tiny steam-engine that set three blades whirling fast enough to deliver a cooling breeze as he laboured over yet another fortune-making design that would, invariably, fail to find a backer. She had once suggested he try manufacturing the fan for sale only to receive an incredulous snort in response. *Fortunes are not won by trinkets, my dear.*

Not petals, she realised, reaching out to play her fingers over the flower's smooth surface. *Blades. The empire has invented a fan that can drive the water rather than the air.*

Lizanne winced as the surrounding chill deepened and her lungs began to burn. She paused just long enough to fix the image of the giant, ship-driving fan in her mind before kicking away and driving for the surface.

An hour later she heaved herself out of the shadowed waters beneath one of Morsvale's many piers, using up the last of the Green to clamber onto a sturdy cross-beam. Dawn had broken to bathe the harbour with a bright morning sun, shafts of light streaming through the pier's planking to splash welcome heat onto her shivering flesh. She had kept to the surface as the *Regal* neared the door, resisting the impulse to inject more product as the cold seeped ever deeper into her bones. Unlike the entrance to Carvenport, Morsvale had but one door, a great iron thing of many riveted plates. The whole edifice was hauled out of the water by means of revolving cogs driven by two steam-engines, of somewhat inefficient design given the clunking racket and copious smoke they emitted.

Lizanne kept to the shadow cast by the *Regal*'s stern as the cruiser turned her paddles and proceeded into the harbour. She waited until the last moment before submerging once more, just as the shoulder of a guard turret came into view. She injected all the remaining Green and Red as she dived, newly invigorated arms and legs working to place her under the warship's keel until her enhanced vision glimpsed the door's trench-like recess below, indicating she had crossed into the harbour proper. She made for a pier directly opposite the one where the *Regal* moored up, crouching amidst the forest of support beams to watch her arrival being greeted by a full company of Imperial troops. The dark red tunics and height of the soldiers, each at least six feet tall, made identification an easy matter: the Scarlet Legion. These were elite regulars, one of the three legions that made up the Corvantine Household Division. They were rarely seen outside the empire's borders, their principal occupation being the subjugation of internal revolt, usually by the most brutal means available. Lizanne could name three separate massacres attributed to the Scarlet Butchers, as Corvantine radicals called them.

She watched as a gangplank was hauled into place and a group of officers made their way from the ship to the pier. There were seven of them, all but one dressed in the uniform of the Imperial Navy. This odd man out was a tall fellow of middling years clad in the dark green uniform of the light infantry, his jacket free of any insignia. Unlike all the other soldiery present he was bare-headed, his hair shaven down to the scalp. She would have taken him for a somewhat unusually aged common soldier but for the obvious deference and respect displayed by all those around him. The tall man acknowledged the salutes of the Legion officers greeting him with a curt nod then gave a dismissive wave as a colonel bowed and gestured at the ranks of waiting legionnaires.

No time for inspections, Lizanne thought, watching the tall man stride past the soldiers to climb into a waiting carriage. *And little interest in ceremony*. She had never seen this man in person before but had read sufficient intelligence reports and seen enough blurred photostats to know his name well enough: Henris Lek Morradin, Grand Marshal of Legions and Victor of the Day of Justice. *The Emperor has sent his favourite attack dog to Arradsia. Why?*

CHAPTER 9

Hilemore

'They call it the Hive, apparently,' Captain Trumane said, tapping the pencilled 'x' on the map with the point of his calliper. The mark sat in a horseshoe-shaped bay in one of the myriad islands forming the north-eastern shoulder of the Barrier Isles. 'A nest of pirates and villains where our prey makes her home. Maritime Intelligence has spent the better part of four years searching for it, and now, gentlemen, it finally lies within our grasp.'

Mr Lemhill rested his hands on the ward-room table, heavy brows drawn as he regarded the map with a practised eye. 'Our speed will count for little in such close confines, sir,' he said. 'And, if this pirates' den is truthfully named, we'll have more than one vessel to contend with.'

'Quite so, Number One,' the captain replied, his tone coloured by a slight smugness. 'Fortunate it is then, that we have no need to enter this particular pit of snakes. Our colleagues in Maritime Intelligence assure me that the *Windqueen* is not currently at harbour. Rather, she is en route via a little-known passage through the dense mass of islands to the south. She is expected to arrive within two days, meaning all we need do is lie in wait. Once she's either sunk or taken as a prize, we will conduct a bombardment of this Hive from a reasonably safe distance before returning to Feros. Even if we don't destroy the settlement completely, the inhabitants will have little choice but to flee in the knowledge that their lair has been discovered.'

'Might I enquire, Captain,' Hilemore said, 'what intelligence we possess regarding the enemy's complement and ordnance?'

'Nothing we can't cope with, I'm sure,' Trumane replied, waving a dismissive hand. 'With our speed and superior armament I see little occasion for concern.'

'Even so, sir,' Hilemore went on, 'most rumours regarding this particular pirate paints her as a blood-burner. Meaning, of course, they will have at least one Blood-blessed on board.'

'Superior gunnery will prove ample antidote to any threat from that quarter,' Trumane said, voice now taking on a tetchy edge. 'And I dare say there are a few marksmen under your command with a keen enough eye to pick off any pirates displaying obvious signs of the Blessing.'

Hilemore recalled the largest battle of the Dalcian Emergency and the huge war-galley that had emerged from the smoke to plough towards his frigate. It was crammed with warriors from bow to stern and, standing at the prow, the last few remaining members of the High King's Blood Cabal. They stood in a dense cluster, bare of clothing and their flesh liberally decorated with garish paint of different hues. Dalcian Blood-blessed continued to attach mystical allusions to their abilities, believing the sigils with which they adorned their skin added somehow to their power. If so, it had availed them nothing that day. Hilemore had leapt atop one of the life-boats, kneeling and taking careful aim with a rifle as Dalcian musket balls buzzed around him. All but one of the Cabal had fallen before the galley drew close enough for their abilities to have any effect. The lone survivor, however, a tall, well-muscled fellow daubed all over in red paint, had clearly imbibed a huge quantity of Green, sufficient in fact to carry him over the rail before he plummeted into the centre of the aft deck. The subsequent two minutes of carnage had provided evidence aplenty of the danger posed by a Blood-blessed at close quarters.

'An effective tactic, sir,' he conceded to Trumane, briefly closing his eyes to clear the images of flaming and dismembered men from his mind. 'However, I would suggest the boarding party's complement be increased as a precautionary measure. Another dozen men should do it.'

'We don't have another dozen men to spare, Lieutenant,' Trumane pointed out. 'Every other man aboard will have his own task to perform when battle is joined.'

'Apart from the cooks and laundry attendants, sir,' Hilemore said. 'And your own stewards.'

He saw Trumane stiffen at that. Most captains made do with one steward, some with none, but Captain Trumane saw fit to employ three. He flushed a little and started to reply but Lemhill, perhaps sensing the onset of an unwise outburst, cut in first.

'I can probably rustle up another six men for you,' he told Hilemore. 'Can't speak for their fighting abilities though.'

Hilemore nodded, glancing at Trumane's reddened features and knowing it was time for a tactical withdrawal. 'Gratefully received in any case, sir,' he told Lemhill. 'If you could have them report to me at first light, I will commence their training.'

Trumane took a moment to regard Hilemore in imperious silence before returning his attention to the map. 'We will proceed at the rate of one half flask a day. By my calculations that will provide an average speed of eighteen knots in fair weather, meaning we should reach the Isles in nine days. We will keep well to the north of this Hive then cut towards the south and find a suitably secluded mooring from which to spring our trap. In the meantime I shall be undertaking regular inspections of the crew, particularly the boarding party, Mr Hilemore. I would hate to administer punishments should you fail to transform your cooks and wash-boys into riflemen in the time available.'

'Fire!' The entire boarding party fired in unison, thirty rifles cracking sharply in the morning air to tear a fresh cluster of ragged holes in the canvas target bobbing a hundred yards off the starboard rail. *Grouping's better*, Hilemore decided upon viewing the results through his spy-glass. *Still falling short of twelve rounds a minute though.* He watched the man nearest to him working the bolt of his Silworth rifle, a single-shot .422 breech-loader that, in the right hands, was deadly up to a mile. Like his fellows, the sailor was a proficient rifleman but hardly expert and Hilemore's experiences in Dalcian waters had provided ample education in the value of expertise.

'Too slow!' he barked as the last man snapped the bolt closed and presented his rifle. It had become a familiar refrain during the voyage south and he saw a couple of the men suppressing weary groans in expectation of his next orders. 'Master-at-Arms!'

The hulking Islander snapped to attention. 'Sir!'

'Three times around the fore-deck, if you please. And let's pick up the pace a bit this time.'

'Aye, sir!' Within minutes Steelfine had them whipped into a column and doubling around the fore-deck, rifles held at port arms and knees raised to hip height with every step. Despite their evident fatigue none of the riflemen faltered, evidence of the depth of respect, or rather fear, with which they regarded their Master-at-Arms.

At the sound of a faint but insistent call Hilemore raised his gaze to the upper reaches of the *Viable*'s only mast where the slender form of Mr Talmant could be seen in the crow's nest. The ensign saluted then waved towards the southern horizon. Hilemore duly turned his glass southwards and it wasn't long before he picked out a faint, grey-green hump rising above the waves.

'Another ship?'

He lowered the glass to find Mr Tottleborn had joined him. The young Blood-blessed rested his arms on the rail, pinched and pale features regarding the view beyond the bows with a mixture of trepidation and weariness.

'No,' Hilemore replied. 'Land. One of the outer islands I expect.'

'Chock-full of savages keen to rape us to death then devour our corpses, no doubt.'

Hilemore cast a cautious glance around to ensure Steelfine wasn't in earshot before giving Tottleborn a closer look. Although the liquor cabinet remained firmly closed to him throughout the ten days it had taken to get here, a perennial redness lingered around his eyes. Added to that, his languid movements and lack of appetite had forced Hilemore to conclude Tottleborn had found some other means of feeding his addiction. As was custom in the Maritime Protectorate, the crew received a daily rum ration but, so far, he hadn't managed to catch any in the act of selling it on. Given that Tottleborn had continued to perform within the bounds of his contract, albeit with an undimmed sullenness and distinct absence of enthusiasm, Hilemore hadn't felt the need to push the matter. However, with their objective now in sight he might have to adopt a less lenient approach.

'It's not the Islanders we need to worry about,' he told Tottleborn. 'Our enemies are likely to be much better armed and a sight more savage.'

He watched the Blood-blessed clasp his hands together to conceal a tremble. 'So it's certain there'll be a battle?'

'Almost certain. Your first time in combat, I assume?'

Tottleborn gave a jerky nod, his thin neck bulging as he swallowed. 'At least fighting isn't specified in my contract,' he said, forcing a smile.

'Quite so. Can't have you swinging over the rail with cutlass in hand, now can we? No, you'll be tucked up nice and safe in the engine room surrounded by several inches of armour-plate.'

Tottleborn's smile faded and his sombre gaze drifted over a sea rendered grey under the overcast sky. 'There's a little known facet of the Blue-trance,' he said in a quiet voice. 'One we rarely talk about. They call it the Shadow.'

Hilemore frowned in puzzlement. He had made it his business to research the nature of the Blessing and its numerous inherent dangers, but this was beyond his knowledge. 'Shadow?'

'Yes. Every Blood-blessed perceives the trance differently. For some it's a storm, for others a forest. Mine is like a corridor of endless doors. I need only open one to access the memory or knowledge it possesses. But sometimes a Blood-blessed will see something in their trance, something dark and formless: a void swallowing light and emitting nothing except a chill sense of finality. It may be mere superstition, but it's said that when you see the Shadow you see a portent of your own death.'

'And you have seen it?'

'My last trance was . . . confused, for reasons best not discussed at this juncture.'

'Meaning you were drunk.'

Tottleborn's eyes flashed at him. 'Meaning it was confused.' He sighed and looked away. 'I believe I saw . . . something. A door that hadn't been there before, its form shifting continually, and it was so very dark . . .'

Tottleborn trailed off as Steelfine brought the boarding party to a halt a few yards away, growling at the sagging men to straighten up before delivering a salute. 'Three laps of the fore-deck completed as ordered, sir!'

'Thank you, Master-at-Arms.' Hilemore turned back to Tottleborn. 'There isn't a pirate vessel afloat with sufficient fire-power to penetrate the armour shielding the engine room. I suggest this shadow door of yours was but a figment born of drink. Now, if you'll excuse me, I have men to train.'

'There's a letter,' the Blood-blessed said before he could move away, 'in my cabin.' He forced another smile. 'For a young lady of my acquaintance back in Feros. Should the worst happen . . .'

'Worry is the enemy of all sailors, Mr Tottleborn,' Hilemore interrupted, finding his patience exhausted. 'Best put it from your mind and concentrate on the matter at hand. I believe a Blue-trance communication is scheduled in less than one hour. Please go and ask Mr Lemhill for the relevant documents. I shall meet you in the ward-room when I'm done here.'

He saw a brief flicker of hurt pass over Tottleborn's narrow features before he nodded and turned away, making for the ladder leading to the bridge.

'Now then,' Hilemore said, raising his voice to address the boarding party and taking a stop-watch from his pocket. 'Let's see if you buggers can do any better with independent fire. An extra quarter measure of rum for any man who manages twelve rounds in a minute.'

The captain chose to anchor in a narrow inlet on the coast of a small island six miles north-east of the Hive. They approached at night, moving at a crawl through the two-moonlit waters, Tottleborn having burned only a tenth of a flask to reduce their speed and engine noise. Hilemore stood at the prow as the *Viable* slowed to a halt, grudgingly impressed by Trumane's navigation. Under his guidance the helmsman had performed a ninety-degree turn exactly ten miles true north and the subsequent passage had been achieved with only minimal corrections. All night the captain stood on the gangway taking repeated readings from the stars and moons with his sextant, every now and then ordering slight changes in their heading to counter the effects of the prevailing current. Hilemore entertained certain doubts about his captain's command ability but his skill as a navigator, like his expert understanding of the workings of the marvellous engine that drove this ship, was unquestionable.

Hilemore also found he couldn't fault the man for his regular inspections of the boarding party; with battle looming men needed a vigilant and sometimes stern commander. However, he wished Trumane would exercise his gift for criticism with greater care, concentrating more on marksmanship and weapons maintenance than uniform infractions. He had come close to ordering one of the cooks flogged for a missing belt buckle but seemed unconcerned by the blunt edge on the boy's bayonet, an infraction for which Hilemore had fined him a month's sea pay before ordering three mornings of close-order drill under Steelfine's instruction.

On the whole he judged the boarding party as ready as he could make them, though only a handful had ever seen combat and they lacked the cutting edge and aggression of the men he had commanded in the Emergency. He could only hope these pirates proved a less ferocious foe than the Sovereignists when the time came.

He turned at the splash of the anchor descending into the still waters of the inlet, soon followed by the soft toll of the bell sounding the commencement of the first watch. He lingered for a moment, his thoughts turning to Lewella, as they ever did when the still hours of the night were upon him. Her letter rested in the breast pocket of his tunic and he couldn't help the feeling that it emitted a certain heat through the fabric, the pain it held warm and irresistible. *Please do not hate me . . .*

As ever, when his thoughts turned to Lewella, they fixed on that first meeting. Whilst young women of the managerial class were typically introduced to their future fiancés at a ball or other suitably chaperoned social gathering, Lewella Tythencroft was destined to meet Lieutenant Corrick Hilemore under very different circumstances. The North Mandinorian port of Sanorah was no stranger to riots, but previous civil disturbances had tended to erupt amidst the ever-fractious and poverty-riven dockside neighbourhoods. This one was different in that the principal agitators were students rather than drunken stevedores enraged at yet another wage cut.

Hilemore had emerged from the post office on Aylemont Road to find himself embroiled in a scene of smoke-shrouded chaos. He could see a line of mounted Protectorate constabulary clubbing their way through a crowd of yelling youths, batons and placards colliding in an ugly melee before the horses broke through and the young people scattered. One, however, remained where she was.

She was tall with auburn hair trailing from a hatless and dishevelled head, her well-tailored clothes marking her out as of managerial station, although the message painted onto her placard spoke of contradictory allegiances. *IRONSHIP MUST BE DISSOLVED!*

'Votes not shares!' he heard her cry out, standing straight-backed and unafraid as her fellow protestors fled on all sides. 'End the corporate tyranny!'

Hilemore found himself transfixed by the sight, continuing to stare even as a salvo of rifle-shots sounded through the thickening smoke. The moment was broken, however, by the sight of a Protectorate constable wheeling his horse about and galloping straight at the object of Hilemore's fascination.

'Votes not shares! Votes no—'

The young woman's chant ended in a hard grunt as Hilemore's charge took her off her feet, horse and constable thundering past, the clatter of iron-shod hooves counterpointed by the whistle of the constable's baton as it came within a whisker of Hilemore's head. They landed a few yards on, Hilemore finding himself staring into the woman's eyes, bright hazel eyes that were angry rather than grateful.

'Get off me!' she shouted, struggling free. 'Corporate pig! Slaver's mercenary!'

Hilemore's attention was dragged away by the sound of the constable attempting to bring his mount around for a second charge. Luckily, the fellow was clearly a novice horseman and took an inordinate amount of time to complete the manoeuvre. Hilemore surged to his feet, covered the intervening distance in a few strides and jerked the constable's foot free of his stirrup, hauling him from the saddle with a heavy shove. He slapped a hand to the animal's flank to send it galloping off through the smoke then turned to find the young woman had regained her feet and was crouching to retrieve her placard.

'Put me down!' she yelled as he forestalled any delay by simply lifting her onto his shoulder and bearing her away at a steady run. 'Unhand me you Syndicate lackey!'

He was obliged to shield her from several more assaults as he skirted knots of conflict where students and constables battled one another with an intensity that he wouldn't see outmatched until the Dalcian Emergency two years later.

Finally the smoke began to thin as they entered a residential street away from the main concourse. The young woman had fallen into a stern silence by now and glared at him as he set her down, lips set in a hard, unyielding line as he touched a finger to his cap. 'Apologies, miss.'

'You, sir,' she said, glare undimmed, 'are a whore to the corporate elite.'

And then she kissed him.

'Cocoa, sir.'

Hilemore blinked and turned to find Mr Talmant confronting him with a steaming tin mug. 'Cookie's compliments, sir,' the ensign went on. 'Says his boys are a lot more obedient since you came aboard.'

'Be sure to thank him for me.' Hilemore accepted the mug, raising his eyebrows as he paused to sniff the steaming aroma. *A tot or two of rum, if I'm not mistaken.* He decided it would be churlish to refuse the cook's gratitude and took a generous sip.

'A wild shore, sir,' Talmant said, nodding at the jungle-thick mass of the island. The light of the double moons played over the dense foliage like a scattering of silver dust that did little to alleviate its ominous appearance. 'Do you think we'll see any Islanders?'

'I've only sailed these waters once before,' Hilemore replied. 'My first posting in fact, when I was an ensign like you. Sailed up and down the whole archipelago in a customs cutter for six months and never caught sight of a native the whole voyage. In fact, Mr Steelfine is the only Islander I've had the pleasure of seeing at close quarters.'

'I believe he's from one of the Vineland tribes that live near the Strait. The only tribe ever to be successfully pacified, they say.'

Hilemore had serious doubts that the word 'pacified' could be truthfully applied to Steelfine but was impressed by the boy's knowledge. 'Are you an educated fellow then, Mr Talmant?'

The ensign gave a cautious smile. 'I had three years of school, sir. Milvale, Explorer House.'

Milvale, Hilemore knew, was one of the more prestigious boarding schools where the Mandinorian managerial class sent their children. Mr Talmant, it seemed, came from successful stock. 'Explorer, eh?' he asked.

'The house was founded by the Explorer's Guild, sir. Back in the days of the old empire. I believe it was their intention to educate successive generations of adventurers.'

'Is that why you joined up? To voyage to the far-flung reaches of the globe?'

'Partly, sir. My tenure at the school came to a somewhat abrupt end, you see.' He paused and Hilemore saw an embarrassed flush on his cheeks despite the gloom. *Money troubles,* he decided. It was a familiar story. The Talmants' stock must have fallen: a bad investment or over-extended credit on the family mansion. Either way the school fees could no longer be met and it was time for the boy to find gainful employment. Though the youth seemed cheerful enough with his lot.

'And you, sir?' Talmant asked. 'The Maritime Academy, I assume?'

Hilemore shook his head. 'My father didn't believe in formal education. Or rather, he resented the expense it required. My brothers and I were taught reading and numbers by my mother. Luckily, my grandfather had schooled her in the mysteries of navigation and I proved an able student. It was of considerable assistance when I applied to the Protectorate, my knowledge of other areas having been so neglected.'

'Your grandfather,' Talmant said, a certain hushed reverence in his voice. 'I overheard Mr Lemhill make mention of him. Truly you are the grandson of Fighting Jak then, sir?'

Fighting Jak, or Captain and later Commodore Jakamore Racksmith to be precise. A man Hilemore had known intimately for but one year of his life, but what a year it had been. The old man had taken them in after his father had finally frittered away the last of the family holdings, necessitating the sale of Astrage Vale to Cousin Malkim, a man of singular odium. Father had taken himself off to the eastern steppes, ostensibly to seek out some fabled lost treasure and restore the family fortune. Hilemore, then aged thirteen and old enough to know a lie when he heard it, had sternly refused to take his father's hand the day he left. Instead he turned his back and walked to the carriage that would take him, his brothers and his mother to their grandfather's comparatively humble home by the sea. He remembered Father calling his name but he hadn't looked back. Whatever became of him Hilemore never knew, though in idle moments he preferred to imagine him tucked up warm and safe in a yurt with a plump nomad woman and a full skin of fermented milk.

'Keen to hear an anecdote are we, Ensign?' he asked Talmant, grinning at the boy's evident discomfort. 'Grandfather rarely spoke of his battles, though my mother had provided me a rich history of his career. No, he preferred to speak of his more peaceful endeavours. It's often forgotten these days but he was as much an explorer as a fighter. I dare say he would have been at home lecturing in your old college.'

'It would have been an honour to hear him, sir.' Talmant fidgeted for a moment before continuing, evidently struggling with the right choice of words. 'Lieutenant, with regards to the boarding party . . .'

'No,' Hilemore interrupted flatly.

'But, sir. It's plain you are short-handed . . .'

'Short-handed or not, I have no place for you, Mr Talmant. You have an allotted role aboard this ship.'

Talmant stiffened a little. 'Shackled to the captain's side, relaying messages whilst my comrades fight is hardly honourable duty.'

'On that point you are utterly wrong.' Hilemore smothered an exasperated sigh, knowing he was looking at himself from ten years before, though even then he had stood half a foot taller than this deluded youth. 'There is no safe place in a sea battle, Mr Talmant,' he said, voice now rich in authority. 'As you will soon discover when we draw within range of our adversary's guns. The captain has done you credit by ascribing you a vital role. I suggest you do not abuse the opportunity with churlishness.'

Talmant's posture abruptly shifted into straight-backed respect, eyes averted as he saluted, replying in a standard tone, 'Very good, sir.'

Hilemore nodded and returned the salute. 'Carry on, Mr Talmant.'

'Sir!'

He watched the lad take a few steps, then sighed again before calling after him. 'A moment, Ensign.'

Talmant halted and about-faced, still maintaining his rigid posture. 'Aye, sir.'

'You and the other junior officers will draw revolvers tomorrow morning and report here for target practice. Bring your swords, too. And I had better not find any with a dull edge.'

He saw Talmant suppress a grin before he saluted again. 'I'll make sure of it, sir.'

'See that you do, Mr Talmant.' Hilemore returned his gaze to the island as Talmant's footsteps faded, watching the moonlight play on the tree-tops and feeling Lewella's letter burn against his breast once more. *Throw it away,* a seductive voice whispered inside his head. *Consign it to the sea and curse her name. Betrayal deserves nothing else.*

If that's true, he answered himself, *I had best throw myself in as well. Still* – he took another gulp of cocoa before upending the mug and emptying the remainder into the still waters below – *in a day or two the pirates may well spare me the trouble.*

CHAPTER 10

Clay

'Told you to leave it be,' his uncle grated through clenched teeth.

'I did,' Clay replied. He glanced across the table at Silverpin busily shovelling fresh scrambled eggs into her mouth, apparently oblivious to the conversation. It became abruptly clear to him that his uncle had no notion of the gift she had made him the previous night. He turned away and left a lengthy pause before replying. 'Man like that had no shortage of enemies. Seems someone saved me the trouble.'

'You think Keyvine's crew will see it that way?'

'Keyvine's crew are already slicing each other to pieces over who gets to sit the throne, or if they ain't they soon will be. Besides, you got Ironship protection now, right?'

'Don't tell me what I got, boy!' Braddon started to rise, stopping only when Fredabel put a hand on his arm.

'He was here all night,' she said softly. 'Lest he sprouted wings, can't see how he could've done this thing.'

There came a light knocking at the door. It was open to receive the fresh morning air but the new arrival lingered outside, awaiting leave to enter with his broad-brimmed hat clutched in both hands. He was a bulky man of New Colonial complexion, closer to fifty than forty with long hair and a heavy beard, the duster he wore and the butt of a shotgun jutting above his shoulder clearly indicating his Contractor status. He gave a respectful nod as Fredabel went to greet him. 'Mrs Torcreek.'

'Mr Skaggerhill.' She took both his hands and drew him inside. 'I've told you many times, just come on in.'

'Yes, ma'am,' Skaggerhill replied with an earnest nod, Clay noting the faint flush on his cheeks. *Seems Auntie won't be wanting for a suitor if anything happens to Uncle,* he surmised.

'Skaggs,' Braddon said, getting to his feet to shake the man's hand. 'Join us for a bite.'

'Eaten already, Captain. But thank you for the consideration.' 'They here?'

'Gathered in the yard, sir.' Skaggerhill gave an embarrassed wince and inclined his head at the door. 'Got a small matter to attend to first, however.'

Loriabeth lay in the back of the wagon, a livid bruise on her cheek and the twin holsters on her hips empty. 'Had to take her guns,' Skaggerhill explained. 'Got a mite rambunctious after the third bottle.'

'What happened to her face?' Fredabel asked, arms crossed tight in concern as she cast a wary glance at her husband's darkening visage.

'She, uh, formed an attachment,' Skaggerhill said, voice heavy with reluctance. 'Young fella from the Trueshots. They danced for a while, then it seems he said something unfortunate. Things got a little hairy for a time. May be politic to go see their captain, smooth the waters like.'

Braddon stared down at his daughter with a barely controlled rage. 'And she wants a place on this expedition,' he said in a low voice.

'Probably just trying to fit in,' Fredabel said, voice deliberately light. 'It's Contractor custom to let loose a little the night before an expedition.'

'She ain't a Contractor,' Braddon grated, turning to his wife in mounting anger. 'She's my daughter. Her actions reflect on me, on this company. This is not some ragbag headhunter mob . . .'

He trailed off as Clay stepped between them, moving to the wagon and taking hold of Loriabeth's arms. He hauled her onto his shoulder and carried her inside without particular difficulty since she weighed next to nothing. She gave a weary moan as he heaved her onto her bed, surfacing from the wine-induced fog and blinking at him with dulled eyes. 'Shit,' she groaned. 'You're still here.'

''Fraid so, cuz,' he replied with a smile. He glanced at the door as his aunt and uncle's argument escalated downstairs. 'Though right now I'm not sure which one of us your pa will kill first.'

'Kill you first,' she mumbled, curling up on the bed and snuggling childlike into the covers. 'Kill you for murdering your pa . . .' After a few seconds she began to snore.

Clay took a look around her room, finding it surprisingly neat and well-ordered with an extensive collection of knives adorning the walls along with several maps and photostats of the Interior. He stepped closer to examine a framed sepia image above her bed, Braddon crouching next to a dead drake, a Red judging by the size. His uncle was maybe a decade younger, clasping his longrifle in one hand whilst balancing a little girl on his knee, her face smudged slightly. Children tended to be blurred in older photostats due to an inability to keep still long enough for the image to set.

'Been waiting for this a long time, huh?' he asked Loriabeth, receiving only a drooling rasp in return.

'Claydon!' Fredabel called from downstairs, voice strained with forced conviviality. 'Miss Lethridge is here.'

Altogether they numbered six and Loriabeth was not counted amongst them. Aunt Fredabel had gone to wake her when the Longrifles assembled in the yard but Braddon forbade it with a command terse enough to leave his wife scowling.

'You really want to leave it like this?' she asked.

'Time she learned some consequences,' he replied before turning to the company, refusing to look as Fredabel stomped off back to the house.

'This here's my nephew, Claydon,' Braddon told the Contractors, jerking his head at Clay. 'If you're familiar with the Blinds I guess you've heard the name and may be wondering why a known killer and thief is part of this expedition. I'm also mindful that I've never before taken a company so deep into the Interior. I ask you to trust my word that this is how it needs to be and the reward is equal to the risk. Any who can't do that are welcome to forego this contract with an assurance that your choice won't affect our future dealings.'

He fell silent, arms crossed in expectation of their answer. Clay was accustomed to the company of dangerous folk but found the scrutiny of the Longrifles more disconcerting than he would have liked. In addition to Skaggerhill and Silverpin there were a man and a woman of New Colonial stock, both possessed of a forbidding appearance and penetrating gaze. The man was tall, with a narrow face and tendrils of dark hair snaking down from a balding scalp. Clay put his age at somewhere past thirty but he could have been older from the deep lines clustered around his eyes. He carried a longrifle in a soft leather bag and rested his powerful hands on the barrel whilst regarding Clay, head tilted, like a cat analysing unfamiliar prey. What caught most of Clay's attention, however, was the sight of the blood-red collar the man wore about his neck. *Cleric,* he realised. *What's a churchman doing in this company?*

'Don't worry, young 'un,' said the woman at the tall man's side, reading Clay's expression. 'Preacher don't do much preaching these days.' She made a stark contrast to her fellow Contractor, being of chunky build and standing only an inch above five feet, the pistols on her hips and carbine on her back a clear indication of her role. *Gunhand.* 'Name's Foxbine,' she said, taking off her hat in greeting and revealing a mass of red hair twisted into thick braids in the style of an Island woman, though the absence of tattoos and her accent revealed her to be of Carvenport origin.

'Pleased to meet you, ma'am,' Clay replied, then nodded at Preacher. 'And you, sir.'

'Well, he's polite enough,' Foxbine said to Braddon. 'And time's wasting, Captain. We wanna make Stockade by nightfall we'd best move out.'

Braddon nodded and shifted his gaze to Preacher. 'You're sure?'

The tall man said nothing, merely casting a final impassive gaze at Clay before hefting his rifle and walking to his horse. 'Well, that gets it said.' Braddon pointed at Skaggerhill's wagon. 'Clay, you ride with the harvester. Thank your aunt for her hospitality and let's get gone.'

Braddon walked to his horse without a single glance towards the house. He mounted up then flicked an impatient hand at Clay as he stood staring in surprise. Shaking his head he went inside and found Fredabel running a cloth over the meal table.

'My uncle . . .' Clay began, unsure of what to say.

'We don't say good-bye,' she told him. 'He always comes back and when he does it's like he's only been gone a day. So we never say good-bye.' She stopped and turned to him with a smile. 'It was good to have you under my roof again, Claydon.'

'And I thank you for the favour, Auntie.'

She gave a furtive glance at the door then moved closer, taking something from the folds of her skirt and pressing it into his hand. 'Don't tell your uncle. The cost of it would drive him mad and those Ironship witches said you were only allowed Blue.'

Clay looked at her gift, feeling his heart lurch in gratitude. A vial, the colour and density of the contents wonderfully familiar. *Black. A full vial of Black.* 'Thank you, Auntie,' he said, quickly consigning the vial to his pocket. 'Rest assured I'll pay you back . . .'

'Oh, hush now.' She leaned close and planted a kiss on his cheek then withdrew a little, hands on his shoulders. 'Knew your mother. Only a little, but I liked her well enough. Knew your father too, more than I wanted to. Sometimes there are men who just need to be taken out of this world. So, regardless of my husband's view on the matter, I see no reason to bar you from this family. When you come back, this house will be your home for as long as you want it to be.' She hugged him close then pushed him towards the door. 'You go on now. And keep close to Mr

Skaggerhill. If there's anyone can keep you alive out there it's him.'

The jungle stank. It wasn't just an odour, or a scent, it was a stink, thick, cloying and inescapable. It assailed his nostrils at every breath, rich with the sweet tang of decay and overripe fruit. Added to the discomfort of the stink was the ominous sight of the jungle itself, a wall of green closing around with every mile passed since leaving Carvenport. The road grew dimmer as they travelled, the trees rising to obscure the sun until the company was completely in the shade and the road had transformed into a rutted track.

'First time beyond the walls makes a fella itch, alright,' Skaggerhill commented, watching Clay fidget, sweat-beaded eyes constantly roving the surrounding curtain of greenery. 'Feels like it's gonna reach out and grab ya, don't it?'

Clay confined his reply to an irritated scowl, striving to stare straight ahead at the two oxen drawing the wagon, but managing only a few yards before the jungle inevitably drew his gaze once more.

'You're right to be wary, young 'un.' Skaggerhill chuckled. 'Fairly shit my pants first time out. And with good reason: Greens are always looking for an easy meal.'

'What Greens?' Clay grunted, gesturing at the surrounding wall of vegetation. 'Haven't seen shit all day.'

Skaggerhill gave a wry chuckle. ''Course you ain't. If you was to see a Green this far north it'll be strung up for harvesting. When we gets farther south though, you find y'self unlucky enough to catch a glimpse of a live one and you'll most likely be dead a second or two later.'

Clay's hand moved unconsciously to the only weapon he had been allowed, a double-barrelled hammer-lock pistol of antique appearance. His uncle had handed it to him as the company mounted up in the stable-yard, reading the disdain on Clay's face with a direct glare that dared him to voice a complaint. 'For protection only,' Braddon said. 'You got two shots and they're both already loaded. You fire this without a reason, you ain't getting any more.'

'Won't do you no good,' Skaggerhill said, nodding at the pistol. 'Jungle Greens are pack hunters, like to swarm over you from several directions at once.'

'So what do I do if I see one?'

'Run like the Seer's ghost is on your heels and scream your lungs out.'

'The noise'll scare them off, I guess.'

Skaggerhill chuckled again. 'No, but we hear you screaming we might come running quick enough for there to be something left worth saving.'

The town of Stockade sat on the eastern bank of the Greenchurn River. At first glance it appeared to consist of a half-circle of spike-topped tree-trunks enclosing a clutch of tents and huts of mean appearance. However, as they approached in line with the bank, Clay found his gaze drawn mostly to the long jetty that extended from the shore into the fast-flowing river. This, he realised, was where the real town lay. Two-storey houses sprouted along its length and a twenty-foot-high watch-tower rose at the junction where the piers split off. He counted half a dozen paddle steamers moored along the piers, mostly small single-wheelers but one side wheeler standing out thanks to the tallness of its stacks and the Ironship pennant flying from its mast.

'The *Firejack*,' Skaggerhill said. 'Only blood-burner to work the river trade. She'll be home for a while till we make the Sands.'

'You ever been there?' Clay asked him. 'The Red Sands.'

A cloud passed over the harvester's usually cheery features and he gave a short nod. 'Just once. They're well named, right enough. Don't seem natural for land to be so truly red. There's a badness to the place, a feeling to the air and it ain't just the dust.'

'But you're still willing to go? 'Cause my uncle asked you to?'

Skaggerhill gave him a sidelong glance. 'Your uncle asked me to walk naked across a southern ice-floe, I'd do it. Twenty expeditions together so far, and I came back whole and a damn sight richer from each and every one. Captains like him are a rare breed.'

The entrance to the town lay open and unguarded, the collection of tents and huts beyond shrouded in smoke. Raucous merriment rose from a large two-storey structure near the jetty but for the most part it was quiet. Men and women in Contractor garb sat around fires, sharing meals or playing cards, a few calling greetings to his uncle as they passed by. 'Only the river folk truly live here,' Skaggerhill explained. 'And they keep to the jetty. Contractors spend a night or two in camp waiting for a boat or trying to find a company, then move on.'

Braddon led them to a vacant patch of ground near the wall and told them to make camp. 'I'll check in with the *Firejack*'s skipper,' he said. 'Clay, help Mr Skaggerhill raise the tents then make supper.' He met Clay's gaze with the same glaring expectation of a challenge. *I do suspect,* Clay thought, *Uncle would quite like to beat me in front of this company.*

'My pleasure, Uncle,' he replied with a smile, climbing down from the wagon.

'Miss Foxbine.' Braddon turned to the gunhand. 'Take a turn around the camp and the tavern. See what the rumour-mill's weaving these days.'

Foxbine tipped her hat. 'Will do, Captain.'

Braddon turned his horse towards the pier, raising a hand to the various Contractors calling out greetings, Clay noting that every voice was coloured by a deep respect.

'You cook?'

Clay turned, finding himself confronted by Preacher. He stood at least half a foot taller than Clay, staring down with the same impassive scrutiny from before.

'Not especially,' Clay replied.

'I don't eat fowl,' Preacher stated, holding Clay's gaze. He was vaguely aware that those who still maintained adherence to the Seer's teachings often held objections to various food-stuffs.

'Seer spoke against it, huh?' he asked.

Preacher blinked, his expression unchanging as he repeated 'I don't eat fowl,' in exactly the same emphatic tone, before adding, 'Nor anything that flies.'

'Yeah, you said.' A familiar heat was building in Clay's chest as the tall man continued to stare, the heat that had come close to killing him as often as it had saved him back in the Blinds.

'He's got it, Preacher,' Skaggerhill said, coming to Clay's side. 'You know I'd never let such a thing touch your plate.'

Preacher looked at the harvester, blinked and walked back to his horse.

'Next time he says something to you,' Skaggerhill told Clay in a quiet voice, 'just nod, real polite-like, and agree. If he says the sky's purple with red dots all over it, you just nod and agree. Understand me, young 'un? This ain't the Blinds. Everything out here, including the people, is worse than anything you ever seen before.'

'A full company of headhunters?' Braddon asked with a sceptical frown.

Foxbine shrugged and nodded. 'That's the word, Captain. Second-generation crew out of Rigger's Bay, over fifty strong they say. Went hunting for Spoiled along the coast and just' – she spread her hands – 'never came out again. Some Contractors went looking and found a few bodies, all marked and cut up the way Spoiled like to do.'

'When was this?'

'About a month back. Seems the whole of Rigger's Bay is squawking about it, demanding more troops from the Protectorate and such.'

'Spoiled getting all riled up is never good news,' Skaggerhill commented. 'But Rigger's Bay is a good sight out of our way.'

'Thought the Spoiled were supposed to be near extinct,' Clay said which drew a hearty laugh from Foxbine.

'They're like rats,' his uncle replied in a grim tone. 'Always more than you think there are.'

'True enough,' Foxbine said, her mirth subsiding into a nostalgic grin. 'You remember that last trip to the Flats? Only time I ever ran out of ammunition.'

Supper was beef sausage and rice, cooked under Skaggerhill's close supervision. Clay had watched Preacher carefully examine his plate before taking a bite, chewing and pursing his lips in apparent satisfaction. Silverpin sat next to Clay, happily gorging herself on the meal in what he was coming to understand as a characteristic lack of moderation, then offering him a wink of appreciation. As Foxbine related her accumulated gossip the bladehand reclined, leaning in Clay's direction and running a whetstone over the narrow blade of a six-foot spear. Clay recognised it as an Islander's weapon, the haft fashioned from ebony and covered from end to end in intricate carvings and tribal symbols. The butt ended in a fist-sized ball which, he knew, made an excellent skull-cracker. If the conversation held any interest for Silverpin she failed to show it, though she did cast an occasional shy smile in Clay's direction.

'Anything else of interest?' Skaggerhill enquired of Foxbine.

'Contractor Company took some losses in the Badlands,' she said. 'More than usual, that is. Seems the Reds are getting a sight boisterous these days.'

'Since when weren't they . . . ?' the harvester began then trailed off as a high, piercing screech came echoing over the wall. Clay saw him exchange an urgent glance with his uncle. 'Can't be. Not so far north, not for years.'

Braddon stood, raising a hand to silence him. Clay rose as the rest of the company followed his uncle's lead. They listened for a while, Clay suddenly aware of the silence as the entire congregation of Contractors strained their ears for another sound. Nothing came for several moments and a murmur of conversation had begun to return when the screech rose again, louder and closer this time, and, if Clay was any judge, it wasn't alone.

'That's a Seer-damned pack,' Skaggerhill breathed.

'Greens?' Clay asked.

'What else they gonna be?' Foxbine grunted, hefting her carbine.

'Best get to the wall,' Braddon said, unsheathing his longrifle from its green-leather covering. 'Clay, stay with the wagon.'

Clay stared after him as he led his people towards the wall, most of the other Contractors following suit with weapons in hand. The casual humiliation caused the heat to rise in his chest again, spawning all manner of unwise notions. 'Fuck this,' he muttered, drawing his double-barrelled pistol and following, though at a discreet distance.

He was surprised to find the entrance still standing open. Apparently no-one had thought to close it in quite a while. 'Not sure the hinges even work any more,' a heavy-set man was saying to Braddon. He wore the peaked cap and overalls typical of river folk and was flanked by two younger men in similar garb. 'Been some talk we should just go ahead and take down the walls, for all the good they do these days.'

'Looks like they'll be doing you some good tonight,' Braddon replied, nodding at the darkness beyond the gateway where the screeching chorus continued unabated. If anything, it seemed to have risen in volume.

'How many, d'you think?' the riverman asked Braddon.

'Full pack and then some.' Braddon worked the lever on his rifle, chambering a round. 'More than twenty, most likely. It's your town, sir, but my advice is you get this sealed up best you can, and the quicker the better. That's a frenzy song they're singing. Frenzy makes 'em unheedful of injury. Just a few get loose in here and it's gonna get ugly real fast.'

The riverman gave a sweaty-faced nod and started barking orders, a clutch of townsfolk running to heave the doors in place, rusted hinges squealing. They buttressed them with some sturdy beams and dragged a wagon across the entrance for good measure. Clay saw Braddon lead the Longrifles up a ladder to a narrow parapet running along the top of the wall. Dozens of Contractors hurried to follow suit amidst a chorus of clicks and snicks as they loaded their weapons.

Clay climbed to a point halfway up the ladder, close enough to hear any conversation, though the Contractors had all fallen into a tense silence. The screeching chorus of the Green pack rose and fell for several minutes, Clay finding it impossible to gauge their distance from the wall. Eventually he heard Skaggerhill say, 'Could throw some torches out there. Get some light on them.'

'Grass is too dry this close to town,' Braddon replied. 'We'd most likely set the walls to blazing. Besides, nothing's more likely to drive them crazy than fire.'

He fell silent at an insistent thumping to his right, Clay risking a glance at the parapet to see Silverpin slamming the butt of her spear onto the planking. She held her finger to her lips and leaned out between the spikes, ear cocked to the darkness. Clay heard it then, a new sound amidst the drake song, though just as chilling. *A horse,* he realised. *Screaming.*

'Someone's out there,' he heard Foxbine say, her judgement soon confirmed by the sharp crack of multiple pistol-shots cutting through the general cacophony.

'Who'd be fool enough to travel the jungle at night?' Skaggerhill asked.

Clay saw Silverpin step back from the wall, grip tightening on her spear as she crouched. 'Don't!' he shouted, clambering up the last few rungs of the ladder. But she was already in the air, vaulting the spikes into the blackness beyond. He reached the wall in time to see her sprint away into the darkness as a fresh salvo of shots rang out.

'Clay.' He turned to see Braddon reaching for him, voice rich in warning. 'Ain't nothing you can do . . .'

Clay took hold of a spike and swung himself over the wall, Braddon's hand flailing at his shirt but failing to find purchase

as he fell. The drop was significant but well within Clay's expertise and he landed without injury, pausing in a crouch to survey
the blankness ahead. The Greens' screeching seemed to have
doubled in intensity, perhaps loud enough to mask any more
shots. His eyes snapped to a sudden flare in the darkness, a brief
gout of bluish flame off to the right. The colour was distinctive,
glimpsed only a few times when business took him to the breeding
pens. *Drake fire.*

'Claydon!' his uncle yelled from above. 'You get your ass back
up here now!'

Clay cast a glance up at the wall, seeing Braddon's furious face
staring down, his arm outstretched and lowering a rope. Clay
gave him a grin before rising and running towards the flames.
He covered perhaps thirty yards when something caught his foot,
sending him tumbling through the long grass. He scrambled to
one knee, pistol aiming at a bulky shape in the grass as his nostrils
detected a thick stench of mingled blood and shit. *The horse,* he
realised, his gaze alighting on a partly severed hoof before finding
the animal's head. It lay with mouth agape, eyes still wide and
frozen in terror.

I may have done a foolish thing, he decided, attention fixed on
the sight of the horse's partially revealed rib-cage, mesmerised
by the white bone jutting from the part-roasted gore. Another
gout of flame to the left tore his gaze away and he caught a glimpse
of Silverpin, silhouetted against the sudden light, leaping into the
air, the blade of her spear flickering as it spun. The flames died
in an instant, the Green's screeching song momentarily faltering
as if in answer to some unspoken command.

Clay ran towards the spot where he had glimpsed Silverpin,
finding her withdrawing her spear from the corpse of a Green.
She had skewered it precisely at the join between skull and neck,
something he had seen harvesters do to old and unwanted stock
in the pens. This Green, however, was nothing like the stunted,
greyish creatures in the pens. It must have been at least eight feet
in length, twin lines of upraised, razor-like scales running the

length of its body from the broad spade-like snout to the spear-point tail. Its legs, thick with muscle, ended in wide, three-toed claws, curved and wickedly sharp. Instead of the wings seen in other species of Drake, it had two curving horns protruding from its back. On pen-bred stock these were usually little more than thumb-sized spikes, but here they were at least a foot in length, indicating an animal of considerable age.

He stepped back in alarm as the Green's jaws snapped closed, its tail twisting convulsively.

'Just a spasm,' came a pained voice to his right. It was Loriabeth, lying in the grass with blood on her leg. She was fumbling with one of her pistols, desperately trying to reload the open cylinder.

'Your pa really is gonna kill you,' Clay told her, moving to crouch at her side, then pausing as the Greens' song rose again. He scanned the long grass, pistol levelled and heart thumping. He whirled at the sound of something rushing through the grass, the pistol coming round to aim directly at a charging Green, legs blurring and tail thrashing as it scythed through the grass towards him. He fired his two shots in quick succession, his fears about the weapon's age proving unjustified by the satisfying roar and thump in his hand as the hammers came down. He saw the shots strike home, blood spouting on the Green's shoulders. It barely slowed. *Frenzy makes 'em unheedful of injury.*

'Shit!' He dropped the pistol and reached for the vial in his pocket, knowing he didn't have time to drink it but neither did he have time to run. He managed to get the stopper off by the time the Green came within arm's length, jaws gaping wide.

Something boomed close to Clay's ear, forcing him to reel away, for one panicked instant nearly losing his hold on the vial though not before a few precious drops had slipped out. Ears ringing, he saw the Green's head snap back, legs tangling beneath it as it collapsed and rolled to lie spasming in the grass.

'The head,' Loriabeth said in an exhausted sigh, on her knees now, smoke trailing from her pistol as she lowered her sagging arm. 'Always the head.'

Clay moved to catch her before she fell, wrapping an arm around her waist. He looked at the vial in his free hand, seeing a bead of product glistening on the glass and fighting down a surge of temptation. He replaced the stopper and returned it to his pocket. 'We gotta go!' he called, casting around to find Silverpin. She rose from the grass less than three yards away, spear in one hand and freshly bloodied knife in the other. She met his gaze and gave a nod.

Fresh flames blossomed as they lifted Loriabeth between them, hauling her back to the wall at a run. The Greens' song had changed, the pitch deeper now so that Clay couldn't help but discern a definite emotion to it. *Rage,* he realised. *We made them angry.* He risked a backward glance, seeing four separate fires burning in the grass, dark, long-tailed shapes flickering amidst a sudden confusion of shadow and smoke. He took a firmer grip on Loriabeth and ran faster.

They were within twenty yards of the wall when the Drake rose from the grass directly in their path. It was the largest Clay had seen yet, its twin horns rising from its back like scimitars. It issued a new sound as they skidded to a halt before it, not a screech but a roar, rich in fury and challenge. Clay was close enough to see the pink tongue and throat, the naptha ducts at the base of the tongue flooding the mouth with a fine mist, ready to catch light when it summoned the igniting gasses from its belly.

Should've drunk that vial, Clay decided.

A hail of gun-shots swept down from the wall, the big Green disappearing amidst fountaining earth and blood as every Contractor with a clear view fired in unison. The barrage didn't let up for what seemed an age, the Green writhing and twitching as bullet after bullet tore at its flesh.

'Over here!' Clay turned at the sound of Skaggerhill's shout and saw a trio of ropes cast from the wall. He and Silverpin dragged Loriabeth to the nearest rope and tied it around her waist. The girl was barely conscious now and could only groan in protest as she was hauled up. Clay watched Silverpin take hold of a rope and begin to climb, then took a final look at the burning field behind. The fires had joined now, creating a thick barrier of flame between the town and the jungle, inching closer by the second. He saw no sign of the Greens and realised their song had fallen silent.

'Claydon!' He looked up to see his uncle above, stern-faced and clearly furious, and wondered if facing the fire might be preferable to climbing the wall. In the end the overwhelming heat made the decision for him and he took hold of the rope, climbing as many hands hauled him to the top. He expected a tirade, or even a blow or two from Braddon, but his uncle merely looked him up and down in critical appraisal before moving away. Clay followed him to where Loriabeth lay on the parapet, wincing as Foxbine secured a makeshift bandage around her leg.

'Tail strike,' the gunhand told Braddon. 'She got lucky.'

Braddon said nothing, meeting his daughter's gaze as she stared up at him, face streaked with sweat and soot. 'You knew I wouldn't stay behind,' she told him, tone rich in accusation.

'Yes,' Braddon replied in a gravelly sigh. 'You didn't get your brains from your mother.'

CHAPTER 11

Lizanne

The house on Careworn Street stood empty, its doors and windows boarded up and an Imperial crest stencilled onto the planks in whitewash. The occupant had been a lifelong Morsvale resident, a clock-maker to trade who also dabbled in antiquities, an expensive hobby requiring more funds than his vocation could provide. Exceptional Initiatives, however, had been more than happy to indulge his interests for the past two decades, in return for certain services. *The best cover,* Lizanne recalled from a lecture at the Division training school, *is no cover at all. It is always preferable to recruit from amongst the local populace. An agent with fewer lies to tell has fewer lies to forget should they ever face detection.*

She paused at a dress-maker's shop opposite the house, ostensibly to gaze longingly at the elegant gown adorning the mannequin in the window, such a contrast to her own dowdy skirt and jacket of plain wool. However, her eyes strayed constantly to the clock-maker's house reflected in the glass. She could see no obvious signs of surveillance in the houses on either side, nor any indication in the street itself, but the Cadre were rarely obvious about anything. The clock-maker had been silent for close to seven weeks. It was improbable they would have kept watch for nearly two months following his arrest, but certainly not impossible. Lizanne had once spent the best part of three months secluded in a hide near an East Mandinorian hunting-lodge before her target appeared.

The clock-maker, she knew, was almost certainly dead. He may have had fewer lies to remember than a Division agent, but would also have had little resistance to the Cadre's highly effective, if unsubtle, interrogation methods. She had been briefed on his activities and knew there was nothing he could have told them that might identify her. As soon as the man failed to make his regular rendezvous his handler followed protocol and made for his extraction point. The fact that there had been no Imperial agents waiting for him indicated the arrest must have been very recent, probably a matter of hours. Regardless of this good fortune Lizanne knew that the clock-maker would have provided his interrogators with a fulsome account of his activities, including the recent purchase of an empty box with an interesting inscription. A box purchased at his handler's insistence, no less. Unsubtle they may be, but the Cadre were rarely foolish. *They have to know Division will have sent someone,* she concluded. *They would watch this place for a year just on the off-chance of snaring me.*

Lizanne decided it best to leave a close inspection for another time, casting a final wistful glance at the gown in the window before moving on. She had a call to make and it would be best not to make it after noon.

'Can you sew?' Housekeeper Meeram asked her. She was a plump woman with severely tied-back hair of jet-black and disproportionately small eyes, resembling dark beads set into the fleshy pillow of her face. They almost seemed to disappear completely as she looked Lizanne up and down, gaze narrowed in estimation.

'Yes, ma'am,' Lizanne replied, eyes downcast. Corvantine servants rarely looked their employers in the eye.

'Show me your hands.'

Lizanne tentatively raised her hands, the housekeeper grabbing her wrists and turning them over. 'Used to work, I see,' she observed. 'But the calluses have gotten a little soft, my dear. Out of practise are we?'

'The voyage from Corvus was long, ma'am. Not many folk in steerage willing to pay for tailoring, or cleaning. Did earn a few pins cooking though. Had to fix our own meals on the ship . . .'

'All right.' Meeram released her hands and moved back to her desk. She wore a heavy set of keys on a chain about her neck, keys that rattled as she moved. Lizanne hoped she wore it throughout the day and into the evening. 'And you were employed in the household of Landgrave Ekion Vol Morgosal for two years,' Meeram said, scanning the letters of introduction Lizanne had provided.

'I was, ma'am. Second maid to Landgravine Morgosal.'

'Yes.' The housekeeper peered closer at the letters. 'Who has done you the kindness of signing these references, I see.'

'The Landgravine was always very pleased with my service, ma'am.'

'I assume you came here in the knowledge that there is a long-standing friendship between the Landgrave and my employer.'

'My former housekeeper's suggestion, ma'am. She said His Honour often received letters from Burgrave Artonin complaining of the lack of decent servants to be found in Morsvale.'

'True enough.' Meeram sighed. 'The last girl kept tripping up the stairs with the master's tea-tray. I suspect there may be something in the water here, a bacterium of some kind that stunts the wits of those born to this blighted land.'

Housekeeper Meeram sat down, clasping her hands together and fixing Lizanne with a hard stare. 'Now, girl, if you expect to find a place here, I will have the truth from you. Why did you leave the Landgrave's employ? I find it scarcely credible a maid of such experience, and such a fortunate situation, would simply pack her things and travel across the ocean on a whim.'

This one's a mite too sharp for my liking, Lizanne decided. She summoned a flush to her cheeks and lowered her gaze farther, shifting in discomfort. 'There was . . . a difficulty in the Landgrave's household.'

'Speak plainly, girl,' Meeram snapped. 'What difficulty?'

Lizanne kept her gaze averted. 'The Landgrave's youngest son. He developed an . . . inappropriate interest in one far below his station.'

'Ahh.' Meeram sat back, grimacing slightly in understanding. 'And was this interest returned?'

'Gracious no, ma'am!' Lizanne looked up with an earnest gaze. 'He was just a boy, with boyish notions. I tried to be polite in dissuading his attentions but his interest became . . . unduly excessive, to the point where it threatened embarrassment to the family.' She was careful to put the correct inflection on the word 'embarrassment,' a term that carried great significance in the upper echelons of Corvantine society. Amongst the managerial class of the corporate world, steeped in its own modes of snobbery and petty gossip, social embarrassment would always be overlooked in light of success. In the empire, however, it could be a family's ruin, especially if word of it reached the Imperial Court.

'So, the Landgravine thought it best if you were placed at far remove,' Meeram said.

'Yes, ma'am. She was very kind.'

'Well you will be free of such entanglements in this household. The Burgrave has but one child, a daughter of fifteen. And fortunately for you, she is in need of a maid. I give you fair warning she is a difficult charge, hence the vacancy.'

Housekeeper Meeram opened a drawer and consigned Lizanne's letters to it with a brisk sweep of her plump arm. 'I shall of course need to verify your references. It should take the better part of eight weeks to exchange correspondence with your former employers. In the interim, you will receive room and board and two crowns a month, rising to three upon confirmation of your status. Is this acceptable?'

Lizanne gave an eager nod. Her research had indicated most servants in Corvus could expect to receive half a crown a month. It appeared servants were indeed hard to come by in Morsvale. 'Very acceptable, ma'am.'

After leading her to the small attic room she would occupy during her service, Meeram had given her a maid's uniform of somewhat archaic appearance and referred her to the extensive list of duties pinned to the door. 'I have an absolute intolerance for tardiness,' she said. 'You are required to be at your allotted task by the fifth hour. Not one second later. As for now, get changed and report to the kitchen. You can take the master his afternoon tea.'

Burgrave Leonis Akiv Artonin was a wiry man of perhaps sixty who greeted Lizanne with a kindly smile as she curtsied before his desk, tea-tray in hand.

'A new face,' the Burgrave said, rising from his chair. Lizanne took the opportunity to steal a glance at his desk as she lowered her gaze, finding it mostly covered in household accounts and frustratingly free of any maps or intriguing antique-related correspondence. 'And who might you be, my dear?'

'Krista, sir.' She curtsied again. 'Recently arrived from Corvus and employed by Madam Meeram on recommendation of Landgrave Morgosal.'

'Oh excellent.' Artonin's smile broadened. 'And how is my old friend? I'm afraid I've sadly neglected our correspondence of late.'

'The Landgrave has been unwell, as you may know, sir. But his condition has improved in recent months.' All true facts gleaned from Division reports on the Corvantine aristocracy. Landgrave Morgosal, an enthusiastic whore chaser, had been laid low by an infection of an intimate nature, recently cured thanks to advances in medicinal Green.

'I am glad,' Artonin said. 'The Landgrave and I served in the cavalry together for several years. It would pain me to think a mundane illness could do what rebel cannon could not.'

'The Landgrave often spoke of your service, sir. He said you saved his life at the Battle of Verosa.' Another well-documented truth. Despite his less-than-imposing physical presence, in his youth Captain Akiv Artonin's courage in rescuing his wounded commanding officer from the teeth of a rebel battery had won him the Emperor's Star for bravery and elevation to the nobility.

'A dimly recalled day,' he said, smile fading a little. 'And best forgotten in any case.' He paused for a moment, scrutinising her face. 'You are from Corvus, you say?'

Her complexion was too pale for a Corvus native. The Burgrave was an observant man it seemed. 'I was born in the city, sir. But my people were of northern stock.'

'Ah yes. The famines drove a great many of your people into the heartland, as I recall. Tell me, do you speak Selvurin?'

'Yes, sir. My grandmother never spoke anything else so I just picked it up.'

'Excellent. Can you read it too?'

This was tricky. She couldn't appear overly educated but suspected Artonin had a particular reason for his question, one that might prove useful. 'After a fashion, sir. Grandmother had a box of old letters. When her eyes got bad she needed someone to read them to her.'

'Then it seems good fortune has brought you to my door.' Artonin went to the heavily laden bookcase behind his desk, scanning the shelves until he extracted the required volume. Lizanne noted how he ignored the upper shelf completely. The row of thick legal-reference works it held were free of dust but appeared mostly unread from the clarity of the lettering and intactness of the bindings.

'Here we are,' he said, Lizanne lowering her gaze once more as he turned to her with a slender tome in hand. 'What do you make of this?' he asked, handing it to her.

She set the tea-tray down on his desk and accepted the book. It was bound in red leather and the gold mostly faded from the embossed title. 'Vizian's Fables,' she read, taking care to labour over the pronunciation. It was a collection of children's stories from the early empire, long before the Selvurin language had been displaced by Varsal. 'Grandmother would tell me these tales,' she said, smiling in fond recollection. 'But I never saw them in a book before.'

She began to hand the book to him but he shook his head. 'Why don't you keep hold of it for a little while. I've attempted my own translation but my Selvurin is sadly not up to the task. I keep losing the nuance. With your assistance perhaps I can capture it.'

'You want me to write all these stories out in Varsal, sir?'

'Oh, I think a verbal recitation will do. Naturally, you will be paid for the additional duty.'

He smiled again and she found herself hoping she wouldn't have to kill him. 'Thank you, sir. I should be very happy to help.'

A series of loud thumps came from beyond the study door as someone descended the stairs with considerable haste. Lizanne saw a wince of anticipation pass across the Burgrave's face an instant before the door flew open and a diminutive figure in a blue-silk dress burst in.

'Tekela,' Artonin said warmly, moving towards the new entrant, arms opening to embrace her. The girl, however, didn't seem interested in a welcoming hug.

'Who's she?' she demanded, pointing a rigid finger at Lizanne.

'This is Krista, your new maid.'

Lizanne gave a curtsy of the appropriate depth. 'A pleasure, miss.'

The girl would have been pretty but for the scowl that transformed her features into a mask of unwelcoming spite. 'Get rid of her!' she said, turning back to her father. 'I didn't choose her. You said I could choose my maid.'

'You chose the last one, my darling,' Artonin reminded her in a gentle tone. 'And she left after two days.'

'She was a thief and a liar and a strumpet.' The girl shot another scowling glance at Lizanne. 'And so's this one. I can tell.'

Perhaps she shares her father's keen eye, Lizanne considered, albeit slightly peeved by the strumpet remark.

She saw the Burgrave stiffen, his patience evidently running thin. 'Do you wish me to force you to apologise to a servant, Tekela?' he asked in a soft voice.

The girl's scowl deepened into a defiant glare as she matched stares with her father, eventually softening into a sullen pout when it became clear this was a battle she couldn't win. 'Sorry,' she mumbled in Lizanne's direction, not meeting her gaze.

'There we are,' Artonin said, smiling once more as he placed a hand on his daughter's cheek. 'Did you find an appropriate dress today?'

'No,' she huffed. 'They were all awful. If only you would let me go to Nizley's.'

'Their prices are ridiculous. Your mother always said so.'

The girl's scowl returned, accompanied by a self-pitying whine. 'Mother wouldn't have sent me to the ball in little more than peasant rags.'

'Keep looking. I'm sure you'll find something. Krista will go with you tomorrow.'

Tekela gave another glance in Lizanne's direction, a frown of suspicion augmenting her aggrieved pout. 'What could *she* know about fashion?'

'I did see a most fine dress this morning,' Lizanne offered. 'In a shop window on Careworn Street. I believe it would suit Miss Artonin very well indeed.'

'Marvellous,' the Burgrave said, stilling his daughter's next objection with a tight hug and a kiss to the forehead. 'Now, off to the drawing room, my dear. Miss Margarid will be here soon for your pianola lesson.'

The girl shrugged free of him and stomped to the door, Lizanne hearing the words, 'Margarid's a tone-deaf old hag,' before the door closed behind her.

'I've survived revolution, war and over a decade on this continent,' the Burgrave reflected. 'But by all the ghosts of the hundred emperors, I think fatherhood will finally do me in.'

As was custom Corvantine servants ate together in the kitchen two hours after serving their masters' evening meal. In addition to Housekeeper Meeram, Burgrave Artonin maintained a staff of three maids, one footman, one cook and one butler. In most noble houses the butler would have exercised authority below stairs but here everyone deferred to Meeram. Mainly, Lizanne assumed, due to the obvious infirmity and wayward memory of the ancient, white-haired fellow seated at the head of the table.

'What is your name, girl?' he enquired of Lizanne for the third time as the cook doled out a dessert of rice pudding.

'Krista, Mr Drellic,' she replied, earning a nod of approval from Meeram for the absence of impatience in her tone.

'Got a look of the north about you,' he observed, as he had once before. 'Best if you don't go wandering too far. Not everyone in Corvus is as welcoming as the Artonin family.'

Lizanne saw the two maids seated opposite her smother a shared giggle. They were several years her junior and prone to girlish ways, though they both had the sturdy look of those who grow up accustomed to daily labour.

'I shall be careful, sir,' Lizanne assured him.

'May I ask, Miss Krista,' the footman said, 'what manner of vessel carried you from Corvus?'

'She was called the *Southern Pride*,' Lizanne replied. 'Biggest boat I ever saw until I caught sight of that warship steaming into the harbour ahead of us.'

'Oh yes, the *Regal*,' the footman enthused. 'A fine sight she makes. Such clean lines. They say she can achieve close to thirty knots.'

Or maybe more, Lizanne thought, recalling the sight of the great steel fan affixed to the *Regal*'s hull. 'You have a liking for ships, Mr Rigan?'

'Indeed I do. It is my ambition to enlist in the navy, once the Burgrave sees fit to sign my letter of recommendation.' Lizanne could see the keenness in Rigan's expression. She put his age at just over twenty and his face had a certain plumpish aspect not dissimilar to Housekeeper Meeram's. His small, dark eyes confirmed Lizanne's suspicion of a maternal relationship, as did Meeram's frown of disapproval at his maritime ambitions.

'I was lucky in catching sight of a famous personage

disembarking the *Regal*,' Lizanne went on. 'Grand Marshal Morradin no less.'

A sudden hush descended as Drellic stiffened, his spoon falling from his hand and all confusion departing his gaze. 'Morradin,' he whispered. 'The Butcher is here?'

'Don't upset yourself, Mr Drellic,' Meeram said in a cautious tone.

'Twelve thousand men dead in a day,' Drellic went on, voice edged with a long-held anger. 'My son amongst them. All on the Butcher's order.'

'I'm sorry if I . . .' Lizanne began then fell silent at Meeram's warning glare.

'And they call him a hero,' Drellic said, teeth clenched now. 'The great commander, no more than a pig grown fat on the blood of wasted youth . . .'

'Now, now!' Meeram said with a strained smile, getting to her feet and laying a firm hand on the old man's shoulder. 'Our new employee might mistake your meaning, Mr Drellic. And we all know where mistaken words can lead. I think you're overly tired. Perhaps an early night will do you good.'

'Bodes ill that he's here,' Drellic muttered as Meeram ushered him to his feet, guiding him to the stairs. 'Means the Emperor has another slaughter in mind. Best if you send your boy away . . .'

'Please don't say such things, Mr Drellic,' Lizanne heard Meeram say as their footsteps ascended the back stairs.

'Well, that's the most sense I've heard out of him since I got here,' one of the maids said. She was the taller of the two with a freckled nose and auburn curls escaping the pale blue cap the maids were required to wear.

'Careful,' Rigan warned. 'The Cadre might forgive a half-mad old man's ramblings, but you don't have that excuse.'

The maid scrunched her nose at him in dismissal before turning her attention to Lizanne. 'I'm Kalla,' she said, then nodded at the girl next to her. 'She's Misha.'

The other girl, clearly the more shy of the two, replied to

Lizanne's smile with an uncertain one of her own. Unlike Kalla, her colouring was more in keeping with Corvantines from the Imperial heartland, light olive skin and black hair, though her eyes were a pale shade of green. 'You have been with the family long?' Lizanne asked her although it was Kalla who replied.

'Five years,' she said. 'Madam Meeram picked us out of the orphanage. Was going to be just me but Misha gave such a terrible bawling at us being separated that she took her too.' She flinched as Misha gave her an annoyed poke in the ribs. 'Well, you did. We should thank you for turning up when you did,' she went on, turning back to Lizanne, 'otherwise it'd be us waiting on the Horror.'

'The Horror?' Lizanne enquired.

'The Burgrave's evil spawn.' Kalla paused to stick her tongue out at Rigan's sigh of reproach. 'Tosh, you don't like her any better than the rest of us. This would be a happy house to work in but for her.'

'Ah, Miss Tekela,' Lizanne said. 'I'm to accompany her tomorrow. She needs a new dress.'

'Then you'd best prepare yourself for a trying day. Once saw her scream herself sick in the milliner's cos they didn't have a blue ribbon for her bonnet.'

'Madam Meeram did warn me she was . . . difficult.'

'Difficult's not the word. She's been a nightmare ever since her mother died. Now there was a woman who knew the value of a good switching now and then. The Burgrave's too kind, is what it is. Forking out for pianola lessons, dancing lessons, sketching lessons, new shoes and frocks every week. All has to be paid for. No wonder the Burgrave's been selling off his old stuff. Won't be long before one of us'll be let go so's she can festoon herself with jewels and such. All so she can snare a nobleman one day, not that there's one mad enough to have her.'

A fter supper, and an hour spent scrubbing dishes at the cook's direction, Lizanne repaired to her attic room to lie on the bed. She removed her shoes but was otherwise fully clothed whilst she indulged in two hours of sleep. Her insomnia would always disappear once a deployment was fully underway and experience had taught her the value of seizing the opportunity to sleep whenever practicable. Inevitably, there would come a time when such indulgence became impossible and she would face a constant struggle with exhaustion, though the Green would help as long as it lasted.

She woke in the small hours, finding the house steeped in a gratifying quietude. Rising from the bed, she filled the bowl on her bedside table and splashed water on her face to banish the lingering fog of sleep then retrieved the Spider and Whisper from their hiding-place in the gutter outside her small window. She went to the door and opened it a fraction, strapping on the Spider and injecting a drop of Green to enhance her senses. She could hear no trace of conversation, though a female voice was whimpering through a nightmare and a loud snoring could be heard from one floor down. *Mr Drellic,* she assumed with some satisfaction; the grating cacophony would help mask any unavoidable creaking from the staircase.

Lizanne made an unhurried progress down the backstairs to the next floor then across the hall to the main staircase. She had the Whisper in hand though hadn't thought it appropriate to load a Redball. Should she encounter an unfortunate night-time wanderer the issue would require a stealthy resolution. She had already identified a narrow, shaded alley-way two streets away where a body would most likely lie undiscovered for sufficient time to facilitate her swift extraction.

She paused at the landing on the first-floor, crouching and scanning the hallway below. The distressed whimpering she had detected before was louder here and she realised it emanated from the room of the Burgrave's daughter. The sounds were mostly indistinct through the door but the ebbing Green enabled her to catch the words 'Please!' and 'I didn't tell!' amidst the babble. *The Horror has horrors of her own, it seems,* Lizanne concluded before moving on.

Haste is the burglar's worst vice, she had been told at the Division school. Her tutor in the larcenous arts was a compact but muscular man she later learned had been the most successful thief in North Mandinorian history before Exceptional Initiatives offered him a lucrative teaching contract. *The thief who rushes towards their object is the thief who will be hanging by a rope the next morning.*

So she moved with a creeping slowness down the final flight of stairs, splaying her bare toes wide for a stable grip on the wood. *There's never been a stair or a floor-board that didn't creak,* the former burglar had said. *Secret is not to fight it, but control it. Lift your foot just as slow as you put it down.* The stairs made a few protesting noises as she descended to the ground floor, but nothing that wouldn't be mistaken for the natural grunts and groans common to all older houses in the quiet hours. After a full ten minutes of careful progress she finally felt the chill marble of the chequer-board floor under her feet.

She paused, eyes roving the shadows, ears alive for anything out of place, moving towards the Burgrave's study only when satisfied the household's slumber hadn't been interrupted. As expected the study door was locked, almost certainly by Artonin himself. It would be a rare Corvantine noble who would allow a servant unfettered access to his study, no matter how trusted.

Lizanne crouched, injecting another drop of Green and peering at the lock. One of the former burglar's more tedious lessons had been the memorisation of every major make of lock employed throughout the civilised world. This was a fairly typical example of an Alebond Commodities Suresafe mortice lock. Like many a Corvantine it appeared Burgrave Artonin was not immune to flouting the Imperial restrictions on purchase of corporate goods. It was an old and uncomplicated design but greatly disliked by the criminal fraternity for its solidity and the weight of its main lever, both of which made it extremely difficult to pick. She injected a half-second burst of Black and closed her eyes, clearing her mind and focusing on the memory of the diagram depicting the lock's inner workings. The main lever was heavy, but light as a feather under the touch of the Black. She remembered to hold it in place at the apex of its arc as releasing it would result in an unwelcome rattle. Instead the Suresafe issued only a faint click as it surrendered its grip on the door. Lizanne slowly worked the door-handle and let herself in, closing it softly behind her.

She briefly checked the desk, finding it clear of papers and the drawers all locked. Using Black to pick the locks was a possibility but also tricky and time-consuming. In any case, she thought it unlikely Artonin would conceal anything of true value or interest in so obvious a location. She quickly switched her attention to the top shelf of his bookcase and the row of thick legal tomes. She reached up and tested the seam between two of the volumes, giving a soft grunt of satisfaction when it transpired the books were actually joined at the binding. In fact, these weren't books at all. A few seconds further exploration revealed twin catches at each end of the edifice, and pressing them in unison enabled its smooth removal.

Any expectation that the revealed hiding-place would contain a delightfully complex artifact of gears and cogs were swiftly dashed, however. Instead, there were papers. A dozen or so tightly bound bundles of letters, some stacked periodicals and several leather-bound ledger-books. Reading it all in the time available was impossible and she could see no obvious clue as to which would offer useful information.

Sighing, she took a moment to memorise the position of the cache's contents before reaching inside and extracting the topmost ledger book. She was expecting merely a mundane list of household expenditures but upon leafing through the first few pages found herself pleasantly surprised. The Burgrave wrote in flowing, elegant Eutherian interspersed with sketches and diagrams of an enticingly technical nature. Skipping back to the first page she found herself whispering aloud the title inscribed at the top: 'Conjectures on the Designs and Inventions of the Mad Artisan.'

Although Lizanne was not habitually given to expressions of

excitement she couldn't suppress a slight increase in the tempo of her heart-beat as she read on:

The true identity of the man, or one might more properly say 'genius,' known to our brotherhood of scholars as the Mad Artisan, has never been fully established. What is known beyond any credible doubt is that he was born in the empire sometime during the late Third Imperium and arrived in the then-nascent colony of Morsvale whilst still a young man in his twenties. It is also known that he made several journeys into the interior of this continent and that his experiences there were fundamental in crafting the many wondrous designs he left to posterity. Chief amongst these devices is, of course, the marvellous Arradsian Solargraph, the exact operation of which still defies our understanding, although the inscription on the box that housed it leads one inevitably to speculate on the Artisan's knowledge regarding perhaps the greatest mystery this continent possesses . . .

The door's hinges were well oiled, but still issued a betraying whine as it opened. Lizanne's arm snapped level with her shoulder, the Whisper straight and unwavering as it centred on the space between the intruder's eyes.

Tekela stood in the doorway, dressed in a silk night-dress, her hand still on the door-handle and staring at Lizanne with wide eyes. For some reason her cheeks were damp with fresh tears. The scowl from that afternoon had vanished now, replaced by an expression of blank incomprehension.

'What are you doing?' she had time to say before Lizanne's finger tightened on the Whisper's trigger.

CHAPTER 12

Clay

The river folk proved to be a resourceful bunch when it came to dealing with fire, anchoring two paddle steamers close to the bank so they could play their pumps over the advancing flames. By morning the river-bank had been transformed into a tract of steaming ash that stopped less than ten feet from the wall. Only one Green corpse remained sufficiently whole to warrant harvesting, the others all no more than blackened humps rising from the cinders. They counted thirteen in all, Braddon estimating at least seven more were still prowling the jungle close to town.

'Worth a day's hunting, Captain,' Skaggerhill suggested. 'Even iffen we bag just the one.'

Braddon shook his head. 'Can't afford the time. Besides, every company in town will be out there within the hour. Get the best price you can for this one.' He nodded at the Green suspended head down from Skaggerhill's harvesting frame. 'Just be sure to have it done before evening. The boat won't wait for us.'

'Come hither, young 'un,' Skaggerhill said, moving to the hanging Green. 'Learn a thing.'

Clay couldn't quite suppress his trepidation as he approached the drake. Dead it may be but its tail, secured to the frame's upper spar by a chain, had an unnerving habit of twitching even hours after the beast's demise. Also, as Skaggerhill had enthusiastically demonstrated, a drake's bite reflex lingered for a good while even without a living brain to command it.

'Hah!' The harvester chuckled as the snapping jaws closed on the thick wooden peg he thrust between them. 'Only beast on the globe that can kill you when it's stone-dead.' He took hold of the drake's lower jaw with a thickly gloved hand, grunting with effort as he prised it apart and twisted the peg so that the jaws remained clamped in an open position.

'The hide ain't gonna be worth much in this state,' Skaggerhill mused, stepping back to survey the multiple bullet-holes and scorch-marks tracing the length of the corpse.

'Had heard they were immune to fire,' Clay said, recalling the sight of the blackened drake corpses outside the wall.

'Popular myth,' the harvester replied. 'Their hide's resistant to flame, that's why Contractors wear these green-leather dusters. But don't expect it to save you from a full blast of drake fire. A hot enough flame and they burn like anything else.'

This was the big Green that had sought to bar Clay's path to the wall, claimed by Braddon due to the fact that the Longrifles had put the most metal into it. Clay found himself even more impressed by it in daylight. Even slackened by death the power of the animal was evident in the bulging muscles of its legs and neck. Also, unlike the pen-bred Greens in Carvenport, its hide retained a complex pattern: a swirl of green and yellow, shot through with streaks of black. It was as if some paint had gotten all mixed up on the scales and frozen before the colours could meld.

'Caught in mid-change when it died,' Skaggerhill explained. 'They can shift their colour somewhat to match their surroundings. Still mostly green, but altered so as to confuse the sight of its prey. Jungle Greens ain't so good at it as their plains cousins though; they can change colour completely so as to disappear into the grass. Yellow in the dry season, green in the wet. The river Greens though, they're like ghosts. Just shadows in the water. It's a brave Contractor works the river trade.'

He pointed to a large steel bucket on the wagon. 'Bring me that, would you? And that big clay jug next to it.'

Skaggerhill removed the cork from the jug and sloshed a good measure of the contents into the bucket before swishing it around.

'White spirit,' he said. 'Kills any mites and impurities that could spoil the blood. Product Brokers will lower the price if they spy any bugs floating about.'

He took a spile and mallet from the tool belt on his apron and had Clay position the bucket directly beneath the drake's head. 'Been hanging for long enough for the blood to pool,' he said, placing the spile's point halfway along the neck. 'Best stand back, it'll gush some.'

He gave the spile two hard whacks with the mallet, driving it deep into the drake's hide. The outflow of blood was immediate, flowing from the spile to the bucket in a thick, dark torrent. 'Should net us a full quart,' Skaggerhill sniffed, stepping back as the blood continued to flow. 'Would be more if I had time. Reckon we'll sell the carcass once it's bled. It'll take too long to skin her and harvest the bones.'

'The bones?' Clay asked.

'Yes indeedy. Bones, organs, eyes, naptha sacs, brains. It's all worth something. Only thing best left to the plasmologists is the heart. Stuff you get from the heart is near black and like to burn you to the bone iffen a drop touches your skin. Well, us non-Blessed folks, that is. Reckon you'd be alright. Though I hear tell even the Blood-blessed can't drink the stuff.'

Clay gave him a sidelong glance. 'My uncle told you what I am.'

'No, but it ain't hard to figure. Why else'd you be here, given your lack of skills and all?'

Clay nodded at the rapidly filling bucket. 'Do I get a share of this?'

'That's up to the captain. And payments are only tallied when the expedition's over.'

'I don't mean money. I meant the product. You know how to dilute it, right?'

'To a usable standard, sure.' His beard parted in a smile, teeth bright and eyes cheery. 'But that, like everything else that occurs in this company, is up to the captain.'

*

He found Braddon with Loriabeth in the tent. Foxbine and Silverpin had been tending to her but he had told them to take themselves off to the tavern. He sat beside her recumbent form, eyes intent on the girl's sweat-covered face, not looking up when Clay entered, though he did offer a muttered greeting. 'That was a damn-fool thing you did last night.'

'You're welcome,' Clay replied, tone hardened by the ingratitude. He took a second to force down his anger before speaking again. 'How is she?'

'The wound is deep but she'll keep her leg. Most who suffer a tail strike ain't so lucky. Foxbine anointed the gash with Green to ward off infection and gave her a tincture of opium for the pain.'

'So she'll live?'

'Seems so.'

Clay found his uncle's face unreadable. Was it anger or concern that drew his brows so? 'You know,' he said, 'if you leave her here she's just gonna find a way to follow.'

Braddon leaned back from Loriabeth's side and gave him a weary glance. 'What d'you want, Claydon?'

'Skaggerhill bled near a full quart from the Green. I want some.'

'Payment for this?' Braddon gestured at Loriabeth.

'Some token of appreciation seems fitting.'

'Fair enough. Thank you for helping to save my daughter's life. Now go help Skaggs unpack the wagon.'

'The Green . . .'

'Ain't for you, Clay. Madame Bondersil added a very particular clause to our contract concerning your employment. You get the requisite amount of Blue only at the allotted time for the trance. Apart from that' – his brows lifted in a mockery of apology – 'you get shit all.'

'I'll be more use to this company if I have a ration of product.'

'Your employers see it differently. They think you'll be more likely to take to your heels the first time we get near civilisation, if not before. The life you chose had consequences, boy. Absence of trust being one of them.'

'The life *I* chose?' Clay felt the unwise heat building again, making him acutely aware of the forbidden vial in his pocket. 'I thought it was you chose it for me, Uncle.'

The faint vestige of humour faded from Braddon's face, resuming his unreadable frown as he turned back to his daughter. 'No place in my house for a boy who kills his own father.'

Auntie thinks different. Auntie thinks your brother was better off dead. He didn't know why he left it unsaid; the truth may have inflicted some additional hurt after all, a little recompense for his lack of product. But something about this felt all wrong, the two of them bickering whilst his cousin lay senseless and wounded just feet away.

'I need a new gun,' he said instead. 'Lost that relic you gave me last night.'

'Carried that piece my first-ever expedition,' Braddon told him, his voice near toneless and oddly lacking in reproach. 'Should've known better than to trust it to you, I guess.' He sighed and glanced up. 'Go find Foxbine in the tavern. She knows the local iron broker. The cost will be deducted from your share.'

They boarded the *Firejack* come early evening, the two tall stacks already belching black smoke into the air as stevedores hauled aboard the last of her cargo. The horses, oxen and wagon would be left within the town stable and sold off if they failed to return within six months. Preacher and Skaggerhill carried Loriabeth up the gangplank on a stretcher, the sight of the unconscious girl provoking an unwise outburst from a youthful deck-hand. 'Ain't signed up to serve on no hospital barge. Ill luck to let some sickly bitch aboard . . .'

Braddon knocked him down with a single punch, moving on without breaking stride or sparing another glance at the boatman, who now lay spitting blood onto the deck. 'He's new, Captain,' the *Firejack*'s First Mate apologised as Braddon approached the ladder to the wheel-house.

'Skipper up top?' he asked.

'Yes, sir.'

'Good. My daughter and Miss Foxbine will have my cabin. I'll bunk with the company.'

'Very good, sir.'

'Clay.' Braddon started up the ladder. 'You're with me.'

The skipper proved to be a compact fellow of Old Colonial stock who, as far as Clay could tell, could have been any age between sixty and eighty. His features, partly obscured by a silver-grey beard, were leathery and wrinkled but there was an evident spryness to him that seemed to deny his years. Like most of the crew his uniform was only partially complete, a blue jacket and peaked cap bearing the Ironship badge. Otherwise there was little to distinguish him from the Independents who worked the river trade.

'This is Captain Seydell Keelman,' Braddon introduced him. 'Master of the *Firejack*. Captain, my nephew Claydon.'

'Welcome aboard, young sir,' Keelman said, a keen scrutiny in his gaze as he looked Clay up and down. 'You ain't a company man, now are ya? Ironship Blood-blessed got a particular look to them. Not you though.'

'I am proudly Independent, sir,' Clay told him. 'And hope to remain so for the rest of my days.'

'Well good for you. Spent two decades on the river without benefit of a company flag, myself. But' – he touched a finger to his cap – 'comes a time when a man has to think on his pension.' He turned to Braddon. 'How much?'

'Half a vial.'

Keelman's hand went to his collar, extracting a chain attached to a bulky key. 'Need you to sign for it,' he said. 'The manager of the River Division is a stickler for balanced books.'

He led them from the wheel-house and along a passageway to a large, well-appointed cabin, complete with a gleaming oak dining-table reflecting the brass chandelier hanging from the ceiling. A number of portraits adorned the walls, each depicting a man in the uniform of a captain in the Ironship Merchant Fleet. 'The *Firejack* tends to use up her captains,' Keelman explained, gesturing at the portraits. 'I'm the sixth skipper since she launched fifteen years ago.'

He went to one of the portraits, pulling it out on a hidden hinge to reveal the safe behind. He worked the heavy key in the lock then twisted the safe's dial, hand moving with an unconscious rapidity which prevented Clay from catching more than two of the six digits in the combination. Hopefully the voyage down-river would afford further opportunities to learn the rest of it.

Once the safe was opened Keelman removed a ledger-book, an empty vial and a flask from the safe. He carefully poured a half-measure of product into the vial from the flask and handed it to Braddon. 'I'll leave you to it,' he said, after Braddon had signed the ledger-book, both it and the flask having been returned to the safe, once again locked and concealed behind the painting. 'We'll be underway within the hour. Be glad if your company would join me for supper tonight. Cookie's gotten us some prime catfish.'

'Happily accepted, Skipper,' Braddon told him.

After Keelman had gone he pointed Clay to one of the chairs ringing the table and produced a pocket-watch from the folds of his duster. 'Two minutes yet,' he said. 'Sure you can do this?'

Clay looked at the vial his uncle had placed on the table. Enough Blue for a trance of some intensity, though, as he had come to understand, the duration did not necessarily relate to the amount of product ingested. He found his palms were sweating and realised for the first time how much his sessions with Miss Lethridge had disturbed him. The ease with which she moved around his mind was disconcerting to say the least, made worse by the evident disdain for what she saw.

'Guess we'll find out,' he replied.

Braddon kept a careful eye on the watch, waiting until the last ten seconds before nodding at Clay. He drank the vial in one gulp and the storm of image and sensation descended in a rush.

Punctual, Miss Lethridge's mind said in approval. *I'm happy to see my lessons weren't entirely wasted.*

Clay surveyed her thoughts, finding the panorama of disciplined whirlwinds largely unchanged though the nearest one was a darker hue than he recalled, flashing red and white and the clouds that formed it seemed to roil with greater energy than the others. *Something wrong?* he enquired.

A minor complication, now resolved, she replied. There was a pause and he felt her undertake a brief voyage through his own recent experience. *Still far too messy in here, Mr Torcreek. You really need to find a coherent visual template. But what's this?* Another pause as she effortlessly prised open the throbbing boil that contained the previous night's memories. *Yes, the first sight of a wild drake is always jarring.* He saw the clouds of her mind darken further in disapproval. *However much your new colleagues might appreciate your heroics, you are not employed to needlessly risk your life. A great deal depends on the success of this expedition.*

He confined his response to a brief flash of lightning, something that happened whenever his anger and resentment flared.

Don't sulk, she chided him, a certain weariness colouring the shared sensation. *Just make your report.*

We're on the Firejack, he told her. *About to leave Stockade.*

On schedule. Good. Apart from last night's excitement, has there been any interest from other parties?

Not so's I've noticed. Uncle's crew is highly respected, feared even. Other Contractors tend to keep their distance.

She gave a pulse of satisfaction before continuing. *When you surface, ask him if he's familiar with any old stories concerning a Corvantine known as the Mad Artisan. I believe he may be important to our endeavour.*

I guess that means you ain't found a map with a nice cross on it telling us where the White's certain to be found?

Our operation is unprecedented and its parameters highly dynamic.

What's that mean?

It means nothing like this has been attempted before and no, I have yet to discover a map or other intelligence precisely identifying the location of our fabled quarry. Nor do I expect to.

So where's that leave us?

Continue to your objective. The Red Sands may offer further clues. The whirlwind twisted somewhat and he experienced a flush of uncertainty mingled with reluctance, two emotions he hadn't felt from her before now.

You sure you're alright? he asked.

Perfectly, she responded, the whirlwind snapping into a more regular shape. *Look to your mission, and mind what I said about further heroics.*

Then she was gone.

'Damn, kiddo.' Foxbine gave a sad shake of her head, gunsmoke fading as the waterspout from Clay's shot cascaded down a yard to the left of the floating branch she had told him to aim for. 'Woulda thought a Blinds boy would know how to shoot.'

'I ain't used to the kick yet,' Clay said in annoyance. 'This thing bucks like a mule.'

'Don't you go blaming your weapon, now. That there's a fine piece of engineering.' She searched the passing river for another target. 'There.' She pointed at a half-submerged tree-stump on the far bank. 'Should be big enough for ya.'

At first glance the pistol Foxbine chose for him appeared just as antique as his uncle's double-barrelled relic. The black enamel on the frame was chipped in numerous places and the mismatched plain steel cylinder an obvious replacement for the original. But at least it was a six-shooter and, if Foxbine's reaction to finding it at the iron broker's was any indication, something of a prized rarity.

'An Alebond Mark One long-barrel,' she said, a faint note of awe in her voice as she spied it through the iron broker's glass counter.

'Yep, she's a treasure to be sure,' the broker said, an elderly man with bushy eyebrows that jutted out over his thick spectacles. 'Would have made a goodly sum on her if she had all the original parts.'

'You got the stock?' Foxbine asked.

'It was all rotted but I made another myself.' He disappeared into the dense racks of rifles and shotguns crowding the rear of his shop, returning after a short delay with what appeared to be the sawn-off stock of a rifle. He took the pistol from the counter and slotted the stock into a brace on the rear of the butt, transforming it into a carbine. 'They made these for the Royal Mandinorian Cavalry,' the iron broker said, holding the weapon out to Foxbine. 'Back when there still was such a thing. Some credit the winning of the Second Spoiled Wars to this beauty.'

Foxbine had held the weapon only briefly before handing it to Clay with a sigh of regret. 'Tempted to buy her for myself, but I'm guessing the captain wants me to arm you as best I can.'

Despite his initial misgivings, Clay had to admit the weapon sat well in his hands. The heft of it was oddly comforting and the length of the barrel, twelve inches rather than the usual six, gave it a more sinister appearance than most pistols. 'They called it the Stinger,' the broker said as Clay peered down the sights. 'Still shoots true, young fella. And the action's smooth as the day she was made. Wouldn't sell her otherwise. Business like this runs on reputation.'

Foxbine raised a questioning eyebrow at Clay, who nodded in approval. 'We'll take her,' she told the broker, not bothering to ask the price. 'Assume you've got a holster that'll fit my friend here. We'll also need two more cylinders, two boxes of .48 short and .52 long, the steel tips if you got 'em.'

'Going after Black, huh?' the broker asked, reaching up to the shelves behind the counter for the required ammunition.

'Iffen there's any to find.' She took one of the boxes of .48

and tossed it to Clay. 'Load her up. Tomorrow we'll have us a lesson.'

The holster was designed to fit under his left arm rather than around his waist, the Stinger being too long to carry at the hip with any comfort. The stock hung from a strap across his back, within reach for a quick assembly. However, at first she had him firing without the stock, standing on the platform on the boat's stern and taking one-handed pot-shots at the various targets she pointed out.

'Better,' she conceded as his bullet took a chunk out of the tree-stump. 'And another.'

After firing off twenty rounds or more she had him practice replacing the cylinder. 'Gotta get so's your hands can do it without thinking. Can't be fumbling around when the Spoiled come boiling over the hill.'

'How long you been at this?' he asked her.

'Oh, fourteen years now, give or take. In my blood, y'see. Like Loriabeth, though never done anything so dumb as that girl.'

'Your people were Contractors?'

'Yep. Ma and Pa both. Second and Third Hands on the Chainmasters crew. Brought in live drakes from far and wide. Was them that caught the Blood-lot Black.' She gave a small, cautious frown. 'Guessing my family owes you for that.'

'Why? Wasn't them that set it loose.' Clay snapped the lever in place, locking the cylinder to the Stinger's frame, then started over at her insistent nod. 'How come you didn't join the Chainmasters?' he asked.

'I did for a time. Never took to the work though. It's a grim business, trapping and hauling beasts across miles of jungle and desert. Most of 'em die during the journey. Just stop eating and wither away. A dying drake is a grim sight but it's the sound that gets ya, keening away for hours on end like a pining dog but pitched low so you can't never blot it out. Besides, the money started getting thin after my second expedition. Just not enough wild ones left in reasonable distance of civilisation. So I went looking for another position. Your uncle and my pa go way back, so he took me on. Had to prove myself, though. Lucky for me the Spoiled came at us in decent numbers that year.'

'They really as ugly as they say? Like men but all twisted up, I heard.'

'They ain't men.' There was a grim insistence to her tone, her affability suddenly vanished. 'Ugly they is, inside and out. But it's evil that makes 'em so. Don't ever mistake a Spoiled for human, and never let 'em take you alive.'

'The White Drake,' Braddon said. The Longrifles had gathered in the *Firejack*'s ward-room, alone save for Captain Keelman. When the stewards had cleared away the dinner dishes Keelman passed round a box of Dalcian cigars. All but Preacher had taken advantage of the offer and soon a thick cloud of sweet-smelling smoke hung over the table as Clay fought the impulse to cough.

'That's what we're after?' Skaggerhill asked, exhaling smoke in a laugh of mingled delight and incredulity.

'Indeed,' Braddon assured him, tossing a neatly folded sheaf of papers onto the dining-table. 'As bonded under contract with the Ironship Trading Syndicate. Fees and shares stipulated. Feel free to read at your leisure.'

'I assume,' Skaggerhill said, barely glancing at the contract, 'this means we have some notion of where to look when we get to the Red Sands.'

'We make for the Crater,' Braddon replied, 'search for any sign of the Wittler Expedition.' He paused to nod at Clay. 'After that, my nephew will provide further guidance from our employers.'

'Pardon me, Captain,' Foxbine said. 'But this ain't a capture crew. We find this thing, iffen it can be found, what then?'

'There's an egg,' Clay said, voice a little hoarse. 'Or there was. Wittler's crew found it before they all died. All but one anyway, if the story's to be believed.'

'All this time, thought it was all just another tall tale,' the gunhand mused.

'Wittler was real enough,' Skaggerhill said. 'Knew him a little, though I was scarcely older than Clay at the time. Fine captain, if a little unbending. Caused quite a stir when the Sandrunners failed to come back and claim their wagon. No-one knew the Badlands and the Sands better than Wittler. If they can take him they can take anyone.'

'Ironship sent a Protectorate expedition in search of them not long after,' Braddon said. 'All they found was bones. We'll be on the lookout for what they missed. Protectorate don't know the Interior like we do.'

'And if we find nothing like they did?' the harvester asked.

'Then hopefully more clues will be passed to Clay. And, fact is, we already have one.' He gave Clay an expectant nod.

Clay took another draw on the cigar, managing not to grimace as he said, 'The Mad Artisan. Any of you ever hear the name?'

The Longrifles replied with blank faces, except for Preacher. He kept his gaze downcast, fixed on his hands clasped on the table before him, speaking softly, 'A figure from Corvantine history. Inventor of many wonders and, in his day, said to be the wisest man in the empire.'

'He have a name?' Braddon asked.

'No-one knows it for sure,' Preacher replied. 'Historians have often confused his tale with the comedy of Cevokas, although the dates don't match up and, if Cevokas ever really existed, they could never have met.'

'Is there any tale that puts the Artisan with the White?'

Preacher shook his head. 'Although he was supposedly a famous explorer in addition to everything else. One story has it that he found a cache of ancient but wondrous devices somewhere and that's where the inspiration for all his inventions came from.'

'What happened to him?' Braddon enquired.

'Stories differ. Some say he fell foul of the Cadre, as many noteworthy personages did in the aftermath of their formation.

Others have it that he just went wandering one day and never came back.'

'How'd you know this?' Clay asked.

Preacher raised his gaze, face as impassive as ever. 'They teach more than scripture in the seminary.'

'That's useful, Preacher,' Braddon told the marksman. 'You remember any more, let me know.' He turned to Captain Keelman. 'How long till we make the Sands, Skipper?'

'Well, we can't follow the path taken by Wittler,' Keelman replied. 'He took a barge down the Greychurn, then followed the fork that leads into the Badlands. The *Firejack*'s too broad in the beam for such a course. We'll stick to the Greenchurn and skirt the Badlands. There's some shallows sixty miles or so south of Edinsmouth offers a decent mooring, far enough from the bank to ward against Spoiled attacks.' He paused for a contemplative puff on his cigar before replying. 'I'd say twenty days altogether, including a stopover for supplies at Edinsmouth.'

'Thought this tub was a blood-burner,' Clay said. 'Can't it go any quicker?'

His uncle's face darkened a little but the wiry skipper seemed to take no offence. 'Our Blood-blessed'll quicken her up some on the straights, young fella. But the river ain't the ocean and it sets its own pace.'

He pushed back from the table and got to his feet. 'I'd best see to the evening watch.' He inclined his head. 'Gents, ladies. Some brandy in the cabinet if you're partial.'

Silverpin had already risen to retrieve the liquor by the time the door closed.

'Guessing I don't have to issue no lectures about circumspection,' Braddon said, accepting a glass of brandy from the bladehand as she shared it out. 'Another crew gets word of what we're after there'll be an army of Contractors on our tail within days.' He fixed Clay with a hard stare. 'Means no getting drunk and spilling your guts to some whore in Edinsmouth.'

Clay sipped the brandy Silverpin passed him and pursed his

lips in appreciation. *Contracting life has its compensations.* He returned his uncle's stare with a hopeful smile. 'They have whores in Edinsmouth?'

Edinsmouth was like Stockade but constructed on a much grander scale with an even smaller shore-based settlement. Dozens of piers and jetties extended out into the river, all crowded with two- or three-storey buildings and many linked by high walkways and cantilevered bridges that rose and fell continually like the bobbing heads of some water-bound herd of beasts. There was a whole fleet of barges and steamers moored up around the jetties, with more arriving and leaving by the hour. Night was coming on by the time the *Firejack* approached its mooring so the whole spectacle was peppered with the yellow orbs of a thousand or more lanterns.

'Seer knows I hate this outhouse of a town.' Foxbine sighed in distaste as the *Firejack*'s paddles slowed to a crawl and the helmsman spun the wheel to align her starboard side to the jetty.

'Don't look so bad,' Clay observed, earning a caustic laugh from Skaggerhill.

'A notion likely to change upon closer inspection,' the harvester said. 'You'd best stay close tonight, young 'un. Sounds to me like the headhunters are in town.'

Clay could hear the raucous laughter rising from the densest part of the stilt town, his Blinds-tuned ear picking out the vicious edge to it. *Just like the Colonials Rest on fight night,* he thought. *Only even more hungry.*

'They're troublesome?' he asked.

Skaggerhill shrugged. 'Some crews are worse than others, but all best avoided when they're off the hunt. They spend months on end out there looking for Spoiled and when they find some there's an even chance they ain't gonna survive the encounter. It's a rare headhunter lasts more than a few years. They'll spend a night or two here, drinking and whoring themselves blind, then go on out and do it all again.' The harvester paused to nod at Silverpin, who stood regarding the town with a grim expression.

'She knows all about it,' Skaggerhill said. 'Used to be a head-hunter, didn't ya', sweetness?'

Clay knew Skaggerhill to be as tough a fellow as he was like to meet, but noticed the harvester couldn't help blanching a little as Silverpin turned her gaze on him.

'Anyways,' he said, coughing a little and turning away. 'Just stay close to us, is all.'

When the steamer had moored up they made their way to a tavern at the far end of the pier. The sign above the door featured a painting of a warship of antique appearance, sails billowing as her broadside blazed cannon fire at a flaming shore. 'The Stupendous' proclaimed the white lettering below the image. It all meant nothing to Clay though he heard Preacher mutter something about the painting's inaccuracy as they made their way inside. 'She only had half that number of guns.'

The tavern was busy but not overly crowded, populated mostly by boatmen and stevedores who clustered in their various crews, playing games of chance or attempting drunken renditions of old shanties. The Longrifles occasioned no particular interest as they took a table near the door.

'Be back by midnight,' Braddon had instructed, himself opting to stay on the boat. 'Anyone who has to be carried back will be fined.'

Skaggerhill bought the first round, placing a clay tankard that nearly overflowed with a frothy dark beer in front of Clay. 'Take it easy, strong stuff this,' Foxbine advised as Clay took his first gulp, raising his eyebrows in appreciation at the taste. It had a fruity tang to it and only a slight edge of bitterness, and the high alcohol content left a pleasing tingle on his tongue.

'They call it Jungle Rot,' Skaggerhill said. 'Barley and hops mixed with three types of fermented native fruit.'

'Don't care what they call it,' Clay said, draining half the tankard in a single, luxuriant swallow. 'As long as there's more.'

He realised he hadn't been drunk in quite some time, the last being a lengthy binge with Derk the day before he started training in earnest for the fight with Cralmoor. They had awoken the next day on the floor of the rented room they shared with Joya, who had kindly refreshed their senses with a bucket of none-too-fresh water. He found himself smiling at the memory of her tirade, rich in words he never realised she knew. She only quieted when he took her face in his hands and planted a long kiss on her forehead. It earned him a slap but at least she stopped yelling.

'Stallwin!' He looked up at Skaggerhill's shout, finding the harvester risen to his feet and pumping the hand of a slim, long-haired man about his own age, evidently another Contractor from the duster he wore.

'Skaggs,' he replied with a grin. 'So bastards never die, I guess.'

He took a seat at Skaggerhill's insistence, laying down a whiskey bottle he was affable enough to share if any wanted. 'Longrifles,' he said, raising his glass in a salute. The others all raised their tankards and Clay sensed a certain gravity to the gesture. He was beginning to understand that mutual respect meant a lot between Contractors, possibly because it was so rare a commodity.

'Riverjacks,' Skaggerhill replied in a formal tone and they all drank, Clay following suit and realising his tankard was near empty.

'This here's Kleb Stallwin,' Skaggerhill said to Clay. 'Second hand to the Riverjacks. Kleb, say hello to Claydon Torcreek, the captain's nephew and our newest hand.'

'A pleasure, young sir.' Stallwin greeted him with a nod. 'Though it seems you've chosen an interesting time to start your career.' He turned back to Skaggerhill, lowering his voice a little. 'These boat-swabs had an interesting story, 'bout a Green pack attacking Stockade. Can't be true, surely.'

'Close enough to truth,' the harvester replied. 'Damn near killed the captain's daughter. Luckily Clay and Silverpin here got her over the wall in time.'

'A whole pack?' Stallwin pressed. 'Full-grown too?'

'Full-grown,' Skaggerhill confirmed. 'And meaner than I've seen in a long time. Would've taken 'em for southern breeds if they hadn't been so far north.'

'Maybe they moved,' Clay said, smothering a belch and searching his memory for the right word. 'Migrated, I mean to say.'

Stallwin indulged him with a smile. 'Greens don't migrate, son. No drake does. They're so territorial they'll kill one of their own brood if it wanders too far. More likely a long-hidden pack, driven to try for human prey by desperation. You may have been privileged to witness the final days of the last pack remaining north of the Badlands.'

Stallwin and Skaggerhill's conversation soon moved on to the exclusive, jargon-filled talk of those engaged in the same profession: the prices being paid for product in various settlements, which company had lost the most hands recently and so on. Clay found himself losing interest as the last of the Jungle Rot slipped down his throat.

'Shit,' he mumbled, contemplating the bottom of his tankard with a grimace.

'Fetch another round,' Foxbine said, sliding a scrip note across the table. 'But get y'self a half-measure this time.'

'Surely,' Clay lied, getting to his feet with note in hand. He made a slow progress to the bar, his way being obstructed by so many boatmen, though he found himself curiously unperturbed by all the jostling. The place was raucous, right enough, but the atmosphere had none of the simmering violence that pervaded nearly every drinking den in the Blinds. Somehow, here in this river-bound stilt town in the middle of a jungle far from what people chose to call civilisation, he felt safer than he had in years.

He found a gap at the bar and waved the scrip note at the serving-woman, who seemed preoccupied with another customer.

'Gotta shout in here, fella,' said the man on Clay's right.

Clay nodded and waved the note again, his call to the serving-woman cut short when she moved to the far end of the bar.

'Too bad,' the man said. 'Don't worry, she'll get to you soon enough. Probably all apologetic when she realises you're Braddon's kin.'

Clay turned to him, taking a closer look. He was a diminutive figure of Old Colonial stock, his skin weathered and lined, like leather stretched over a frame of sticks. Clay took note of the pattern of scars and tattoos that had been etched into the flesh around his eyes and mouth, and the row of pointed teeth he revealed when his lips parted in a smile. *File tooth,* he thought, recalling some of the aged drunks who congregated in the Blinds and claimed allegiance to long-defunct headhunter crews. Those that still had teeth often looked like this, though this one wore a plain woolen coat of dark blue, just like the boatmen.

'How is the great captain?' the man asked, laying his elbow on the bar and turning to face Clay. As he moved his coat parted to reveal a necklace, a leather string adorned with what appeared to be greenish-yellow pegs, all sharpened to a point. He also wore a short-barrelled revolver at his right hip and a long-bladed knife at the other.

'You know my uncle?' Clay asked him, edging back from the bar a little, so as to unhinder the holstered Stinger.

'Met him once,' the man said. 'Though I dare say he wouldn't remember. Can't expect a great mucky-muck Contractor like him to spare a glance or a word for scum like me.'

'Headhunter, huh?' Clay's eyes flicked around, seeking the man's companions. Apart from his accoutrements everything about this man's bearing was familiar, and his type never picked a fight without allies.

'That's right.' The man rattled his necklace. 'Gotta hand in the heads or y'don't get the bounty. Teeth's the only way to keep a true score.' He gave a shallow bow. 'Tadeus Ellforth, at your service. Although,' he paused to chuckle, 'in all truth, young fella, tonight I'm engaged to be very much the opposite.'

Clay needed no further encouragement and began to reach for the Stinger. *Put this one down and hop over the bar before his friends start shooting* . . . His arm didn't move. He knew what was happening in a single, dreadful instant. He had never been on the receiving end before but had dished this treatment out enough times to know it for what it was: muscles bulging with the strain as he fought the invisible grip, sweat breaking out all over his skin as every part of him throbbed under the pressure. *Black.* He met Ellforth's eyes as the headhunter chuckled again. *Bastard's a Blood-blessed.*

'Had me a right interesting Blue-trance recently,' Ellforth went on, stepping closer, his tone and posture convivial, like they were two old friends sharing a story. 'With a fella I know in Morsvale. Offered me fifty thousand in exchange notes to come here and wait for you to show up.' The headhunter gave an apologetic grimace. 'Guessing you know what he wants me to do next, and we'll get to that. But, it occurs to me there's additional value to be had here. I mean to say, fifty thousand just for your sorry hide. Raises some pressing questions in a man's mind.'

Ellforth leaned closer still and Clay felt his gorge rise at the stench of the man's breath, rich in smoke and recently chewed meat, worse even than the jungle. 'So, how's about you tell me what your famous uncle is looking for, and maybe I'll make it quick. Snap your neck and you're gone before you know what's happening. Or, I could crush your liver and you'd linger for days, screaming all the while whilst your skin turns yellow and you shit your insides out.'

Clay felt a single bead of sweat trace down his face as the headhunter stared into his eyes. He knew now the truth of Skaggerhill's words: *Everything out here, including the people, is worse than anything you ever seen before.* Whatever lived behind Ellforth's gaze was beyond madness or cruelty, an implacable mis-shapen thing of pure will and greed. It couldn't be bargained with, bought or persuaded. He was going to die here in this shitty bar in this shitty town. The only thing that remained was to decide the manner of his passing.

'So?' Ellforth asked in a gentle whisper. 'What y'got to tell me, Mr Torcreek the younger?'

Clay felt the Black's grip loosen a little, just enough to free his mouth. 'Came looking for your mother,' he told Ellforth in a spittle-rich rasp, 'didn't fuck her enough last time.'

Ellforth blinked and moved back. He stared at Clay for a long while, long enough to stir the faint hope that the Black might burn out. But something told him Ellforth had the skill to string this out for a few minutes more, certainly long enough to make good on his threat. 'Well now,' he said, a grin forming on his lips. 'Ain't you just the perfect nephew. Think he'll weep over your grave, boy?'

Clay started to reply with another insult but his mouth clamped shut, teeth snapping together so fast he nearly bit off the tip of his tongue. Ellforth took a slow deliberate step backwards and began to laugh, lips drawn back over the yellowed spikes of his teeth as he gave voice to rich and genuine hilarity.

He was still laughing when his head exploded.

CHAPTER 13

Hilemore

'Signal from the crow's nest, sir.' Ensign Talmant straightened from the speaking-tube to address the captain. 'Mast sighted due west. Five points off the port bow.'

'Bang on time,' Trumane observed with an anticipatory smile that forced Hilemore to the relieved conclusion that cowardice, like navigational incompetence, was not amongst his captain's vices. 'Considerate of these scum to be so punctual. Helm, five points to port. Number One, signal the engine room to engage the main power plant. Two flasks, if you please, and tell Mr Bozware to stand by to add another at my order.'

'Aye, sir!' Lemhill relayed the order via the communicator before adding further instruction via the speaking-tube. Within a minute the paddles had begun to churn with blurring rapidity, doubling the *Viable Opportunity*'s speed to eighteen knots. They were in deeper waters now, well clear of shore and the sea mostly becalmed under a light breeze, meaning the cruiser's unique abilities could be exploited to the full, much to the captain's evident delight.

'I find it's a little like flying, don't you, Lieutenant?' He raised an eyebrow at Hilemore, gesturing at the onrushing sea beyond the bridge window.

Hilemore had to admit there was a certain intoxication to the experience of traversing the ocean faster than a man could run. 'An invigorating sensation, sir,' he agreed.

'Indeed.' The captain turned back, clasping his hands behind his back, fists clenching and unclenching. From the absence of a tremble Hilemore judged the gesture as more a signal of eagerness than fear. 'But I suspect we are about to experience something even more stirring.'

'Crow's nest has her fully in sight now, sir,' Talmant reported. 'A one-stack side wheeler of narrow beam, Corvantine lines. Grey-and-black paint scheme.' The boy paused, ear glued to the tube as he listened further. 'She's flying Briteshore Minerals colours.'

'Just as Intelligence promised,' Trumane observed with a satisfied chuckle. 'Number One, sound battle stations, if you please. Signal Guns to load fragmentation shell and aim for her paddles and upper workings. All guns to fire as she bears until ordered to cease.'

'Aye, sir!'

Hilemore could see the gun-crews running to their pieces as Lemhill pulled three long blasts from the steam-whistle's lanyard, the signal for imminent action. The First Officer then moved to the speaking-tube at the rear of the bridge to relay orders to Lieutenant Bilforth, the gunnery officer stationed on the lower deck. Although he carried a bullhorn, Bilforth, like most experienced gunnery officers, preferred to relay messages in person. Hilemore could see his blocky form running from one gun to another on the fore-deck, crouching to deliver orders to the senior hand in charge of each piece.

The *Viable* was equipped with four twenty-four-pounders on each side, arranged in pairs fore and aft of the paddles, with another half-dozen twelve-pounders on the upper decks. They were all relatively modern weapons, smooth-bore muzzle loaders with long barrels and reinforced breeches that gave them a bottle-like appearance. A well-drilled crew could fire perhaps one round every hundred seconds to a range of three miles, though this would inevitably reduce in battle due to fouling of the barrels. However, the *Viable*'s most impressive piece of ordnance was the brand-new rifled pivot-gun on the fore-deck. Officially it was known as a Falcontile Mark One, in honour of its inventor, but Protectorate sailors had been quick to dub it the Irondrake for the impressive gout of flame its muzzle produced with every shot. It was slower to load than its smaller forebears, taking two full minutes to heave the sixty-pound shells into the barrel, but it outranged any smooth-bore gun by at least a mile and, at sufficiently close range, could punch a hole clean through six-inch armour-plate. Added to this was the novel pivot mechanism on which it sat, enabling the crew to swiftly bring the Irondrake to bear on any target within a one-hundred-and-eighty-degree radius of the fore-deck.

'Smoke on the horizon, sir,' Talmant reported, pointing dead ahead.

'I see it,' Trumane replied in a murmur, training his glass on the plume of grey-black smoke. 'I believe our prey has made note of our approach.'

Hilemore raised his own glass for a better view, frowning at the odd pattern described by the smoke. It should have been streaming either north or south according to the wind or the direction of the vessel that produced it. Instead it appeared to be rising and falling in a chaotic, back-and-forth motion. Also, the plume was thicker than it should be, even for a vessel moving at top speed. 'She's putting up a screen,' he said. 'Seems they intend to make a chase of it.'

'Quite so,' Trumane agreed. 'Helm, another five points to port if you please.'

'No sure way to tell which way she'll turn, sir,' Lemhill cautioned. 'Could strike out to the north.'

'She'll be low on coal and product,' Trumane replied without lowering his glass. 'So it's of little matter which course she chooses. If she makes for open water we'll catch her in a day rather than an hour.'

Hilemore watched the smoke-screen grow thicker as they approached. It soon broadened to a good three hundred yards in length, swirling this way and that as the *Windqueen* moved about inside it, her course rendered unknowable and the gunners deprived of a target.

'A clever opponent,' Trumane observed, a small smile on his lips as he lowered his glass. 'I do appreciate an interesting engagement. Number One, slow to one-third. Helm, take us directly towards the smoke.'

A hush descended as the *Viable* reduced speed, the roar of the paddles diminished to a regular swishing thrum as the smoke roiled ever thicker. They had drawn to within a half-mile of it when two quick flashes lit the swirling fog like lightning in a heavy storm.

'Incoming fire!' Hilemore barked, his words soon drowned out by the whining groan of approaching shot. The first fell wide by several yards, raising a towering spout off the starboard paddle that gave the gun-crews a liberal dousing. The second, however, slammed into the *Viable's* starboard bow just above the anchor mounting. The iron-clad hull rang like a bell, loud enough to make Hilemore wince as the ship shook from bow to stern. Despite the power of the impact, the shot had no chance of penetrating the hull. However, it had more than enough force to shatter the thinner armour that covered the rail to the right of the Irondrake, scattering it across the fore-deck in a cloud of steel splinters. Hilemore saw all but one of the Irondrake's gun-crew fall, limbs and torsos shredded by the deadly cloud, Mr Bilforth amongst them.

'Seer-dammit all.' Trumane sighed before raising his voice to address Lemhill. 'Number One, gather men from the port guns and take charge of the Falcontile.'

'Aye, sir!' The First Officer saluted and ran for the gangway.

'Maintain course,' the captain told the now-ashen-faced helmsman staring fixedly at a fresh spider-web crack in the glass directly in front of his station. He was scarcely older than Talmant and evidently shared his lack of experience. Nevertheless he duly straightened up and took a firmer hold on the wheel, though Hilemore saw the sweat he left on the handles. Talmant seemed only marginally less perturbed, face bleached and eyes wide, though he did manage to offer Hilemore a weak smile in response to his glance, mouthing something as he did so. 'No safe place.'

'Sir!' Hilemore turned at the helmsman's shout, seeing a sleek shape emerging from the smoke.

'Impudent swine,' Trumane observed, though his tone remained cheerful. 'I do believe she intends to ram us.'

The *Windqueen* came on at full speed, her blood-burner status confirmed by the white foam billowing beneath her churning paddles. Hilemore could see figures moving about on her fore-deck and made out the bulky shapes of two cannon positioned on either side of the prow. 'Bow chasers, sir,' he reported to Trumane. 'Looks like Corvantine thirty-two-pounders.'

'Noted, Mr Hilemore,' the captain said. 'Ensign Talmant, signal the engine room to increase to full ahead. Helm hard-a-port. Lieutenant, please remind the starboard crews of their orders.'

Hilemore made for the hatchway, stumbling as the helmsman spun the wheel and the *Viable* listed. He hauled himself outside as two more shots came from the *Windqueen*, their gunners' aim spoilt by the captain's manoeuvre and the two balls passing harmlessly over the aft deck, albeit low enough to make the crews duck. Cupping his hands around his mouth Hilemore yelled the order at the gun-crews below. 'Stand to, lads! Let's give her a broadside!'

He fancied there may have been a ragged cheer in response, though it was difficult to tell above the resurgent roar of the paddles. The *Viable*'s shift to port placed her at a right angle to the on-coming pirate, whilst her speed easily rendered any ramming attempt a fruitless enterprise. The *Windqueen*'s narrow profile would have made aiming a difficult task if she had been at a decent range, but her abortive attack had put her at less than three hundred yards distance; any Protectorate gunner contriving to miss at that range would deserve a flogging. The two guns fore of the *Viable*'s starboard paddle fired in unison, one shell impacting on the pirate's hull to little obvious effect. Luckily the other was aimed with more care and exploded just behind her bows in a cloud of flame and shattered decking, Hilemore discerning the mangled shapes of several crewmen amidst the descending wreckage. He gave a grunt of satisfaction at the sudden absence of the pirate's bow chasers through the fading smoke.

The *Viable*'s two aft guns fired one after the other, one shell wrecking a life-boat and the other shredding the casement of the *Windqueen*'s starboard paddle. Hilemore quickly trained his glass to gauge the damage. He could see that one of the blades had been split in two and several others badly damaged. However, the wheel was still turning, though at a slower rate, and the *Windqueen* had begun to sheer to port due to the paddle's reduced grip on the water.

'Good work, lads!' he called to the gun-crews below. 'Keep at it!'

He returned to the bridge and saluted Trumane before making his report. 'She's badly winged, sir. Damage to the starboard paddle, though she's still able to make headway.'

'For a short time only,' Trumane replied, turning to the helm. 'Hard-a-starboard. Mr Talmant, slow to one-third.'

'Slow to one-third. Aye, sir.'

'Now then.' The captain's gaze shifted from the *Windqueen*, now pouring on what speed she could with a thicker plume of black smoke streaming from her stack, to the Irondrake, fully loaded and ready under Lemhill's supervision. 'Let us see what our new toy can do.'

Mr Lemhill was clearly no stranger to the arts of gunnery or the workings of the novel weapon he now commanded. His ad hoc gun-crew had loaded the piece with powder and shell and now knelt to the rear of the gun, hands clapped over their ears as the First Officer peered down her sights, hand-working the wheel that altered the angle of the pivot. After a few seconds, as the smoke from the *Windqueen*'s stack began to drift over the fore-deck, he pulled the gun's firing lever. The blast of noise and flame that issued from the Irondrake banished the gathering smoke in an instant, the gun recoiling on its spring mounting like a rearing horse. Hilemore turned his gaze to the *Windqueen* in expectation and, after a second long interval, was rewarded with the sight of her upper works disintegrating in a ball of fire: the bridge, stack and crew quarters all blasted apart in one fiery instant.

'Seer's balls,' the helmsman breathed, eyes wide as he took in the sight of the near-ruined vessel heaving to port as her starboard paddle finally stalled and she began a slow circle. Hilemore's glass picked out the sight of burning men on the deck, some crawling, others casting themselves over the side in desperation.

The captain ordered an increase to two-thirds speed and the *Viable*'s starboard guns soon found the range for the pirate's port paddle. Two volleys proved sufficient to put it out of action and see the *Windqueen* adrift and burning.

'Ever the way with pirates,' Trumane commented as another flaming man threw himself from the *Windqueen*'s stern, thrashing briefly before going under and leaving a smoking patch on the water. 'Can't stand up to a real enemy.'

He turned to Hilemore. 'I'll lay us alongside to port, Lieutenant. Muster your party and take her in hand. She may still be worth salvaging and prize money should never be sniffed at. And there's bound to be some loot in her hold.'

'Very good, sir.' Hilemore saluted and made for the exit, sliding down the ladder for a rapid descent to the deck. 'Master-at-Arms!'

'Sir!' Steelfine materialised out of the thinning smoke no more than three feet away, standing at rigid attention. 'Boarding party mustered and awaiting orders!' Hilemore made note of the barely suppressed eagerness in the Islander's voice.

'Stand to at the aft port rail,' Hilemore ordered. 'Ladders and ropes at the ready, bayonets fixed. Sharpshooters to lie prone atop the life-boats.'

'Aye, sir!'

Hilemore took the opportunity to check his revolver as the *Viable* manoeuvred into position, turning the cylinder and thumbing back the hammer to blow grit from the mechanism. The smoke grew thicker as they drew near to the *Windqueen*.

Whatever vitals Mr Lemhill's shot had found continued to blaze and Hilemore knew it may have been wiser to simply let her burn down to the water-line then witness her sinking in the log. However, like Trumane, he wasn't immune to the lure of a prize In addition to a welcome share in the spoils, one-twentieth of the vessel's total value for a second lieutenant, it added considerable lustre to an officer's record.

The captain ordered the *Viable*'s pumps into action when they got to within forty feet of the pirate, the gun-crews taking up the hoses to play jets of water over the stricken vessel. They were required to stay at it for a good ten minutes before the flames and smoke had dampened sufficiently to allow boarding.

'Away the grapples!' Steelfine shouted as the *Viable* drew even closer to the *Windqueen*, the range now no more than twenty feet. There was no sign of any opposition, nor even a glimpse of the crew beyond the few charred corpses littering the wreckage. The boarding party threw their ropes with practised accuracy, the grapples biting into the pirate's timbers as the ropes were drawn tight. 'Haul hard, lads!' Steelfine called, continuing to exhort them to greater efforts until they finally bumped hulls with the other ship.

'Ladders up!' Hilemore ordered, moving to the rail with Steelfine at his side. 'Once we're aboard,' he told the Islander, who, he saw, now stood with a sea-axe in hand, 'take ten men and sweep belowdecks. Subdue any opposition and make efforts to secure whatever cargo they may have stolen.'

'Aye, sir.'

Hilemore drew his sword as the last boarding ladder slammed into place, hopping up onto it and waving for the men to follow. 'Time to earn your sea pay, lads!'

He led them over in a rush, the men yelling at his back, either in eagerness or a desire to conquer their fear. Once aboard, however, he found there was little reason for trepidation, save the danger posed to a weak stomach. A man lay dead on the fore-deck, his torso separated from his lower half and guts liberally strewn about in a tangled red smear. Curiously, although much of the corpse was scorched and blackened, his face remained unmarked and free of soot. *Varestian,* Hilemore decided without surprise, noting the angular features common to those born to the Red Tides. *Was there ever a more piratical race?*

'Chuck it up if you're going to, lad,' he told a green-faced youth standing near by and staring at the carnage with wide, unblinking eyes. 'Better out than in.'

He glanced over to see Steelfine's squad descending into the smoking guts of the ship then conducted a thorough search of the wreckage. They found another dozen corpses in various states of mutilation and one that appeared to be completely untouched, a muscular fellow of Dalcian lineage who was quite dead despite no obvious signs of injury.

'It's the blast, sir,' one of the riflemen said, a veteran judging by his age and the way he held his Silworth. 'Smushes up the innards but leaves the outers be.'

Hilemore turned at a shout from another man, seeing a diminutive figure being hauled from a smoking pile of timber. 'Caught us a fish, sir,' the rifleman said. 'Only a tiddler, though.'

The captive couldn't have been more than twelve years old, stick-thin arms visible through the ragged clothing he wore. He stumbled to his knees as the sailor dragged him to Hilemore, breathing in hard, choking sobs, face averted. Hilemore knew it was custom for Varestian youth to take to the seas at an early age but could scarcely credit why they would take one such as this on a pirate cruise.

'Sea-brother,' Hilemore said in his basic but passable Varestian. The captive's face abruptly snapped up, eyes wide in surprise and fear. A brief scan of the delicate if besmirched features told Hilemore his mistake. 'Sea-sister,' he corrected. 'Where is your captain?'

The girl said nothing, though a hard narrowing of her eyes indicated it was more due to defiance than shock.

'What d'you want done, sir?' the veteran rifleman enquired.

'They didn't strike their colours and pirates got no protection under the law. No consequence to just slinging her over the side.'

Hilemore ignored him and cast his gaze about the deck, watching his men poke the smoking wreckage with their bayonets. It was all quiet but for the rustle and clatter of untended rigging. 'There's nothing else here,' he said then nodded at the kneeling girl. 'Take this one back to the *Viable*. I'll question her later. Tell the captain the rest of the crew appears to have been accounted for.' He moved towards the hold, speaking over his shoulder. 'I'll be taking inventory of the cargo with the Master-at-Ar—'

Something large and bulky exploded from the hold in a cloud of splinters, ascending to a height of near twenty feet before crashing back down onto the deck with a sickening thud. *Steelfine*, Hilemore realised, watching as the Islander tried vainly to rise, teeth bared in a snarl and axe still in hand, eyes fixed on the figure emerging from the hold.

'Arms up!' Hilemore barked, too late as the wave of force swept over them, sending rifles spinning and several men over the side. He himself was thrown from his feet and sent crashing into the part-ruined paddle casement. The air rushed from his lungs, forced out by the impact, leaving him gasping. His vision dimmed as he slid to the deck, seeing a shadowy figure move away from the hold on unsteady legs. He watched one of the fallen rifles rise into the air and fly towards the figure who raised a hand to catch it with almost casual ease.

At least one Blood-blessed on board, Hilemore thought, watching the figure raise the rifle and point it at Steelfine.

CHAPTER 14

Lizanne

Kill her. Lizanne's finger had stalled just a fraction short of the Spider's firing point. The girl continued to stare at her, mouth open and eyes wide. Perhaps it was her eyes that did it, bright and uncomprehending, so free of the spite she had shown earlier. Or perhaps it was the fresh tears still glistening on her cheeks. *Kill her!*

From beyond the door came the sound of movement on the first-floor landing followed by Burgrave Artonin's tired call. 'Who is abroad at this time of night, pray tell?'

I'll have to be quick, Lizanne decided. *One shot for her then another for him from the foot of the stairs. Tricky but not impossible.* Then she would gather up all these wonderfully enlightening papers and be on her way. It would be prudent to set fire to the house as well. The servants would be sure to provide an excellent description of the mysteriously vanished maid who started work only that morning.

Instead she just stood there, aiming her pistol and finding, much to her surprise, she was quite incapable of shooting a fifteen-year-old girl.

'Well?' came an impatient query from upstairs.

Tekela blinked and turned slowly to the doorway. Her first attempt to speak ended in a cough but she swallowed and tried again. 'It's just me, Father,' she called, voice thin but loud enough to carry. 'I mislaid my slippers.'

Lizanne heard the Burgrave sigh an exasperated curse. 'Well, look for them in the morning.'

Tekela turned back to Lizanne before replying, voice smaller now. 'Yes, Father.'

Lizanne heard Artonin's door close and waited a few seconds before lowering the Whisper. 'Close that,' she whispered, nodding at the study door.

The girl hesitated then slowly swung the door closed, wincing at the slight squeal from the hinges. Lizanne saw her take a deep breath before turning back to confront her. 'My father is a good man,' she said. 'You won't hurt him, will you?'

Lizanne closed the ledger on the desk and returned it to the hiding-place in the bookcase, making sure the contents matched her memorised glance before securing the concealing edifice in place.

'He is not a traitor,' Tekela said. 'No matter what lies are spun against him. He is loyal to the Emperor.'

She thinks I'm Cadre, Lizanne realised, her regard for the girl's courage going up a notch. She turned back to meet her gaze, eyes lingering again on her still-damp cheeks. 'Bad dream, miss?'

Tekela flushed and wiped at her eyes with the sleeve of her night-dress. Lizanne saw that her hands were trembling. 'Please,' she said. 'I don't know what you've been told, but . . .'

'We'll talk further in the morning, miss.' Lizanne moved to the girl's side, pausing to whisper in her ear. 'Speak of this and I will kill everyone in this house. Now, follow your father's instruction and go to bed.'

*T*he Mad Artisan. The drifting clouds of Madame Bondersil's mindscape flickered as she searched her memory. *Not a tale I'm familiar with. You've passed it on to Mr Torcreek, I assume?*

Yes, Madame. Not less than two hours ago. His command of Blue is improving but still lacks discipline.

And the Longrifles' progress?

Safely aboard the Firejack, *not without some drama apparently.*

Drama?

A pack of wild Greens attacked Stockade. I'm afraid Torcreek indulged in some unwise bravado. Rest assured I cautioned him against any repetition.

Greens attacking Stockade. Madame's clouds took on a reddish tinge of surprised concern. *Not an occurrence I ever thought I'd hear tell of again.* There was a pause as she reordered her thoughts, the clouds soon taking on the same familiar, serene drift.

I'll start delving into the archives, she told Lizanne. *See if there's any mention of this mysterious Corvantine genius.*

There is another matter, Madame, Lizanne told her, forming one of her whirlwinds into an accurate depiction of the fan-like device she had seen affixed to the *Regal's* hull.

What is that? Madame asked.

I was hoping you would know. Or, if not, then I suspect Jermayah would.

She saw Madame twist one of her clouds into a near-exact copy of the image Lizanne had provided. *There are other warships at harbour in Morsvale, I assume?*

Ten that I saw.

Do they also feature this device?

I didn't have the opportunity to conduct an extensive reconnaissance. However, I doubt it. The Regal *is a recent arrival and the other vessels appear to have been stationed in Arradsian waters for some time. Also, she was carrying a passenger of some importance. Grand Marshal Morradin is now in Morsvale. He was greeted on arrival by a full company from the Scarlet Legion.*

Madame's clouds grew red once more, their drift transformed into a sudden roil. *Troubling,* was her only comment.

Quite, Lizanne agreed. *A ship of the* Regal's *power in Arradsian waters is concerning enough. But the presence of Household troops coupled with Morradin's arrival . . .*

Duly noted, Lizanne. Rest assured your intelligence will be passed to the Protectorate as a matter of urgency. In the meantime you have a primary objective and we cannot allow any distractions, however pressing they may appear.

Her mindscape was now a simmering storm, dark with

authority and shot through with something Lizanne hadn't seen before. This was their first shared trance for the best part of a decade, and the colour and shape of Madame's thoughts remained much the same as she remembered. But now she saw dark tendrils spreading throughout the clouds in brief, convulsive spasms, tendrils that had started to grow at mention of a development that might impede her pursuit of the White. *Indeed, Madame,* she assured her mentor. *I have several lines of enquiry to pursue.*

The storm lessened, the tendrils shrinking into small, flickering vines. *Good. I await your next report with interest.*

Thank you, Madame. She began to close the connection then stopped at Madame's insistent thought.

And, Lizanne?

Yes, Madame?

You know the girl has to die.

Madame's mindscape vanished, leaving Lizanne adrift amongst her whirlwinds and pondering the folly of trying to hide anything from someone so well versed in the trance. More troubling, however, was the lingering image of the tendrils coiling through Madame's clouds. *So,* she thought. *That's what obsession looks like.*

Tekela was waiting by the carriage after breakfast, pale of face and somewhat red-eyed beneath her bonnet. Despite her countenance Lizanne found herself struck by how pretty she was now that all vestige of a scowl had vanished, thinking her face as close to being genuinely doll-like as she had ever seen. 'Apologies for my lateness, miss,' she told the girl with a curtsy. 'I do hope you haven't been waiting long.'

Tekela said nothing, simply staring at her in numb silence.

Lizanne gave a brief glance at Rigan, who stood with crop in hand next to the carriage's duckboard, regarding Tekela with a puzzled frown. Lizanne moved to her side, offering a hand and gesturing at the carriage. 'Shall we be about it then? I truly think you will like this dress.'

The girl gave a stiff nod and took the proffered hand, Lizanne leaning close as she climbed into the carriage. 'Rebuke me,' she whispered in Eutherian.

She met the girl's startled glance and gave a barely perceptible nod accompanied by an insistent glare. 'You . . .' Tekela began, stumbling over the words and attempting to imbue her tone with the customary waspish edge. 'You will not last long in my father's house like this,' she managed, though her words were coloured by a slight stammer. 'Any further lateness and you'll be turned out . . . Turned out into the street with no pay. Wouldn't like that would you?'

'No, miss,' Lizanne assured her with deep solicitude. 'I surely wouldn't.'

'Enough dawdling.' The girl waved a hand at Rigan. 'Let's be away, boy.'

Rigan tipped the peak of his cap and climbed onto the duck-board, setting the horse to motion with a gentle swish of his crop over its rump. Tekela sat in rigid silence as they made their way along Hailwell Gardens towards the northern quarter, her gaze fixed on Lizanne, who sat opposite engaged in a careful exam-ination of the passing buildings. Morsvale was much more uniform in architecture than Carvenport, each house closely resembling its neighbours with their pillared porches and high, sloping roofs. In the poorer districts people lived in long rows of terraced brick-built housing, their walls dark with decades of accumulated soot. Lizanne doubted there was a building in the city less than fifty years old. *They've stagnated here,* she decided, recalling one of the many mantras beloved of the managerial class: *progress through competition, competition through progress.*

'Are you a thief?' the girl burst out finally, though with suffi-cient presence of mind to speak in Eutherian. 'Or a spy?'

Lizanne turned to her, lowering her voice. 'Not so loud, if you please, miss.'

Tekela flushed under the weight of her stare, then replied in a softer tone. 'The boy doesn't understand us.'

'No. But he might wonder why a maid can speak the noble tongue.'

'So you're a spy then. A thief wouldn't know Eutherian.'

Lizanne looked at her in silence, wearing an expression of placid expectation.

'I know you're not Cadre,' Tekela said. 'They would just arrest us all. Which makes you a corporate saboteur. I know about your kind, you want to destroy the empire and make us all slaves.'

Lizanne replied with a raised eyebrow.

'I know you won't kill my father,' the girl said, a note of triumph in her voice. 'Or the servants, or me. If you were going to you'd have done it last night.'

Horror she may be, stupid she is not. 'And if you were going to expose me you would have done it by now,' Lizanne returned.

Tekela's brow took on a sullen frown and she looked away. 'I hoped you'd be gone this morning,' she mumbled. 'And the Cadre . . . Father doesn't like them, and they don't like him.'

'Why?'

The girl hesitated and Lizanne heard the lie in her muttered response. 'I don't know.' Tekela's face tensed and her eyes flashed at Lizanne in wary accusation. 'But if they knew you had even set foot in our house . . .'

'They won't. And as for destroying the empire, I'm afraid my objective is far more modest and I suspect you may be in a position to help me achieve it.'

'And why should I do that? Since you're not going to kill me, or anyone I care about, what threats can you make?'

Lizanne scrutinised Tekela's bearing closely for a moment, discerning less anger and uncertainty than she would have expected from a young girl finding herself ensnared in so dangerous a circumstance. There was a glimmer of something in her gaze, something more than fear or adolescent self-interest. *Excitement,* Lizanne realised. *All her tantrums are just a mask for boredom and now she's found a new game.*

'The servants seem to think your father is likely to place himself in the poorhouse,' Lizanne said. 'The cost of your education and wardrobe being so exorbitant.'

The ghost of a habitual pout played over Tekela's lips. 'Is that what spies do? Pay heed to commoners' gossip?'

'Yes, it is frequently what spies do. Useful information comes from a wide variety of sources and snobbery can be a fatal indulgence in my business.' She realised her voice had taken on an impatient edge, not dissimilar in fact from the inflection adopted by Madame Bondersil when her students failed to grasp the simplest of lessons. 'What if,' she went on in a more moderate tone, 'you could have all the dresses, shoes, bonnets and jewels you want? And your father could have a whole mansion full of books and ancient artifacts to puzzle over? Would you like that?'

Tekela was silent for some time, small lace-clad hands fidgeting and a variety of emotions flicking across her doll-like face. 'Your employers are wealthy then?' she asked.

'Wealthy is a supremely inadequate term with which to describe my employers.' Lizanne smiled and leaned closer. 'Your father owned a box, very old and valuable. It had a Eutherian inscription on the lid referring to the White Drake. I know he sold it at auction recently. Did you ever see it?'

The girl frowned, eyes narrowing in calculation. 'What do you want it for?'

Lizanne shook her head. 'Oh no, miss. If we are to enter into an arrangement information will flow but one way.'

Tekela's mouth took on a downward curve, as if she were about to embark upon another tantrum. However, a glance at Lizanne's steady gaze seemed to cure her of the temptation. 'Plague take bonnets and dresses and jewels,' she said. 'I want passage out of this dreary city and a house in Feros for Father and me. I hear it's a very interesting place.'

No mention of money, Lizanne noted. *Even though stepping beyond the bounds of Imperial territory without express permission is punishable by death, she's prepared to take the risk. Why?* 'All eminently achievable,' Lizanne assured her, putting the question aside for now. 'But also dependent on results.' She leaned back, eyebrows raised in expectation.

'I recall the box well enough,' Tekela said. 'Though I was only eight or so when he brought it home. Mother was angry he spent so much and they had a terrible row. After that he rarely took it out. Mother didn't like to be reminded of it.'

'Did you ever see inside?'

'Once. There was a jumble of cogs and spindles in it, like the workings of a clock. Father said it showed the passage of the three moons but I couldn't see how. Then Mother came home and got angry. Father sent me upstairs to play.' A sad frown bunched Tekela's smooth brow. 'I could still hear them though. Mother could say very bad things when she was angry.'

And not sparing with the switch either, Lizanne recalled, thinking this girl and her father may have been better served by the woman's absence. 'Did he ever speak of it again?' she asked. 'Explain what it was for?'

Lizanne shook her head. 'I never saw it again until the day he took it to the auction house. He seemed very sad, now I come to think on it.'

'The device it contained had been removed before he sold it. Do you know what became of it?'

Tekela moved her slim shoulders in a shrug. 'I don't really pay much attention to his enthusiasms. It may still be in the house, though I couldn't say where.'

'Does he have other hiding-places like the one in his study?'

'I didn't even know about that one.'

Lizanne smothered an exasperated sigh. She didn't doubt the girl's honesty but this was hardly worth the promised expense. She was calculating how to combine the right amount of threat with encouragement when Tekela spoke again.

'Uncle Diran might have it, I suppose.'

'Uncle Diran?'

'I call him "uncle," but he's really just Father's old friend. Diran

Akiv Kapazin. He works at the museum. They spend endless hours together waffling about old things.'

The museum. Where better to hide it? 'You are close to this uncle?' she asked.

'Not especially.' A smug smile curved Tekela's lips. 'His son's regard, however, is of a higher order.'

'His son?'

'Sirus. He works as Uncle's assistant, when he's not penning yet more inept verse to send me. Last time he rhymed "the gentle wind blows" with "your tiny bud nose."'

'So if you were to visit the museum it wouldn't appear out of place?'

'I only go when Father drags me there for some tedious function. Although, Sirus is always offering a guided tour so it would be an easy matter to arrange it.'

Lizanne returned her gaze to the passing streets, pondering the information and ignoring Tekela's insistent gaze. As they made their way past Victory Park she saw something she had noticed the previous day when making her way to the Burgrave's house, her eyes being attuned to seeking out high points in any landscape. A tall spire rose from what appeared to be a temple of some kind. Religious observance varied widely throughout the empire, as did forms of belief, but she knew this to be an oracle site, a place where those with the supposed gift of reading the future had once dwelt, growing fat on the offerings of gullible supplicants. Oracularism had fallen into disuse in recent decades, largely because the Imperial family had eschewed it in favour of a return to the once-defunct Imperial Cult which elevated the emperor to near-godlike status. But here and there the old temples lingered on, though most, like this one, were long since unoccupied.

Her eyes tracked the length of the spire and, given its position, she judged it would offer no view of the clock-maker's house. However, it would afford a clear line of sight to the dress-maker's.

'What do you want me to do?' Tekela asked, as they turned a

corner into Careworn Street. The excitement Lizanne had noticed earlier was back now, the girl's gaze more intense, eager even. *Already she begins to enjoy the game,* Lizanne thought, feeling a twinge of self-recognition. She hadn't been much older when an Exceptional Initiatives agent had first piqued her interest in covert matters.

'For now,' she replied as Rigan brought the carriage to a halt outside the dress-maker's, 'try on the lovely dress I've found for you. You will buy it, after an appropriate amount of fussing, then make a scene and take the carriage. You will tell Madam Meeram you have sent me on an errand to find shoes to match the dress and she should not expect me until after dark. You understand?'

Tekela's eyes flicked to the shop beyond the carriage window. 'There's something here, isn't there? Something you want.'

Lizanne leaned forward, taking hold of Tekela's small hand and squeezing hard enough to make her gasp. 'Information flows but one way, miss. Now' – she released her and opened the carriage door, slipping back into Varsal and raising her voice – 'let us do some shopping.'

Tekela's second attempt at an intemperate outburst was considerably more convincing than her first, albeit a trifle overplayed. 'I'll have Father order Madam Meeram to cane you,' she said, wagging a finger in Lizanne's face, tone shrill with shrewish zeal. 'You see if I don't! Ungrateful slattern!'

Lizanne lowered her gaze and glanced back at the dress-maker's shop in apparent mortification. She could see the elegantly attired woman inside offering a sympathetic wince through the window. They had spent the better part of an hour in the shop as Tekela tried on the dress, a narrow-waisted arrangement of pleasingly complementary silks and lace. She appeared quite fetching to Lizanne's eyes but the girl was evidently practised in finding fault with even the most skilled work. 'The hem's too low,' she told the elegant woman. 'Don't you know the fashion is now an inch above the heel?'

'A detail easily remedied, miss,' the woman replied. 'The alteration should take only an hour or two.'

'The sleeves also,' Tekela said, straightening her arms and angling her gaze at the tall mirror. 'Too plain.'

'Perhaps a touch of silver braid about the cuffs,' the woman suggested. 'If it were to be matched with appropriate earrings and necklace, the effect would be quite breath-taking. However, the price would also require modification . . .'

'Then modify it,' Tekela said, waving a dismissive hand. 'And take the waist in another half-inch. I'm not a sow. Bill to Burgrave Artonin, Hailwell Gardens. My girl here will collect on the morrow.'

'Very good, miss.' The woman moved behind the counter to write up the transaction. She appeared every inch the proprietress of a dress shop, from the impeccably arranged hair to the finely made but otherwise unadorned gown she wore; anything too elaborate might outshine the customers. But something was off: her back a little too straight and stride a little too precise, like steps learned on a parade-ground. Military training had a tendency to seep into the soul and was consequently always difficult to mask. Also, her hands, whilst as elegant as the rest of her, were possessed of an evident strength that went beyond the seamstress's arts.

Cadre, Lizanne decided. *But is she Blessed?*

'During your walk home,' Tekela said, climbing into the carriage with Rigan's assistance, 'you would do well to ponder if you truly deserve a place in my father's house.'

She slammed the carriage door closed and sat with her nose raised to a near-exact forty-five-degree angle. 'Sorry,' Rigan whispered to Lizanne in apology. She favoured him with a small smile of understanding before he climbed up onto the duckboard and set the carriage in motion. She stood watching them depart for a moment then sighed and began a weary southward trudge.

*

She spent an hour or more wandering the park, ostensibly smiling at flower-beds and partaking of the roasted chestnuts or iced creams offered by various vendors. In reality she was conducting a thorough reconnaissance of the area surrounding the oracular temple and its useful spire, taking note of the patrol routes and routines favoured by Morsvale's constabulary. She was unsurprised to find this city more heavily policed than Carvenport, the constables patrolling in pairs at annoyingly regular intervals and regarding their fellow Imperial citizens with often glowering scrutiny. She was, however, gratified by their uniform absence of any obvious sign of true intelligence or individual initiative; a stupid enemy was always easier to evade, or kill.

She filled the final hour before nightfall by throwing bread-crumbs to the ducks and swans occupying the park's boating lake, then secluded herself in a suitably dense cluster of bushes whilst the park-keeper hustled lingerers to the exits. She lay prone on the dirt, uncaring of any stains to her dress, stirring only when the last rattle of keys in the iron gates had faded to nothing. She took the Spider from her handbag and strapped it to her arm before hoisting her skirt and drawing the Whisper from the holster fastened to her thigh. In idle moments she often wondered how ordinary women went about their daily business encumbered by the ridiculous under-garments they were obliged to wear in these supposedly modern times.

She found the temple boarded up and adorned with various signs warning against intrusion and proclaiming the place due for imminent demolition. A small drop of Green was enough to enable a swift removal of boards from one of the smaller windows and she climbed inside to find a gloomy interior of dust-shrouded marble. She made her way to the south-side of the building where a narrow flight of winding stairs led upwards into the spire, the Green facilitating a rapid ascension to the top. The spire was crowned by a roofed viewing platform, the rafters of which were busy with the annoyed cooing of pigeons unsettled by her appearance. She climbed outside onto a narrow ledge to avoid the constant patter of bird droppings, considering that, for all its excitements and rewards, the life she had chosen was rarely a glamorous one.

She crouched, ingesting more Green to enhance her vision and ward off the inevitable ache to her muscles. She could see a light inside the dress-maker's, flickering a little as the occupant moved about. After a few minutes the light abruptly faded and the elegant woman emerged from the shop, pausing to secure a grating over the window and door before locking them in place. She then made an unhurried progress north to the junction with Needlecraft Row, turning right and making for the more spacious streets of the town's western quarter. Lizanne's suspicions were confirmed by the woman's progress, pausing at every corner, frequently doubling back on herself, all standard practice for an operative proceeding towards a secure location. For a few moments Lizanne was worried she might lose her as the distance between them broadened, but fortunately the woman came to a halt at an apparently nondescript house on Ticker Street. It was a neighbourhood mostly occupied by what the Corvantine noble class termed 'the middling sort,' the bookkeepers, lawyers and petty government officials who provided the bureaucratic glue for the empire's myriad workings. She watched the woman approach the front door and knock three times, pause then knock twice more. The door opened after a short interval and she disappeared inside.

Lizanne took a moment to scan the surrounding roof-tops, picking out a guard positioned on the house opposite, lying prone with a repeating carbine at the ready. The house behind was obscured from her sight but it was a safe assumption another marksman had been placed there also. *Safe house,* she decided. *Anything more important would be better guarded.* Her gaze returned to the shop and the boarded-up clock-maker's house opposite. She still saw no sign of surveillance which meant whoever had charge of this operation was far too skilled for her liking and the risks of mounting a close inspection were too great.

She huffed in frustration, leaning back on her haunches. It was aggravating but not disastrous; the Cadre had provided her with intelligence on their organisation and she had uncovered one of their agents. Also, she now had a keen new asset to exploit. Lizanne smothered the upsurge of nostalgic recognition provoked by the memory of Tekela's earnest gaze. Sentiment was always unwise and here would most likely prove fatal. *You know the girl has to die . . .*

CHAPTER 15

Clay

For a second everything was red, the grip of Ellforth's Black lingering for a few heart-beats despite the sudden absence of his head. Clay could only stand rigid as blood, brains and skull fragments spattered his face. Release came when what remained of Ellforth slumped against the bar and slid to the floor, the last vestiges of Black leaking from his body. Clay's every muscle seemed to spasm at once, the world reeling around him as his legs gave way and he collapsed onto the headhunter's corpse, retching and quivering.

'Longrifles up!'

Clay turned his twitching head to see Uncle Braddon standing near the tavern door, jacking a spent cartridge from his rifle. There came the scrape and tumble of chairs as his company scrambled to obey. Braddon unslung a second rifle from his shoulder and threw underhand, Clay tracking the weapon's arc towards Preacher. The rifleman caught it with almost casual ease, worked the lever and brought it to his shoulder, aiming at something to Clay's left. Foxbine had both pistols drawn and aimed in the same direction whilst Skaggerhill stepped to her side and thumbed the hammers back on his shotgun. His old friend Stallwin was backing towards the corner, one hand on the revolver at his side.

Clay blinked bloody grit from his eyes and swivelled his gaze to the right. Most of the boatmen who had been engaged in such raucous merriment only seconds before now lay flat on the floor, hands over their heads, whilst others were scrambling under tables or clambering out of the nearest window. However, there was a group of ten figures in the centre of the tavern who seemed content to bide awhile longer. They were all dressed in the same kind of blue riverman's coat worn by Ellforth, though like him they were all adorned with tooth necklaces, each face featuring a unique pattern of scars. *Ellforth's crew,* Clay realised, taking dim satisfaction in his own judgement. *Fella like him never makes a move on his own.*

The headhunters, three women and seven men, stood with hands on their weapons, carbines and pistols half-drawn or half-raised, every face hard with a keen desire for retribution. One, a tall Old Colonial with a large-calibre pistol gripped at his side, bared his filed teeth in evident eagerness for the coming confrontation.

'Lawful killing,' Braddon said, his tone absent any note of conciliation. If anything he seemed mightily angry. 'Your man should've expected nothing different. Any of you worthless shit-heels don't want the same, leave your weapons on the floor, find a window and crawl your sorry behinds on out of here.'

Although the tall headhunter's grin broadened yet further at the warning, Clay saw a flicker of uncertainty flash across the faces of his companions. Glances were exchanged and they began to edge backwards, weapons lowering. The tall man, however, was having none of it. 'Fuck the law, Captain,' he told Braddon in an oddly conversational tone. 'And fuck you t—'

His head snapped back in a blur, his final word choking off into a hacking gurgle, blood streaming down his face from the short-handled knife buried in his eye-socket. Clay turned to see Silverpin drawing her arm back for a second throw. This one sent the knife into the tall man's other eye, evidently buried deep enough to find the brain from the way he fell to the floor, all vestige of life suddenly drained from his limbs.

A multiple thudding sounded as the remaining headhunters dropped their weapons and began to back away. 'I got a long memory and an unforgiving nature,' Braddon told them. 'Catch sight of any of you again, I won't be minded to be so nice. Now get gone.'

The headhunters fled, battering their way through the tavern's rear windows in their haste to be elsewhere.

'Clay,' Braddon called to him. 'Time to go.'

Clay tried to rise then slumped back onto Ellforth's corpse, arms and legs still suffering the after-effects of the Black's grip. 'I'm alright,' he said, waving a hand as Skaggerhill moved to help him up. He lingered for a second, fighting his gorge at the stink and sight of the headhunter's shattered skull, then got unsteadily to his feet.

'They got sharpshooters on the roof-tops outside,' Braddon said. He caught Silverpin's gaze and pointed her to the corpse of the tall headhunter. She moved to it, quickly drawing her blades from his eye-sockets then unsheathing the broad knife at the small of her back. Clay turned away as she went about her work, though the sound of it was enough to finally make him spew.

''Salright, kiddo,' Foxbine said, rubbing his heaving back. 'It's what he would've wanted.'

This made the others laugh, apart from Preacher, who stood at his uncle's side, keen eyes scanning the darkness beyond the door. The tumult that had covered the town on their arrival had faded now, leaving a palpable and expectant silence. 'One opposite,' Preacher reported. 'Another hunkered down by those barrels on the wharf. Can't see the others.'

'Headhunters move in packs of twenty or more,' Braddon said. 'Means at least a half-dozen we can't see.' He raised his voice, casting it out into the dark. 'Your captain and your Blood-blessed are dead! There's no profit to be had here!' He nodded at Silverpin and the Islander tossed her grisly trophy through the doorway. Braddon let it lie on the board-walk for a good few seconds before speaking again. 'We're coming out! You know me and you know what's like to happen if a single bullet comes my way!'

He turned to the company, speaking low. 'Preacher, take the

lead. Miss Foxbine, Silverpin, keep Clay between you. Skaggs, you and me bring up the rear.'

Skaggerhill nodded then turned to raise a hand to Stallwin. 'Wish we coulda talked longer, Kleb. You know how it is.'

The Riverjack shrugged and holstered his pistol. 'Always a pleasure, Skaggs. Any messages to take up-river?'

'Call in on my Lousille when you get to Carvenport. Let her know her old pa's still kicking. Maybe make sure she's not wanting for essentials.'

'That I will.' Something in Stallwin's gaze told Clay there was more to this exchange than just the parting of old friends. Skaggerhill had asked for a favour not granted lightly. 'You take care now,' the Contractor said as they began to troop out the door.

'Always do, Kleb.'

They moved at what seemed a crawl to Clay, Preacher a few steps ahead with rifle stock firm against his shoulder and eyes constantly roving the walkways and bridges. Silverpin and Foxbine kept Clay tight between them the whole while and he felt a certain shame at voicing no objection. He had drawn the Stinger, though from the way his hands continued to tremble he doubted it would do him much good if any shooting started up. As they neared the wharf the *Firejack*'s whistle began to sound, casting a plaintive call across the town.

'Seems the skipper got word of our trouble,' Skaggerhill said. 'Calling the crew back from their revels.'

'They better be quick about it,' Braddon grunted. 'We ain't lingering here a second longer than we have to.'

Preacher came to a halt as they came to the walkway leading to the *Firejack*'s mooring, sinking into a crouch and staring intently at the board-walk ahead. 'What ya got?' Foxbine asked him in a whisper.

Preacher said nothing, his rifle tracking the walkway in a slow side-to-side sweep. The moment stretched and Clay had begun to ponder reaching for Auntie's gift when Preacher fired. The shot sounded like a roar in the stillness, a plume of powdered wood erupting from the walkway. For a second there was no sound save the fading echo of the rifle-shot, then the tell-tale splash of something heavy falling into the river.

'Bastards are underneath,' Foxbine said, raising both pistols and firing off all twelve shots faster than Clay would have thought possible. Splintered wood rose in a cloud the length of the walkway, accompanied by shouts of alarm and more splashes from beneath the planking. A pair of dark figures began to clamber up as Foxbine's guns fell silent and she went into a crouch, hands moving with unconscious speed and precision as she replaced the cylinders. Preacher fired again, two shots in quick succession, the climbers tumbling into the water.

'Let's go!' Braddon shouted and they ran the remaining distance, Skaggerhill snapping off a shotgun blast at a shadow glimpsed beneath the board-walk. Keelman greeted them at the gangplank, his weathered features grim and not entirely welcoming.

'Company orders didn't say anything about this kinda trouble,' he said to Braddon as they came aboard in a rush. Foxbine and Preacher hunkered down at the rail, weapons aimed at the town.

'It's the Interior, Skipper,' Braddon told him. 'There's always trouble. Best you cast off now.'

'Still got four men unaccounted for. My Second Mate amongst them.'

'They ain't here yet, they ain't coming. Likely the headhunters grabbed them up and are already wringing what they can outta them. We can't wait.'

As if to underline his point a shot came from the town, the bullet whining past the skipper's head to smack into the bulkhead behind. He barely flinched, though the anger that coloured his shouted order to cast off indicated a reluctant acceptance of Braddon's advice. The *Firejack* soon pulled away from the wharf, paddles churning the water white. A few more shots were fired before they drew out of range, doing no damage beyond a shattered window. Preacher fired only one shot in response, though his grunt of satisfaction indicated he had hit his mark. They were soon steaming south at a brisk pace, Edinsmouth fading into the distance then disappearing completely as they rounded a bend.

Clay turned as Braddon laid a hand on his shoulder, finding his uncle looking him over in close inspection. 'I ain't hurt,' Clay said, shrugging off the hand. He returned the Stinger to its holster, finding to his annoyance his hands still hadn't stopped shaking. 'How did you know? About the Blood-blessed.'

'Saw the headhunters taking up position around the tavern,' Braddon replied. 'Someone always takes the watch, tonight it was my turn.'

'Uncle, the Blood-blessed, he said . . .'

'Somebody hired his crew to kill you, and the rest of us into the bargain I'm guessing. Headhunter rarely spends a bullet without someone paying him first. Seems there's a bounty on us now.'

'Morsvale,' Clay said. 'He said he Blue-tranced with someone in Morsvale.'

'Corvantine bastards,' Skaggerhill said, spitting over the side.

'Ironship warned me it might come to this,' Braddon said, turning to address them all. 'Seems we're not just on a hunt now. Now we're in a race and we just missed our last chance to turn back.'

Somehow the others all managed to fall asleep the moment they hit their bunks, whilst Clay lay awake for hours. He had reason enough to ensure there were no eyes or ears to witness what he needed to do, but the lingering effects of Ellforth's grip ensured sleep was denied him in any case. Added to the palsy was the lingering image of the headhunter's leering face, the evident delight in what he was doing, not to say the stench of his breath. It all combined to raise a singular question in his mind: *Was that me?* He thought back over all those vicious back-alley confrontations in the Blinds, the times he had used Black to settle a score or collect a debt. He had been cruel at times, he knew that, but never needlessly and those on the receiving end had been more than deserving. He hadn't been an Ellforth but after a few more years, and a war with Keyvine, who knew what he might have become?

He slipped from his bunk when Skaggerhill began to snore; that the cacophony failed to wake Preacher or Braddon was ample sign they were sound asleep. Outside the night was clear and the sky lit with a vast panorama of stars. Only Nelphia was visible tonight, denied the company of her smaller sisters as she made her imperceptible progress across the twinkling back-drop. He remembered that Joya had liked to sit out on the roof and gaze up at the heavens, for hours at a time some nights. He had often felt the urge to go sit with her but never did, thinking it an intrusion; this was her time and they asked enough of her as it was. So she would watch the moons and he would watch her; it had seemed a fair trade at the time.

He chose a spot near the port paddle casement, glancing around to ensure there were no crewmen in sight before reaching into his shirt to extract his prize. He was gratified to find Ellforth's lack of personal hygiene didn't extend to his vials. The padded green-leather wallet was shiny from regular wiping and the glass tubes themselves free of any besmirching grease that might contaminate the contents. He checked each one in turn, grunting in annoyance at the meagre stocks. There was barely a drop of Black left, meaning the bastard had taken a full dose before approaching Clay. He supposed it was flattering. The Blue was similarly denuded but there was about a quarter vial of Green and Red. Added to Auntie's gift he now had a half-decent supply of product, not counting Blue but he doubted he'd be making much use of that when the time came.

He took only the smallest sip of Green, letting it settle on his tongue before swallowing it down. As expected the tremble imme-diately vanished from his hands and the residue of nausea still clutching at his guts loosened then faded completely. He swept the river with his enhanced vision, finding the waters now transformed into a swirling mist through which clouds of small fish darted, gleaming like fire-flies. He raised his gaze to the lonely moon and an involuntary gasp escaped him. So clear, he wondered, eyes tracking over Nelphia's surface. Usually monochrome, now it stood revealed as a pleasing patchwork of crimson mountains and vermilion valleys, the sparsely cratered plains a soft shade of azure. It was mesmerising, capturing his complete attention for the full sixty seconds it took for the Green to fade and lodging a memory he knew was unlikely to dim.

As the last of the Green ebbed away and Nelphia's surface resumed its grey-black pallor, he recalled Miss Lethridge's advice to find a visual template for the trance, a mindscape she called it. He decided it was worth a try. The moon was as good an image as any and compelling enough for him to sustain a facsimile during the trance. Also, it might spare him another lecture.

He added Auntie's gift to the wallet and returned it to his shirt, knowing he would have to find a better hiding-place come the morning. He made his way back to the hatch leading to their shared cabin then paused at a new sound from the stern. It was soft but high-pitched, like the whimper of a pup in distress. Keenly aware of the fact that he had left the Stinger in the cabin he briefly debated going back for it before moving towards the stern; he had the wallet after all. More whimpering came as he neared the cluster of crates and barrels lashed to the aft deck, the sound clearly human but also possessed of a wince-inducing fear.

He found Silverpin lying on a large coil of rope, clutching herself tight as if chilled, her tattooed features alternately slack then tense in response to whatever horrors lurked behind her closed eyes. She bared her teeth as she whimpered again, the sound transformed into a snarl as she lurched and lashed out. Her hand was empty but he saw that it gripped an invisible knife, jabbing and thrusting with expert savagery before it fell limp onto her side.

Clay watched as her heaving chest slowed to a regular rhythm and her shivering subsided, feeling a surge of guilty arousal at the sight of her sweat-beaded skin. He switched his gaze to her face, seeing the features take on a placid, almost serene cast. He retrieved an unused tarpaulin from the deck and draped it over her, taking care to do so at arm's length lest she awaken with a start, this time with a real blade in hand. He sat on a crate and watched her sleep for a while, thinking it odd how harmless she appeared. Despite the tattoos and the predatory leanness, he saw now that she was scarcely older than he. He wondered how old she could have been when, if as Skaggerhill had claimed, she took up with a pack of headhunters. As old as he had been when Uncle cast him out into the Blinds maybe? Younger even. If so, it was hardly surprising she might suffer the occasional nightmare.

Feeling the tug of sleep he rose from the crate and started back to the crew quarters, pausing when he saw Silverpin's lips moving. No sound came from them but it was clear she was speaking, the lips forming words in a silent torrent. He could make little sense of it, but he did detect one word, repeating over and over. *Mother . . .*

After a short while the flow of words stopped and she became serene and apparently content under the tarpaulin with no trace of distress to mar her features. He stared at her for some time but she slept on in tranquil silence, her lips free of the slightest twitch. Eventually, as Nelphia slid farther to the west and his eyelids began to droop, he turned away and started back to his cabin, a single question defying his fatigued mind. *What is she?*

'There,' Skaggerhill said, pointing a stubby finger at a patch of swamp land off the starboard bow. In the five days since leaving Edinsmouth the surrounding jungle had thinned, giving way to large tracts of grassy, bug-misted swamp. Clay followed the harvester's finger, picking out a cluster of dome-like forms amidst a less grassy patch of brown-tinged water. For a moment he thought some river folk had come to grief, perhaps thanks to one of the fabled but yet unseen river Greens, upturned boats the only sign of their demise. But looking closer he saw the forms were moving, each producing a subtle but visible wake in the water.

'What are they?' he asked

'Glyptids,' Skaggerhill replied. 'Though most folk call 'em shell-backs. You'll get a better look when we pass by some dryer land. Though you probably won't credit your eyes when you do. They're the most unlikeliest-looking beast I ever did see, next to the drakes that is.'

'They dangerous?' Clay asked, then realised it was a stupid question. *Everything out here is dangerous.*

'They ain't meat-eaters,' Skaggerhill replied. 'But you don't wanna get too close, especially when they got young 'uns around. Glyptid's got a tail like a hammer. They'll crack you open from neck to balls with a single sweep. Seen it happen once.'

A shout came from the upper deck, Clay glancing up to see a deck-hand pointing to the sky. He shaded his eyes against the sun and searched the sky until he found it, a cruciform shape, black against blue. He knew instantly it was no bird. Even at this distance he was able to gauge some measure of its size, an impression confirmed when the shadow of a wing swept over the steamer, shading it from bow to stern. The *Firejack*'s whistle gave a long, insistent blast which sent the crew running. Uncle Braddon and Preacher soon appeared on deck with rifles in hand.

'Ain't after us,' Skaggerhill told Braddon as the drake angled its wings, its neck forming an elegant curve as it peered at the river below.

Braddon's gaze went to the cluster of humps in the swamp and he nodded, turning and cupping his hands to yell at the wheel-house. 'Steer to port and pile on the steam! It's going for the shell-backs!'

The *Firejack*'s paddles were soon churning at a greatly increased rate as the steamer put a good distance between them and the shell-backs. If the drake had any care for their presence it failed to show it, sweeping around in a slow descending circle. Clay could make out its colouring now, seeing the sun glint on its jet scales.

'Fifteen-footer,' he heard Skaggerhill say. 'He's a long way from home.'

The Black levelled out then abruptly shortened its wing-span, plummeting down at a steep angle until it was no more than five feet off the water. It spread its wings again, talons skimming the river. On reaching the shell-backs it reared up, the claws of its rear legs slashing downwards. The swamp water erupted into a white maelstrom for a few seconds at it took a firm hold on its prey, Clay feeling the wind-rush as it fanned its wings. It gave a piercing squawk of triumph as it rose higher, something thrashing in its grip. Clay assumed it had taken a juvenile from the size of it, smaller than the others. The shell-back had a blunt, block-shaped head, its mouth agape as it screamed in distress, club-headed tail whirling in panic. The other shell-backs cried out in unison, blocky heads raised from the water to issue a chorus of plaintive dismay as the drake flew away with its prize. It rose to a great height in the space of a minute, soon becoming no more than a speck in the sky.

'He'll find some rocky ground to drop it on,' Skaggerhill said.

'Ever see one so big this far north?' Braddon asked him.

'No, Captain.' Clay saw there was a troubled cast to the harvester's gaze. 'Not ever. Younger Blacks sometimes venture farther afield in search of a mate, but full-grown males keep to their hunting grounds and guard their females close.'

'So what's it doing here?' Clay asked.

Skaggerhill grunted a laugh and clapped him on the shoulder. 'I'll be Seer-damned if I know, young 'un. First Greens attacking Stockade now Blacks hunting in swamp country. Could be this land is trying to tell us something.'

The swamp grew more shallow with each passing mile and disappeared completely after another three days. The Greenchurn now snaked its way through a mix of arid plains and scrub bush-land. As Skaggerhill promised, Clay was afforded plentiful opportunity to view shell-backs out of the water. They moved in herds of twenty or more, raising copious dust clouds that covered their leathery shells in a reddish-brown shroud. They seemed placid creatures for the most part, happy to munch away at the dense bushes clustering around the river's numerous tributaries. Occasionally though, two of the larger beasts would go at each other, mouths gaping to roar as they circled around, twisting to deliver thunder-crack blows with their club tails. With little else to do Clay kept watch on the shell-backs and the sky, looking, or perhaps hoping, for another sight of the Black. So far, however, the lumbering herds had remained unmolested.

'Pa says they taste like mutton.'

Clay turned to find Loriabeth limping to his side. She had finally emerged from her cabin the day before, thinner in face and body and incapable of walking more than a few steps at a time, but otherwise healthy to Clay's eyes. She also seemed less inclined to habitual insult. 'Says I can hunt us one if we get a chance,' she went on, resting her slender arms on the rail and sighing a little from the effort of walking.

'Would've thought they taste like turtle,' Clay replied. 'Thought that's what they are, just big turtles.'

'Maybe. Guess we'll find out before long.' She paused, throat working and gaze guarded. 'I ain't thanked you for what you did at Stockade.'

'Thank Silverpin. Get the feeling she didn't need my help.'

'Thanked her already. She just nodded and went back to honing her blades. Known her for four years now and she barely seems to see me. Awful puzzling why she'd risk her neck for mine.'

'Uncle brought her into the Longrifles?'

She shook her head. 'Was Skaggs that found her back in some shit-hole tavern in Carvenport. Seems she was in the midst of a disagreement with her old headhunter crew. Her skills impressed him enough to make an introduction.' She shifted, wincing a little and clutching at her leg.

'You alright?' he asked.

'Aches now and then is all. Foxy says given time it should heal enough that I won't limp my whole life.'

He watched her massaging her thigh, seeing the suppressed pain in her face. 'Was it worth it, cuz?' he asked. 'Coming after us was the most fool thing I ever saw, and I saw plenty in the Blinds.'

'Pa told me what we're after. Damn right it was worth it. We're the luckiest Contractor crew to ever track the Interior, Clay. The White Drake, a thing no living soul has ever seen. Think on it.'

Her eyes had taken on a gleam not dissimilar to the one he had seen in Madame Bondersil's gaze when she had first explained the objective of this enterprise. They all had it to some extent, even Preacher. Something about the prospect of the White Drake had a power to capture the heart, and it wasn't just the reward. By now he had seen enough of the Interior to conclude that Contractors were not drawn here solely by lust for profit. The risks involved in traversing this land meant there had to be more to it. They lived for the mysteries that lurked here, the basic need to explore and find what others hadn't.

'I'd rather think on the reward I'm due,' he said. 'And there's a chance some living soul has seen it. Your pa tell you about the Wittler Expedition?'

'He told me. But Wittler wasn't my pa and the Sandrunners weren't us.'

The Badlands came into view later that day, the plains on the western bank giving way to a dense panorama of jagged chalk spires and cliffs that ascended from the river like castle walls from one of the old books Joya liked to read. Clay could see taller peaks to the west, rising like black teeth against the dimming sky. There was something strange about the peaks, a mottled surface that accentuated their already unnatural appearance. Also, there seemed to be some kind of cloud lingering over the summits.

'They volcanoes or something?' he asked Skaggerhill, who laughed.

'Different kind've fire birthed in those peaks.' He offered Clay his spy glass. 'Take a look.'

It took a moment to focus the glass, Clay working the eyepiece back and forth until the blurred image coalesced into something that almost made him drop it. *Reds. The sky's full of Reds.*

They wheeled around the peaks in a crimson swarm, flame gouting from their mouths in short bursts. Most were smaller than those he had seen in the Carvenport pens, albeit possessed of considerably more vitality. Here and there a larger specimen soared through the shifting swarm to land atop one of the innumerable ledges that covered the peaks, usually with something formless and bloody dangling from its talons. Wherever they landed a clutch of the smaller Reds would detach from the swarm and descend on the newly arrived meal, heads bobbing as they tore and rent the flesh to nothing in a matter of seconds.

'Hatchlings at play,' Skaggerhill explained. 'They fly about and burn off their naptha before bedtime.'

Clay focused the glass on one of the youngsters as it sidled up to an adult. The full-grown Red was about two-thirds the size of the Black he had seen, presumably mother to the infant nestling against its flank from the way it licked the blood from its face and drew it closer with an enveloping curl of its tail. He saw now that the peaks' jagged appearance came from the numerous ledges and holes carved into their surface by what he guessed was centuries of talon scrapings. It resulted in something that resembled a giant tooth-shaped honeycomb, blackened by soot born of generations of drake breath.

'Guess you know where to come when you need Red,' he said to Skaggerhill, handing back the glass.

'Oh no. Ain't nobody made it to the heart of the Badlands and lived to tell of it. Reds live in hives and they don't like visitors. Get within a mile and they'll come at you in a swarm no amount of bullets can stop. No, you want to hunt Red you gotta be smart about it, set live bait at the edge of their territory and be patient. They live in swarms but hunt alone.'

'Live bait?'

'Goats work fine, mostly. Though they prefer horse. Closest thing to a Cerath, their usual prey.'

'Cerath?'

'Imagine a horse that mated with a bull and gave birth to a freakishly giant foal, and you've got a pretty good picture. You get Lesser Ceraths living close to the Badlands to the west, great herds of the things. More every year since there are fewer drakes to eat 'em.'

Clay returned his gaze to the distant peaks and their cloud of juvenile Reds. 'Fewer?'

'Surely. Time was the swarm was so thick it'd blot out the sun.' Skaggerhill's tone took on a note of sombre reflection as he added, 'One day there won't be no more drakes, and no more Contractors. Makes a fella wonder what the world'll look like then.' He gave Clay a rueful grin before moving away, casting a final comment over his shoulder. 'We reach the Sands tomorrow, young 'un. Might wanna clean and oil your weapon in the meantime. It's likely to see some service out there.'

CHAPTER 16

Lizanne

'"... and so the third and fairest daughter of the Diamond Realm went willingly with the King of the Deep,"' Lizanne recited, '"carried away and down into the depths of the ocean never to return. Though on that same day every year her kin gather on the shore-line, for it's said her song can be heard on the sea-breeze and it is the song of a queen well pleased with her husband."'

'Ah.' The Burgrave nodded, his pen moving across the page in eager but precise strokes. '"Diamond Realm," you say? I've been translating it as "The Bejewelled Kingdom."'

'Yes, sir,' Lizanne said. 'A lot depends on how you say it.'

'And the title,' he went on. '"The Third Daughter's Sacrifice."' Accurate would you say?'

'"Marriage" would be better, sir. In the northern provinces parents talk of sacrificing their daughters at the wedding ceremony. It's a tradition, y'see.'

'Sacrifice,' he repeated softly, pen stalled on the page. 'I see more wisdom in these fables every day.'

Lizanne lowered the book as he returned to his scribbling, soon losing himself amongst the words. She was pondering whether to ask permission to withdraw when the door-bell gave an insistent jangle.

'Shall I go, sir?' she asked.

'Better not,' the Burgrave replied. 'Answering the door is the only duty Mr Drellic remembers to perform with any efficiency. I'm loath to upset him.'

She nodded and curtsied. 'I'll be about my duties then, sir. Since you're about to have company.'

'Thank you, Krista. Ask Cook to send up some tea, would you?'

'Certainly, sir.' Upon exiting the study she caught sight of Mr Drellic making steady if glacial progress along the hallway. She made a brief visit to the kitchen to relay the Burgrave's tea order then returned to the ground floor to find that Drellic had finally reached the door. She busied herself dusting a vase situated close to a convenient mirror which afforded a clear view of the visitor, her cloth pausing as Drellic opened the door to reveal a tall man in the blue uniform of the Imperial Dragoons. Her momentary concern dissipated, however, when the man offered the butler his cap with a familiar smile.

'Mr Drellic,' he said. 'How are you today?'

'Well, Major. Very well, thank you.' Drellic stood aside, head bowed as the officer entered. 'The Burgrave's in his study, sir. Go right on in.'

Lizanne averted her eyes as the officer approached the study, hearing a momentary pause in his footsteps as he caught sight of her. 'New blood?'

Lizanne turned and stood with her head lowered, deferring to Drellic to make the introduction. 'Quite so, Major,' the ancient butler said, gesturing a quivering hand at Lizanne. 'This is . . .' He paused, brows furrowed and eyes unfocused. 'This . . . is . . .'

'Krista, sir,' Lizanne said, bobbing a curtsy.

'That's not a Morsvale accent,' the officer observed, angling his head slightly. 'Corvus. Am I correct?'

Studying his face she discerned a similar confidence to that of the unfortunate Mr Redsel, though his military bearing and lean features also put her in mind of Commander Pinefeld. It was an appealing combination but she knew this mission had already accumulated sufficient complications. 'Indeed so, sir,' she said in a neutral tone, lowering her gaze. She had the satisfaction of feeling his eyes track her from head to toe; reciprocated or not such interest could always be useful.

'And how is the old dung heap?' he asked. 'Haven't been back for nigh on a decade.'

'Please stop quizzing my employees, Arberus,' the Burgrave said, appearing in the study doorway beyond the major's shoulder 'She's not one of your troopers.'

The officer inclined his head at Lizanne. 'Major Arberus Lek Hakimas, miss. Seventeenth Dragoons. At your service.' He glanced over his shoulder at the Burgrave's insistent cough then inclined his head at her once again and grinned before making his way into the study. The Burgrave closed the door, muting their conversation, though from the convivial tone she discerned a long-standing friendship.

'This is . . .' Drellic said again, still standing in the hallway with his face drawn in confusion.

'Come on, Mr Drellic,' Lizanne said, taking his arm. 'Cook's got some fresh honey cakes baking.'

She began to guide him towards the kitchen then paused at the sight of Tekela's pale face appearing at the top of the front stairs, beckoning urgently. 'You go on, Mr Drellic,' she told the butler, patting his shoulder. 'I need to finish my chores.'

'Krista!' he said, face alight with mingled triumph and joy. 'Your name is Krista.'

'Yes, sir,' she said, planting a kiss on his wrinkled cheek. 'Yes it is. Go on now. Cook baked them special for you.'

She watched him proceed to the backstairs, muttering her false name over and over, then ascended to the landing where Tekela waited. 'Come,' the girl whispered, taking hold of Lizanne's hand and leading her towards a room at the front of the house.

'What is . . . ?' Lizanne began but the girl rounded on her with a fierce scowl.

'Shhhh!'

The room she led her to was small, the walls a faded shade of yellow and decorated with hand-painted flowers. An infant's cot stood against the wall and a small rocking-horse rested under the window. 'My old nursery,' Tekela said in a whisper, pulling

Lizanne towards the fire-place. She knelt and began to work her small fingers into the join around the grating, grimacing with the effort as she prised it free. 'Listen,' she mouthed to Lizanne, gently laying the grate aside and leaning close to the hearth, head angled and ear cocked. Lizanne followed suit and was instantly rewarded with the sound of the Burgrave's voice, as clear as if she were listening through an open window.

'. . . and yet another warship crowding the harbour, I hear. Quite the fleet they're gathering.'

'Indeed,' came the major's voice. 'Three blood-burners amongst them.'

'And the garrison?'

'Swollen to over twenty thousand men.' There was a pause and Lizanne discerned the sound of smoke being inhaled from a cigarillo. 'My friend, I believe you were right. War may well return to these shores very soon.'

She heard the Burgrave utter a bitter sigh. 'Are all refuges to be denied us, then? Even here in this blighted continent of jungle, desert and drakes. Is there nowhere the regnarchy won't look to sate their lust for conquest?'

Lizanne found herself leaning closer at mention of the word 'regnarchy.' She knew it to be a term not heard in Corvantine society for the better part of two decades, at least not openly. A term coined by one Morila Akiv Bidrosin, philosopher, radical and ideological mother to the revolutions that had nearly torn the empire apart a generation before.

'Please,' came Arberus's sigh via the grate, 'no speeches, Leonis. I come for instruction, not enlightenment. That happened years ago, as you are well aware.'

There was a pause before the Burgrave replied, Lizanne finding his voice very different from the affable, indulgent noble she had taken him to be. Instead he sounded more like the soldier he had once been, his tone decisive and hard with authority. 'Have you met with Morradin yet?'

'A brief conference only, attended by several dozen officers of senior rank. Seems I was invited because he remembered me from Jerravin. Sometimes it pays to win a medal in an ignoble cause. He didn't say anything, leaving it all to his adjutant.'

'And the object of this conference?'

'Training, mostly. We have been given a new regimen to follow, and I must say, it's a considerable improvement on the old one. Less drill, more marksmanship and field manoeuvres, plus a twenty-mile forced march every ten days. Also, the list of punishments has been extended and the rate of floggings doubled. It appears he intends to turn our colonial garrison into a real army.'

'There can be only one objective for so large a force.'

'I know.'

'When?'

'No plans have been issued, but any offensive will have to be launched well in advance of the wet season. Meaning perhaps a month, maybe less.' Lizanne heard the major take another puff on his cigarillo. 'Should we warn them?'

'*They* are as much our enemy as the Imperial brood.'

'They have helped us in the past. Supplied arms and intelligence . . .'

'But never enough to ensure victory. It suits them to succour a thorn in the Emperor's side, but ultimately they have just as much reason to obstruct our goals. A world freed from the twin tyrannies of regnarchy and corporatism is hardly in their best interests. No, we will allow the two monsters the opportunity to destroy one another. If the Emperor believes he can seize this continent's riches with impunity he's madder than I imagined. The Ironship fleet will strangle the empire's trade and famine will result, along with riot and dissent. Fresh soil to plant the seeds of freedom.'

'You are aware, old friend, that I will be required to fight in this war?'

'And you shall, Arberus. As I once hardened my heart and fought for those I despised. Fight well, lead your men with courage and skill. Gain the marshal's notice and who knows how high you might rise? To have one of our own so close to him . . . We have never been so graced by opportunity.'

'And I had hoped I might have time to make better acquaintance with your new maid.'

Lizanne exchanged a glance with Tekela, seeing her mouth twitch in amusement as Arberus continued, 'Tell me, do you judge her worthy of recruitment? Can't tell you what a bore it is spending time with these hollow-skulled society wenches.'

'Our sisters awaiting freedom from traditional subjugation,' Artonin corrected with the air of someone imparting an oft-told lesson. 'She's bright enough, but it's too soon to judge her character or sympathies. And I wouldn't put it past the Cadre to place a spy in my house.'

'That delightful creature?' Arberus scoffed. 'Never. I know a spy when I see one.'

Lizanne was obliged to give Tekela a warning nudge as the girl covered her mouth to smother a giggle.

'And the other matter?' Artonin enquired. 'Any progress to report?'

'Called on Diran yesterday,' Arberus replied. 'Says he's close to a breakthrough, but he's been saying that for the past two years. Sometimes I think we came here on the greatest of fool's errands.'

'It's worth the risks. Think what we might accomplish if we had such a thing in our grasp . . .'

'You put too much faith in legends, old friend. Diran asked after you, by the way. Perhaps a personal visit might gee him up a bit.'

'He imagines we're all just a merry band of harmless scholars attempting to solve a historical riddle. Any urging to greater efforts might arouse his all-too-keen mind to suspicions best avoided. Besides, after the spectacle Sirus has been making of himself recently, a certain distance is required.'

'The boy is smitten, true enough.' Arberus voiced a rueful chuckle. 'Poor little bugger.' There was a pause and the sound of rustling paper. 'Diran did pass on his latest jottings though . . .'

He fell silent at the sound of knocking. 'Ah, Misha,' he said as they heard the door being opened, 'Would you care for some tea, Arberus? I see Cook has been kind enough to provide honey cakes as well . . .'

Lizanne gestured for Tekela to replace the grate and rose from the fire-place, lost in momentary contemplation of what she had heard. *I imagine this must be what it feels like to strike gold,* she thought.

'You,' she said, keeping her voice low and turning to Tekela, 'have not been entirely honest with me, miss. I believe you know exactly why your father doesn't like the Cadre.'

There was a brief spasm of what may have been contrition on Tekela's face before it transformed once again into a pout. 'Well, you know all about it now,' she muttered, then brightened. 'And all information is valuable, is it not?'

'Its value varies, as does its danger.'

'I'm not afraid.'

So much fun to be had in this new game, Lizanne thought, reading the girl's eager expression. 'Do you share your father's convictions?' she asked. 'Are you eager for the fires of revolution to burn anew?'

Tekela shook her head. 'No, and neither was Mother. She lost her father and three brothers in the wars. I think . . . I think Father had other reasons than love for marrying her.'

I dare say you're right, Lizanne decided. 'What can you tell me about this Major Arberus?'

'He's been calling at the house as long as I can remember. He acts like my big brother but I can tell he doesn't mean it. He buys me birthday presents but they're always the wrong thing. Last year he got me a Palaver set. I don't even know how to play.'

Palaver was a board-game played with tiles of varying values placed face-down on a grid. The players would attempt to identify each piece based on a series of ten questions where the opponent was only permitted to lie three times. With a hundred tiles on the board success in Palaver depended as much on a facility for obfuscation as it did arithmetic.

'You should learn,' Lizanne told Tekela. 'I think you'd be very good at it.' She fell silent, thoughts churning this new glut of information. 'I believe,' she said eventually, 'it's time for that trip to the museum.'

The Imperial Museum of Antiquities was situated in the middle ring of the concentric, circular arrangement of buildings forming the centre of Morsvale. In common with the architecture Lizanne had witnessed so far, every building was of archaic construction and would have benefited from some organised maintenance; tall marble columns stood partly blackened by accumulated soot and she saw more than a few cracked window-panes sitting in rotting frames. The district was home to the town's administrative and military headquarters and known, without apparent irony, as 'The Imperial Ring.' However, amongst the Burgrave's servants, and Lizanne assumed most other commoners, it was better known as 'The Emperor's Arse.'

'Krista's taking the Horror to the Arse today,' Kalla commented over breakfast, a meal eaten a good hour before the Burgrave and Tekela rose from bed. 'Gonna see that museum fop keeps mooning over her. Can't think why, she's never gonna marry the poor sod.' She bit into a crumpet and gave Misha a nudge. ''Member that night he climbed the garden wall and started singing up at her window? Had flowers and everything. She threw her piss-pot at him.'

The two maids shared a giggle then quieted at Madam Meeram's disapproving frown. 'You know the rule, girls. No gossip at this table.'

'Yes, Madam,' they replied in unison.

'You'll have to take a cab, I'm afraid,' Meeram told Lizanne, gesturing to the empty chair where Rigan normally sat. 'My son is off pursuing his maritime ambitions once again.'

'The Burgrave signed his letter?' Lizanne asked.

'No, but we are acquainted with a senior supervisor in the Custom House. Rigan believes his signature may carry sufficient weight to facilitate entry to the Naval Academy.'

'He wants to be an officer?' Lizanne was surprised. The Imperial Armed Forces were notorious for their snobbery and rarely gave commissions to members of the lower orders, and certainly not to servants.

'Ambition will be the boy's ruin.' Meeram sighed. 'His father was the same. Always signing up with some expedition or other, each one supposedly destined to yield more profit than the last. Rigan was five years old when he went off on the last one. We haven't seen him since.'

'I've heard many tales of the Interior,' Lizanne said, frowning in sympathy. 'It holds countless dangers, so they say.'

'Not for the Burgrave,' Kalla said around another mouthful of crumpet. 'Him and the handsome major go off expeditioning every year.'

'Really?' Lizanne asked. 'Didn't have the Burgrave down as an adventurous type.'

'It's just a few weeks when the wet season ends,' Meeram said. 'The Burgrave believes it refreshes him for the year ahead.'

'Misha thinks they're off treasure hunting,' Kalla said, nudging her companion once more. 'Don'tcha?'

The maid gave a tremulous smile in Lizanne's direction. 'They had a map spread out yesterday,' she said in her barely audible voice. 'Saw them going over it in the study when I came for the tea-tray.'

'Doesn't mean they're looking for treasure,' Lizanne said. 'Could just be working out their route for the next trip.'

'They was talking when I came in,' the girl replied. 'Saying that's the best place to look for it. Anyway' – she gave Kalla a brief scowl – 'was Rigan said it might be a treasure map, not me. Don't wanna poke my nose in the Burgrave's business.'

'A creditable attitude,' Meeram said, a note of finality in her voice. 'One we would all do well to emulate.'

There was no map in the hidden compartment, Lizanne recalled. Diran did pass on his latest jottings though . . . Uncle Diran who works at the museum. The handsome major came bearing his most recent contribution to the Burgrave's scholarly endeavours, meaning it's likely still in the house.

'Whatever you do,' Tekela said as the cab pulled up outside the museum, 'don't mention poetry, even if he asks you.'

A slender, dark-haired young man stood waiting for them on the museum steps. He was dressed in a newly bought suit, the collar tight about his neck and his hair carefully arranged and oiled. Despite his preparations, however, his youth and the nervous smile he offered Tekela made him resemble a boy playing dress-up.

'Tekela,' he said with a bow, voice betraying a slight quiver. 'You have honoured me . . .'

'Yes, alright, Sirus,' she told him, Lizanne gaining the impression she was restraining an habitual scorn. She waved a hand at Lizanne. 'This is Krista, my new girl.'

'My pleasure, miss.' Sirus bowed to her also, a significant breach of manners he clearly didn't know he was making.

'Your note said something about jewellery,' Tekela said.

'Oh yes. A cache discovered in a grave-site on the west coast only a few months ago.'

'Grave-site?' Tekela's mouth took on a curl of distaste. 'You want to show me dead people's jewels?'

'They're remarkably well-preserved,' he assured her. 'And the craftsmanship is extraordinary. Far above anything we've seen before. The expedition also found clay tablets engraved with writing. Such things have been unearthed elsewhere but never in so much quantity . . .'

'Fascinating,' Tekela interrupted in a tone that combined boredom with impatience.

'Well, I hope so.' Sirus turned and gestured at the museum door. 'Shall we?'

The museum had a grand if besmirched edifice, tall columns supporting a triangular block of marble upon which a scene from Corvantine antiquity had been carved in relief. Lizanne recognised it as the Divination of Caranis the First, the moment some fifteen hundred years before when a senate-ruled commonwealth was transformed into an empire. The theme continued inside with numerous frescoes and statues, all depicting a somewhat one-sided view of Imperial history. There were battles aplenty but no massacres; happy crowds cheered victorious generals but none suffered starvation or torture. Naturally the revolutionary wars, the most important event in Corvantine history, were conspicuous by their absence.

She followed behind Tekela as Sirus led them along a broad, echoing hallway lined with paintings of monumental proportions. The young man made continual attempts to engage Tekela in conversation, his gambits ranging from enquiring after her father's health to a commentary on the oddly inclement weather. She responded to it all with non-committal shrugs, Lizanne having warned her against any uncharacteristic displays of interest or affection.

'I sent flowers with my note,' he said, a desperate tone creeping into his voice. 'I trust you got them.'

'You sent white roses,' Tekela replied. 'They're for funerals.'

'Oh.' His face clouded only for a second and Lizanne found herself admiring his resilience as he forced a smile and ploughed on. 'Red next time then. Once my new verse is complete.'

Lizanne saw Tekela smother a caustic reply and take a calming breath. *How bad can his poetry be?* she wondered.

Sirus came to a halt before a set of solid double doors and extracted a bunch of keys from his jacket pocket. It took a long moment's fumbling before he managed to unlock the doors, swinging them wide as he bowed, flourishing his arm in an elaborate and practised gesture. 'It is my honour to finally welcome you to my sanctum. I give you the vaults of the Imperial Collection of Arradsian Artifacts.'

Tekela just sniffed and marched through the doors with her nose raised. *He's far too good for you,* Lizanne decided. *Though you'll probably be in your sixties before you realise it.* Any amusement occasioned by the thought soon expired under the weight of another. *You know the girl has to die . . .*

The room beyond the doors was cavernous, their footsteps echoing through seemingly endless rows of stored curiosities. A variety of stuffed and mounted creatures stared out at Lizanne from behind glass cases alongside pinioned beetles of alarming size. Beyond them were cabinets full of pottery shards and collections of shaped flint. Sirus led them through the maze of exhibits with accustomed speed, Lizanne making careful note of the route. So far she hadn't caught sight of any guards but assumed that would change come nightfall.

'Here we are.' Sirus stopped at a tall wooden cabinet of many thin drawers. 'I've just finished cataloguing all the finds. The Imperial Actuary will be round tomorrow to value it all.'

'So you won't get to keep it?' Tekela asked.

'Some pieces will remain with us, no doubt. The less valuable, of course. The Emperor deserves his due.' The slight edge to Sirus's voice as he said this made Lizanne wonder if he might share some sympathies with Burgrave Artonin.

'We'll start with the sapphires, I think.' Sirus pulled one of the drawers from the cabinet, carefully setting it down on a near by table then removing the thin paper covering.

Lizanne managed to stifle her own reaction but Tekela gave an involuntary sound that was part awe and part greed. The necklace was arranged in a circle, a chain of silver adorned with four sapphires. The stones were set in ornate mountings of unfamiliar design, sharing no motifs with either Mandinorian or Corvantine craftsmanship. There was an appealing fluency to it, the individual links of the chain and the mountings moulded into twisting, organic forms, appearing almost to have grown around the stones.

'This was dug out of a grave?' Tekela asked, her hand reaching out to touch one of the sapphires as if drawn by some invisible magnetism.

'The grave of a female between eighteen and thirty years old,' Sirus said and Lizanne noted all hesitation had now left his voice. 'Though the deformation of the bones made ascertaining the age difficult.'

'Deformation, sir?' Lizanne asked, then lowered her gaze at Tekela's glare. Speaking out of turn was risky but curiosity was always her greatest vice. 'Your pardon, miss,' she said.

'Oh it's quite all right,' Sirus said, offering her a smile. 'Yes, miss. The owner of this necklace was undoubtedly a member of what is commonly termed the Spoiled.'

'I thought the Spoiled were savages,' Tekela said, returning her hungry gaze to the necklace. 'They couldn't have made this, surely.'

'Our findings indicated they did, and much more besides. Whatever they are now, it seems they were something very different in the past.' He turned and extracted another drawer from the cabinet. This one held a bracelet of white gold inset with rubies and a clasp fashioned into a tiny and near-perfect facsimile of a drake's head.

'The drake is a common motif in their designs,' Sirus said, seeing Lizanne's interest. 'Understandable, given they must have encountered them on a daily basis. Curiously, we have found no evidence that they hunted drakes; if anything the artifacts indicate a near-religious reverence.'

Tekela wasn't listening, playing her fingers over the bracelet before desire overcame caution. 'Just for a second,' she told Sirus, placing the bracelet on her wrist and fumbling with the clasp. 'There,' she said, extending her arm and angling the wrist so the rubies caught the light. 'As if it were made for me, don't you think?'

'Quite,' Sirus agreed softly.

'Here, girl.' Tekela turned and presented her back to Lizanne. 'Put the necklace on me.'

Lizanne glanced at Sirus, who gave a nod of assent, then took the necklace and carefully fastened it around the girl's neck. She laughed and whirled about in delight, the jewels glittering. Lizanne had to admit she did look fairly stunning. A view evidently shared by Sirus, who stared in unabashed fascination.

'What's this!' a booming voice echoed through the maze of curiosities accompanied by heavy and rapid footsteps. A very large man soon hove into view, advancing towards them with a purposeful stride, his bearded face flushed an angry red. Lizanne guessed his age at somewhere past fifty though the way he moved indicated a considerable vitality. 'What are you doing, boy!' he demanded of Sirus. 'This is not a playground.'

'Father . . .' Sirus stammered. 'I-I was . . .'

'Fawning, boy!' The large man jabbed a finger at Sirus before turning his glare on Tekela. 'That's what you were doing.'

Tekela seemed utterly unconcerned by the fellow's anger, smiling and standing on tiptoe to peck a kiss to his cheek. 'Hello, Uncle Diran.' She stood back, adopting a regal pose in her finery. 'Don't I look marvellous?'

Diran issued a low, rumbling sound that put Lizanne in mind of a well-stoked boiler. However, Tekela must have had some hold on his heart for his tone was more measured when he said, 'Indeed you do. Now take those off before a guard happens by and shoots you.'

Tekela responded with one of her best pouts but dutifully beckoned Lizanne forward to divest her of the jewels. 'Pity there's no photostatist on hand.' She sighed as Sirus hastily returned the items to their cabinet. 'I should have liked an image of myself suitably adorned for once. You should see the drab beads Father makes me wear.'

'Your father is deserving of more gratitude,' Diran snapped in rebuke, his glower gradually softening under her wounded frown. 'Come on,' he said in a resigned tone, striding off towards the doorway and gesturing for them to follow. 'As you're here you may as well have some lunch.'

He led them from the vaults, standing with arms folded and

face stern whilst Sirus locked the doors, then proceeded via an elegant marble staircase to the upper floor. 'New maid?' he asked Tekela, nodding at Lizanne. 'Hope she lasts longer than the last one.'

'Oh,' Tekela turned a judgemental glance on Lizanne, 'so far she's proving tolerable enough.'

The room he led them to was part office and part workshop, though considerably more ordered than Jermayah's den of cluttered knick-knacks. A bench near the window held a number of diagrams, all neatly arranged side by side and, sitting in the middle, an intricate device of some sort. A device of numerous cogs and gears that would have fit neatly into a box Lizanne had seen recently. Before she could get a closer look, however, Diran ordered Sirus to clear the bench and the device was swiftly consigned to a locked cabinet along with all the diagrams.

'Go and tell the porter to bring us some sandwiches,' Diran instructed his son. 'Ham, I think. And a selection of cakes for our guest.'

After Sirus had gone he settled into the leather chair behind his desk and reached for a pipe. 'So, how's your father?' he enquired, piling tobacco into the bowl. 'Haven't seen him in an age.'

'Scribbling away as always,' Tekela replied, taking a spare chair and smothering a yawn. 'He sends his regards, of course.'

'As I send mine.' Diran held a lit match to the tobacco and reclined, smoke billowing as his gaze took on a more serious cast. 'You know my son's in love with you, I suppose?'

Tekela stiffened a little. 'As his many poems would seem to indicate.'

'Coming out in a few months, aren't you? Dare say there'll be more poems in the offing, from more appropriate authors.'

'Provided Father doesn't persist in dressing me in rags.'

'It'll be hard on Sirus, seeing you on the arm of another.'

'I have never encouraged him. Quite the opposite, in fact.'

'And yet here you are, feeding his obsession.'

Tekela shrugged. 'I wanted to see the jewels.'

Diran exhaled a cloud of smoke, shaking his head. 'Never able to walk past a mirror. Just like your mother.'

Lizanne saw Tekela stiffen yet further, her tone taking on an icy quality as she replied, 'Is that a topic you really wish to explore, Uncle?'

The subsequent silence stretched as they regarded each other through the haze of pipe-smoke. Lizanne saw how Tekela's hands had bunched into small, angry fists in her lap. *What is it between these two?*

'There will be no more poems,' Diran said finally. 'I'm sending Sirus to Corvus. A vacancy has opened up in the Imperial Archives. In time, and with luck, he'll find a more suitable recipient for his verse.'

'I sincerely hope he does.' Tekela got to her feet. 'I shan't be staying for lunch, after all, Uncle. Say good-bye to Sirus for me. And pass on my best wishes for his future endeavours.'

Tekela was silent for most of the ride back, staring at nothing as the cab rattled over the cobbles. Lizanne resisted the urge to ask for clarification of her conversation with Diran, knowing it would risk indulging in yet more sentiment. *The game is nearly over,* she reminded herself.

As if reading her thoughts Tekela stirred from her torpor, speaking in dull Eutherian, 'That was it wasn't it? The device on the bench.'

'I believe so.'

'So you plan to steal it, I assume?'

Lizanne evaded the question. Revealing her intentions would be an excessive risk at this juncture. 'You should prepare yourself to reveal our agreement to your father in the next few days,' she said instead. 'Once my mission is complete, there will be no room for delay.'

'He'll be angry.' Tekela's voice betrayed only slight concern at the prospect. 'Being forced to abandon his studies and his plots.'

'I expect so. Though he'll have little choice once the Cadre learn of our activities, as they surely will before long.'

'How will it be done? Getting us to Feros safely?'

'It's better if you don't know. However, you should have a bag packed and be ready to leave at a moment's notice.'

Tekela nodded, her listlessness dissipating now as the joy of the game reasserted itself. Lizanne found herself unable to meet the girl's gaze for the rest of the journey.

Back at the house she returned to her allotted chores with customary diligence, though the work-load had increased since Rigan had as yet failed to return from his trip to the Custom House. 'He'll be in some dock-side tavern,' Meeram said at the evening meal. 'Palling around with sailors and pestering them for stories.'

Lizanne retired to bed early, complaining of a headache brought on by Miss Artonin's taxing company. In her attic room she divested herself of her maid's uniform in favour of the clothes she had arrived in. Ostensibly no different from the garb typical of a young Corvantine woman of mean station, the ensemble was in fact carefully tailored so as not to impede her movements. She wore a pair of thin cotton leggings under the skirt to guard against cold and her shoes were flat-soled and gripped to facilitate athletic activity. She strapped the Whisper to her thigh where it could be easily drawn via a slit in the skirt, then affixed the Spider to her forearm, each vial fully charged.

She opened the window and climbed out onto the roof, viewing her chosen route to the museum. It was a winding path and likely to exhaust nearly half her Green, but that couldn't be avoided if she was to complete her task before morning. *Whereupon I'll have another to perform . . .*

She pushed the thought away and focused her mind, depressing the middle-finger button to inject a good measure of Green into her veins. Such a high dosage was dangerous, producing a sense of physical invulnerability and euphoria that could only be countered by the most deeply ingrained training. She stood, limbs seeming to thrum with the new-found energy, fixed her gaze on the successive roof-tops and walls that would lead her to the museum, then launched herself into space.

CHAPTER 17

Hilemore

The Blood-blessed fired the rifle, the bullet smacking into the planking just to the left of Steelfine's head. Hilemore shook the fuzz from his vision, seeing the Blood-blessed stagger again and nearly fall before straightening with a loud curse. It was a woman, he saw, long hair tied in braids and clad in silks of various colours, though much besmirched and torn. Only a captain would dress in so many colours. He watched as she cast the rifle aside and summoned another from the deck, bringing it to her shoulder and taking unsteady aim at Steelfine once more.

Hilemore surged to his feet with a shout, ignoring the screaming pain in his back. He drew his revolver and caught hold of the captive, who squirmed in his grip but soon quieted when he pressed the muzzle of the revolver to her temple. 'Captain!' he called to the Blood-blessed in Varestian.

The woman turned to him and froze, her eyes lighting with fury then frustration as she fixed them on Hilemore.

'There is no hope for you in this,' he told her. 'But I promise safe passage and freedom for this one.' He tightened his hold on the girl, who squirmed again, voicing an angry snarl. Hilemore kept his gaze fixed on the woman. He was gambling, hoping she had nearly exhausted her Black and used up all her Red in feeding the *Windqueen*'s engine.

The woman's mouth twisted into an ugly sneer as she said something in Varestian, an insult rarely heard for it was the worst her kind could utter. 'Oath-breakers! What trust could I ever give you?'

'You can trust this one will live!' He pressed his revolver harder against the girl's temple. 'And I'll guarantee a trial for you in Feros. Are your colours struck?'

The woman's gaze shifted to the girl and Hilemore saw an unmistakable similarity in their features, and the near-frantic concern in the woman's eyes. She staggered again, a patch of blood spreading across her midriff, muttering a curse in Varestian before letting the rifle fall from her grasp. 'My colours are struck, you treacherous bastard!' she cried out, sinking to her knees and casting a forlorn gaze around the smoking ruin of her ship.

Steelfine lay unconscious in the doctor's cabin, blood-stained bandages on his head, arms and legs. There didn't seem to be any inch of him that wasn't bruised, grazed or cut. Although deaf and blind to the world he still retained enough vitality for the occasional bout of dangerous thrashing, obliging Dr Weygrand to have his orderlies strap him down.

'Can't rightly explain his survival,' the doctor advised Hilemore. 'Big and strong as he is, he should be conversing with the King of the Deep right now.'

All told the engagement had cost them six dead and twelve wounded, the latter resulting from the Blood-blessed captain's attentions on the *Windqueen*'s deck. In accordance with Protectorate custom the dead had been consigned to the sea at the first opportunity, sewn into a canvas shroud, weighted and slipped over the side after a brief recitation of the Order of Thanks by the captain. Of the wounded, only Steelfine remained bedridden despite his inhuman resilience.

'How much Green has he had?' Hilemore asked.

'One-tenth of a flask. I would like to have administered more, but regulations . . .'

'Bugger regulations,' Hilemore said. 'Increase the dosage, as much as he needs. I'll sign the order.'

Dr Weygrand was a veteran Protectorate physician of near as

many years service as Mr Lemhill. A tall man with silver-grey hair, he projected an air of calm authority and clearly wasn't about to surrender it to a second lieutenant. 'Medicinal use of product lies within my purview, Mr Hilemore. Exhausting our stocks treating one patient will serve us ill should we suffer further casualties.'

Hilemore bit down on his frustration. That the doctor's judgement was undoubtedly correct did little to alleviate an angry guilt. *I should have sent more men with him. Should've known a Blood-blessed would have survived the blast.*

'If he worsens,' Weygrand went on, voice softening a little, 'I'll administer another dose, heavily diluted however.'

Hilemore nodded, knowing this was more than he could have expected. 'Thank you, Doctor.'

'And you?' Weygrand asked. 'Heard you took a pretty bad knock over there.'

Hilemore shrugged his shoulders, concealing a wince at the flaring ache in his back. 'Just a bruise or two.'

'Off.' The doctor tapped his stethoscope to Hilemore's tunic, his tone brooking no argument. 'Let's take a look.'

'If the point of impact had been a tenth of an inch to the right,' Weygrand said a short while later, making Hilemore gasp as he pulled a bandage tight about his torso, 'you'd be paralysed from the sixth thoracic vertebra down.'

'A comforting thought, Doctor,' Hilemore grunted. 'Have you checked on our prisoner?'

'Yes. Numerous lacerations and minor burns plus a puncture wound to the upper abdomen. Nothing fatal, though, and I'm confident she'll make a full recovery in time for the hanging.'

'The girl?'

'Completely unharmed, but I can't speak for her mental state.'

The speaking-tube in the upper corner of the medical bay gave a high-pitched whistle before Ensign Talmant's voice came through. 'Lieutenant Hilemore to the ward-room, please.'

'Seems you're wanted.' Weygrand finished tying off the bandage and gave Hilemore a small bottle of pills. 'For the pain,' he said. 'Two in the morning, two at night. And don't skimp.'

'A higher butcher's bill than I would have liked,' Captain Trumane said, looking over the list of casualties. 'Still, couldn't be helped. And it always does the crew good to be properly blooded early on.'

He put the list aside and lifted a glass of claret from the wardroom table, Hilemore and the other officers present following suit. 'Gentlemen,' Trumane said, raising his glass in a solemn toast. 'To victory.'

'To victory,' they echoed, drinking in unison. It was another Protectorate custom for a ship's officers to toast a victorious engagement before the captain went about allotting the various prize-shares and honours.

'The quartermaster has completed his survey of the pirate's cargo,' Trumane said, lifting another document from the table. 'It appears she's been busiest on the Corvantine trade routes. We have two full chests of Imperial crowns, plus sundry liquors, spices and tea. An impressive haul indeed, coming to an estimated two hundred and fifty thousand in Syndicate Scrip. Shares will be allotted according to rank, with a one percent bonus for Mr Lemhill and a half percent for Mr Hilemore. The boarding party and gunners will also receive individual grants of two hundred scrip per man.'

There was a general murmur of appreciation around the room as each officer present calculated his sudden upturn in fortune.

'I should like to donate my bonus to the Ship's Fund, sir,' Hilemore said, his mind lingering on the sight of Steelfine's bandaged form. The Ship's Fund was a pool of donations maintained by the quartermaster to provide succour to maimed crew or assistance to the families of those who had fallen. It was expected, but not required, that officers contribute a small amount of their share to the fund.

'Quite so, Lieutenant.' The captain raised his glass to him.

'Naturally, I'll be making my own contribution as well. Now then.' He turned to Chief Engineer Bozware, still clad in his oily overalls as he appeared to be the only man on the ship's roster immune to Trumane's obsession with the uniform code. 'You've looked over our prize, Chief. Can she be saved?'

'Not without a dry-dock and a few months' work, sir,' Bozware replied. 'Too much warping of the hull due to the fire. Plus her engine's a wreck. They overloaded her with product trying to get away, blew every gasket.'

'Pity,' the captain mused. 'Rarely seen a one-stacker with cleaner lines. Mr Hilemore, oversee the transfer of her guns, plus any other armaments you can gather, then soak her in oil and burn her.'

'Aye, sir. And the enemy dead?'

'What of them?'

It was Lemhill who replied, his tone possessed of a certain, emphatic conviction. 'Pirates or not, those who die at sea belong to the King of the Deep. We burn them, we deny him his due.'

'Doesn't do to anger him, right enough,' Bozware agreed. 'And the men are like to get antsy if we fail to observe custom.'

'Very well,' the captain said, evidently wearied by his officers' superstitious attachments. 'Mr Hilemore, ensure the enemy dead are consigned to the sea with due ceremony. Once the *Windqueen* is safely burned we have a bombardment to deliver. Number One, I shall require you to operate as gunnery officer for the remainder of the voyage. Transfer any duties you feel appropriate to Mr Hilemore.'

'Very good, sir.'

'Excellent. I shall require a plan of bombardment by tomorrow morning. Let's see if we can't level this den of sea-rats, shall we?'

'Words?' the pirate captain asked him, face striped by the shadows of the brig's iron bars. She sat slumped on the narrow, mattressless bunk with her daughter curled up by her side. The girl's eyes were bright as she stared over her mother's shoulder, whether in accusation or fear Hilemore couldn't tell. Both were barefoot and dressed in engineer's overalls: free of any laces or belts that might cheat the hangman. 'What words?'

'Words for the dead.' Hilemore struggled for the right translation. His Varestian was adequate but mostly limited to matters sea-related. 'Prayers,' he said in Mandinorian, knowing the woman could speak it; all sailors did. 'What prayers do you want said for your crew?'

'None.' She turned away from him, face set in hard dismissal as she slipped back into her own tongue. 'Words spoken by an oath-breaker are piss on the breeze. The Lords of Sea, Salt and Wind would shield their ears against them.'

'I have broken no oath to you,' Hilemore insisted. 'You will face trial and the girl will be freed when we arrive in Feros.'

The woman gave a harsh, disgusted laugh then sobered when she saw his serious gaze. 'You don't know, do you?' she asked with narrowed eyes, switching back to softly accented Mandinorian. 'Why they sent you after us.'

'You are pirates.'

'No.' She leaned forward on the bunk, face coming closer to the bars. He noticed for the first time how young she was, barely older than he in fact. Despite her comparative youth there was an undoubted strength to her features, accentuated by the keen intelligence he saw in her eyes. Seeing her up close he could understand how she had commanded a ship of cutthroats with such success.

'I have been a pirate, in my time,' she told him, 'until a more lucrative offer was made me. What do you know about the *Windqueen*, Lieutenant? Scourge of the trade routes, phantom of the seas, striking wherever the cargo was richest. The most successful and feared pirate ship in years. Why do you think we were so successful? Why do you think your captain found us with such ease?'

'Sound intelligence and expert navigation.'

A very small grin played over her lips. 'Intelligence, yes. But from where?'

'What are you saying?'

'One man's pirate is another's privateer. Would it interest you to know, Lieutenant, that the *Windqueen*, during all the years she hunted the waves, never once took an Ironship vessel?'

She's a liar, and a murderer to boot. But something in the woman's bearing gave him pause, the soft reflection in her voice and absence of anger told of a resignation to her fate. *She knows no words will save her. So why lie?*

'It was that little favour we did the Protectorate in Carvenport, I assume,' she said when he didn't respond, slumping back on the bunk and putting an arm around the girl. 'Who would have thought witnessing the slaughter of a few Blinds cutthroats was worth all our lives? Or perhaps they decided our success had become too much of a potential embarrassment.'

She looked away and lapsed into silence, hand tracing through her daughter's hair as she snuggled closer. Realising the fruitlessness of further questions, Hilemore turned to go.

'A coin,' she said as he rapped his knuckles on the heavy door for the guard to let him out.

'What?' he enquired, glancing back.

'They need to carry a coin into the depths. Payment to the Lord of the Sea for all they took from him in life. One copper crown each should suffice.'

'I'll see to it.'

'And a gold one for the *Windqueen*.'

'I doubt my captain would agree to that.'

'There's a cache of Dalcian sovereigns hidden in the hold. I'll tell you where to find it if you spare one for my ship.' She raised her gaze once more, anger shining clear for the first time. 'Gold might persuade the Lord to find a home for her soul in his dominion. Since I am to be denied it, I would like her to take my place. So speak my name when you cast it forth.'

Hilemore raised himself up on the bow and threw the coin into the roiling smoke as the *Windqueen* slipped below the waves, leaving a flaming patch of oil on the swell. As she had bidden he spoke the pirate's name when the coin splashed into the burning waves, 'Zenida Okanas.' The *Viable*'s paddles began to turn soon after, taking them westwards towards the pirate den. His gaze lingered on the blaze as it faded into the darkening horizon. Pirate she may have been but it was always sad to watch a ship die, especially one so finely made. When the last flicker of flame had vanished he made his way to the engine room.

He found Tottleborn seated on his platform, engrossed in another product of the vulgar press. This one bore the title *Slave of the Spoiled* and featured an appropriately lurid cover. An improbably muscled and anvil-jawed man of North Mandinorian complexion attempted to shield a buxom and barely clothed woman from an advancing mob of mis-shapen savages. Hilemore had never set eyes on a Spoiled but, from the vagueness of the illustration, doubted the artist had either.

'I have a chest full of real literature if you'd care to borrow some,' he told Tottleborn, ascending the gangway to his platform. The auxiliary power plant was in full clattering swing, obliging him to shout. 'Scirwood, Dasmere, all the greats.'

'Great and turgid in equal measure,' Tottleborn replied, not looking up from the book. 'I will thank you to allow me to pursue my own literary path, Lieutenant.'

Despite the continuing resentment that coloured his tone Hilemore discerned an upturn in the Blood-blessed's mood today. The reason was not hard to divine. 'It seems your portent was mistaken,' he said, raising his arms to gesture at the undamaged engine room. 'I told you no harm could come to you in here.'

'Indeed you did. Didn't stop me nearly pissing myself when the guns started up though.'

'A natural and very common reaction.' He produced his pocket-watch and flipped the case open to display the time.

'Do we have to?' Tottleborn groaned, laying his book aside. 'We did this only yesterday.'

'Regulations. The emergency Blue-trance will be observed after every combat action. The Sea Board needs to know the condition of its ships at all times. It's only sixty seconds, Mr Tottleborn. You will relay our casualty figures and the value of cargo seized. Then you can return to your' – he cast a caustic glance at the book – 'literary pursuits.'

A few moments later he stood watching as the young Blood-blessed sat eyes closed in the ward-room, hands clasped before him on the table. He had ingested only a small measure of product, his face taking on the serene aspect that seemed to be typical of the trance, as if all emotion had either been suppressed somehow or had fled the body. Hilemore kept count of the seconds with his watch, glancing up in expectation when the second hand ticked past the minute. However, Tottleborn's trance continued. Hilemore frowned, returning his gaze to the watch and counting off another full minute, then another. Thirty more seconds elapsed before the Blood-blessed issued a loud, convulsive gasp. He seemed to deflate in his chair, head lolling forward and hands splayed on the table. His back heaved as he drew in a series of long, retching breaths, finally raising his head to regard Hilemore with a face bleached of colour.

'Didn't take enough,' he rasped. 'Had to cling on as long as I could.' He jerked convulsively and vomited, nearly falling from his chair. Hilemore rushed forward to keep him upright, settling him back into his seat.

'What is it?' he demanded.

'New orders from the Sea Board.' Tottleborn grimaced, wiping his mouth and rubbing at his temples before offering Hilemore the weakest of smiles. 'It appears that, as of yesterday, we are at war with the Corvantine Empire.'

CHAPTER 18

Clay

The Red Sands smelled like blood. The wind carried a fine crimson haze from the shore to the *Firejack*, possessed of a sharp, metallic sting that stirred a faint nausea in Clay's gut. It was late morning and the sun had risen to a clear sky, revealing just how aptly named this desert was. 'It's really red,' he commented, eyes tracking over the dunes, finding only the slightest variation in hue and no hint of any vegetation. 'And it tastes like iron,' he added, scraping his tongue along the roof of his mouth.

''Cause that's what it's made of,' Skaggerhill said. He held a hand up to the wind for a few seconds then showed it to Clay, tiny red flakes visible on the callused skin. 'It ain't sand, it's rust. Educated fella I knew in Carvenport said it must've been a mountain range once, all filled up with iron ore. One day thousands of years ago some great catastrophe turned it into a desert. Wind carried off the rock sand, it being lighter, leaving this. Here.' He tossed Clay a pack that seemed to be two-thirds comprised of full canteens. 'No water on the Red Sands. Gotta carry our own. You be sure to ration it. And tie a kerchief about your face, don't want this shit in your lungs.'

The Longrifles crowded into one of the *Firejack*'s boats and rowed to shore, jumping clear in the shallows and wading the rest of the way. Clay looked back at the *Firejack* as the others all pulled on their packs, seeing Loriabeth raising a hand in farewell. She had accepted Braddon's stern refusal to let her come along with a stoic calm, though Clay saw how it pained her. 'He's right, cuz,' he told her the night before as the steamer moored up close to the shallows. 'You ain't anywhere near healed enough yet.'

Braddon gave his daughter only the briefest glance before turning his back on the river and unfurling a map. 'A mite over thirty miles to the Crater,' he said, aligning a pocket compass to the chart and checking his bearing against the sun. 'I want to be there by noon tomorrow so we'll be pushing hard. We move in single file. Clay, make sure you keep to the steps of whoever's in front of you. Don't want the Spoiled getting a notion of our numbers. Preacher, take the rear. Everyone else, eyes on the flanks. Let's go.'

They moved in a south-westerly direction, Braddon setting a punishing pace and allowing only a five-minute stop per hour. There was little talk, Clay noting how each of his companions kept their gaze on the surrounding desert. Braddon and Preacher had their rifles ready and Foxbine marched with carbine in hand.

'How can the Spoiled live out here?' he wondered aloud when they had finally stopped for the night. They clustered round a somewhat puny fire fuelled by the small sack of coal Skaggerhill had brought along. Whilst the absence of shade made the day a heat-hammered trial, night on the Red Sands brought a cutting chill. 'What's there to live on?'

'Each other, iffen they're hungry enough,' Foxbine grunted, her eyes roving the dunes, transformed into a dark crimson sea under the light of the moons.

'Spoiled live on the fringes,' Skaggerhill said. 'Hunting Cerath and shell-backs. But they come here regular, and in numbers. No-one's sure quite why.'

'It's sacred to them,' Preacher said, provoking a surprised silence due to the rarity of the occurrence. 'One of the early expeditions described a ceremony they witnessed here. The Spoiled come here to pray. We're walking across their church and desecrating it in the process.'

'Fuck their church,' Foxbine said, lifting the kerchief that covered her mouth to spit on the rust grains beneath her feet.

'We see any o' those bastards, I'll be happy to desecrate them too.'

They made the Crater just after noon the next day. It lay in a broad depression free of any dunes and at first it seemed like a low, flat-topped hill but soon revealed itself as a circular hole in the desert, sixty feet wide and ten deep.

'Where's all the nesting White Drakes?' Foxbine asked, a sardonic lilt to her voice. 'Stories I heard about this place, you'd think there'd be more to it.'

'Clay, Silverpin, you're with me,' Braddon said, sloughing off his pack and hefting his rifle. 'Take your shovels. The rest of you keep watch.'

Clay sighed in relief as the pack slid from his shoulders, then took a long pull from a canteen. 'You want us to start digging now?'

Braddon ignored him and strode off towards the lip of the crater with Silverpin at his side, spear in one hand and shovel in the other. Clay pressed a hand to the comforting weight of Ellforth's wallet inside his shirt, then drew the shovel from his pack and followed with a muttered curse. The crater walls were steep but had enough of an incline to allow them to slide down to the floor.

'Just more rust,' he said, kicking a small mound of the stuff as his uncle moved about, eyes roving the ground. *No great skeleton to take back to Carvenport in triumph. And certainly no shiny egg.* 'It'd take months to dig through all this,' he called to Braddon, who didn't seem to hear.

Clay turned to see Silverpin crouched near the centre of the crater, hand splayed on the rust. After a second she took her shovel and started scraping at the surface. Clay moved to her side, watching as she carefully worked the tool's blade through the metallic soil. His heart took a sudden lurch at the sight of something smooth, pale and round emerging from the flaked dirt.

'Seer-damn me to the Travail,' he breathed. *The egg . . .* The thought died, however, as Silverpin's shovel dug deeper, revealing a crack in the pale shape. A few more scrapes and two rust-filled eye-sockets stared up at them from the hole.

Like it would ever have been that easy. Clay straightened, calling to his uncle, 'Got us a skull here.'

'Female,' Braddon said a short while later, fingers tracing over the smooth brow of the skull. 'Young too, I'd guess.'

'Ethelynne Drystone?' Clay suggested.

Braddon shook his head. 'There was a lady gunhand with Wittler's crew. Madame Bondersil said Ethelynne saw her die here when the powder from the White's bones made them all crazy.'

'Speaking of which.' Clay rose and spread his arms out to encompass the barren floor of the crater. 'Where is the great mucky-muck?'

Braddon retrieved his shovel from the ground and tossed it to Clay, voice hardening with impatience. 'Ain't gonna find it without a little digging, now are we?'

They dug for an hour, finding more bones, all human. 'Look at this poor bastard,' Clay said, lifting a skull from the dirt. He guessed this one was male from the heaviness of the brows, a single neat hole punched plumb between.

'Pistol-shot twixt the eyes,' Braddon surmised, glancing up from a partially exposed rib-cage. 'Rules out the Spoiled doing all this.'

In all they uncovered the remains of one woman and three men, each with evidence of having suffered death by gun-shot. 'Accounts for all of them 'cept Wittler and Drystone,' Braddon said. 'Skaggs said he was a good deal taller than his crew. No clothing nor weapons either, which means the Spoiled must have happened by afterwards and taken it all. Stands to reason they took the drake bones too.'

'No bones, no egg.' Clay emptied the last of his canteen down his throat, glancing up at the near-dark sky. 'Seems to me we came a long way to prove this thing can't be found.'

'No, we proved it can't be found here. And we proved Ethelynne didn't perish with the rest of them, Wittler either maybe.' Braddon started back towards the lip of the crater. 'We'll dig proper graves for these folks in the morning. Preacher can say the words, if he's so minded.'

'Then back to the boat, right?'

Braddon kept walking.

'Uncle,' Clay persisted, stalking after him. 'We're going back to the boat in the morning, right?'

'We know they came via the river and Badlands to the north,' Braddon replied. 'Could be more sign there.'

'And how many more miles is that . . .'

'As many as I say we walk, Clay!' Braddon rounded on him, face dark with menace. 'I say we walk across this whole Seer-damn continent, we do it.' He glanced at the empty canteen in Clay's hand, gaze softening a little. 'And go easy on that. I ain't asking the others to go short for you.'

He volunteered for first turn on watch, preferring to stave off fatigue for two hours in order to enjoy an uninterrupted sleep. Preacher shared the shift, sitting on the far side of the fire, rifle in his lap and staring out at the darkened dunes in customary silence. Clay found it surprisingly easy to stay awake, partly due to the icy chill. He was obliged to wrap his duster tight around him and drape a blanket across his shoulders. Unlike Preacher he stayed on his feet, pacing back and forth across the newly frosted ground, breath misting in the air. At Skaggerhill's advice he had drawn his Stinger but kept it within the folds of his duster, close to the warmth of his body so the workings wouldn't seize in the cold.

Thirty miles back to the boat, then . . . what? His mind had been busy with calculations since they climbed out of the crater. With a decent gulp of Green he could cover thirty miles in a couple of hours. Tell the Skipper they all perished on the Sands. Then back to Edinsmouth and on to Carvenport . . . where the

Protectorate were likely to carve a smile into his throat within a day of arrival. Plus it meant leaving the Longrifles to perish in this desert, something that might not have concerned him before but, one way or another, he owed them all now, especially Silverpin. He had other options: bypass the *Firejack* altogether and make for the Alebond enclave at Rigger's Bay on the coast, a plan that involved a two-hundred-mile trip through the jungle. Even with Ellforth's product his brief exposure to the realities of traversing the Interior left him in little doubt as to the likely outcome.

Fact is, you're stuck, he told himself. *Just as stuck as you were back in that Protectorate cell.*

He was pondering the gleam he had seen in his uncle's eye in the Crater, that same hunger for the White they all seemed to share, when something moved out in the desert. The Stinger came free of his duster in a blur, the stock going to his shoulder and the sights aligned with his eye in a smooth movement that said a lot for Foxbine's teaching. A small, upright shape stood just above the Stinger's fore-sight. For a moment he took it for a tree-stump, surely an impossibility in these wastes, but then saw it was a man. Small and swaddled in thick coverings, his face hooded and a shoulder-high walking-stick in his hand. Unmistakably a man.

'Preacher!' Clay hissed, thumbing back the Stinger's hammer.

He heard the scrape of the marksman's boots as he rushed to his side, then blinked as the man with the walking stick *shifted*. It was just a small, jerky movement then the crimson rust around him erupted into a plume of dust that twisted and drifted to the right.

'What is it?' Preacher demanded, appearing at his side with longrifle raised.

'There's someone out there,' Clay said, tracking the whirl of dust with the Stinger.

Preacher was silent for a moment then slowly lowered his rifle. 'Just a dust-devil,' he said.

'There's a man in it,' Clay said. 'He raised it. Must be a Blood-blessed.'

The swirling plume drifted on a few more yards then split into a half-dozen smaller, whispy vortices. They faded in a few heart-beats, revealing nothing but empty air.

Clay felt the weight of Preacher's stare as he lowered the Stinger. 'He was there,' he insisted. 'Spoiled maybe, come to scout us out.'

The expression on the marksman's face indicated a realisation he may not be the only crazy man in this company. 'Spoiled don't walk alone.'

'Still, we should wake the others.'

'Feel free.' Preacher cradled his rifle between crossed arms and returned to his station on the far side of the fire. 'Be sure to tell your uncle it was your idea though.'

In the morning he went over the ground where he had seen the swaddled man, finding only vague tracks in the flakes that could have been left by a gust of wind.

'The Sands do this, young 'un,' Skaggerhill said, watching with a faintly amused expression as Clay scoured the ground. 'Play with a fella's brain. Seen a man go crazed my last trip here, blazing away at shadows he swore were the ghosts of his kin.'

'Wasn't no ghost,' Clay said, raising his gaze. 'It was a Blood-blessed and I'm betting he's on our trail now.'

Skaggerhill shrugged and inclined his head at the camp where the company were packing up. 'Then he's got a long walk ahead. Best not keep the captain waiting.'

As they tracked north Clay kept just as close a watch on the landscape as the others. The swaddled man, however, failed to reappear, not during the day and not at night. Clay stayed awake past his watch, wandering around the fire in a wide circle, hand clutching the Stinger beneath his duster. 'Sit still awhile, will ya', kiddo,' Foxbine said in annoyance. 'That's awful distracting.'

He sank onto his blanket, unable to shake the certainty the small man with the walking-stick was out there in the dark, watching, waiting. *But for what?* He knew a measure of Green might help, enhance his vision enough to pick out their pursuer amongst the dunes, but with Foxbine so close there was no way to take it without her knowing. Sleep came slowly and proved fitful, leaving him heavy of head and no less fearful come the morning.

They pressed on for three hours, trekking over a flat expanse devoid of dunes that ended abruptly in the chalk labyrinth of the Badlands. 'Keep it tight,' Braddon ordered. 'No more than two feet from your neighbour. Get lost in here you got lousy odds of making it out again.'

He kept his compass in hand as they made their way through the narrow maze of thin, conical tors and winding channels. The landscape often forced a deviation from true north but the compass kept them moving towards the Greychurn River. There was little warning before it came in sight, just a slight cooling in the air before the Badlands fell away into a steep slope of red sandstone, descending into dark, swift-flowing waters.

'Can see why folks tend to avoid this stretch,' Foxbine commented, looking down at the churning current.

'In full spate due to the rains,' Braddon said. 'Wittler made the journey earlier in the year, when it was calmer.'

'Can't see nowhere they coulda moored up,' Skaggerhill said, shielding his eyes to scan the course of the river.

'Well, we know for a fact they did.' Braddon pointed east. 'We follow the bank. See what turns up.'

The going was treacherous, the stone forming the bank soft and liable to give way under a heavy footfall. More than once Clay found himself coming perilously close to dropping into the swift waters below. It took another two hours before they found a small inlet with a gently sloping bank, the kind of place where a company might moor up a raft if they intended to make for the Red Sands. On the bank lay the skeleton of a large drake, the bones bleached white and long denuded of flesh. At first Clay entertained the faint hope they had found the White's bones but Skaggerhill pronounced it a male Red.

'Dead a good long while,' Skaggerhill judged, looking over the skeleton and poking a finger into the hole in its skull. 'Longrifle shot took it down, but that don't account for this.' He crouched, pointing to the creature's shattered sternum. 'Looks almost like it burst from the inside.'

'Ethelynne,' Braddon said. 'In the final trance she had with her, Madame Bondersil told her to make for this corpse and use the last of her Black to draw out the heart. The blood it held was her only chance against Wittler.'

'She drank heart-blood?' Skaggerhill gave a low whistle. 'Little wonder no-one's seen her since.'

'Over here, Captain,' Foxbine called, her boot nudging at something a short ways off. It was so shrouded in chalk-dust Clay initially assumed it must be more of the drake's bones but a quick waft of Foxbine's duster revealed it as a human skeleton, though far from complete. Unlike those in the Crater, this one retained the long-rotted rags of its clothes and the dry, papery remnants of a boot enclosed its only foot.

'Wittler,' Braddon said, eyes tracking the body from end to end. 'Too tall for anyone else. Looks like he contrived to lose an arm and a leg.'

'Drakes've been at him.' Skaggerhill peered closer at the arm-bones. 'Got teeth marks here, too small for a full-grown. Juvenile Reds must've come by and had themselves a feast.'

'They ate his arm and leg off?' Clay asked.

Skaggerhill shook his head. 'Reds don't eat bones. Ain't got the teeth for it.'

'Only cannon fire can bust up a body like that,' Foxbine said.

Braddon straightened, casting his gaze around the surrounding landscape. 'Spread out. If there's anything else to find here I want it. Sweep two hundred yards out then come back. Stay in pairs. Clay, go with Silverpin.'

The bladehand took the lead, moving with spear lowered through the narrow channels of chalk and sandstone. Clay's eyes strayed continually to the tops of the stunted cliffs that surrounded them, wondering if the hooded head of the swaddled man might pop up. Climbing these walls would have been difficult, perhaps impossible given the softness of the stone, but not for a Blood-blessed and he remained convinced that's what the man had been.

'I did see him,' he muttered, drawing a glance from Silverpin. 'I saw a man,' he repeated. 'Wasn't just some figment.'

She nodded, face devoid of any mockery or scepticism, then moved on. *At least somebody believes me,* he thought.

They had made a slow progress through the maze for maybe a hundred paces when Silverpin came to a sudden halt, eyes narrowing as she peered at something to her right. Clay tracked her gaze, seeing a channel descending then broadening into a steep-walled canyon. His gaze immediately went to a deep crack in one of the walls, more than wide enough for a man to gain entry, and stacked at the opening what could only be more bones. They had been collected into a cylindrical structure some ten feet high, skulls, thigh-bones and ribs all fused together somehow and woven into a macabre monument, to what only the Seer knew.

Silverpin approached in a slow, half-crouch, spear at the ready. Clay followed at a short interval, Stinger drawn. Such a thing could have been crafted by human hands, and for all they knew the artist was still in residence. Silverpin flattened herself against the stone before darting her head around the edge of the crack. Clay heard her take a few sniffs before she relaxed, moving away from the stone and shaking her head at him.

'No-one home, huh?' he asked, peering into the gloom, seeing nothing but blackness and his nose detecting only dust. Even so, he had no intention of stepping inside just yet, not without the rest of the company in front. He turned to the bone stack, frowning at the first skull he saw. It didn't seem quite right, the chin too prominent and the brows featuring small, spiky protrusions. 'Spoiled,' he realised, eyes flicking from one malformed skull to another. The deformity differed in each case, some with spikes growing out of their cheek-bones, others with what could only be called horns jutting from their jaws or temples.

A scuff of boot leather drew his attention away from the bones and he had time to see Silverpin disappearing into the black void of the crack. 'Wait!' he called out, moving to follow then hesitating as his boot stepped into the all-consuming shadow. 'At least take a light.'

He waited, heard nothing then cursed, slipping off his pack to retrieve the small lantern it held. It took several seconds of fumbling and cursing before he got it lit, the yellow beam it cast reaching only a few yards into the crack. There was no sign of Silverpin. He spent a full ten seconds voicing the foulest language he knew, then took a firm hold on the butt of the Stinger and made his way into the dark.

The air was musty but cool, soon becoming dank as the light revealed dampness on the walls. The passage had a slight but discernible downward slant, becoming wider the deeper he went until finally it opened out into a large chamber. It was maybe twenty feet across, the ceiling too high to be made out by the lamplight. After a few seconds of casting the beam about he voiced a sigh of relief as it played over Silverpin's slim form in the centre of the chamber. She stood in a circle of stones, head cocked as her eyes tracked over it, keen and unblinking.

'Fool thing you did,' Clay admonished her, though she didn't seem to hear. 'How'd you find your way without a light?' Again no reaction; she seemed completely engrossed in examining the stone circle. He moved closer, the lamplight revealing the stones to be densely packed together in a ring about three feet high, held in place by some form of mortar. He saw it was covered by something, some kind of dried liquid that had accumulated over several years until the stones were rendered near black with it. He cast the light over the surrounding rock, finding it liberally streaked with more of the same stuff. *Blood*, he realised, his thoughts returning to the stacked bones outside. *Killed here and piled up out there. But by who?*

Despite several more enquiries Silverpin remained apparently oblivious to him, enraptured by whatever she saw in the stones. He moved away, playing the lantern over the cavern walls, finding more blood, some of it splashed higher than his head. *Not just killed,* he realised, glancing back at the circle. *Ripped apart . . . feasted upon.*

'It nested here,' he said aloud, realisation dawning in a rush. Wittler's blasted body, not a cannon-shot, an egg, bursting apart in flame and fury as they did when their mothers bathed them in the waking fire, setting free what waited within. 'She used the Red's heart-blood to birth the egg. The White hatched, ate up what was left of Wittler and came here where the Spoiled fed it, fed it with their own flesh.'

He realised Silverpin was looking at him now, her fascination with the stones transformed into a keen, almost scary scrutiny. 'Right?' he asked, finding the weight of her gaze uncomfortable. She gave no response, stepping from the stones and walking towards him with a purposeful stride. He drew back, Stinger gripped tight though he didn't raise it as her hands remained empty. 'What's . . . ?' he began as his back bumped up against the wall, falling silent as she leaned close and planted a kiss on his mouth, a long kiss.

'Um,' he said when she drew back. It was all he could think to say. 'Maybe . . . maybe we should go get my uncle.'

She angled her head, raising an eyebrow, mouth forming a small smile.

He moved to her, drawing her close, mouth finding hers again. There was a ringing sound as she began to discard her blades. 'Yeah,' Clay breathed as she pressed herself against him. 'He can wait awhile, I guess.'

II

ALIGNMENTS
AND ANOMALIES

It is not the purpose of this tome to explore in detail the many superstitions, frauds and fallacies that surround the subject of plasmology. It is true that lesser cultures beyond the Corporate Sphere, particularly in Dalcia but also in certain regions of the Corvantine Empire, continue to look upon the Blessing as a manifestation of divine favour or conjuration resulting from ancient ritual magics. However, the rational mind is quick to spot the logical inconsistencies and flaws in such beliefs. Whatever nonsense may be claimed by the adherents of the sadly still-extant, but thankfully much-denuded Church of the Seer, there is no credible evidence that use of the Blessing was ever demonstrated beyond the confines of the Arradsian continental mass prior to the opening of the Strait and the first phase of Mandinorian Colonisation. And, to answer a question oft put to the author, I do not consider the fabled White to be anything more than a conglomeration of outlandish tales arising from those frequently chaotic and costly days, when as many lives were lost to madness as to the attentions of the Spoiled.

———

From *A Lay-person's Guide to Plasmology* by Miss Amorea Findlestack. Ironship Press – Company Year 195 (1579 by the Mandinorian Calendar).

CHAPTER 19

Lizanne

Lizanne sprinted to the end of the roof-top and leapt, somer-saulting over the museum railings to land on the gravel beyond. Without the benefit of Green such a leap would probably have left her with two fractured ankles; as it was her legs only betrayed a slight burning as she crouched. Lizanne had the Whisper in hand and a Redball loaded into the top barrel; tonight she could afford no half-measures. She had foregone the luxury of prolonged surveillance of the building's environs. The urgency was too great and the Green had already burned down to its last vestiges thanks to her enjoyable but strenuous journey across the roof-tops of Morsvale. Instead she had waited only long enough to gain a fair idea of the guards' patrol schedule before vaulting the railings.

Finding no sign of detection she rose and ran for the side entrance. It was a curious facet of her experience that those responsible for the security of important buildings would expend considerable energy in securing their main access points whilst paying only marginal heed to those used by the people actually employed within. Also, doors used with any constancy, especially by poorly paid functionaries, were rarely as well locked as they should have been.

Lizanne was obliged to inject a modicum of Black to undo the side-entrance, secured by a heavy padlock-and-chain arrangement rather than the excellent double mortice with which it had been equipped. Padlocks were her favourite kind of lock, the mechanism standardised across all makes and swiftly undone by a few seconds' concentration. The tricky part was reattaching it once she had gained entry, requiring her to reach through the door with the Black and reassemble it from memory. She re-attached the chain but didn't engage the locking mechanism; it should be enough to fool a casual glance and she might have need of a swift exit.

She recharged with a small amount of Green before proceeding through the basement store-room where she found herself, just enough to enhance her senses. There were a few more doors between the basement and the ground floor, but nothing overly troublesome. On emerging into the marble-floored lobby she crouched to remove her shoes, leaving them in a shadowed recess by the door. Lizanne paused for a moment as her bare feet cooled on the marble, expecting to hear the footfalls of a night watchman echoing through the museum's many halls, but instead her augmented hearing detected only the faint murmur of voices from the floor above.

Someone's working late, she decided, stealing across the lobby to the staircase. It wasn't necessarily a problem provided this dutiful scholar kept to their own business. However, she was obliged to stifle a groan of frustration as, upon reaching the top of the stairs, she realised the voices came from Diran's office.

She crouched behind the balustrade, her ears revealing the conversation in full, albeit-brief detail.

'I don't . . .' Diran's voice, hesitant and lacking the bluster and surety from before. The tone and cadence were all too familiar to Lizanne: a man in desperate fear of his life. 'Don't have it,' Diran managed, Lizanne picturing the sweat covering his face. 'Not here.'

'You didn't make a copy?' another voice asked, the tone hard and demanding though the speaker was careful to keep it muted.

'N-no. I can . . . redraw it though. I have my notes.'

'Where?'

'The cabinet.' Diran's voice took on a slight note of relief. *And*

I thought him a clever fellow, Lizanne mused in grudging sympathy. 'Just there. If you'll allow me pen and paper . . .'

'No need.' The gun-shot was muffled, probably by a suppressor of some sort. 'The notes should suffice.'

She had only seconds to process the significance of this, her mind soon fixing on some inevitable and unwelcome conclusions. *They know what he was working on. They know of his association to Burgrave Artonin. And they know he has the map.* She had only a matter of hours before being compromised. Protocol was clear in such circumstances: compromise at any stage requires immediate extraction. It was the only rational course.

Lizanne kicked the door to Diran's office off its hinges and entered in a roll, hearing the thump of a suppressed pistol followed by the whip-crack of a bullet missing by inches. She came to one knee, sighted the Whisper on the man standing beside Diran's desk and fired twice, one shot to the belly, one to the arm. The man fell across the desk with a pained yell, pistol falling from his spasming hand.

She stood up, using the Black to lift the assassin from the desk and slam him against the wall. A demonstration always saved time on explanations and any tediously prolonged threats. Lizanne moved to the desk, pausing to glance at Diran and finding him predictably dead with a hole in his temple, the paper-strewn desk covered in blood that seeped over the edges.

'Can't say I liked him overmuch,' she said, turning back to the assassin. 'But still, I think he deserved better.'

The man gasped, arms and legs spread flat on the wall, blood flowing freely from the wound in his belly. Despite his evident agony and imminent death she could see him fighting to retain his discipline, dragging breath through clenched teeth, his gaze averted. *Cadre through and through,* she decided. *No freelancers here.*

'I realise this is probably a pointless exercise,' Lizanne said, casting a meaningful glance at his bleeding abdomen. 'But formality dictates I at least make the offer. Quick and painless or slightly slower and infinitely more ugly. And I'll crush your larynx so you can't scream.'

No reaction. Gaze fixed and averted, breath laboured but still regular. *Never engage the interrogator,* she recalled from the Protectorate school. *Not in thought, gesture or deed. Any form of engagement involves communication, and communication inevitably involves the exchange of information.*

She applied a gentle pressure to the wound, widening it a little, a fresh torrent of blood seeping forth to spatter the floor beneath his dangling feet. She fixed her eyes on his, gauging the reaction as she spoke a single word, 'Artonin.'

It was barely a flicker, just a slight twitch in his fevered gaze, but she caught it. *They know.* 'Thank you,' Lizanne said and used the last of the Black to crush his skull.

She let the body fall and moved to the cabinet behind the desk, wrenching it open. The device lay where Sirus had placed it, the dim light from Diran's lamp catching the edges of its many cogs and levers. A stack of note-books sat alongside the device but, as he had told his killer, there was no sign of any map. She consigned it all to her pack, gratified to find that the device weighed only a few pounds. She would need to conserve her Green and the journey back to the Burgrave's house was already likely to prove taxing without additional weight.

Proceed to extraction. The thought spoke in Madame's voice, as the rational side of her brain often did. She ignored it, moving to the door and closing it softly behind her. *You are compromised,* Madame's voice insisted. *Proceed to extraction.*

The map, she replied, running down the staircase and moving to the alcove where she had left her shoes.

You have the device and the notes. Proceed to extraction.

She pulled on her shoes and returned to the basement, calculating the most efficient ground-level route to the Burgrave's house. She paused at the side-door, taking a deep breath and focusing her mind for the task ahead.

This is not about the map, Madame accused, summoning the image of Tekela's eager, doll-like face.

Lizanne ignored her and stepped out into the fading night.

There will come a time, one of her instructors had said several years before, *when a covert operation will transform into a tactical engagement. Whilst such a circumstance should be avoided wherever possible, you should be prepared to shift your operating parameters accordingly. However, this does not mean an abandonment of careful planning or pursuance of only the most realistic objectives.*

She counted three Cadre agents in the street with another standing in the open doorway. They all wore the same long dark overcoat and a flat-topped hat. The Cadre tended to a uniform appearance when they emerged from the shadows; it discouraged any unwise curiosity from the populace. Lizanne approached at a sedate walk, carrying her pack as if it contained newly bought groceries and frowning in apparent puzzlement at their presence. The three agents moved to confront her as she neared, one in front, the other two taking up positions on either side, edging closer.

'You work here, miss?' the one in front enquired.

'I am maid to Miss Artonin,' she said, suitably fearful eyes moving from one to the other.

'Ah,' he said, 'recently arrived from Corvus, are you not? Bearing a personal recommendation from Landgravine Morgosal, I believe.'

'Why yes, sir.' Her gaze swivelled to the house in apparent bemusement.

'Curious then,' the agent went on, stepping closer, 'that our recent trance communication from Corvus reveals that the good lady has never heard of you.'

His thin smile held a certain triumphant confidence, though his lack of outright alarm indicated that, regardless of what intelligence they had obtained, the most pertinent aspect of her identity had not yet been discerned.

'You shouldn't have let me get so close,' Lizanne told him, drawing the Whisper from the slit in her skirt and shooting him in the forehead. She used Black to freeze the agents on either side and delivered a single round into each of their heads in a swift switchback motion. The agent in the doorway was quick, pistol already drawn and sweeping towards her. She threw his arm aside with a surge of Black and shot him twice in the chest. He gave a groan as she ascended the steps to the door, obliging her to put another round into his skull.

She crouched in the hallway, Whisper held out in a two-handed grip, scanning for targets and ears alive for any sound. *Nothing, not even a creaking board.*

She checked the study first, finding Burgrave Artonin slumped on the floor behind his desk, leaking blood onto the carpet from half a dozen exit wounds in his back. An old-model cavalry revolver lay under his hand, his thumb frozen in the motion of drawing back the hammer. *He forced them to kill him,* she deduced, uncertain what that might mean for Tekela's fate.

The girl's room was empty but disordered, drawers upended and sundry clothes and girlish accoutrements strewn about. She went from room to room and floor to floor, Whisper gripped tight and ready, finding the general untidiness resulting from a cursory search but no more agents, or servants.

She found them in the kitchen, all seated at the table, heads slumped forward, each with a single gun-shot to the back of the head. Madam Meeram had been tied to her chair, indicating she at least put up a struggle. Misha and Kalla were holding hands, heads lying on their sides so they seemed to be staring into one another's empty eyes. Mr Drellic was seated next to Cook, his expression displaying as much confusion in death as it did in life. *Krista . . . Your name is Krista.*

Tekela and Rigan were not amongst them.

Lizanne returned to the study and tore open the Burgrave's hiding place. The Cadre clearly hadn't had time for a proper search as she found the papers intact. Amongst the ledgers and sundry documents lay a tubular leather case typically used for the storage and transport of maps. She resisted the impulse to open it then and there. Despite the early hour the agents' bodies would soon be noted and all manner of discord was about to erupt in the street outside. She exited through the garden, leaping the wall and striding towards the northern quarter.

The sharpshooter had no time to react beyond glancing up with wide, fear-filled eyes as she plummeted towards him, the Green enabling her to cover the distance from the edge of the roof in a single leap. Lizanne landed with her knees on his shoulders, pinning him down as she plunged a knife into the base of his skull. She snatched up his carbine, a long-barrelled model with an optical sight, and trained it on the roof-top of the safe house opposite. *Nothing,* she surmised in satisfaction, setting the carbine aside and recalling one of Madame's favourite axioms: *overconfidence is frequently fatal.*

She climbed down to the street via a drain-pipe and walked to the safe-house door, fingers depressing three buttons on the Spider and flooding her with an intoxicating mélange of Red, Green and Black. Half her remaining supply used up in a single dose, though she expected to need every drop of it. Efforts had been made to disguise the nature of the door but the Green revealed the iron bracings reinforcing the edges and the lock would have taken all morning to unpick. There was also a small, glass peep-hole at eye-level. She knocked on the door three times, waited then added two more knocks before retreating a good twenty yards and drawing the Whisper from her skirt.

Lizanne focused her gaze on the peep-hole and waited. After a short interval she detected the slight shift of colour indicating someone had responded to the knock, raised the Whisper and summoned enough product to unleash the Redball. She aimed for the peep-hole, reasoning it was the only weak point, and was gratified to see the door disintegrate in a fiery ball of burning splinters and melting iron. She entered in a run, leaping the mangled remains of whoever had come to answer the door and putting two rounds into a figure stumbling about in the smoke-filled hallway. Two more agents came thundering down the staircase at the end of the hallway, pistols drawn. She shot the one in front and dragged the other off his feet with Black, crushing his gun hand and holding him suspended in mid air as she came closer.

'Where's the girl?' Lizanne demanded, squeezing his throat. Like the assassin in the museum he strove to cleave to his training but the shock of her assault had clearly unnerved him. His eyes gave a downward flick and his mouth sputtered around a hope-less plea.

Keen to conserve her Black, she let him fall and shot him through the temple. She found a sturdy door at the end of the hallway, another one with a lock too complex to pick in a reason-able time. Luckily, this one didn't have any iron bracings and it gave way after two hefty shoves with the Black, though it left her with a fast-diminishing reserve. The busted door revealed a dimly lit stairwell descending into the bowels of the house, the sound of curious and alarmed voices emanating from below. She paused to slot another Redball into the Whisper's top barrel before proceeding down, coming to a halt at the sight of a half-open door at the foot of the stairs.

'I am a Blood-blessed operative of the Ironship Protectorate!' Lizanne called out. 'If you wish to survive this encounter, disarm yourselves and stand aside!'

The response was so swift it nearly caught her off guard, the bulky form of a Cadre agent bursting through the door with a pistol in each hand, blazing away and filling the stairwell with a fog of flame, gunsmoke and powdered plaster. Lizanne leapt, her back connecting with the ceiling as the agent's continuing barrage tore at the steps where she had been standing. The excitement of it all instilled a slight loss of control, causing her to reply with two rounds from the Whisper where one would have sufficed. The agent crumpled, issuing a faint death-rattle as Lizanne landed and stepped over him into the chamber beyond.

It was a large, windowless space, walls, floor and ceiling all covered in white tiles. The floor had been constructed with a slight incline towards a grated drain in the centre. Rivulets of blood traced from the drain to a figure tied to a chair, a slender young man, head slumped forward and the signs of recent torment covering his bare torso. *Sirus.* From the sight of him he hadn't lasted very long. Tied to the chair opposite was the more substantial form of Major Arberus, similarly slumped and abused. Tekela had been secured to a third chair between the two men, positioned so as to afford a clear view of proceedings. She appeared unharmed though her unblinking, perhaps unseeing eyes and bleached features told of more internal wounds. Two men stood back from the ugly tableau, unremarkable in stature or appearance as men of their occupation often were in Lizanne's experience. They wore aprons and thick leather gloves, stained red naturally. The various implements of their trade lay on a small, wheeled cart. Both stood with their bloodied gloves raised, plainly terrified.

'You've seen my face,' Lizanne told them by way of explanation. Luckily she still had two rounds left in the Whisper.

Tekela had been secured to the chair by a pair of steel cuffs fastened to a brace. Lizanne retrieved the key after a brief search of the torturers' bodies.

'I didn't . . .' The girl spoke in a whisper as the cuffs came free of her wrists. 'Didn't tell them anything.'

'It doesn't matter.' Lizanne took her elbow and guided her to her feet.

Tekela gaped at her with her unblinking eyes. 'They killed Father . . .'

'I know.'

'Made me watch what they did to Sirus . . .'

'I know, miss, but we really have to go now.'

'That woman, the dress-maker. She made me watch . . .'

Lizanne paused, frowning. 'Dress-maker?'

An invisible hand gripped her like a vice, lifting her off her feet and slamming her into the rear wall of the chamber, the

Whisper flying free of her grasp as she connected with the tiles. She struggled but the grip tightened, forcing the air from her lungs and spinning her about to face her assailant.

The dress-maker was clad in simpler attire today, dark waist-coat and skirt, cream-sleeved blouse. She might have been taken for a mid-level manager back in Carvenport. But here her status was obvious, made more so by the silver Imperial crest pinned to her breast. *Blood Cadre. How did I miss it?*

'Hello again,' the dress-maker said in perfect Mandinorian, a slight smile on her lips.

Do not engage. Lizanne averted her gaze, clamping her mouth shut.

'Quite the mess you've made,' the woman continued, casting a rueful glance at the torturers. 'Skilled employees don't grow on trees, you know.' She moved a few steps closer, eyes scrutinising Lizanne's frozen form. 'Where are they?' she asked, noting the absence of Lizanne's pack. She had concealed it behind a water-tank on a near by roof-top before coming here, knowing the chances of success were only about fifty percent. *A miscalculation,* she realised now.

'The map and the solargraph,' the dress-maker said, voice hardening and the grip tightening on Lizanne's chest. She felt her ribs begin to strain from the pressure. 'Your little friend here doesn't seem to know. And I assume that was your handiwork at the museum.'

Do not engage!

'I will kill her before I kill you,' the woman promised with affable sincerity. 'Eventually.'

A series of dry clicking sounds came from the left and Lizanne strained her eyes to see Tekela backed into the corner, the Whisper held in her small hand. The barrel was trained on the dress-maker, the mechanism clicking as her finger repeatedly pulled the trigger on an empty cylinder.

'Thought we'd ruined her,' the woman mused, turning back to Lizanne. 'People are always so delightfully surprising, don't you find? Now, as you must know my Black is close to expiry, so I'm afraid a disabling injury is in order. A fractured pelvis always seems to do the trick . . .'

Lizanne wasn't listening, her eyes focused on the Whisper still held outstretched in Tekela's hand, and the Redball sitting in the top barrel. She unleashed more Red than necessary, the explosion of flame causing the girl to release her hold on the weapon, but not before the Redball had escaped the barrel. Lizanne was denied the spectacle of the dress-maker's demise, though the resultant debris was more than sufficient evidence of its finality.

She slid down the wall, leaving a clean space on the tiles amidst the abstract mural of red and black. She felt the last dregs of product dwindle away, leaving the familiar aches and strains that resulted from intense use. Her limbs shook and her chest hurt with every breath. Tekela appeared at her side, face earnest now, reason returned though tears fell freely down her cheeks.

'Sorry about your father,' Lizanne told her.

Tekela shook her head. 'It was Rigan,' she said. 'They told him he would have a commission in the navy. The dress-maker made him tell it all to me before she killed him. He'd been their spy for over a year.'

Lizanne nodded, recalling Rigan's absence the previous day. 'That makes sense.' She tried to get up, groaned and slumped back down.

'Here.' Tekela put an arm around Lizanne's shoulders, helping her to rise after several seconds' effort. 'What do we do now?'

A loud, hacking cough filled the chamber, causing Tekela to whirl about, snatching the now-useless Whisper from the tiles and waving it as if it had the power to ward off all dangers. Major Arberus jerked in his chair, spitting blood onto the tiles before turning to them with a baleful glare. 'A very good question, my dear.'

'A governess once told me this place was haunted,' Tekela said, eyes roving the interior of the oracular temple. Like Lizanne, she wore a skirt and blouse stolen from an upstairs room in the safe house, presumably belonging to the unfortunate dress-maker. They were at least two sizes too big, making her appear even more childlike, though Lizanne knew her childhood had come to an end in that tiled room.

'She would take me to the park sometimes,' the girl went on. 'I think she was trying to frighten me into better behaviour.' She issued a short giggle, far too shrill and bordering on hysteria for Lizanne's liking. 'It didn't work.'

Major Arberus gave a pained groan from atop the stone bench where they had laid him, head lolling in his sleep and face betraying a fearful wince. Lizanne had been obliged to dose him with Green to get him here, trussed into the clothes of one of the dead agents and walking stiffly between them as they made a hurried progress to the park. Fortunately, it was still early and the only folk about were street-sweepers, who quickly averted their gaze at the sight of the major's garb. He had collapsed on reaching the temple, sinking into a sleep so absolute Lizanne wasn't entirely sure he would wake. His wounds were grievous but healing quickly thanks to the Green, but she knew there were other wounds that cut deep enough to lay a man low no matter how strong the medicine.

'He said nothing,' Tekela said. 'The whole time. Not one word. Sirus wouldn't shut up, begging them to let me go . . .' She trailed off into another shrill giggle, sinking onto a bench and falling silent.

Lizanne had been cataloguing the supplies looted from the safe house, a decent but not copious stock of product from the dress-maker's room plus two pistols and ammunition. The product appeared to be of decent quality but the slightly dull colour indicated the Cadre's plasmologists were still somewhat behind their corporate adversaries in the fields of dilution and refinement. Still, it was a lucky find given the reduced state of her own stocks. She had also taken a moment to secure some food and water.

'Here,' she said, moving to Tekela's side with a water bottle. 'Drink.'

'I'm not thirsty . . .'

'Drink.' Lizanne held the bottle to her lips until she took it 'None of this is your fault,' she said, watching the girl gulp down the water. 'This was always going to happen, from the moment the Cadre recruited Rigan as an informant. You did not cause this.'

Tekela lowered the bottle, eyes taking on the unblinking stare once more, her voice listless. 'I so wanted to tell him, to see the look on his face when he found out what I'd done. What manner of creature am I?'

Lizanne said nothing. She briefly entertained slapping the girl, but doubted she would even feel it. Instead she placed one of the stolen pistols in her lap, saying, 'I need you to keep watch for a short time. I have to consult with my employer.'

Tekela stared at the gun in bafflement. 'If they find us I won't be able to fight them off. Not with this.'

'It's for you, not them. I'll be at the top of the spire.'

Night was coming on as she emerged onto the spire's ledge, the pigeons once again cooing in alarm. She ingested a small drop of Green and fixed her gaze on the harbour. As expected the warships were abuzz with activity, sailors hurrying to allotted tasks and smoke rising from the stacks as engineers stoked the engines. The harbour door was in place to ward off the nightly tide, but as soon as it receded the fleet would sail. Turning to the Imperial Ring she saw columns of troops mustering on the various parade-grounds, regiments of cavalry already trooping south towards the city gates. *That's why the Cadre moved against Artonin,* she decided. *Clearing the decks in advance of Morradin's great offensive.*

She sat on the ledge, crossing her legs beneath her, and injected a two-second burst of Blue.

*

I *cannot vouch for its accuracy,* she told Madame Bondersil as the black tendrils of the woman's obsession slavered over the image of the map. *All I know is it was drawn by a respected Corvantine scholar after careful examination of the Mad Artisan's solargraph.* She summoned an image of the device, revolving it to display its complex workings.

Most excellent progress, Lizanne, Madame complimented her, more tendrils emerging from her storm to explore the solargraph. There was no communication for several moments as the tendrils did their work, becoming so thick it seemed as if both map and device were swallowed by a pulsating black fog.

And the other matter, Madame? Lizanne prompted eventually.

Mmmm? Oh, the impending war. I will of course pass on the intelligence to the relevant parties. However, it is vital I collate all available data on the White. More tendrils, this time reaching for the few pages from the Burgrave's notes Lizanne had had time to memorise. *With all this I suspect Jermayah may well be capable of building a replica solargraph.*

Forgive me, Madame, but the absence of urgency seems inappropriate. War between the Corvantine Empire and the Syndicate essentially means world war.

One that will end the moment we have the White in our possession. This is not my first war, Lizanne. In time you will realise they have a tendency to rage and then fade, like unseasonal storms. Commerce, however, remains constant regardless of the weather.

Another few moments' scrutiny and the tendrils receded, the clouds of Madame's storm taking on a brisk, swirling energy. *Are you prepared for extraction?*

As prepared as I can be in the circumstances.

The girl . . .

Is coming with me. So is the major. I believe they may be useful. The sudden, dark ferocity of Lizanne's whirlwinds left little room for further discussion.

And you do this in full knowledge of the consequences? Madame enquired, a note of weary resignation colouring her thoughts.

I do.

A brief, convulsive spasm of frustration set Madame's storm roiling for a second before she reasserted control. *Very well. I dare say, with the war and all, Exceptional Initiatives may prove more forgiving than usual. You shouldn't count on it, however.*

Understood.

I hope so. Your next communication with Mr Torcreek is in eighteen hours, correct?

Yes, Madame.

Do not proceed to extraction until you have passed your intelligence to him. Omit mention of the war. I believe the captain would benefit from a lack of distractions at this juncture.

CHAPTER 20

Clay

'Well, it's a nest sure enough.' Skaggerhill crouched, running a hand over the blood-black stones. 'Ain't seen one quite like it before, though. Looks almost man built.'

They had all come to take a look at the discovery, though Foxbine got antsy after only a few seconds in the cave and announced she would go stand guard at the entrance. Silverpin stood with her head resting on Clay's shoulder, something his uncle took full notice of but kept any comment to himself. For the time being at least the nest had captured his full attention.

'The Spoiled?' he asked the harvester.

'Nah, Captain. See here.' Skaggerhill pointed to the mortar holding stones in place. 'Bile straight from the second stomach. They cough it up to melt rock when they craft a nest. Only drakes do that, but never so neatly.'

'So it eats up Wittler then finds a place to nest.' Braddon wandered the cave, scanning the stained walls. 'Then the Spoiled obligingly come along and feed themselves to it.'

'It's more than a mite strange,' Skaggerhill admitted.

'Worship,' Preacher said. He stood near the chamber entrance, apparently unwilling to proceed any farther. There was a new tension in his face, a certain animation that hadn't been there before. It made Clay wonder what it might be about this place that aroused fear in a crazy man.

'What's that?' Braddon asked.

'They came to worship it,' Preacher said.

'Getting ate for their trouble,' Skaggerhill pointed out.

'Worship takes many forms.' Preacher turned and left the chamber without another word.

'Worshipped or not,' Braddon said. 'It ain't here now. Nor do we have any sign where it went.'

'Got big enough to fly off, I'd guess.' Skaggerhill climbed out of the circle. 'All winged drakes can fly the moment they're hatched, but it takes a good while before they can cover any real distance. About six years for a Black. Guessing this one's a sight bigger though.'

'It's twenty-seven years since the thing hatched.'

Skaggerhill spread his arms helplessly. 'Then, Captain, I guess we still got us a lotta searching to do.'

Silverpin stayed at Clay's side when they made camp that night, having trekked out of the Badlands and on to the Sands once more as they retraced their steps to the *Firejack*. She seemed completely unconcerned by the stares of the others, his uncle's being particularly rich in disapproval. Clay took some small enjoyment in watching Braddon's frown deepen when he put an arm around Silverpin's shoulders, drawing her closer still. What had happened in the cave left him in a fugue of confusion and lust. Lurid tales abounded about the wanton ways of the Island tribes but she hadn't been wild, pressing herself against him with evident passion but no biting or scratching, pulling away his clothes with insistent rather than frenzied hands. All so different from the whores he had occasionally indulged in back in the Blinds. A whole world of difference in fact.

'So where's this leave us?' Skaggerhill said, poking at the coals in their miniature fire. Of them all he seemed the most inclined not to notice Clay and Silverpin's altered relationship.

'Richer in knowledge, if nothing else,' Braddon replied, keeping his gaze on Clay. 'And entirely reliant on our contracted Blood-blessed.'

'Next trance is in two days,' Clay said. 'We'll just have to see what the lady's got to tell me. If the Corvantines ain't got her yet.'

'That likely?'

'They knew about this little jaunt. Who's to say they don't know about her? Looks like we may have to call an end to this whole venture, Uncle.' *With any luck,* he added inwardly, though the thought made him wonder if his one hundred thousand scrip would still be forthcoming should the expedition prove a failure.

'I say when we call an end, boy.' A deep, barely controlled anger had crept into Braddon's voice. *It's back,* Clay realised, seeing the familiar hungry glint in his uncle's eye. *Worse now he knows the great myth ain't a myth. Now he's got something real to chase.*

'Preacher,' Clay said, turning to the marksman. 'You're a book-learned fella. Just how big is Arradsia, would you say?'

'One point eight million square miles,' Preacher replied without hesitation.

'One point eight million,' Clay repeated, turning back to his uncle. 'Lotta ground to cover with no real idea of where to look.'

Braddon got slowly to his feet, staring down at Clay and speaking in slow, emphatic tones. '*I* say when we call an end, *boy.*'

Silverpin suddenly stiffened against Clay's side, her hand snatching up the spear at her feet. 'It's alright . . .' Clay began to soothe her but she sprang away, panther fast, leaping over the fire and bearing Braddon to the ground.

'Don't!' Clay shouted, surging to his feet then reeling away as something buzzed past his ear, leaving a stinging pain in its wake. It thudded into the sand just beyond where Silverpin had his uncle pinned to the flakes. Clay put a hand to his ear, staring in shock as it came away bloody.

'Spoiled!' Foxbine called out, whirling to face the darkened dunes, carbine at her shoulder. Silverpin rolled off Braddon to crouch with spear in hand, glancing over at Clay and urgently beckoning him to her side. He could only stand gaping with blood running down his neck.

'Dammit, young 'un!' Skaggerhill sent him sprawling with a

sweep of his leg, the harvester lying prone, shotgun at the ready. 'Skin that iron. We got work to do.'

Clay fumbled for the Stinger, wincing as Skaggerhill's shotgun sent a loud, booming blast into the darkness beyond the fire. Clay managed to work the weapon free, cursing the whole while. He reached for the stock on his back then flattened himself to the flakes as the air above thrummed with multiple unseen projectiles. One sank into the ground a bare six inches from his face, an arrow, shuddering with the impact. It was fashioned from bone, he saw, sparsely fletched with dried grass. A series of harsh guttural shouts dragged his attention from the arrow and he turned in time to see half a dozen ragged figures charging out of the darkness, clubs and knives in every hand.

Skaggerhill fired again, cutting down one, then a salvo from Foxbine's carbine felled two more. The Stinger bucked in Clay's hand and another collapsed just yards away. He couldn't remember aiming or drawing back the hammer. He thumbed it once more and fired again, the Spoiled taking the bullet full in the chest less than an arm's length short. Clay ducked as the last one swung at him, the club whistling over his head. A flurry of shots from the rest of the company sent the Spoiled jerking and spinning until he collapsed onto the fire, his blood drawing a sizzle from the coals.

Multiple snicks in the gloom as they reloaded, Clay marvelling at the absence of a tremble as his fingers fed fresh rounds into the Stinger's cylinder. He finally managed to get hold of the stock and slotted it into place, pulling it tight against his shoulder as he hunkered down, using the body of the last Spoiled he shot as cover. He could see its face in the meagre light, scales and spines contrasting with an oddly peaceful expression.

'We get 'em all, y'think?' he hissed at Skaggerhill.

The harvester snapped closed the breech of his shotgun and rested it on his pack. 'Just scouts. Take a sniff and you'll get an idea.'

Clay frowned in bafflement but nevertheless widened his

nostrils to taste the air, face soon bunching in disgust at the thick scent carried by the westerly wind. It smelled worse than Ellforth's breath, rich in a corruption that warned of deep and lasting sickness. 'Stinks like product gone bad, don't it?' Skaggerhill commented. 'I'd say we got us a full war-party out there, at least.'

'How many's that?'

The harvester's face was grim, as was his tone. 'Too many.'

Clay's hand stole into his shirt, clutching Ellforth's wallet. He had begun to open the flap when the Spoiled charged again. For a while everything was a whirl of gun-shots, war-cries and falling Spoiled. The Stinger bucked repeatedly in Clay's hand as he aimed and fired on pure instinct. They came on so fast there was no time to think. He gave an involuntary shudder as the Stinger's hammer clicked on an empty chamber, the Spoiled he had been aiming for charging on, teeth bared and the spiny ridge of his forehead gleaming. Clay reversed his grip on the pistol and got to his feet, stepping close to trap the Spoiled's club arm and hammering the butt into his forehead. The Spoiled reeled back a few feet then twisted into a bloody pirouette as Skaggerhill sent the contents of both barrels into his chest.

A lull descended, Clay sinking down behind the corpse once more as he reloaded, casting a glance around the camp. They were all still breathing and apparently unharmed. Silverpin crouched at his uncle's side, spear blooded down to her fist whilst Braddon methodically slid fresh cartridges into his longrifle. Foxbine had apparently emptied her carbine and had both pistols in hand. Just in front of her lay the bodies of seven Spoiled. From her expression, equal parts rage and hunger, Clay judged she didn't think her haul sufficient.

'Don't suppose we scared them off, huh?' he asked Skaggerhill.

'They don't scare. Just keep comin' till we're outta bullets or they're outta bodies.'

A sudden rush of wind brought another wave of the Spoiled's stench, even thicker than before. *Seer-dammit, there's more gathering out there.* He abandoned any hope of secrecy and reached for Ellforth's wallet. *All of it,* he decided. *Not a time for half-measures.*

He had begun to pull Auntie's vial free when a great roaring sound erupted out in the darkness. He looked up to see a wall of flame rising fifty yards out, birthed by a jet of fire cast down from above. The Spoiled were dancing, not in celebration but agony, their screams cutting through the roar of the flames. A gust of wind swept across the camp and Clay saw the stars above blacked out for an instant as something large passed overhead. A few seconds later another jet of flame swept down fifty yards to the south. More dancing Spoiled, more screams. Clay caught sight of the drake's wing outlined against the rising flames as it swept low over the desert.

It made several more attacks, circling to cast its flames down at the milling Spoiled until the camp was entirely ringed by fire. No-one spoke, Clay seeing only dumb amazement on every face save Silverpin's. She alone stood regarding the spectacle with narrow-eyed suspicion. A cry echoed down at them from the sky as the flames began to die leaving behind a glowing orange ring of melted iron: the piercing scream of a triumphant drake.

'There!' Foxbine said, pistols pointed at something out on the sands. It stood just outside the glowing circle, a small figure swaddled in rags clutching a walking-stick. For a second Clay's swaddled man stood regarding them in stillness. None of the Longrifles fired, some primal instinct telling them they looked upon their saviour. The small figure hefted its stick, turned and walked off into the darkness. After a few moments they heard the rush of wind and thrum of wings that told of a drake alighting on the earth. A moment later it took to the sky, Clay catching a glimpse of its silhouette as it passed across the face of Nelphia. *The Black from the river.* Somehow he knew it, knew the beast and whatever commanded it had tracked them from the *Firejack* to the Badlands and back again. And, although it was just a small speck, he could have sworn he saw the swaddled man perched on the drake's back before it angled its wings and disappeared from view.

That is certainly very curious, Miss Lethridge commented as he shifted his mindscape to replay the events on the Sands, the intervention of the swaddled man and his apparently tame Black being a particular point of interest. Clay showed her the piled bodies of the Spoiled, all twisted up and scorched, some forged together by the heat of the drake's fire.

The remainder of your journey was uneventful, I trust? she enquired.

Saw no more sign of the Spoiled, nor the man. The trek back to the *Firejack* had been a mostly quiet affair, each of the Longrifles marching in preoccupied silence whilst Clay tried not to fiddle with the bandage Foxbine had secured over his ear. Although Clay knew they all prized discovery above most things, he wondered if what they had witnessed the night before had been one wonder too many, a thing best left unseen.

You may not have found the egg but your uncle should still consider this a success, Miss Lethridge told him. *At least we now have confirmation of Ethelynne Drystone's account. I expect Madame Bondersil will be very pleased.*

I'll be sure to tell him, he replied, pausing to take in the sight of her whirlwinds. They spun with considerable energy but lacked the cohesion he had seen before, and there seemed to be a lot more red in the mix. *More complications?* he asked.

The past two days have been . . . eventful, but productive. Look here. She pulled a small, pale twister closer, opening it out into a sheet of paper.

That a map? he asked.

Indeed it is. I have reason to believe it holds clues to the where- abouts of our quarry. Be sure to memorise it as I taught you.

He scraped a copy of the map into the dirt of his mindscape, a colourful re-creation of Nelphia's surface, his various mem- ories formed into valleys and mountains. *A considerable improvement,* she had complimented him when the trance was joined.

You any idea what all this means? he asked when the drawing was complete. *The drake saving us like that? The Spoiled feeding themselves to the White?*

Perhaps, if as your Preacher opines they truly worship this thing, they felt they had no choice. As for the drake's actions, that is one of many things currently beyond my understanding. However, with the wealth of documents and the device in my possession, hopefully answers will be forthcoming when I return to Carvenport.

Mission's over, huh?

This part of it, at least. Though extraction is likely to prove hazardous so don't be too surprised if I fail to appear at the next trance.

He didn't like the matter-of-fact tone to her thoughts and was surprised to find he actually cared if she made it out safely. He put it down to some side-effect of the trance, mutual concern being inevitable when two minds were joined.

You be sure to take care, he told her. *The Corvantines've got a lead on both of us now, don't forget.*

Her thoughts betrayed a faint amusement, though also a small glimmer of gratitude. *Why thank you, Mr Torcreek. And congratulations, by the way.*

For what?

The Island girl. Though you may want to have a care. I hear they mate for life. With that she was gone, leaving him pondering a means of better guarding his secrets in the trance.

'The Coppersoles.' Skaggerhill grimaced as he straightened from the map Clay had drawn. 'That's Briteshore holdings, Captain,' he said to Braddon. 'And they ain't partial to trespassers.'

'They rarely venture more than twenty miles from shore,' Braddon replied, fists resting on the table and gaze fixed on the map. 'Too busy digging treasure out of their mines. Can't see them bothering us none.'

He touched a finger to the map, tracing the dotted route that ran south from Morsvale, skirting the Badlands and the Red Sands until it intersected the Greychurn on the other side of the Badlands from where the *Riverjack* was currently moored up. From there the dotted line continued on, tracing around the Red Sands and the southern Badlands before coming to Krystaline Lake. From there it continued south in the dense confines of the Coppersole Mountains. Upon reaching the foothills, however, the line abruptly ended in a symbol Preacher confidently translated as the Corvantine equivalent of a question mark.

'It's a long way,' Clay observed, wondering if he shouldn't have sketched a different route, one that led them to a settlement with a decent-sized port and ships available for charter. However, he was aware his uncle knew him far too well to allow for any deception. 'And, seems clear whoever drew this ran out of clues just short of the mountains.'

'But at least we have us a due date for arrival.' Braddon tapped a finger to the note scrawled alongside the question mark. Clay had copied it exactly as it appeared in Miss Lethridge's shared memory, finding it meaningless since he didn't know any Corvantine. His uncle, however, was apparently more learned. 'The tenth of Margasal,' he translated then glanced up at Preacher.

'Twenty-seventh Verester in the Mandinorian Calendar,' he supplied, adding after a pause, 'the date of the next alignment.'

'Alignment?' Clay asked.

'Visible in the southern hemisphere only once in every twenty years,' Preacher said. 'The three moons in alignment with the planets. The moons cause a total eclipse, allowing the planets to be viewed in daylight for only the briefest instant.'

'What's that got to do with the White?' Clay wondered.

'Breeding cycle, maybe,' Skaggerhill suggested. 'All the drakes breed at certain times of year. The Blues only spawn when the three moons are visible in the sky, f'r instance.'

'Ain't gonna know one way or the other till we get there,' Braddon said, rolling up the map and turning to Captain

Keelman. 'We make for the Falls. After that, it's on to Krystaline Lake.'

'**D**ammit, kiddo. Sit still, will ya?'
　　Clay stalled a reflexive jerk of his head and bit down on an unmanly whimper as Foxbine put another stitch in his ear. She had painted the wound with a few drops of Green, making it sting like the fires of the Travail, but that had been a picnic compared to this. 'How much longer?' he asked through gritted teeth.

'Sheesh, from all this wailing you'd think the damn thing had been torn away entirely.' He could hear the smile in her voice. 'Just a couple more. Try not to blub now, your lady-love's watching.'

They were on the *Firejack*'s fore-deck, Silverpin sitting near by and observing the gunhand's work with keen scrutiny. Loriabeth had also paused in her daily constitutional to partake of the scene. 'Really neat work, Foxy,' she said. 'Looks like Cuz won't have much've a scar to boast about.'

'The lower half of my ear was dangling,' he muttered.

'Trust you to be the only one to get scarred up.' She delivered a playful punch to his shoulder and sat down on a barrel, rubbing her leg. 'Got bad, huh?' she asked the gunhand.

Foxbine hesitated before replying, her casual tone sounding somewhat forced to Clay. 'Bad as I've seen it. Never had to take down so many at one time before, and there was plenty more lining up behind. Still.' Clay winced at another tug to his ear. 'Always glad to increase my count. Takes me up to over ninety now.'

'You've killed ninety Spoiled?' Clay asked.

'Ninety-two, to be exact. And before this expedition's done, I expect I'll make my century.' Her scissors gave a soft snick and she moved back from him. 'You're all done. Don't go picking at it now. The skipper ain't likely to spare us any more Green just to save your ear from dropping off due to infection.'

It was a six-day haul to the settlement of Fallsguard, Clay

noting Captain Keelman was now more inclined to set his Blood-blessed to firing the engine whenever possible. *Keen to off-load us,* he deduced, seeing the skipper's stern countenance whenever he had cause to speak to Clay's uncle. *Didn't sign on for this kind of trouble.*

Clay spent his days scanning the skies for the reappearance of the Black and its swaddled rider, without result. He did see a few solitary Reds prowling the banks and the plains for prey, and on one occasion a glimpse of the elusive river Green. It exploded from the waters of an inlet shadowed by a thick canopy of over-hanging trees, a flickering spectre of white and green, something dog-sized thrashing and screaming in its maw.

'Got himself an otter,' Skaggerhill observed as the drake dragged its prize below the surface. Clay saw its colour change as it passed beneath the *Firejack*'s hull, from white to greenish brown to match the river-bed. But for the still-struggling otter it would have been invisible.

'Remind me not to go for a swim,' he told the harvester, who bared his teeth in a grin.

'Seems young 'un's finally learning.'

At night Silverpin would lead him to one of several more private alcoves in the vessel's bowels. Behind the main boiler in the engine room seemed to be her favourite spot, possibly because the noise obscured the sounds she made in the midst of passion. For a woman who couldn't talk, she certainly knew how to give voice to certain sensations. The night before they were due to reach Fallsguard she proved particularly vocal, gasping out hard, ragged breaths as she straddled him, face close to his so their breath mingled.

Clay stroked a hand through her blonde locks as she relaxed against him. He always felt like he should say thank you at times like these. They lay on a pile of sacking in the shadow cast by the boiler. There was only one engineer on duty at night, an aged, bespectacled fellow who had yet to notice their regular visits, or failed to care if he had. The blood-burning engine was off, as it was only employed in the daylight hours, and the racket of the main power plant was something awful, obliging him to speak in fierce whispers close to her ear.

'Miss Lethridge says Islanders mate for life,' he said. 'That true?'

She raised herself up a little resting her chin on his chest. In the drifting steam and the yellow half-light cast by the engineer's lantern her tattoos seemed to dance as she raised an eyebrow.

'I mean to say,' he went on, 'are we . . . married now, or something?'

She raised both eyebrows.

'It's not like I mind. Just, nice to be asked is all.'

Her teeth flashed white for a second and she turned her head, slim, ink-covered shoulders shaking in amusement.

'Guess that's a no,' Clay muttered. He stroked her hair some more until her mirth subsided, then gently raised her face up. 'I never said thank you, for Keyvine.'

She shrugged, face expressionless. *Not important. Just a small favour to a colleague.*

He hesitated, unsure of the wisdom in voicing what he had to say next. Their intimacy had enhanced his ability to read her moods, but there were times when he sorely wished she could talk. 'You ever ponder the wisdom of all this?' he asked. 'Whether traipsing around the Interior looking for this thing is really the best idea?'

Her tattoos danced again as her brow creased into a frown.

'I know you care about my uncle,' he went on. 'But there's other means of earning a living. Other places we could be.'

Her frown deepened and she drew away from him, sitting up and turning her gaze to the floor.

'You saw that thing's lair,' he persisted, reaching for her. 'Whatever grew there wasn't just some dumb beast, it could *think*. And if it's still out there, what size d'you imagine it is now? And what's it gonna think of us?'

She stood up, reaching for her clothes and pulling on her shirt.

'We don't have to do this.' He moved to her, putting his hands on her shoulders, lips brushing her ear. 'Fallsguard offers a chance to get on another boat. And I have product . . .'

She stepped away, slipping from his hands and pulling on the rest of her clothes. Her gaze was guarded now, all intimacy abruptly vanished.

'I ain't gonna watch you die,' Clay said.

She strapped on her knife belt and paused, face tense but also a little regretful as she met his gaze and shook her head. Some measure of hurt must have shown on his features for she sighed and came close, pressing a kiss to his cheek before making for the exit.

Seer-dammit, he thought, hating a sudden grim realisation. *I can't leave her.*

It was midday when they heard it, a faint, irregular crackling echoing through the jungle, like many dry twigs being snapped all at once. The trees had begun to thicken in the last few days, scrub-land and marsh disappearing as the river narrowed and the current grew swift. The surrounding country had also steepened so that they were constantly overlooked by tall, densely forested hills. Clay found it ominous, the unbroken mass of the jungle canopy and the mist-shrouded peaks combining to convey a sense of being watched. His unease grew as the crackling increased in volume and rapidity, rising to a crescendo of sorts before subsiding to silence.

'That what I think it is?' he asked Foxbine.

'Gun-fire,' she confirmed, carbine in hand and eyes scanning the bank off the port rail. 'Sounds like somebody's had themselves quite the party.'

Fallsguard came into view as they rounded a bend, Clay surprised to find it a fortress rather than a town. Unlike Stockade or Edinsmouth it was constructed almost entirely from stone, perched atop a rocky outcrop that jutted into the river and connected to the bank by a narrow wooden jetty. It was a truly massive structure, the walls rising from a thickly buttressed base to a height of over a hundred feet, complete with crenellations and narrow slits just like in one of Joya's old books. Though the castles in those tales were usually all white walled with colourful pennants flying from minarets. There were no pennants here, the walls dark with long-accumulated grime and streaked with variously hued effluent. Presumably the inhabitants were content to cast their waste into the river in the safe knowledge it would soon carry it away and over the landmark from which the place derived its name.

The source of the gun-fire became clear as another barrage erupted, smoke pluming on the fort's east-facing wall. Clay tracked the direction of fire, drawing up in alarm at the target. They milled about at the edge of the tree-line, waving clubs, spears and bows, garbed more sparsely than those they had killed on the Sands. Spoiled bodies littered the ground between the trees and the bank with more lying still on the jetty, reaching a point halfway along and no farther.

'Get the sense we came at a bad time?' Clay asked his uncle.

The *Firejack* moored up on a narrow stone quay at the foot of Fallsguard's west-facing wall, Clay finding it significant that there were no other boats in attendance. They were greeted at the gangplank by a man in the uniform of a major in the Ironship Protectorate Infantry. From the thickness of his beard and the weariness in his gaze it appeared neither sleep nor ablutions had troubled him for some days.

'Thank the Seer!' he said, pumping Braddon's hand as he stepped onto the quay. 'Wasn't expecting you so soon.'

'Expecting us, sir?' Braddon asked.

'Our emergency trance communication,' the major said. 'Sent four days ago. I assume you were diverted here in response.'

Braddon shook his head and handed the officer an envelope bearing the seal of the Ironship Board. 'I'm afraid we're here on a different purpose.'

The major broke the seal and read through the letter, his soot-stained brow creasing. 'Render every assistance,' he muttered after a moment, voicing an appalled, humourless laugh as he read on. 'Provision of an escort?' He raised his weary gaze to Braddon. 'Allow me to show you something, Captain Torcreek.'

Once inside, Fallsguard transformed from fortress to town. There were taverns, shops and dwellings all arranged in successive tiers rising the height of the great building. Numerous walkways traced from one tier to another, sometimes intersecting to produce the impression of an inverted tree growing into itself. It was brightly lit with hundreds of lanterns hanging from the walkways, conveying a celebratory appearance at odds with the evidently subdued mood of the inhabitants. They seemed to be mostly old people and children, staring down at the new-comers with mingled hope and trepidation.

'Had to conscript all the able-bodied,' the major explained, striding towards a cage of some kind, heavy chains ascending from its roof through the criss-crossing walkways above. 'Got them manning the walls in shifts.' He opened the cage's door and stood aside, motioning for Braddon to get in.

'Preacher, Clay,' Braddon said. 'With me. The rest of you find a tavern. Don't get drunk.'

Once they were all in the major gave a hard yank on a lanyard, the wail of a steam-whistle sounding far above. After a few seconds' delay the cage began to rise swiftly, Clay clutching at the sides in barely concealed alarm as the castle's various tiers sped past in a blur.

'Counter-weights,' the major explained.

The cage came to a sudden jerking halt as it drew level with the topmost tier, two men reaching out to secure it in place. The major led them along a short corridor and out onto Fallsguard's upper battlements. There were about fifty people arranged along the parapet, some Contractors in evidence but the others mostly townsfolk, all armed with longrifles of varying makes and calibres.

'We're averaging two thousand rounds a day,' the major told Braddon, offering him a spy-glass and pointing to the edge of the jungle below. Clay followed his uncle to the parapet, peering down at the ground. The Spoiled seemed almost comical at this distance, capering about like two-legged ants. But there was nothing funny about the bodies, more than he had thought on the river. The largest mass lay in the space between the trees and the jetty, piled in three distinct clumps.

'How long?' Braddon asked the major, handing back the spy-glass.

'Two weeks now. Night and day.'

'Must be a thousand corpses down there.'

'More than that. We got most of them on the first night. They came out of the jungle in a wave, overrunning the outer pickets before we knew what was happening. Colonel Montfelt died leading the counter-attack, held them long enough to secure the jetty, though it cost us half our riflemen.'

'You have cannon?'

'Six guns, but we've expended half the canister and two-thirds of the shells. I'm husbanding the rest for their next charge. They try it at night, mostly.'

'Jungle Spoiled,' Braddon mused, resting his hands on the parapet. 'Never seen them in such numbers before. Usually they fight each other more than they fight us. In Stockade we heard talk of a headhunter company out of Rigger's Bay getting wiped out. Guess now we know why.'

He straightened and turned to Preacher, inclining his head at the Spoiled far below. 'Twenty rounds only. No steel tips.' The marksman nodded and began to unsheathe his rifle from its green-leather case.

'Consider it our mooring fee,' Braddon said to the major, putting a hand on his shoulder and steering him away from the wall, speaking quietly. 'I have every sympathy with your situation, sir. But you saw the orders, our mission is a Board priority and we need to get down to the lake.'

'I can't spare a single man.'

'I see that.' Clay saw his uncle force a smile, gripping the

Ironship officer's shoulder tight enough to make the man wince. 'But I'm sure you can spare a few cannon shells.'

They had a few hours to kill before Uncle Braddon's clever scheme kicked off, Clay opting to spend it in a tavern, contemplating a half-measure of ale in morose silence. Foxbine had gone to join Preacher aloft, no doubt keen to make her century before they left. Silverpin had gently disentangled her hand from Clay's then gone to help Loriabeth carry her gear from the *Firejack*. The steamer was already heavy with refugees, the decks crowded with old people and children awaiting safe passage back to civilisation. Most of the children were crying or staring at their former home in pale-faced shock, their parents being compelled by virtue of contract to stay and defend this valuable company installation. Captain Keelman had exchanged the briefest handshake with Braddon before turning and striding back up the gangplank, face set with a keen determination to be gone from this place and the dangers of this mission as soon as possible. The tavern had a narrow window in its stone wall that afforded a good view of the *Firejack* steaming away north, the Blood-blessed in the engine room clearly put to work once more from the steady progress she made against the current.

'Pardon me, young sir.'

Clay turned, finding himself confronted with a slightly built young man, only a few years his senior but with round spectacles and a stubbled chin that made him look older. From his complexion Clay judged him as a South Mandinorian, with an accent that told of managerial education if not lineage, though his less-than-edifying appearance bespoke considerable recent hardship. His jacket, well tailored though it was, had many small tears in the sleeves and could have benefited from a prolonged laundering. The man also had a green-leather bundle under his arm, filled with books from the shape of the bulge, and a long case over his shoulder, too bulky for a rifle sleeve.

Clay met the fellow's gaze, saying nothing and sipping some more ale.

'Orwinn Scriberson,' the young man introduced himself. 'Principal Field Astronomer to the Consolidated Research Company. At your service. Might I join you for a moment?'

Clay stared at him in silence, watching him fidget. He didn't seem any threat but Ellforth had left him wary of tavern encounters with strangers.

'Purchase you another ale, perhaps,' Scriberson went on valiantly. 'I feel there is a matter we could discuss, to our mutual advantage.'

'I have more than a half before nightfall, my uncle will shoot me,' Clay said, nodding at the seat opposite. 'But feel free to discuss away. Got shit all else to do right now.'

'You arrived this morning, did you not? With the Contractor company?'

'The Longrifles Independent Contractor Company. Going south in search of Black.'

'Quite so.' The young man gave a smile, earnest and hopeful to the point of desperation. 'And hence the crux of my enquiry. You see, I too wish to journey south in pursuit of a contractual obligation. Tell me, have you heard of the impending alignment?'

CHAPTER 21

Hilemore

'I'd take it for some kind of ornamentation, but for its size and position.' Mr Lemhill squinted suspiciously at the sketch Tottleborn had provided. 'Is he sure the dimensions are correct?' he enquired of Hilemore. 'Seem a little outlandish to me.'

'Mr Tottleborn lacks the imagination for exaggeration, sir,' Hilemore replied. 'Whatever this is, Protectorate Intelligence has confirmed it has been fitted to the underside of the INS *Regal*, the most powerful Corvantine vessel in Arradsian waters.'

'I'll send for Chief Bozware.' Lemhill moved to the speaking-tube. 'If anyone can tell us what the confounded thing is . . .'

'There's no need,' Captain Trumane interrupted. He stood at the ward-room's port-hole, hands clasped behind his back as he stared out at the sea. He had taken only a brief glance at the sketch, Hilemore noting how his recent good humour evaporated immediately. 'That, gentlemen, is a stolen treasure. A near-exact copy of the prototype proposed to the Sea Board by a good friend of mine near five years ago.'

'Sir?' Lemhill asked, plainly baffled.

'Professor Widdern's Patented Revolving System for Marine Propulsion,' the captain said. 'Or screw propeller for short.'

'I am to understand, sir,' Hilemore said, 'this device can push a ship through the water?'

'Indeed it can, at considerable velocity I might add. Professor Widdern's experiments indicated a twenty percent increase in speed, and that with a Mark One thermoplasmic engine. If the *Regal* boasts a modern power plant she could out-run even us.'

'If this device was proposed to the Sea Board . . .' Hilemore began then fell silent at the captain's grim countenance.

'The Board is comprised of old men clinging to old ways,' he said. 'Though to their credit they did purchase the professor's invention, then promptly locked it away and suppressed all publication of the designs. It appears the Cadre's agents have not been idle in the meantime.'

'If they've outfitted the *Regal* with this thing,' Lemhill said, 'it stands to reason they didn't stop there.'

'Indeed it does. We may well be facing an entire fleet capable of outpacing every other Protectorate vessel afloat.'

The silence heralded by this observation lasted several seconds, Lemhill and Hilemore exchanging a cautious glance as the import of the captain's words sank in. 'The vaunted commodore should have concentrated on Feros instead of the Strait,' the captain said, more to himself than them. 'Then we might have had a chance to gather enough strength to break through later. Still, orders are orders.'

He moved to the map spread out on the ward-room table, eyes narrowed in concentration. 'Mr Hilemore,' he said. 'Have Mr Tottleborn burn one full flask at first light. Once it's expended Chief Bozware is to squeeze every ounce of power from the auxiliary engine.' His finger tapped the cross pencilled onto a point fifty miles north of the Strait. 'With any luck we should make the rendezvous point within three days.'

'Very good, sir.'

'And the pirate settlement, sir?' Lemhill asked.

'It seems fate has conspired to grant them a reprieve,' the captain replied. 'We can afford neither the time nor the ammunition for a bombardment.' He paused in contemplation. 'Though we could hang the pirate woman. Leave the noose around her neck and rig the body with floats so it washes ashore. A fine warning, don't you think?'

'She was promised a trial, sir,' Hilemore said.

'Sea law provides for summary justice, in the right circumstances.'

'I gave my word, sir.'

A sudden sharpness in the captain's gaze told Hilemore his tone must have contained more force than he intended. 'Besides,' he added, 'I believe she may be willing to impart further intelligence on the activities of her associates. In return for preferential treatment for her daughter once we reach Feros.'

'A company orphanage will be more than the brat deserves,' the captain said, then gave a tired shake of his head. 'Very well, Mr Hilemore. Far be it from me to impugn your honour.'

'Thank you, sir.'

'We can allow no other indulgences, however.' The captain looked at both of them in turn. 'The men will be drilled in gunnery and combat every spare hour from now until we make the rendezvous. I suspect easy victories are now behind us.'

'What was that?' Hilemore enquired of Ensign Tollver, a lanky youth with the most refined accent on the ship. He straightened from his lunge, offering Hilemore a weak smile as he gave another swish of his sword.

'The Sylian Flourish, sir,' he said. 'My fencing master at school assured me it can blind and disable in a single lunge.'

'Your fencing master?'

'Yes, sir. Master Farstaff. He had studied the art of the sword all over the world . . .'

Tollver trailed off as Hilemore returned his own sword to its scabbard, unbuckled it and dropped it on the deck. He took up position a few feet in front of the ensign, standing with arms open. 'Show me again,' he said.

Tollver glanced uncertainly at the four other ensigns gathered for the morning practice. 'Sir?'

'I am your opponent,' Hilemore told him. 'Blind and disable me with the Sylian Flourish.'

The youth hesitated further then made a slow repeat of the move, the blade failing to come close to Hilemore's face. 'Again!' Hilemore commanded. 'Your best effort, if you please. Unless you'd like ten strokes of the scabbard before supper.' It was custom to punish ensigns by beating them across the buttocks with a scabbard as they bent over the mess-room table. The humiliation, as Hilemore knew to his cost, was far worse than the pain.

Tollver flushed and made another lunge, faster this time, the blade sweeping down before flicking at Hilemore's eyes. He ducked under it, caught hold of the ensign's wrist, dug his thumb in hard to force the sword from his grasp then twisted his arm behind his back.

'I am not teaching you to fence,' Hilemore told Tollver, wrapping his other arm around the youth's neck and steadily increasing the pressure. He turned about so they faced the other ensigns, now backed away in alarm. 'I am teaching you to fight,' Hilemore told them as Tollver gave a harsh, choking rasp. 'In the midst of battle you will have no time for flourishes or pirouettes or the perfect parry. Use your sword for what it is, a sharp implement designed to kill. Thrust and hack at the enemy's face and arms until he falls then find someone else to thrust and hack at. If your sword breaks, use the stump as a dagger. If you lose that, pick up a rifle or anything else to hand and use it as a club.'

He released Tollver, letting him collapse to the deck, gasping as he massaged his throat. 'Within days,' Hilemore continued, stepping past the choking ensign, 'we are likely to be in combat with the Corvantine fleet. You may consider yourselves seasoned by our recent engagement, but that was a mere scuffle compared to what we face next. The crew will be looking to you for an example of courage and leadership. Fail them and you fail this ship and the service.'

He looked down at Tollver, meeting the boy's gaze until he got to his feet, standing stiffly at attention. 'Draw revolvers and stand at the rail,' Hilemore ordered. 'We'll see if your marksmanship is any better than your sword-play.'

After ten minutes of their blazing away at the various jetsam he cast over the side he concluded their enthusiasm might compensate for a lack of expertise, though Talmant proved to possess a keen eye.

'Good,' Hilemore said as the ensign blasted another bottle to pieces from a distance of twenty yards. 'Teach you fire-arms at the Explorer's School did they?'

'Yes, sir. Pistol and rifle both.'

'We'll see what you can do with a Silworth tomorrow. Having another marksman to call on is always useful.' He turned towards the mid-deck as something caught his eye. Master-at-Arms Steelfine emerged from below clad in his full uniform and moving with stiff-backed deliberation as he saw Hilemore and saluted. 'Mr Talmant, you have the class. Another twenty-four rounds apiece, if you please.'

'Aye, sir.'

'I find it scarcely credible the doctor has released you,' Hilemore greeted Steelfine, returning his salute.

'Didn't give him much choice, sir,' the Islander replied. His face still bore numerous bruises along with a stitched cut on his slab-like forehead, but Hilemore was gratified to find that his voice had lost none of its vibrancy. 'Permission to return to duty, sir.'

Hilemore stopped himself asking after Steelfine's condition; he doubted the man had much room in his soul for such notions as uncertainty or the willing acknowledgment of weakness. 'Granted,' he said instead. 'I believe the armoury would benefit from a close inspection. With battle looming I'd like to be sure all small arms are in working order.'

'I'll see to it.' Steelfine hesitated a moment, staring straight ahead without meeting Hilemore's gaze. 'Honour requires I give you notice, sir.'

'Notice, Master-at-Arms?'

'Yes, sir. The pirate ship, that Blood-blessed bitch . . . I owe you a life.'

'Merely doing my duty, Mr Steelfine.'

'Such debts are not taken lightly amongst my people. From now until the debt is paid you will find me at your side.'

Hilemore saw no empty melodrama here. If anything Steelfine's expression was one of marked reluctance, his bearing that of a man forced into an unwanted obligation. He knew little of the Barrier Isles tribes but they were renowned as a people with scant understanding of such civilised notions as dishonesty or an empty promise. Also, he doubted he had much choice in accepting the Islander's commitment.

'Within a day or two,' he said, 'you may well get the chance.'

They sighted the first Protectorate ship a day later, a sleek if aged Marlin class frigate named the *Contractual Obligation*. Captain Trumane was obliged to reduce speed to one-half to allow the other vessel to cruise alongside as Ensign Talmant related the message conveyed via her signal lamp. 'Greetings from the *Obligation*'s skipper, sir,' he said. 'In accordance with standing battle orders he notifies you of his seniority and commission date, which reads as follows . . .'

'Yes, yes,' Trumane snapped. 'Presumably he has some orders for us.'

'We are to take up station five hundred yards off their port side and continue to the rendezvous in formation. Should we encounter the enemy we are to fire flares and await orders.'

Hilemore saw the captain's face flush red with poorly concealed anger, hearing him mutter, 'Time-serving tub-thumper,' before curtly telling Talmant to send an acknowledgment. They steamed westwards for another day, three more Ironship vessels joining their small flotilla before nightfall. Two were frigates like the *Contractual Obligation* and one a large supply ship lumbering along at a top speed of thirteen knots, obliging the other vessels to trim their speed in order to maintain formation.

'He should cast that laggard loose,' the captain said, training his glass on the supply ship. It was one of several criticisms he had voiced about their new commander in the preceding hours. 'Fat lot of good she'll be when the shells start flying.'

'Ships ahead, sir,' Talmant reported. 'Crow's nest counts twenty plus.' He hesitated, ear glued to the speaking-tube as his face betrayed a deep relief. 'All flying Ironship colours.'

Hilemore hadn't seen such a large gathering of warships since the Emergency, and even then the fleet hadn't featured so many heavy units. Four cruisers were in attendance, along with several Sea Wolf class light cruisers and Marlin class frigates. Sitting in the centre of the fleet was the dark bulk of the *Consolidation*, her pennants proclaiming Vice-Commodore Norworth as overall Fleet Commander.

'Signal from the *Consolidation*, sir,' Talmant said, reading the distant flicker of the cruiser's signal lamp. 'All captains to report for council of war by the tenth hour tomorrow.'

Hilemore heard the captain voice another mutter, 'More delay,' before adding a quotation he recognised as penned by an ancient scholar from the Old Imperial days, though the name escaped him, '"What a trial it is to submit to the whim of fools."'

Vice-Commodore Norworth was a barrel-chested man of South Mandinorian descent, his impressive array of battle honours forming a multi-coloured square on the broad canvas of his tunic. The other captains of the fleet stood around the table of the *Consolidation*'s cavernous ward-room to listen to his plan of battle. As was custom each was attended by a junior officer of his choosing and Trumane had surprised Hilemore by selecting him for the honour. 'If you're going to command one day I suppose you should witness a poor example as well as a fine one,' the captain offered by way of gruff explanation.

'Emergency trance communication from yesterday,' the commodore said, speaking in an accent only slightly more refined than Mr Lemhill's, 'confirms the Corvantine main battle fleet assembling off Corvus. The Sea Board has ordered the Protectorate High Seas Fleet to proceed to Feros with all dispatch. However, it will be at least two weeks before a major battleship arrives in Arradsian waters, meaning the prosecution of this war resides solely in our hands for the time being and it doesn't require a strategic genius to identify our enemy's primary objective.' He turned to the huge map covering the ward-room wall, slapping a hand to the Strait. 'Here, gentlemen, is where we find the enemy, and here is where we sink him.'

A general murmur of assent swept around the room, some captains clearly enlivened by the prospect of action as peacetime offered so few chances for prizes and advancement. 'We proceed south at twenty-one hundred hours,' the commodore went on. 'Standard battle formation, frigates in front, light cruisers guarding the flanks, main units in the centre. If the enemy is in possession of the Strait we will retake it. If they are not we will hold it against all attacks until relieved. Any questions?'

The silence lasted only two seconds before Captain Trumane stepped forward. 'If I may offer an observation, sir?'

The commodore's narrowed gaze and flaring nostrils told Hilemore much of what he thought of any observation Trumane might offer. However, it would be poor form to ignore him in front of so many witnesses. 'Of course,' Norworth grated.

'There are ten blood-burners in this fleet,' Trumane began, 'the *Viable Opportunity* being by far the fastest. If our objective is to secure the Strait then I suggest they be formed into a separate striking squadron and sent ahead of the main body.'

'A bold stratagem indeed.' Norworth raised his thick brows, apparently impressed. 'Remind me, Captain. How many actual commands have you held in your career?'

Hilemore saw Trumane stiffen a little. 'Two, sir. Though I would point out my battle honours . . .'

'Look about you, Mr Trumane.' The commodore gestured at the assembled captains. 'Battle honours abound in this room, as do observance of duty and sensible tactics. Sending our entire complement of blood-burners off on a mad charge into the Strait will avail us little.'

Trumane flushed but ploughed on. 'I am sure we are all by now familiar with the new propulsion devices fitted to the enemy's vessels. It is entirely possible they have already seized the Strait or are at least close to doing so.'

'One device,' Norworth pointed out, 'fitted to one ship.'

'As far as we know, sir. Thanks to certain decisions made by those senior to myself, the Corvantine Imperial Navy has had five years to improve their fleet whilst, with the notable exception of my ship, we have done little more than stagnate.'

The annoyance on the commodore's face transformed into a simmering anger and he stared at Trumane for several moments of taught silence. 'You there,' he said finally, Hilemore concealing a start as Norworth's gaze switched to him. 'Hilemore, isn't it? I pinned a medal on you after that Dalcian mess last year.'

'Yes, sir,' Hilemore said, snapping to attention.

'I served alongside your grandfather,' the commodore went on, returning his gaze to Trumane. 'Fighting Jak Racksmith, the finest battle commander in the Protectorate's history. What do you imagine he would make of your captain's daring scheme?'

Hilemore was tempted to offer only a short and non-committal reply, but as ever the tug of duty compelled him to speak his mind. 'My grandfather rarely spoke about his battles, sir,' he said. 'But once I asked him about his tactics at the Battle of Rigger's Bay, considered his greatest victory by many. He just said, "Bugger tactics, lad. Thinking is a luxury when the guns start up."' He met the commodore's gaze squarely. 'In short, sir, I believe he would counsel doing exactly what my captain has suggested.'

The captain waited until they were in the launch being rowed back to the *Viable* before giving full vent to his anger. 'Consigned to the rear by that half-brained dullard!' he fumed, tossing the envelope containing their orders into Hilemore's lap.

'The rear, sir?' Hilemore enquired, unfolding the orders and the diagram containing the formation the fleet was to adopt. The *Viable*'s original position as one of the lead vessels had been conspicuously crossed out and a new one scrawled just behind the lumbering supply vessel they had escorted to the rendezvous. He kept silent, knowing the blame for this particularly humiliating outcome lay as much with him as it did with Trumane. The captain, however, saw only one target for his ire.

'Opposed me at every turn,' he fumed. 'Opposed my promotion. Opposed my recommendations to the Board. Opposed the refit of this ship. It's hidebound relics like him that will bring us to ruin.'

'Sir,' Hilemore said, casting a meaningful glance at the crewmen manning the oars.

The captain mastered himself with an effort, face retaining a quiver as he tugged his tunic straight. 'In any case, your . . . honesty was courageous, and appreciated, Lieutenant. It won't be forgotten.'

Four more ships steamed to join the fleet before the allotted hour, swelling their force to thirty vessels of varying types, though none was as slow as their closest neighbour. The supply ship was named the *Mutual Advantage* and was clearly of civilian origins, broader across the beam than any of the other ships and her half-dozen guns perched on her deck like incongruous afterthoughts. Her crew seemed a cheerful lot, however, waving at the *Viable* as she steamed in their wake, possibly in mockery though Hilemore suspected it owed more to an enhanced sense of security at having a modern ship close at hand.

The tension grew thick the farther south they steamed, the crew taking on a grim aspect under the looming prospect of battle. Hilemore kept up a steady routine of drills throughout the day and much of the night, as much to occupy their minds as to enhance their efficiency. Despite his efforts and their evident tiredness as the watches switched over and they trooped below-decks to their bunks, he doubted any would sleep. He filled up the remaining hours before the Strait came into view by inspecting the armoury with Steelfine, finding every weapon in immaculate condition. The Islander had regained some vitality in the preceding days, possibly enlivened by the imminence of combat.

'Six years, sir,' he replied in answer to Hilemore's question as to how long it had been since his last engagement. 'Not counting the pirates of course.' He lifted another rifle from the rack and slid open the bolt for inspection of the mechanism, giving a sorrowful shake of his head. 'In the Isles such an interval would cause a man to call himself a coward and his wives and husbands to find one more worthy.'

Wives and husbands? Hilemore left the question unasked. It appeared Islander customs were even more bizarre than he imagined. 'Have you ever been back?' he asked instead, taking the rifle and inspecting the chamber before peering down the barrel. 'To your home island?'

Steelfine's gaze clouded and he accepted the rifle from Hilemore in silence, returning it to the rack and hefting another. For several moments it seemed he wouldn't give any answer but it appeared his continuing sense of obligation to Hilemore compelled some form of response, albeit softly spoken. 'A dead man has no home.'

In the early hours Hilemore roused Tottleborn from his cabin, finding it neater than before, the man's extensive collection of tawdry reading matter now stacked in an orderly pile and no sign of a bottle anywhere.

'Four?' Tottleborn asked around a yawn, eyeing the flasks in Hilemore's hands.

'Half our remaining supply,' he said. 'Captain's orders. Action is imminent, after all. I shall require you . . .'

'To stay in the engine room for the duration of the coming unpleasantness.' Tottleborn reached for his shirt. 'Rest assured, Mr Hilemore, I've no intention of showing my head above decks until the last echo of gun-fire has faded.'

With the Blood-blessed safely ensconced in the engine room, Hilemore proceeded to the bridge, finding the captain already in attendance. 'Morning, Lieutenant,' he said, his previous fury apparently cured by the advent of a new day.

'Good morning, sir.' Hilemore saluted. 'Mr Tottleborn is at his station and Chief Bozware reports all mechanicals in working order.'

'Excellent.' Trumane gestured at the spectacle of the fleet beyond the window, all steaming south with paddles churning and smoke rising from their stacks, streaming away swiftly thanks to the stiff northerly breeze. 'At least we'll have a decent view of the unfolding debacle, eh?'

'Quite so, sir,' Hilemore replied, divining that the captain's improved mood could well have arisen from the prospect of witnessing Commodore Norworth's plan come a cropper. So it was with scant surprise that he watched Trumane's visage darken some four hours later when Talmant related a signal from the *Consolidation*. 'Advance units report Strait clear of enemy vessels. All ships to proceed to allocated stations. Enemy action remains imminent.'

'Blind luck,' the captain sniffed, then sighed as he addressed the helmsman. 'Steer south-south-east. Ensign Talmant, relay the message to Mr Lemhill if you will. Lieutenant, relevant entry to the log.'

'Aye, sir.'

Hilemore had just finished scribbling the course change into the log when another signal came from the crow's nest. 'Enemy vessels in sight, sir.' Talmant's voice was calm though his face betrayed a sudden loss of colour Hilemore found worrisome.

'That was quick,' Trumane observed with some satisfaction, raising his glass to peer at the southern horizon. 'Beat them here by the barest margin. As I said, just luck.'

'Beg pardon, sir,' Talmant went on, a palpable quiver now creeping into his tone. 'The enemy approaches from the north, and in numbers. Estimate of forty-plus vessels, all men-of-war and flying Corvantine colours.'

'Seer's-teeth!'

Hilemore followed the captain as he rushed from the bridge, glass now trained on the north. Even without benefit of an optic

Hilemore could see them already, smoke rising from small black lumps on the horizon, growing in number by the second.

'Fire flares!' the captain barked, Hilemore hurrying back inside to jerk the lever that launched their signal rockets. They streamed into the sky a second later, screaming then exploding in a thunderous cacophony. He then gave three successive heaves on the steam-whistle's lanyard, the crew running to battle stations in response. He had a glimpse of Mr Lemhill through the bridge window, hounding his crews to their guns, before Trumane ducked his head into the doorway, barking more orders.

'Reverse propulsion on the starboard wheel, bring us about. Ensign, signal the *Mutual Advantage:* Enemy approaching in large numbers from the north. Relay to flagship. Am engaging.'

One of the advantages offered by a paddle-driven ship was the ability to turn, as Hilemore's grandfather had put it, on a copper scrip. Within two minutes the *Viable* had reversed course and was steaming north, Trumane ordering three vials into the engine. 'They're moving too fast,' he said, voice soft as he continued to observe the approaching enemy fleet. 'Some don't even have paddles. We face the future today, and it's likely to kill us.'

Behind them the sea was filled with a discordant symphony of shrieking whistles and exploding rockets as the fleet reacted to the *Viable*'s signal. The *Mutual Advantage* wallowed as she came about, wheels turning the sea white and her crew scurrying to and fro with what seemed to Hilemore a singular lack of proper direction. Off to port the *Contractual Obligation* moved with much greater purpose, making her turn with almost as much alacrity as the *Viable* though her comparative lack of speed soon saw her falling behind.

'Waited until we entered the Strait,' the captain was saying. 'They must have cleared it at least a day ahead of us then turned about.' He met Hilemore's gaze, raising his voice. 'It appears we have the misfortune not to be facing a foolish admiral today, Mr Hilemore.'

Hilemore replied with a grim smile. 'Indeed it does, sir.'

'Still.' Trumane rested an affectionate hand on the bulkhead. 'At least they won't be expecting *us*. See if we can't throw a wrench in their works, eh?'

Hilemore's reply was drowned out by the familiar, grating roar of something very large passing overhead. His gaze snapped to a tell-tale flash rising from one of the approaching ships as another shell was fired. He had time to watch the first plunge into the sea just to port of the *Mutual Advantage*'s bow, the resultant spout rising a good sixty feet into the air, before the second slammed into the supply ship's stern. Lacking armour, the hit was instantly ruinous, the shell penetrating all the way to the lower decks before exploding, ripping her apart from bridge to rudder. Men and bits of men were visible amidst the falling debris. Within less than a minute she had foundered, the sea flooding into her shattered hull to claim her for the Deep. The bow swung high as she went down, Hilemore glimpsing a knot of men clinging to the forward anchor mounting before she slipped beneath the swell.

'This,' Captain Trumane observed, turning away and lifting the glass to his eye once more, 'is going to be a very trying day.'

CHAPTER 22

Lizanne

It was five days before they were ready to move. The major's wounds were so severe that, despite Lizanne expending two-thirds of their remaining Green in repeated doses, two days went by before he was able to walk, and even then only due to urgent necessity. The Morsvale constabulary had made numerous sweeps of the park but, thanks to either basic indolence or lack of imagination, had failed to search the oracular temple. Near the evening of their second day in hiding, however, it appeared they had decided, or more likely been ordered, to be more thorough. Fortunately, Lizanne had not been idle in the interim. A thorough inspection of the temple revealed a subterranean chamber complete with a marble font and bench, presumably reserved for the oracle's private meditations. Her decision to enhance her search with a modicum of Green paid dividends when the unnatural perception detected a false wall in the chamber, behind which she discovered a cache of dusty scrolls. *The Oracular Scriptures*, she decided, thinking Tekela's father would have made much of such a discovery. *Hidden away from the fires of persecution.*

The space was small but, once she had removed the scrolls, of sufficient dimensions to accommodate both her and her companions. They had huddled together in the dark as the constables searched the temple, forced into intimate entanglement by the confines. If the major felt any arousal at finding himself in such close proximity to two young women, it was well hidden behind a pale, sweat-covered mask of pain. He lay deepest in the space, pressed up against the far wall with arms braced and teeth gritted to guard against any gasps or grunts of discomfort. Lizanne assumed he knew she had the Whisper in hand beneath her skirt, ready to silence him should it become necessary. Tekela, by contrast, threatened no revealing sound or fidgeting, lying curled about Lizanne in relaxed quietude, like a kitten cuddling up to its mother.

It occurred to Lizanne that, had she followed her first impulse that night in Burgrave's study, it would have been the first time she had taken an innocent life. There had been a few over the years less deserving of their fate than others, but none whose demise hadn't improved the world in some small way. Tekela was certainly spiteful, selfish and spoiled, but also still curiously innocent in many ways. Lizanne had never had much truck with notions of ingrained female maternalism, but she had to admit that sparing the girl had engendered a protective instinct, or at least a desire not to see so much effort wasted.

The constables had stomped around for a good two hours, their progress through the temple marked by the crash of upturned pews or the thud of tumbled marble as they vented their boredom on the temple's statuary. Booted feet had echoed in the chamber for only a short time, two searchers by Lizanne's estimation, exchanging grunted profanity as they kicked the walls, either too ignorant or indifferent to catch the slight change in pitch as their boots found the false panel. After the boots had faded Lizanne insisted on a prolonged wait before they emerged.

'What did you do with the scrolls?' Arberus asked a short while later. It was evening and he sat with a blanket wrapped about him, shivering a little as they could not risk a fire.

'Ripped into the smallest pieces Tekela and I could manage,' she replied. 'Then scattered about amongst the dust piles. Anyone seeing them might have wondered where they could have been stored.'

'Historical treasures, lost forever. Leonis would have wept.' She detected no real regret in his voice; if anything he seemed to find the scrolls' fate amusing.

She glanced over at the staircase to the spire where Tekela kept watch with a revolver in hand. 'He certainly was a scholarly man,' she agreed, keeping her voice low. She didn't want the girl hearing any discussion of her father. 'For a spy.'

'He was scholar and spy both,' Arberus replied. 'Though he would have called himself an agent of change.'

'So which is it?' she enquired. 'Corvantine Liberation Army? Republic First? Co-respondent Brotherhood?' She saw his gaze betray a slight flicker at that. 'So, the most radical of the bunch.'

'I expect the notions of personal freedom and representative government would appear radical to a slave of the corporate world.'

'A slave receives no compensation for their labour, whereas I find myself fairly wealthy despite my youth. Besides, the pursuit of profit can be quite liberating, whilst ideologues often find themselves enslaved by their dogma.'

'Tired corporatist rhetoric.' He shook his head in mock sorrow. 'I had expected better of you. You are, I assume, operating far beyond your mission remit? If you weren't, the girl and I would be dead by now. Unusual for a corporate operative to display such compassion.'

'I had an agreement with Miss Artonin. My employers and I take such things seriously.'

'What will become of her?'

'In her father's absence it appears the role of guardian falls to me. She will be well provided for.' *I am wealthy after all.* 'As for you' – she gave a reluctant smile – 'I am compelled to arrange my own extraction, events having developed at such a pace. No doubt you and your associates have resources which will prove useful.'

'For all I know every Brotherhood agent in this city is dead or undergoing torture as we speak.'

'No, they are not. Burgrave Artonin engineered his own demise to prevent such an outcome, and Tekela tells me they hadn't yet wrung any information from you. Impressive endurance, by the way.'

He looked away, face clouding at the resulting memory. 'Your offer?' he asked after a moment.

'Residence in an Ironship holding of your choice, plus a reasonable financial settlement.'

'I don't care to live in your world of greed and self-interest, nor do I give a damn about your money.'

'Your alternatives do not appear particularly appealing at this juncture.'

He thought for a moment longer, eyes meeting hers in steady determination. 'The interests of the Brotherhood and your employers seem to coincide at the moment, war being imminent after all.'

'Your point?'

'Assisting us will assist you. Increased discord in the Emperor's homeland will hardly help win his war. With sufficient arms, and funds, there is much we could achieve.'

'I can promise no such aid. However, I will guarantee a meeting with the appropriate Ironship officials. But, trust is only earned through reciprocation and you have information I need regarding the Burgrave's scholarly pursuits. I believe you had occasion to explore the Interior together?'

He raised a knowing eyebrow. 'Servants are such great resources, aren't they? Did any of them live, by the way?'

'No.' She fell silent, holding his gaze in expectation.

'So,' he said, a fresh realisation creeping into his voice, 'that's your mission. The grand, endless quest for the enigma lurking somewhere in this continent. I had assumed you were sent to ascertain the Emperor's intent in sending Morradin here.'

'A fruitful adjunct, as it transpired.'

He sighed the smallest laugh then shrugged. 'Every summer for the past five years we would charter a boat and go off downriver in pursuit of his latest clue, rewarded, if we were lucky, with a ruin or two. Last year though . . .' He trailed off, his gaze becoming distant, brow furrowed in consideration of a troublesome memory.

'What?' she prompted.

'One of the Mad Artisan's scrawlings told of a place, the Spearpoint Isle, he called it. Much of his description was gibberish, but one phrase kept repeating: "The Place of Offering to the Provider." Leonis believed it to be a translation of hieroglyphs found on the island, despite the fact that no scholar has ever succeeded in translating the inscriptions left by Arradsia's ancient inhabitants.'

'You found it?'

'There's an island in the middle of the Volkarin River, where it widens about two hundred miles south-west of Morsvale. It's a narrow oval of jungle a few hundred yards long now, but Leonis thought it must once have been much larger, its mass eroded by the river's current over the ages. The jungle was so thick we spent days hacking through it until we came to the rocky core of the island, a solid slab of granite overgrown with vines, but beneath them we could see carvings in the stone, pictograms and hiero-glyphs, clearly ancient from the wear of them. It seemed as if every inch of the rock had been carved and etched over the course of what must have been a century or more. There didn't seem to be anything else to find there, no artifacts, certainly no clue as to the possible existence of the great enigma, but then we climbed it.'

The creases on his brow deepened as he summoned uncom-fortable memories. 'The stone, it transpired, was hollow. A great circular opening had been hewn into its crest and continued down to such a depth the bottom was lost to the gloom. We dropped a torch in and it fell at least a hundred feet, revealing what could only be a pile of bones. After that there was no holding Leonis, he had to investigate and I had little choice but to follow.

'We had our bearers rig ropes to lower us down. It was an . . . unnerving experience I must say, like descending through a place of nothingness, a void that might swallow a man whole. It was something of a relief when my boots finally touched rock, but the relief didn't last long. The bones we had seen from above were arranged into some kind of stack, or rather a sculpture. Skulls, arms and legs all fused together by means unknown, so many it stood taller than I am. At first I took the bones for human but soon realised they were Spoiled from the many deformities. There must have been thirty or more of them all twisted into that horrid monument, and they weren't alone. We lit more torches, scattering them about and the full scale of the cavern was revealed, extending away on all sides, the walls unseen beyond the glow, and everywhere there were more of these hideous sculptures. They stood in rows extending from a central pit, a perfect circle carved into the rock about sixty feet in diameter, ten feet deep . . . and it was stained to the point of near blackness.

'Leonis told me a curious fact about blood. It seems that, over time and in sufficient quantities, it will stain rock, seeping into the pores of the stone so deeply that no amount of rain or wind will wash it away. And there was no rain or wind in that cavern. An ocean of blood had been spilled in that pit, and whatever spilled it had made play with its victims.'

'The Provider,' Lizanne said.

'Yes. A curious choice of translation, wouldn't you say? But they didn't name him the Mad Artisan for nothing.'

'Did you find anything else?'

'Only more bones. We counted over two hundred stacks before the dwindling torch-light forced us back. There were no artifacts that we saw, no revealing pictograms, just a place of wanton slaughter and mystifying art. Leonis made copious notes, of course, passing it on to his circle of scholars on return to Morsvale. There were a dozen of them, learned men and women like Diran, all duped into assisting the Brotherhood under the guise of scholarly curiosity.' His face tensed in a spasm of poorly controlled guilt and he pulled his blanket tighter around his shoulders. 'I dare say the Cadre is busy interrogating them all as we speak.'

'I assume the Burgrave intended to return to the island?'

'Yes, armed with the results of Diran's labours. It was to be our most ambitious expedition to date. Who knows where it might have led us.'

Hopefully the same destination as Mr Torcreek's merry band, she thought. 'It's time we discussed extraction,' she said. 'I find it hard to believe the Brotherhood didn't have a contingency for a circumstance such as this.'

'There is someone we could approach. Someone with a ship, of sorts.'

'A member of the Brotherhood?'

He shook his head. 'A vile, self-serving rogue whose one redeeming feature is a refusal to welch on a debt.' A faint grin played over his lips. 'I think you and he will get on famously.'

Contact and sometimes collusion with the criminal element is one of the more distasteful tasks undertaken by a field operative, Lizanne recalled reading in a Division training manual. *But it will often become necessary in order to complete a given objective. Studies commissioned from the Customer Demographics Faculty of the Ironship University consistently demonstrate that the criminal element in any coastal city will invariably be concentrated in and around the port facilities.*

Morsvale's dock-side district wasn't quite as irredeemable a slum as the Blinds, but it was close. The houses were mostly wood rather than stone and the streets narrow and winding. It was in many ways a mirror to the vast, unpoliced and poverty-wracked districts of Corvus and the other Corvantine cities she had seen, and equally noisy at all hours. Drunken revelry sounded from many a tavern, angry or inebriated voices blasted from open windows and here and there rose the shouts and running feet of fight or theft. Lizanne noted how Tekela stared about with wide eyes, arms crossed and one hand on the revolver beneath her jacket. She had come close to drawing it once already when an amorous drunk lurched out of an alley, slurring an enquiry over the price for the young one to Arberus. A vicious shove from the major had been enough to send him on his way, muttering curses as he staggered off.

A few other shadowy predators had dogged their progress for

a while, but Arberus's size seemed to be sufficient to keep them at bay. Eventually they came to a tavern where he paused. Unlike every other drinking den they had passed this one was quiet, the sign hanging above the door faded to unreadability and a dim glow visible through the dirt-covered window. Arberus turned to Lizanne, gaze intent and tone entirely serious. 'Say nothing. He'll only listen to me in any case, and his people don't react well to opinionated women.'

With that he pushed the door open on squealing hinges and went inside. The reason for the tavern's comparative quietude became obvious as Lizanne followed the major into an empty room. A single unoccupied table with four chairs was positioned near the door with a small lantern suspended above it. Beyond the table a bar could be made out amidst the shadowed interior. It was only when something large and bulky shifted in the shadows that Lizanne realised they weren't completely alone. Arberus went to the bar as the bulky shape moved into the light, a hulking, shaven-headed man resting two meaty arms on the bar and staring at them in naked suspicion. Lizanne made note of his light bronze complexion and high cheekbones. *Dalcian.*

Arberus gave no greeting to the man, simply saying the words, 'Varestian brandy,' before turning and moving to the table. He sat down and gestured for Lizanne and Tekela to follow suit. Lizanne guided the girl to a chair beside the major and took the one opposite, angling it so as to maintain a good view of both door and bar.

They waited, Lizanne finding it significant that no brandy was forthcoming in the interval. Finally, after ten minutes or more, as Tekela grew visibly more agitated and Lizanne had been obliged to place a calming hand on her forearm, a man came striding out of the shadows. He moved to the table and sat down without a word, casting his gaze at each of them in turn, flame pluming from a match as he lit a cigarillo. He wore sailor's garb, sturdy boots and canvas trousers with a plain cotton shirt, leather brace-lets on his wrists and both ears pierced with several rings. Like the hulking bartender, he was Dalcian, though considerably smaller in size. In fact, in terms of height he was barely taller than Lizanne, but the lean muscle of his forearms and chest revealed by his half-open shirt bespoke an individual of considerable physical strength. Also, the earrings, Lizanne knew, signified mastery in several of the martial arts for which the Dalcians were famed.

'You're not dead,' he observed to Arberus in perfect Eutherian, giving a complimentary incline of his head.

'Neither are you,' the major returned in a neutral tone.

The man revealed white teeth in a smile. 'The Cadre isn't after me.' He gave a small laugh when Arberus didn't respond, blowing smoke up at the lantern. 'Word flies quickly, my friend. You're worth five thousand crowns at the last count.' His gaze swept over Lizanne and Tekela. 'These two considerably more.'

We can pay triple that amount, Lizanne wanted to say, but kept silent. She knew well the truth of Arberus's words; Dalcian men had a marked aversion to doing business with women. Adherence to their patriarchal customs was a matter of near-religious zeal.

'And you, my friend,' Arberus said. 'What is your life worth?'

The humour faded from the Dalcian's face, the tip of his cigarillo glowing as he took a deep draw. 'My youngest brother said I should kill myself,' he reflected after a lengthy pause. 'The debt I owe you being so great. "One day it will dishonour the entire clan," he said. "Your death will wash it away." He even offered to do it himself. His funeral was more expensive than I would have liked, but I was fond of him. He did speak a lot of sense, after all.'

Arberus said nothing and the Dalcian crushed his cigarillo onto the table, finger smearing the embers into ash as he asked, 'Where?' in a tone of dull acceptance.

'Carvenport,' Arberus said. 'Or as close to it as you can get without running afoul of the Corvantine fleet.'

The Dalcian gave the slightest of nods. 'Tomorrow. Earliest

tide. There's a room upstairs. Food will be brought to you.' He got up and walked back into the shadows without another word.

'What did you do for him?' Lizanne asked Arberus in a low voice.

'I killed his father.' He got to his feet, bowing and gesturing at the tavern's interior. 'Ladies, shall we?'

The steamer was little larger than a tug-boat, equipped with a single rear paddle and one thin stack rising behind the wheel-house. Her paint-work was old and peeling and the stack blackened with years of accumulated soot. Barely legible Eutherian painted on the prow proclaimed her the *Wave Dancer*, though to Lizanne's eyes she seemed capable of no more than a stumbling jig.

'Appearances deceive,' Arberus murmured to Lizanne, seeing her sceptical frown. 'Those in Kaden's profession know well the value of disguise. She's a sturdy boat and quick into the bargain.'

Kaden stood on the fore-deck, muscular arms crossed and face impassive as they came aboard. Night had yet to fully fade and the becalmed harbour waters were a mirror to the dock-side lamps. There were no warships at anchor now, Lizanne saw, only a scattering of Independent freighters and patrol boats. Somewhere, she knew, the Corvantine fleet would be battling the Protectorate for control of the Strait. She could only hope it meant they had no vessels to spare for antismuggling patrols.

At Kaden's terse command a pair of crewmen led them to the hold, pulling up some planking on the keel to reveal a hiding-place. Tekela couldn't contain a whimper at the sight of a black rat swimming through the bilge-water. 'We have no choice,' Lizanne said. 'They'll be searching every vessel leaving port.'

The crewman tossed a canteen of water to the major before slotting the planks back in place, the meagre light streaming through the gaps soon extinguished as they hauled crates to fully conceal the hiding-place. There was sufficient room to sit but not enough to move more than an inch or two. Once again Tekela curled herself against Lizanne's side, stifling a gasp as a rat came sniffing about their feet. Lizanne sent it scurrying with a swift kick.

'Sorry,' the girl whispered, clearly fighting a sob. 'Make a poor spy, don't I?'

Lizanne grinned in the darkness. 'You're doing well enough.'

The engine started up an hour later, its clanking soon accompanied by the rhythmic swish of the paddle as they got underway. Lizanne abandoned all attempts at keeping any vestige of her clothes dry as the bilge-water shifted with the boat's movements. They came to a halt a few moments later, a commanding whistle sounding through the bulkhead followed by a muted shout. 'Heave to for inspection!'

Lizanne took hold of the Whisper as multiple boots drummed on the decks above. She gently disentangled herself from Tekela and pressed the middle finger button on the Spider to inject a drop of Green, her boosted hearing soon revealing every word spoken above. 'You didn't used to be so greedy,' Kaden was saying in Varsal.

'There's a war on,' came a gruff reply. 'You see this place? Trade's halved in two days.'

'Keep demanding this much and it'll halve again. I'd hate to have to advise my clan to avoid Morsvale in future.'

'Don't threaten me, slit-eye.' A tense silence, then a grudging, 'Twelve hundred, and that'll cover you for the return trip. And I want two boxes of cigars this time.'

'Fairly spoken, Captain.'

Despite the agreement the search continued, presumably so the corrupt captain could make a show of a thorough inspection. After a few more minutes, however, the thunder of boots receded and the shifting bilge-water and increased engine noise indicated they had moved on towards the harbour mouth. Tekela tensed as a rumbling squeal resounded through the hull like the death agonies of some great sea-beast.

'It's just the door,' Lizanne whispered to her. 'We'll be at sea soon then we can get out of here.'

Some two hours later, as they still huddled in the stinking wetness, Lizanne felt justified in giving Arberus an impatient jab with her toe. 'I said he owed me,' he responded in a resigned tone. 'I didn't say he liked me.'

'Couldn't take a chance we might happen upon a patrol boat,' Kaden explained some four hours later. Lizanne couldn't detect any particular contrition in the smuggler's voice; if anything the faint twitch of his lips as he looked Arberus up and down told of a malicious enjoyment of their discomfort. Come midday they had been released, in a state of chilled bedragglement, from the hiding-place and allowed to take a turn about the deck. The *Wave Dancer* cruised towards the east keeping within a mile of the coast, chugging along at a decent clip which confirmed the major's claims about her misleading appearance. The north Arradsian shore-line was rich in inlets and coves, perfect refuges for the various smuggling conglomerates keen to take advantage of the disparity in duties between Imperial and Corporate holdings.

Tekela leaned on the rail, gripping it tight, her face raised to breathe deeply of the fresh sea air. 'Only been to sea once before,' she said. 'Father took me on a short cruise once, when I was still very young. A storm blew up and I got so scared he told me a story to calm my fears.' She lowered her gaze to the passing waves, a catch creeping into her voice. 'About the King of the Deep.'

'"The Third Daughter's Marriage,"' Lizanne said. 'An old Selvurin tale. Here.' She opened her pack and extracted a small book, handing it to Tekela. 'I think he would want you to have this.'

'I don't know this language,' Tekela said, fingers tracing over the embossed letters on the cover.

'Vizian's Fables,' Lizanne told her. 'A compilation of Selvurin folk-tales. The story he told you came from this.'

'You took this from his library?'

'I didn't steal it. He gave it to me to help with his translation.'

'You speak Selvurin?'

'It's one of six languages I can speak fluently. I can get by in five others well enough for basic communication. The Blue-trance makes learning such things easier. Understanding is enhanced by shared thoughts.'

Tekela sighed and shook her head. 'You know so much. Whilst I can do little but pick out a dress.'

'There are few skills that can't be learned. If you want to read the book I can teach you.'

Tekela consigned the book to the inside pocket of her jacket, her hand then moving to the butt of the revolver tucked into her belt. 'There's something else I'd rather learn first.'

'All in good time.' Lizanne cast a glance up at the sky, finding the clouds thickening and feeling an edge to the wind. 'We'd best get below. I believe it's about to rain.'

The next two days were spent in the hold with only brief excursions above deck. They were brought meals and water at regular intervals but otherwise the crew mostly ignored them, bar the occasional lustful glance at Lizanne or Tekela. Whatever dark deeds might cloud their thoughts, however, it seemed the crew's fear of their captain was enough to keep them in check. She noted their obedience to him was absolute, rarely speaking in his presence except to acknowledge an order, and always with a respectful bob of the head.

'A clan-leader is close to being a king in Dalcian society,' Arberus explained. 'There are several thousand people who owe him fealty.'

'Then why doesn't he live in a palace instead of this dingy crate?' Tekela asked.

'His family have been smugglers for generations. If Kaden didn't smuggle they would lose respect for him. It's what his clan does, and not just here. The Jade Tigers have affiliates all over the world.' He gave Lizanne an apologetic smile. 'He's probably even richer than you, miss.'

'Wealth only has meaning if it is either enjoyed or invested,' she returned. 'A miser is merely a pauper with fewer friends.'

'Misquoting Bidrosin at me, now.' He gave Tekela a warning glance. 'Don't let this one fill your head with corporatist notions, my dear. Your father . . .'

'Is dead,' Tekela cut in, 'All his books and his plotting couldn't save him, or you for that matter.' She nodded at Lizanne. 'But she did.'

'You think this woman is a hero of some kind? Ask her how many people she's killed for her corporate masters. For *money*, Tekela.'

'As opposed to killing for redundant ideology,' Lizanne said. 'Your empire's history is a thousand-year epic of war, revolution, genocide and corruption, much of it committed in the last hundred years thanks to Bidrosin and her ilk. Since the advent of the Corporate Age there has been nothing like that in any of our holdings. People are fed, educated and employed.'

'A happy slave is still a slave. And if the corporate world is such a paradise, why do they need people like you?'

'Because of people like you . . .'

She trailed off at a sudden sound from above, a faint crump followed by a whining groan and a booming splash.

'Cannon-shot,' Arberus said, getting to his feet and running for the ladder. Lizanne paused to strap on the Spider and pull the pack over her shoulders before following, telling Tekela to stay close. The *Wave Dancer* tilted as she climbed up on deck, the boat's prow swinging southwards as Kaden barked out orders. She joined Arberus at the rail where he stood staring at something to the north. 'Patrol boat?' she asked.

'Frigate,' he said, shielding his eyes against the sun. 'One of the new ones, sadly. I suspect the Cadre tranced an order to the fleet to send her to intercept us. One of their dock-side informants must have made note of Kaden's departure.'

The ship was perhaps three-quarters of a mile off, the sea white around her bows as she cut through the waves faster than any vessel Lizanne had seen. She was narrow across the beam with a sleek, angular appearance enhanced by the absence of paddles.

'Twenty knots?' she guessed, her mind returning to the device she had seen fixed to the *Regal*'s hull.

'Closer to twenty-five,' the major said. 'Oh, the wonders of technology.'

A flash appeared on the frigate's bow, followed seconds later by the faint report of a cannon and the grating screech of an approaching shell. The *Wave Dancer* heaved to starboard, the suddenness of the change in course throwing Lizanne and Arberus off their feet. The shell came down less than twenty yards to port, raising enough water to deluge the deck in a brief rain-storm.

'Those weren't warning shots,' Arberus said, rising and shaking the water from his hair. 'It appears they've given up trying to capture us.'

Lizanne turned her gaze to the south, seeing the shore less than half a mile distant now as the *Wave Dancer* piled on more steam. She could see the narrow inlet Kaden was aiming for and knew it offered only a slim chance of refuge as the confines would make them a sitting duck for the frigate's gunners. She rushed to the wheel-house, finding Kaden at the tiller, eyes fixed on the inlet.

'Keep straight,' she told him in Dalcian. 'No more weaving. We need to maintain a steady course.'

The look he turned on her was part fury and part disdain. Even in this extremity it appeared his people's arcane customs held sway. 'Women are forbidden the voice of command!' he grated.

'Steady your course.' She injected a burst of Red and heated the air between them, taking satisfaction from the alarmed surprise in his gaze. 'Or I'll dispense with your services and have the major do it.'

He glared at her in a moment of helpless rage then swung the tiller to midships, training the bows on the inlet. 'They're too fast,' he said, voice quivering. 'Soon their gunners won't miss.'

'Just maintain the course,' she told him and went outside.

She climbed onto the wheel-house roof, grimacing amidst the smoke billowing from the stack and injecting both Green and Black, half a vial of each; enough to make her stagger a little. She gritted her teeth against the disorientation and locked eyes onto the fast-approaching frigate, awaiting the next flash from her cannon. She had read of this being done, but only in history books pertaining to the age of sail when guns cast balls slow enough to track their flight with the naked eye. Modern guns fired at a much higher velocity, but with the Green she might have a chance.

The frigate was perhaps five hundred yards off now, close enough to see the vague shapes of the gunners servicing the long-barrelled gun on her fore-deck. It fired a second later, Lizanne's altered vision perceiving the shell as a streak of white against a dark blue sky. She waited until it was at the apex of its arc then unleashed the Black as it began a downward plummet. She had intended to divert it but the wave of force she released was enough to trigger its percussion fuse, transforming it into a black cloud of combusted explosive that peppered the sea with a hail of shrapnel.

Focus, she told herself, a statue-like stillness gripping her as she concentrated all attention on the frigate. She was close enough now to make out the individual forms of the gunners, scurrying to haul another shell into the breech. The next shot was fired at a lower trajectory from a distance of just over three hundred yards. She unleashed all her remaining Black a split-second after it was launched. This time it failed to explode in mid air, the force wave throwing it wide and disturbing its flight sufficiently to make it tumble in the air before ploughing into the sea twenty yards to port. The power and proximity of the explosion sent a shuddering tremor through the *Wave Dancer*, throwing Lizanne onto her back.

Lizanne lay on the wheel-house roof, chest heaving and vision dimming as the Green faded. Exhaustion was the inevitable price for expending so much product in such a short space of time. A brief glance at the shore-line told her they were almost there, the jungle rising on both sides, but they still had another hundred yards to traverse before a bend in the river would shield them from more shells. She groaned, getting to her feet and injecting more Green and Black, leaving only a small amount of the former and draining the latter, but moderation would be folly now.

A small, gleaming streak buzzed past her ear as she straightened, her well-attuned senses instantly recognising it as the passage of a rifle-bullet. Another came a second later, plucking at the sleeve of her jacket, the Green muting the resultant flare of agony as it grazed her flesh. The Corvantine gunnery officer, evidently a resourceful fellow, had gathered a half-dozen marksmen at the frigate's prow. They blazed away with more enthusiasm than expertise, bullets striking the *Wave Dancer* from paddle to wheel-house, though one shot did smack into the board an inch from her left foot.

Focus. Lizanne centred her gaze on the gun, a rifled ten-inch model of modern design, now aimed straight and level as the range was so short. She watched a gunner swing the breech closed before locking it in place and taking hold of the lanyard attached to the firing mechanism. She waited until his arm had begun to pull the lanyard taut, time slowing as her gaze found the firing lever. She unleashed all her remaining Black the moment the lever moved, the gun swivelling about on its mounting, the long barrel sweeping the gunners aside before coming to a sudden, juddering halt, trained directly on the frigate's bridge, whereupon it fired.

The explosion ripped through the bridge and crew quarters, transforming them to scrap in a heart-beat and birthing a rising blossom of orange flame roiling amidst a pall of black smoke. The frigate immediately fell away as her rudder lost all trim, the bows swinging to starboard and her deck listing sufficiently to cast several crewmen into the sea. Flame must have found her magazine for Lizanne was treated to the sight of her exploding a few seconds later, her hull broken into two swiftly sinking pieces before the *Wave Dancer* turned the bend in the river and she was lost from view.

'Miss?' Arberus had climbed up to join her. She saw that he had a rifle in hand, presumably taken from the smugglers. From the smoke rising from the barrel he must have been trying to ward off the Corvantine sharpshooters.

A fresh wave of exhaustion seized her and she found herself collapsing against him, the vestiges of Green dwindling away and her vision dimming into an all-consuming void.

CHAPTER 23

Clay

'It has long been theorised that there are in fact four other planets in close orbit around the sun, rather than three. And with this' – Scriberson patted his long green-leather case – 'I may well be in a position to prove it.'

Braddon exchanged a glance with Clay. He had led the astronomer to the Falls' quay-side where the Longrifles were gathered to await the commencement of his uncle's scheme. He had made no comment so far upon hearing Scriberson's tale, but now his gaze betrayed a slight glimmer of interest. 'What you got in there, young man?'

'This, sir' – Scriberson set the case down on the flagstones and began to undo its straps – 'is the pinnacle of modern optics. The product of extensive analysis and experimentation in the Consolidated Research workshops.' He undid the case, splitting it in half. It contained two items nestling into recesses of cushioned velvet. One a folded-up wooden stand of sturdy appearance and the other a long brass tube, or rather three brass tubes fitted together in order of diminishing size. The smallest tube had an eyepiece that resembled that of a spy-glass.

'I give you' – Scriberson stood back a little, a note of pride in his voice as he gave a somewhat dramatic flourish at the tube – 'the New Model Consolidated Research Astronomical Field Telescope. Capable of three times the magnification of any other portable optic currently available.'

'A remarkable and valuable item to be sure.' Braddon inclined his head in appreciation before turning a less-than-impressed gaze on the astronomer. 'But I'm bound to ask, what in the Travail's it got to do with me or my company?'

'Mr Scriberson,' Clay said, 'why don't you tell my uncle about the place where you intend to train this here device on the alignment.'

He saw Braddon's interest deepen at mention of the alignment as Scriberson spoke on. 'There is a place spoken of in the records of the earliest expedition to venture into the Coppersoles. The account was written by a somewhat erratic Corvantine and has often been dismissed or ignored due to its often impenetrable and rambling language, all set down in an archaic derivation of Eutherian. However, a research project commenced at my behest managed to confirm many of the historical and geographic details in the documents, adding considerable weight to its veracity. It relates how a Corvantine expedition made its way to a ruin atop a tall mountain, fighting off Spoiled attacks along the way as one might expect. The account becomes confused at this point, but one aspect that remains clear is that the explorers witnessed an alignment upon reaching the mountain top, "a view of such clarity and majesty as never glimpsed by civilised eyes," apparently. Arradsia is well known for the unique spectacles its sky-line offers the astronomer, but this appears to have been something very special indeed.'

'And you came out here all on your lonesome to see it?' Braddon's voice conveyed equal parts scepticism and grudging admiration.

'Well, not initially.' Scriberson shifted a little in discomfort. 'I arrived in Rigger's Bay with six companions some three months ago. All Consolidated Research employees of good standing and varying areas of expertise. The expedition was intended to encompass botany, biology and geology as well as my own discipline.'

'And where's these experts now?'

'Sadly, expertise does not equate to courage. We were obliged to employ an escort from Rigger's Bay, a Contractor company recommended by the local Consolidated office. Unfortunately, they proved unworthy of our trust.'

'Robbed you and left you adrift in the jungle, huh?'

'Quite so. They took all our funds and equipment, though they were kind enough to leave us alive. It seems they were not so lucky. We found their bodies when making our way back to Rigger's Bay. From the state of them I deduced the indigenous denizens of this continent felt they had a grievance to settle. They left most of our equipment intact, however.'

'Your company sent you into the Interior with a bunch of headhunters.' Braddon's chuckle was echoed by the other Longrifles. 'You any idea how lucky you are to be alive, young man?'

'Fully aware, sir. As were my companions, who decided their adventuring days were at an end. I alone chose to proceed.'

'You walked through the jungle all the way to the Falls?' Loriabeth asked.

'Actually, miss, I constructed a raft and made most of the journey by river. There were difficult moments, I'll not deny, but I had ample provisions and a keen sense of purpose. There will be but one chance in my lifetime to witness the alignment from such a vantage point. I had intended to seek passage south on arriving at Fallsguard but, sadly, the Spoiled have contrived to imprison me here for the past ten days.'

'May I assume,' Braddon said, 'you're in possession of a map to guide you to your destination?'

'Lost to the thieves and the Spoiled, sir. However' – Scriberson tapped a finger to his temple – 'I am blessed with a very efficient visual memory.'

Seeing the calculation on his uncle's face, Clay said, 'Mr Scriberson offers a generous fee if we escort him south, Uncle. Plus, he says he knows a way into the Coppersoles, an old trail that leads into the heart of the mountains. Lotta Black nesting in the highest peaks, right, Skaggs?'

'So they say,' the harvester agreed. 'Never been there myself, though.'

'Fee?' Braddon asked Scriberson.

'Indeed, Captain. I can offer fifty thousand in exchange notes.'
He went to one of his leather-wrapped bundles and extracted a
wallet bulging with currency. 'The Spoiled saw no use for the
thieves' booty.'

'What makes you think we won't just steal it like they did?'
Loriabeth enquired, offering the astronomer a bright smile.

'I took the precaution of asking around before approaching
Mr Torcreek. Your company has a creditable reputation for
honesty, amongst other attributes.'

'That we do,' Braddon said, casting his gaze over Scriberson's
gear. 'If you're gonna travel with us, most of this will have to go.
Be quick about choosing what to take, only what you can carry
in comfort. We leave as soon as it gets dark.'

'Where's your weapon?' Clay asked Scriberson as they
hunkered down in the boat. It was one of the *Firejack*'s
life-boats left behind at his uncle's insistence, shallow-hulled and
of sufficient size to carry them all. The astronomer sat down at
Clay's side, his telescope case clutched tight and a small pack of
sundry belongings on his back. He had been visibly perturbed at
leaving most of his books behind, though Loriabeth had agreed
to carry one, professing herself curious as to the contents.

'*A Natural History of Arradsia*,' she read, squinting at the title.
'That mean there's an unnatural history out there somewhere?'

'I don't carry a weapon,' Scriberson told Clay, the sweat on his
face shining in the gathering dark. 'I have rather an aversion to
such things.'

'Can't walk the Interior without a weapon,' Clay said.

'He ain't getting none of mine,' Foxbine muttered, perched at
the boat's prow with carbine in hand. ''Sides, if he ain't shot before
he'll be more a danger to himself and us than any Spoiled or
drake.'

'Very true, miss,' Scriberson said. 'I'm sure I shall be perfectly
fine, Mr Torcreek. Having survived one jungle sojourn without
need of a fire-arm, I'm sure I can survive another.'

Braddon emerged from the shadowy bulk of Fallsguard and strode towards the boat, climbing in and settling himself next to the tiller. 'The major's agreed to a short barrage only, so we'll need to be quick. Anyone falls, they get left. No exceptions.'

'The lift?' Skaggerhill asked.

'Still intact, least as far as my spy-glass can make out. Prob'ly should've made use of Mr Scriberson's tellyscope doodad.'

'Assistance I'm happy to render, sir,' Scriberson offered, relief colouring his tone as he half rose from his seat.

'Ain't got time.' Braddon jacked a round into his longrifle's chamber and laid it across his knees. 'Let's get gone. Barrage starts precisely one half-hour from the second we set off.'

They pushed away from the quay and were soon speeding down-river, having no need of oars thanks to the swiftness of the current. Braddon worked the tiller, guiding them into the centre of the flow and past the foam-ringed boulders that proliferated along this stretch. It wasn't long before Clay heard it, a faint hiss at first that soon rose to a murmur, then a roar. He could see a fine mist rising ahead as the river opened out once more before seeming to disappear way short of the horizon.

'Oars out!' his uncle barked. Preacher and Skaggerhill heaved their paddles into the rowlocks and began to pull as Braddon steered them towards the eastern bank. They scraped to a halt amidst a cluster of rocks, Foxbine leaping clear with rope in hand, quickly joined by Clay. Together they held the boat in place whilst the others climbed out, Scriberson coming close to disaster when his foot slipped on the damp stone. Skaggerhill managed to grab him before he tumbled into the river, telescope and all.

'Anything?' Braddon asked, crouching at Foxbine's side as she peered at the shadowed bank. The jungle was sparse here, only a few patches of tree and bush littering the rocky ground.

'Seems quiet, Captain,' the gunhand replied. 'Maybe they missed us . . .' She trailed off at the sound of many voices rising from the left, a great hubbub of excited rage. 'Then again.'

'Get low,' Braddon told the rest of them, crouching behind a broad boulder and pulling the rim of his hat down about his ears. 'This is gonna be quite the kerfuffle.'

Clay saw the Spoiled come boiling out of the tree-line, an anonymous charging mass, raised spear-points gleaming in the moonlight. It seemed to him there were significantly more than they had faced on the Sands, more in fact than they had bullets to kill. They had charged to within a hundred yards when the first cannon shell hit, slamming into the ground just left of the main body, a dozen or more thrown high by the blast. Clay had time to glimpse the flashes lighting Fallsguard's south-facing wall before five shells arced into the ranks of Spoiled in quick succession, Clay shielding his eyes against the blast of flame and wind as the flat, hammer-blow sound of the explosions slapped against his ears. Around them waterspouts rose as debris rained down. When he looked again the ground was carpeted with still or crawling bodies and beyond them the dim shapes of surviving Spoiled fleeing back into the jungle. There was a pause as the gunners adjusted their aim then a fresh salvo fell amongst the trees, presumably to keep them running.

'Up!' Braddon shouted, surging to his feet. 'Won't take them long to gather for another try.'

They had to hop from rock to rock before making the bank whereupon Braddon led them at a run towards the roaring fury of the Falls. The ground fell away into a sheer cliff where it flanked the great tumbling cascade of water, Clay finding himself momentarily enraptured by the sight of it. A quarter-mile-long crescent where uncountable gallons rushed over the edge every second to plummet into blackness. Stretching out below was the mirror-like expanse of Krystaline Lake, a broad blade of silver extending to the horizon and beyond.

'Clay, over here, dammit!'

He turned and trotted towards his uncle's voice, finding him wrestling with the lock on a cage similar to the one they had used to ascend to the Fallsguard battlements. However, this one was much larger, hanging suspended by chains fastened to all four corners of its roof. The chains looped through a series of pulleys fixed to a large T-shaped scaffold above. The cage hung from one arm of the T whilst a larger chain hung from the other, its length swallowed by the gloom below the cliff-edge. *Counterweights,* Clay thought.

'It's seized,' Braddon said, stepping back from the lock and drawing his revolver. A single shot was enough to shatter the lock and soon he and Preacher had hauled the cage's door wide. Clay turned to cast a glance behind them, realising the barrage had stopped. He could see a fresh swarm of Spoiled rushing along the river-bank, war-cries audible even above the roar of the Falls. Silverpin gave an insistent tug on his arm and he followed her into the cage where Braddon was hammering the butt of his longrifle against a long lever that descended from the cage's ceiling.

'Rusted,' Braddon grunted, teeth clenched as he pounded harder. 'Ain't been used in months.'

'Time's pressing, Captain,' Foxbine warned, carbine raised as she stood at the open cage door, the war-cries coming closer by the second.

Clay, seeing every eye fixed on his uncle as he continued to assault the lever, turned away and drew his wallet from his shirt. He extracted Auntie's gift and gulped down a decent-sized drop before returning the wallet to his shirt. 'Here,' he said, moving to Braddon's side and taking hold of the lever. He made a show of heaving at it, fists tight on the handle and teeth gritted, but his gaze centred on the mechanism to which it was fastened.

'Captain!' Foxbine called, her carbine snapping off three quick shots.

Clay shut out the distraction, focusing on the dense patch of rust visible on the lever's fulcrum. Two concentrated bursts of force were enough to turn it to powder, the lever jerking forward in his grip. An involuntary shout rose from each of them as the cage plummeted down, chains and pulleys squealing, Foxbine reeling back from the blurring rock rushing past the open door.

For one dread-filled moment Clay thought the cage had been freed from all constraints, their fall being so rapid, but then noticed the relief on Silverpin's face as she entwined her hand with his. From the rate the cliff face slid past the door it was clear they fell at a goodly rate, but not near enough to prove fatal.

'Nicely done, young 'un,' Skaggerhill breathed, gripping the bars to gaze out at the growing spectacle of Krystaline Lake. 'Seer-damn me if a sight like this wasn't worth the trip.'

The cage descended to a small, fortified tower carved out of the base of the cliff. They came to a juddering halt some ten feet short of the tower's upper battlement, indicating the gearing on the scaffolding above must have seized as the counterweight reached the apex of its ascent. They dropped down one by one, finding a deserted structure. Four cannon were arrayed around the battlement but were unloaded and showed no signs of recent firing. Their descent through the tower revealed no occupants though it was clear a company of Protectorate troops had been in attendance. Two criss-crossed flags adorning the mess-hall indicated the garrison consisted of the Third Company of the Seventeenth Light Infantry and the Twelfth Battery of Mobile Artillery. However, there were no rifles in the armoury and a brief inspection of the stores found them mostly empty.

'Gathered up what they could carry and took to their heels,' was Skaggerhill's guess.

'Still plenty of powder and shell in the magazine,' Foxbine said. 'Enough to hold this place against the Spoiled for a good while.'

'Maybe it wasn't the Spoiled they fled from.'

'Find a billet and rest up,' Braddon ordered. 'We move on at first light. I want four on watch, two below, two up top, three-hour shifts. Clay, you and Mr Scriberson can enjoy the best view.'

Clay watched Scriberson set up his telescope, finding a certain fascination in the way it all fitted together and the expert precision with which the astronomer aligned it. 'Brionar is in the ascendant tonight,' Scriberson said. 'Its rings should be visible.'

'Rings?' Clay asked. Thanks to Joya he knew Brionar to be the largest planet in the solar system, but didn't recall anything about rings.

'Brionar has an extensive ring system,' Scriberson explained, adjusting the telescope's eyepiece a little. 'Would you like to see?'

Clay put his eye to the optic, blinking in confusion until it found the focus. He could see a bright spherical smudge in the centre flanked on either side by two smaller spheres. 'Looks like it's got ears to me.'

'The focus must be slightly off. Allow me.' Scriberson turned the eyepiece a fraction and the blurred image abruptly resolved into a green-blue ball ringed by a silver disc.

'Well, that's something to see, alright,' Clay said. 'Must be some size of a thing if we can see it so clear.'

'Thirty times the size of our own world. With ten moons of its own.'

'Makes you wonder if there's some fella out there looking back at us.'

'It's doubtful. Brionar is believed to be composed mostly of gas so there would be nothing for him to stand on.' Scriberson paused and gave an uncomfortable but determined sigh. 'How much product do you have left?'

Clay glanced up at him, memories of Ellforth suddenly at the forefront of his mind. But he could see no threat in Scriberson, just guarded necessity. 'See a lot, don't ya?' Clay asked.

'Observation is my profession. Do your companions know what you are?'

'They know. But they don't know I got product of my own. A secret I'll oblige you to keep, since you got me to thank for bringing you along.'

'Of course. I just . . . It's very important I complete these observations. If you could guarantee my safety, I have additional funds . . .'

'I been out here only a short time, Scribes.' Clay returned his eye to the optic, smiling a little at the stark beauty of the distant world and wishing Joya were here to share it. 'But that's long enough to learn there's no guarantees to be had in the Interior.'

They spent three days trekking through the jungle fringing the eastern bank of the Krystaline, Braddon setting a steady but not exhausting pace. Skaggerhill had advised moving with a cautious step as the climes south of the Falls were said to be rich in wild Greens. Silverpin took the lead, keeping a good dozen feet ahead of Clay and moving with the kind of natural grace that made her appear at home in this place. He had grown used to the stink of it by now, not so fearful of every shadow or unexpected sound, even finding the occasional glimpse of beauty amongst the crowding green walls. Birds of vibrant colours and large hooked beaks glided among the tree-tops. Lower down small chattering monkeys were sometimes to be seen hopping from trunk to trunk, long tails curled like whips as they arced through the air.

It was late afternoon on the third day when Silverpin came to a sudden, rigid halt. She stood absolutely still for a second then slowly lowered herself into a crouch, gaze centred on a shaded patch of jungle to her right. Clay held up a hand to halt the rest of the company then drew the Stinger and moved to her side. 'Something?' he whispered.

She didn't look at him, keeping her eyes on the shadow and drawing a thumb across her throat in an unmistakable gesture. *Dead thing. Human too, since why else would she stop?*

He turned and beckoned Foxbine forward, pointing to the shaded spot. She knelt and trained her carbine on the jungle as he and Silverpin went to take a look. The bodies lay in a circle just beyond the wide trunk of an ancient tree, rifles lying close to hand, some with the bolts drawn back. They were several days gone by Clay's reckoning, flesh blackened and sloughed off the bones, mostly eaten away by the swarms of flies still abuzz over the scene. What remained of the uniforms, however, was strangely well-preserved though torn and scorched in many places.

'Greens,' Skaggerhill pronounced a short while later. 'Looks like those Protectorate soldier boys from the tower made a stand here.' He gave an irritated glance at Scriberson, who was loudly engaged in losing his lunch near by.

'I count twelve,' Braddon said. 'There's near eighty men in a full company. And they had the artillerymen with them too.'

'Got separated maybe. Greens'll do that. Split smaller groups off from the herd.'

'They ain't been ate,' Loriabeth said, face thickly sheened in sweat and evidently fighting a rising gorge with admirable determination. 'Still . . .' She swallowed as Scriberson gave another heave. 'Still got most of their flesh and all.'

'That's a curiosity, true enough.' Skaggerhill shook his head, grimacing in consternation as he surveyed the bodies. 'Skulls intact also. Greens like to crack 'em open and scoop out the brains. Never known a pack not take time to feed.'

'No drake bodies either,' Clay pointed out.

'Soldier boys ain't Contractors,' the harvester replied. 'Probably wasted their ammo shooting at the body 'stead o' the head. Means this musta' happened awful fast though.'

'We'd best check 'em for papers,' Braddon said. 'Might find some clue why they lit out from the fort.'

Clay concealed a groan, stepping forward in anticipation of the order.

'Not you,' Braddon said, turning to the bent-over form of their newest member. 'Mr Scriberson. Time to start earning your keep, young man.'

'Just letters from wives and sweethearts,' Scriberson said. He sat close to the camp-fire, thumbing through the blood-stained papers he had taken from the corpses. Braddon had them cover another few miles before making camp on a shingle beach on the lake-shore, a well-chosen spot that gave them only one flank to guard come nightfall. Scriberson's face was haggard from prolonged vomiting, though he had taken to his grisly task without complaint. 'No diaries or orders. No clues as to what they were doing out here. I took these also.' He held up a brace of copper discs, each bearing a name and a number. 'So at least the Protectorate can notify their families.'

'Provided you live long enough to hand them in,' Foxbine muttered. She sat facing away from the fire, carbine resting in her lap and gaze ceaselessly scanning the jungle. Clay saw his uncle frown at the gunhand's fatalistic tone though he said nothing.

'I got a question,' Loriabeth said to Scriberson, patting the book she had carried from Fallsguard. 'Says here no-one knows for sure where we all come from.' She paused to leaf through a few pages, stumbling over the pronunciation of a particular phrase, 'The Evo-, erm, Evalootnary Paradox.'

'Evolutionary,' Preacher said, breaking several days' silence, though he appeared content to leave it at a single word.

'That's quite true, miss,' Scriberson said. 'There is no general consensus on the evolutionary origin for the higher orders of animals inhabiting this planet. Thanks to the fossil record we know that some microbial and insect species have clearly developed into their modern form over countless centuries of adaptation. Whereas, larger species, including our own, have left behind no ancestor more than ten thousand years old, and those are virtually identical to their modern descendants.'

'Ten thousand years is a long time,' Clay said.

'In human terms, yes,' Scriberson replied. 'But in evolutionary terms it's not even the blink of an eye.'

'Somebody must have a notion,' Loriabeth insisted. 'I mean we can't all just have sprung up from nowhere.'

'There are various theories. Dr Avaline, the biologist who accompanied my expedition, was an advocate of the Arradsian Progenitor hypothesis. He believed that all the so-called "orphan species" have ancestors which simply haven't yet been found, but may well one day be unearthed in the unexplored wilds of this continent. He had hoped to find some supporting evidence in the mountains, but failed to appreciate that scientific progress is rarely made by fearful souls.'

'The heavens torn asunder,' Preacher said, leaning forward to meet the astronomer's gaze across the fire.

'I am a scientist, sir,' Scriberson returned in a curt tone. 'Not a theologian.'

'What's that?' Loriabeth asked.

'And from the great tear in the world poured forth all manner of foulness,' Preacher went on, his voice possessed of a strident cadence, as if he were back in his pulpit. 'The drake being the most vile, for its blood is rich with the taint of wickedness.'

'Mere legend dressed up as visionary insight,' Scriberson said, though Preacher kept on, his voice becoming louder with every intonation.

'Hear my words and heed my warning for I tell all who have the wisdom to know truth, the drake will make us its slaves. Eternal bondage its sole promise. Know that the Travail is coming. Know that twenty-one score and ten years from the day of my passing will come the days of fire and iron . . .'

'Preacher,' Braddon said. It was softly spoken but apparently carried sufficient weight to cause the marksman to abandon his sermon. He had risen to his feet and stood blinking in the fire-light, as if waking from a dream. After a second he reached for his rifle and stalked away into the dark without a word.

'Shouldn't someone . . .' Clay began but Braddon shook his head.

'He'll be here come the morning.'

'That was Seer Scripture, right?' Loriabeth asked.

'The Prophecy of the Travail,' Scriberson said. 'Gibberish scribbled down by a madman, or a Blood-blessed if you believe his more deluded followers.'

'The Seer was a Blood-blessed?' Clay said. He hadn't known

this. In fact, most of what he had heard about those who followed the teachings of the Seer seemed to regard the Blessing with considerable suspicion, if not outright hostility.

'It's just one theory amongst many,' Scriberson said 'Conceived in an effort to explain the more outlandish claims made about his life. The claim is that, despite the fact that he lived and died two centuries before the opening of the Strait, he somehow gained access to drake blood and the Blue-trance gifted him with visions of the past and the future. Hence his vision of drakes falling out of some great tear in the sky, and his many lurid descriptions of the Travail. The fact that no Blood-blessed in history has ever experienced such a thing would indicate delusion rather than prophecy, even if he did secure himself a supply of product, which seems doubtful.'

'Thought some of it came true,' Clay said. 'He predicted the fall of the old empire, right? And he said ships would one day cross the seas without sails.'

'An educated guess, in both cases. The Mandinorian Empire was in the process of a long decline in his own day and early experiments with steam locomotion had already been conducted.'

'Remind me,' Braddon said. 'When exactly did he die?'

'The most reliable accounts relate that he expired of plague during the great outbreak of eleven seventy, by the Mandinorian calendar . . .' The astronomer trailed off, a frown of annoyed realisation creasing his brow.

'Yes, young man,' Braddon said with a sombre grin. 'Exactly twenty-one score and ten years ago.'

They came upon more bodies the following afternoon, similarly scorched and mutilated to those found the day before but lying singly or in pairs. The surrounding ground was liberally seeded with spent cartridge cases and discarded kit. 'Running battle, I'd reckon,' Skaggerhill said, hefting a half-empty pack. 'Casting off anything that might slow 'em down.'

They heard the shots a few miles on, faint cracks echoing

through the trees from the east. 'Still some kicking, at least,' Foxbine said, raising a questioning eyebrow at Braddon.

'If they're busy with the soldiers they're less likely to come for us,' Skaggerhill pointed out.

'Seems they'll be done with them before long,' Clay said. 'Then they'll be on our trail anyways.'

Braddon thought for a moment longer then unshouldered his rifle. 'Silverpin, Preacher, you're in the lead with me. Miss Foxbine, Skaggs on the flanks. Clay, Lori, keep Mr Scriberson company in the rear. Eyes on the trees.'

They moved at a sedate walk rather than a rush which might spoil their aim. Clay had the Stinger drawn and stock in place, mimicking his uncle by moving with it already at his shoulder so the barrel pointed wherever he looked. As ordered he continually swept his gaze over the branches above, eyes alive to anything that might betray the presence of a drake and trying to ignore Scriberson's heavy, fear-laden breaths at his side. 'Betcha wish you had a weapon right now, huh?' Clay asked in a whisper.

Preacher claimed the first kill. They had covered another two hundred paces or so, the distant cracks of rifle fire becoming louder with each step, when the marksman stopped and fired a single shot. Thirty yards away a bulky form slumped down amidst a patch of dense jungle. There was a second's frozen silence, the jungle's myriad voices suddenly stilled as the echo of the bullet faded, then a bellowing roar sounded directly ahead and a large Green exploded from the jungle. It charged towards them in a blur, shredding foliage in its wake, jaws agape and its hide a whirl of shifting hues. Braddon put a bullet through its mouth from fifteen paces.

'Rear-guard,' Clay heard Skaggerhill mutter as they moved past the Green's twitching corpse.

Another twenty yards on saw the jungle open out into a broad glade, whereupon they all came to an abrupt and astonished halt.

'What is that?' Loriabeth breathed.

'A city, miss,' Scriberson replied, all trace of fear now vanished from his voice. It was overgrown by vines, the stones cracked by roots and age, but it was still, unmistakably, a city. Spires, unfamiliar in construction and thickly shrouded in leaves, rose on all sides, some over thirty feet high. Partly ruined steps ascended to broad avenues and promenades flanked by numerous one-storey buildings with low, sloping roofs. They could see no sign of the drakes or the soldiers but the rifle fire continued to echo unabated somewhere amidst the ruins, now accompanied by the angry baying of a large pack of Greens.

'Guessing this place ain't on your map?' Clay asked Scriberson, who nodded, gaze still enraptured by the sight of the city.

'Ain't got time to gawp,' Braddon said, moving forward. 'Look lively. There's work to be done.'

They found more bodies littering the ruins as they made their way into the weed-infested maze. Clay counted over twenty by the time they had cleared the outer ring of structures, finding themselves in a broad, rectangular plaza, the tallest tower they had yet seen rising from its centre. The source of the continuing rifle fire became clear as soldiers could be seen on the tower's upper tiers, maintaining a dwindling barrage at the pack of drakes swirling around the base. Clay was struck by their size, larger than those he had seen in the north, larger even than the two they had just killed. Their hides had taken on a grey-green hue that matched the mossy surface of the plaza and they seemed to shimmer as they made repeated attempts to climb the tower. Two or three would separate from the pack to scrabble their way up, claws tearing at the ancient stone, until they were close enough to cast their flames at the defenders before losing purchase or being forced back by a flurry of rifle-shots. There were a number of Greens lying dead or close to it around the tower, indicating the soldier's aim had improved a little during their journey to this place.

'Preacher.' Braddon pointed the marksman to a near by roof-top. 'No point waiting. Just kill as many as you can. Miss Foxbine, Skaggs, go with him. The rest of you with me.'

They followed him as he ran to what appeared to have been a building of some importance, featuring two storeys rather than the one that seemed typical of the dwellings here. They found a part-destroyed stairwell inside that led up to the roof. He set Loriabeth to guarding the stairs and had Silverpin and Clay stand alongside him at the roof's edge.

'They'll be coming for us when the killing starts,' he said, flipping up the rearsight on his rifle and taking aim. 'You need to keep them off me.'

He fired without further preamble, Clay glimpsing a flash of red amongst the mass of Greens followed by an immediate change in the pitch of their roaring. It sounded more like a scream now as the entire pack ceased its assault on the tower and turned to face the new threat. A shot came from the left and another Green collapsed, blood pluming from its skull.

'Steady now,' Braddon said, jacking another round into the chamber.

Instead of the expected charge, however, the pack fled, still pealing out their weird, screaming roar as they streamed away to the south and were soon lost in the mass of the jungle, though the echo of their cries seemed to take an age to fade.

'Seen some strange sights on this trip,' Braddon said, lowering his rifle. 'But that surely beats it all.'

CHAPTER 24

Hilemore

'Hard a-port!' The *Viable Opportunity* heaved over with a groan of protesting ironwork as the hull strained against the swell. They were already at full ahead and it was no time to reduce speed. A bare five seconds after making the turn the salvo of Corvantine shells slammed into the sea no more than thirty yards distant. To starboard the *Contractual Obligation* wallowed adrift and burning, smoke billowing from her wrecked upper works to drift across the *Viable*'s path, providing a welcome smoke-screen in the process. Despite the poor visibility the *Viable*'s guns continued to fire at every target within range.

Hilemore watched as Mr Lemhill ordered the pivot-gun into action once more, the crew crouched and hands clapped to ears against the now-familiar flash and boom. Their efforts had clearly borne fruit judging by the sudden appearance of a ball of flame amidst the swirling smoke ahead, though he couldn't identify the target or the damage caused. It was their seventh successful hit of the action, a more frenzied engagement than Hilemore had ever known, lasting just under twenty minutes since the first Corvantine salvo had claimed the *Mutual Advantage*. In that time he had seen the *Contractual Obligation* take a dozen hits before falling out of line, and two more frigates suffer a similar fate before the mingled fog of cannon-smoke and burning ships had frustrated all attempts to follow the course of the battle. From the continuing roar and whistle of shot, however, it was clear the matter remained undecided.

Regardless of the confusion, he knew with some certainty that they had crossed the Corvantine line of battle, perhaps the only Protectorate vessel to do so. Captain Trumane had steered a winding course amongst the fast-moving shadows of the enemy's fleet, ordering all guns to fire at any target that presented itself and exploiting the *Viable*'s speed to the full. 'See if we can't shake 'em up a bit, eh?' Trumane had said. 'Give the rest of the fleet a chance.'

Hilemore remained uncertain how much of an advantage they had won for their comrades. There had been two huge explosions only minutes ago, lighting up the haze with the kind of energy that could only result from the exploding magazine of a cruiser. Though he tried to push the grim suspicion aside, instinct told him they had to be Protectorate vessels. The Corvantine ships were so fast, matching the *Viable* in many cases, and the accuracy and rapidity of their gunnery bespoke years of training. *This was a trap,* he knew. *Long laid and well-planned. And we strolled right into it.*

'Enemy cruiser dead ahead, sir!' Ensign Talmant reported from the speaking-tube. His earlier fear seemed to have evaporated in the urgency of battle and he spoke in a clear, strident voice.

Hilemore and Trumane went outside to train their spy-glasses on the smoke wreathing the sea beyond the bows, a tall shape soon resolving into view. Like many of the other Corvantine vessels, she had no paddle casements though her lines were markedly less sleek than those of their newly built ships.

'The *Regal*,' Trumane said. 'Heavily modified, but it's her.' Hilemore followed the captain back to the bridge, watching him stare at the approaching cruiser with an unwavering concentration. After thirty long seconds he barked, 'Ten degrees to starboard!' just as a tell-tale flash blossomed on the *Regal*'s prow. The shell landed just wide of the *Viable*'s port bow, close enough to send a quaking shudder through the entire ship. Hilemore was sent sprawling along with Talmant and the helmsman, though Trumane somehow managed to remain upright.

Hilemore heard the answering roar of their own forward

battery and scrambled to his feet in time to see the shell impact on the *Regal*'s upper works, scattering shrapnel across her fore-deck and, with any luck, killing some of their gunners. Talmant gave voice to an involuntary shout of triumph, echoed by the helmsman. Trumane, however, saw no reason to celebrate. 'She's turning,' he said, watching the cruiser heave to starboard. As the *Regal*'s side was revealed Hilemore saw the rows of guns arrayed along her middle and upper decks, counting at least thirty.

'Seems we're in for an old-fashioned broadside,' the captain observed. 'Ensign, signal the engine room to add another flask to the main power plant.'

'Aye, sir.'

Five flasks. Hilemore was unable to recall an instance when such a quantity of product had been burned at once. The results of unleashing so much power in a single burst were unpredictable to say the least, but, given the impending danger, like the captain he couldn't see an alternative.

Time seemed to stretch as the *Regal* sought to complete her turn, enough time in fact for Mr Lemhill to loose another shell from the pivot-gun and score a hit on the cruiser's mid-section. The effect was difficult to judge but Hilemore assumed, or rather hoped, they had at least disabled a gun or two. The *Viable* gave a sudden, jerking lurch, Hilemore coming close to losing his footing once more as she leapt forward, the paddles roaring and the needle on the speed indicator swinging past its maximum.

'Five degrees to starboard,' the captain ordered, unable to risk a sharper turn but presumably hoping to present less of a target to the *Regal*'s gunners. They had cleared two-thirds of her length by the time the first gun fired, the broadside sweeping along the hull in a booming cacophony of flame and smoke. Hilemore switched his gaze to the bridge's aft window, finding the sea beyond the *Viable*'s stern roiling with multiple impacts. For a brief moment he entertained the delusion they might have suffi-cient velocity to emerge unscathed, instantly dispelled when a shell slammed into the port railing just ahead of the rudder. He had time to watch the rearmost battery torn to pieces by the resultant hail of shrapnel before a thick pall of black smoke concealed the grisly sight. Despite the hit, the *Viable*'s speed seemed unaffected and they cleared the sights of the *Regal*'s gunners without further injury.

'Bring us to midships,' the captain commanded before turning to Hilemore. 'Damage report, if you please, Lieutenant.'

'Aye, sir.'

He slid down the ladder and ran to the stern. Two men were stumbling about in shock, uniforms ripped and flesh scored by numerous cuts though neither appeared to have suffered fatal injury. He shook them both back to sensibility then ordered them to the sick-bay. A brief inspection of the impact site confirmed the loss of the battery and most of its crew, their remains scattered in red and black clumps around the ruined gun. Fortunately, he found no sign of a hull breach and the rudder appeared undamaged.

'Look to your piece!' he shouted to the nearest gun-crew, who stood regarding the scene in wide-mouthed horror. He pointed to the dim shape of a Corvantine frigate four hundred yards to starboard. 'Target in range!'

He hurried towards the bridge, gratified by the sound of renewed firing, and had begun to clamber up the ladder when the *Viable* abruptly veered off course. The deck pitched beneath his feet as she slewed to port, the vibration of the engine suddenly absent from the planking. He turned to the port paddle casement, his guts lurching at the sight of the whirling blades coming to a halt.

'Get to engineering!' Hilemore glanced up to see Trumane staring down at him from the top of the ladder, face flushed with mingled anger and alarm. 'There's no answer from the tube. Find out what in the Travail is happening down there.'

Hilemore went below, shouldering his way past men hauling fresh ammunition from the magazine and navigating the various obstacles that always seemed to accumulate belowdecks when a ship was in action. He found the engine room filled with steam. One of the stokers lay next to the hatch, a jagged blade of shattered iron protruding from his upper chest, face slack and eyes staring vacantly in death. For the first time since Feros the place was possessed of an unnerving quiet, absent of both the harsh clatter of the auxiliary and the steady thrum of the blood-burner. In fact the only sound was the harshly spoken profanity coming from Chief Engineer Bozware's throat somewhere amidst the vapour.

'Chief!' Hilemore called, making his way forward.

There was no answer, just more cursing, now accompanied by the ringing sound of a hammer. Hilemore climbed the steps to the platform where the main power plant rested, drawing up short at the sight of Tottleborn. The Blood-blessed sat slumped in his chair, one of his beloved periodicals resting in his lap, mouth open as if frozen in the act of speaking, and a large iron rivet skewered through his temple. *Sometimes a Blood-blessed will see something in their trance, something dark and formless . . .*

Hilemore tore his gaze away, turning to find the plasmothermic engine dead, the fire behind the glass extinguished and a gaping rent in the combustion chamber. It looked as if some feral monster had hatched from the thing, punching its way out in a violent frenzy. A fresh bout of cursing drew his attention to the scene below. The Chief stood astride the gearing of the auxiliary power plant, swinging a hammer with concentrated ferocity at a piece of jagged metal embedded deep in the cogs. Hilemore didn't need a detailed explanation to gauge their predicament. Both engines were off-line and the *Viable* was dead in the water.

'It blew almost exactly six minutes after adding the fifth vial,' the Chief said through gritted teeth as he continued to swing the hammer. 'In case you want to make a note in the log.'

'We had no choice.' Hilemore returned his gaze to the blood-burner, noting that the rent in the combustion chamber was severe but also narrow. 'Can you seal this?' he asked.

'Aye, but what's the point?'

'How long?'

Bozware ceased his hammering, comprehension dawning as he met Hilemore's gaze. 'Half an hour at least, but it'll be a bodge.'

'Do it. I'll be back directly.'

He went to the ward-room first, unlocking the safe to extract all the remaining flasks of Red then ran along the corridor to the bridge. The hatch to the bridge stood open, affording him a clear view as it disintegrated in a blaze of flame and splintered metal. The blast lifted him off his feet and threw him the length of the corridor, a jarring impact with the bulkhead leaving him senseless.

He surfaced to the sound of panicked shouting and the smell of burning fabric. His hands were suffering repeated flares of agony and someone appeared to be punching him in the chest. After a few seconds, enough of his senses had returned to reveal the shouts as his own and the punches in fact blows delivered by his hands as he attempted to beat out the burning patches on his tunic. A large shape loomed out of the smoke and Hilemore found himself hauled upright, staggering a little as broad hands slapped away the flames.

'Are you injured, sir?' Steelfine asked, narrow gaze tracking him from head to foot in appraisal.

Hilemore shook off the Islander's grip before taking a deep breath of the tainted air, coughing and straightening his back. 'I must get to the bridge.'

They found it a shambles, the walls and roof vanished though the wheel remained mostly intact. The only sign of the helmsman was the red stains covering the woodwork. Captain Trumane lay under a pile of fallen debris, blood streaming from his ears and nose. Hilemore checked his pulse and found it faint but present, though from the amount of blood staining his tunic his injuries were evidently severe. Incredibly, Ensign Talmant still stood next to the speaking-tube, his uniform ragged and liberally covered in blood and, whilst he seemed completely unharmed, his eyes were empty of all comprehension.

'Ensign!' Hilemore took hold of the boy's singed tunic, shaking him until a vestige of life returned to his eyes. He blinked and cast a panicked gaze around at the wrecked bridge.

'The captain , , ,'

'Is incapacitated.' Hilemore realised the sound of cannon fire had faded completely and looked towards the bow, taking in the awful sight of the forward pivot-gun. It swung on its mounting, most of the breech shot away, surrounded by the mangled remains of its crew. He could see the bulky but mutilated form of Mr Lemhill amongst them. 'It appears command now falls to me. Take the wheel. The engines will start up again soon.'

'Sir.' Hilemore turned to see Steelfine pointing to something to port. A Corvantine cruiser had come to a stop some three hundred yards off. She was one of their new-builds, sleeker and more compact in design than the *Regal*, but apparently well-supplied with marines. They stood along the rail in battle-order whilst the cruiser lowered boats over the side.

'Seems they want a prize,' Steelfine observed. His voice held a definite note of good humour, even anticipation.

'They want our engine,' Hilemore said. 'The *Viable* is the fastest ship they've faced today. I assume their admiral is keen to find out why.'

He went to the gangway and surveyed the sea. The fog of battle had faded to a thin mist, revealing a long row of burning hulks. Guns could still be heard in the distance but the rate of fire was desultory; the day had been lost. He turned his gaze to the *Viable*, counting the bodies littering the deck and noting that all her guns were now silent. Further resistance was a hopeless prospect.

'Mr Steelfine,' he said. 'Muster the riflemen and prepare to repel boarders. See if you can't get the starboard guns loaded and ready, but don't fire until my order. I'll be there directly.'

He had expected some hesitation, a desperate entreaty not to throw their lives away perhaps. But instead Steelfine simply snapped off a salute and turned to descend to the deck, his voice casting out a barrage of orders as loud as any siren. Talmant also just continued to stand at the wheel, wordless and unbowed, though he did spare a glance for the captain.

'We've no time to deal with him, Ensign,' Hilemore said. 'Stay at your station. Once we're underway steer north-north-east.'

'Aye, sir.'

The guard standing outside the brig greeted Hilemore with a pale face, though was smart enough not to ask any questions as he handed over his keys. 'The captain is injured,' Hilemore told him, turning to unlock the door. 'Get to the bridge and transfer him to sick-bay. When you've done that draw a rifle and join the Master-at-Arms on deck.'

Inside, Zenida Okanas stood at the bars, her daughter at her side, slim arms clutching her mother's waist and regarding Hilemore with an accusatory frown.

'Our Blood-blessed is dead,' Hilemore told the pirate woman, seeing little point in preamble. 'I am now acting captain and hold full authority.'

She angled her head, a single eyebrow raised as she awaited his next words.

'Name your price,' he said.

She pulled her daughter closer for a second then pointed her to the bunk, repeating the gesture with stern insistence when the girl hesitated. 'Full pardon,' Zenida Okanas said. 'And the return of my sovereigns.'

Hilemore unlocked the cage door and stood back. 'Done. I'll provide a witnessed agreement when matters are less pressing. As for now however . . .' He gestured at the corridor.

The woman turned to her daughter, speaking softly but firmly in Varestian. 'Stay here. If this tub starts to sink make your way up top and swim east. The current may take you to the Isles.'

The girl gave a short nod of affirmation and Zenida Okanas briskly walked from the brig, striding ahead of Hilemore as they made their way to engineering. They found the Chief Engineer at the blood-burner, hammering a final rivet in place with a bulky, steam-driven hammer. He had cannibalised the auxiliary engine for iron plates of sufficient dimensions to cover the rent in the combustion chamber, making it resemble a blistered injury to metal skin. Hilemore saw a row of tarpaulin-covered bodies near the door, Tottleborn's presumably amongst them.

'Another twenty minutes,' Bozware said, groaning as he and the stokers set the steam-hammer down. 'Got to reconnect the steam lines.'

Hilemore handed the three flasks to Zenida Okanas. 'You know what to do, I assume?'

She gave the engine a brief glance and nodded before addressing a question to Bozware. 'Is this thing likely to blow again?'

'We'll find out, won't we?' the Chief replied, not raising his head as he went about fastening a steam line to the engine's outflow valve.

'"Caution favours no-one in battle,"' Hilemore said in Varestian, quoting an old proverb.

'If I die,' she replied, 'I will expect you to see my daughter home. The Highwall, in southern Varestia . . .'

'I've heard of it.' He turned and made for the hatchway. 'Though if you die, I expect we'll all join you in the Deep shortly after.'

'Keep down, you no-balled swine!' Steelfine shouted to the assembled riflemen, all crouched about the fore-deck at Hilemore's order. He had managed to get three of the remaining guns into action, all loaded with chain-and-canister-shot rather than shells. Such archaic munitions were no longer carried by many Protectorate vessels but, once again, Trumane had proven himself a prescient captain. Hilemore had the guns set back from the rail and concealed behind piled wreckage, the gunners all under strict orders not to fire until his command. He crouched at Steelfine's side, the three surviving ensigns at his back with swords and revolvers drawn. He had named them his personal bodyguard, hoping a sign of favour might stiffen their spirits somewhat. However, despite some forced smiles, they all shared the bright-eyed and rigid expressions common to youth who witness far too much carnage in a single dose.

All in all, the *Viable*'s defenders numbered some thirty-three souls, what remained of the original riflemen plus the surviving crew. It wasn't enough to defeat a full company of Corvantine marines but it may well suffice to delay them whilst Bozware got the blood-burner back on-line. There was the added risk that, once it became evident they intended to fight it out, the captain of the Corvantine cruiser might simply decide to pull back his marines and blast them out of the water. *In which case you will have scored a victory,* Hilemore reminded himself. *In denying them the* Viable's *engine.*

He moved to the rail and peered through the assembled debris to observe the approach of the Corvantine launches. There were two in front with another six behind, each carrying fifteen marines. Two launches from the rear echelon had separated from the formation and begun to circle around the *Viable*'s stern, presumably to assault the port side whilst the remainder assailed them from starboard.

'Take ten men and cover the port rail,' Hilemore told Steelfine. 'No firing until they're climbing the ropes.'

He saw the Islander's hesitation, no doubt pondering the chances of fulfilling his obligation if he didn't remain at Hilemore's side. 'It'll all be blades and fury soon enough,' Hilemore told him. 'Come find me then.'

Steelfine gave a nod and moved away, keeping low as he picked out the ten men who would accompany him. Hilemore returned his gaze to the approaching launches. The marines rowed with sedate but disciplined dips of their oars, a small cannon perched on the prow of each launch where their officers stood watching the silent and smoking hulk ahead with more vigilance than Hilemore would have liked.

'Make ready,' he told the gunners, sending them scrambling to the pieces, removing the chocks from the wheels in preparation for rolling them forward. Hilemore moved down the line of guns in a crouch, checking the sights and speaking just loud enough for them to hear. 'Go for the men, not the boats. There will only be time enough for one shot, so aim true. When it's done, pick up your weapons and join the fight.'

He was gratified by the general murmur of assent and the determination on every face. He had made a brief speech on ascending to the deck, promising escape if they could stand off the assault for only a few minutes. Fortunately, it seemed they had believed it more than he did.

He returned to his vantage point and held up a hand, watching the nearest launch approach until it was so close he could make out the features of the officer on the prow. He was dismayed to find the man of similar age and height to himself, a veteran too judging by the scar that traced along his jaw-line. The officer peered at the *Viable* with an intense scrutiny, eyes narrowing farther and Hilemore knew he had detected some sign of warning, a glimpse of one of the guns or a bayonet raised a fraction too high. In either case, the game was up and the fight was on.

Hilemore brought his hand down just as the marine officer began to open his mouth in a warning shout. All three guns fired at once, Hilemore seeing the marine officer's tall form shredded into several pieces by the hail of canister and chain, along with approximately half the marines behind. Smoke momentarily obscured the neighbouring launch but when it cleared he was rewarded with the sight of it listing in the water, waves lapping over its side and oars hanging limp. The marines aboard lay in a twitching ruin.

The response from the other launches was immediate, their small cannon slamming three high-explosive shells into the *Viable*'s upper rail. The damage to the ship was slight but the resultant explosions cast enough splintered wood and metal into the assembled crewmen to leave at least half a dozen writhing or dead on the deck.

'Leave them!' Hilemore barked at one of the ensigns, who was attempting to haul away a wounded man. 'Time for that later.' He stood, raising his voice to a roaring pitch. 'Riflemen up! Independent rapid fire!'

The riflemen moved to the rail and began firing immediately, the initial volley scything through the ranks of the marines in the third launch as it attempted to navigate the channel between the two ruined boats. Hilemore saw several Corvantines fall into the sea as their comrades attempted to find cover in the confines of the boat. He allowed the riflemen a few more seconds' fire before ordering them to shift their aim to the other launches. However, the marine officers had been annoyingly quick to react, ordering the oarsmen to increased efforts and closing the distance. One had drawn up to the *Viable*'s side just fore of the paddle casement and another was casting ropes at the stern.

Recognising the greatest danger lay where the defenders were thinnest, Hilemore ordered the ensigns to fall in behind and moved forward, gathering the gunners along the way. A marine was already clambering onto the rail when they got there, teeth gritted as he hauled himself up the rope towards the iron grapple hooked onto the *Viable*'s side. Hilemore shot him in the face, the body tumbling back onto the boat below. Another marine managed to get a foot on deck before the combined fire of the ensign's revolvers sent him over the side in a welter of blood. Hilemore leaned over the rail and emptied his revolver into the dense ranks of marines below, near oblivious to the shots that came in response, one whipping close by his ear and another shattering the jaw of a gunner who had rushed to his side.

'Keep firing,' he told the ensigns, ducking back down to reload. The three youngsters responded immediately, their fear now replaced by the fury of combat as was often the case once battle became joined and all uncertainty fled. The gunners moved up to add their rifles to the barrage, all whooping in excitement or casting obscenities at the unfortunate marines below as they poured out a desperate barrage. When Hilemore raised himself to fire again, a fresh cylinder in his revolver and eyes alive for targets, he saw a boat filled with corpses or wounded. A few survivors were swimming away, making for the cruiser where their most likely reception would be a noose. The Corvantines were notoriously intolerant of cowardice.

A fresh upsurge of rifle fire tore his gaze back to the stern. The riflemen had evidently fired a final volley before moving in with the bayonet, thrusting at the wall of green-clad bodies now clambering over the side. Fresh firing had also erupted to port, indicating Steelfine's men were now battling the other two boatloads of marines.

Hilemore holstered his revolver and drew his sword, ordering the ensigns to follow suit and ensuring the gunners had fixed bayonets. 'With a will, if you please, lads,' he said, moving forward at a steady run. The marines had managed to force back the riflemen by a few yards by the time he led his small band into their flank, laying about them with his sword. He hacked down a marine desperately attempting to slot a fresh round into the chamber of his rifle, then slashed open the face of another who raised his bayonet a fraction too late to ward off the blow. Seeing his charge the *Viable*'s crew gave a savage shout of defiance and launched themselves at the marines with renewed vigour, bayonets stabbing and rifle-butts clubbing. The marines were forced back to the rail, though their sole remaining officer proved a valiant fellow. Standing straight and immune to either injury or fear, he steadied his men into a tight defensive knot around the aft anchor mounting, taking careful aim with his revolver as he dispatched three riflemen in quick succession.

'Pull back!' Hilemore told the crew, drawing his own side-arm. 'Reload and finish them with a volley.'

His order had clearly drawn the marine officer's attention, for he fixed him with a keen eye before his revolver swung round for another carefully aimed shot. Hilemore's arm came up in response, blurring with the speed of it, his shot loosed in tandem with the marine's, the two bullets passing each other in mid air. He felt something pluck at his shoulder, numbing the flesh beneath his tunic, but stopped himself looking at the wound. Instead, he stepped to the side and drew back the revolver's hammer for another shot, only to find it wasn't necessary. The marine officer had slumped back amidst his men, a large red hole in the centre of his forehead. An instant later the riflemen fired a single deafening volley, blood pluming in crimson blossoms on the tunics of the remaining marines as they were driven lifeless to the deck.

Hilemore turned to the port rail, finding Steelfine's men engaged in a frantic struggle with two boat-loads of marines. The Master-at-Arms had eschewed a rifle for a sea-axe and could be seen in the thick of the fight, the axe blade trailing blood from his tireless blows. His face had taken on an oddly serene expression, for all the world a man content in his labour.

Hilemore opened his mouth to order the surrounding crew into a firing line, intending to warn Steelfine to drop to the deck whilst their volley sent the marines reeling over the side. At that moment, however, the *Viable Opportunity* lurched into renewed life.

Those marines still clambering up the *Viable*'s side were jolted into the sea as her paddles swung into motion and a gout of steam rose from the stacks. A cheer rose from the crew and they immediately launched themselves at the remaining Corvantine marines, most of whom took the prudent course of jumping over the side. Within seconds the remainder were dead, each pinned to the deck by a clutch of bayonets, some in the act of surrendering.

'You there, Tollver,' Hilemore called to the lanky ensign who stood staring at his bloodied sword in dim-eyed fascination. He snapped to attention quickly, however. 'Get to the engine room. Tell Mr Bozware to make smoke, as much as he can.'

'Aye, sir.'

Hilemore paused to order the marine bodies cast over the side and the guns reloaded then made his way to the bridge. 'North-north-east, sir,' Talmant said, hands firm on the wheel.

'Very good, Ensign.' He checked the speed indicator, finding that the *Viable* had already accelerated to twenty knots. Clearly, the Chief's repair had been less of a bodge than he warned. He found the captain's spy-glass lying undamaged on the floor and trained it towards the south. Those Corvantine vessels in sight had evidently come to a near halt in the aftermath of battle, either to claim prizes or pluck prisoners from the sea. Some were piling on steam for a pursuit, including the sleek cruiser that had launched the marines. Clearly, their admiral was still keen to get his hands on the *Viable*'s engine for none of the Corvantines fired a shot.

'Mr Talmant, make ready to turn hard a-starboard at my signal,' he told the ensign.

'Aye, sir.' The boy hesitated. 'Won't that take us into the islands, sir?'

'With any luck.'

The smoke-screen blossomed from the stacks a few moments later. They were fortunate with the winds today, the relative stillness of the air allowing the smoke to settle over the *Viable*'s wake in a thick grey blanket. 'Make your turn, if you please, Ensign.'

The boy swung the wheel as ordered until the compass-needle settled on dead east, whereupon he brought the rudder back to midships. Whatever restraint had curtailed their pursuers had evidently been lifted and the flat boom and whine of shells could be heard through the smoke, though none came within a hundred yards. The Corvantine gunners had assumed they would maintain a northerly course and laid their fire accordingly. *After all,* Hilemore reflected, *only a madman would take his ship into the Isles. A madman . . . or a pirate.*

CHAPTER 25

Lizanne

'As close to Carvenport as I could get without running afoul of the Corvantine Fleet.' Kaden smiled thinly and tossed Major Arberus another canteen.

'It's fifty miles away,' Arberus returned. 'With who knows how many Corvantine scouts patrolling the jungle.'

'Then you had best not linger. I now consider our debt settled and will certainly kill you the moment I see you again. You can keep the rifle.' With that the smuggler turned and strode back to the wheel-house. A few moments later the *Wave Dancer* pulled away from shore and began to turn about. Night was coming on and her stack glowed a little in the gloom as she made her way back up-river, fading from sight a short while later.

'He didn't even say thank you,' Tekela observed.

Lizanne shouldered her pack and held up one of the canteens they had been given. 'I think this is the sum of his gratitude.' She glanced at the dark wall of jungle crowding the river-bank. She knew every drake pack in this vicinity had been hunted to extinction over a decade ago, but her brief experience of the Interior had bred a healthy respect for the many uncertainties lurking beyond the walls of civilisation.

'We'd best put in some miles before it's too dark to see,' she said, starting forward. 'Miss, do not stray more than two feet from my side.'

'I surely won't,' Tekela replied in a small voice, her gaze bright with alarm as it roved the jungle.

They managed only an hour's travel before darkness forced a

halt. Lizanne had found a trail of sorts, presumably a track left by some of the small deer that populated this region in ever-increasing numbers since there were no drakes to thin their herds. The trail led to a small glade where they made camp for the night, Tekela huddling close to Lizanne for warmth as the major had been vocal in forbidding a fire.

'Morradin will have his cavalry well ahead of the main body,' he said, rifle cocked and ready as he sat scanning the jungle. 'I should know, I would have been amongst them.'

'Do you know his plan of attack?' Lizanne asked.

'Only the broad strategy. Morradin is not a particularly verbose man, nor particularly trusting. The army will advance en masse from Morsvale, screened by cavalry and skirmishers, and approach Carvenport from the south-west. The fleet, provided they manage to secure the Strait, will bombard the town in preparation for the final assault. Hardly subtle, I know, but he's not the most subtle commander. His record speaks for itself, however.'

'How many troops in total?'

'Two full divisions, plus the Morsvale militia companies. I'd say twenty-five thousand, altogether.' He glanced over at her. 'You intend to trance this to your contact in Carvenport, I assume?'

'The next scheduled trance is tomorrow evening. Hopefully, I'll give the Protectorate some prospect of organising a defence.'

'The Carvenport garrison numbers no more than three thousand troops, and only four batteries of artillery. They'll be lucky to last a day.'

'The empire's spies have been busy, I see.'

He gave a humourless laugh, muttering, 'Spies are always busy.'

She watched him closely as she spoke another word, resisting the impulse to partake of some Green to enhance her sight as she had precious little left. 'Truelove,' she said.

Nothing. No reaction beyond a faintly puzzled glance in her direction. 'What?'

He's not that good an actor, she decided. *The name means nothing to him.* 'Never mind.' She settled next to Tekela, putting an arm around her shoulders to ward off her shivers. 'Wake me when you get tired.'

There has been no word from the Protectorate Fleet for two days, Madame told her, mindscape simmering like an unappetising soup on the boil. *A decidedly ominous development that forces me to conclude the Strait has been lost to the Corvantines. Nevertheless, the Board has ordered Carvenport held at all costs pending relief, which they promise will arrive within the month.*

A month may as well be a year at this juncture, Lizanne replied. *Morradin has a full picture of our strength, not to mention agents at large in the city.*

Reduced in number as of this morning, I'm happy to say. All known Cadre operatives were arrested at dawn. The interrogations have revealed another four agents previously unknown to us.

There are undoubtedly more.

Certainly, but hopefully this little demonstration will be enough to keep them quiescent, at least for now.

Truelove?

Not a sign nor a clue. The name is unknown to any of the operatives we arrested. A now-familiar black web appeared in Madame's mindscape, the tentacles spreading and coiling about the clouds with a vibrant energy before she reasserted control. The web froze but lingered and Lizanne was unsurprised by the next question. *The device is intact?*

Quite intact, Madame. As are the documents I was able to retrieve.

Excellent. I have a select group of scholars awaiting their arrival. We should have a much clearer picture to communicate to Mr Torcreek within days.

Presuming we can hold the city that long.

Allow me to worry about the military tedium, Lizanne. The grand marshal will find we have a few surprises for him. In the meantime, make your way here with all haste, safe delivery of the device being your sole priority, sentimental attachments notwithstanding.

'Hateful, stinking, bloody place!' Tekela groaned. She was on all fours, her foot having tangled itself in a vine. Watching her climb wearily to her feet Lizanne could see only a small vestige of the scowling, tantrum-prone girl from a few weeks before. Her overalls were besmirched from the filth of the smuggler's boat and the attentions of the jungle. Her hair had been tied back into a severe bun but lank, unwashed strands hung across her face like emaciated snakes. Then there was the grief, of course, the pain of it deepening now that she had time to dwell on the series of events that had brought her here. She tried to hide it, fixing her face into a mask of quiet determination for the most part, but Lizanne saw it plainly; the haunted cast to the eyes and the inability to smile that told of deep-seated loss shot through with guilt.

'We'll rest a moment,' Lizanne said, pointing Tekela to a near by fallen branch.

'I'm not tired . . .'

'Just sit, miss.'

Arberus glanced back at them then rested his back against a tree, drinking deeply from his canteen. In contrast to Tekela, much of his vitality had returned in recent days, though his occasional winces told of scars not yet healed. Also, Lizanne saw no grief in him, just a persistent anger and unwavering purpose. *Fanatics are useful,* she recalled an instructor saying once, *but should always be regarded as disposable resources.*

'Here,' she said, rolling up her sleeve and turning to Tekela. She removed the vial of Green from the Spider and handed it to the girl. 'Two sips. It's the dress-maker's stock so it's not as potent as I'd like, but it'll keep you on your feet for a few miles.'

Tekela regarded the vial with a suspicious frown. 'I've never . . . Father didn't like it, wouldn't have any in the house.'

Lizanne stared at her expectantly until she brought the vial to her lips, cautiously drinking down the allotted two sips and grimacing at the taste. 'That's awful . . .' She trailed off as the effects took hold, colour flooding her cheeks and her slumped shoulders straightening. 'Oh,' she said, voice just a little below a squeak.

'Come on.' Lizanne patted her hand and got to her feet. 'Two more days and we'll be in sight . . .'

A faint but strident note sounded from the south, echoing through the trees with urgent warning. 'Hunting horn,' Arberus said, instantly on his feet with the rifle stock at his shoulder. 'Imperial Rangers.' He raised his gaze to the sky, peering through the trees at something far above.

'What is it?' Lizanne asked.

'They know where we are.' He pointed at two small winged silhouettes visible through a gap in the canopy. They were directly above, circling lazily. 'Hawks. The Rangers prefer them to hounds.'

The horn sounded again, closer this time.

'Half a mile?' Lizanne wondered.

'More like a third. And they're on horseback.'

She turned to Tekela, watching her clutch her revolver with a fresh sheen of sweat on her face. The Green had added some colour to her cheeks but the fear in her eyes was palpable. *Sentimental attachments notwithstanding . . .*

'Take this,' she said, sloughing off her pack and handing it to Arberus. 'When you reach Carvenport you're to place it in the hands of Madame Lodima Bondersil. No-one else. She is aware of our arrangement.'

She drew the Whisper and moved to Tekela, briefly clasping her hand. 'Go with the major, miss.'

'Wait!' The girl's hand tightened on Lizanne's, refusing to let go. 'We go together or not at all.'

'I can hold them long enough for you to get away,' Lizanne replied. 'The major can't.'

She gave Tekela's hand a final squeeze then firmly pulled herself free, turning and running towards the south without further pause. Tekela called after her, the desperate entreaties turning to frustrated anger as Arberus began to haul her away. Lizanne injected a brief burst of Green and increased her pace.

The first trooper came into sight barely a minute later, trotting his mount forward at a steady clip through a sunlit clearing. He rode with a carbine in one hand and the reins in the other, clad in the grey-green uniform of the Imperial Light Horse. From his weathered features, and the way his eyes constantly roved the surrounding jungle, Lizanne judged him a veteran and no stranger to the Interior. She found a suitable tree and quickly climbed to a third of its height, perching on a thick branch from where she could observe both the trooper and the company following behind at a professionally cautious distance. She put their number at a dozen, though there were certain to be other squadrons near by. However, only this one was likely to pick up the trail left by Tekela and the major.

She allowed the lead trooper to pass beneath unmolested; dispatching him wouldn't have been especially difficult but the real danger lay in the squadron as a whole. She voiced a soft sigh of frustration upon glancing at the Spider and the parlous state of product remaining in the vials. Only a quarter-vial of Green remained and all the Black gone. Fortunately, she still retained nearly half a vial of Red, and another four of Jermayah's delightful munitions.

She slotted a Redball into the Whisper's top barrel and waited, fingers poised over the Spider's buttons as the cavalry troopers came closer. Only when the last trooper had passed beneath the branch did she inject all her remaining Green along with half the Red. The disorienting effect was immediate and only barely suppressed, her fatigue having sapped her concentration some-what. Despite the sudden nausea she managed to keep her gun arm steady as she trained the Whisper on the middle of the troop and lit the Redball.

The munition impacted on the upper back of a trooper, birthing a satisfyingly large explosion. The unfortunate Corvantine was killed outright, along with his horse, whilst two of his comrades were sent tumbling from their saddles to writhe screaming in a welter of flame. Lizanne shot another as he attempted to control his bucking mount, then flinched as a carbine bullet smacked into the branch barely a foot to her right. Her Green-boosted eyes fixed on the source immediately; the veteran lead scout, galloping back along the trail at full pelt, carbine at his shoulder as he skilfully worked the lever for a second shot.

Lizanne leapt from the branch, tumbling end over end to land amidst the still-rearing horses as the scout's next shot cut the air above her head. She shot down two more troopers in quick succession, then ducked as a third swung at her with a sabre, the tip of the blade coming close enough to snick a few hairs from her flailing pony-tail. He proved an annoyingly adept horseman, keeping his mount in check and dancing it closer, sabre drawn back for a killing thrust whilst he kept low behind the horse's neck to prevent her putting a bullet into his forehead. Lizanne unleashed the Red in a single, instinctive blast. The horse's scream choked off as the heat ate through its throat in an instant, the rider faring little better. His uniform, skin and much of his bone turned to ash. The ghastly remnant of horse and rider, one-half flesh the other a charred ruin, collapsed as Lizanne scrambled away and whirled to face the still-charging veteran.

He was nearly upon her now, weathered face set in a mask of furious triumph behind his levelled carbine. Lizanne's gun hand came up in a blur, exhausting her reserves of Green in a reflexive aim-and-fire motion of such speed and accuracy no non-Blessed could ever be expected to match it. The bullet took the scout in the eye just as his finger tightened on the carbine's trigger, the shot going wide as he tumbled lifeless from the saddle.

Lizanne staggered amidst the carnage she had created, all but a few dregs of product in her veins as she scanned for more targets, finding only dead and dying. She sagged, relief and exhaustion mingling to bring forth an unusual and unfamiliar sound from her throat. It took a moment's puzzled reflection to recognise it as a sob. *How many years since that happened?* she wondered, thumbing a tear from her eye as the sob turned into a rueful laugh.

All humour abruptly vanished at the arrival of a fresh tumult of galloping horses and she found herself voicing a weary groan at the sight of another cavalry troop approaching along the trail. They came on at a cautious canter, halting a good fifty yards short to survey the smoking ruin of their comrades. From the exchange of wary glances she concluded they had deduced her nature, but would also soon divine the fact that she was all but out of product. She sighed, taking a firmer grip on the Whisper and drawing the stolen Cadre revolver from the pocket of her overalls. Getting to her feet she stood with both weapons held at her sides, head cocked in expectation.

The cavalrymen exchanged a few more wary glances before one gave an impatient bark of command, a sergeant from the bullish tone of authority in his voice. In response the troopers all drew their carbines from the scabbards on the saddles and spread out, each taking careful aim as they moved closer in a slow walk. Lizanne thought she might be able to get two before they shot her down and scanned their line, choosing which one to kill. She chose the sergeant, a wiry fellow as cavalrymen often were, his lean features grim and eyes dark behind the sights of his weapon. She was raising both pistols when the sergeant's face disappeared in a red-and-white cloud of sundered flesh and powdered bone.

Gunfire erupted from the jungle to the trooper's right, at least twenty weapons firing at once, a mix of carbines, shotguns and longrifles judging by the discordant mix of cracks and booms. The troopers withered under the weight of fire, none managing to loose off a single shot in response before they were brought down. *Impressive marksmanship,* Lizanne thought, noting the empty saddles on the mostly unscathed horses as they circled about their fallen riders, whinnying in alarm.

A chilling wave of exhaustion swept through her and she found herself on her knees once more, arms sagging to rest her pistols in the mud. 'You're alive!' She raised her lolling head to find Tekela running towards her, Major Arberus close behind. 'I knew you would be!' Lizanne groaned as the girl crushed herself against her.

'Miss Lethridge?' a voice asked in a gruff Old Colonial accent.

Lizanne's gaze went to the stocky figure standing next to Arberus, a woman of middling years with a shotgun resting in the crook of her green-leather-clad arm. Beyond her Lizanne could see other figures in dusters moving amongst the Corvantine dead and crouching to retrieve any valuables or weapons with practised efficiency.

'Griseld Flaxknot,' the woman introduced herself, touching a finger to the rim of her broad-brimmed hat. 'Captain of the Chainmasters Independent Contractor Company. Madame Bondersil is very keen for us to see you home.'

She woke to the jangling of chains, her befuddled mind instantly conjuring visions of a Corvantine torture chamber. *The smugglers, the jungle, all a dream . . . The dress-maker captured me in Morsvale . . .*

'Krista?' Tekela's breath was soft on her ear, coaxing her back to awareness. Lizanne groaned and forced her eyes fully open, finding the girl's face poised above hers, brow bunched in concern. Something hard jolted beneath Lizanne's back and she realised they were in motion, her eyes going to the swaying chains above Tekela's head.

'Drake-catcher's wagon,' she realised aloud.

'Yes.' Tekela helped her into a sitting position, resting her against the thick iron bars that formed the wagon's walls. Major Arberus sat at the far end of the wagon, gazing out at the mounted Contractors riding alongside. Lizanne noted that his rifle was gone.

'They wouldn't let us stop,' Tekela went on. 'Even though there was no waking you. Just piled us into this thing and set off.'

'How long?'

'Two days. I . . . did wonder if you were ever going to wake.'

Lizanne's tongue scraped around the inside of her mouth, making her grimace at the acrid dryness of it. 'Water, please.'

Tekela held a canteen to her lips, though Lizanne soon took it from her, holding it up and gulping down the blessed contents in convulsive heaves. Intense use of product often had unpleasant side-effects, dehydration and fatigue chief amongst them, though she couldn't recall experiencing such a profound reaction before now. Her limbs felt like benumbed rubber and there seemed to be an iron bar skewered through her skull from temple to temple. 'Lizanne,' she said, finally lowering the canteen and wiping a weak hand across her mouth.

'What?' Tekela asked.

'My name. Lizanne Lethridge.'

She saw Arberus shift at that, shooting her a guarded glance that told of instant recognition. *A famous family can be a disadvantage in certain occupations,* she knew, but felt the girl deserved to know the name of her self-appointed guardian. She turned to her, switching to Mandinorian. 'You know this language?'

Tekela gave a half nod, her reply faltering and heavily accented. 'It was the one . . . lesson Father would not . . . allow me to . . .' She fumbled for the right word.

'Shirk?' Lizanne suggested.

Tekela smiled and nodded. 'I . . . am not . . . fluent.'

'That will change.' Lizanne raised herself up farther, gazing out at the passing country. The jungle was thinner now and the trees not so tall, meaning they were nearing the partially settled bush-country south of Carvenport. 'It's likely to be all you'll speak for many years to come.'

They passed by several homesteads before nightfall, one-storey houses with wide, sloping roofs surrounded by a clutch of barns and corrals. All were abandoned, the livestock gone or recently slaughtered. The Chainmasters reported all wells had been spoiled with animal carcasses and any harvested crops either left to rot or deliberately burned.

'Company orders,' Captain Flaxknot commented when they stopped for the night. She had kept them moving until the sun finally dipped below the horizon, posting guards in a tight perimeter and sending two of her marksmen to watch the southern approaches. 'Don't wanna leave nothing for the Corvantines. Recall my grandpap saying he saw the same thing happen once, musta' been eighty years ago. Guess that makes this, what, the Third Corvantine War?'

'Fourth,' Lizanne said. 'Not counting the occasional skirmish in between.'

The captain turned a hard-eyed gaze on Major Arberus. 'Guess they never tire of getting beat.'

'I have a feeling this will be the last one,' Lizanne said, her thoughts returning to Grand Marshal Morradin and the impossibly swift frigate she had destroyed. The Ironship Syndicate had made itself perhaps the most powerful organisation in the world on the basis of innovation, but in the process had burdened itself with an ever-more-complex and extensive bureaucracy and a Board given to tortuous deliberation. The Corvantines had no Board; they had the Emperor. Scion of an erratic and often corrupt line he may have been, but apparently possessed of sufficient wit and singular vision to at least put the corporate world on the back foot within a few days of launching his grand military gambit. Much depended on the Board's willingness to adapt and throw off deeply enshrined company regulations. Somehow, she doubted the process would be anything but a long and painful one.

Unless Madame's scheme comes to fruition, she reminded herself. *Perhaps her obsession will save us after all.*

A faint, plaintive shriek echoed from the tree-line to the south, Captain Flaxknot instantly coming to her feet in response, along with every Contractor in sight. Lizanne was concerned by the expression on the woman's face, a mix of deep surprise and unaccustomed fear. 'Can't be,' she heard her whisper.

'What . . . ?' Lizanne began, only to be waved to silence. Flaxknot moved to the camp's south-facing flank, beckoning one of the Chainmasters to her side, a sturdy young man with a similarly shaped nose to his captain's.

'You heard it?' she asked.

'We all did, Ma,' he replied, Lizanne gauging his expression as even more fearful than his mother's. 'Weren't no phantom. What in the Travail can it be doing here?'

A bright, expanding mushroom of flame erupted in the trees a half mile to the south, lighting up the country as it ascended into the air. Another shriek sounded as the flames faded, louder this time and possessed of an unmistakable note of triumph. Some trees continued to burn bright enough to reveal the sight of men and horses running, all of them aflame.

'What they always do,' Flaxknot said. 'Hunt and kill.'

'Greens?' Lizanne asked, moving to join the captain.

'Wrong call,' she replied without turning, her eyes reflecting the flames. 'Too much fire all at once. We just witnessed a Red fry up a company o' Corvantines. Guessing they picked up our trail and were angling to creep up on the camp in the darkness.'

'It saved . . . us?' Tekela asked in her broken Mandinorian.

This made Flaxknot turn and regard the girl with an amused twist to her mouth. 'Surely, young miss. Outta the goodness of its heart, no doubt.' The captain strode to her horse, voice raised in command, 'Saddle up! We're moving out. No more stops till we make the city.'

True to her word, Captain Flaxknot allowed no rests and they moved through the darkened bush with the aid of a few torches, pressing on without pause come daybreak until the hazy mass of Carvenport appeared on the northern horizon. Lizanne was initially puzzled by the haze. Carvenport's atmosphere was never as polluted as Morsvale's, but as they drew closer she saw that it was in fact dust. It rose in a fine, grainy mist, born from the labour of at least a thousand people hard at work amidst a network of newly dug trenches, spades and picks rising and falling with urgent energy. A troop of mounted Protectorate soldiers soon emerged from the brown fog to greet them, the presence of three riderless horses indicating their arrival had been expected.

'Madame Bondersil requests you join her at the Academy, miss,' the lieutenant in charge told Lizanne, hand quivering a little as he snapped off a precise salute. 'Your companions, also.'

'My thanks for your diligent care, Captain,' Lizanne told Flaxknot as she climbed into the saddle, gesturing for Tekela to follow suit.

'Never failed to fulfil a contract,' the woman replied. She glanced back at the bush country, her unease evident in the way she flapped her hat against her thigh. 'You be sure to tell her what we saw,' she said, turning back to Lizanne. 'The Red last night . . . It was all wrong, a thing that shouldn't be. I suspect we got more than Corvantine trouble at our door.'

'I'll tell her,' Lizanne promised. She tightened the pack's straps across her shoulders, feeling the weight of the device shift against her back and recalling the black web infecting Madame's mindscape. *Though I doubt if she truly cares a damn for anything else just now.*

'I've never ridden,' Tekela was saying, still unmounted and eyeing the tall war-horse with some trepidation.

'It's easy,' Arberus said, taking hold of her waist and lifting her onto the horse's back. 'All you have to do is try not to fall off.'

As they made their way towards the city Lizanne soon gained an appreciation for the extent of the fortifications. It appeared every Carvenport resident was now engaged in digging trenches, from stevedores to managers, labourers and accountants. All hands had either answered the call to work in the city's defence or, judging by the sullen expressions of a few, been pressed to the task against their will. The speed with which the entrenchments had been constructed was partly explained by the presence of several Blood-blessed. Some toiled away at the earth with Green-fuelled industry whilst others shifted great stacks of sandbags with the aid of Black.

'Morradin will have to spend two thousand lives at least to take this place,' Arberus commented as they came to the final set of breastworks. An interlinked line of artillery emplacements had been constructed close to the walls, all raised to afford clear fields of fire for miles around, each one connected to its neighbour by a zig-zig line of trenches, some already manned by Protectorate infantry.

'Do you expect that to dissuade him?' Lizanne asked.

'On the first day of Cortanza he sent four thousand men to die in a diversionary attack so he could advance his guns a bare fifty yards. On the second day, another twelve thousand died in a frontal assault against the rebel centre. Apparently, he still sleeps soundly every night and enjoys a hearty breakfast on waking. Make no mistake, Miss Lethridge, whatever the cost, Morradin will take this city.'

Madame Bondersil's hands trembled a little as she rested them on the solargraph, a thin sigh escaping her lips, eyes rapt and unwavering as she drank in every cog and lever. 'Have you attempted to activate it?' she asked Lizanne. They were in her office at the Academy, now transformed into a de facto military headquarters as the Board had been quick to name Madame as Executive Manager of the Arradsian Holdings. It was a rarely used position, affording near-dictatorial powers to the holder and therefore only employed in times of crisis. The fact that so many Protectorate officers were waiting outside was an indication that the balance of power in the city had abruptly shifted away from the local corporate managers. However, Lizanne knew this was merely a public demonstration of a long-hidden reality; Madame had long been the true power here.

'More pressing matters precluded any experimentation,' Lizanne replied. She stood at formal attention before the desk, having not been offered a seat. Arberus and Tekela had been obliged to wait downstairs, the Protectorate soldiers who had accompanied them from the trenches still very much in evidence. 'Also, I was worried I might break it.'

'Yes.' Madame's fingers lingered on the device, twitching a little. 'It is good to see your judgement hasn't completely failed you.'

Lizanne stiffened, her burgeoning resentment stoked somewhat by the fact that this was the closest thing to a compliment Madame had offered since her arrival. 'Every decision taken was born of necessity,' she said, casting a pointed glance at the papers spread out on the desk next to the solargraph. 'And I believe my results speak for themselves.'

Madame's gaze snapped up, dark with anger. 'Your identity is forever compromised now. You do realise that, I trust?'

'Everyone who saw my face in Morsvale is now dead, save for the smuggler and I doubt he'll be returning there for a very long time.'

'Not everyone.'

Lizanne found herself gritting her teeth to forestall an unwise reply. She knew this meeting was a milestone in both her career and her relationship with her most cherished mentor, the future of which greatly depended on what she said next. 'I gave assurances to secure the assistance of local resources,' she said, keeping her voice as even and uncoloured by emotion as possible. 'A tactic employed in many covert operations. I will attest to the correctness of my actions should the Board require a fuller enquiry. Also, I believe Major Arberus may have more to say about our overriding mission, being so familiar with the Interior and the studies of Burgrave Artonin.'

'And the girl? Is she, perhaps, also an expert in her father's work?'

Lizanne's hands were clasped together behind her back and she found herself flexing her fingers over the buttons on the Spider. Captain Flaxknot had generously provided a half-vial of Green as a restorative and she still had a third of it left. 'Miss

Artonin,' she said, meeting Madame's gaze and speaking in a deliberately soft tone, 'remains under my protection.'

Madame straightened, blinking in either surprise or disappointment. 'You were always such a cold child,' she said. 'So distant from the other girls. When you went off to join Exceptional Initiatives, I must confess to a certain trepidation as to what I might have unleashed upon the world.'

She returned her gaze to the solargraph, lifting her hands from it with a visible effort. 'Take this to Mr Tollermine. The papers will be copied and distributed to my coterie of experts. Your next trance with Mr Torcreek is tomorrow, I believe?'

Lizanne waited a moment before replying, searching Madame's bearing for some sign of continuing threat, then slowly removed her finger from the Spider. 'Yes, Madame.'

'Convey to him whatever Mr Tollermine is able to discern. He's been busy crafting various deadly devices with which to greet our Corvantine visitors, but that must be set aside now. You will ensure he doesn't allow himself any distractions.'

'I will, Madame. Major Arberus and Miss Artonin?'

'Keep them with you. I can't spare anyone to guard them in any case.'

'There is the other issue I raised . . .'

'A Red this far north is certainly unusual.' Madame's tone held a certain weary note as she turned to her window, arms crossed as she gazed out at the harbour. It was full of merchant vessels unable to sail now the Corvantines held the Strait. The sailors had either volunteered to assist in the city's defence or were hiding themselves belowdecks to wait out the coming storm. 'But, as ever, I find our human enemies a more potent threat.'

'Mr Torcreek's last trance communication indicated unusual activity in the Interior, breeds of drake hunting beyond their usual habitats and the Spoiled even more aggressive than usual. I can't but wonder if it isn't somehow connected.'

'This continent is dying,' Madame said, her tone absent any particular alarm. 'Or rather, the drakes are dying. We have hunted them to the point where their eventual extinction is now inevitable and we are witnessing their death throes. We should consider ourselves privileged, for future generations will come to think of the drakes as the legends of a less-civilised age. Unless, of course, we find the White.'

The White, Lizanne thought. *Her every thought circles back to it. The answer to all our ills.* 'I should make haste to Jermayah's,' she said, moving to the desk and returning the solargraph to her pack. Madame didn't turn, merely nodding as Lizanne went to the door, though she did have a few parting words.

'Should the girl or the major prove to have been unworthy of your trust, I assume you retain sufficient stomach to handle the matter in the appropriate manner.'

CHAPTER 26

Clay

The sergeant who greeted Clay's uncle at the base of the tower was unshaven and hollow-cheeked, pale features concealed beneath a mask of mingled soot and blood, his uniform stained, ripped and charred in numerous places. Nevertheless, he still managed to deliver a respectful, straight-backed salute, the bandage on his hand leaking blood as he did so.

'Since when d'you salute civilians?' Braddon asked him.

'Since they saved my life, sir.' He stepped forward to extend his uninjured hand to Braddon. 'Eadsell, Sergeant . . .'

'. . . Seventeenth Light Infantry,' Braddon finished, briefly clasping the man's hand. 'We found your colours back at the fort. I'm bound to say, Sergeant, it don't seem too dutiful to me. Abandoning your post like that.'

Clay saw Eadsell stiffen a little and cast a hard look back at the tower. 'My duty is to follow orders,' he said. 'However mad and driven by greed they might be.'

There were only seven soldiers left, all exhausted to the point of near collapse and none without at least one bandaged wound or burn. They stood or sat slumped about the tower's uppermost tier, regarding the Longrifles with either glassy-eyed exhaustion or sagging relief. An eighth figure rose from a huddled position on the floor as they climbed up the narrow stairwell, a portly, middle-aged fellow in bedraggled civilian clothes and possessed of a certain wild-eyed animation.

'How many in the main body?' he demanded of Braddon, apparently feeling no need to offer a greeting.

'Main body?' Braddon asked.

'The reinforcements,' the man said, his tone rich in petulant insistence. 'You are but a vanguard, I assume.'

'No, sir. It's just us.' Braddon angled his head, looking the man up and down in scrutiny. 'And who might you be?'

'This is Dr Erric Firpike,' Sergeant Eadsell said when the man stiffened into an aggrieved silence. 'Contracted Archaeologist to the Consolidated Research Company.' The sergeant's tone said much for his opinion of the doctor.

'Really?' Braddon said, turning an enquiring eye to Scriberson. 'Then I guess you two must be acquainted.'

Clay watched as the young astronomer regarded Firpike with a stern aspect that spoke of recognition mingled with palpable dislike. For his part, Firpike exhibited a distinctly odd agitation at the sight of an apparent colleague. 'By reputation only,' Scriberson said in a quiet voice before turning to the sergeant. 'What has this man told you?'

'He came down the Falls a few days before all communication ceased with Fallsguard,' the sergeant replied. 'Bearing a joint contract between the Ironship Interior Exploration Division and Consolidated Research. He had Protectorate orders compelling our assistance in his mission.'

'Which was?' Braddon asked.

The sergeant gestured at their surroundings, his voice taking on a distinctly bitter note. 'This place. A lost city rich in wondrous treasures.'

'Might I see these orders?' Braddon enquired, extending a hand to Firpike. The man looked as if he might object but a glance at the rest of the company soon cured him of any hesitation. 'Well, ain't that pretty,' Braddon said after looking over the sheaf of papers Firpike produced from the folds of his jacket. 'Got the company crests just right. See, Skaggs?'

The harvester took the papers and gave a grunt of amused appreciation. 'Expensive work. Pity about the signature.'

'Are you saying they're forged?' the sergeant said, his gaze now fixed on Firpike's rapidly paling face. The other soldiers began to stir at this, coming to their feet and stepping closer, each one with a rifle in hand. From their expressions, Clay deduced their fondness for the doctor matched that of their sergeant.

'Those orders are signed, stamped and duly witnessed,' Firpike stuttered, taking an involuntary step back before forcing himself to remain still. He had nowhere to run in any case. 'I met personally with . . .'

'Mr Jonnas Greymount,' Braddon noted, retrieving the papers from Skaggerhill. 'Head of Ironship Interior Explorations, signed some six weeks ago, I see. Mr Greymount was well-known to me. Can't pretend to being his friend as such, but I did respect him enough to attend his funeral a year and a half ago. Since then, Interior Explorations has been in the hands of Madame Bondersil.' He held up the papers. 'Can't see her name here anywhere.'

'You piece of filth!' Sergeant Eadsell lunged for the doctor, grabbing him and forcing him to the tower's parapet. 'Seventy men dead!' Eadsell grated as his men closed in, a couple raising rifles with fixed bayonets. 'All on the promise of lies!'

'I . . . I didn't force anyone to come,' Firpike protested, voicing a panicky yelp as Eadsell forced him back farther, his head dangling over the parapet. The drop was about fifty feet onto hard stone and, even if he survived it, he had to know there would be no hand lifted to help him. 'Your captain could have provided just a small escort . . .'

'You knew, you bastard!' Eadsell shouted, spittle flying as Firpike jerked in his grip. 'You knew once that greedy fool heard the word "treasure" he'd do anything to get it.' An angry growl rose from the soldiers, a couple crouching to take hold of Firpike's legs.

Clay turned to his uncle, speaking quietly, 'They keep talking about treasure. And Scribes here had no notion this place existed.'

'We didn't come for trinkets,' Braddon said.

'Knowledge, Uncle. Knowledge is a treasure.'

He saw Braddon think it over, waiting until the soldiers had begun to tip the doctor over the edge before barking out, 'Stop that!'

They took some persuading, but Braddon's air of authority, not to mention the guns of his Contractors, was enough to compel Firpike's release. They left him on all fours on the floor, retching with fear.

'Young man,' Braddon said to Scriberson. 'Why don't you tell us what you know about this fella?'

The tower had a pit in the centre of its topmost floor with a gap in the ceiling above. It made for a fine fire-place which Clay guessed must have been its original purpose. When night came they huddled round the blaze to hear the astronomer's story, Foxbine and Preacher posted on the parapet to keep watch on the ruins. Firpike sat a little apart from them, unbound despite Sergeant Eadsell's protests. 'He runs off, he'll be dead within the hour,' Skaggerhill said. The archaeologist had said nothing since his rescue from the soldiers' vengeance, sitting with his knees drawn up and face set in a mask of self-pity.

'There's a figure from history,' Scriberson said. 'The man who wrote the account that brought me here, in fact. We don't know his name, but he has become known as the Mad Artisan in most scholarly circles.'

Clay watched his uncle shrug. 'Never been one for history. What's it gotta do with the charlatan here?'

'Dr, or rather, former Dr Firpike was one of the most accomplished non-Corvantine authorities on the Artisan. Veteran of several expeditions to the Arradsian Interior and author of three books describing the Artisan's various wanderings. His principal achievement, however, was the discovery of a design for a mechanical compass, one which worked perfectly when reconstructed.'

'Mechanical compass?' Loriabeth asked with a frown.

'A device that will always point true north without benefit of magnetism. It's all due to the arrangement and dimension of various cogs. The story goes that the Artisan got lost in the Interior and, lacking a traditional compass, navigated his way home by constructing the device. Though there are those who claim he simply found it, along with most of the other novelties ascribed to him. The invention itself has been lost but *Mr* Firpike was able to unearth a design, said to be the work of the Artisan's own hand. It was the subject of his last book and saw him awarded an honorary doctorate and elevated to the position of Chief Archaeologist to the Consolidated Research Company.'

Braddon spared a glance at Firpike's huddled form. 'Guess it didn't take.'

'No,' Scriberson said, voice rich in sour judgement. 'Other researches into Artisan lore, including some of my own, revealed no corresponding mentions of this device. Unusual given the Artisan's almost manic love of repeatedly describing his own achievements. However, a journey through the company's most ancient archives did uncover a Dalcian instrument of remarkably similar design, one that predated the colonisation of Arradsia by at least two centuries.'

Loriabeth gave a wicked chuckle, turning to slap Firpike on the back. 'You sly old dog, Doc.'

'Doctor no longer,' Scriberson said, clearly peeved at her appreciation for the charlatan's ploy. 'He was, of course, duly stripped of his doctorate and his contract cancelled. Legal moves were also instituted to recover the lucrative research grants paid to him, whereupon he disappeared, along with the money. In the unlikely event I ever heard of him again, I must confess I expected it to involve a lurid demise in a gambling den or whore-house.'

Clay saw Firpike stir a little, head raised as he muttered a toneless retort. 'I was duped by unscrupulous rogues.'

'Rogues who shared your handwriting and could never be found,' Scriberson replied. 'How very curious.'

'Alright, Doc,' Braddon said, giving Firpike an insistent nudge. 'Time to spill it. What brings you here? And have a care not to give voice to any lies. I got a keen ear for 'em and right now my company is your only ticket back to civilisation.'

Firpike hesitated a long while before shifting himself to face them, his fearful misery still etched into his face, though the prospect of survival did appear to have returned some animation to his voice. 'Not all my . . . acquisitions were sourced from forgers,' he began, drawing a disgusted snort from Scriberson, though he ploughed on with only a faint tic of irritation. 'The Artisan collected many stories from others who roamed the Interior; Contractors, headhunters and the like, though they were all called hunters in those days. A fragment of one of his collections turned up in a Mandinorian antiquary emporium, though the owner had little idea of its true worth. It related a conversation with a hunter, a fellow seemingly almost as unhinged as the Artisan himself. His company had been engaged in hunting aquatic Greens on Krystaline Lake but had contrived to snare an overly large and aggressive specimen which overturned their boats and left them stranded on the shore, minus several unfortunates who became a meal for their erstwhile prey. Weeks of wandering the jungle saw them beset by Spoiled and Greens alike, until a lone survivor happened upon a city.' Firpike paused to raise his arms in a weak, almost dismissive gesture at their surroundings. When he spoke again his voice had taken on a bitter tone, the tone Clay recognised from gamblers who threw everything into the pot on a sure-fire hand only to see it vanish to a better one. 'A city rich in all manner of treasure, there for the taking.'

'So,' Braddon said, 'you thought a little jaunt out here would restore your fortunes.' He glanced at the grim-faced soldiers on the other side of the fire. 'And got these poor bastards to come along as insurance.'

Firpike gave a small shrug. 'Their commanding officer was a . . . pragmatic man.'

'Now a dead one,' Clay pointed out, deciding he didn't much like Mr Firpike. It was plain in the faintly self-satisfied cadence of his voice and the aggrieved victimhood in his face: a man who cared nothing for the lives lost in pursuit of his dream of regained eminence. 'So where is it?' he asked. 'This great treasure.'

'For obvious reasons,' Firpike replied in a tone that did nothing to improve Clay's opinion of him, 'a fulsome investigation of the ruins has not yet been possible.'

'More's to the point,' Braddon said. 'What exactly is it? There's all kinds of treasure.'

'The Artisan's account was vague in regards to that,' Firpike said. 'However, if his other writings are anything to go by, it will certainly be worth finding.' He paused, neck constricting as he swallowed and gathered some fortitude for his next words. 'However, I can assure you it won't be found without my assistance. I have memorised the Artisan's account and no copies will be found on my person. Your assistance in fulfilling my mission will, of course, entail a substantial reward . . .'

He trailed off as the Contractors all broke into laughter, save for Preacher, who kept his gaze on the ruins. Seemingly, Firpike's tale held no interest for him. Clay had also noted that he hadn't said a single word since his outburst on the lake-shore.

'I'll make you a counter-offer, Doc,' Braddon said to Firpike, now sunk into guarded sullenness by their amusement. 'We'll tarry a day to search for this wondrous prize of yours, and if we find it we let these here soldiers decide who gets what. Seems the fairest outcome, all things considered.'

The vastness of the city became clear during their initial survey the next morning. Braddon forbade any division in their strength and they moved as a crowd, sweeping first north then south to find the edge of the ruins. It soon became clear that the buildings they had encountered so far were but a small part of a much larger whole, most of it so overgrown as to be near invisible amidst the thick jungle. However, now they could recognise the various forms of the city's architecture, the vine-encrusted towers and houses became obvious landmarks amongst the trees.

'Must go on for miles and miles,' Skaggerhill said. 'We'd have to hack our way into every building.'

'How did this get missed for so long?' Clay wondered. 'I mean Contractors have hunted here before, right?'

'Not so often as elsewhere. The lake's always been a tricky place to get to. Besides, those that do make it here ain't looking for no lost city, especially when it's damn near claimed by the jungle. Another year or two and this place would've been hidden for good.'

'It would have been very different in the Artisan's day,' Scriberson said. He moved with pencil and notebook in hand, jotting down a hasty note or sketch whenever they paused. 'The buildings more intact, the inscriptions not so faded.' He crouched to peer at something carved into the base of a plinth of some kind, a flat-topped stone so cracked and weathered it appeared about to collapse at any second.

'That's some kinda writing, huh?' Clay asked him.

'I believe so. There have been examples found at other sites, though never as extensive. These symbols appear similar in form, but no-one has yet found a way of translating them.'

'Maybe the Spoiled can read them?' Loriabeth suggested. 'I guess it was their forebears that built the place.'

'Spoiled ain't got the brains to read nothin',' Foxbine insisted. 'And it's a certainty they could never have made a place like this. Shit, folks today couldn't make a place like this.'

Braddon called a halt soon after, standing to regard Firpike in wordless expectation. 'The Artisan's account spoke of a bridge across a broad canal,' he said. 'Leading to a great temple of some kind. The hunter maintained the bulk of the treasure would be found there.'

'Can't see no bridge,' Skaggerhill said, voice rich in impatience. Clay could tell he found their dalliance here a pointless distraction from pursuit of the main prize.

Firpike pointed at something in a swathe of jungle to the south. 'But there is the canal.' It was only a shallow depression in the mass of vegetation but on closer inspection it became clear that it extended in a straight line into the depths of the overgrown city. 'It was always my plan to follow it to the temple.'

They had to hack their way through in several places, the wall of vines and new-grown trees being so thick. Silverpin and Clay shared the duty, cutting a path with long-bladed knives. Unlike the others, she seemed unperturbed by this place, the prospect of imminent riches failing to enliven her at all. If anything she appeared bored, the fascination that had seized her in the White's cave back at the Badlands now replaced with disinterested labour.

'You think this is all horse shit, right?' Clay asked during a pause, lifting a canteen to let the water cascade over his sweat-slick face. She replied with only a rueful grin, twirling her knife in a brief but expert flourish before returning to her work.

They found the bridge after what felt like twenty miles of cutting but, in fact, couldn't have been more than two. Clay surmised it must have been quite a sight in its day; a tall, elegant arc spanning a fifty-foot gap. But now the central span had tumbled into the weed-filled canal below, the remaining structure resembling the stunted and deformed arms of some vine-covered giant. Off to the left the temple rose out of the jungle, the most majestic building they had seen so far. It appeared to be a four-sided structure of five tiers, each smaller than the one below so as to form a huge pyramid. The jungle had claimed the two lowest tiers, making it appear like an island partly swamped by a sea of green.

'Guess you're not wholly a liar, after all,' Clay told Firpike, though the man seemed not to hear, gazing up at the temple in rapt fascination.

'The Artisan tell of any way in?' Braddon prompted as the archaeologist continued to stare.

Firpike blinked and tore his gaze from the temple with a visible effort. 'The hunter's account became confused when he spoke of the temple,' he said. 'He had been confined to an asylum by the time the Artisan sought him out. Much of what he said about the place was rambling nonsense, though he kept repeating the word "treasure."'

'In Eutherian, presumably?' Scriberson asked.

'The Artisan wrote in Eutherian,' Firpike replied, a little stiffly. It seemed to Clay he resented the presence of another scholar at his great discovery.

'But did the hunter speak it?' Scriberson pressed.

Firpike remained silent for a moment, frowning in reluctant consideration. 'The Artisan describes him as a one-time Steppe nomad, come across the ocean in search of his fortune in this fabled land.'

'Meaning his primary tongue would have been unintelligible to outsiders, so he would most likely have spoken West Mandinorian to anyone not of his tribe. Probably an archaic form to boot.'

'Failing to see the import of this discussion, gents,' Braddon said.

'Translation,' Scriberson said. 'Meanings often become confused due to multiple translations. From the nomad's tongue to West Mandinorian to Eutherian. Much could have changed in the process. "Treasure" in Mandinorian is often translated into Eutherian as any item of value or importance.'

'You mean,' Clay said, 'we may not be finding ourselves knee deep in gold and jewels when we get in there.'

'Indeed,' Scriberson said, regarding Firpike with the same suspicion he had maintained since first setting eyes on him. 'Though we do know that whatever the nomad found here eventually landed him in the madhouse.'

A moment's silence descended, soon stretching into several more as the soldiers exchanged nervous glances and the Longrifles did likewise. 'Well,' Braddon said eventually, moving towards the temple with a purposeful stride, 'we've come this far. Besides, if anything I saw in the Interior was gonna send me mad, it woulda happened years ago.'

They could find no way in at ground level, the vines proving too thick and the great expanse upon which the temple had been constructed cracked and sundered in many places by the trees that had grown through the stone. Loriabeth volunteered to climb to the upper tiers, demonstrating how well her leg had healed by scaling the wall of close-packed greenery with a lithe ease. She cast a rope down from the second highest tier and the Longrifles climbed up one after the other.

'We'd best stay here,' Sergeant Eadsell said, to the evident relief of his fellow soldiers. The sergeant's face shone with more sweat than could be accounted for by mere exertion and his voice betrayed the strain of a man nearing the limits of courage. 'Makes sense to guard the escape route.'

'Sound military thinking,' Braddon assured him, taking hold of the rope.

Loriabeth had already found a way in, a decent-sized gap in the vines on the temple's north-side. She crouched at it with pistol in hand, peering at the gloomy interior with uncharacteristic reluctance. 'Smells funny,' she said as Clay clambered to her side. 'Like something old and long dead.'

A quick sniff confirmed it, Clay finding the smell had an unpleasant mustiness to it. He could see a broad beam of sunlight streaming through the darkness beyond the gap, indicating the temple roof had fallen in at some point. He glanced back, finding Silverpin close by and inclined his head at the gap. 'Shall we?'

After the clamminess of the jungle the temple interior felt blessedly cool, Clay standing in a void of shadows until his eyes accustomed themselves to the gloom. The floor was uneven in several places, causing him to move with a cautious step, Stinger at his shoulder and Loriabeth and Silverpin close by on either side. This tier was a single space free of walls, the ceiling supported by rows of octagonal pillars. Clay was inevitably drawn to the sunlit centre of the space, the beam streaming down through a wide opening into the depths of the temple. Like the pillars, the hole was eight-sided and ringed by a balustrade. Clay leaned over to glance up then down, confirming each successive tier also featured an identical hole. The base of the temple, as revealed by the bright octagon of sunlight, appeared just a jumble of fallen stone.

'Well, it's surely big enough,' Skaggerhill murmured, appearing out of the gloom alongside Braddon and Preacher.

'Big enough for what?' Clay asked.

'A winged drake.' The harvester leaned on the balustrade, gazing down. 'Red, Black or . . .' He trailed off at a warning cough from Braddon.

'They paid homage to it, here.' Preacher stood back from the hole, keeping to the shadows though the light glinted on his eyes. Clay felt his unease deepen at the tone of the marksman's voice: possessed of the same stridency as when he had quoted scripture. 'Bowed down to worship a harbinger of destruction.'

'Don't appear to have done them much good,' Loriabeth said, kicking a loose stone across the floor so it tumbled over the edge of the hole. It was two full seconds before they heard the faint clatter as it found the bottom.

'Nevertheless,' Scriberson said, 'I believe our devout friend may be right. About this being a place of worship, at least.' He had stopped at one of the pillars, playing the light from a small lantern over its surface. Clay joined him, making out the symbols etched into the stone.

'More writing that can't be read?'

'Partly, but not all. See here.' Scriberson angled the lantern a little, revealing a series of images carved into the stone. They were simple in form but had been crafted with considerable precision; a group of human-like figures stood with arms raised below what could only be a drake, flying aloft with wings spread wide and flame blossoming from its gaping jaws.

'That a Red?' Clay wondered.

'A Black,' Skaggerhill said, coming to join them. 'You can tell by the spines along the neck. Reds don't have so many.'

'They worshipped the Black,' Clay said, exchanging a glance with his uncle. 'Perhaps that wasn't all.'

'Look around,' Braddon said. 'Every pillar.'

The inscriptions varied on each pillar, both in length and complexity, but the basic motif remained: people in supplication to a Black drake. 'Maybe it's different on the other floors,' Skaggerhill suggested and Braddon soon had them hunting for a stairwell. They found it set into the western wall, the way down blocked by fallen stone but the way up clear and intact. As before, Clay and Silverpin went first, finding a small chamber with fewer pillars, though once again all identically decorated.

'Guess they just really liked the Black,' Skaggerhill said.

'Got something here,' Foxbine called, lowered to a crouch with her torch held close to the floor. Clay lowered his own torch, revealing a complex arrangement of small, square tiles, many of different hues.

'Mosaic,' Scriberson said, voice pitched a little high in excitement. 'We need more light.'

Clay and Silverpin were obliged to return to the lower tier to cut vines for more torches, laying them out on the floor to reveal the mosaic in full. It was similar in form to the carvings on the pillars but much more detailed. The Black had been rendered with an unnerving accuracy, the jet scales glittering bright in the torch-light. The people crouched below in worship were similarly convincing, though their form proved unexpected.

'That ain't no Spoiled,' Foxbine said, tapping a boot on the figure in the centre of the bowing humans, a young woman in a light blue robe. Like the others, she had skin of bronze and an elaborate mass of dark hair. Though the band on her head set her apart, a spiky contrivance fashioned from feathers, gems and what could only be gold.

'An indigenous Arradsian,' Firpike said, crouching to play a hand over the figure before casting a somewhat triumphant glance at Scriberson. 'An unspoilt forebear, just as I predicted in my second book.'

'Merely an expansion of theories already advanced by more accomplished scholarship,' the astronomer replied, though Clay felt his dismissive tone was a little forced.

'You mean the Spoiled weren't always Spoiled,' Loriabeth said.

'Quite so, young lady,' Firpike said, returning a hungry gaze to the mosaic. Clay noted how his hand lingered on the woman's crown; the only evidence of treasure they had so far found. 'The deformities typical to the native inhabitants of this continent have long puzzled biologists, given that they are found nowhere else on the planet. It has been theorised that their line became corrupted somehow, leaving them prone to deformity and reduced intelligence. A theory never validated, until now.'

'So what corrupted them?' she asked.

'Another great mystery awaiting an answer. But, at least now we know it happened long after the building of this city.'

'Got another one here,' Braddon called from the other side of the hole. This time the torches revealed a different image, though the woman from the first mosaic remained. She stood holding aloft something large and red that dripped a crimson cascade into her mouth. The Black that had been the object of worship lay dead beside her, its chest rent open, whilst another smaller drake emerged from a sundered egg near by.

'Heart-blood,' Skaggerhill whispered, shaking his head. 'They drank its heart-blood when it died.'

'Thought that stuff was fatal,' Clay said.

'To us, certainly,' Firpike said. 'But perhaps not to them. We know modern-day Spoiled have been witnessed eating raw Drake flesh without suffering fatal consequences. It could be they had some inherent immunity to its effects, like Blood-blessed today.'

'Heart-blood will still kill a Blood-blessed,' Skaggerhill pointed out.

'Not in every case. There are stories of some who survived. Receiving gifts beyond that of a normal Blood-blessed in the process.'

Clay returned his gaze to the woman in the mosaic. 'Makes you wonder what gift she received,'

'There's another stairway back here,' Foxbine called from the gloom.

*

'So,' said Braddon, 'I'm guessing this is what the mad fella meant by treasure.'

The pyramid's summit was open to the elements and featured a single pillar next to the octagonal hole in the centre. The jungle had reached even to this height and the pillar was wreathed in vines but not so thickly as to conceal the nature of its construction. Clay reached through the vegetation to press a hand to the untarnished yellow metal beneath, feeling the indentations of an engraving.

'Half a ton's worth of gold at least,' Skaggerhill surmised. 'Though how in the Travail you'd get it down from here and back to civilisation, I don't know.'

'There are ways,' Firpike said, gazing at the pillar with bright-eyed agitation. 'Now proof has been found, there isn't a corporation in the world that wouldn't fund an expedition.'

'You're forgetting our deal, Doc,' Braddon said. 'This don't belong to you.'

'What?' Firpike laughed in genuine astonishment. 'Captain, you must see the value of this discovery. Beyond the mere profit to be had from the gold, the historical importance . . .'

'All up to Sergeant Eadsell and his men to decide. You can make your case for their consideration and I'll stand witness to a contracted outcome. But, make no mistake, Doc. They decide to throw you in the lake and keep this all to themselves, I ain't standing in their way.' He turned away as Firpike began to sputter, glancing around at the otherwise barren platform. 'Ain't nothing for us here. Mr Scriberson, Doc, you got a half-hour to take what notes you can, then we're climbing down.'

Clay went to Braddon's side as he moved to the edge of the platform, gazing out towards the blue expanse of the Krystaline to the west. 'All Black and no White,' Clay said in a soft murmur.

'It was worth the trip, just on the off-chance of finding another clue. I do wonder if we ain't missing something here, though.'

'It's a big city. Could be other temples.'

'No.' Braddon gestured at the surrounding jungle. 'Nothing

comes close to this in size. Preacher's right, these people were in thrall to the Black . . .'

He fell silent as a sharp, cracking sound echoed from below, quickly followed by a half-dozen more. 'Eadsell,' Braddon said, shielding his eyes to peer down at the base of the temple. At first the soldiers were hard to make out amongst the varying hues of green but then Clay saw them, two clambering desperately up the rope whilst the others maintained a rapid fusillade at the tree-line. He couldn't make out what they were shooting at but then he heard it, the same piercing scream from when they had first found the city. *Greens*. He could see them through the canopy, skin flickering as they raced through the patchy sunlight. They came boiling out of the jungle a few seconds later, far more than had been assaulting the tower, too many to easily count.

'Preacher, get over here!' Braddon called, unshouldering his longrifle. He began to fire immediately, the rifle booming out three rapid shots, Clay seeing Greens tumble as they began to scramble down the far bank of the canal. All but two of the soldiers had made it up the rope to the second tier now, Sergeant Eadsell and one other continuing to fire at the onrushing Greens.

'Eadsell!' Skaggerhill called, cupping his hands around his mouth. 'Forget it! There's too many! Just get up here!'

The sergeant glanced upwards and gestured for his comrade to make for the rope, fired a final shot then followed. A Green clawed its way out of the canal and sprinted in pursuit, leaping with claws raised and mouth gaping. Preacher's shot caught it in mid air, its head snapping back in a red cloud. Braddon and Preacher continued their barrage as the soldiers climbed, aiming with a precision that belied the rapidity of the shots. Clay counted at least a dozen Greens felled by the time both marksmen stopped to reload.

'What in the Travail is this?' he heard Foxbine breathe, gazing down at the tree-line in blank astonishment.

For a second Clay could only see yet more Greens, emerging from the jungle in a seemingly endless tide, but then amongst the rushing drakes he saw them, moving slower though seemingly in equally large numbers. *Spoiled.*

They came to stand at the edge of the jungle as the last of the Greens charged clear of the trees. Clay had no notion how many, a thousand, two thousand? For a short time they just stood there, gazing up at the temple in silent contemplation. The Greens were roiling about at the base of the temple, still baying out their screams without any regard for the copious prey at their backs.

'I'm guessing this is new,' Clay said, flexing his trembling hands on the Stinger.

'Greens eat Spoiled just like they eat everything else,' Skaggerhill said. 'But not today. Today, seems like they both just want us.'

A ripple ran through the long line of Spoiled, all of them moving with a parade-ground precision as if in response to some unspoken command. Clay could see most had raised their arms, thinking perhaps a homage to this place, but then a closer look saw they all held something.

'Down!' he shouted, whirling away, snagging Braddon's duster to drag him along. The arrows rose in a black cloud, some striking the edge of the platform whilst others described a narrow arc to plummet down. Clay huddled behind the golden pillar, making himself as small as possible, hearing the sharp raindrop-like clatter of flint striking stone all around. Someone issued a pained grunt near by and he winced as a fleck of shattered flint stung his cheek.

He raised his head as the clatter faded, eyes instinctively seeking out Silverpin. She was crouched at Foxbine's side, the gunhand's face tensed in pain as she gave forth a torrent of profane fury, bloodied hands clamped around the arrow embedded in her thigh. 'Sons-a-bitching fucking freaks!'

Clay moved to where his uncle stood staring down at the spectacle below. Eadsell and his men lay scattered about the second tier, pierced all over by arrows. Below them the Greens had begun to climb, making slow but steady progress as they latched their claws on the blanket of vines, still screaming all the while.

'That Product you got hidden,' Braddon said to Clay, slotting a round into his longrifle. 'I'm thinking now would be a good time.'

He moved away before Clay could say anything else, barking orders. 'Preacher, you and me will take the front. Lori, cover the right. Skaggs, on the left. Silverpin, look to the rear. Clay, choose your own ground. Mark your targets and make 'em count. Ammo costs money.'

He and Preacher immediately resumed their barrage at the Greens below, the steady boom of their longrifles punctuating the increasingly loud chorus of drake screams. It wasn't long before they came within range of Loriabeth's pistols and Skaggerhill's shotgun, and for a few moments all was noise and rising gunsmoke, dimming occasionally as the Longrifles reloaded.

Clay saw Firpike huddling at the base of his beloved pillar, eyes closed tight against the din, and hugging the vine-encrusted gold as if worried it might be snatched away. Clay considered hauling him off the thing but then saw Scriberson raising himself up to cast a curious glance over the edge of the roof. The astronomer reeled back almost immediately as a blast of drake fire licked the edge of the platform. Clay rushed to Scriberson's side, helping him pat away the patch of flame on his sleeve. Clay took out Auntie's vial and gulped down some Black before risking a glance over the edge.

Two Greens clambered straight towards him, claws blurring and smoke rising from their snapping jaws. He raised the Stinger and began firing, loosing off two shots to no good effect before forcing himself to take a calming breath. *The head, always the head.*

His next shot impacted on the snout of the Green on the left, forcing it to halt but failing to kill it. He raised his aim a fraction as the beast shook blood from its snout, slotting a round cleanly into its skull and sending it tumbling onto its brethren below.

Clay shifted his sights to the other Green, which had now

scrambled to within a dozen feet. It sprang to the side as he fired, the bullet tearing a chunk of flesh from its foreleg but failing to dislodge it from the vines. It launched itself upwards as he fired his final round, tail whipping and jaws gaping as the bullet impacted on its belly, drawing blood but barely slowing it down. It scrambled up the remaining distance in a blur of shifting colours, claws shredding vines and calling out its piercing scream. Clay fought panic and locked his feet in place, fixing his gaze on the drake. There was no time to reload and he had only one weapon left. He waited until it came within a yard of the temple's summit then unleashed the Black in a single blast. The Green's head jerked back from the force of the wave, Clay hearing the crack of breaking bone before it was cast off into the air, tumbling end over end to disappear into the jungle.

'Down to my last ten rounds, Captain!' Preacher called out. Clay turned to see him methodically reloading his longrifle, smoke streaming from the barrel, which had taken on a reddish glow from furious use. Near by, Skaggerhill loosed off both barrels of his shotgun then drew his revolver and snapped off two shots. Foxbine had evidently refused to let her wound lay her low and stood with her back propped against the golden pillar, bloodied bandage on her leg and a revolver in each hand.

Clay glanced down, seeing another half-dozen Greens begin the long climb to the summit, with more still clambering out of the canal behind. The Spoiled continued to stand at the tree-line, still as statues. Clay couldn't know what they were waiting for but doubted it was anything good. He checked the vial in his hand, finding less than half left.

He reloaded the Stinger and took careful aim at the leading Green below. The range was long but worth a shot. *It'll have to pause whilst it clears the second level; there's a gap in the vines . . . The vines.* He watched as the Green clambered up, noting how brittle the vines were under its claws. *Dry as tinder,* he realised.

He lowered the Stinger and hurried to Braddon's side. 'Got an idea,' he said. 'Get everybody back from the edge.'

He ran for the stairwell, ignoring the shouted query his uncle cast after him, sprinting down the steps and into the second tier before reaching for his wallet. It was the scratch of claws on tile that saved him, pure instinct sending him sprawling. The flames missed him by inches, the heat of the blast singeing the hairs on his arm as he rolled away. The Green screamed, the shadow that concealed it lingering on its skin as it leapt for him, teeth gleaming amidst the black. The Stinger roared and red blossomed in the descending silhouette. The Green landed atop him, leaking enough product to have killed an unblessed. As it was, the burn of it on his neck was sufficiently painful to make him yell and kick free of the corpse in a scramble. He shot it again as he got to his feet, more out of spite than necessity.

He took a moment to wash away the blood with the water from his canteen, then reached for the wallet once more. 'Right,' he gasped, extracting a vial and looking around at the many gaps in the walls and the vines beyond. 'Let's see if Skaggs is right about you fuckers burning like anything else.'

He drank a quarter of the Red, staggering a little as it mingled with the lingering Black in his gut. Ellforth's stock wasn't the best quality and the dilutions didn't mix well with the more refined product Auntie had given him. The combination made for a nauseous gut and a thumping headache, but it couldn't be helped. Once his vision cleared, he concentrated on the biggest gap in the wall, the vines beyond bursting into flame instantly. He cast his gaze around in a slow circle, fire blossoming wherever it lingered, pausing to gulp down more Red as it dwindled in his blood-stream. Within minutes the fire had taken hold and the heat was fast becoming unbearable. He ran to the next tier and repeated the process, lighting several more fires that soon merged with the flames rising from below. He stopped when the smoke thickened into a choking fog and made his way back to the summit, fatigue rising due to the intense use of so much inferior product, forcing him to crawl the last few steps.

Braddon and Silverpin rushed to him as he clawed his way

free of the smoke, dragging him to the edge of the octagonal hole in the centre of the platform. They were all huddled there, forced back by the heat. Clay could hear the drakes screaming through the swirling fog, in pain now rather than rage. One came clambering up, heaving itself over the edge with difficulty, hide blackened and blistered. It made an effort to crawl towards them, jaws opening and closing spasmodically until a shot from Loriabeth put it out of its misery.

'Seems you saved us and killed us both, young 'un,' Skaggerhill commented. The flames were now licking above the summit's edge and the smoke grew thicker by the second, so it seemed likely they would choke before they burned.

'Do—' Clay began then fell to coughing, the fit violent enough to see him retching. He grunted, gesturing frantically at the hole and pointing downwards.

'Skaggs, Lori,' Braddon said, rising from Clay's side. 'Fix ropes to the pillar.'

The smoke was near blinding by the time they had two ropes fastened in place. Mr Firpike apparently saw little need to observe a chain of command by immediately lunging for one of the ropes and commencing a rapid but inexpert descent. 'Can't we just shoot him now?' Loriabeth asked her father.

'Too low on ammo.' He gestured for her to go next then told Foxbine to follow, the gunhand's descent accompanied by a loud chorus of profanity as she forced animation into her wounded leg.

'You ready?' Braddon asked, crouching at Clay's side when the others had all climbed down.

'Guess I'll have to be.' Clay groaned as his uncle hauled him upright, head thumping fit to burst and the gut ache worsened by the stink of smoke and burning flesh.

'Take it slow,' Braddon cautioned as he took hold of the rope and swung himself over the edge of the hole. A good five yards of rope slipped through Clay's grip before he found purchase, letting out a yell from the effort and the burn to his hands. He hung there for a short while, gasping the slightly clearer air, then began to descend, arms and legs shuddering as he inched his way down. He knew he wasn't going to make it after only a few more seconds of effort; there simply wasn't any more strength left in him. He stopped, wrapping his legs and arms around the rope, head lolling as he turned to Braddon, now hanging at his side.

'How'd you know?' he asked. ''Bout the product?'

'Thief's a thief,' Braddon replied with a shrug. His face darkened as he took in Clay's evident exhaustion and drooping eyes. 'Wake up, boy! We ain't done here!'

Clay could only manage a slow shake of his head. 'Wasn't lying,' he said, his voice sounding faint and far away to his own ears. ''Bout Keyvine. Wasn't me . . .'

'Claydon! You hold on, now!'

'She made me a gift . . . Take good care of her, Uncle . . .'

He was aware of the rope slipping through his grasp, of his uncle's shouts being drowned out by something else, presumably a concoction of his fading and befuddled mind. A drake's call, far louder and deeper than the screams of the Greens, the sound cutting through him, forcing his eyes open as he fell, staring up at the pale, smoke-shrouded octagon above and the dark shadow growing in its centre. The sound intensified as the shadow grew in size, sprouting wings that banished the smoke with a single flap before it descended into the temple. Clay's exhaustion finally overtook him just as the shadow came into focus and he knew he was greeting death with a fever dream, so impossible was the image. A Black drake, streaking towards him with mouth wide and talons outstretched, and perched on its back, a small figure swaddled in rags.

CHAPTER 27

Hilemore

'Fifteen effectives,' Dr Weygrand reported. He sat at the ward-room table, grey-faced with fatigue and his shirt richly decorated with a spatter of red and brown. It was customary for officers to don full uniform and remain standing when making after-action reports, but Hilemore saw little need to observe tradition at this juncture. 'Another twenty wounded. I expect eleven will survive, five are possibles, the other four won't last two days.'

'The captain?' Hilemore asked.

'One of the possibles. He remains comatose, though his pulse is regular and he shows occasional signs of movement. He's lost a good deal more blood than I'd have liked, though.'

'Green stocks?'

The doctor shook his head. 'All gone within an hour of joining battle. Unless some of the crew had a private stock.'

'A good point. Mr Steelfine.' Hilemore turned to the Islander, the only one present who had opted to remain standing. He had also found the time to change into a clean tunic. 'Please conduct a search of the crew quarters, see what you can unearth. Wouldn't be the first crew to hide a little product aboard.'

'Aye, sir.'

Hilemore shifted his attention to Chief Bozware, who appeared to share the doctor's state of near exhaustion. 'How long until the auxiliary is back on-line?'

'Another day, at least. And we're down to a quarter vial of Red.'

Hilemore suppressed a frown of annoyance. They had followed a slow, winding course through the Isles until nightfall forced a halt. As he had expected, Zenida Okanas proved capable of navigating these channels without falling afoul of reefs or sand-bars, guiding them to a sheltered bay where they could drop anchor. Despite making a successful escape from the Maritime Protectorate's worst military debacle, Hilemore knew their immobility counted as a failure. *The Corvantines badly want our engine,* he knew. *And what chance their admiral won't risk some smaller vessels to get it?*

'Very well,' he said, forcing a brisk note into his voice. 'We remain at anchor until the auxiliary is repaired. In the meantime we shall heal the *Viable*'s other injuries and see to our fallen. Mr Talmant, notes for the log, if you please.'

'Aye, sir.' The ensign lifted his pen and held it poised over the open log-book.

'The following appointments are made under my authority as acting captain of the IPV *Viable Opportunity*. Master-at-Arms Steelfine to receive a battlefield commission and brevet promotion to the rank of second lieutenant. Accordingly, he will undertake the duties of First Officer.'

The Islander's only apparent reaction was a slight stiffening to his back, though Hilemore saw him blink a little more than was customary.

'Ensign Talmant is also promoted to the rank of third lieutenant and will undertake the duties of Second Mate.'

Talmant's pen slipped, spilling ink onto the log which he instantly began to blot away. 'Apologies, sir.'

'It's quite all right, Lieutenant. The former prisoner Zenida Okanas has been contracted as Blood-blessed to the *Viable Opportunity*. She will also undertake the duties of navigation officer. The terms of her appointment will be appended to the log in due course.'

There were some exchanged glances across the table but, either through agreement or weariness, none of those present felt compelled to voice an objection to allowing a pirate onto the ship's list. Hilemore got to his feet, obliging the others to follow suit.

'Doctor, Chief,' he said. 'I am also ordering you to take at least five hours' sleep. Can't serve this ship if you're dead on your feet.'

He had given Tottleborn's cabin over to Zenida Okanas and her daughter. The girl opened the door at the fifth knock and Hilemore was surprised to find her holding one of the fallen Blood-blessed's periodicals, this one even more lurid than usual. 'She-Wolf of the Isles' the cover proclaimed, the letters emblazoned in red and carefully arranged so as to cover the breasts and nethers of the implausibly proportioned and muscular warrior-woman it depicted.

'That isn't for you,' he told her in Varestian, reaching for the publication. The girl jerked it out of reach, mouth taking on a defiant grimace as she glared back.

'She likes the pictures,' her mother said. She lay on the bunk, a forearm across her eyes and voice weary. 'Can't read the words in any case.'

'The content is unsuitable,' Hilemore stated.

The woman voiced a soft laugh. 'I'll wager my daughter's seen more unsuitable things than you have. Varestians don't coddle their children.'

'Nor teach them to read?'

'She can read a compass and a map. My people rarely have other uses for writing.' She groaned and sat up on the bed. 'More orders for me, Captain? I've already plotted you a course through the Isles that'll see us to open water in three days. What more do you want of me?'

'Open water will be our grave without product to fire the blood-burner. Corvantine patrols will intercept us before we've covered half the distance to Feros.'

'I have no product.'

'I see that. But we both know there is a place where it might be obtained. A place where only one of us will find welcome.'

The pirate's face clouded a little in realisation. 'The Hive.'

'Quite so.'

'I may have found welcome there once, when I had a ship and loot to fence. The only welcome I'm likely to receive upon stepping ashore from a Protectorate launch will be a lynching, if I'm lucky.'

'They might be less aggressive if our guns were to cover your landing. And much of your loot still rests in our hold.'

The woman's eyes flicked to her daughter and Hilemore saw something pass between them, the girl's face taking on a warning cast. 'He's right,' Zenida said, slipping into Varestian. 'We have little choice.'

'He'll kill you and steal me,' the girl said, the first words Hilemore could remember her speaking. In fact, he had come to suspect she might be mute.

'I will never allow that,' the pirate told her daughter in emphatic terms.

'I have no intention of causing harm to either of you,' Hilemore said, somewhat puzzled.

'We weren't talking about *you*,' the girl sneered in oddly cultured Mandinorian.

'Really?' Hilemore looked at her mother. 'Then who?'

Zenida Okanas gave no reply, merely coming to her feet with a tired groan. 'I'll need to plot a fresh course.'

Bozware's estimate proved to be overly optimistic, the repairs to the auxiliary engine taking two full days and even then the *Viable* could only make five knots at full clip. Fortunately, the confined waters of the Isles required more manoeuvrability than speed, as well as an expert hand on the wheel. Hilemore had soon come to appreciate the pirate woman's gift for angling the rudder precisely so as to take full advantage of the fast-flowing currents between the islands, and her deftness in avoiding the many hidden treacheries in these waters.

'First sailed here when I was nine,' she said on the evening of the second day. She had just steered them past the shoulder of a coral reef that appeared nowhere on any Ironship chart of the region. 'My father's boat, *The Silver Dart*. First blood-burner owned by the Okanas family.'

'And you fired the engine, presumably?' Hilemore asked.

'Of course. Father was able to borrow enough to buy her the day after the Blood-lot revealed my Blessing. He made it all back with interest on our first voyage. Aren't many freighters can out-run a burner. By the time I was sixteen we had funds enough to buy two more ships, and timber to build a port of our own.'

'Your family built the Hive?'

'It was more of a joint enterprise. Pirates tend not to compete with each other if it can be avoided, those that survive for any length of time that is. Feuding makes for poor profits.'

'Is it your father that waits there now? Is he the man your daughter fears?'

Her face took on the stern aspect he had come to realise meant she had no more words for the time being. It was therefore a surprise when she replied after a lengthy silence, 'No, just his bitter seed.'

They gave the last of the dead to the Deep the following morning, the four doomed men on Weygrand's list plus two of the possibles who had expired overnight. Hilemore said the appropriate words and formally crossed the names off the ship's list whilst the honour guard stood at rigid attention in newly laundered uniforms. He had insisted on a strict observance of dress code today. With the ship in its current state and so many comrades fallen, the crew needed the reassurance of discipline and ritual. Steelfine dismissed the men after the last body had slid over the side, and Hilemore had him linger to survey the *Viable*'s works.

'Battle-scarred but unbowed, sir,' was the Islander's estimation.

'Battle-scarred indeed,' Hilemore said, taking in the numerous scorch-marks in the decking that were too deeply ingrained to be scrubbed away. The upper works had been partly reconstructed thanks to the diligent work of the ship's carpenter, the timber provided by a tree-felling expedition ashore whilst they had been at anchor. At Steelfine's urging Hilemore had permitted only one tree to be taken. 'My people will know we are here,' he had said. 'And they don't appreciate greed.'

'Then why do your people tolerate the Hive?' Hilemore asked. 'It strikes me there must be greed aplenty there.'

'Pirates have been traversing the Isles for a hundred years or more. They learned early on the value of reaching an accommodation with any tribes they encountered. I imagine the Hive is tolerated because its leaders pay annual tribute, and the price will be steep.'

'Gold?'

Steelfine gave a rare smile, teeth bright in the morning sun. 'Weapons, sir. Plus a few sundry luxuries, but mostly weapons. The only currency in the Isles.'

The Hive came into view in late afternoon, heralded by the sight of smoke leaking into the darkening sky from a cluster of tight-packed dwellings halfway up the slope of the island's highest peak. Instead of a dock, the few ships in attendance were moored to a series of tall posts, each at least sixty feet high. 'Mooring ropes are fixed to a ratchet that slides up and down with the tide,' Zenida explained. 'Couldn't afford a wall to guard against the three moons. Works well enough as long as there's no storms.'

The *Viable* moored up just within cannon-shot of the town. Hilemore ordered a red flag with a white circle hoisted above the wheel-house; the universal signal requesting truce and negotiation. 'Don't expect it to be a shield if this goes against us,' the pirate woman advised as she and Hilemore climbed into the launch. 'It's just a rag on a stick to the man you'll meet tonight.'

Hilemore turned to Steelfine, who stood staring at the town with undisguised suspicion, his jaw clenched in suppressed anger at being ordered to remain behind. 'Remember,' Hilemore said. 'Not one second past the twelfth hour. Confine the bombardment to the ships then make all speed north. No delays, Number One.'

He held Steelfine's gaze until he received a curt nod then sat down to grasp the oars. Zenida Okanas spared a glance at her daughter standing at Steelfine's side, saying nothing but Hilemore saw the brightness in her eyes before she blinked and looked away. 'You haven't told me her name,' he said, starting to row for the shore. They were alone in the boat at her insistence, also unarmed, which made his back itch with every pull of the oars.

'Why would that interest you?' she replied, gaze fixed on the approaching town.

'The ship's log for one. I like to keep accurate records.'

She remained silent as they came level with the moored ships, the crewmen coming to the rail to watch them pass. A few held rifles and shotguns, though none was aimed in their direction. From the straightened backs of a few, Hilemore discerned they recognised his passenger.

'Akina,' Zenida said when they had cleared the ships. 'It means jewel.' Her voice was hoarse and Hilemore kept his gaze from her face to spare her embarrassment, knowing she was fighting tears. *She expects to die tonight.*

The shore-line consisted of a broad beach, crowded with boats and piled cargo awaiting transport or sale. There were numerous onlookers as they grounded the boat and strode free of the surf, however the small group of armed men barring their path captured most of Hilemore's attention. They were led by a stocky man of middling years and North Mandinorian origin, judging by the red hair crowning a face tanned from many years under the southern sun. In contrast to the men at his back he wore an affable, even jovial expression. 'Captain Okanas,' he greeted Zenida in a rumbling baritone. 'So glad to find you're not residing with the King of the Deep, after all.'

'Constable Tragerhorn,' she replied, taking off her hat to return the bow. 'May I present Captain Hilemore of the Ironship vessel *Viable Opportunity*. Come ashore in search of honest commerce.'

One of the pirates gave a scornful snicker at that, soon echoed by his fellows, though Hilemore took note of the speed with which they fell silent at Tragerhorn's backward glance. 'Captain,' he said, turning back, and maintaining his genial tone. 'Constable Kaylib Tragerhorn, charged with maintaining order in this port by its duly appointed government. Your flag has been noted and will be respected. However, any breach of the customary rules of parley will result in swift punishment.'

'I understand, sir,' Hilemore replied in as neutral a voice as he could manage. Treating with pirates was not a circumstance he relished, but honour must be set aside in the face of dire necessity.

'How many are present?' Zenida asked Tragerhorn.

'Three of the five,' he replied. 'More than usual, in fact. Recent events have gotten everyone in a bit of a tizzy, as you might imagine.' He stepped aside, gesturing at the winding track stretching away from the beach. 'They're waiting, and given their mood, we'd best not tarry.'

As with any land regularly beset by the three-moon tide, the slope beyond the beach was mostly rock and sparse bush, ascending at a sharp incline until it levelled out when they came to the town. There were considerably more onlookers here, clustered in doorways and alleys or peering down from windows and balconies. Also, unlike the pirates on the ships, they were less shy in giving voice to anxiety.

'What you doin' with 'im, Captain?' a woman demanded of Zenida as they passed by one of the larger dwellings. She glared down from a balcony amidst a number of other women, sparsely dressed and liberally painted as befit their profession. 'Take your ship away and it turns out you're more a whore than I am!'

'Clamp down on that shit-mouth, Lirra!' Tragerhorn warned, pausing to fix the woman with a hard stare that soon had her shrinking back into the protective huddle of her sisters. Tragerhorn lingered to regard the surrounding townsfolk with a challenging glare, gaze tracking from face to face, each abruptly finding somewhere else to look. After a few seconds, he moved on and they proceeded along the muddy thoroughfare that formed the Hive's Main Street, this time without any accompanying catcalls.

'Glad to see your authority hasn't waned, Constable,' Zenida said, 'I assume the One Rule is still in force?'

'That it is, Captain,' Tragerhorn replied. 'Been a good six months since I had to enforce it though.'

'One Rule?' Hilemore enquired.

'Those that founded this place were a pragmatic lot,' Tragerhorn said. 'As us seafarers tend to be. There's only one rule if you break a law here.'

He paused again and gestured ahead where the street opened out into a square of sorts. Rising from the centre of the square was a tall scaffold resembling a gallows but with four arms instead of one. From each arm there hung a narrow cage inside which Hilemore could see the dull white glimmer of bone or skull amidst the shrunken bundles of rags and desiccated flesh.

'They can last a good while, sometimes,' Tragerhorn commented. 'Folk throw food at the cages, apples and such, all rotten naturally. Surprising how long a man can subsist on other people's leavings.'

He led them past the scaffold to the largest structure Hilemore had seen so far, an oddly elegant reproduction of the kind of mansion favoured by the higher echelons of the Mandinorian managerial class. It stood three storeys high, complete with rectangular columns and tall windows, though the modern aspect was spoilt somewhat by the classical statuary adorning the rooftop.

'My father had the good fortune to happen upon an accomplished architect aboard a liner out of Carvenport,' Zenida said. 'He built this in return for his freedom. Oddly, when it was done he decided he'd rather stay. Too many bad debts, apparently. Spent his remaining years whoring and drinking, all at my father's expense.'

'I'd say he got his money's worth,' Hilemore replied, his eyes lingering on the statues, long-forgotten gods and goddesses standing as dumb sentinels over this den of scum. It put him in mind of the crumbling pile at Astrage Vale and the many marble figures that littered the grounds. They were all antique and retained considerable value though his father had always resisted selling them, no matter how many times the bailiffs came knocking. Hilemore doubted that Cousin Malkim would share the same scruples.

'Best not make them wait, Captain,' Tragerhorn advised, gesturing to the steps ascending to the mansion door. It was opened by a hulking South Mandinorian fellow clad in archaic servant's livery of satin waistcoat and an elaborately cuffed lace shirt. The near-comical appearance was offset somewhat by the pistol on his hip and the Dalcian tulwar strapped across his back. Two more men stood in the corridor beyond, not so large but both similarly attired and armed.

'Constable.' The hulking fellow greeted Tragerhorn with a respectful nod.

'Mr Lockbar,' the constable replied. 'Captains Hilemore and Okanas to see the Directors.'

Lockbar stepped aside to allow them entry then courteously requested they raise their arms and stand still whilst he searched them both. 'I was welcome in this house long before you,' Zenida said, face paling with anger as the man patted her down.

'My contract is with the Directors,' Lockbar replied in a neutral tone.

When satisfied they were unarmed he turned and led them through a marble-floored hallway, the two other guards falling in behind along with Tragerhorn. 'Leave all negotiation to me,' Zenida murmured to Hilemore as they proceeded to a set of double doors. 'Speak only in response to a direct question.'

Lockbar swung the doors open and bid them enter. The space beyond was cavernous and lit by a row of six chandeliers suspended from a ceiling of moulded plaster. *Ballroom*, Hilemore decided, taking in the floral pattern on the tile floor. Three people sat in chairs next to the cavernous fire-place, long shadows stretching away in the orange glow. They stayed seated as

Hilemore and Zenida came closer, stopping a dozen feet away at Lockbar's order.

The seats were occupied by two men and a woman. The man on the right was portly and balding, with a bulbous nose so reddened from burst veins he appeared almost clownish, an impression countered by the deep scars tracing across his hairless head and the sharp calculation in his eyes. The woman on the left was perhaps fifty years old with thin, handsome features and hair tied back in a severe bun. She was elegantly dressed in a black mourning gown free of any adornments or jewellery. She regarded Hilemore with only the barest flicker of interest before fixing her gaze entirely on Zenida. Hilemore saw a weight to that gaze despite the woman's expressionless features, whether born of malice or warmth he couldn't tell.

But it was the man in the centre who captured most of his attention, his honed instincts attuned to seeking out the most salient threat. He was a few years Hilemore's senior and not particularly tall, nor especially muscular. He wore sailor's garb of good quality and had his hair worn long as was customary with Varestian men-folk. Unlike the bald man he bore no scars but Hilemore took one look at his face and knew he looked upon a killer. The eyes were steady as they traced from him to Zenida, taking in every detail and seeing more than most could. It was always the way with predators.

'Aren't you going to introduce your new friend?' the man in the centre asked Zenida in slightly accented Mandinorian.

'Captain Hilemore of the IPV *Viable Opportunity*,' Zenida replied, keeping her voice on an even keel.

'Ah yes.' The man turned to Hilemore with a smile. 'The ship that came to pound us to dust then just sailed away. That was your mission was it not, Captain?'

Hilemore saw little reason to lie, knowing deception would be wasted on this man. 'It was. More pressing matters compelled us on another course, however.'

'More pressing matters, yes.' The man laughed. 'In particular, this war you appear to be in the process of losing. It seems we owe the Corvantines a considerable debt.'

'If they come here, I doubt you'll get the chance to repay it.'

'Why should they come here? Unless in search of you.' The man's smile faded and he turned back to Zenida. 'You haven't finished your introductions.'

'Captain,' Zenida went on, face flushing a little as she gestured to the bald man. 'This is Captain Kordwine of the *Osprey*, Co-Director of the Eastern Isles Trading Conglomerate. This' – Zenida's discomfort visibly deepened as she turned to the woman – 'is his fellow Co-Director Ethilda Okanas, my esteemed step-mother, and this' – she gritted her teeth upon facing the man in the centre – 'is Director-in-Chief Arshav Okanas . . . my brother.'

Arshav's smile returned, though only for an instant as he said, 'Half-brother,' very precisely.

Zenida said nothing, face now tense with anger and, Hilemore was disturbed to see, a definite measure of fear.

'Where is my niece?' Arshav asked in a tone of soft intensity. 'Aboard the Ironship tub, perhaps? Or are you going to claim she died at this one's hands? Which would, of course, beg the question, why are you willing to sell yourself to him . . . ?'

'Arshav,' Ethilda Okanas said, her voice not overly loud but possessed of a sharp note of command. Arshav fell silent, though Hilemore saw a spasm of resentment flick across his face.

'She *is* well, I trust?' the woman enquired of Zenida, casting a brief but loaded glance at Hilemore. 'And not held hostage to your conduct here?'

'I am pardoned and contracted under the captain's authority. Akina is not here by my choice.'

'You have no ship,' Arshav stated. 'The law is clear.'

'I am contracted as crew,' Zenida returned. 'Therefore, I have a ship.'

Her half-brother abruptly slipped into Varestian, a snarl creeping into his voice. 'A corporate ship. A slaver's ship.'

'But still a ship.'

'Enough of this,' Captain Kordwine said in Mandinorian, speaking for the first time. 'Your family disputes are a private matter, and this is conglomerate business.' He gave Hilemore an appraising stare before speaking again. 'From the look of your ship it seems you've been in the wars, Captain.'

'Indeed we have, sir.'

'As our Chief Director says, we had chance to see you sail by recently. She's a blood-burner, isn't she? Fastest I ever saw, in fact. It doesn't take a brilliant mind to reckon out what you came here for.'

'We have a hold full of valuable cargo.' Hilemore glanced at Lockbar before slowly reaching into his tunic and extracting the list of the hold's contents. 'If this is truly a commercial enterprise, then I'm sure a price can be agreed.'

'There's only one price I'll agree to,' Arshav said, still staring at Zenida. 'I'll not see my niece given over to corporate scum . . .'

'We will need some time to consult,' Ethilda broke in, Hilemore noting the annoyance colouring her tone and surmised she was either aggrieved by her son's intent or peeved at his lack of guile in revealing it. 'Mr Lockbar, escort the captains to the Shell Room and provide appropriate refreshment.'

The Shell Room was aptly named, a large study in which the walls and ceiling had been inset with sea-shells of varying sizes, some painted in brightly coloured enamel or adorned with semi-precious stones. Hilemore found its garishness at odds with the rest of the house, thinking it doubtful that this had been in the drunken architect's plans. 'My father had curious tastes when it came to decoration,' Zenida explained. 'The older he got the more curious they became.'

Lockbar had placed a bottle of wine and two glasses on the broad, oak-wood writing-desk set back from the window. Zenida had poured a small measure into a glass, sniffed it once then set it aside. 'No whiff of poison, but we'd best not trust it.'

Hilemore went to the window, finding scant surprise at the

sight of another two armed guards standing amidst the flower-beds outside. 'Why is possessing a berth on a ship of such import?' he enquired, turning back.

Zenida sat and rested her elbows on the desk, lowering her head to massage her forehead. She said nothing for some time but then, apparently deciding there might be some value in sharing knowledge, said, 'A Varestian without a ship is homeless. A homeless parent cannot care for a child.'

'This is your law?'

'Yes. We do have them, you know.'

'So, if you cannot provide a home for your daughter . . . ?'

'Law dictates she be placed with her closest relative, who will undertake the duties of guardian, along with certain responsi-bilities regarding the administration of her property.'

Hilemore frowned in puzzlement. 'Akina has property?'

'Akina is one of the wealthiest individuals in the southern seas, thanks to my father.' She sighed, leaning back in the chair, hands gripping the edge of the desk. 'Towards the end of his life our bond . . . diminished. He didn't approve of my accommodation with your Syndicate. "Privateer is just another word for whore," he said, an observation that did little to improve matters between us. So, when he managed to get himself killed during some mad treasure-hunting jaunt to the Interior, his will made for interesting reading. My beloved half-brother and I each received one twen-tieth of his estate, a tenth going to my stepmother whilst the entire remainder was left to Akina. He remained very fond of her despite our estrangement.'

'So, if your brother claims her, he claims her wealth.'

'Yes. And I have grave doubts he will administer it with her best interests in mind.'

Hilemore paused, fumbling over the best way to phrase the next question, but she pre-empted him. 'Akina's father died three years ago.' She paused to glance around the room. 'Two years to the day after completing his last great architectural work.' She looked up at Hilemore, grinning a little at his expression. 'He wasn't always such a complete drunk, and I was more easily impressed when younger.'

He nodded and looked away, thinking to spare her blushes but she merely seemed amused by his discomfort. 'You Mandinorians and your rigid customs,' she said with a faint laugh that soon faded. All mirth had vanished when she spoke again. 'Arshav will demand we hand over Akina in return for product. I need to know, will you allow this?'

'Certainly not,' he replied, more curtly than he intended as the suggestion had chafed his honour. *What does she imagine I am?* 'Tell me,' he said, leaning against the desk. 'How seriously does your brother take Varestian customs?'

She angled her head, eyes narrowing. 'Do I sense a stratagem brewing, Captain?'

'It seems to me the solution to this dilemma is obvious, providing your brother responds as custom requires.'

'This is not a prospect to be entertained lightly. He's a very dangerous man.' She looked away for a moment, brow furrowed in contemplation. 'But not one I'll miss. Ethilda will take it badly, though I can't say that troubles me much either.'

'The rest of the town?'

'If it's a properly conducted affair I doubt they'll be overly troublesome. Arshav is a man surrounded by employees, not friends.' She paused, face entirely serious now. 'You appear strangely certain the outcome will go in our favour.'

Hilemore shrugged, recalling something his grandfather had said, 'A captain is always certain.'

Lockbar came to fetch them an hour later. The three Directors sat in the same chairs, though now Captain Kordwine's posture was more slumped, his face the sullen grimace of a defeated man. *The Chief Director's greed outweighs sensible commerce,* Hilemore decided as Arshav Okanas got to his feet, ignoring Hilemore to address his half-sister.

'We'll not be bought by this corporate hireling,' he said. 'But he can have his product, and you to fire it. My niece, however, requires a secure home . . .'

Hilemore moved in a blur, darting forward too fast for Lockbar to react, covering the distance to Arshav in a heart-beat and delivering a hard back-hand cuff across his face. The pirate reeled back, blood on his face as his mother scrambled to her feet with a shout of outrage.

Hilemore stood back, hearing a tulwar scrape from its scabbard an instant before the sharp point began to press into his back. He fixed his gaze on Arshav, kneeling and wiping the blood from his nose as he glared up at Hilemore, face quivering with rage. Hilemore smiled and spoke a single word in Varestian, 'Challenge.'

CHAPTER 28

Lizanne

'Squeeze the trigger, don't jerk it.'

Tekela tried again, keeping a solid, two-handed grip on the revolver and placing the shot dead in the centre of the target's chest. Lizanne had been pleased to discover Shiny Man had been resurrected in her absence, remolded now into an advancing Corvantine infantryman complete with lowered, bayonet-tipped rifle and peaked cap. 'Raise your aim,' she told the girl. 'Your weapon is low-calibre and one bullet is unlikely to stop a charging man when his dander's up.'

Tekela aimed again and fired, the bullet leaving a hole in Shiny Man's copper cheek. Her hands had proven too small for the Cadre pistol she had carried since Morsvale, the recoil nearly snatching it out from her grasp the first time she fired it. Lizanne had obtained a smaller-calibre piece from Jermayah's armoury, a seven-shot .22 revolver with a six-inch barrel. What it lacked in power would hopefully be compensated for by its accuracy, and Tekela was proving an adept student.

'Reload and do it again,' Lizanne told her. 'Faster this time.'

'Can't we have some lunch?' Tekela grumbled, slipping into Eutherian as she tended to do when tired.

'Speak in Mandinorian,' Lizanne reminded her, gesturing impatiently at the girl's revolver. 'Lunch later.'

She glanced over at Jermayah as Tekela reloaded. In the three hours since she handed him the solargraph he had barely issued more than a grunt, sitting hunched at his work-bench with a dizzying array of intricate tools placed within reach. He only stirred once, raising his head to bark a warning when Major Arberus began a close inspection of one of his new inventions, a multi-barrelled gun of some kind mounted on a wheeled carriage.

'Keep practising,' Lizanne told Tekela. 'Fifty rounds then you can take a rest.'

The girl gave a faint groan but nevertheless dutifully raised her revolver and loosed off another salvo at Shiny Man. Lizanne left her to it and moved into the darker recesses of the workshop, finding the alcove where Jermayah made his home. It featured a small bed and side-table, piled high with various technical manuals, the only reading he ever seemed to indulge in. Lizanne sank onto the bed and lay back, taking a vial of Blue from her skirt pocket. She went through the usual pre-trance ritual of controlled breathing, visualising her mindscape before checking her wrist-watch and raising the vial to her lips.

'Not there?' Madame Bondersil's scowl put Lizanne in mind of one of Tekela's tantrums, as did the waspishly impatient tone. 'What do you mean, not there?'

'Mr Torcreek failed to make the connection at the allotted time,' Lizanne replied, her tone possessing more placidity than she felt. 'There could be any number of reasons for his absence.'

'Death by far being the most likely.' Madame sighed, turning back to view the trench-works below. Lizanne had found her on the city walls accompanied by a gaggle of Protectorate officers, all now retired to a respectful distance. Lizanne was struck by their uniformly haggard faces, all drawn in fatigue and anxiety as they cast repeated glances at the country beyond the trenches, as if Morradin's horde might appear at any moment. Carvenport had never been a choice posting for the Syndicate's soldiers. The garrison tended to be officered by those either too lacking in courage or competence to merit a more active command, or those in search of a quiet billet in which to await retirement and pension. It didn't augur well for their prospects of holding the city. She was, however, heartened by the extensiveness of the trenches, the web of emplacements and dug-outs seeming to have doubled in size since yesterday. A few of Jermayah's newfangled guns were positioned to cover the more obvious approaches and she was gratified to see a large number of Contractors occupying the outermost trenches. *At least they can shoot straight.*

'Any fragments?' Madame enquired, dragging her attention away from the defences. Fragments was a catch-all term for the vestiges of deceased trance-mates that sometimes appeared in a Blood-blessed's mindscape, but only when they had died in mid-trance. Lizanne counted herself fortunate she had never experienced one.

'No, Madame.'

'You schooled him in the emergency procedure, I trust?'

'Contact to be attempted the following day at exactly the same time, and repeated until established.'

Madame nodded, frowning in contemplation for several minutes, apparently uncaring of the officers fidgeting near by. 'Has Mr Tollermine made any progress?' she asked finally.

'He is entirely focused on the task, but the device is yet to be made functional. Your coterie of scholars?'

Madame shook her head in mild disgust. 'Spend most of their time arguing with each other. They do seem impressed with the late Burgrave's canon of work, however.'

'He was an impressive man, in many ways. I'll quiz the major again, see if he can share more about their expeditions . . .'

Her words were abruptly drowned out by a loud boom that reverberated over the walls to echo through the streets beyond. Lizanne's gaze instantly went to the rising plume of earth fifty yards beyond the trench-works. The Contractors ran for cover as another shell descended, this one closer by ten yards, quickly followed by a dozen more. The barrage continued, sweeping over the outer trenches in a spectacle of churned earth, birthing a thick brown fog that soon obscured all from sight. The last shell came down barely a hundred yards from the walls, landing near an artillery position. When the fog faded Lizanne could see the corpses of three gunners lying beside their dismounted piece whilst others writhed and screamed near by.

'Marshal Morradin is clearly no laggard,' Madame observed. The last of the smoke drifted away, revealing the sight of Corvantine soldiers advancing from the tree-line to the south. Lizanne judged them to be skirmishers from the looseness of their formation and the way they scurried from cover to cover. A crackle of rifle fire erupted from the Contractors, proving the barrage had done little to thin their numbers. Lizanne counted a dozen Corvantines felled before they retreated back into the trees. *Just a probe,* she decided. *The marshal gauges our numbers and willingness to fight.*

'Return to the workshop,' Madame told her. 'Continue to report any progress to me. Regardless of the fate of this city, the device must not fall into Corvantine hands, nor any knowledge that might enable them to reconstruct it.'

She held Lizanne's gaze until she gave a nod of affirmation, the implacability in her once-cherished mentor's gaze birthing a thought as she walked away, surprising in the depth of anger that accompanied it. *You vicious old bitch.*

The artillery started up again after midday, a slow, steady bombardment rather than another lightning barrage. The regular crump of exploding shells resounded through the workshop, making Tekela wince and the major pace back and forth in poorly controlled agitation. Jermayah, however, still didn't raise his gaze from the solargraph.

'Morradin did the same at the siege of Jerravin,' Arberus commented. 'Three solid days of pounding before the main assault. Frays the nerves as well as the defences.'

Keen to keep Tekela distracted, and sensing the girl had had enough of target practice for the day, Lizanne began to teach her the basics of unarmed combat, conscripting the major as a reluctant participant.

'Keep low,' she said, moving in a crouch towards his back. 'Under his line of sight. When you're close enough . . .' She lunged, fixing a hand over Arberus's mouth, forcing his head back and sinking an invisible knife into the base of his skull. 'Make sure you wiggle it about to churn up the brains.'

Tekela frowned. 'That doesn't seem fair.'

'You are barely five feet tall and any man you meet, and many women, are likely to possess twice your strength. Fairness is not an option for you, my dear.'

She turned to the major, watching him thumb a spot of blood from his mouth. 'Sorry,' she said.

'Strong even without product,' he replied with a small grin that reminded her of their first meeting in the Burgrave's hallway.

'Seer-dammit to the Travail and back again!'

They turned to see Jermayah on his feet, a hammer raised in his fist as he glared down at the solargraph in wide-eyed rage. 'This cursed thing was surely crafted only to vex me!'

'Mr Tollermine!' Lizanne said, employing her most corporate voice. 'You forget your contract, sir.'

His gaze swung to her, the fury fading slowly as he lowered his hammer. The expression that covered his face as he looked again at the solargraph was one of abject defeat. 'It's beyond me,' he said tonelessly, tossing the hammer onto the bench. 'I can't make it work.'

'I simply do not believe that,' Lizanne said, moving to his side. She leaned down to peer at the device on the bench, blinking in surprise as she noted that it remained completely intact, not a single screw or bolt undone. 'I had thought your explorations might be more extensive.'

'If I take it apart, I might never be able to reconstruct it.'

'How do you know you can't repair it if you don't?'

'This is not some child's toy in need of a new spring.' He extended a hand to the device, fingers splayed and hesitant, as if he were reaching to touch a candle-flame. 'There is more here . . . More than is known by us.'

'It was crafted by a man's hand two hundred years ago, and he was mad. If such a man could make it, surely you can fix it.'

He shook his head, features drawn in mingled frustration and bafflement as he pointed to a bolt in the centre of the device. 'This is the fulcrum of the entire mechanism, and it's locked.'

'Then pick the lock.'

'I don't even know what manner of lock this is.' He turned the solargraph, taking up a small steel probe and tapping it against a row of eight cylinders set into its side. 'See these,' Jermayah said, touching the probe to the thin strips of metal fixed to the top of each cylinder. 'They are all connected to the fulcrum. I suspect they must be triggered to release it, but I see no method as to how.'

'Can't you remove them?'

'Not without breaking the connection and that will seize the entire mechanism.' He huffed out a low, rumbling sigh, tossing down the probe where it clattered against the cylinders, producing a series of sharp, almost musical pings. 'There's nothing else for it.' Jermayah turned away, running a hand through the shaggy mass of his hair. 'It'll have to be taken apart, each component recorded, itemised and copied. Then I'll attempt a reconstruction.'

'How long?' Lizanne asked him.

'It took me six months to reconstruct the blueprints from the shadows in the box.'

'We do not have six months, Jermayah.'

'And I do not possess miraculous powers . . .'

He fell silent at the sound of several more pings from the device. They turned to find Tekela tapping the probe to the cylinders, producing a simple but recognisable tune in the process. 'Chimes,' Tekela said, slipping into Eutherian once more. 'My mother left me a music box that sounded much the same. It would play the "Emperor's March."'

Lizanne expected some irritated outburst from Jermayah but instead his face took on a frown of deep concentration as he moved back to the bench. 'Continue,' he told Tekela when she began to step back.

'Eight . . . chimes,' she said in her halting Mandinorian, playing the same tune at a faster clip. 'Different notes. Eight notes make an . . .' She fumbled for the right term, turning to Lizanne and speaking a word in Eutherian.

'An octave,' Lizanne translated. 'The foundation of all music.'

'Music,' Jermayah repeated, extending a finger to the chimes. 'Of course. Play the right tune, and it unlocks the fulcrum.'

'But which one?' Lizanne wondered. 'There are many tunes in the world.'

'"The Leaves of Autumn,"' Major Arberus said, now standing beside Tekela and regarding the device with much the same fascination as the rest of them. 'I always thought this thing a waste of time, if not money. But Leonis had such faith in it. "The Key to the Interior's treasures," he said.'

'"The Leaves of Autumn"?' Lizanne enquired.

'It's the only reference to music in the Artisan's surviving correspondence,' he said. 'Whilst we don't know much about him, it seems he was engaged to be married at one point, a union never fulfilled thanks to his endless obsession with the Interior's mysteries. However, a fragment of a letter to his sweetheart does survive, and in it he makes reference to the tune to be played at their wedding, her favourite.' He turned to Tekela, speaking in Eutherian. '"The Leaves of Autumn." You know it? It's very old.'

'My music tutor liked the old ones,' Tekela said, frowning in concentration as she held the probe poised over the chimes. 'Tedious old trout, that she was.' After a few seconds she tapped the probe against the chimes in a precisely executed sequence that made Lizanne wonder if the girl might have an innate talent for something after all. Tekela played the first eight notes, then paused when nothing happened. Jermayah waved an impatient hand at her and she tried again. The tune she produced was slow in tempo and conveyed a definite sense of melancholy despite the high pitch of the chimes. The melody was so sombre in fact, Lizanne couldn't help but think it a decidedly strange choice for a wedding.

'That's the first . . . movement,' Tekela told Jermayah in Mandinorian as the last note faded, her tone apologetic as she lowered the probe and the device remained stubbornly inert.

'You didn't hit every chime,' he said. 'I suspect the tune needs to include every note.'

'The main theme,' Arberus said. 'It's fairly complex as I recall.'

Tekela thought for a moment then tapped out the sequence, the notes from the eight chimes overlapping to produce a lilting harmonic resonance. The bolt in the centre of the solargraph issued a loud click then made a one-hundred-and-eighty-degree turn counter-clockwise. Another series of clicks emerged from the device as the three levers on the top began to move, then came to a halt as the final chime fell silent.

'Seer's balls,' Jermayah breathed. 'It's powered by music.'

'He's calling it "kinetic resonance,"' Lizanne said, then gave an involuntary crouch at the whining growl of a shell passing overhead. 'The conversion of sound to energy. I must say it's a fascinating phenomenon to observe.'

Madame had established her headquarters in a large Old Colonial residence near the south wall. Apparently, it had been the home of the Contractor's Guild, who had generously gifted, or more likely surrendered it to her needs. Much of the grounds and surrounding houses had been converted to makeshift hospitals where doctors, nurses and volunteers tended the growing number of wounded carried back from the trench-works as the Corvantine bombardment continued to take a steady toll. It had been nearly midnight when Lizanne made her way here, passing through rows of tents from which a chorus of pained voices could be heard, a chorus she knew would only grow louder with every passing day.

Madame had moved her private quarters to the house's basement after a few Corvantine shells had made it over the wall to smash some neighbouring homes to splinters. She sat at her desk from the Academy, presumably moved here with the aid of Black, the voluminous stacks of reports and messages arranged into neat but tall piles on either side of her. For now, however, her full attention was fixed on Lizanne.

'So, it's working?' she said.

'When the right combination of notes is played, yes. We're having to guess which tunes to play. It appears the Artisan was clever in his choice of music. "The Leaves of Autumn" unlocks it, whilst the three dials indicating the orbits of the moons will respond to an old Corvantine ditty called, "Dance of the Heavens." The other two dials remain inert but Miss Artonin and Major Arberus are compiling a list of likely candidates. Jermayah is of the opinion they relate to geography, as their dimensions correspond to the old Corvantine reckoning for latitude and longitude.'

'Excellent work, Lizanne.' Madame's tone was free of any triumph, possessed of a pre-rehearsed formality Lizanne recognised as signifying the end of a contract. 'Tomorrow, Protectorate officers will collect the device and notes for examination by my scholarly associates. Please instruct Jermayah to resume construction of his deadly novelties. You and your associates may assist him in this regard if you wish. From now on your only role in this mission will be as conduit to Mr Torcreek. If, as I expect, he fails to make contact during tomorrow's trance, you may consider your mission complete. Any accommodations you wish to make with Exceptional Initiatives regarding Major Arberus and Miss Artonin are your concern alone.'

Lizanne was glad of her decision to leave the Whisper at Jermayah's for some maintenance work; otherwise the temptation to shoot Madame between the eyes would have been hard to resist. As it was, she could only stand at rigid attention as she sought to maintain a suddenly fragile composure. *She thinks the Longrifles dead,* she realised. *But, provided this city remains standing, another expedition can be sent, an expedition firmly under her sole control.* Even without benefit of the trance she knew Madame's black web of obsession to be fully grown now, leaving no room for shared profit. The White was to be hers alone.

'I assume,' Lizanne began in as carefully modulated a tone as she could manage, 'Madame has confirmed this course of action via trance with the Board.'

'The Board are frightfully busy at the moment,' Madame replied, her voice as colourless as before. 'You may have noticed why.'

Was this always your plan? Lizanne wondered. *Have the war provide a cloak for your ambition? With the Corvantines at our throats the Board will accede to any notion that might offer salvation.* 'What do you imagine will happen if it's ever found?' she asked. 'Every clue uncovered by Mr Torcreek and every scrap of evidence provided by the late Burgrave Artonin, it all speaks of something best left in peace.'

'Cowardice and profit are rare bedfellows,' Madame replied.

'Profit is dependent on a successful outcome to this siege. As yet, I have seen little reason for optimism.'

Madame smiled, a spectacle Lizanne once saw as merely unusual but now found chilling. 'You under-estimate Jermayah's abilities,' Madame said. 'Ask him to show you some of his new toys. He has been *very* busy.'

'A magazine of fifty rounds,' Jermayah said, slotting the component into a port on the top of the weapon's barrel-shaped breech, a long narrow box containing a stack of standard rifle-bullets. He worked a lever to chamber the first round before taking hold of the handle extending from the machine's underside. 'Best cover your ears,' he said and began to wind, the weapon's six barrels blurring into motion.

Even though Lizanne clamped her hands firmly over her ears, the blast was near deafening, like a whole platoon of infantry firing at once. Shiny Man had been spared this demonstration though the sandbag-covered wall behind his usual standing-place received some fearful punishment, a faint hiss of escaping sand accompanying the echo of fading gun-fire.

'Rate of fire depends on how fast you turn the handle,' Jermayah explained, tugging tufts of cotton wool from his ears. 'A well-drilled crew can manage over three hundred a minute.'

'What do you call it?' Major Arberus asked, staring down at the weapon with an expression that told of keen if somewhat awed appreciation.

'Officially, "Rapid-fire Device Mark Four."' Jermayah gave a shrug. 'Been calling it the Growler.'

'Should call it . . . monster,' Tekela said, regarding the smoking barrels with obvious dislike.

'This monster might save this city,' Lizanne reminded her before turning to Jermayah. 'How many do we have?'

'Got a half-dozen finished before the siege began. There's more being made under contract at other shops along with the plentiful stocks of ammunition they need. It's a slow process though, since the designs are so new. Still, they should take a fearful toll on the Corvantines. Would've liked a chance to finish Mark Five though.'

'Mark Five?' Arberus asked. 'You improved on this?'

'Not really an improvement.' Jermayah moved away, leading them to a large, tarpaulin-shrouded lump in the deepest recesses of the shop. He gestured to the major to take hold of the covering and together they hauled it free. 'More like an enlargement. I call it the Thumper.'

This one really is a monster, Lizanne decided, eyeing the revealed contraption. It stood taller and broader than its younger sibling with four barrels instead of six, and of a calibre at least five times the size.

'Fires this,' Jermayah said, holding up a bullet that appeared to be suffering from some form of elephantiasis. 'Point-eight-inch explosive shell. Thought the Maritime Protectorate might have a use for it but never got the chance to demonstrate it.'

'So it might not work?' Arberus asked.

'All my devices work, sir,' Jermayah replied, his tone slightly peeved. 'Put three rounds through her and she worked fine. Would've been more but I was worried the shop might come down. Had to contract a bricklayer to repair the damage as it was.'

'Can you make more shells?' Lizanne asked.

'Got stocks of brass, steel and propellant enough for maybe two hundred. Take a while though, and it's delicate work.'

Lizanne took the shell from him, feeling the weight of it and the smoothness of the projectile. *One shell could bring down four men at once . . .* A recent memory rose in her mind, flames blossoming in the darkened jungle and Captain Flaxknot's fearful countenance. *Or, perhaps even a full-grown drake.*

'What else have we got to do?' she said, handing the shell back. 'Show me.'

CHAPTER 29

Clay

It was a nightmare Clay hadn't had for many a year, though it had haunted him for a time in the Blinds, fading when he found Joya and Derk. The scene was much as it had been in life, though whatever vicious corner of his mind crafting this version had added a few details; the blood covering his father's hands for example, and the rent and torn body of Clay's mother on the card-table before him. A stack of scrip and exchange notes were piled atop the corpse, stained red but otherwise unnaturally rigid and neat. Clay's father turned, cigarillo poised before his lips as he regarded the boy standing at the tavern-door with a less-than-welcoming grin. Clay could see the faces of the cards in his other hand, a winning hand in Mourning Jacks, unbeatable. He was about to become a rich man, though give him another day and he'd be poor again.

'Ma's dead,' Clay said, as he had when this hadn't been a dream.

'So your uncle tells me,' his father replied, turning back to the table and adding another hundred scrip to the blood-stained pot, the notes sticking to the blood on the dead woman's face.

'Heard you were back,' Clay said. 'Been looking for you.' Another truth, coloured by a high, desperate tone that tore at his insides now. 'For more than a week.'

'Been busy.' His father jangled the tooth necklace about his neck. 'With a goodly haul, too, I might add.'

'How much were you gonna give to Ma?' The desperate tone had gone now, though Clay didn't recall his voice being so utterly devoid of emotion.

'She showed me the door.' His father laughed as one of the other players upped his bet. 'Ain't no obligations twixt us, boy. Go on back to your uncle.'

'How much were you gonna give to Ma?' The pistol was an aged one-shot hammer-lock and felt heavy in his boy's hands. His uncle kept a chest of old weapons in his basement, securely locked but Clay knew where he kept the key. He chose the pistol because it was the only one with ammunition that seemed to fit, though he wasn't too sure he had loaded it right. Even so, he had every intention of finding out.

His father froze as Clay drew back the hammer with a loud click. 'Showed you the door 'cause you broke two of my ribs after you broke her nose for the second time,' Clay said. 'Showed you the door because you're a mean drunk and a lousy gambler.'

His father didn't turn and Clay always believed he knew what would happen next. It was in the forced shrug of his shoulders as he unfroze himself, and the overly mannered way he added more money to the pot. A man maintaining a lifetime's façade in the face of death. 'She,' he said, nodding at the corpse on the table, 'was a fine woman who deserved better. She had a kindness and grace rarely seen in this place, and I always knew I wasn't worthy. It made me hate, and drink and seek death in the Interior. I know this is my end, I know my own son will kill me this night, and I know it to be fitting.'

He hadn't, of course, said any of this. These words were born of the nightmare. In fact he had said, 'Your ma was a whore. Fucked if I ever knew you were even mine.' It didn't matter, though in the succeeding years Clay would often lie to himself that it had been these words that sealed his father's fate. But the fact was, nothing was going to save him.

He remembered the pistol-shot being louder than it was now, more a roar than the dry hiss and crack of hammer finding powder to send the ball into the back of his father's head. He also recalled the place erupting into panic and discord as the mingling of headhunters and Blinds scum decided how to react to another murder. But now there was no commotion. They all just sat drinking or carousing and the other players at the table kept on with their game. Clay's last glimpse of his father had been of him slumped across the table, blood and brains leaking from the front and rear of his head, just before he turned and ran, losing himself in the maze of street and alley. But now he stood, still and fascinated as his father rose from the table, face streaked with blood from the hole in his forehead as he turned to his son, fond smile on his lips. Clay began to scream when he started to speak.

The screaming kept on until it choked him, making him retch and flail. It took a while before two thoughts surfaced amidst the confusion and sputter: *I'm alive. This ain't no dream.*

He stopped flailing, lying with chest heaving on what he realised was something soft. A few seconds' blinking brought his eyes into focus and he found himself staring at a stone ceiling. *The temple?* he wondered, recognising the pattern of stonework as similar to the great pyramid. It couldn't be. The place was surely still burning or charred black as coal by now. He tried sitting up, finding the ache of his limbs so severe the task defeated him. Grunting, he tried again, his surroundings swaying as he came upright, head abuzz with the fugue of recent awakening.

He was in a circular chamber of broad dimensions, the lines of the columns that supported the ceiling and the tiles on the floor convincing him this was another structure in the city. The thick wall of vines that covered the exterior and excluded sunlight also indicated it was as heavily overgrown as everything else. An opening in the centre of the floor revealed a spiral stairwell descending into gloom. To his right sat a desk of basic construction, clearly fashioned from locally harvested timber judging by the bark still clinging to its roughly finished edges. It was piled high with papers, stacked into neat beribboned bundles. A pen sat in an ink-well beside an unfurled sheet half-covered in an artful, flowing script. Clay sat up straighter upon noting the freshness of the ink and the two-thirds-melted candle that sat next to the paper.

He realised he was fully clothed, though his boots were gone. Casting around he saw them placed at the foot of the bed on which he sat, his duster rolled up beside them and, sitting propped against the wall, the holstered Stinger complete with remaining ammunition. A quick exploration found no injuries beyond the scrapes to his hands, though there was a cluster of pale spots on his forearm, presumably the result of the Green he shot in the temple. He got up, staggering as the chamber tilted again and the buzz in his head rose to a greater pitch of intensity. He stumbled towards his belongings, snatching up the Stinger and checking the cylinder to find it empty. He began to reload it immediately, cursing as his trembling fingers sent bullets skittering across the floor.

'Shit!' He bent to chase after one wayward round then stopped as his eyes found something more.

It had been arranged around the back of a chair of similarly crude construction to the desk, a coat of some kind, a coat fashioned so as to resemble a thick swaddling of rags. Sitting on the chair was a long walking-stick, the bulbous head of which bore the signs of extensive and inexpert whittling.

The Black, plunging down out of the smoke . . . The Black with someone perched on its back . . . Someone he had last seen on the Red Sands . . .

'So, you're finally awake.'

He whirled, Stinger coming round to aim at the figure emerging from the stairwell. She was a diminutive woman of perhaps forty, hair cut short to frame a fine-boned, pale-featured face of North Mandinorian origin. There were some lines in her forehead and around her eyes but she seemed to Clay to possess a vitality that belied any age, an impression fortified by the brightness of her smile.

'Probably best if you don't do that,' she advised, climbing the last few steps, Clay tracking her with the Stinger. He noticed she bore a tray with a bowl of something that steamed and gave off a hunger-inducing aroma.

'Don't move!' he ordered, his commanding tone undermined somewhat by a fresh wave of dizziness that saw him take a stumbling step to the right.

'Really,' she said, smile unfaltering and showing an absolute absence of fear, 'that's not the best idea . . .'

She trailed off as a deep, rumbling sound came from outside. It wasn't particularly loud but the tone of it sent a tremor through him and he felt the stone beneath his feet throb with it. A dark shadow passed by outside the wall of vines, air whooshing as it swayed back and forth with slow deliberation.

'You're making him nervous,' the woman said.

Clay slowly lowered the Stinger, the rumbling noise and whooshing shadow stopping as he did so.

'Guinea fowl soup,' the woman said, holding up the tray.

'Who . . .' He staggered again, coming close to falling. The woman set the tray down on the desk and came to his side, guiding him back to the bed. 'Who are you?'

She stood back, smile less bright now, a little sad in fact as she extended a hand. 'Ethelynne Drystone, sir. And you are?'

He sat at the desk eating soup with a mis-shapen steel spoon he guessed she must have carried with her from Carvenport all those years ago. He asked no questions of his own, for she seemed to have plenty enough for the both of them. 'And Madame Bondersil seemed well to you?' she enquired, eyes bright with a keen desire for knowledge, though not so hungry for it as he might imagine her to be. Just an old pupil asking after a fondly remembered teacher.

'She's vital enough, alright,' he said and gulped down another mouthful. It may have been due to his hunger, but the soup seemed just about the best thing he had ever eaten. Rich in flavour and seasoned with pepper and wild thyme. 'Though I gotta say, she has a somewhat severe disposition.'

Ethelynne Drystone gave a nostalgic laugh, clasping her hands together as she reclined on the bed. 'A thing unlikely to ever change. She still runs the Academy, I assume?'

'That and more. Got the Protectorate dancing to her tune now.'

She inclined her head, smile lingering as she studied him. 'But you, I would guess, are not drawn from that august body. Are you, Mr Torcreek?'

Blinds don't wash, he reminded himself. *No matter how far you get.* 'No, ma'am.'

Her eyes went to the unscarred skin on his right hand. 'And unregistered too, I see. What a terribly interesting young man you are.'

He inclined his head at the ceiling from which a few more rumbling sounds had been heard as he ate his meal, accompanied by the scrape of what could only be claws on stone. Very large claws. 'Not so interesting as you, ma'am.'

She just smiled some more, watching him eat for a time until she asked what he knew she would. 'She sent you for the White, didn't she?'

He saw little point in lying, since he suspected she already knew most of what he could tell her. 'And you, if you could be found. Seems she never gave up hope you might be out here somewheres. Makes me wonder why you never tranced with her. Would've been an easy matter for her to send a company to bring you back.'

'Which presupposes that I wished to go back.'

'Seen more of the Interior than I ever wanted to. And if I could get myself off this Seer-damn continent tomorrow, I surely would. Yet you chose to stay out here all these years.' He shook his head and scraped the last of the soup into his mouth before setting aside the bowl. 'Thank you for your hospitality, ma'am.'

'Call me Ethelynne. Formality is a wasted commodity in this place.'

'Alright, Ethelynne.' He turned to face her. 'Where's my company?'

'Where you left them.' She got up from the bed and moved to one of the vine-covered openings between the pillars. 'Come, I'll show you.'

The patch of vines she took hold of turned out to be a door of sorts, cunningly crafted so as to merge with the blanket of vegetation outside. She gave it a push and it swung out on a hinge, revealing a narrow balcony affording a view of the jungle that told Clay he was at a far higher elevation than even the temple's summit. Krystaline Lake was a thin blue line far off to the left, indicating he was viewing it from the south. His attuned eye tracked across the verdant sea of jungle, picking out the overgrown towers and canals of the city before it came to rest on the bulk of the temple, except it wasn't so bulky now. The top three tiers had gone, the building seemingly tumbled in on itself leaving only a blackened stump.

'The jungle had become one with the structure,' Ethelynne said, stepping out onto the balcony and resting her elbows on the balustrade. 'When you burned it, the stones began to crumble.'

After tapping a tentative toe to the balcony floor, Clay went to join her. He looked down at the jungle below, fighting off another bout of dizziness. He turned his gaze to the ruined temple, wishing for some Green to enhance his scrutiny as all he could see was charred stone. 'My company . . .' he began, surprising himself by immediately stumbling over the words, a catch in his throat.

'There is a network of tunnels under the temple,' she said, touching a reassuring hand to his forearm. 'They strike me as a resourceful bunch. Though they may need a little help digging themselves out.'

He nodded, head lowered as he mastered himself. The thought of them all lying crushed under tons of rubble had been hard to endure, though he couldn't claim any particular concern over Firpike. 'You saved us before,' he said. 'On the Red Sands. Why?'

'It only seemed polite. I've taken to visiting the Sands at regular intervals in recent years. Having espied your sojourn, it wasn't especially difficult to guess your intent.'

'You know what we found there?'

All humour abruptly vanished from her face and she turned away, gaze flicking involuntarily to the south. 'Yes.'

He was unable to keep the accusation from his voice when he said, 'You let it live.'

'I had just drunk the heart-blood of a Red drake and used it to birth something far worse, killing a man I had begun to fall in love with in the process. It's fair to say my reasoning was somewhat impaired. I got back on the raft and let the river take me away.'

'You and Wittler . . . ?'

She gave the smallest laugh and shook her head. 'I was just a girl then, with silly notions. And he was a very impressive man, though considerably older. I'm often given to pondering what might have been if Clatterstock hadn't powdered that confounded bone.' Her expression became grim, shot through with the pain of reluctant remembrance. 'He saw, you know? Wittler breathed in the powdered bone and saw what I would do to him to survive. That's the great secret Madame has sent you in search of, Mr Torcreek. The White holds the future in its veins.'

He waited before speaking again, watching her thumb a small tear from her eye with an embarrassed grimace. 'We think it's in the Coppersoles,' he said. 'We think the alignment might be a way to find it.'

She pursed her lips and gave a slight nod. 'A fair deduction.'

He knew then he was looking upon a woman with a wealth of knowledge far beyond anything Skaggs, Scriberson or Firpike might possess. He also knew her desire to share it was limited, shaped by whatever she had been doing out here all these years. 'Madame thinks it's the key to everlasting profit,' he said. 'My uncle, the others, they just hunger for a glimpse of it, like it's hooked their souls somehow.'

She turned to face him, smiling again, a knowing smile. 'And you, Mr Torcreek? Do you lust for it, also? Or is it merely greed that drives you?'

He thought for a while before replying, everything he had seen and heard since leaving Carvenport babbling in his head like water on the boil. 'Seen a lot on this trip,' he said. 'What it left behind on the Red Sands, this place, what the mere thought of it does to otherwise clear-sighted folk. None of it bodes well for when we find this thing.'

She said nothing for a long time, standing and regarding him with the same knowing affection. Eventually she turned and glanced up to the roof of the tower, Clay following her gaze and immediately drawing up in shock. His alarm was such he came close to tipping over the balustrade, Ethelynne reaching out to steady him with a laugh. 'It's alright. He only bites when I ask him to, or when he's particularly angry.'

The Black stared down at Clay with narrowed eyes, small tendrils of smoke leaking from its nostrils as it gave another low, rumbling growl. It sat perched on the tower's stepped, pyramidal roof, sickle-like claws latched onto the stone and wings folded as its tail swayed gently behind. *Blue eyes,* was the only coherent thought to pop into his head. *It has blue eyes.* But these eyes were so different from the eyes of the Greens that had assailed them at the temple. There was no hate in them, no desire for blood or death. Looking at the way the light caught them, the way they *gleamed*, he knew he was looking into the eyes of something that looked back and understood what it saw. *This beast can think.*

'Well, that's a relief,' Ethelynne said. 'It seems we are all of like mind.'

'You drank heart-blood,' he said a short while later as they descended the tower's seemingly endless stairs. She had paused to gather some choice belongings into her swaddling of rags, which she rolled up and slung across her shoulders. 'That's supposed to be fatal, even for us.'

'For some of us, I'm sure,' she replied. 'But not me, apparently. I've done it twice now.'

Twice. 'Don't it hurt?'

'Certainly. The last time was the most agonising experience of my entire life.'

'Then why'd you do it?'

'Because the reward outweighed the cost.'

'Reward?'

She laughed a little. 'All in good time, Mr Torcreek.'

'Claydon, or Clay if you like. Since we're being informal and all.'

They emerged from the base of the tower onto a broad platform. It was much like those that formed the ground level of the rest of the city except it featured considerably more statuary. They all sat about gazing up at the tower, cracked and wreathed in jungle but still recognisable as representations of drakes and people.

'Guessing somebody of importance lived here once,' he commented, nodding at the tower.

'They called him "The Ordained,"' she said. 'A quasi-religious figure of great learning and wisdom. Part scientist, part shaman.'

'How could you know that?'

'The inscriptions.' She pointed her stick at the unfathomable script etched into the tower's base. '"Know this as Home to the Ordained. All must show him honour."'

'You can read this stuff?'

'Much of it. It's been my principal project for much of the last five years.'

'Scribes said no-one can read it.'

'Scribes?'

'Scriberson. A Consolidated Research scholar who got attached to us on the way.'

'Well, Scribes and his fellows don't enjoy my advantages when it comes to Interior artifacts.'

He nodded at one of the human statues. 'Got another fella travelling with us says these weren't Spoiled. Said the spoiling came later.'

'Yes, much later.' She paused to cast a wistful glance up at the tower. 'Pity,' she murmured. 'One of my more favoured homes.'

From her tone he deduced she didn't expect to return, something that added an ominous shadow to their next course.

'You didn't live here the whole time?' he asked.

'Only the last few years. I tend to move around a fair deal. Sometimes I'll even venture north to a trading post to buy sundry comforts and necessities. Ink and paper mainly, though I'll confess a weakness for the occasional small cask of brandy.'

'They don't ask who you are?'

'I make efforts to disguise myself. To them I'm just a madwoman who got separated from her company and kept roaming the Interior. Which, when you think about it, is fairly close to the truth.'

A gust of wind blew across the platform making Clay close his eyes against the stirred grit. When he looked again the Black had come to rest a short distance away. It opened its mouth to issue what he assumed to be a hiss of welcome as Ethelynne strode towards it, taking hold of one of the spines at the base of its neck to haul herself onto its back with accustomed ease. She wiggled her hips a little to wedge herself firmly between two spines then turned to Clay with an expectant glance.

'You must be crazy,' he stated, unmoving.

'I need to show you something,' she said. 'It's a long walk and, spry as I am, my knees are not what they were.'

'My company . . .'

'Aren't going anywhere, and it's only a short diversion.'

'Fine. Tell me the way and I'll meet you there . . .'

He trailed off as the Black flexed its wings and coiled its neck to gaze at him, mouth opening to issue an unmistakably impatient squawk. 'Best hurry up,' Ethelynne advised. 'He might conclude you don't like him.'

Somewhat to his surprise, Clay found his feet taking him towards drake and rider, heart rate seeming to double with every step. 'He got a name?' he asked, halting at the beast's side and keen to explore any avenue for delay.

'Yes, but it wouldn't make any sense to you. I call him Lutharon for convenience. It's from an old Mandinorian legend about a shadow demon.' She smiled again and inclined her head to the position just behind her.

'He able to lift both of us . . . ?'

'Just get on, you baby!'

He took a breath and reached for the spine behind her, finding it rough under his grip, like old shoe-leather. It took a few tries before he managed to haul himself into place, the sweat building on his brow the whole time as his heart kept on its steam-hammer rhythm. He sat as she did, wedged between two spines. It wasn't exactly comfortable, but neither was it unbearable. In fact, it reminded him of his first time on a horse outside the Protectorate gaol-house. *Except horses got no wings,* he thought as Lutharon rose from a crouch, Clay feeling the muscles of the beast's neck shifting beneath the skin.

'Hold on!' Ethelynne advised as the drake turned about, making for the tower. He was perturbed by the joyful anticipation in her voice. 'Tight as you can!'

He took her advice, gripping the spine with both hands, worrying that the unabated sweat leaking from his palms might dislodge them at any second. An involuntary yelp escaped him when Lutharon leapt, Clay finding himself staring up at the length of the tower as the drake's talons found purchase on the vines and began to climb. 'His kind are mountain dwellers!' Ethelynne told him, voice raised to a cheery pitch above the loud scrabble of claws and flexing wings. 'Prefers to launch himself from an elevated perch.'

'Uhh!' Clay replied, fighting a rising gorge and resisting a strong impulse to close his eyes.

Lutharon climbed to about half the tower's height, paused to angle his head and regard them with one bright blue eye, as if checking they were both still aboard. He gave a hiss of satisfaction then tensed before propelling his bulk away from the tower with a push of all four limbs. Clay always wondered why he didn't scream as, instead of gliding gently away over the jungle, they plummeted straight down until he could see the cracks in the paving-stones that made up the platform below. Perhaps he was just too scared to scream, though at least he did finally manage to close his eyes. A lurching heave to his stomach told of a change in direction and when he forced his eyes open he saw they were now ascending, the jungle canopy dipping below his eye-line for a moment before Lutharon angled his wings and they levelled out.

Ethelynne gave an excited giggle and patted a hand to the drake's neck, craning her own to call to Clay above the rushing wind. 'No matter how many times, I never get tired of it!'

Clay could only nod and choke down vomit.

Lutharon gave two beats of his wings, sending them higher, Clay wincing at the chill though he found the view an increasing distraction from his fear. They were higher than any mountain now, higher than a human could ever get, and the world revealed below was rendered new. *So small and so big,* he thought as the jungle merged into a single emerald blanket. Off to the north the Falls were a mist-shrouded wonder, seeming to sparkle as they fed the mirror-like breadth of the Krystaline. He could even see Fallsguard, a narrow black spike jutting above the misted cascade. He wondered if it had fallen by now or if the major had somehow contrived to fend off the Spoiled. In either case, he could see no boats on the river.

Lutharon angled his wings once more and Clay looked down to see what remained of the temple. Evidently the fire hadn't contained itself to the pyramid; black tendrils of ruined foliage snaked out into the canopy of trees so that it resembled the charred remains of a colossal squid. Lutharon flew over the ugly spectacle to take them west for a mile or more where he began to circle a small clearing, descending with every bank of his wings. Clay scanned the jungle for any sign of drake or Spoiled, seeing only yet more ruins through the trees and gaining an appreciation for how huge the city below must have been. He saw Ethelynne smooth a hand over Lutharon's neck and the drake turned again, shortening his wings to bring them lower still, the ground flashing beneath before Clay's stomach gave another lurch as the drake spread his wings and reared back for a landing.

'It's this way,' Ethelynne said, lifting a leg to slip from Lutharon's side and striding off into the trees. Clay's dismount was less elegant and accomplished by expedient of the drake's twisting his body to dump him onto the ground. One of Lutharon's blue eyes gleamed down at him for a second before he trotted off in pursuit of Ethelynne. *Not altogether sure he's taken to me,* Clay mused as he followed in the drake's wake.

Ethelynne led them on a winding course through yet more ruins, even more overgrown and hard to discern than those Clay had seen during the trek to the pyramid. From the many shattered columns and levelled dwellings he judged that whatever had brought the city low had been particularly destructive here. He still saw no sign of any Greens or Spoiled but kept the Stinger drawn as a precaution.

'That's not really necessary,' Ethelynne told him, turning as she paused at the foot of a stairway so thickly covered in vines and tree-roots it was barely recognisable. 'They rarely come here.'

She continued to linger at the base of the steps, gazing upwards with both hands tightly grasping her carved walking-stick. Clay followed her gaze and saw that the steps ended on a raised platform extending away on either side, the ends of it lost to the trees.

'What's up there?' he asked.

Ethelynne took a few moments to answer, and when she did her voice was soft. 'Memory.'

She started up without another word, clambering over vines and roots with an energy that made Clay question her claims of infirm knees. He and Lutharon duly scrambled up after her, the drake's talons shredding much of the foliage encasing the steps in the process. Coming to Ethelynne's side Clay found himself looking down into some kind of rectangular bowl-shaped structure. It was at least three hundred yards long and about two hundred wide, the enclosing walls arranged in descending tiers to a flat surface. A large cylindrical tower rose from the centre of the surface, standing perhaps thirty feet high and twelve feet thick. It was heavily overgrown but, through the gaps in the vegetation, Clay determined that it had been fashioned from much paler stone than that used elsewhere in the city.

'The inscriptions I found here indicate it was some kind of sporting venue,' Ethelynne said. 'People would gather in their thousands on festival days to watch athletes compete in foot-races and tests of strength. I believe it was as much ritual as entertainment.'

Beside her, Lutharon gave a low, ominous growl. His blue eyes were narrowed as he looked upon the arena and his tail scraped yet more foliage from stone as it swished in agitation.

'Drakes have many mental limitations that humans do not,' Ethelynne said. She put a hand to Lutharon's snout which calmed him somewhat, though his tail continued to swish. 'But,' she went on, 'when it comes to memory they are our undoubted superiors. You see, drake memory does not die with the individual, but rather accumulates down the blood line over many generations. Not everything remains, of course, even they have limits, but locked in every drake's mind are memories from its forebears that span centuries.'

Clay followed as she started down into the arena, leading him to the tower in the centre where she stopped and gestured for him to take a closer look. *Not stone,* he realised, peering through the gaps in the shroud of vines. A skull stared out at him from a wall of fused bone, just like in the Badlands but on a much grander scale, and a great deal older. He stood back, his gaze tracking the tower from base to top. *How many bones would it take to fashion such a thing?*

'The last of my Blue,' Ethelynne said, and he turned to find her holding up a vial of product. 'The connection won't be strong given the brevity of our association, but it should be enough.'

Clay glanced back at Lutharon, now lowered to a defensive crouch, eyes fixed on the tower and wings half-spread as if in readiness for a quick flight. 'You can share memories with him?' Clay asked. 'Like in the trance?'

'The differences between a human mind and a drake's are considerable, so complete understanding is impossible. But yes, we have shared memories. One I should now like to share with you.'

'He knows what happened here,' Clay realised. 'One of his ancestors saw it.'

'Yes.' She held the vial out again, eyebrows raised expectantly.

'Can't you just tell me?'

'I have a task to perform, Clay, one I shirked almost thirty years ago. I believe I shall need your help to complete it.' She removed the stopper from the vial and drank half the contents, holding it out to him once more. 'But I won't ask you to join my course without a full understanding of what lies ahead.'

Clay's gaze returned to the empty eyes of the skull peering out at him from the vines. The compulsion to know, to find answers to so many questions, was strong, but tempered with an awareness that this was a decision he may well regret for a long time.

'Well, I guess a memory can't kill me,' he said, taking the vial and draining the remaining product.

Ethelynne's mindscape took the form of a library, Clay finding himself surrounded by tall shelves, each crammed with more books than he could count. The books came in various sizes, the colour of each binding different. Some were bound in board of faint pastel shades whilst others, usually the larger volumes, were bound in leather of more vibrant hues.

The Academy library where I spent so much time as a girl, Ethelynne explained. *Madame Bondersil was forever dragging me out of here. Naturally, I had to make a few modifications to fit everything in.*

Clay perceived her as a vague, ghostly shape gliding through the maze of shelves, eventually coming to a stop. *Here we are.* She reached out a translucent hand to pluck a book from the shelf, one of the larger volumes, bound in shiny, black leather. *Are you ready?* she asked, spectral fingers poised to open the book. Noting the way her hands had begun to shimmer he wondered if she wasn't more nervous about opening it than he was.

When you are, ma'am, he told her.

She opened the book and the library disappeared, replaced in the blink of an eye by a swirl of confused colour and sensation. Clay grunted as the discordant mess of images birthed an ache in his head. *What in the Travail is this?* he demanded.

The world as seen through the eyes of a Black drake, she said. *I told you, their minds are different, as are their eyes. They do not see as we do. Relax, let your mind adjust.*

He tried to calm himself, allowing the ache in his head to subside into a dull throb as the confusing morass gradually resolved into recognisable shapes. *People,* he realised, seeing what he initially took as a cluster of flames but now realised were running figures, red silhouettes against a dark background.

They see heat rather than light, Ethelynne said. *It is often a uniquely beautiful way to perceive the world . . . But not today.*

The red silhouettes were engulfed by something so hot it appeared like a pale yellow jet. When it cleared they lay on the dark ground, flame rising from their crumpled remains in an orange fog. Through the shimmering heat Clay could see more figures, a great mass of them in fact, boiling over the walls of the arena in a fiery tide. He realised he was seeing this from near ground level, the view shifting as the drake that had captured it tried to rise, then faded for a second as it failed, eyes closed in pain.

Wounded, Clay realised as the vision cleared and tracked over a massive body riven with fresh scars, all leaking blood. He could feel the animal's agonies, muted and bearable but still fierce enough to make him reconsider his decision to let Ethelynne show him this.

The wounded drake's gaze swung about, revealing that the

mass of people descending the tiers had now reached the arena floor. By now Clay's mind had adapted to the change in perception sufficiently to allow him to make out details. He could see the faces of the onrushing figures and recognise their deformities. *Spoiled.*

Yes, Ethelynne confirmed. *The first generation of Spoiled. Countless people taken and twisted into a horde intent on destroying those with whom they had once lived in harmony.*

The pale yellow jet streamed out once more, engulfing the leading Spoiled in flame. The vision shifted to the left, revealing a Black drake, a huge male even bigger than Luthoran. His mouth gaped wide to spew more flames before he spread his wings and launched himself directly into the midst of the on-coming horde, teeth, claws and tail wreaking bloody havoc. Clay felt something then, a rush of warmth through the pain and knew his host was looking upon its mate. The male Black must have cut down fifty or more before they swarmed over him, clubs, hatchets and spears rising and falling in a frenzy.

His host gave a faint despairing cry as the male Black's tail cut down another few Spoiled before it fell limp and his huge body disappeared under the seething mass. The view swung away from the Spoiled and fixed on something small, something Clay realised had been sheltering behind his host's body. The boy was perhaps twelve, and looked up into the eyes of the wounded drake with an expression of such trust and affection it was hard to bear. Beyond the boy he could see evidence of battle, the bodies of Spoiled and un-Spoiled humans lying tangled together in death, the fierceness of their struggle clear in the dismembered limbs and sundered entrails littering the ground. There were a great many bodies, enough, he understood now, to craft a tower eighty feet high from their bones when this was over.

They were protecting him, he thought, returning his attention to the boy.

Apparently so, Ethelynne replied. The memory froze at that point as she focused all her attention on the boy. *This city, and others like it, once they were mighty and the Black was revered; understanding grew as one Blood-blessed in every generation drank the heart-blood of a dying drake. This boy, I believe, was the last Blood-blessed born to this city, a precious soul they sacrificed themselves to preserve. It seems not all humans here fell under his sway.*

His?

She unfroze the memory and a vast piercing cry sounded in the sky above the arena, the horde of Spoiled all freezing in place as if in response. Clay's drake host shuddered as a very large shadow swept the structure from end to end. Her gaze shifted to the sky as it grew dark, the sun blotted out by a huge, winged shadow. She tried once more to rise as the thing landed a short distance away, its claws shattering the stone floor of the arena. Its colour was not revealed by the heat-vision but from its size Clay knew this could be only one breed of drake. It glowed with energy, shining brightest in the upper belly where it stoked its fires. Behind the massive drake the Spoiled horde all stood, as still and silent as Protectorate riflemen on parade.

Clay's host succeeded in raising herself up, the vision swaying as she staggered and stumbled her way towards her enemy. It peered down as she approached, head tilting from side to side in apparent curiosity. The female Black came to an unsteady halt a few yards short of her foe, raising her gaze to meet its eyes. They blazed back at her like two glowing coals and Clay felt something new stir in her pain-wracked body: defiance.

The female Black launched herself at the White, the vision blurring as she coughed out a jet of flame, fading to reveal her claws latching onto its neck, talons digging deep. For a few seconds all was a confusion of flame and heat, then a new pain, sharp and deep enough to make Clay cry out. The vision flickered, clearing for a moment to show the White stepping over its victim and making an unhurried progress towards the small boy who now stood amidst a mound of corpses, lacking all protection.

Clay was forever grateful that the vision descended into blackness at that point, for he had no desire to see what came next.

Lutharon brought them down on the temple's western side, alighting just beyond the canal on a patch of ash-grey ground littered with tree-stumps and the twisted remains of Greens. What remained of the Spoiled lay along the canal bank, a long, straight line of blackened bodies, all twisted up. *They just stood there and burned,* he realised. Strangely, he felt no triumph at the sight; it was too ugly for that. Instead, there was only a sense of grim satisfaction at the necessity of it and, though he fought it, an undeniable flare of guilt.

Lutharon folded his wings and issued a low, rattling sound that Clay initially took for a growl but Ethelynne seemed to take as a reassuring sign. 'It seems there are no enemies close by,' she said, slipping from the drake's back. Clay followed quickly before Lutharon could tip him off once more.

'So it rose once before,' he said. He had to hurry to keep up with Ethelynne as she strode towards the east, away from the temple. Lutharon lumbered along behind, pausing now and then to sniff at the corpses of his lesser relatives.

'It would appear so,' Ethelynne replied. 'And in so doing, either killed every human on this continent or transformed them into its mindless servants.'

'Which means something must have brought it down. Otherwise, its descendants would still be ruling this place.'

'Sound reasoning, Claydon. Well done.'

'You know what it is, don't you?' Clay persisted. 'That's why you stayed out here all these years. You've been looking for a way to bring it down.'

'Actually, I haven't the faintest idea what brought about its prior demise. But, perhaps with your help, I might finally find out.' She kept striding across the ash without further explanation and he realised she was done answering questions for now.

After a hundred paces the ash gave way to thick jungle,

Ethelynne disappearing into the trees without hesitation. Clay drew the Stinger and hurried after her, eyes roving the shadowed surroundings for signs of an enemy. Despite her assurance, the Interior had ingrained a caution in him that didn't fade easily. He found her halted before what he initially took to be just an overgrown rocky mound but soon recognised as another ruin. Surveying the fragments of tumbled stone he was able to envision the arch they must once have formed, his gaze tracking along the mound to see it disappear into the earth a short way off.

'They called it the "Supplicants Path,"' Ethelynne said, tapping her walking-stick on the stones. 'Those hoping to ascend to servitude in the temple would gather once a year to walk it. Any who navigated their way to the temple would graduate to the next set of tests.'

'What if they didn't?' he asked.

'Most just made their way back here and went home, greatly shamed by their failure and obliged to do penance. Though some inscriptions speak of supplicants becoming lost in the tunnels, never to emerge.' She crouched, leaning close to the stones with ear cocked. 'Nothing,' she said, after a moment.

'Are there other ways in?' he asked, a certain desperation creeping into his tone.

'There were, but the Krystaline swallowed them centuries ago. The coast-line was very different when this city rose tall.' She straightened, looking expectantly back at the trees. There soon came the sound of cracking branches and Lutharon landed a short distance away, the ground shuddering with the weight of his arrival.

'Drake hearing is perhaps ten times that of a human,' Ethelynne said as the Black sniffed at the stones before cocking his head in a manner unnervingly similar to hers. Lutharon became very still, blue eyes closing in concentration before he huffed a loud grunt and moved back. Woman and drake exchanged a long look, Clay sensing the passage of information between them.

'Is it heart-blood that does it?' he asked Ethelynne. 'Lets you command him like this?'

'Command him?' She laughed. 'What an absurd notion. But, you are partly correct. Heart-blood brings about certain changes in a Blood-blessed, provided one survives the experience of drinking it.'

'But he's a Black, and you drank Red.'

'What an astute observer you are, Claydon. Your friends are there.' She tapped her stick to the stones. 'But it seems they're in a bad way. The air in the tunnels isn't very good. Pockets of gas have built up over the years.'

Clay moved to the stone, pulling away a hefty boulder then immediately reaching for another. It soon became apparent, however, that shifting so much rock would take more time and strength than he possessed. 'Can he help?' he asked, panting and pointing at Lutharon.

The great black turned to Ethelynne and once more Clay sensed their unspoken communication. 'He's . . . understandably reluctant,' she reported eventually.

'Reluctant?' Clay fought down a surge of anger. 'Can't you just tell him to do it?'

Ethelynne's face took on a severe aspect that would have put Madame Bondersil to shame. 'He is not some beast of burden bound to obey my every whim. He is a thinking and feeling creature, and, as you have seen, his kind have a very long memory. He can smell your people; he knows what they are. He was barely ten years old when I found him, Clay. Starved nearly to death and nuzzling at the corpse of his mother, his mother who had a longrifle bullet embedded in her skull. I assume the body tumbled into too difficult a place for the Contractors to harvest her. Most of her blood had seeped away, but some still lingered in the heart.'

Lutharon issued another rattling hiss, his gaze still locked on Ethelynne's and Clay knew they were engaged in some kind of unspoken communication. 'You drank his mother's heart-blood,' he realised. 'That's how come he's bound to you.'

'It enabled a certain mutual understanding,' she answered.

'Then he knows you need me to find the White.' He jabbed a

finger at the piled stones and stared up into the Drake's eyes. 'And I need them. I've seen what you've seen. Do you want to see it happen again?'

Ethelynne moved to Lutharon's side as the drake's hiss faded, smoothing a hand over his flank before closing her eyes and pressing her forehead to his hide. Clay heard her whisper, 'I'm sorry,' before moving back. Lutharon's gaze swivelled back to Clay for an instant, eyes betraying a certain reluctance, if not resentment, then he turned about, tail whipping. For a moment Clay thought he would take flight once more but instead the drake raised his tail and brought it down in a blur. The spear-point-like tip must have possessed the hardness of iron from the way the stone shattered under the weight of the blow. Clay moved back as Lutharon repeated the action over and over, the tail whipping in a rising cloud of powder. After several minutes Lutharon turned about and began to dig at the sundered stone, gravel rising in a fountain as he burrowed with forelegs and back legs. He stopped when something noxious rose from the hole he had dug, scooting back and waggling his head before sneezing out a plume of flame. Whatever miasma had escaped the hole caught the spark and blossomed into a brief but bright column of blue fire.

Clay stepped to Lutharon's side and crouched to peer down at the hole he had dug. For a long moment he heard nothing, but then came the sound of echoing voices, faint and clearly near exhaustion, but still alive. He sagged in relief then turned to Ethelynne. 'Best take him back a ways. This is gonna take some explaining. And as for the White, that all stays twixt us for now.'

She nodded and Lutharon abruptly bounded away, launching himself into the tree-tops once more. Clay turned back to the hole, cupping his hands about his mouth to call out, then pausing as a fresh thought crept into his head. *Leave them here. They'll find the way out soon enough. What d'you think Uncle'll make of your purpose?* He forced the notion away with ruthless conviction as Silverpin's face loomed large in his mind. *Ain't leaving them adrift in the jungle. Got from now until the Coppersoles to make him see sense.*

'Uncle!' he called into the hole. 'This way! Got someone you'll be glad to meet!'

CHAPTER 30

Hilemore

Duels, as Hilemore knew all too well, were a very serious business in Varestia. Although the peninsula was renowned for the warlike and unwelcoming nature of its inhabitants, the region hadn't seen a full-blown civil conflict for the best part of two centuries, even during the tumultuous years of the Revolution which had seen Varestia transformed into a de facto autonomous state. Duelling remained the principal reason for this uncharacteristically lengthy period of peace. If one clan found itself in dispute with another, the matter would normally be resolved either through an arranged marriage or single combat. Similarly, petty feuds between individuals could be settled with a duel before they could escalate into something worse. In consequence, the formalities surrounding such occasions were numerous and subject to a rigid code, successive decades having evolved a system that prevented any claim of unfairness or skulduggery that might defeat the entire purpose. Duels were overseen by a neutral party with a detailed knowledge of the varied technicalities who would be handsomely paid for the task. In the Hive the duty fell upon the shoulders of Constable Tragerhorn who, despite not being of Varestian origin, took a rigorous approach to his responsibilities.

'Your exact age, if you please, Captain?' he enquired, a pair of half-moon reading spectacles perched on his nose and pen poised above an open leather-bound book. He had already jotted down Hilemore's height and approximate weight along with a signed annotation that he had suffered no recent physical impairments and was not likely to expire from some hidden ailment within the next year.

'Twenty-eight and four months,' Hilemore replied, taking a long drink from the water bottle handed to him by Ensign Tollver. They had returned to the *Viable* after the meeting with the Directors the day before. He sat on a stool on the aft deck, sweating freely from recent exertion. Steelfine stood near by with sword in hand and, despite their shared bout of practice, didn't appear to be sweating at all.

'Do you have any relatives likely to question the legality of this proceeding, or pursue vengeance and feud in the event of your death?'

Hilemore's thoughts flicked briefly over his brothers and the complete absence of correspondence between them. 'No.'

'You are not married?'

Lewella's eyes the last time they met, tearful, regretful, but also so very angry . . . 'No.'

'How many enemies have you killed in single combat? An approximate figure will do.'

'Is this really necessary?'

Tragerhorn merely raised his thick eyebrows above his spectacles, a polite smile of expectation on his lips.

Hilemore sighed. 'Battle does not count as single combat, I assume?'

'No, sir.'

'Then one. I fought a duel in Varestia seven years ago.'

'Just one, sir?'

'Just one.'

'Mmmm.' Tragerhorn scribbled in his book before playing the pen on his lips in contemplation.

'Problem?' Hilemore asked.

Tragerhorn shook his head in apology. 'I am unable to approve this contest, Captain. It being so unequal.'

'Unequal?'

'Indeed. You see, Director-in-Chief Arshav has fought over

thirty duels, killing twenty-three men in the process. To match you against him would violate the Duelling Code, and prove tantamount to murder in my opinion.'

'Put me in the circle with him and I'll show you murder!' Hilemore's face reddened as he surged to his feet, Tragerhorn blinking as he leaned close to shout into his face. 'You think me some managerial milksop, sir?'

'Captain!' Zenida appeared at his side, casting a wary glance at the constable, who used a kerchief to wipe Hilemore's spittle from his face as she tugged him away. 'This won't do any good. He's too much a stickler. It's why Father hired him all those years ago.'

Hilemore took a moment to calm himself, resting clenched fists on the rail. 'If he won't approve the duel, what then?'

'Since you are the challenger, the contest will be declared in Arshav's favour and any status and property you hold rendered to him. However' – she paused to cast a pointed glance at Steelfine – 'in cases where the contestants are not equally matched, nomination of a proxy is acceptable.'

'Twenty-four,' Steelfine stated a few minutes later, brows furrowing as he thought further. 'No, twenty-five. I was forgetting my second cousin. It wasn't a very long contest.'

Hilemore raised an eyebrow at Tragerhorn, who thought for a moment then gave a nod. 'The ninth hour tonight. Captain Okanas will guide you to the venue. Please be sure to bring a fully itemised cargo manifest, and the little lady in question. The Directors are insistent upon this point.'

The Conglomerate had established a dedicated arena for duels on a bluff overlooking the harbour. It was just a circular pit with a sand-covered floor though, from the hushed reverence of the Varestians present, it could well have been a Church of the Seer. The non-Varestian townsfolk, however, evidently viewed the occasion as an opportunity to indulge in public drunkenness and gambling. Hilemore saw numerous bets placed and a few brief fist-fights break out as they waited. The crowd voiced a ragged cheer as Tragerhorn strode into the pit, falling to murmured anticipation as he raised a hand.

'Challenge has been made and accepted,' Tragerhorn said in a tone of strident formality. 'These men,' he pointed in turn to Arshav and Steelfine who stood at opposite sides of the pit, bare to the waist and sword in hand, 'come to settle a grievance through blood. This fight is theirs and theirs alone. The contest will continue until death or yielding. Any who interfere will be subject to the One Rule.' He strode to the edge of the pit and climbed out, raising both arms above his head. 'Begin!'

Hilemore watched Steelfine stride towards his opponent with unhurried confidence, whilst Arshav immediately dropped into a fighting crouch. Zenida stood close to Hilemore with her daughter between them. From the way she clutched the girl to her side he thought that, whatever the outcome this day, the idea she would ever hand her over to Arshav was a patent absurdity. He had seen her slip something into her trouser pocket back on the ship, the light catching metal before she concealed it from sight. The bulge in her pocket was signature enough, however. *Corvantine revolver,* he judged. *She must have scavenged it from the deck after the battle.*

'You won't need that,' he said as they clambered into the launch.

Her hand went to the revolver in unconscious reflex and she met his gaze with feral resolution, speaking softly. 'She stays with me, even if I have to slaughter everyone in this shit-pit.'

'It won't come to that.'

'You can't be sure. My brother's skill matches his spite.'

Hilemore had glanced over at Steelfine standing at the prow of the launch, features placid as he raised them to let the evening breeze play over his tattooed skin. 'I have every confidence in our champion.'

He returned his attention to the pit, watching Steelfine come to a halt a few feet short of Arshav, standing at a slight angle to his opponent but making no effort to raise his blade. 'This is not an order,' Hilemore had told him back on the *Viable*. 'We'll find another way . . .'

'Our debt is not settled, sir,' the Islander reminded him. 'But today it will be.'

Arshav lunged, moving with a cobra-like speed that made Hilemore wonder for an instant if Tragerhorn might have done him a service. Steelfine, however, possessed plentiful speed of his own. He twisted, allowing the point of Arshav's blade to jab the air where his shoulder had been, then twisted the other way as the pirate tried another lunge.

Arshav stepped back, breathing deep, calming breaths, though Hilemore could read the growing frustration and anger on his face. He tried a slashing attack next, swinging his sword first at Steelfine's legs then his neck in a display Hilemore suspected Ensign Tollver would have admired greatly. Steelfine stepped over the slashing blade then ducked the back-swing, seeming to move with a preternatural slowness Hilemore knew came from his ability to read his opponent's moves.

'Mother,' Hilemore heard Akina say in a small voice.

'Don't worry,' Zenida said. 'All be over soon.'

Arshav spat a florid curse in Varestian and attacked again, flicking his sword-tip at Steelfine's eyes, then his belly before leaping into a mid-air pirouette that, in the normal course of events, should have laid the Islander's neck open below the jaw. Steelfine's sword came up for the first time, steel ringing as it met the pirate's blade, sending his arm wide and leaving his face open. The pirate saw the danger and tried to back-pedal but the Islander was far too quick. He performed a leap of his own, leg extending into a kick that found Arshav's nose. Blood flew as the pirate's head snapped back and he landed hard, sword flying from his grip. He scrabbled for it as Steelfine strode towards him, issuing a pained yelp as the Islander's boot came down on his wrist. He began to assail Steelfine with a barrage of Varestian profanity as the Islander leaned lower. Arshav fell to abrupt silence as the tip of Steelfine's sword touched his neck.

'Mother!' Akina repeated, more urgently now.

'Hush!'

'Yield!' a voice called out from the crowd, loud and commanding. It was Ethilda, struggling free of the crowd despite their restraining hands. 'Yield, damn you, Arshav!'

The pirate, however, said nothing, face set in a defiant glare as he raised his chin to allow the blade a better target. Steelfine paused and turned to the crowd, his gaze soon finding Hilemore, brows raised in a question.

Hilemore was about to nod when he felt an insistent tugging on his sleeve and glanced down to see Akina, face pale and stricken with alarm. 'It's custom,' he told her. 'I did order him to spare your uncle if he yielded.'

'Not that!' she said in disgusted exasperation, turning and pointing out to sea. '*Look!*'

He turned, following her finger. The crowd behind them was relatively thin, allowing a fine view of the sea. It was a clear day, sunlight shafting through the sparse cloud to play over the two smaller islands to the north and, between them in an arrowhead formation, a flotilla of Corvantine frigates. They were perhaps three miles off, wakes thinning as they slowed and made a turn to port, a turn that could mean only one thing.

Hilemore bent and lifted the girl, turning and running for the pit as her mother followed close behind. He jumped into the pit and reached Steelfine's side just as the first shell landed in the town. The crowd convulsed at the thunder-clap report of the explosion, screaming panic soon taking hold as another shell landed on the hillside barely twenty yards away.

'Get to the beach,' Hilemore said, pushing Akina into Steelfine's arms. 'Guard the launch. Give me ten minutes. If I fail to arrive, return to the ship and take command. Head south at best speed.'

Arshav Okanas had regained his feet by now and stood near by, blood pouring from his ruined nose as he railed at his sister. 'You brought them here!' he yelled as three more shells tore into the Hive, flame and smoke blossoming amidst shattered wood.

'Everything our father built, soon to be pounded to ruin! You did this, Zenida!'

She drew the Corvantine revolver and levelled it at Arshav's head. He quailed for a moment then stood firm, refusing to yield to her any more than he had to Steelfine.

'Don't!' Ethilda struggled free of the churning crowd and rushed to stand in front of her son, arms spread to protect him as she stared at Zenida in desperate entreaty. 'Please, Zenida! For your father's sake.'

Zenida hesitated, glancing down the hill to the harbour where a fresh salvo of Corvantine shells could be seen raining down on the anchored pirate vessels. One was already burning, whilst the others spewed steam from their stacks in a frantic effort to put to sea. 'Soon you will have no ship,' she told her step-mother and half-brother. 'Then perhaps you will know what it feels like to beg aid from those you hate.' She gave a dismissive flick of the revolver and they fled, Ethilda pushing her son into motion. He cast a single, hate-filled glare at his sister then ran after his mother.

'Go!' Hilemore slapped a hand on Steelfine's shoulder, the Islander overcoming his reluctance with a visible effort as he bore Akina away, skirting the now-burning town as he made for the beach.

'Where do they keep it?' Hilemore asked Zenida. 'At the mansion?'

She shook her head. 'Tragerhorn has charge of it.'

Hilemore cast about, seeing the constable making for the town at a steady run. They set off after him, ducking repeatedly as the Corvantine barrage continued. When they neared the town the flow of panicked people reversed, those who had run towards imagined safety realising their error whilst those who had already seen the effects of the bombardment had taken to their heels. Hilemore found himself forcing his way through the throng, the thickness of which thinned abruptly when Zenida fired a shot in the air and yelled out a firm promise to kill the next scum-sucker to bar her way.

They had lost sight of the constable in the fray but Zenida knew the route to the gaol-house where he held office. They had to throw themselves flat several times as they made their way through the town, flaming debris and broken glass raining down and filling the streets with a growing pall of smoke. Various ugly sights greeted them as they ran on, a child screaming at his decapitated mother, a pig digging its snout into the entrails of a disembowelled man. Hilemore could only close his eyes to it all and keep following the pirate woman as she led him through the smoke. The gaol-house came into view a few moments later, apparently untouched though the buildings on either side were burning fiercely. The door was open and they found Tragerhorn inside, busily filling a leather satchel with copious amounts of scrip and exchange notes from an open safe.

'Fines, I assume?' Zenida asked him.

'My contract has just been terminated by the Corvantine navy,' he replied, barely glancing up as he continued to pile notes into the satchel. He stopped when Zenida raised her revolver.

'We won, fair and legal,' she said. 'Where is it?'

The former constable tensed, eyes narrowing as he looked at them both in cold calculation. *A true mercenary,* Hilemore decided. *Dutiful only up until the point where his life is in the balance.*

'There's another safe in the back,' Tragerhorn said. 'But only I have the combination.'

Another shell landed outside, shattering the windows and scattering glass across the room. Tragerhorn cursed, clutching at the fresh cut on his arm, though Zenida barely noticed, stepping closer and pressing the revolver's barrel into his forehead. 'Then tell me!' she grated.

Tragerhorn's eyes flicked to Hilemore. 'I have six Corvantine warrants on my head,' he said. 'So, when they land I'm dead anyway. I want a berth on your ship.'

'Done,' Hilemore said and Zenida lowered the revolver. They followed Tragerhorn into the recesses of the gaol, past the barred cages where two men were imprisoned. They screamed at the constable for release, hands clutching at him through the bars. 'Don't waste your compassion, Captain,' Tragerhorn advised, reading Hilemore's expression and working a key in the lock of a heavy door. 'Child rapers, the pair of them.'

He pulled the door open revealing a safe of much more sturdy construction than the one in the outer office. 'This will take a moment,' he said, kneeling to touch his fingers to the dial. 'It's a lengthy combina—'

His last word was drowned out by an explosion that wrecked the forefront of the gaol-house, Hilemore finding himself blinded and deafened as the blast threw him against the cages. He came to his senses with a tongue of flame licking its way up the sleeve of his tunic. He scooped up powdered stone from the floor and patted the fire out, dragging himself to his feet and trying to shake away the bombastic orchestra that seemed to have taken up residence in his head. The sound of laughter brought him back to full sense, his vision focusing on the two prisoners. The blast had evidently torn the doors of their cages free and they stood amidst the ruins of the gaol-house, joyful at their good fortune.

Two pistol-shots sounded and the prisoners fell, Hilemore turning to see Zenida lowering her revolver. 'Child rapers,' she said with a shrug.

They found Tragerhorn slumped next to the safe, a jagged wooden splinter speared through the centre of his face. 'Seerdammit!' Hilemore kicked the safe then ducked as another shell screamed overhead to slam into the whore-house up the street. 'We need to go,' he told Zenida. 'We'll head deeper into the Isles on auxiliary power. I daresay you know a hiding-place or two . . .' He fell silent as she held up a small vial of product.

'Black?' he asked.

'Fortunately,' she said, stepping past him to crouch at the safe.

'Where did you get it?'

'I always had it.' She removed the stopper and drank the vial's contents in a single gulp before tossing it aside. 'Your men are overly bashful when searching women, Captain. You should talk to them about that.' She closed her eyes and laid a hand on the safe, frowning in concentration. 'It's a rare thing for a ship not to carry a safe. One reason why having a Blood-blessed aboard always made my father's voyages so profitable.' She gritted her teeth, grunting with effort as the safe gave a satisfying clunk.

The safe proved to hold an embarrassment of riches, Tragerhorn having evidently exploited every opportunity his position afforded. Alongside a goodly supply of product, there were stacks of scrip notes and Dalcian sovereigns plus a small chest piled with varied jewellery. Ever the pirate, Zenida took the lot, sweeping it all into Tragerhorn's satchel before retrieving the constable's revolver and handing it to Hilemore. 'I have a sense you'll need this on the beach.'

Her prediction proved all too reliable. Steelfine stood before the prow of the grounded launch laying about with an oar at a group of half a dozen pirates intent on seizing any means of escape. Two men lay dead at his feet, one with a broken neck and the other with the Islander's sword buried in his guts. Akina sat in the launch, beckoning frantically to her mother. Hilemore and Zenida were obliged to hurdle several corpses as they ran towards the launch, the Corvantine gunners having made plenty of sport with the flood of pirates seeking return to their ships. Hilemore could see two more vessels burning and another in the process of slipping beneath the harbour waters. The smoke was too dense to make out the state of the *Viable* but he could at least confirm she was still afloat and seemed to be underway, though at very low speed. *Clever lad,* he silently complimented Mr Talmant. *A moving target is harder to hit.*

Zenida came to a halt a short distance from the launch, levelling her revolver at the pirates. He had expected her to issue some form of warning but whatever solidarity she might feel for these men had apparently disappeared when they posed a threat to her daughter. She fired all four remaining bullets, taking down two pirates and wounding a third. The others rounded on her, terror and desperation banishing reason as they charged, knives and cudgels raised. Hilemore emptied the constable's hefty revolver as fast as he could, the weapon giving an uncomfortable jerk with every bullet fired. Despite its clumsiness, the large calibre proved effective. Three more pirates lay dead by the time the hammer fell on an empty chamber and the only survivor wisely dropped his knife and sprinted off into the swirling haze.

'Apologies for the delay, Number One,' Hilemore said, moving to put his shoulder to the prow of the launch.

'Unnecessary, sir.' The Islander grunted, adding his own weight to the effort and soon they had pushed the launch free of the sand. Zenida leapt aboard and took the tiller whilst he and Steelfine slotted the oars into the rowlocks and began to haul. 'I take it,' Steelfine said between pulls, 'our business here is concluded?'

'Yes, and quite successfully I must say.' *Though whether I can legally divide the prize money is another matter.*

Zenida was obliged to steer them around and through the burning hulks of the unfortunate pirate vessels and the occasional survivor still bobbing in the water. One managed to latch a hand onto the launch's rail only to withdraw it with a howl as Akina pounced, teeth rending at the knuckles. They were forced to slow on clearing the hulks, the smoke so thick it appeared they were lost amidst a sea fog.

'There, sir.' Steelfine pointed to a bulky shape off to starboard and soon they came in sight of the *Viable*. She appeared to be circling at dead slow, rails crowded with look-outs despite the continuing shell-fire from the Corvantines. The crew gave a hearty shout upon seeing the launch, casting a veritable web of ropes over the side.

'Tell Mr Talmant to make speed full ahead!' Hilemore called up to the crew as Steelfine and Zenida caught the ropes. 'Steer course for the harbour mouth!'

Hilemore leapt clear of the launch as the crew hauled it level with the *Viable*'s rail, sending Zenida to the engine room with orders to Chief Bozware to fire up the blood-burner immediately. 'Man the guns,' he told Steelfine. 'Load shell only. Fire as she bears.'

'Aye, sir!'

He caught sight of Ensign Tollver as he ran to the bridge. 'Muster the riflemen, if you please, Mr Tollver. Sharpshooters to the rail.' He returned the boy's salute and climbed the ladder, finding Talmant at the tiller.

'She's at seven knots, sir,' the lieutenant reported. 'The Chief did some more tinkering whilst you were ashore.'

'She'll soon be doing a damn sight more.' Hilemore peered through the smoke clouding their course, making out the dim hump of the sloping headland forming the western edge of the harbour. 'Two more points to starboard, Mr Talmant. We'll need to shave this as fine as we can.'

'Aye, sir,' Talmant replied just as the port-side guns opened fire to drown out his voice. Hilemore could make out the sleek shape of a Corvantine frigate through the haze, briefly illuminated as one of the *Viable*'s guns found the range and slammed a shell into her fore-deck. The frigate veered away as her own guns boomed a reply, raising waterspouts on either side of the *Viable* but doing no damage.

Hilemore turned his gaze to the speed indicator, finding the needle stubbornly stuck on seven knots. *Come on, Chief,* he prayed inwardly whilst clasping his hands behind his back and affecting as unperturbed a demeanour as he could. *A captain is always certain.*

His patience was rewarded barely three seconds later when the *Viable* gave a now-familiar lurch and the needle began a rapid climb, past ten, then fifteen, then twenty, all in the space of a few seconds. *What a marvellous machine this is.* 'Steady the course, Lieutenant,' he told Talmant as the prow drifted slightly to starboard. 'Be prepared to turn at my command.'

He waited until they cleared the headland, the course so close to the shore they could feel the slight diminution of speed as the

Viable's hull scraped a sand-bar. Then they were clear, open ocean beckoning them north. 'Slow turn ninety degrees to port, Lieutenant,' Hilemore ordered.

'To port, sir?' The lad frowned at him. 'But that'll , , ,'

'Take us south and back into the Isles. I'm well aware, Mr Talmant. Make your turn, if you please.'

'Aye, sir.'

When the turn had been completed he went to the speaking-tube and called down to the engine room. 'Captain Okanas to the bridge immediately, please,' he said before going to the hatch and casting his gaze to the stern. The smoke was thinning now and most of the Corvantine guns had fallen silent. Three frigates were labouring in pursuit of the *Viable* but the distance was increasing by the second. *Not a blood-burner amongst them,* he concluded. He could see only burning ships in the harbour and, on the hillside beyond, the Hive appeared to be just a mass of flaming buildings. Had Trumane delivered their own bombardment it would have wrecked a large portion of the town, perhaps compelling the occupants to establish their villain's den elsewhere. The Corvantines, however, were more interested in complete destruction, raising two pressing questions in his mind. *How did they know of this place? And did they come for us?*

CHAPTER 31

Lizanne

She's alive?

Very much so. Sane and healthy, too.

Lizanne could feel her mindscape shifting in reaction to the revelation. Ethelynne Drystone, living in the Interior all these years. *Madame will be . . .* Her thoughts clouded, the last meeting with Madame looming large. Lizanne couldn't escape the conviction that, whatever her prior sentiments, Madame's principal reaction to this news would be one of suspicion. The lost pupil's reappearance was a complication, and with the object of her obsession so close, any complication would be unwelcome. She could also sense Clay's reluctance to share the information. His encounter with the Corvantine hireling at Edinsmouth was a barely suppressed memory that left a lingering distrust beneath the surface of his mindscape.

You alright, miss? Clay asked. *Getting dark in here.*

Apologies. She reasserted control of her mindscape, though the whirlwinds were still a little ragged. *I appreciate your trust in me, Mr Torcreek.*

Gotta trust somebody if we're gonna survive this. Can hardly keep it from you anyhow.

True, but I thank you for the honour of your confidence, in any case.

She had a decision to make, the import of which could not be under-estimated. *What does she know of the White?*

There was a short delay before he replied, his thoughts coloured with a reluctant resolve. *I could tell you.* He opened one of his memories, displaying the image of an overgrown tower rising from the floor of an arena. *But it'll be easier to show you, though I doubt you'll thank me for it.*

When it was over she took quite some time to reorganise her whirlwinds into respectable order. She wasn't used to being flustered and resented the disharmony it caused to her mindscape, although she couldn't argue with his logic. A simple retelling wouldn't have been enough.

You appear to have decided to break your contract, Mr Torcreek, she observed, referring to his discussions with the miraculously revived Ethelynne Drystone.

Yes, he replied simply, pausing to read the reaction of her storms. *Thought there'd be a different response, if I'm honest.*

She summoned one of her whirlwinds and extracted the memory of Major Arberus's account of his last expedition with Burgrave Artonin. *My own investigations have gone some way to corroborating your findings.*

So, you agree? You'll help us?

The decision was too enormous for her to conceal the shiver that ran through her storm, new whirlwinds sprouting from the clouds whilst others withered and died. When it settled the storms had taken on a reddish hue, the colour of conflict . . . and fear. *Yes,* she told him. *I take it your uncle and fellow Contractors know nothing of this change of heart?*

Reckon I might be sporting a few bullet-holes if they did. They got a real hankering for this thing now.

You know what that might mean further down the road?

I know. Just have to find a way to make sure it don't come to that.

Seeing the firm conviction colouring his thoughts, she decided not to pursue the point. *This astronomer you picked up in Fallsguard. You trust him?*

Seen no reason not to, as yet anyways. You think I should be worrying about him?

His appearance at that juncture seems a little convenient, having survived a journey through the Interior alone to boot. It may be my ingrained paranoia, but he'll bear close scrutiny.

His mindscape pulsed with agreement before he summoned another memory: a handsome woman of Old Colonial stock standing on a porch. *Your aunt,* Lizanne recalled.

Yeah. Be grateful if you could check and make sure she's alright, what with the war and all.

If I can. This place is about to become very hectic. And I suspect Madame will be keeping a close eye on my activities from now on.

She sensed his acknowledgment before his thoughts twisted into a more pressing question. *What you gonna tell her?*

That you failed to make today's trance and can therefore be presumed dead. From now on we shall be pursuing our own contract, profitless though it's likely to be. I will endeavour to obtain what information I can, though from now on it would be better if you advised your uncle that the information I have provided confirms the wisdom of your current course. How much Blue do you have left?

A quarter-vial, more or less. Got a good supply of the other colours, thanks to Ethelynne, but she used up the last of her Blue to share the drake's memory.

Very well. From now on you will conserve your stocks and refrain from making contact until you reach the Coppersoles. I will resume trancing for a short time at the allotted hour in five days. Hopefully, by then I will have more information to guide you.

Seems to me a lot depends on you making it through the coming battle.

She found herself touched by the concern evident in the sombre hues of his mindscape, so different now from the ill discipline and self-interest of their first trances. *Fortunately,* she replied, *thanks to an old friend of mine, I may well have the means to do just that.*

'Eight hundred in four days.' Jermayah surveyed the stacked cannon shells with an appreciative shake of his head. 'Wouldn't have thought it possible.'

'Lizanne did most of the work,' Tekela said, pausing in the midst of polishing the latest batch. Her face was besmirched with grease and she wore a pair of ill-fitting overalls and a headscarf, making her resemble a line girl from one of the huge Syndicate manufactories.

'You performed a creditable amount of labour too, miss,' Lizanne told her from her makeshift resting-place atop Jermayah's work-bench. Prolonged use of Green had indeed greatly increased their productivity, but the cost in fatigue was proving steep. Major Arberus could be heard snoring from his newly constructed bunk in the recesses of the workshop. He had completed a ten-hour shift mixing propellants to Jermayah's exacting recipe. The process had a tendency to befuddle the mind due to chemical exposure, as demonstrated when he had sunk to one knee the night before, taken Lizanne's hand and slurred his way through a proposal of marriage.

'Marry a radical anticorporatist?' she scoffed, hauling him upright and pointing him to his bed. 'I think not, sir.'

'Probably for the best,' he mumbled, stumbling away. 'Marriage is an archaic institution. Grams always said so. Look at Leonis and Salema. Never a happy word between them.'

Lizanne gave Tekela a cautious glance, though the girl seemed not to have heard. She spoke rarely of her father now, and her lapses into Eutherian had diminished in concert with her increased use of Mandinorian. The day before, Lizanne had spent a brief rest from manufacturing to compose her formal report to Exceptional Initiatives, complete with recommendations regarding the future employment of both Tekela and the major. So far, however, she had resisted the urge to seek out the local Agent-in-Charge and submit it for approval. The management of Exceptional Initiatives lay in the hands of those whose absence of sentiment made Madame Bondersil appear the paragon of compassion.

They'll probably find a use for Arberus, she decided, gaze lingering on Tekela as she performed the delicate task of screwing a percussion cap into a shell casing. *But they'll kill her, even if they don't kill me.* The conclusion left her calculating alternatives. War, as she well knew, bred the kind of chaos that might well facilitate an unquestioned disappearance. She was well schooled in the art of discarding an identity and there were places in the world where even the Protectorate's arm couldn't reach. Although, few could be said to be conducive to the secure housing of a young lady and her self-appointed guardian. Some regions of Dalcia retained a good degree of stability despite the recent disturbances. Or, if desperation became a factor, there was always the vast East Mandinorian steppe where, even within living memory, whole armies had disappeared without a trace.

Did I do you a kindness? she wondered, watching Tekela and thinking of that night in her father's study, the inability to pull the trigger. *What did I spare you for? Even if this city stands against Morradin, what then? What happens if we fail and the White rises?*

She closed her eyes, reasserting control over her thoughts with long-practised discipline. *Uncertainty is the field agent's lot,* she reminded herself. *Confine your consideration to practicalities. Action is the antidote to fear.*

When she looked again she found Tekela had stopped and stood amidst the rows of gleaming shells with her head raised. 'It's different,' she said. Lizanne's tired head took a moment to comprehend her meaning, then she heard it; the ever-present artillery barrage had changed, a new faster rhythm underpinning the slower clock-work regularity they had grown accustomed to over the preceding week.

'Naval guns,' Arberus said, tugging on his overalls as he emerged from the shadows. 'The Corvantine Fleet is here. Morradin will attack before the end of the day.'

'What in the Travail is that?' The Protectorate artillery captain regarded the Thumper with equal parts bafflement and disdain as they trundled it up to the forward battery.

'Rapid Fire Device Mark Five,' Lizanne told him before adding a brisk string of lies. 'Myself and these technicians are contracted employees of Exceptional Initiatives, Experimental Weapons Division. This device has been approved for deployment by Madame Bondersil. You are ordered to render all assistance in positioning it for maximum effect against the enemy.' She handed over an envelope containing a set of recently forged orders that would be unlikely to bear more than cursory scrutiny. Fortunately, the captain had more pressing matters on his mind this evening.

'I have no men to spare,' he said, briefly scanning the orders before giving the Thumper another baffled glance. 'Will this thing really help?'

'Give us a clear field of fire,' Arberus said, careful to moderate his accent into a gruff semblance of Arradsian-born tones, 'and you'll see soon enough.'

The captain's scepticism didn't seem to have been overcome to any great degree, but he dutifully pointed them to a position a hundred yards or so to the left of his battery. 'We're thinnest there. Got a bunch of conscripted townsfolk manning that stretch, plus a few sailors mixed in. Don't expect them to stick around too long when it starts in earnest.'

Lizanne nodded her thanks and the four of them began pushing the Thumper towards the allotted position. The network of intervening trenches was too narrow to navigate so they were obliged to traverse the shell-holed overground gaps between the defences. Jermayah had sacrificed his beloved thermoplasmic carriage to provide a movable mounting, and the advanced suspension he had designed made the task of wheeling the thing over rough ground so much easier. Marshal Morradin had also been kind enough to shift the full weight of his artillery away from the defences to the city itself, the tempo of the bombardment increased to match that of the fleet now crowding the waters beyond the unbreachable giant edifice of the mole. The journey from Jermayah's shop to the south wall had been a perilous one, Lizanne pulling Tekela into cover more than once as the shells came down on Old Town, shattering houses that had stood for centuries and igniting numerous fires. She had considered ordering, or more likely, confining Tekela to the workshop but knew the security it offered was illusory; there were no more safe places in Carvenport.

'Protectorate business! Make way!' Lizanne greeted the defenders in the trench, a distinctly unmilitary bunch judging by their non-uniform clothing, though the sailors were easily recognised, as much because of their truculence as their sea-boots.

'Piss off, deary,' one replied with a yellow-toothed smile. 'This stretch of line is spoken for . . .'

He trailed off when Arberus jumped into the trench, looking down at the stocky sea-dog with a stern demeanour until he shuffled away. 'Here,' the major said after a quick inspection of the trench, pointing to a slightly raised hump near the centre. 'Gives us a clear field all the way to the trees.'

He and Jermayah took charge of sighting the Thumper whilst Lizanne and Tekela sorted the ammunition. They had only managed to carry half in the carriage, though Jermayah seemed confident it would be enough. 'Get the shock of their lives when she starts to sing,' he said, slapping an affectionate hand on the weapon's barrels. Arberus's military persona re-emerged with a vengeance and he was soon ordering the defenders to fill additional sandbags with which to shield their position. None of the conscripts seemed willing to voice an objection. If anything, many seemed relieved to hear an authoritative and competent voice, albeit one with a peculiar accent.

'Your place is here,' Lizanne told Tekela, guiding her to a spot next to the rear wheel of the Thumper's carriage. 'You load the magazines. You do not do anything else and you do not raise your head above the edge of this trench. Do you understand?'

She received only a brief, pale-faced nod in response, the girl's wide and overly bright eyes indicating she was all too aware of the dangers they faced today. 'There will be explosions,' Lizanne said, taking a roll of cotton wool from her pocket and pressing it into Tekela's hands. 'Put some in your ears, and open your mouth wide when the shells start falling. You have your revolver?'

Tekela nodded again, reaching into her overalls to pull the pistol from the holster Jermayah had given her. Lizanne saw how her hand was shaking and reached out to clasp it, forcing a smile and meeting the girl's eyes until the tremor faded. 'Only if you have to,' Lizanne said, squeezing her hand before moving to Arberus's side. He stood scanning the distant tree-line whilst Jermayah continued to tinker with the Thumper, Lizanne suspected more out of nerves than necessity. Like Tekela, he had never seen combat before.

'Anything?' Lizanne asked the major.

'It'll be a while yet,' Arberus replied. 'He'll keep pounding the town to spread as much fear and panic as possible. May not even launch his assault until nightfall, though that's always a risky option. It's hard to control an army in the dark.'

Lizanne studied his face for a moment, seeing only the focused gaze of the professional soldier facing battle. 'No qualms, Major?' she asked. 'Once this starts you'll be killing your own people.'

He replied with a quote, something she noticed he often did when notions of moral difficulty were raised, as if the mere repetition of dogma was enough to banish all doubts. '"True change has never been bloodless."'

'Bidrosin again. Do you know all her writings by heart, I wonder?'

Arberus's eyes remained fixed on the tree-line but his voice took on an oddly nostalgic tone. 'Oh yes. Even the poetry. That was her profession, you see, before the First Revolt. She found herself cast into prison for penning an amusing ditty concerning the Emperor's excessive fondness for the company of young boys. Rather than kill her, the Emperor thought it more amusing to strip away all her family's wealth. Every sibling, cousin, uncle and aunt reduced to poverty with a stroke of a pen and she cast out from prison, destitute. A singularly vindictive act I suspect he came to regret in time.'

'She changed her name,' Lizanne said, realisation dawning as she recalled her own history lessons. 'Bidrosin was merely a pseudonym, adopted when her husband divorced her.'

'Indeed, though for a time she went by her maiden name until finding love with a fellow radical as her unending torrent of anti-Imperial pamphlets drew more and more attention. Her children adopted the name, partly to honour her but also to disguise their association.'

'Arberus.' Lizanne shook her head, voicing a laugh that drew a start from the surrounding conscripts. 'So, you were born into revolution.'

He shrugged, his mouth forming a rueful grin. 'Grandmother was a difficult woman, but also made some very compelling arguments. Certainly more compelling than the vapid Imperial bombast they drummed into us in school.'

'What became of her? The histories I've read are ambiguous regarding her fate.'

'Despite numerous unwise adventures during the Revolution, she survived to grow old hiding in my parents' attic, eventually losing her sight which proved a great trial for she so loved to read. It was one of my chores to read to her, though in time I came to understand it as an honour. She died when I was fifteen, quietly in bed and as comfortable as we could make her. We laid her to rest in a grave crowned by a stone carved with a false name. One day I hope to replace it with the real one.'

Still, Lizanne thought but left unsaid, *she had a better death than the millions who died in pursuit of her nonsensical scribblings.*

'Leonis came to the funeral,' Arberus went on. 'He had been one of her earliest acolytes. The whole notion of his joining the Imperial army had been Grandmother's idea. It was hoped that he would win enough renown on the battlefield to place him in proximity to the Emperor one day. Sadly, the day never came. My parents were leery of any further involvement with the Brotherhood but Leonis found a willing accomplice in me, especially when he began to tell me of a great and powerful secret lurking in the depths of this continent, a secret that might resurrect our cause, provided we got to it first.'

Lizanne gave a mirthless laugh. 'If you had found it, I suspect the result would have been anything but resurrection.'

'So, you think it best left buried? A wondrous discovery shunned by humanity, despite all it can teach us?'

'I have come to believe it should not be left buried, but destroyed. I believe the wonders that did indeed once flourish on this continent were brought down by the very thing we seek.' She stared at him until the weight of her gaze made him turn. 'My employers do not share my concerns. When they come to light, I may need your assistance.' She cast a meaningful glance at Tekela, now busily engaged in arranging the Thumper's magazines into a neat stack.

She saw calculation in his gaze rather than sentiment as he looked at the girl, though there was perhaps a small glimmer of affection. 'Our prior arrangement?' he asked.

'To be negotiated with the Board. But I will need to appeal to them directly, in Feros. Once they hear my full account of this endeavour, I'm hopeful rational measures can be agreed.'

'Meaning, at some point, we will have to contrive an escape from this port, in the midst of a siege no less.'

Lizanne looked back at the city, realising the combined barrage of fleet and army had faded. There remained four hours until nightfall, which indicated Marshal Morradin had decided not to await the cover of darkness after all. 'Meaning,' she said as they both crouched down beside the bulk of the Thumper, tensing in anticipation, 'the city has to still be standing for us to escape it.'

He nodded as the first shell came down, tearing a hole into the earth just south of the outer trenches, quickly followed by a dozen more. Arberus's reply was lost amidst the din, but she read his intent readily enough as he patted an affectionate hand to the base of the Thumper.

*

The barrage seemed to last an eternity but in fact couldn't have gone on for more than a half-hour. The cotton in Lizanne's ears did much to shield her from the noise but she could still feel it, the earth quaking with the continuous rain of destruction. The depth of the trench protected them from much of the shrapnel but not from the fountains of displaced earth and boulders which soon had them covered in dirt and wincing from bruising encounters with falling stone. Worse than the physical effects, however, was the gnawing uncertainty that grew into fear and then terror as the barrage continued. All in the trench quickly understood it to offer only a partial refuge when a Corvantine shell scored a direct hit on a neighbouring position occupied by Protectorate Regulars. Limbs and partially destroyed torsos had been amidst the debris that rained down, the ghastly sight enough to send one of the conscripts screaming for the rear, casting his rifle and ammunition away as he pelted off into the smoke. A few others had clearly been tempted to follow his example, edging closer to the rear of the trench and tensing for a rush. Their determination faded when one of them poked his head up to scan for an escape route only to have it split down the middle by an inch-long shard of shrapnel.

When it seemed it might never end, Tekela reached out a hand to Lizanne. She sat with knees drawn up and her back against the Thumper's base, eyes closed tight and trembling arm extended. Lizanne took her hand, holding it tight, watching the girl's lips move in an unheard prayer, or was it a song? The suspicion was confirmed when at last the final shell came slamming down and a thick wall of silence descended on the trenches, the sudden, almost shocking stillness broken only by Tekela's song. Lizanne's estimation of her musical talents deepened upon hearing her voice. She recognised the tune, 'The Leaves of Autumn,' the Eutherian lyrics sung with a captivating sweetness at odds with the landscape that greeted their gaze.

The defences had been transformed into a semblance of Morvia's surface, every square yard seemingly cratered and pitted.

In some places the barrage had been so intense the shell-holes overlapped. Predictably, the Protectorate artillery positions had borne the brunt of the fire, Lizanne seeing one in a state of near-complete destruction whilst the nearest battery lay in a shambles of shattered wheels and dismounted guns. She could see the harassed captain busily ordering his dazed men to rebuild the position and found herself impressed that he managed to get one piece sighted and ready by the time Arberus's shout dragged her attention to the south.

At first she could see nothing but drifting smoke and the dim shadow of the tree-line, but then came the piercing wail of multiple bugles and the ominous growl of thousands of men charging into battle. The smoke seemed to vanish all at once, revealing the dark mass of Corvantine infantry emerging from the trees. They moved at a steady run, rifles levelled and bayonets fixed, sword-waving officers out in front, each blowing a shrill whistle. A ragged volley of shots came from the outer trenches as the Contractors recovered their dazed wits, a score or more Corvantines falling, mostly officers as far as Lizanne could tell. The Contractors evidently knew how to pick their targets. Despite its accuracy, their fire lacked the weight to stem the tide of onrushing infantry and soon dozens of duster-clad figures could be seen running to the second line of trenches.

The Protectorate artillery seemed to take this as the signal to open fire. Their numbers had been thinned by the Corvantine barrage but they still possessed enough fire-power to take a fearful toll on the attackers. Large rents were torn in the Corvantine ranks as they neared the trenches, men and parts of men cast into the air amidst the flame and exploding earth. But still they came on, at least a full brigade by Lizanne's estimation, driven onward through the rain of shell and bullets either by blind duty or fear. As they came to the edge of the outer trenches the Protectorate infantry and Contractors manning the second line unleashed a deafening blast of rifle fire, cutting down the first rank of Corvantines like a scythe through wheat. Lizanne could hear the distinctive roar of Jermayah's Growlers amidst the general cacophony, their worth proved by the mounds of dead piling up among the shell-holes.

Some Corvantines escaped the blizzard of lead to take shelter in the trenches vacated by the Contractors, whereupon they began to return fire, Lizanne ducking down as the bullets whined overhead.

'You lot waiting for something?' Arberus demanded of the conscripts, most now cowering beneath the lip of the trench. Some of the sailors duly bobbed up to fire an unaimed shot or two but the rest just gaped at him, the combined effects of the barrage and this new onslaught breeding a paralysis that couldn't be shaken by a stern word. Arberus swore in Eutherian and strode towards the nearest conscript, a managerial type judging from his well-tailored hunting jacket. He stared at Arberus in whitefaced shock as the major pressed his pistol against his head. 'Get up!' Arberus ordered.

Some primal instinct seemed to warn the manager that this was no bluff, for he immediately got to his feet, albeit somewhat shakily. 'Fire your rifle!' Arberus ordered, keeping his pistol pressed to the man's temple until he raised his rifle to his shoulder and fired off an inexpert shot. 'Again!' Arberus said. 'And aim this time!'

The manager worked the bolt to open the breech, fumbled his first attempt to slot a bullet in place, succeeded at the second try and fired again. He flinched when a Corvantine bullet smacked into the ground near by, but nevertheless continued to fire as Arberus stepped back and pointed his revolver at the stillcrouching conscripts. 'All of you. If you want to live, get on your feet and start fucking fighting!'

Lizanne moved to the major's side, fingers poised over the Spider's buttons and Whisper in hand. However, further encouragement proved unnecessary as they all slowly got to their feet and began to fire at the Corvantines in the trenches below. Their position had been cleverly constructed at a greater height than the outer trench lines, allowing the defenders to fire down at the now-densely-packed Corvantines. The conscripts' lack of expertise mattered little when presented with such an unmissable target. More than a dozen Corvantines fell at the first volley, quickly followed by many more as the conscripts realised they had the upper hand and their rate of fire increased.

'Not yet,' Arberus told Jermayah as his hand went to the Thumper's lever. 'This is just the first wave.'

Gazing down at the dreadful spectacle unfolding below, Lizanne thought of poor Mr Drellic's words regarding Grand Marshal Morradin and concluded the old butler hadn't been so mad after all: *The great commander, no more than a pig grown fat on the blood of wasted youth.*

The trench below was now crammed with the dead or dying, in some places the corpses so densely packed they remained upright, the mass of bodies twitching continually under the unrestrained rifle fire. Yet more bodies littered the ground beyond, the wounded crawling or staggering about amidst the storm of shell and bullet. She saw one officer propping himself up on an upturned rifle, his leg missing below the knee but still waving his sword and blowing his whistle until a burst of Growler fire tore him apart.

The conscripts, blood-lust now stoked to full and not yet sated, continued to pour bullets into the mass of bodies below until Arberus barked at them to stop wasting ammunition. All along the line the crackle of gun-fire slowly ebbed as it became apparent the Corvantine assault had been stopped at the outer trench. A few shocked and wounded men could be seen through the haze, staggering or crawling back towards their own lines.

'I suppose they'll ask for a truce now,' Lizanne commented. 'To gather up their wounded before renewing the assault.'

Arberus's laugh was hollow, his gaze fixed on the ground beyond the trenches in tense expectation. 'Clearly, you don't know our enemy that well, Miss Lethridge.'

A few seconds later came the tumult of a fresh assault, bugles, whistles and the shouts of charging men echoing through the smoke before they appeared. *Another two brigades,* Lizanne realised as she gauged their numbers, her unease deepening at the sight of the dark red tunics of the men directly in front of their trench. *The Scarlet Legion.*

Arberus had also been quick to spot the presence of the Imperial Elite, moving to the Thumper and patting Jermayah on the shoulder. 'It's time. You turn the handle, I'll aim.' Jermayah had constructed an ingenious mounting for the weapon that enabled it to be swivelled about on lateral and vertical axes with minimal effort. Arberus took a second to align the Thumper then nodded at Jermayah. Lizanne had time to fumble some fresh cotton into her ears before the weapon began to roar. Its rate of fire was slower than the Growler's but the harsh, percussive bark that accompanied the departure of every shell from the multiple barrels still made for a jolting experience. She was surprised by how little smoke it produced, Jermayah apparently having concocted a new form of propellant that allowed the gunner to observe their target as they fired. She was therefore treated to a full demonstration of the Thumper's effectiveness as the first shells tore into the ranks of the Scarlet Legion.

Much of the first rank simply disintegrated, a line of tall men, maintaining impressively disciplined order as they charged with rifles levelled and bayonets gleaming, transformed into bloody ruin in the space of a few seconds. She saw four men explode in quick succession, the men behind and to the sides reeling away from the flying shrapnel and fragmented bone. It seemed that for every man the Thumper killed directly it took down three more with the force of the resultant explosion. By the time they had exhausted the first magazine, the centre of the Scarlet Legion's line had been stopped completely. The legionnaires on the flanks, however, continued to charge on despite the shock of the Thumper's attentions, rallied by sword-wielding officers to increase their pace.

'Reload!' Arberus said.

They had practised this over and over again in the workshop; Jermayah opened the breech, Lizanne removed the empty magazine and Tekela replaced it with a full one. All done in less than four seconds.

Arberus traversed the Thumper to the right as Jermayah began to turn the handle once more, then worked the weapon slowly from side to side to concentrate fire on the Legion's flanks. More exploding men, more gaps torn in their ranks, but still, somehow, the survivors came on. Perhaps four hundred made it to the outer trench where they began to clamber over the bodies of those killed in the first assault. The Protectorate troops and Contractors in the second line opened a withering fire, exacting a heavy price for the legionnaires' courage. But the Imperial Elite were not easily daunted, struggling on over the mounds of corpses and ascending the slope towards the second line. They were close enough for Lizanne to make out their faces now and they all seemed to be screaming, either through rage or madness, running forward as their comrades died around them.

Arberus ordered another fresh magazine and depressed the Thumper's barrels by several inches before firing again. At this range the effect was too much even for the surviving legionnaires; whole platoons were wiped out at once, some men suffering multiple hits so that they were simply blasted out of existence. The Thumper's shells raised a dust-storm, concealing the final moments of the Legion's assault as Jermayah exhausted the last of the magazine. The pall settled slowly, revealing a scene of utter carnage. Men lay in pieces, heads, limbs, legs and rifles tangled up together like discarded meat from an abattoir.

'Fuck me,' Lizanne heard one of the sailors say before he choked off into a retch.

Incredibly, one man remained standing amidst the slaughter, a great barrel-chested fellow with the grizzled look of a veteran sergeant. He stood staring down at what remained of one of the proudest regiments in the empire, face expressionless but tears streaming down his craggy cheeks. After a moment he straightened, squared his shoulders and hefted his rifle, then began a slow deliberate advance towards the second line of trenches. Arberus took a rifle from one of the conscripts and shot the man in the head, his body collapsing onto the piled remains of his men.

'A trifle harsh, Major,' Lizanne commented as Arberus lowered the rifle.

'When the Scarlet Legion took Jerravin,' he said, 'they chained up all the surviving defenders and made them watch as their wives and daughters were raped and beheaded. Then they doused them in oil and burned them alive. I stood and watched them do it, laughing along with all the other butchers, because that was my role then.' He turned and handed the rifle back to the conscript, the manager he had forced to his feet earlier. 'You asked if I had any qualms,' he said to Lizanne. 'I trust this stands as sufficient answer.'

CHAPTER 32

Clay

'Madame Bondersil says we should trust her, huh?' Braddon spoke quietly, his gaze lingering on Ethelynne as she sat with Lutharon on the lake-shore. The drake had curled up on the shingle beach come nightfall, tail curving to form a protective barrier around the small woman nestled against his massive chest. Whilst she seemed at ease, the drake's eyes remained bright in the gloom, his gaze sweeping over them all in continual and wary scrutiny. Upon emerging from the tunnels, Preacher and Braddon had immediately begun to raise their longrifles at the sight of a large male Black standing barely twenty feet away, only lowering them when Clay rushed to stand in their sights. Even then, it had taken some while before the knowledge that he had discovered the fabled personage of Ethelynne Drystone fully sank in.

The Longrifles sat around a makeshift camp in various states of dishevelled hunger, much of their supplies having been lost at the temple. Scriberson seemed the least affected, his fascination with Lutharon apparently banishing any mere physical wants. Firpike, still alive somewhat to Clay's annoyance, regarded the animal with a mixture of barely controlled fear and naked calculation; the ability to control a drake was worth more than all the gold and knowledge now buried beneath several hundred tons of charred stone.

Predictably, the Contractors were considerably more agitated by Lutharon's presence, their wary observance the equal of his, and all keeping their weapons close as they huddled around the fire the beast had raised for them at Ethelynne's request. Their suspicion had only been slightly allayed when Ethelynne treated Foxbine's leg wound with her stock of Green. The injury had begun to fester in the dank confines of the tunnels but a hefty application and ingestion of Green had done much to start the healing process, though the gunhand was still obliged to lean on Skaggerhill as she walked.

Clay took some solace from the comparative lack of concern displayed by Silverpin. She had clambered out of the tunnel and rushed towards him, crushing herself to him in relief, then drawing back to cast a curious glance at Ethelynne and Lutharon. 'It's complicated,' he had said, which, from the lengthy kiss she then pressed to his lips, seemed explanation enough for the time being.

'So Miss Lethridge tells it,' Clay told Braddon, still a little fog-headed as he was not long out of the trance. 'She's back at Carvenport now.' He glanced over at the others, lowering his voice and deciding some truth would make the lies slip down easier. 'The Corvantines have it under siege, Uncle. Sent a whole army from Morsvale to take it. They're holding out for now, but their cannon are pounding the place day and night.'

Braddon's gaze abruptly lifted from Ethelynne, eyes widening in concern.

'I asked her to check on Auntie,' Clay assured him. 'She said she would.' He paused, watching his uncle fold his arms, face clouded with uncharacteristic indecision. He stayed quiet for a good while, features set in a frown that Clay knew must be masking considerable turmoil. *How strong is the White's pull?* he wondered. *Enough to make you turn your back on your wife?*

'If we start back now,' Braddon said finally, 'assuming we can find a means to make it up the Falls, then the river, whatever's gonna happen will have happened by the time we get there.'

'That's Madame's thinking too,' Clay said, hoping his quiet tone concealed his disappointment and the ominous realisation that accompanied it. *It's really got him now. Nothing I say is gonna turn him around.* 'She says the war can be ended if we find the

White. Securing an egg or a live specimen will be enough to make every corporation in the world throw their lot in with Ironship. Corvantines'll have to come to terms then. So she says, anyways. And Miss Lethridge thinks they can hold out for a good while yet.'

Braddon nodded, his gaze tracking to Skaggerhill then Loriabeth. 'Say nothing of this to the others. Piling on another load of worry won't help anybody. We got us a contract and I aim to fulfil the terms; that's all they need know for now.' He looked again at Ethelynne and Lutharon. 'Why's she so keen to help us?'

'She ain't one for revealing her intentions, but I sense she's got a hankering to see the White again. Spent more than twenty years out here pondering the mysteries of the Interior. The White's still the biggest one of all. Also,' he added with a grin, 'seems she knows a way we can get to the Coppersoles that won't take the best part of two months trekking through the jungle.'

'I found it four years ago,' Ethelynne said as Lutharon's claws tore away another patch of vegetation from the mound. Come the morning she had led them south along the shore, covering five miles before midday. They halted at a small lagoon fed by a narrow inlet in the shore-line. Lutharon immediately plunged in and began tearing away at what appeared to be a large moss-covered mound in the centre of the lagoon.

'I only found one of the crew,' Ethelynne went on. 'Half-dead from a Green bite and delirious. He kept rambling on about salvaging some lost treasure from the lake-bed. There's an air-pump of some kind on board, so I suspect his companions met their end beneath the depths.'

'Lost treasure?' Firpike asked, a keen glint in his eye.

'Yes,' Ethelynne replied. 'Some outlandish tale of a fabulously jewelled ship of ancient origin lurking beneath the waters of the lake. I must say, my own research has uncovered no mention of it, but' – she gave Clay a sidelong glance, a small but mischievous grin on her lips – 'the Interior has ever been a magnet for those in search of the unfindable.'

Lutharon tore away another patch of moss, revealing the unmistakable shape of a river-boat hull. A few moments more and the craft was fully revealed. She had a single paddle at the stern and one stunted and multiply holed stack rising from the wheel-house. Clay gauged her size as perhaps a quarter that of the *Firejack*, but that still left plenty of room to carry them all, provided they could get her engine working.

'She could do with a good sprucing up,' Ethelynne said as Lutharon nudged the heavily besmirched vessel towards the bank. 'But she's been untouched since I found her.'

'Did he say what manner of ship?' Firpike persisted, stepping closer to Ethelynne then promptly stepping back as Lutharon issued a warning rumble.

'The poor fellow expired the night after I found him,' Ethelynne replied. 'There are some documents aboard, the captain's log and such. They held little interest for me, but if you'd care to . . .'

Firpike ran to the bank and leapt aboard without another word. Soon they could hear him rummaging around in the wheel-house.

'*River Maiden*,' Skaggerhill said, wiping a hand along the hull to reveal the boat's name-plate. 'Her timbers must still be water worthy, otherwise she'd have sunk by now. We should still check her over for leaks though.'

'See to the engine first,' Braddon said. 'If we can't get it working, won't matter how tight the hull is.'

To their surprise the *River Maiden* proved to have two engines, one a coal-burner, the other a much smaller arrangement of pipes and combustion chamber. 'Damned if she isn't a blood-burner,' Skaggerhill said, crouching to run a hand over the power plant in appreciation.

'Can you make it work?' Braddon asked.

The harvester shrugged and shook his head. 'I know a little about boats, and less about engines.'

'If I may?' Scriberson said, stepping forward. Skaggerhill made way for him and the astronomer crouched to run a careful eye over both engines, hands exploring the various components with practised familiarity.

'Done this before?' Clay asked.

'Engineering has always been my secondary passion,' Scriberson replied, grunting a little as he gave a hard twist to the gears connecting the coal-burner to the main drive-shaft. 'I was Chairman of the Consolidated Research Amateur Artificers Club. We would hold a contest every year for the most outlandishly pointless kinetic apparatus.' He sighed as the gears refused to budge then lifted the lid on the engine's exhaust tube to peer inside.

'Too much rust, Captain,' he told Braddon. 'It's seized beyond repair. This beauty, however' – he nodded at the blood-burner – 'is a sealed unit and should still run if fed sufficient product. I'll need to make sure the main shaft will still turn the paddle, however. And the water reservoir will need to be cleaned out and refilled.'

'Get to it,' Braddon told him, nodding at a box in the corner of the engine room. 'Looks like the boat's grease monkey was kind enough to leave his tools behind. Skaggs will help out best he can.' He turned to Clay, nodding at the hatchway. 'Let's see if Miss Drystone will share some of her riches.'

Ethelynne seemed to attach little value to the product she carried and handed over a full vial of Red without demur. 'Naturally,' Braddon assured her, 'there'll be a full accounting of expenses when our contract's fulfilled. You will, of course, receive a full share . . .'

He trailed off as she laughed, covering her mouth and turning away as her mirth continued unabated for several minutes. She laughed for such a long time that Clay found himself worrying over what conclusions his uncle might draw from such a display. 'Forgive me, Captain,' she said eventually, having sobered some-what and wiping tears from her eyes. 'It's just been a good long while since I heard talk of such things, and said with such sincerity too.'

Seeing her mouth twitch in anticipation of another outburst, Clay cut in quickly, 'We got other pressing matters. There's maybe a day's rations left between all of us. And then there's the scarcity of ammo.'

'I can help with one,' Ethelynne said, turning and striding towards Lutharon. 'But not the other. I've had no need of guns in all my days here.' She climbed onto the drake's back, calling out as he flexed his wings and tensed for the launch, 'I'll be back before nightfall!'

Watching drake and rider climb into the air and glide away over the lake, Braddon shook his head, his features displaying both wonder and wariness. 'Mad as a bag of cats, but that beast follows her like a love-lorn hound.'

'It starts out rationally enough,' Firpike muttered, perched on the fore-deck with the boat's log resting on his knees as he pored over the mildewed pages. 'But then descends into gibberish a few days before the entries end.'

'That's truly fascinating,' Clay told him, casting another armful of moss over the side. 'How's about you lend a hand here and do your pondering later?'

'Oh, leave him be,' Loriabeth chided from the prow where she was scraping the worst of the muck from the hawser. 'I'm all fired up and curious about this treasure ship, myself. What's it say about that, Doc?'

'Precious little,' he replied, thumbing back a few pages. 'It seems this boat was chartered in Rigger's Bay by a fellow referred to only as Mr O. The captain was paid five hundred in exchange notes up front and promised a thirty percent share in whatever treasure was retrieved from the lake. He does give a position for the likely site of the discovery though.' Firpike paused to favour Braddon with a hopeful glance.

'Forget it,' the captain told him. 'Though I'll be happy to drop you off on the way south, Doc.' He turned to Foxbine, sitting on the mid-deck engaged in an inventory of the remaining ammunition. 'What's the count?'

'Twenty-two rifle rounds,' she replied. 'Mostly steel-tips, which is good, I guess. And sixty-three of the .48 short, which most surely ain't. Plus, Skaggs only has six shotgun shells left. We run into any more trouble, Captain . . .'

'I know,' he said. 'Guess we'll just have to be extra circumspect from now on. Keep thirty of the .48s and parcel out the rest equally between Clay and Lori. Me and Preacher'll take equal shares of the .52s.'

A sudden shift in the deck made Clay stagger a little, his gaze going to the engine-room hatch from which a low steady hum could be heard. 'Seer-damn me if they didn't fix it,' Foxbine said, starting to rise. Clay paused to help her up and they joined the others in the engine room where a grease-stained Scriberson stood next to the vibrating thermoplasmic engine.

'Lad's a genius, right enough,' Skaggerhill told Braddon.

'It's running on kerosene just now,' Scriberson said, tapping the dim glow behind the glass window of the combustion chamber. 'It'll need product to turn the paddle.'

'Your share just went up three points, young man,' Braddon told him. 'And I'll add another three if this thing holds out all the way to the Coppersoles.'

'You still intend to press on?' the astronomer asked. 'Not that I'm displeased, the alignment is my life's work after all. But with so little ammunition, how profitable could this expedition be for you now?'

'Let me worry about that. There's mining settlements in the mountains, bound to have some ammo to trade. Besides, you and me have a contract.'

As promised, Ethelynne returned in the evening as the sun began to dip. Lutharon descended out of the sky to flare his wings and hover over the camp they had established next to the lagoon, opening his claws to drop two enormous fish close to the fire. 'That salmon?' Loriabeth wondered, giving one of the fish a dubious poke. 'Never seen one so big.'

'Looks like good eating to me, whatever it is,' Skaggerhill said, drawing a knife to start the gutting.

The fish did indeed prove to provide a hearty meal, the flesh only slightly bony and the supply fulsome enough to fill their growling bellies. 'Just got fed by a drake,' Skaggerhill said when the meal was done, rubbing his stomach and looking over at Lutharon who had curled up a good distance away. 'And I thought this place was done surprising me.' His gaze shifted to Ethelynne sitting on the opposite side of the fire. 'I gotta know, miss. How's it done? All my years on this continent, I ain't never seen this.'

Ethelynne gave one of the faint smiles Clay had come to recognise meant she had no answer to give and the silence stretched until Preacher spoke up. 'It worships her.' His gaze was fixed on Lutharon and had that same focused animation as when he started quoting the Seer. Also, Clay noted his rifle lay unsheathed across his lap. 'And you it,' Preacher went on, turning to Ethelynne. 'You drank of the drake's heart, just like the Witch Queen in the mosaic.'

Ethelynne gave a lengthy laugh, seemingly finding almost as much amusement in Preacher as she had Braddon. 'She wasn't a witch,' she replied after a while. 'Or a queen for that matter. And you mistake love for worship.'

'"Ware the witch,"' Preacher quoted, his stridency increasing by the word. '"For she will conspire with the drake towards our ruin."'

Ethelynne gave a girlish giggle, as if she were engaged in some delightful game, then replied with a quote of her own. '"And the sun became a man, and spoke to me in the voice of an eagle commanding that I not eat of any winged beast, for they are all in secret thrall to the drake." You appear to put great faith in the words of a man who was patently insane.'

Clay saw the marksman's hands tense on the stock of his rifle, as did his uncle. 'Easy now, Preacher,' he said. 'Let's not offend a lady who's been so generous with us.'

Preacher continued to stare at Ethelynne, Clay slowly lowering his own hand to the Stinger as he saw the way the man's fingers twitched on the rifle. *Like a drunk wary of reaching for his last drink.* The twitching stopped, however, when Lutharon voiced a growl and rose from his resting place to come to Ethelynne's side. He moved without haste, tail swishing as he rested his great head on her shoulder, closing his eyes as she reached up to scratch his nose. *Love, not worship,* Clay thought.

Preacher rose to his feet, staring at woman and drake in naked disgust, then abruptly turned about and walked away, pausing at the edge of the fire-light when Braddon spoke up. 'If you're not here come the morning, I understand. But if you are, leave your scripture behind when you step on that boat. I ain't got the patience for it no more.'

Clay soon came to understand that the Krystaline was more a sea than a lake. The surface that seemed so placid from a distance was in fact prone to swells and choppiness when the wind rose, often causing the deck of the shallow-hulled *River Maiden* to heave at alarming angles. 'Pardon,' Skaggerhill called from the wheel-house when Clay and Silverpin came perilously close to tipping over the rail as they crested a particularly large swell. 'She takes a bit o' steering, for sure.'

Once they had completed all the repairs they could, Lutharon had taken to the water once more to push the craft out of the lagoon and onto the lake. Firing the engine proved to be a less complicated matter than either Clay or Scriberson expected. The astronomer simply injected a quarter of Ethelynne's vial into a nozzle on the engine's topside whereupon it flowed into a small chamber covered by thick glass. 'Now what?' Clay asked.

'You burn it.' Scriberson handed him the vial. He took a sip then focused on the product behind the glass, stepping back in instinctive alarm when it burst into fiery life. The drive-shaft began to turn immediately, giving off a loud squealing that only abated when Scriberson poured some oil over it.

They endeavoured to keep to true south since departing the lagoon, Preacher still aboard much to Clay's surprise. He sat at the prow, staring fixedly ahead and not once glancing up at the drake and rider overhead, not even when they came swooping down to deposit another pair of over-large salmon on the deck.

Firpike had made one more abortive attempt to persuade Braddon to pay a brief visit to the supposed location of the fabled treasure ship, sternly refused despite Loriabeth's enthusiastic support. 'C'mon, Pa,' she pleaded. 'Let's have us an adventure and maybe get rich into the bargain.' It had been to no avail and Firpike was reduced to leaning over the side to peer into the depths of the lake, as if some glimmering clue might catch his eye.

'Wouldn't do that,' Foxbine advised the disgraced scholar. 'Krystaline's famed for its river Greens. Grow big as Reds they say, and they ain't shy.'

'I know well the fauna of this lake, madam,' Firpike sniffed. 'The Greens here are known to be nocturnal hunters and to steer clear of boats.'

'Tell that to the poor bastard who wrote that,' Clay said, nodding at the log-book Scriberson had taken to keeping close at hand.

'In point of fact, young man,' Firpike replied, 'the unfortunate skipper's account supports my research. They were attacked when they foolishly conducted a diving expedition at night.' He gave a wistful sigh and returned his gaze to the water. 'So much knowledge to hand and yet so far away.'

'Doesn't it say anything about what manner of ship it was?' Scriberson asked. He had taken a break from tending the engine and sat on the deck regarding Firpike with his habitual suspicion, though now it was augmented by a reluctant curiosity.

'The description is vague,' Firpike replied, taking up the log-book and holding it to his chest, reminding Clay of a child worried his playmate might steal his toy.

'Spill it, Doc,' Loriabeth said. 'We all found this boat, so we all got a stake in the treasure.'

Firpike's gaze tracked over them, the recurrent awareness that he was not amongst friends looming large in his face as he sullenly opened the log-book and extracted a loose page. 'This appears to be a copy of an ancient Dalcian text. It is known that the Dalcians managed to navigate the eastern flank of the Barrier Isles and the Razor Sea long before Queen Arrad discovered the northern strait. However, their numbers were always too small to establish a colony and few expeditions ever returned. Those that did were often dismissed as madmen or liars with their fanciful tales of fire-breathing beasts and great cities rising from the jungle. This' – he held up the page – 'appears to be a fragment from an account describing one such voyage. The language is so archaic it defies accurate translation. However, it seems this Mr O., whoever he was, spent considerable time and money seeking out Dalcian calligraphers who could help decipher its meaning.'

'The period?' Scriberson enquired.

'Early Satura Magisterium.'

The astronomer gave a sceptical frown. 'That's over two thousand years ago.'

'Closer to three, in fact.' Firpike's tone was more than a little smug.

'What's it say about the ship?' Loriabeth said.

'This is where it becomes most obscure.' Firpike looked again at the loose page. 'It seems the best interpretation the calligraphers could come up with was "a vessel of wonder, unbound by earth or sea, come to rest with precious cargo 'neath the silver waters." There are some additional geographical references that I assume led Mr O. to this lake.'

'Seems a slight thing to risk so much for,' Clay said. 'Just a few lines from an age long-gone.'

'Precious cargo,' Loriabeth said. 'Could be anything down there.'

'More likely nothing.' Clay looked up to see Braddon standing with his arms crossed and visage more fierce than any worn throughout the whole journey from Carvenport. 'We went wandering off after one distraction already,' he said. 'And it damn near did for us all. That ain't happening again. We're heading south to the Coppersoles where we will fulfil our contract, and that's all there is to it. Any of you wanna disagree, you're welcome to depart this company right now and enjoy the swim.' He turned his glower on Firpike, pointing at the log-book. 'You do what you want with all that guff when we part ways. But I don't want any more talk of it in this company.'

Braddon's gaze softened a little as he settled it on Scriberson. 'Young man, how about you and Clay seeing if you can get a knot or two extra out of that engine. I don't relish being on this lake a moment longer than necessary.'

They were able to increase speed to a creditable fifteen knots by the simple expedient of adding a third of their remaining product to the combustion chamber. Even so, the southern horizon remained stubbornly free of mountains by the time the sun began to fade. Lutharon came swooping down as sunset cast an orange tint over the eastern sky. Ethelynne could be seen pointing emphatically at the shore-line to the west.

'Seems she don't think it's a good idea to be out here come nightfall, Captain,' Skaggerhill noted and Braddon gave the reluctant order to find a mooring for the night.

'The Green packs become more numerous in the lake's southern reaches,' Ethelynne explained over a supper of yet more fish, enlivened somewhat by Skaggerhill's inventive use of seasoning. He had steered the *River Maiden* into a shallow bay just as the last light fled the sky. Ethelynne insisted they vacate the boat and wade to shore, making sure not to leave any lights burning on board. 'They're attracted to bright things.'

'They really grow big as Reds here?' Skaggerhill asked her.

'Certainly, some even bigger, and decidedly more aggressive in defending their territory. The southern shallows are rich in manatees, dolphins and other sundry beasts for them to hunt.'

'What about Spoiled?' Braddon asked her. 'We likely to find any when we reach the mountains?'

'The coastal tribes were wiped out by Briteshore's Contractors years ago. However, there remain some populous enclaves in the higher peaks.' She paused to offer an apologetic smile. 'I'm afraid they aren't very welcoming to visitors.'

As usual, Clay volunteered for first watch along with Silverpin. They sat together on a large rock close to the shore that offered a decent all-round view, Silverpin resting her head on his shoulder as he ran a hand through her blonde locks. They hadn't made love since leaving the *Firejack* and he found himself resisting the foolish notion of suggesting a surreptitious assignation in the jungle. Somehow though, the very absurdity of the idea made it more alluring, the thought of them pressed together in the under-growth, rolling around in the dark . . .

He came to his senses as she abruptly straightened, disentan-gling herself and coming to a crouch with spear in hand. The reason for her alarm soon became obvious. Lutharon was breathing fire. The drake stood at the shore-line, silhouetted by his own flames, tail thrashing in obvious agitation as he cast repeated jets of flame out over the lake. In between each breath he would move from side to side, growling as his wings flared then folded.

'What in the Travail is he doing?' Clay wondered aloud.

'Warning.'

Clay turned to find Ethelynne standing near by. She was wearing her swaddle-coat, the hood drawn back to leave her face bare, revealing an altogether more serious expression than any he had seen her display before.

'Warning what?' he asked but she said nothing, her gaze entirely fixed on the Black as he continued his fiery display. A sudden movement on the lake caught Clay's eye, a flash of white as something broke the surface, something large and fast. Lutharon immediately became even more agitated, rearing back on his hind legs to raise himself, standing well over twenty feet off the ground as he spread his wings and roared. More white flashes erupted on the lake and Clay realised whatever was out there wasn't alone. He could hear screeching now, high-pitched and loud enough to cut through Lutharon's warning roar. It was different from the scream of the jungle Greens but possessed much the same ability to leave a chill in the soul. Lutharon, however, remained uncowed.

He launched himself into the air, still roaring, a mighty flap of his wings taking him out over the water where he cast a torrent of flame down at the thrashing water. Clay could see them in the glow of the drake's fire, jaws snapping and tails thrashing as they spat their own fire in response, though the flames seemed slight in comparison. Lutharon's wings thrummed as he hovered, roaring and jetting flame until the foaming water beneath finally subsided into a steaming calm. He beat the air to gain more height and circled the spot for several minutes, head swivelling about as he scanned the water for enemies. Apparently satisfied, he returned to the shore where Ethelynne was waiting. She pressed herself against his flank as he shielded her with a wing, gaze still roving the lake.

'Doesn't make sense,' Clay heard Ethelynne say from beneath the ebony curtain of the wing. He moved closer, motioning for Silverpin to stay put. He had expected some sign of aggression from Lutharon but the drake barely spared him a glance before lifting a wing and allowing him to move to Ethelynne's side.

'What doesn't make sense?' he asked.

She had pressed her face into Lutharon's flank and when she turned to him he was appalled to see tears shining on her cheeks. 'He says they've gone mad.'

The next day dawned behind a heavy cloud that continued to thicken throughout the morning. By midday the *River Maiden* paddled under a grey-black sky and thunder could be heard rumbling to the south. 'Storm coming,' Skaggerhill pronounced, somewhat redundantly. 'Best get any bailing gear ready. This tub handles poorly at the best of times. Can't speak for how she'll steer all filled up with rain-water.'

'The bilge-pump seems to be in reasonable condition,' Scriberson said. 'With Clay's help I should be able to get it working.'

The pump's pipe-work had more than a few blockages which Clay was able to clear with a small amount of Black. It was delicate work, but well within his expertise. 'I've only ever seen it used for large-scale manufacturing,' Scriberson said as Clay carefully drew out a glob of congealed engine grease. 'Quite the talent, sir.'

'And I got plenty of practice lifting coins and watches from manager's pockets back in Carvenport.'

'Oh.' Scriberson blinked and looked away in discomfort. 'You were . . .'

'Blinds scum all the way,' Clay finished, enjoying the astronomer's embarrassment. 'Or a notorious thief and killer, according to my uncle.' He returned his attention to the pump, fingers exploring the thick rubber tube protruding from the main valve and detecting a hard lump. 'Knew a fella back in the Blinds,' he went on, concentrating on the lump and summoning the modicum of product he had swallowed to inch it along the tube, 'had such a knowledge of a man's innards, he could reach inside with the Black to stop a heart or pinch a vein. Didn't even have to see it. He used to bribe a morgue attendant to let him in so he could practice on the corpses.'

'A valuable skill, I assume,' Scriberson said, plainly appalled but keeping any disgust from his face.

You acting now? Clay wondered, thinking back on Miss Lethridge's warning to watch this one closely. 'Right,' he replied, still guiding the lump through the tube. 'Cost you a packet to hire Black Bildon. Always wondered if I should try to learn his tricks, ask him for an apprenticeship or some such. Somebody killed him before I could.' He laughed as the lump came to the end of the tube, revealed as a rusted iron bolt as it popped into his hand. 'Can't think why.'

If it's an act, it's a good one, he decided, seeing the expression on Scriberson's face: repugnance mixed with pity.

'I'm glad such things are behind you, Clay,' the astronomer said.

Clay tossed the bolt aside and rose to his haunches, shuffling closer to Scriberson and speaking softly. 'Neither of us are stupid men, Scribes. So, I'm given to think you already guessed we ain't going to the Coppersoles to hunt for Black. Am I right?'

Scriberson glanced at the hold's open hatch then nodded slowly, keeping his voice low. 'It seemed unlikely Miss Drystone would be assisting you if that were the case. And I do know her story.'

'Then you know the best thing you can do the moment we get anywhere near a settlement is take off and don't look back. Forget the alignment. Forget whatever prizes, medals or bonuses they'll pile on you for looking through that tube of yours at the right moment. What's in those mountains ain't worth your life.'

'Is it worth yours?'

Clay thought about how he had clung to life back in the Blinds, when every day was a battle. Now, here he was moving ever closer to something he knew would most likely see him dead, and yet he had no real thought of turning back. 'There's a thing needs to be done,' was all he could think to say.

A shout came from outside, Foxbine's voice raised in alarm. Clay took a moment to strap on the Stinger's holster and followed Scriberson onto the deck. The gunhand stood at the prow, hopping on her good leg and pointing at something directly ahead. The rain had started by now, masking the horizon in a thick haze of vapour, but Clay could make out a dark shape in the water. For a moment he thought it might be a drake but soon discerned it as wreckage. 'Stop the engine,' Braddon ordered and Scriberson rushed off to comply.

The *River Maiden* slowed as the engine died, Braddon going to the starboard rail to latch onto the wreckage with one of the pole-hooks they had found on board. 'Thick planking,' he commented, Clay taking a moment to recognise the flotsam as a ragged chunk of a boat's hull, scorched black in most places.

'Happened recently,' Skaggerhill judged. 'Timber rots if it's more than a few days in water.'

'There's more here,' Foxbine called from the prow. They found further sundered planking, plus some barrels bobbing in the swell, all showing signs of recent burning. Then, as they continued to drift south with the current, Loriabeth spotted a man clinging to a piece of wreckage a hundred yards off the port side. Keen not to use up all their product Braddon had them turn the *Maiden*'s paddle by hand whilst Skaggerhill steered them towards the survivor.

'Hey!' Loriabeth called to him as they drew within reach. 'Wake up, mister!'

There was no response, the man remaining slumped in apparent exhaustion, his lower half beneath the water. Braddon used the pole-hook to draw the wreckage closer but this immediately upset the balance, tipping the man loose. Loriabeth immediately turned away, retching as the man bobbed in the water, his entrails splaying out from his severed torso like the tentacles of some sea creature. He stared up at them with empty, milky-white eyes, mouth open in a strangely baffled expression.

'Briteshore Minerals,' Skaggerhill said, pointing at the lettering stencilled onto the wreckage.

'It must have been a survey craft,' Scriberson said. 'The lake-bed is believed to be rich in mineral deposits.'

'Seems they found something more than just rocks,' Clay observed.

'Greens.' Skaggerhill nodded at the bobbing man. 'Bit him clean in half.'

'Can't do nothing for him now,' Braddon said as they continued to stare. 'Let's set about gathering up these barrels, see if there's anything we can use. Clay, Mr Scriberson, see to the engine.'

'Erm.' Loriabeth stared down at the barrel she had just levered open with her belt knife, taking a long step back. 'Pa.'

'Well, that's a turn-up,' Braddon mused, stroking his chin as he regarded the barrel's contents. It appeared to Clay to consist of a dozen brown tubes, all packed tight in a binding of cotton wool and sealed against the water with oilskin.

'What's that?' he asked, moving closer only for his uncle to gently push him back.

'Twelve sticks of Briteshore's finest accelerating agent,' Braddon said, adding, 'Explosives, boy,' when Clay shrugged in bafflement.

'Might be best to tip it over the side,' Foxbine said, keeping well back and eyeing the barrel with considerable suspicion. 'Seen a fella get turned to powder by just an inch worth of that stuff.'

'We're too low on ammo to be cautious now, Miss Foxbine,' Braddon told her, crouching to carefully replace the barrel's lid.

They looked up at a loud squawk from Lutharon. The rain had abated an hour after they traversed the wreckage of the Briteshore vessel, finding more barrels on the way, some packed with greatly welcomed foodstuffs, others tools and equipment of little use, and one with brandy which Braddon refused to let on board, much to Firpike's annoyance. The sky cleared a little after noon, the clouds fading to reveal the black shadow of Lutharon's cruciform shape above. It seemed he and Ethelynne had encountered little trouble tracking them through the rain-storm.

The drake described a slow, descending circle and they could see Ethelynne pointing to the south-west. Skaggerhill duly altered course and they saw it after only another mile, faint and formless at first but soon resolving into the jagged grey mass of a mountain range. They were finally at the Coppersoles.

III

THE BLESSED
AND THE DAMNED

The Blessing remains perhaps the most baffling mystery as yet unsolved by modern science. Even in this new age dominated by the rational pursuit of profit, the answer to this question still eludes our best minds: Why is only one in every thousand born to each generation afforded the ability to make use of the wondrous properties found in the blood of the Arradsian drake? Extensive research, most recently the exhaustive statistical analysis produced by Professor Skylar Blackfold of the Consolidated Research Company, has uncovered no shared physical characteristics between the Blessed. Height, pigmentation, eye-colour and the new science of blood grouping, reveal no commonalities between subjects. The phenomenon is also not hereditary; Blessed parents do not produce Blessed children. Social research has also provided no useful insight as personality amongst the Blessed is as varied as the rest of the population. Depending on their beginning station in life, a Blood-blessed is just as likely to embark upon a career of base criminality as they are to find productive and responsible employment. The Blessing, it appears, is as random as the weather.

From *A Lay-person's Guide to Plasmology* by Miss Amorea Findlestack. Ironship Press – Company Year 195 (1579 by the Mandinorian Calendar).

CHAPTER 33

Hilemore

'The northern route is suicide,' Hilemore said. 'As the Corvantine attack on the Hive demonstrated. Fast as we are, we can't out-run every ship likely to bar our path, and enemy patrols will grow ever more numerous as we draw near Feros, assuming we even get that far.'

He was alone with Zenida in the ward-room, having unfurled a map of the eastern Isles on the table. He had given the tiller over to her upon clearing the Hive's harbour mouth, keeping the *Viable* at full speed and trusting her to navigate a course through the winding channels to the south. It had been a perilous enterprise, even with her knowledge. Steering a vessel of such size through so many narrow passages was a considerable challenge and they had come close to running aground more than once. However, as the sky grew dark and the way behind remained free of any pursuers, he knew his trust hadn't been misplaced.

He ordered Bozware to switch to auxiliary power and reduced speed to dead slow. Zenida, face slick with sweat from her exertions at the wheel, guided the ship to the south-side of a tall, rocky islet whereupon she collapsed. Hilemore caught her as she fell, carrying her back to Tottleborn's old cabin and laying her on the bed next to Akina.

'I wish she'd killed Arshav,' the girl said, pulling a blanket over her mother.

'Killing one of your own blood is not an easy thing,' Hilemore replied, thinking back over the many times he had been tempted to plunge a knife into his father's back during yet another drunken catastrophe at the dining-table.

'It won't be for me,' the girl said before none-too-gently pushing him from the cabin and firmly closing the door.

Zenida didn't re-emerge for a full day, and when she did it appeared the rest had done much to restore both her vitality and facility for caustic observation. 'So, we will simply sail around the Isles until the war ends? Forgive me, Captain, but the pleasure of your company is not so alluring and I have pressing family matters in Varestia to attend to. My darling brother will no doubt be doing everything in his power to get there before I do.'

'Assuming he survived the attack.'

'Oh, he survived, you can be sure of that. And the bitch that whelped him.'

'In any case,' he said, forcing a patient tone into his voice, 'the southern course offers certain opportunities.' He traced his finger along the eastern edge of the Isles to where they curved towards Arradsia's south-eastern coast-line. 'Hadlock,' he said, tapping the dot at the head of an inlet that stretched into the Coppersole Mountains from the south-eastern coast.

'A Briteshore holding,' she said.

'With an Ironship concession and berthing rights for Protectorate Vessels. Also, we should be able to purchase sufficient product to carry us to Varestia.'

Zenida raised an eyebrow. 'You wish to take me home, Captain?'

'I wish to save my ship and, if possible, continue to prosecute this war. Varestia will put us close to the Corvantine home waters and maritime trade-routes, with which I'm sure you are highly familiar. With most of their fleet concentrated around Arradsia, the pickings are likely to be rich, wouldn't you say?'

Her lips twitched in amusement, though he saw the definite glimmer of interest in her eyes. 'I thought I was the pirate here.'

'Privateer,' he reminded her. 'And also now contracted crew of an Ironship Protectorate Vessel in time of war.'

'Your entire Protectorate can perish from the black pox for all I care. They did try to kill me, if you recall.'

'Purely a matter of business, I'm sure. And so is this.'

She returned her gaze to the map, sighing and shaking her head. 'It's a very long way.'

'It's either this or we strike out for Dalcia. Hundreds of miles of open ocean and I doubt we'll find much welcome at the end of it.'

'It's not so much the passage through the Isles that concerns me.' Her finger circled the apparently open water between the tail-end of the eastern Isles and the south Arradsian coast. 'They call it the Razor Sea for a reason. More hidden reefs than can easily be counted. And there's nothing between it and the waters off Carvenport. Who's to say the Corvantine Fleet isn't already patrolling the region?'

'A risk we'll have to run. Unless you wish to sit out the war here whilst your brother rebuilds his fortunes in your homeland.'

She glared at him for a second then stood back from the map, folding her arms. 'I believe it's time to renegotiate my contract,' she said. 'Equal shares in all prize money. Half for me, half for the ship. Think of it as compensation for your Syndicate's betrayal.' Seeing his burgeoning anger, she added. 'Or perhaps you'd like to fire the engine and navigate both the Isles and the Razor Sea yourself?'

It took two days of careful piloting to reach the Razor Sea, Hilemore using the time to return the *Viable* to some semblance of military readiness. The worst of the damage to her decking and upper works was repaired and Ensign Tollver given the task of overseeing an application of fresh paint which obscured much of the blackening she had received. Hilemore reinstituted daily drills for the gun-crews and riflemen, something that aroused little grumbling now that they had all gained a hard education in the rigours of battle. His principal worry remained their diminished numbers. So far, Dr Weygrand had returned only two men to active duty and maintained a rigid determination not to release more until sure of their recovery.

'The ship is your charge,' the doctor reminded him during a visit to the sick-bay. 'These men are mine.'

Hilemore paused at the bunk where Captain Trumane lay, still insensible after so many days. 'No change, then?'

'Actually, he started shouting in his sleep last night,' Weygrand said. 'Not for very long, but it's a good sign.'

Hilemore surveyed the captain's slack features, wondering whether it would be for the best if he did return from whatever depths had claimed him. Although Hilemore knew Trumane's handling of the ship during the battle had saved them from destruction, he had severe doubts the man would approve of his accommodations with Zenida, or his chosen course of action. *Another worry best set aside,* he told himself, turning to the doctor. 'We have a copious stock of Green, now. Wouldn't that speed the recovery of these men?'

'Not everything is cured by Green, sir. If it was, there'd be no need for doctors.'

He checked on the engine room next, finding the Chief in surprisingly cheerful spirits. 'Both my babes in fine working order,' he said, grease-black cheeks bunching in a smile as he gestured to the two engines. 'After all the punishment they've had, it's a Seer-blessed miracle.'

'If so, you wrought it, Chief,' Hilemore told him, then frowned at the sight of a small figure in much-modified overalls moving about the auxiliary gearing with an oil-can. 'What's she doing here?' he asked.

'Her mother brought her down yesterday, told me to put her to work. Got a sense she's tired of having her cooped up in that cabin.'

Hilemore briefly considered ordering the girl up top but, seeing the keen animation in her face as she tended the machinery, decided to leave her be. *Better this than spending more time with Tottleborn's collection of filth,* he thought. 'If we encounter any more action, make sure she's taken aloft,' he told the Chief,

'Aye, sir.'

They reached the southern tip of the Isles that evening where Zenida insisted they anchor and wait for morning. 'Running the Razors in darkness is madness,' she told him.

'I trust your knowledge will see us safely through,' he said, frowning as she replied with only a vague nod. 'You are familiar with these waters?'

She didn't look at him. 'I've sailed them before.'

'How often?'

He watched her hands twitch on the wheel. 'Once, when serving on my father's ship.'

'You mean you weren't even in command?'

She rounded on him, eyes flashing. 'Have you ever sailed here, Captain?'

He thought about retrieving their reworded contract and burning it in front of her, but instead took a turn about the deck to calm his anger. The fact that he had no alternative but to trust his ship to her knowledge, meagre though it was, did not sit well. *No good choices in war,* he reminded himself, another of his grandfather's observations. *War is a storm, lad. With a good crew and a good ship, maybe you can ride it out. But there's never been a ship didn't take a battering in a storm.*

Hilemore ran a hand along the *Viable*'s scarred timbers, seeking to banish his worries with as much certainty as he could muster. *A good ship I have, and a crew to match it.*

At first glance the Razor Sea seemed like any other stretch of ocean, a little more prone to wayward currents than some, but hardly unusual. It was only when they had covered the first ten miles that Hilemore came to appreciate the dangers lurking beneath the surface. The sea had a tendency to transform from placidity to swirling eddy or frothing swell in a matter of seconds, without any change in weather or wind to provide a warning.

Zenida insisted they remain on auxiliary power and kept the *Viable* at no more than one-third speed throughout the first day, making several dramatic course changes whilst teams of crewmen fore and aft took soundings with lead weight and rope.

'Eight fathoms!' the ensign in charge of the forward team called out, soon echoed by the team at the stern.

'The most shallow stretch yet,' Hilemore commented to Zenida, who barely nodded, her concentration fixed entirely on the course and the bridge instruments. She had spent much of the preceding night engaged in a close study of the *Viable*'s charts, scribbling down and memorising the series of manoeuvres that would, he hoped, see them safely through this most perilous region.

'Dead slow,' she ordered, maintaining her course. 'And tell them to check for sand.'

Hilemore duly relayed the order, watching the sounding teams swing the lead once more, this time with a dab of tallow smeared on the end of the weight. 'Six fathoms!' the ensign at the bow reported, checking the fragments sticking to the tallow. 'Sand and coral beneath!'

'We're on top of it,' Zenida commented, correcting course as a sudden current began to push the bows to port.

'On top of what?' Hilemore asked.

'See for yourself,' she replied, nodding towards the side. Hilemore went outside and leaned over the railing to peer down at the sea. The water was unusually clear and he could see a school of fish darting about near the port paddle, and below them the multi-hued, jagged shapes of close-packed coral. She had steered them directly over a reef.

'Four fathoms!' the sounding team called out.

Hilemore returned to the bridge and spoke quietly into Zenida's ear. 'What in the Travail are you doing?'

'It goes on for four hundred miles north and the same distance south,' she said, spinning the wheel once more to compensate for the current. 'There's no way around it if you want to make Hadlock in anything like reasonable time.' She checked the bridge clock then the compass. 'Trust me, Captain. If I meant to wreck this ship I could have done so a hundred times in the Isles.'

'Three and one half fathoms!'

Twenty-one feet of depth, he thought. The *Viable*'s draught at her current loading was nineteen. 'We could off-load some cargo,' he said. 'Reduce the weight.'

'Unnecessary,' Zenida replied.

'We have only two feet of clearance.'

She said nothing for some time, her gaze flicking continually between compass and clock. When the sounding team reported again the result was a surprise. 'Ten and one-quarter fathoms!'

'Ten,' Zenida repeated, pursing her lips. 'It was a good twenty fathoms deep a decade ago. It must have grown back.'

'Grown?' Hilemore asked in bafflement.

'My father had a very robust approach to obstacles,' she said. 'If something was in his way, he tended to knock it down. We spent the best part of a summer here lowering explosive charges to blow a hole in this reef. It proved its worth soon enough. Briteshore ships sailing from Hadlock were always a rich prize, and they were poorly armed in those days since what pirate would risk the Razors to get at them? My share was sufficient for me to purchase my own ship, much to Father's annoyance.'

She gave a weary sigh and relaxed her hold on the wheel, turning to Talmant. 'Take her for me, lad. It's clear water for the next sixty miles.'

Hilemore awoke to the hard feel of the cabin deck beneath his cheek, his bleary vision clearing to see a spy-glass rolling towards him across the planking. He tried to get up and realised he was tangled in his bed-clothes, the continual pitching of the deck frustrating his attempts to get free. A quick glance at the port-hole confirmed his suspicion. The rain lashed against the glass and lightning flashed to throw stark shadows onto the wall. *Storm.*

He stumbled onto the bridge a bare five minutes later, liberally soaked from the water cascading over the rails as tall waves pounded the immobile vessel. They had come to a halt at nightfall as per Zenida's instruction. She advised they had one more reef-maze to traverse the following day before reaching open water, an impossible task at night. The sea had been relatively placid then, but for a few squalls on the western horizon. As ever, the sea proved an erratic mistress.

'Blew up only a quarter hour ago, sir,' Ensign Tollver said, clinging desperately to the wheel. Talmant had been sent below at change of watch for some much-needed rest.

'And why are we still at anchor?' Hilemore demanded, but the boy could only gape at him in white-faced incomprehension. Hilemore cursed and went to the lanyard, pulling the six long blasts that signified a ship-threatening emergency.

'Look alive down there!' he yelled into the speaking-tube, being rewarded a moment later by the dull voice of one of Bozware's stokers.

'Sir?'

'Get the Chief out of bed,' Hilemore ordered. 'And Captain Okanas. The blood-burner is to be brought on-line with all haste.'

He went outside, receiving an immediate dunking from another pounding wave as he clambered down to the main-deck. 'You there!' he called to a pair of crewmen clinging to one of the life-boat hawsers. 'Get the stern anchor raised or we'll be swamped!'

They displayed some initial hesitation but evidently had enough discipline and experience to see the wisdom in following his order and were soon staggering towards the stern. Hilemore made for the fore-deck, finding himself swept from his feet more than once as the waves continued to pound at the *Viable*. At one point he found himself pressed up against one of the starboard guns, the raging sea only a few feet from his face as the ship wallowed under the pressure. He was trying to regain his feet when he saw it, something out in the storm, something that caught a gleam as lightning flashed again. It was only for an instant and gone too soon to convince him it had been more than just a figment of his excited mind; an impression of speed and fluidity, knifing through the roiling swell. Then it was gone.

It can't be, he thought, still staring out at the storm. *Not in these waters surely.*

'Sir?' Steelfine's meaty hands gripped him and pulled him upright, the Islander's tattooed face rendered momentarily demonic by a lightning flash as he leaned in to hear Hilemore's order.

'The forward anchor!'

The *Viable* gave an abrupt lurch to starboard as they reached the fore-deck, indicating the aft anchor had either been raised or come loose. They struggled on, reaching the winch. The job of raising the anchor was usually done by a team of four sailors, but thanks to Steelfine's strength they managed to make the three turns of the winch needed to dislodge the great iron grapnel from the sea-bed. For a few seconds the *Viable* swung about wildly, at the mercy of wind and wave, but then the paddles jerked into life and the bow settled to something resembling a course.

'Rouse every man not yet awake!' Hilemore yelled to Steelfine as they locked the winch down. The anchor wasn't fully raised but it couldn't be helped. 'Ensure all hatches are secured and make sure provisions are made ready if we have to take to the boats.'

He made his way to the bridge, a less perilous journey now that they were underway and the danger of swamping had passed. He was relieved to find Talmant at the wheel, Tollver standing at the speaking-tube, head lowered in shame.

'We didn't sink, lad,' Hilemore said, patting his shoulder. 'That's all that matters.'

Zenida arrived, shaking the water from her hair before taking the wheel from Talmant. 'There's no way to chart a course in this,' she told Hilemore, then spun the wheel to turn the *Viable* into an on-coming wave, the bow rising and falling in a stomach-churning heave. 'We'll just have to ride it out and hope.'

She stayed at it for over an hour, steering the ship with an expert's eye for the chaos raging beyond the bridge window. However, the wind defied prediction this night, whipping up waves from all directions, one of which proved too tall and too swift to turn into in time. The *Viable* took the full force of it on the starboard side, Hilemore hearing the clang of sundered iron as the armour on the paddle casement gave way under the blow and the *Viable* was shunted to port. The impact threw Zenida off her feet and Hilemore lunged for the now-rapidly-spinning wheel. He caught it and began to spin it to midships but then felt a hard, grinding vibration course through the ship accompanied by the scream of protesting metal.

Zenida regained her feet and retook the wheel as he rushed to the speaking-tube. 'All stop!' he shouted. 'We're aground!'

'I know!' came Bozware's reply. 'Got half the bloody sea rushing in down here!'

'Plugged up the worst of it,' the Chief said, a feverish hour later. His stokers, in company with a dozen crewmen, were busy pounding timbers into place between the starboard hull and the engine-room deck. They worked in three feet of water, moving with an energy born of survival that negated the water's chill. The buckled hull plate had been hammered into a rough semblance of its former shape then buttressed with timber before Bozware went about securing it with his steam riveter. Even so, water continued to seep in as the repair was far from perfect.

'Luckily the reef seems to have lifted us clear of the worst of it,' the Chief went on. 'Otherwise . . .'

'I know, Chief,' Hilemore told him, steadying himself as the ship rocked back and forth. The reef they were perched on was unwilling to let them go, but also didn't make for a comfortable resting-place as long as the storm raged on.

'Got the pumps working full tilt,' Bozware said. 'Should keep the levels from rising too fast. But she's still taking on way too much.'

'I'll organise a bailing line,' Hilemore told him, making for the hatch. On the way he spied Akina busily sorting out a box of fresh rivets and scooped her up, carrying her under his arm as he made his way up top. She yelled abuse in Varestian all the way to the bridge, falling silent only when Hilemore deposited her at her mother's feet. Zenida pointed her to a corner with an expression that promised dire consequences should she move again.

They worked through the night to ward off the sea, the Chief's crew labouring away to seal every leak whilst a line of crewmen passed buckets of sea-water from engine room to rail. The storm began to ebb with the first glimmer of morning light, and by sunrise had faded into a harsh but blessedly rain-free gale.

'Levels falling, sir,' Bozware reported via the speaking-tube. 'Looks as if we might actually float today.'

'Good work, Chief. Get the men and yourself fed then take an hour's rest.' Hilemore straightened and looked out at the rough seas, pondering the best means to work themselves loose from the reef. *Reverse paddles, perhaps. But that'll use up a good deal of product. Could unship the launches and try hauling her off . . .*

'Crow's nest reporting, sir,' Talmant said, breaking into his thoughts.

Hilemore's irritated response died as he saw the boy's pallor shift from pale to grey. 'Enemy vessel approaching from the north, at speed.'

The Eutherian letters on her side proclaimed her as the INS *Imperial*, a light cruiser with no paddles and far too many guns for Hilemore's liking. *Blood-burner too,* he judged gauging her speed through the spy-glass. *Twenty-five knots at least.* Even if the *Viable* hadn't been shackled to this confounded reef it would have been an unequal contest, though they might have stood a chance of out-running her. He raised his spy-glass to the Corvantine's masts. The signal contained in her pennants was easily read, it being universally recognised. *Strike your colours and prepare to be boarded.*

'Mr Talmant,' he said, lowering the glass.

'Aye, sir.'

'Gather the ship's books and charts into a weighted bag and throw it over the side.'

The boy hesitated but a glance from Hilemore was enough to see him scurrying off. Hilemore went to the speaking-tube. 'Chief?'

'Sir?'

'How long would it take to disconnect the blood-burner?'

'Disconnect, sir?'

Hilemore gritted his teeth and gripped the speaking-tube hard. 'I am about to surrender to a Corvantine cruiser and would prefer not to do so with an intact engine.'

There was a long pause, then a weary reply. 'She can't be disconnected, sir. Not without tearing the guts out of the ship, and that'd take the best part of a week.'

Hilemore nodded. 'Gather whatever diagrams and blueprints you have and give them to Mr Talmant for disposal. Then await further orders. Mr Steelfine will be there directly.' He straightened and turned to Steelfine. 'Number One. Proceed to the magazine and transport our gun charges to the engine room. The Chief will rig a fuse with a ten-minute delay. We will abandon ship and destroy the *Viable* in place.'

Steelfine betrayed no hesitation, though his jaw muscles did give the now-familiar bunch of reluctant anger. 'Aye, sir.'

He sent Ensign Tollver to the sick-bay with orders for Dr Weygrand to prepare his patients for transfer to the life-boats and turned to Zenida. She stood staring at the approaching cruiser in strangely rapt fascination.

'Captain Okanas,' he said. 'It seems our contract is destined to remain unfulfilled. It might go better for you if the Corvantines think you're a prisoner.'

She said nothing, continuing to stare at the Corvantine, though he heard her whisper, 'Impossible,' in Varestian.

'Captain?' He moved to her side, drawing up short at the sight that confronted him. The sea around the *Imperial* seemed to be boiling, churned into a white fury by something beneath, something moving swifter than any ship.

Both Hilemore and Zenida gave an involuntary shout as it erupted from the sea directly in front of the cruiser, rising amidst a mountain of spume, blue scales glinting in the sun. It rose to tower over the *Imperial*, massive jaws gaping and the mane of spines on its neck flared red and angry as it delivered a stream of white fire onto the cruiser's fore-deck. Hilemore could see the crew running in panic or fear as the fire swept over the ship, catching light wherever there was something to burn. The cruiser slewed to port in an apparent effort to evade the assault but the Blue drake hauled itself free of the water in response, wrapping its massive, snake-like bulk around the ship's works then lowering its great head to spew more fire into the ship's guts. A flat boom told of a cannon being fired, the Blue convulsing in response, its coils slackening as it gave a roar of pain and a tide of blood cascaded across the cruiser's deck. It clung on, however, spitting more fire at its enemy, possessed of a seemingly unreasoning fury.

The *Imperial* had drawn close enough now for Hilemore to hear the screams of the crew, maddened by pain as the Blue's blood touched their skin or they fell burning into the sea. Cruiser and passenger passed in front of the *Viable*'s bows, wreathed in smoke, whereupon an ear-paining roar told Hilemore the flames had found the vessel's magazine. A tall flower of yellow-orange flame leapt high into the air, accompanied by another roar from the drake. The *Imperial*'s keel had been shattered by the explosion, the ship held together only by the straining iron of the upper works to which the Blue still clung, thrashing and biting at its hated adversary as the waves rose to claim them both. Within seconds all that remained was a patch of burning oil and a slick of blood, soon faded to nothing by the wind-chopped waves.

'That did happen,' Zenida said in a small voice. Hilemore noted that Akina had emerged from her corner to take her mother's hand.

'It did,' he replied.

'It wasn't some imagining or nightmare,' Zenida went on.

'No,' he said. 'It surely wasn't.'

'Mother!' Akina said, clutching Zenida's hand more tightly and for once sounding like the little girl she appeared to be. The reason for her distress soon became obvious. There were more shapes moving in the sea, more long, blue-scaled forms catching the sun as they knifed through the waves, more than Hilemore found he could count, and all were heading north.

CHAPTER 34

Lizanne

Marshal Morradin launched another assault just after midnight. A short but furious bombardment pounded the defences covering Carvenport's western approaches followed by another massed ground assault, this time with three full brigades of infantry. The battle raged out of sight of Lizanne's position but its fury could be gauged by the intensity of rifle and Growler fire, frequently accompanied by the flat crump of a Protectorate cannon. It wore on for more than an hour, flares launched by the artillery spotters illuminating the steady stream of wounded or maddened Corvantines staggering back to their own lines. When the firing finally died down word swept along the line of another Corvantine calamity; five hundred dead or more were piled up in front of the trenches. It seemed the stretch of line Morradin had chosen to attack was held by Protectorate Regulars and, although the Corvantine infantry had managed to fight their way to the third defensive line, the Syndicate troops' discipline had held in the face of savage hand-to-hand fighting.

'You were right,' Lizanne observed to Arberus after the last sputter of rifle fire had petered out. 'Morradin doesn't appear to have much regard for the lives of his men.'

'Also, I suspect he knew nothing of the Growlers,' the major said, patting the Thumper's breech. 'Or our friend here.'

'If he keeps on like this there won't be an army for him to command.'

'Don't under-estimate him. A brute he may be, a fool he is not. We can count on a change of tactics at some point.'

Lizanne looked down at Tekela, curled up next to Jermayah as they slumbered beside the Thumper's carriage. The need to get herself and the girl away had begun to gnaw at her as the day ground on and the death toll mounted. But every plan that flitted through her mind foundered on the inescapable knowledge that there were but two ways out of this city, and both remained firmly blocked.

'I must say she continues to surprise me,' Arberus commented, smiling a little as he regarded Tekela's sleeping form. 'Always thought she'd grow up to be another version of her mother, but it seems there's as much Leonis in her too.'

'What was her mother like?' Lizanne asked. 'The Burgrave's servants led me to believe she could be cruel.'

'Cruel? At times. But Tekela was never an easy child, and Leonis dragging them to Morsvale had never been in Salema's mind when she married the newly ennobled Burgrave with all his medals and, apparently, enjoying the Emperor's favour. It didn't make for a harmonious home.'

'Did she know? About the Brotherhood?'

Arberus gave a soft but appalled laugh. 'Oh no. Salema was old-money Imperial nobility, but without the money. She used to say the Emperor's biggest mistake was not depopulating Varestia when he had the chance, and she didn't say it in jest.'

'She was cover,' Lizanne realised. 'What better wife for a man seeking to infiltrate the noble class?'

'You're judging him according to your own standards. Leonis could be ruthless, for what revolutionary isn't? But he married Salema because he loved her, despite my strong advice.' His gaze grew more sombre as it returned to Tekela. 'Even if he had known of her betrayal, I think he would have forgiven her.'

'Betrayal?'

'Salema's attitude to marital fidelity mirrored that of her class, in that it was mostly a matter of appearance. It's how the Corvantine aristocracy while their days away, indulging in affairs and enjoying the associated gossip. I suppose you can't really blame her for simply following her conditioning.' He caught the calculation in Lizanne's gaze and shook his head. 'She made . . . an approach. When I refused her she looked elsewhere.'

Lizanne looked down at Tekela, recalling the less-than-pleasant meeting at the museum. 'Diran,' she said.

'Yes.' Arberus sighed. 'Dear old Uncle Diran. Tekela had the misfortune to happen upon them at the wrong moment. Diran came to me in a right old state, worried what it would mean for his friendship with Leonis, not to say access to all his valuable documents and artifacts. I made it very clear to him that this unwise assignation had to end. Salema . . . didn't take it well.'

Lizanne crouched down at Tekela's side, drawing the blanket up to better cover her shoulders. *The nightmare that woke her that first night,* she remembered. *I didn't tell . . .*

'I had to pay a sizable bribe to the doctor and the coroner,' Arberus went on. 'Leonis was near mad with grief as it was. If he had known it was an opium overdose rather than a lesion of the brain . . .' He shrugged. 'What else could I do?'

'But she knew,' Lizanne said, rising from Tekela's side. 'Didn't she?'

'I expect so. It seems carrying the knowledge did little to improve her temperament.'

He looked up as the last flare guttered and died in the sky, the pink illumination it cast replaced by the steel-blue light of the two moons. 'I believe we may be done for the night,' he said. 'You'd best get some sleep.'

She felt the denial die on her lips, the strain and exertion of the day suddenly weighing on her with irresistible pressure. 'As should you,' she said, sitting down at Tekela's side and pulling the blanket across them both. The girl mumbled something and shifted, a distressed frown forming on her smooth brow until Lizanne pulled her closer and she subsided into sleep once more.

'I'll be alright for a while,' Arberus said, turning to run a rag over the Thumper's breech. 'Besides, Bessie here needs some attention.'

'Bessie,' Lizanne repeated, eyelids drooping as her lips formed a smile at the ridiculous notion of naming such a terrible thing. 'Bessie . . .'

She was woken by what felt like twin hammers being rapidly pounded into both her ears at once. She blinked until her vision cleared, finding herself face-to-face with an equally alarmed Tekela.

'Magazine!'

They looked up to see Arberus and Jermayah at the Thumper, wreathed in smoke rising from the open breech. Lizanne shook the vestiges of sleep from her head and reached for the stock of magazines, handing one to the major as she came to her feet to view the scene beyond the trenches. The vision that greeted her made her suspect she might still be dreaming.

'I think I was over-generous in my estimation of the marshal's abilities,' Arberus said, adjusting the Thumper's aim as Jermayah slammed the magazine in place.

'Cavalry!' Lizanne breathed, still unable to quite believe the spectacle before her. They came on at the gallop, more horsemen than could easily be counted, streaming from the trees in a charging mass, sabres and lance-points glinting in the morning sun. Dozens of horses and men already lay dead or dying a good two hundred yards from the outer trench where the contingent of Contractors were maintaining a steady and rapid fire, more horses falling by the second, but still they came on.

'Sending cavalry against an entrenched position.' Arberus's voice was rich in disgusted bafflement. 'He must be mad.'

Jermayah drew back the lever to chamber the first shell and patted the major's shoulder before turning the Thumper's handle. Arberus had elevated the weapon so the rain of shells arced down just short of the tree-line, tearing through the ranks of on-coming cavalry in a spectacle of exploding horses and men. An enterprising Protectorate officer had clearly sensed an opportunity by quickly shifting more Growlers to cover this sector, their criss-crossing fire adding further decimation to the Corvantine ranks. Soon a wall of sundered horse-flesh seemed to have formed in a bloody crescent around the trenches. Lizanne could only guess at what threats or promises compelled the cavalry troopers to keep charging, galloping forward to leap the corpses of their comrades only to be cut down, some torn to shreds in mid air.

The Thumper fell silent once more and they began to repeat their well-honed reloading procedure, Lizanne sighing in frustration when Tekela failed to hand her the fresh magazine. 'Look lively, if you would, miss.'

Tekela didn't appear to be listening, standing and staring at something off to the left of their position. 'What is that?' she wondered.

Lizanne followed her gaze, grunting in realisation as she saw a small man-shaped figure descending through a cloud of smoke towards the trenches, a leap that could only be accomplished by one thing. As the man neared the ground the air before him shimmered with unleashed heat, a sudden upsurge of flame concealing the sight of his fall, but from the bodies and limbs being cast into the air shortly after his landing, Lizanne deduced he had imbibed a large amount of Green and Black. She could see more of them, at least twenty dark figures leaping their impossible leaps and descending on the defenders in a fury of destruction. *Blood Cadre.*

'This was just a diversion,' she told Arberus, gesturing at the slaughtered cavalrymen then checking to ensure the Spider was firmly secured to her forearm. 'Get word to Madame Bondersil to send every Blood-blessed she can to the eastern sector.'

Tekela clutched at her arm as she started to clamber out of the trench. 'Don't!'

'Stay with the major,' Lizanne told her, the impending violence making her tone harder than she intended and she winced at the hurt she saw in the girl's face. 'Keep your revolver handy,' she added, forcing a smile. 'I'll be back shortly.'

She turned away and injected half-second doses of Black, Green and Red, gritting her teeth against the rush of sensation then vaulting from the trench and sprinting towards the eastern sector. She leapt as she neared the scene of the worst destruction, the trenches littered with the corpses of Contractors and conscripts, those left alive fleeing in panic as flames and carnage raged at their backs. The leap took her high enough to see the havoc wrought by the Blood Cadre in just a few minutes, trenches filled with fire, cannon dismounted and their crews torn apart, the dark-uniformed figures of the empire's most feared servants busily wreaking yet more destruction as they descended on the few knots of defenders unwise enough to linger.

She saw one in mid-leap just beneath her, flames blossoming beneath him as he unleashed a blast of Red onto a Growler crew. Keen to husband her product, she put two rounds from the Whisper into his back and had the satisfaction of seeing him plummet to the ground. A half-second later her own leap brought her down directly in the path of a trio of Cadre, all clad in insignia-free plain black uniforms. They had been engaged in dismembering a group of conscripts, one tearing the arm from a screaming man whilst his two comrades blasted the others with Black. Their momentary shock at her appearance gave her time to put a Whisper round in two of their foreheads in quick succession. The third dodged as she adjusted her aim, sinking to the ground and scuttling to the right in a crab-like blur. She felt the air around her thicken with heat as he let loose with a surge of Red, but the fire was weak, indicating he was near the end of his ingested product. She leapt again, sailing over his head and slamming down with a hefty release of Black, the force of it enough to crush his spine.

A bullet whisked by her head as she landed, her Green-attuned eyes instantly snapping to the threat. A woman twenty yards away with a revolver, moving with the aid of Green as she leapt, seeking the advantage of height and firing off a rapid salvo. Lizanne whirled away, raising dust in a concealing screen, and replied with a focused blast of Red, the woman twisting and thrashing in the air as her uniform took light. Lizanne sprinted towards her as she fell, writhing in the dust to extinguish the flames. She was clearly a veteran, however, her recovery swift and near fatal as she swept Lizanne from her feet with a concentrated burst of Black, then raised her pistol for a killing shot. Lizanne saw the woman curse as the revolver was jerked from her grip. It hovered in mid air in front of her face for a second then spun around and fired, the woman's face shattering like glass.

Lizanne tracked the pistol's flight, watching it descend into the hand of a beefy man some twenty yards away. He wore the garb typical of a stevedore, hardy dun-coloured dungarees and a peaked cap. He caught Lizanne's gaze, grinned a little and touched a finger to his cap. Behind him she could see a dozen more people in varied garb emerging from the fog of dust and smoke, some with weapons, most not, spreading out as the air around them seemed to shimmer with suppressed power. Carvenport's Blood-blessed had answered the call.

Lizanne turned, seeing a ragged line of Blood Cadre ahead. For a moment both sides stood regarding each other in silent appraisal, then as if in response to some unspoken command, they all leapt. Lizanne managed to shoot one Corvantine before the two sides collided in an instantaneous release of power. The air itself seemed to have been sundered by the combination of so much Black and Red unleashed at once. Lizanne found herself tumbling through the air, flames licking at the sleeve of her overalls and blood leaking from her nose, seeing a grey haze at the corners of her vision warning of imminent loss of consciousness. She depressed the Spider's middle button an instant before colliding with the ground, the rush of Green sufficient to suppress most of the pain and prevent serious injury.

She found her feet quickly, the Whisper coming up to dispatch two Corvantines crawling about near by, both evidently nursing broken limbs. She saw the stevedore who had killed the Cadre woman, whirling in a miasma of raised dust as he used Black to swing a dismounted cannon around like a club, swatting a

Corvantine out of the air before crushing another into the ground with repeated blows, like a mallet pounding on a splintering peg. A salvo of pistol-shots rang out and the stevedore's furious pounding ceased abruptly, Lizanne watching him stare unbelieving at the holes in his chest before sinking to the ground.

She could see his killer, a tall hatchet-faced man holding a revolver in each hand. He was older than the other Cadre operatives, eyes narrowed in the determined yet shrewd gaze of the seasoned professional. Lizanne pressed three buttons on the Spider, refreshing her product reserves, then leapt again. The hatchet-faced man was quick to spot the danger, jerking aside as she fired her last two Whisper rounds. He rolled then performed his own Green-assisted leap, pistols blazing. Lizanne twisted in the air, feeling the bullets thrum around her, one plucking at the leg of her overalls but failing to find flesh. She sent a blast of Black at the Cadre agent, throwing his aim wide as he fired again, pistols clicking empty as he drew near. Lizanne twisted again, bringing her leg around in a kick that would have done her instructors proud. She felt it connect hard with the agent's ribs, feeling the bones give way under the unnatural pressure. She turned to watch him fall as she landed, blood trailing from his mouth, then spouting high in a red fountain as he connected with the earth. Lizanne saw him twitch then lie still.

She reloaded the Whisper, hands moving with accustomed speed as she cast around for another target, finding only corpses and the dazed figures of the surviving Carvenport Blood-blessed wandering the scorched and part-demolished trenches.

'You there,' she said, spying one in a Protectorate uniform, a young man staring at the blackened body of the agent he had killed. He swung towards her, face momentarily pale and uncomprehending with shock, but straightened a little when she identified herself. 'Exceptional Initiatives. Find an officer and get some riflemen down here to cover these trenches.'

He nodded and ran off. Through a mixture of jostling and sheer force of personality, Lizanne managed to gather the rest of the survivors into a dense knot around a Growler position, instructing them all to replenish their product as she went about restoring the weapon to working order. It was dented and blackened but fortunately the windling lever and firing mechanism remained undamaged, as did the magazines.

'Uh, miss,' one of the Blood-blessed said, a bespectacled woman of middling years in managerial garb. Lizanne assumed her usual responsibilities consisted of daily trance communications with Home Office. From the way her arm trembled as she pointed at the ground beyond the trenches, the trials of the day were evidently coming close to stripping away her self-control. A long line of Corvantine infantry could be seen advancing through the lingering smoke, their dense ranks indicating that Marshal Morradin still had some tactical lessons to learn.

'Stand ready,' Lizanne said, closing the breech on the Growler.

'Shouldn't we . . .' another Blood-blessed began, this one a sailor and just as unnerved as the managerial woman. He had probably been recruited from the engine room of a blood-burner and cast into this maelstrom with little understanding of the consequences. He trailed off at Lizanne's glance, giving a helpless shrug.

'Run?' she finished for him, before training the Growler on the on-coming infantry. 'Where to?'

She didn't wait for an answer, ordering them all to take shelter in the nearest trench and make sure they had gulped down some Black. 'Don't release it until my order,' she said. 'We need to hold them.'

She gripped the Growler's lever and waited until the first rank had closed to within ten yards of the trench, just when their cohesion began to waver as the excitement of seizing an apparently undefended trench took hold. 'NOW!' she shouted. She was gratified to see most of the Blood-blessed in the trench respond to the order, though a couple had clearly reached their limit and remained huddled on the duckboards. The others all stood and unleashed their Black as one, the first two ranks of the lead

Corvantine battalion coming to a sudden and frozen halt as their collective grip took hold.

Lizanne stared at her hand on the lever, wondering why it hadn't moved. The thought came unbidden, treacherous and deadly: *There are so many.* It was the same paralysis that had gripped her in the Burgrave's office; years of experience and training falling away when confronted with a too-awful reality. It was the memory of Tekela's face that unfroze her, the knowledge of the girl's most likely fate if Carvenport fell.

She screamed as she turned the handle, a cry of revulsion swallowed by the growl of multiple barrels sending bullet after bullet into the immobile ranks of infantry. They were held so completely they even failed to twitch as the rounds tore through them, like man-shaped meal-sacks, leaking blood instead of grain, faces unable even to register the pain of death.

She exhausted the Growler's magazine and quickly slotted in a new one, seeing the first signs that the collective hold was starting to falter. The soldiers in the next ranks were trying to force their way past the statue-like corpses of their comrades, some pushing their rifles through the gaps to fire at the Blood-blessed. Lizanne saw the managerial woman take a bullet in the head before tearing her gaze from the slumping corpse and turning the Growler's handle. She worked the flaming barrels along the line of infantry, sights raised slightly to lash at the roiling jam of men trying to press forward. The Growler emptied in short order, however, and, from the many screams of rage and pain, the Corvantines had suffered greatly from her attentions. Still they sought to press forward, the line of frozen corpses prised apart like an old fence then giving way completely as the Blood-blessed's reserves of Black ran out.

The Corvantine infantry surged forward in a howling mob, dead and wounded borne along in the tide, covering the distance to the first trench in a few seconds, fury and blood-lust on every face . . .

The first shell left a thin trail of smoke as it slammed down to destroy the leading company of Corvantines, sundered bodies blown away like rags. Another four shells came down in short order, the great mass of infantry breaking apart under the bombardment. Lizanne glanced back, seeing a newly arrived battery of Protectorate artillery on the rise behind her. The gunners scrambled to reload as what was left of the Corvantine attack milled about just short of the trenches. Still it wasn't over. Dazed or wounded men were being shoved into a semblance of order by officers and sergeants, exhortations rising for a final effort and bugles pealing out anew.

Lizanne slotted a magazine into the Growler, aimed at the most conspicuous officer and turned the lever until the firing mechanism clicked on an empty chamber. The Protectorate artillery resumed firing as she let her hand fall from the lever. The shells were launched with less frequency now the danger had passed. After a five-minute barrage the guns fell silent.

Lizanne didn't look when the smoke cleared, instead slumping down next to the Growler as the last dregs of product fled her system. The screams and the appalled exclamations of the surviving Blood-blessed told the tale well enough. A chill shudder ran through her, making her clutch herself tight until it passed, resisting the temptation to inject a drop of Green. *I earned this pain.*

After a moment, when the shaking had faded, she rose and walked away from the Growler, ignoring the proffered hands and expressions of appreciation from Blood-blessed and soldiers. An officer appeared at her side asking for her name. She muttered 'Exceptional Initiatives' then walked on, coming to a halt at the body of the hatchet-faced man she had killed, idly pondering the question of who he had been. She knew searching the body would prove fruitless as no Cadre agent would ever carry anything that might identify them. But looking at his face and the lines of experience around his eyes, she couldn't help but conclude he must have been a senior figure in the Blood Cadre. *Pity,* she concluded, *he might have had something enlightening to say.*

She was about to move on as she noticed something else, a faint glimmer of metal on the man's wrist. Kneeling, she lifted his sleeve, frowning in baffled surprise until realisation hit home with a jolt.

'This is not my work,' Jermayah said, his nimble hands turning the Spider over in careful examination. 'The materials are far too flimsy. I make devices that last.'

'The design,' Lizanne said, watching his face intently. 'It's identical, wouldn't you say?'

Jermayah pursed his lips in consideration. 'Pretty much. I'll have to have a word with Madame, farming out my designs to inferior craftsmen. It's not on.'

'You showed her the prototype?' Lizanne asked.

'Months ago,' he said. 'Everything has to cross her desk these days. Been waiting to hear back about the patent, actually.'

'Just her?' Lizanne pressed. 'No-one else?'

Jermayah gave her a quizzical look. She had led him to a secluded corner of the trenches to quiz him on the device she had found on the Cadre agent's wrist. 'No-one else,' he said, tone cautious now. 'Where'd you get this?'

'From a dead man who had no business wearing it.' She stood, injecting a drop of Green to banish her lingering fatigue and turning towards the city. 'There is about to be a change of management in Carvenport,' she told Jermayah. 'It may have unfortunate consequences for the girl and the major.'

'Built myself a shelter under the shop years ago,' Jermayah said. 'In case something like this ever happened.' He gave a sheepish grin at her expression. 'Only as a last resort. They're welcome to share it.'

'Go there if it looks like the city is about to fall. I'll find you.' *If I live,* she added silently, running for the city gate with a determined stride.

*

'Where is she?'

The young Protectorate officer outside Madame's office quailed a little under Lizanne's gaze. She had marched past him to kick the office door open, revealing an empty desk. 'Her current whereabouts are classified,' the officer began, then fell to abrupt silence as the tip of the Whisper's barrel pressed into his nose.

'Where?' Lizanne said, summoning enough Red to make the man sweat as she stared hard into his eyes.

'Th-the harbour,' he stammered. 'The Corvantine fleet raised a signal requesting a truce. She's gone to negotiate a cease-fire.'

Lizanne's gaze swept over the office and she knew with instinctive certainty that if she ransacked it a very important item would be found missing. 'Oh, I'm sure she's gone to negotiate.'

She rushed outside, eyes roving the makeshift camp until she found a horse. She leapt into the saddle and kicked the animal into a gallop. It was a somewhat lumbering beast, probably a cart-horse pressed into military service. However, it carried her through the city fast enough to prevent her exhausting her supply of Green, something she expected to have need of very soon. The streets were mostly empty, those citizens not called to the trenches no doubt huddled in basements and with good reason. Most of the Corvantine shelling seemed to have come down on residential areas, and with far too much accuracy and quantity to have been accidental. *Morradin hoping to spread enough terror to provoke rebellion,* she decided. *Little did he know all he had to do was wait and the place would be handed to him on a platter.*

She reined the horse to a halt at the docks, eyes roving the silent and mostly crewless ships before alighting on the great edifice of the mole where three figures could be seen: Madame and two Protectorate guards. Lizanne galloped for the steps where the mole joined the eastern extremity of the docks, leaping clear of the saddle then injecting enough Green to sprint to the top in the space of a few seconds. She could see them clearly now, Madame flanked by two men, covert operatives from the look of them. Beyond the mole the sea was filled with the

Corvantine fleet, frigates and cruisers all at anchor with guns raised and angled towards the city. A small motor-launch was making its way towards the mole, a truce pennant fluttering from its mast and a contingent of Corvantine officers on board. It was a two-moon tide today and the sea was high against the mole, only six feet short of the top, meaning the Corvantines would have a relatively easy time clambering up to receive the city's surrender.

Lizanne injected nearly all her remaining Red and Black, the burn as it mingled with the Green adding fuel to the unfamiliar mix of emotions raging in her breast. She drew the Whisper, sprinted forward and leapt, a yell of unrestrained fury escaping her as she plummeted down a few yards from Madame, remaining in a predatory crouch as the two guards rounded on her, revolvers levelled. They were both Blood-blessed, and had clearly imbibed almost as much product as she had.

Lizanne ignored them, her gaze fixed entirely on Madame, now regarding her with an incurious glance. 'Truelove,' Lizanne said.

The guards both took a step forward, the air beginning to thrum as they summoned their product.

'Enough of that!' Madame ordered sharply, both guards turning to her in surprise. 'Lower your weapons,' she ordered. 'Miss Lethridge and I have business to discuss.'

She favoured Lizanne with a very slight smile as the guards stood aside. 'You look terrible,' she said.

Lizanne rose from her crouch, glancing down at the multiple blood-stains and scorch-marks on her overalls. 'I just killed at least a hundred people,' she replied, lowering the Whisper and stepping between the guards to come to Madame's side. 'Of course I look terrible.'

Madame's face grew sombre and she turned, nodding at the approaching launch. 'Fortunately, such extremes will no longer be necessary.'

Lizanne's eyes went to the canvas bag in Madame's hand, and

the distinctive rectangular bulge of what it contained. 'You really think they'll just sail away and leave us in peace if you give them that?'

Madame shook her head, a thin sigh of exasperation escaping her lips, once again the teacher aggrieved by her pupil's lack of comprehension. 'For all your experience, all your travels, your vision remains so frustratingly narrow. The agreement I am about to negotiate goes far beyond this petty war. We stand on the cusp of something far greater, Lizanne. Something I sincerely hope you will share in.'

'Did they pay you so much then?' Lizanne's fingers flexed on the Whisper as she felt the product in her veins begin to thin.

'Pay me?' Madame's sigh was more of a laugh this time. 'Do you think I did all this for a *bribe*? They didn't buy me, I bought them, and this city into the bargain.' She turned, raising her arm to the docks and the streets beyond. 'You are privileged to witness the birth of the Carvenport Free Trade Company.'

'If you think Morradin will just hand this place over to you . . .'

'Morradin is a dog doing his master's bidding. He'll come to heel when whipped. My accommodation was never with the dog, but the master. In return for exclusive rights to the White, he'll give me Carvenport and half the world if I ask.'

Not obsession, Lizanne realised, her mind suddenly flooded with the image of the black web coiling through Madame's mindscape. *Ambition.* 'All on the promise of something that hasn't even been found,' she said. 'We don't even know what power lies in its blood, if any.'

'Oh, but we do, Lizanne. Or at least, I do, and now so does the Emperor. It wasn't so very hard to deduce, once I had pondered the information from Ethelynne's last trance. Wittler pursued her across the Red Sands, determined to kill her. But why? Was it simple madness, brought on when he breathed in the White's powdered bone? Or was it more? "I ain't gonna burn," he told her, and yet he did. As confirmed by Mr Torcreek. She burned him, as he knew she would. The *future*, Lizanne. The ability to discern the future. For that, the Emperor will give me all I ask.'

'And what will he do with it?'

'As long as he leaves me in peace to run my new enterprise, anything he likes. Empires rise and fall, wars come and go. But, without the Board to fetter me, I'm confident we'll weather the storms and profit in the process. Ironship has stagnated under the weight of its bureaucracy. It's every bit as corrupt and bloated as the monarchies it displaced. It's time for a new age, a post-corporate age where we no longer mire ourselves in the minutiae of governance.'

Lizanne nodded at the bag. 'You needed that,' she said, 'to convince him. That's why you sent me to Morsvale.'

'At first the Cadre had no notion of who Truelove actually was,' Madame said. 'Just that they now had a very useful stream of intelligence tranced to them via a well-paid and well-guarded intermediary firmly positioned in neutral territory. Convincing them to trust me wasn't so very hard: designs for some of Jermayah's more effective innovations, the identities of a few Exceptional Initiatives operatives in Corvantine territory, the location of an Ironship-sponsored pirate den in the Isles. Then, as time went on, reports containing subtle indications that the Protectorate had taken a renewed interest in the fabled White Drake. It all stoked the Emperor's naturally avaricious tendencies to the required pitch. Your little excursion to Morsvale was a tricky thing to engineer, but I trusted your ability to navigate the various difficulties. After the Cadre's spectacular failure to capture you, and prevent the successful retrieval of the solargraph, my intermediary reported that the Emperor was now much more amenable to negotiation. Especially since Captain Torcreek's company had successfully negated a Cadre attempt to stop them at Edinsmouth and appeared to be drawing ever closer to their goal. Sadly, I was obliged to allow this military farce to play out for a time until I could trance with my contact. Still, all those infantrymen piling up outside the walls did focus their minds.

With a global war to fight, they can't really afford to prolong their campaign here.'

Lizanne's gaze returned to the approaching launch, now barely a hundred yards away. 'Mr Redsel?' she asked. 'He wasn't in Corvantine employ, was he?'

'I needed a means of eavesdropping on your trances with Mr Torcreek, or whatever unregistered ne'er-do-well we managed to scrape from the Blinds. It seemed I over-estimated Mr Redsel's abilities and under-estimated yours. Incidentally, is Mr Torcreek truly dead? I find I can't suppress the nagging suspicion that your veracity has been somewhat lacking of late.'

The launch was twenty feet away now, a Corvantine sailor at the prow standing ready with a rope as one of Madame's Protectorate guards moved to catch it. 'Mr Torcreek and I are in agreement regarding what needs to be done with the White,' Lizanne replied, taking a firmer grip on the Whisper.

Madame glanced at her, and blinked.

The Black gripped her instantly, no change of expression in Madame's face that might have warned her. An effortless display of power and expertise that left Lizanne standing there, limbs flaring with agony as she strained against the invisible vice.

'Yet more narrowness of vision,' Madame said, apparently genuine regret on her face as she came closer to cup Lizanne's cheek. 'I had hoped you might succeed me one day. The Carvenport Free Trade Company will need an intelligence arm, after all. You would have been a co-Director, destined for great things.'

She removed her hand and plucked the Whisper from Lizanne's frozen fingers, tossing it into the sea. 'My finest student, and also my greatest disappointment. Unfortunately, I can't kill you. My Corvantine associates are keen to speak to you regarding Major Arberus and his revolutionary comrades. I was going to call for you later today, explain that Miss Artonin's continued good health depended on your agreement with my aims. The major would still have had to be handed over but I might have been able to save the girl. But I see now our positions are too far apart to allow for a workable arrangement.'

She stepped away, her regretful visage transforming into a business-like smile as she turned to greet the Corvantine officers. Lizanne prepared to summon all the Red she could, but Madame's control was so absolute she couldn't even move her eyes. It would probably have been futile in any case. The two guards would have crushed her the moment she tried. But there was so much rage inside her and so much fear. *They will take Tekela when they take Arberus.*

Sweat bathed her as she strained to move her eyes, expending all her remaining Green and managing a slight tick, just enough to catch the edge of Madame's skirt. Lizanne's gaze faltered as something flickered amongst the masts of the Corvantine fleet. At first she thought it a flare, but then saw it was fire. A bright stream of white fire. Another flicker, then more fire. It seemed to be streaming from several directions at once, converging somewhere amongst the mass of ships. The flash came first, then the flat, ear-splitting boom of an exploding ship accompanied by the red-black cloud rising from the sea. A chorus of whistles and sirens resounded through the fleet, guns traversing and water churning as engines sprang to life.

Two more explosions followed in quick succession, accompanied by the thunderous boom of multiple cannon. Madame's control lessened enough for Lizanne to turn her head, her gaze sweeping across the now-chaotic mass of ships then stopping as something caught her eye, something impossible.

The Blue rose from the sea, crest flaring and mouth gaping, sending its fire down at the deck of a Corvantine cruiser. Lizanne had only ever seen dead Blues, and those the steel-net-enmeshed remains hauled from the hold of a Blue-hunter freshly returned from the southern seas. *I never knew they grew so big,* was her only thought as two more Blues appeared on either side of the cruiser, their collective fire descending with such intensity every crewman on the cruiser's deck was instantly engulfed. The Blues' fire died after a moment and they turned in unison, sinking back into the water, the snake-like bodies knifing through the waves towards another victim. The cruiser continued to burn in their wake and Lizanne realised with shock that it was the *Regal*, the same ship she had inspected in Morsvale harbour. Whatever novel modifications she might have gained wouldn't save her now. The fires raged unchecked across the *Regal*'s decks for another minute then she gave a shudder, geysers of fire erupting from her stacks as the flames found her magazine. She blew apart a heart-beat later, the debris raining down all around, fragments of iron and men splashing into the sea and impacting the mole. The launch containing the Corvantine officers took a direct hit from a burning chunk of machinery, its own boiler exploding from the force of the impact, killing all on board along with the Protectorate guard who had caught their rope.

Madame and the other guard shrank back from the destruction. She had never been given to shock but evidently this was a sufficiently close brush with death to slacken her control, just for an instant, but it was enough.

Lizanne focused on the bag in Madame's hand, lashing out with Black to drag it from her grip. She caught it then used the last dregs of Green in her veins to leap as Madame replied, Black churning the air where Lizanne had been with the force of a hurricane. Lizanne sailed over Madame's head, unleashing a wave of Red that forced the woman to leap aside. The Protectorate guard hadn't been as wise, lingering a fraction too long to aim his pistol at Lizanne and taking the full force of the Red. The fire covered him from head to toe in an instant and he whirled, screaming towards the edge of the mole and careering into the sea.

Lizanne landed hard, clutching the bag to her chest and crouching as Madame rose to her feet some twenty yards away. 'Give that to me!' she commanded in a rasping cry, all vestige of discipline seemingly having fled now as she advanced towards Lizanne with a face rendered ugly by frustration and malice.

Lizanne depressed the first three buttons on the Spider, using up the small amount of remaining product and instantly unleashing the Black. Madame was ready for her, however, her own Black meeting Lizanne's and birthing a thunder-clap of displaced air. Lizanne continued to use up her Black, seeking to prise open Madame's defences, but it was like trying to batter her way through granite.

'Give this up, Madame!' she called out, casting a hand towards the sea where Corvantine ships exploded with every passing moment and ever more Blues rose from the waves. 'Look at what's happening here! Your schemes don't matter now!'

Madame, however, proved deaf to all entreaties, summoning a blast of Red and forcing Lizanne to roll to the side as the heat-wave rushed past. Madame followed with a surge of Black, presumably all her remaining product released at once as Lizanne felt the blow like a hammer, the force of it sending her sliding across the mole. An involuntary yell escaped her throat as the agony of snapped ribs cut through the effects of the Green with dreadful ease. She could only cast the last of her Red at Madame as she lay there, but it was a feeble thing, just a shimmering passage of air the older woman side-stepped with ease.

Madame came to a halt a few feet away, staring at Lizanne with a certain grim satisfaction on her face as she took a vial from her pocket and gulped it down. 'You,' she said, shaking her head sadly as she looked down on Lizanne. 'You were . . .'

The Blue moved in a blur, snaking up from below the mole to grasp Madame Bondersil in its jaws. It slowed as it bit down, Lizanne fancying she heard a muffled scream from behind its jagged wall of teeth. The Blue shook its prey briefly then swallowed it down, throat bulging as the meal was conveyed to its stomach with a few convulsive jerks. It gave a satisfied rumble, nostrils flaring then angled its head to stare down at Lizanne.

She didn't hesitate, rolling towards the harbour as the flames streamed down, feeling the heat and a flaring pain as the fire found her hair, her clothes. A brief sensation of falling then the chill embrace of the harbour waters. Fatigue and pain conspired to prevent her kicking for the surface, though she held tight to Madame's bag as she sank ever lower, what it contained being so very important.

CHAPTER 35

Clay

He was watching the dolphins when the settlement came into view. These creatures were smaller than those he had seen in the waters off Carvenport harbour, their skin darker on top, but no less playful. Loriabeth gave a delighted laugh as one leapt clear of the lake just ahead of the *River Maiden*'s bows, spinning in the air before plunging back down. More could be seen shimmering beneath the water as they rode the boat's wake.

'A freshwater variety,' Scriberson said, adding yet another jotting to his note-book. 'Their numbers must be curtailed through predation, but obviously they maintain a viable population. This lake is more well-stocked with marine life than previously suspected.'

'And way too well-stocked with Green for my liking,' Foxbine said, eyeing the surrounding waters with carbine in hand, a habit she had acquired since they found the wreckage of the Briteshore vessel.

'Look there!' Loriabeth called from the prow, pointing at a column of grey smoke rising from the shore-line a few points off the starboard bow. The land beyond the lake-shore rose in a gentle incline of green hills before abruptly transforming into the steep, steel-grey slopes of the northern Coppersoles. Clay had only ever seen pictures of mountains and found the real thing an ominous sight, the vast walls of rock ascending so high their summits were veiled in cloud. The prospect of navigating such a landscape was not a pleasant one.

Braddon ordered the engine slowed then had Scriberson

assemble his telescope on the fore-deck, wary of landing without reconnaissance. 'It doesn't look good, Captain,' the astronomer reported upon peering through the eyepiece. 'It *was* a settlement of some kind. Defensive walls and a jetty. But now . . .' He stood back, gesturing Braddon towards the telescope.

'Burned black and half–torn down,' he said after a moment. 'Can't see no Greens about though. No people, either.' He straightened, face drawn in contemplation.

'Could be some ammo in there, Captain,' Foxbine said.

'I'm aware.' Braddon raised his gaze as Lutharon swept low overhead, gliding towards the smoking settlement in a straight and unerring line. 'Seems the choice has been made for us,' he said. 'Mr Scriberson, fire her up, if you would.'

The jetty was a wreck of blackened pilings and splintered beams, forcing them to ground the *River Maiden* on the thin stretch of shingle alongside. 'Seems a shame to just leave her here,' Scriberson commented as they clambered over the side to wade ashore.

'What else we gonna do with her?' Skaggerhill said, though there was a faintly wistful note to his voice as he afforded the boat a final glance of farewell. 'She served us well, right enough. Got me a mind to come back for her one day. See if we can't find that treasure ship, eh?' He gave Firpike a nudge though the scholar seemed more interested in clearing the water as quickly as possible, as if a Green might come lunging up at him even in these shallows.

Ethelynne stood beside Lutharon at the gate to the settlement, her face betraying a palpable distress. 'I watched them build this place,' she told Clay. 'Only a year ago.'

'Briteshore Minerals, sure enough,' Skaggerhill said, nodding to the scorched sign above the gate. The lettering had been burned away but the Briteshore crest could still be made out. 'Guess they built it as a port for their surveying ship.'

Ethelynne turned and climbed onto Lutharon's back. 'I've no wish to see any more of this. We'll scout ahead for a time.' With that, rider and drake galloped towards the edge of the lake where Lutharon spread his wings and they took to the air, soaring high in a wide circle before striking out for the south.

'Woulda thought she'd have a stronger constitution,' Loriabeth commented. 'Being out here so long.'

'Get the sense this is all new to her,' Clay said, nodding at the smoking settlement. 'Drakes ain't done nothing like this before.' He stole a glance at his uncle who stood regarding the place with an unreadable expression. 'Makes you wonder what could've forced such a change in them.'

'Clay, Silverpin,' Braddon said, drawing his revolver and stepping towards the gate. 'With me. The rest of you, watch the lake.'

The gate had been barred and buttressed but its lower half lay shattered, probably by a flailing drake tail. Clay and Silverpin stooped low as they entered, weapons ready. The scene that confronted them had Clay fighting a convulsive retch. Bodies lay everywhere, part-burnt and savaged, several in pieces. From the tattered remains of clothing he concluded they were a mix of labourers and Contractors. Spent shell casings were liberally scattered about, indicating that at least they went down fighting. The thin smoke still rising from the ruins was evidence that this had all happened recently.

'Greens,' Braddon said, halting beside one of the bodies and eyeing the pattern of bite marks that had torn out the man's insides from belly to neck. 'Guess they dealt with the survey ship then came here. No eating, just killing. Just like the soldiers in the jungle.'

Clay surveyed the settlement, seeing mostly just ruination. It seemed the settlement had featured a couple of bunk-houses and a meal-hall, all torn down and reduced almost to ash. The store-houses and workshops were in a similar condition though he did spy a large structure still standing towards the rear of the enclosure. 'Warehouse, maybe?' he asked his uncle.

'Let's take a look.'

The structure turned out to be another workshop, spared destruction by virtue of its corrugated iron walls and containing something Clay had never seen before. A great, multi-wheeled engine of some kind sitting on a pair of rails. It had another wheeled contraption attached to its rear, a large open-topped tender piled high with coal. The rails on which they sat traced to the rear of the structure and then under a set of twelve-foot-high doors. The engine showed signs of considerable burning, the metal covered in soot and some its workings part-melted. A blackened skeleton lay on a platform just behind the huge iron cylinder that formed the bulk of the engine's mass.

'Trying to fire her up when the Greens broke in,' Braddon said, eyes roving the engine with considerable interest. 'Looks like we got us another job for Mr Scriberson.'

'What is this thing?' Clay asked.

'A railway-traversing locomotive, if I'm not mistaken. Seems Briteshore put a sizable investment in this place. Must have been expecting to shift a whole lotta ore to the coast.'

'Why not do it by boat?' Clay wondered. 'The lake connects to the sea, right?'

'The water-way's choked with rapids for much of its length. The main reason why this region's been so sparsely explored till now.' Braddon's gaze shifted to the rails and he followed them to the doors at the rear of the structure. They were buttressed and barred like the main gate and would clearly take considerable effort to open.

'Go get the others,' Braddon told Clay. 'And check the bodies and store-rooms for ammo, plus anything else we can use.'

They scavenged another three hundred rounds of ammunition from the settlement, though some of it had to be discarded as it failed to match the calibres of their weapons. Still, Clay took no small measure of comfort from the additional twenty rounds Foxbine handed him. Scriberson spent a good hour going over the locomotive engine before pronouncing it functional but in need of slight repair. 'Then don't dawdle, young man,' Braddon told him. 'I aim to be gone from here by nightfall.'

The doors proved to be so well buttressed that Braddon quickly called an end to their attempts to hammer apart the reinforcing beams and resorted to making use of the bounty provided by the lake. 'Been a good while since I did this,' he said, carefully cutting an inch-long segment from one of the sticks of explosives. The others had been quick to retreat from the shed but Clay lingered to observe, reasoning this to be knowledge he may have use for when they got to their destination. 'First thing to learn is make all your movements real slow,' Braddon told him, slotting the segment into the gap between beam and door. 'This stuff don't take too well to any herky-jerks.'

He repeated the process with the other three beams, using up half a stick in the process, then uncoiled a roll of black wire Skaggerhill had found in one of the storehouses. 'This here's the fuse,' he explained, cutting four equal lengths from the wire and braiding them together at one end. 'Makes it go boom.'

'Where'd you learn all this, Uncle?' Clay asked him.

'Once took a job escorting some bone-hunters to the western plains. Ironship and Consolidated Research both pay good money for the bones of long-extinct creatures. There's a plateau in the plains rich in such things, but you have to blast them out of the rocks.'

'Drake bones?' Clay asked.

'No, like Mr Scriberson says, you don't find drake bones that old. Hold this.' He handed Clay the braided length of fuse and then pushed the other ends into each of the segments of explosives. After that he tied the braid to the remaining length of wire and spooled it out as they backed towards the entrance to the shed.

'Everybody best find something to get behind and hunker low,' Braddon told the others as they emerged into the light. 'Cover your ears too.' He and Clay took shelter behind a stack of scorched wood where he snipped the fuse from the coil and lowered a match to it. The fuse lit immediately, Clay watching the smoking cluster of sparks trace along it, leaving a trail of ash behind as it disappeared into the shadowed recesses of the shed. The explosion came a heart-beat later, sending a wave of displaced dust through the settlement accompanied by a boom powerful enough to make Clay glad he had jammed his fingers in his ears.

'Briteshore sure has been busy,' Skaggerhill commented as they surveyed the track leading away from the now-shattered doors. The gleaming steel rails made an incongruous contrast to the landscape they traversed, winding across the grassy slopes in a series of gentle inclines before disappearing into a steep-sided valley some three miles away.

'Gives us a path to follow,' Braddon said, then turned to where Scriberson stood atop the engine platform fiddling with a dial. 'Young man, time to point the way.'

They had found some Briteshore charts amidst the wreckage but they were badly burnt and only partially complete. Fortunately, Braddon had had the foresight to pack some Ironship charts of the region, though they lacked the more fulsome detail of those produced by the mining concern.

'So we know where we're at,' he said, pointing to a dot on one of the Briteshore maps, clearly identifiable as the settlement from its position on the lake-shore and the bisected line tracing away from it towards the south. His finger followed the line into the mountains to the point where it ended in a charred edge. 'Gives us maybe forty miles of charted country.' He unfurled one of the Ironship maps and pointed to an area circled in pencil. 'Best as I can figure this is where we'll end up when the Briteshore map runs out. Question is, does it take us where we need to be?' He looked expectantly at Scriberson.

For the first time since meeting him, Clay detected a marked reluctance in the astronomer's demeanour. Before he had tended to exhibit an endearing if unwise confidence, but now, watching him lower his gaze and shift from foot to foot, Clay knew he was looking on a young man suddenly out of his depth. 'I don't know,' he said in a low voice.

'I beg your pardon?' Braddon straightened from the map, a hard glint creeping into his gaze. 'Say that again, if you please?'

'I don't know exactly where it is.' Scriberson raised his eyes and quickly lowered them again on catching sight of Braddon's expression. 'Just what it looks like.'

'I see.' Braddon's voice was way too even and reasonable for Clay's liking. He took a step closer to the astronomer's side as his uncle went on, 'I seem to recall, however, you telling of a lost map of the region your exceptional memory had captured so well you didn't require a copy.'

'It wasn't a map.' Scriberson swallowed. 'It was a sketch, of the point where the alignment could be viewed. It's a very distinctive place. I'm sure if I caught sight of it . . .'

'Caught sight of it?' Skaggerhill said, his voice holding none of Braddon's deceptive calm. 'You thought we were just gonna wander about these mountains for however long it took you to catch sight of it? You any idea the size of this range, boy?'

'The account states that it's close to the highest peak.' Scriberson gave a hopeful and short-lived grin, adding in a mutter, 'Shouldn't be too hard to find that.'

The silence that followed was long, broken only by Firpike's dry comment: 'And I'm supposed to be the fraud here.'

'We need him to drive the engine,' Clay reminded Braddon, increasingly perturbed by his stillness.

'I can drive the Seer-damn engine,' Skaggerhill stated, levelling a stubby finger at Scriberson. 'We had a contract based on honest statements now revealed as false. That ain't a small matter for folks in our profession.'

Clay's gaze roamed the other Longrifles, finding disappointment and judgement on every face; even Silverpin's tattooed brow had taken on an uncharacteristically stern frown. Loriabeth, however, appeared the most crestfallen, folding her arms and refusing to look at the astronomer, her face taking on the sullen, girlish aspect he thought she had lost on the trail. *A contract is more than just a piece of paper to them,* Clay realised, wondering why it hadn't occurred to him before. *It's what they live and die by.*

'Apologise,' he told Scriberson in a soft but insistent murmur.

Scriberson looked up at them all, blanching visibly under the weight of their collective judgement, all confidence apparently vanished. Now he wasn't the most educated mind amongst a group of people who had hardly ever lifted a book. Now he was a scared and weaponless youth confronted by five angry and very dangerous people. 'It . . . wasn't my intention to mislead,' he stammered after a moment. 'I just . . . need to observe the alignment. It's all I've thought about for the better part of a decade. But, for any offence caused, I offer my sincere apologies.'

'Don't fix it, son,' Skaggerhill replied before turning to Braddon. 'I vote we leave him here, Captain.'

'Seconded,' Loriabeth said, still not looking up.

'Be kinder to put a bullet in him first,' Foxbine put in.

Loriabeth's eyes flashed at Scriberson for a second. 'Got no mood to be kind.'

'Wait.' Clay stepped between them, turning to Scriberson. 'This sketch of the viewing point, you recall it well enough to draw it?'

Scriberson gave a wary nod.

'Then,' Clay said, addressing Braddon, 'we don't need a map. We got us a pair of eyes up aloft, remember? The lady can find this place.'

'The range is vast, Clay,' Braddon replied. 'Even her pet drake couldn't cover it all before the alignment.'

'There's Miss Lethridge also,' Clay ploughed on. 'I'll trance with her tomorrow. See if there's any fresh pointers from that device she brought back from Morsvale.'

'Device?' Firpike asked.

'Mind your own, Doc,' Skaggerhill told him in a tone sufficiently threatening to make the scholar retreat, though not so far as to stray from earshot.

'It's your choice, Uncle,' Clay told Braddon, moving to Scriberson's side. 'But I seen enough wrong on this trip. You leave him here, you're leaving both of us.'

Braddon said nothing for some time, though his previously

placid features had taken on a decidedly grim aspect. When he spoke his words were addressed entirely to Clay, and they brooked no discussion. 'He's your charge now. You vouched for him so you're responsible. Any more *misleadings*, and I'll expect you to deal with it.'

Clay glanced at Scriberson, noting the sheen of sweat on his skin, and nodded. 'I understand, Uncle.'

Braddon switched his gaze to Scriberson. 'Guess you better get drawing.'

Scriberson, possibly in a well-reasoned effort to curry favour, proved as capable with the railway engine as he had with the *River Maiden*'s blood-burner. They were obliged to off-load a good deal of the coal in the tender to accommodate the others, but the astronomer reckoned they still had enough for a good hundred miles' travel. Clay joined him on the platform, taking on the task of shovelling coal into the flaming maw Scriberson had named a fire-box. After a long vigil spent in close examination of the few undamaged or unmelted dials, during which time a thick pall of smoke had filled the shed to near-choking levels, Scriberson raised the largest lever amongst the bewildering array of controls. The engine issued a great hiss, steam blossoming to mingle with the smoke, as it began a slow exit from the shed. There being no way to turn the thing around, they were obliged to push the coal carriage ahead of them, the engine reversing along the track and away from the ruined settlement.

'Nicely done, Scribes.' Clay complimented the astronomer with a clap to the shoulder.

Scriberson, however, was plainly too tense to do more than nod. 'Your words of advice back on the boat,' he said, just loud enough for Clay to hear over the engine's huffing and clanking. 'About taking off. I think I've come to see your point.'

'Little late now.' His uncle was engaged in a careful examination of the sketch Scriberson had provided. It showed an expansive, flat ledge protruding from the flank of a tall, conical mountain. Clay had been somewhat disappointed to find it lacking any other distinguishing landmarks and the others remained singularly unimpressed.

'You really intend to shoot me, Clay?' Scriberson had forced a jovial tone but Clay saw the fearful cast to his eyes.

'You heard the captain.' Clay attempted a reassuring grin. 'Only if you're lying again.'

The engine made steady if ponderous progress up the successive inclines towards the valley. Scriberson's keenness as a driver didn't prevent him misjudging the speed needed to successfully traverse the repeated bends in the track, seeing them forced into an unwanted backslide or two before they finally came to level ground. Once free of the slopes the engine seemed to leap forward, smoke streaming from its stunted stack and the surrounding landscape becoming a blur of green, soon transformed into grey as they entered the valley. The track formed a straight line as the mountains rose on either side. Clay felt a rush of exhilaration as the engine fairly pelted along, experienced only once before when he had ridden on Lutharon's back.

They covered over ten miles before the track began to wind once more, following the course of the narrow stream that traced along the valley floor. Braddon waved his hat upon sighting something up ahead, a small cluster of buildings surrounding a squat wooden tower of some kind. Scriberson duly reduced speed and they glided to a gradual halt alongside the tower, Clay recognising it as a water tank from the pivot and spout affixed to its side. A half-dozen sheds and storehouses had been constructed nearby, all revealed as unoccupied after Loriabeth and Skaggerhill conducted a brief reconnaissance.

'No bodies,' the harvester reported. 'No burning either. Looks like whoever Briteshore posted here just took to their heels.'

Braddon cast a glance at the dimming sky. 'We'll lay up here tonight. Clay, I'm expecting to hear something of use come the morning.'

*

She wasn't there. All he could see was his own increasingly detailed rendering of Nelphia's peaks and valleys. He fought down an unfamiliar sensation, taking a moment to recognise it as panic. The trance, it transpired, could be a scary and lonely place without the company of another mind. His memories stirred in response to the momentary loss of control, dust rising from the moon's surface to form into the varied images conjured seemingly at random from the recesses of his mind. His father's head beyond the old pistol's sights. Derk counting loot. Speeler's murder at Bewler's Wharf. And Joya, of course. Joya dancing . . .

He reasserted control with some reluctance, wanting to watch her dance but knowing it an indulgence he couldn't afford. He had to think of what to tell his uncle. The dust settled and Nelphia's surface reverted to its usual serene starkness, spoilt only by a passing shadow, expanding and contracting as it traced across the moonscape.

At first Clay assumed it to be some vestige of memory that had escaped his control, Lutharon's silhouette perhaps, but then saw it to be a formless thing, its shape constantly changing. Also, it was dark. Dark enough to swallow all light wherever it passed.

A faint warning began to sound in Clay's head as the shadow came closer. Something Miss Lethridge had said back in Carvenport, an answer to a question he raised during their first lesson. A dumb question he realised when she replied in a tone that had been partly amused but mostly dismissive. 'It's in the nature of the trance to give birth to outlandish notions. Please set aside whatever silly stories you have heard from a drunken mouth. There are no portents in the trance, Mr Torcreek.'

Portent . . .

The shadow grew as it came closer, its edges becoming less diffuse, the shape re-forming, coalescing into something recognisable. It stretched out before him, a human figure, the proportions distorted as if cast by a low evening sun, the shape comprehensible but still vague, his mind fumbling towards recognition as it became more real. *It's holding something,* he realised. *It's holding* . . .

The trance shattered around him as the last of the Blue dwindled to nothing. The abrupt shift in sensation made him convulse and cry out from the shock of it, like being plunged into ice-cold water but much worse.

'Claydon?' He felt his uncle's hand on his shoulder as he hunched over, drawing in deep ragged breaths. 'Something happen in there?'

'Ran out of product sooner than expected is all,' he replied after a moment, forcing a smile.

'What'd she have to say?'

Clay lowered his head farther, groaning as he played for time. He had hoped to linger in the trance whilst he concocted the right lie. 'Madame has people working on the device,' he said, sensing Braddon's growing impatience. 'They ain't got anywhere yet, but she says they may have something by tomorrow. In the meantime we're to keep going, trust to Scribes's sketch.'

Braddon gave a grunt of frustration and went to the door of the small shed they had retired to till the morning. Outside Scriberson was replenishing the engine's reservoir with water from the tower, balancing on the huge cylinder as he held the spigot over the port without any offer of assistance from the others. Ethelynne had returned the previous night, Lutharon finding them with ease as he followed the tracks from the settlement. She looked over Scriberson's sketch of the viewing point with a careful eye before cheerfully announcing she had never seen it before.

'We'll scout ahead in the morning,' she promised. 'The highest peak isn't hard to find, but it is a good way off. It'll be at least a day before we can return to you.'

Clay checked the vial of Blue Ethelynne had given him, finding only a few drops left. *Enough for maybe two more trances.* 'Might be better to wait for her to come back,' he suggested as his uncle continued to linger in the doorway.

'Could be she never comes back,' Braddon replied. 'No, we keep going. Stay on this track. It's gotta lead somewhere.'

The track grew ever more winding the farther into the mountains they went and, although Clay hadn't noticed until they found themselves traversing the edge of a deep ravine, they climbed higher with every mile. The stream they had followed since the settlement had grown into a frothing torrent and the valley walls now rose in sheer cliffs, the heights veiled by the perennial mist that seemed to plague the Coppersoles.

'This is really quite the feat of engineering,' Scriberson commented as they neared the end of the ravine. 'The expense of building it must have been enormous.'

'Equal to the reward, I'm guessing,' Clay replied. His gaze lit on something up ahead, a row of posts following the course of the track. The engine moved slow enough for them to gain a full appreciation of the sight as they passed by. *Spoiled,* Clay realised, eyes flitting from one part-rotted and impaled head to another. He counted over sixty by the time they came to the end of the row.

'A warning,' he explained to a perplexed Scriberson. 'Looks like this feat of theirs wasn't managed without some trouble.'

The ravine grew wider as they moved on, transforming into a canyon whilst the ledge they traversed narrowed considerably. 'Best slow it right down, Scribes,' Clay said as his gaze followed the course of the track. Two hundred yards ahead it made a sharp turn to the right where a long cross-beam wooden bridge spanned the canyon. He took the fact that the bridge was still standing as a good sign, however, the blackened state of its woodwork did much to undermine his confidence.

'Can't be drake fire,' Skaggerhill said. They had come to a halt just short of the bridge, dismounting to assess the damage. 'It'd be ashes already.'

Clay saw his reasoning. The burning suffered by the bridge was irregular, dark in one place, lighter in another, speaking of many small fires rather than the continual blast of flame delivered by a drake. 'Spoiled,' he said. 'Revenge for that horror back there.'

'Seems they made a lousy job of it,' Braddon said before turning to Scriberson. 'You're the closest we got to an engineer. Will this thing make it over?'

Scriberson gave the bridge a long moment's scrutiny before replying simply, 'There's no way to tell.'

'Whole heap of use you are,' Skaggerhill said, rolling his eyes.

'You're insistent upon my honesty,' Scriberson pointed out. 'And the fact is, I can't judge if it'll bear the weight of the engine. The beams seem sturdy and unbowed, which is encouraging. But hardly conclusive.'

'So we leave the engine here,' Clay said.

'Wandering through these mountains on foot ain't a notion I relish,' Braddon said.

'The risk's too great, Uncle . . .'

He was interrupted by the boom of a longrifle. They all spun as one, sinking into an instinctive crouch. Preacher stood atop the coal tender, rifle smoking as he jacked another round in the chamber and aimed it back down the track, speaking a single word, 'Spoiled.'

At first it seemed to Clay there were only a few dozen of them, a knot of warriors in buckskins charging along the track, bows and spears raised as they vaulted the body of the one Preacher had shot. Then he saw the great mass following behind, so many some were forced over the edge of the cliff and into the canyon. Unfortunately, this didn't seem to dampen the ardour of their onrushing comrades one bit.

'Seems we're out of options,' Braddon observed, raising his rifle to fire off a quick shot before rushing to the engine. 'Everybody aboard! Young man, all speed if you please!'

Clay scrambled onto the platform alongside Scriberson, shovelling coal into the fire-box as fast as he could whilst the astronomer got the engine in motion. Preacher and Braddon stood tall atop the piled coal in the tender, firing regular aimed shots to conserve ammunition whilst Loriabeth and Foxbine moved to lean from the sides, guns at the ready. Steam blossomed in a thick cloud as Scriberson sought to increase the speed, the engine taking a full agonising minute to reach more than a walking pace, by which time the first of the Spoiled had reached them. One leapt onto the boiler and clawed his way towards the platform, scaled and misaligned features made even more ugly by a snarl of fury. Loriabeth put a bullet through his head before he could get within striking distance, but another two followed, with more sprinting alongside, bows raised to launch their arrows. Foxbine cut them down with a rapid salvo from her carbine, but not before a flint-tipped arrow had thrummed within an inch of Clay's head.

The two remaining Spoiled on the boiler leapt onto the platform, flint-bladed knives flashing. Clay dodged back as a blade left a nick on his forearm, drawing the Stinger and lashing out with a kick at the same time. The Spoiled recoiled then renewed his attack with barely a pause, Clay still attempting to pull the Stinger clear of its holster and wishing he had had the foresight to swallow some product. A loud clang sounded as the coal shovel came down on the Spoiled's head, making him stagger. Firpike gave a somewhat hysterical and high-pitched cry as he brought the shovel down again, but this time the Spoiled was quick enough to parry the blow, forearm stopping the shovel blade short of his head and drawing his knife back for a thrust. The Stinger finally came free of Clay's holster, bucking in his hand as he blasted the Spoiled off the platform.

He turned in time to see Scriberson haul the other Spoiled away from Loriabeth, his arm fixed on the warrior's throat in a choke hold as he thrashed. Loriabeth put the muzzle of her revolver against the Spoiled's head then cursed when the hammer fell on an empty chamber. She flipped the revolver, catching hold of the barrel and repeatedly clubbing the Spoiled until he sagged, whereupon she and Scriberson wrestled his limp form off the engine.

A shout dragged Clay's attention to the coal tender and he whirled to see Braddon grappling with a large Spoiled almost his equal in stature whilst Preacher and Skaggerhill were fully engaged in methodically shooting the archers running alongside. Silverpin leapt towards Braddon, spear-point lancing out to skewer his assailant neatly through the neck. Another clambered over the side at her back, raising a flint-bladed knife for a killing strike then falling dead as Clay put two shots into his back.

He turned back to the engine, Stinger ready as another group of Spoiled attempted to launch themselves on board. However, Scriberson had built enough steam now to out-run them and the Spoiled could only howl in frustration as their arrows clattered against the engine's iron flanks. The firing died down as they drew away from the pursuing mass, Clay realising they were about halfway along the bridge's span.

Something flickered in the corner of Clay's vision and he turned to see a cascade of fire-arrows arcing away from the massed Spoiled at the edge of the canyon. He prepared to duck but quickly realised the arrows were aimed at something else. Following the stream of flaming shafts he saw them streak below the span of the bridge, impacting on something ahead of the engine. After a moment a large wall of smoke began to blossom and Clay leaned out from the platform to peer through the bridge's beams.

'Stop!' he shouted, seeing the burgeoning flames below. They spread quickly up the bridge's criss-crossed timbers, unnaturally quickly it seemed to him. 'Stop, dammit!' he yelled at Scriberson.

The alarm in his voice clearly held sufficient weight for the astronomer to haul on the brake-lever, sparks flying as the engine began to slow. Watching the flames rise ever higher Clay knew with sickening certainty that they weren't going to make it.

'Jump!' he cried out, pushing Loriabeth off the platform. Luckily she proved too surprised to combat the hard shove he gave her, falling free with a sudden and profane exclamation. Firpike had evidently already seen the danger and jumped clear without any urging, quickly followed by Silverpin and Scriberson.

Clay was about to jump himself when he saw his uncle and Skaggerhill crouching at the rear of the engine platform. 'We gotta get off this thing!' he said, rushing towards them then drawing up short at the sight of Foxbine. She lay on her back, revolver in one hand whilst her other clutched the arrow embedded in her chest. Her face was drained of all colour though some life lingered in her eyes. Skaggerhill and Braddon made ready to lift her but she gave a soft shake of her head, lips moving as they formed a smile. Clay couldn't hear the words above the growing roar of flames but could read the meaning. 'One hundred and twenty of the bastards. Who'd have thought it?'

'Uncle!' Clay said as Braddon and the harvester continued to kneel, even though Foxbine's eyes had closed.

Braddon glanced up at him before gently disentangling Foxbine's revolver from her hand and nodding at Skaggerhill. Clay didn't linger, launching himself from the platform with what proved to be an unwise amount of energy. He skidded over the beams towards the edge of the span, arms windmilling as he gaped at the rushing water far below. Someone grabbed the scruff of his shirt and dragged him back.

'Hope you got some product left,' Braddon said, releasing him and nodding at the engine. It had drifted into the flames now, a barely discernible bulk amidst the roiling smoke. After a few seconds a great cracking noise rose from the bridge, accompanied by a shudder that made the beams tremble beneath their feet. The span beneath the engine gave way with a shriek of rent metal as the rails buckled, locomotive and tender plummeting down into the gap, taking Foxbine with it.

'Must've coated the bridge in oil,' Braddon mused, turning to regard the Spoiled who were now standing in a large cluster at the far end of the bridge. 'Chased us right into a trap.'

'Never suspected they'd have the brains for a thing like that,' Skaggerhill muttered.

Clay peered through the beams once more, watching the fire leap from timber to timber, building all the while. He looked at the gap left by the engine's fall, judging the distance as a good twenty feet and then another twenty feet of bridge to reach the other side. Easy for him, not for them. He took the wallet from his pocket, extracting one of the two Green vials and casting a desperate glance at his uncle.

'Loriabeth and Silverpin,' Braddon said, gaze steady and brooking no argument.

Clay nodded and drank a full vial. The others had all come running to stand nearby, the expectation of imminent death writ large on each face. Clay strode towards Loriabeth, grabbing her about the waist without preamble and hoisting her over his shoulder. 'What in the . . .' she began, starting to struggle then stopping as he squeezed her tight enough to force the air from her lungs.

'No time, cuz.'

He sprinted for the gap and leapt, covering the distance easily. They landed hard enough to jolt Loriabeth from his shoulder. She lay gasping on the rails, staring up at him in blank amazement. 'No lingering, Lori,' he told her, pointing to the edge of the canyon ahead.

'Pa . . .' she began but he had already turned away. Another leap brought him down next to Firpike who babbled a desperate entreaty before Clay ran to Silverpin. He found her face more confused than he could remember, mingling anger and reluctance but his Green-borne speed gave her no time to object. He felt the product ebbing quickly as he landed the second time. He paused only for a second to press a kiss to Silverpin's cheek before making the return leap, landing amidst a flurry of arrows. The Spoiled had seen what he was about and didn't like it.

Braddon and Preacher were firing their longrifles at the few Spoiled who had chosen to charge across the bridge, willing to die rather than allow their escape. Clay took Scriberson next, batting away Firpike's clutching hands before launching himself across once more.

'You don't have enough, do you?' Scriberson asked, coughing as the flames and smoke rose ever higher.

Clay just pointed him towards the far end of the bridge and drank his last vial of Green. Skaggerhill had to be wrestled into submission before Clay could convey him across whilst Preacher simply shouldered his rifle and stood in expectant silence. On landing he got to his feet and strode wordlessly towards the other side.

'Uncle . . .' Clay began upon his next landing, casting a pointed glance at a now-hunched and weeping Firpike as Braddon fired off another longrifle round. 'I don't have enough left . . .'

'Take him,' Braddon said.

'Uncle . . .'

'On your way, Claydon.' Braddon jacked another round into the chamber and raised the rifle to his shoulder. Clay knew he could over-power him, carry them both over then watch Firpike's fiery demise as the bridge finally gave way. But he couldn't. His uncle was the captain after all.

'Get up, you bastard,' he told Firpike, jerking him to his feet. The scholar was all tears and thanks as Clay launched them into the air, choking off as they landed. Flames were licking up through the beams now so he used up the last of the Green by throwing Firpike towards the others, now gathered on hard ground where the bridge met the canyon edge.

He turned back, fumbling for the wallet and peering through the smoke to find Braddon's shadowy form. His gaze snapped towards the faint report of a rifle-shot and he pulled the vial of Black from the wallet; Auntie's gift, still almost half-full. He threw it down his throat, grimacing at the burn and casting the force out like a whip. He felt rather than saw it take hold, concentrating hard. He had lifted heavier things than his uncle before but this was still tricky. Blood-blessed rarely used Black on other people unless to do deliberate harm, the force unleashed being so powerful and hard to control. Relief surged through him as Braddon rose clear of the smoke, staring down at his nephew as he passed overhead with the only expression of surprise Clay had ever seen on his face. He guided Braddon over the rest of the span then released him a few feet above the ground.

A wave of nausea made him stagger, sending him to his knees, coughing in the smoke. *The shadow,* he thought, recalling the trance and feeling the bridge shudder as something vital gave way. *Seems some stories ain't so fanciful . . .*

Something looped over his head and drew tight around his chest. He had time to recognise it as a rope before it tightened yet further, drawing an involuntary yell as the cord dug into his flesh. The bridge issued a final, almost plaintive moan accompanied by the matchwood-like cracking of multiple timbers, then he was falling, heat washing over his skin in brief but painful waves before he met the unforgiving embrace of the canyon wall. He hung there for a time, gazing down at the bridge's remnants, smoking timbers and mangled rails cascading into the white water to be swept away in a cloud of steam.

He passed out as they began to haul him up the rock-face with hard, jolting heaves. *Silverpin,* he knew. Somehow it could only have been her. *What is she . . . ?*

CHAPTER 36

Lizanne

Waves. She drifted for a time, lost in the numbing grasp of the harbour depths. She thought she must have died, for there was a memory of darkness, a moment when all sensation fled and she felt the beating of her heart slow to a weak, arrhythmic flutter. But then came hard, insistent jolts and a flaring agony in her chest as something pressed down into her sternum, shoving and shoving. After a while it all went away again and she lost herself in the water's welcoming chill, and now she could see waves up above, the surface seen from below, catching the light of a fading sun. A pleasing sight to take to wherever she was going . . .

A grating catch caught in Lizanne's throat, provoking a coughing fit. She convulsed as the cough continued, tears streaming from her eyes and chest aching from the effort. When it faded she lay back, feeling something soft beneath her. *The sea-bed,* she decided, looking up at the waves once more. She blinked and the waves were abruptly transformed into the wind-ruffled canvas of a tent roof. Further frantic investigation revealed that she was in fact lying on a narrow cot rather than the mud of the harbour floor.

'I'm alive,' she tried to say, but instead the words birthed another round of coughing.

'Easy now, young miss.' Soft but insistent hands on her brow and her back, easing her down onto the cot. Lizanne blinked again, the tears clearing to reveal a kindly face of Old Colonial complexion, a face it took her a moment to recognise.

'Mrs Torcreek,' she said, the words scraping from her throat like wood on sandpaper.

'Indeed so.' Fredabel stepped away for a second then returned with a cup of water. 'And you are Miss Lethridge. Here, drink this.'

The liquid slid down her throat bringing blessed relief, and also a rush of memory. 'The Blues!' Lizanne jerked upright, mind filling with the sight of the Corvantine fleet facing destruction. 'They were at the mole . . .'

'Still are. Swimming back and forth and roasting anyone fool enough to venture out there.'

'The Corvantines?'

'All their ships are either sunk or fled. And their army ain't in any better shape. Never been so thankful to live in a city with walls.'

'Their army?'

Fredabel glanced at the tent-flap behind her. 'Got folks waiting to tell you all about it. But you need a sight more rest first.'

'The device,' Lizanne said, pushing the woman's restraining hand away and pulling back the blankets. 'I had a device . . .'

'Big Corvantine fella's got hold of that, don't you worry. Same one fished you outta the harbour.'

The jolts to her chest . . . *He brought me back*. 'I can't stay here,' she insisted, but Fredabel quickly dispelled any notions of rising by the ease with which she pressed her back onto the mattress. 'Green,' Lizanne said, feeling her vision dim. 'Give me a vial of Green.'

'Oh no.' Fredabel shook her head and firmly tucked the blanket around Lizanne's limp form. 'You've had enough of that for now. Dealt with the worst of your breaks and burns, but I seen folks die if they partake of too much.'

She gave a tight smile as she smoothed the hair back from Lizanne's forehead. 'Miss, I gotta know. You have anything to tell me about my family?'

'They were alive,' Lizanne said, the words emerging in a murmur as the wall of sleep descended. 'When last I looked . . .'

'Y̶ou would have me believe Madame Bondersil was in the employ of the Imperial Cadre?'

Garrison Commander Stavemoor was a bewhiskered man of portly dimensions. Lizanne estimated his age as closer to sixty than fifty and could see the greyness of his skin beneath the voluminous facial hair, the complexion of a man nearing exhaustion. In addition to the commander, the Ironship delegation consisted of a reed-thin woman Lizanne knew to be the Exceptional Initiatives Agent-in-Charge in Carvenport, and two senior managers, one of Accounts, the other Personnel. These last two were both so nondescript and cravenly avoiding of responsibility her mind hadn't bothered to retain their names.

'What you believe is a matter for you,' Lizanne replied, sinking wearily into the chair behind Madame's vacant desk. She was barely an hour from her hospital bed, Mrs Torcreek having released her only after a full day's rest. The makeshift hospital that now crowded the parks of Colonial Town seemed to have become a personal fiefdom for the Contractor's wife, a measure of the respect in which her family was held and a reflection of the woman's formidable organisational talents. Doctors and nurses alike deferred to her in most things and the many wounded soldiers and townsfolk regarded her with a deep affection. Consequently, she had little trouble in forcing what was left of Carvenport's senior management to wait before allowing Lizanne to be questioned.

'You presume a great deal,' the commander went on, casting a pointed glance at the chair.

'I just need a place to sit.' Lizanne reclined, settling into the leather padding. It was cool against her neck, much of her hair having been shorn away so that she now sported a ragged bob that did little to enhance her appearance, as did the partially laundered overalls she wore. Her education had been rich in lessons on the value of proper attire and personal ablutions but now she found she couldn't care one whit for such frippery.

The Agent-in Charge placed a restraining hand on the commander's arm as he bristled yet further. 'Miss Lethridge,' she said in a gentle tone, offering what Lizanne assumed to be an uncharacteristic smile. 'You have an overdue report to make, if you recall.'

You've been out of the field too long, Lizanne deduced, noting the ill-fitting expression of interested concern on the woman's face. 'I made my report to Madame Bondersil on arrival,' she said. 'The fact that she failed to pass it on is telling, wouldn't you say? As is the fact that since my return to this continent I haven't set eyes on you until now.'

The woman stood a little straighter, though Lizanne heard the barely suppressed quaver in her voice as she replied, 'Madame was given full authority by the Board. Any unfortunate actions on her part were performed without my knowledge . . .'

'It doesn't matter,' Lizanne interrupted, waving a weary and dismissive hand. 'Don't you understand? None of this matters now. You have seen what transpired outside the harbour, I assume? And, I'm given to understand, a similar calamity has befallen the Corvantine forces beyond our walls. Our time on this continent is coming to a swift end. Its former owner is keen to reclaim possession and evict the current tenants.'

'How could you know that?' Stavemoor demanded. 'Certainly recent occurrences have been . . . dramatic and very strange. But we still hold a strong position. And have plentiful supplies.'

Lizanne's eyes drifted to the solargraph. It sat on the desk where Arberus had placed it before being escorted from the room, gears and cogs gleaming in the dim light offered by this subterranean refuge. *What were you trying to tell us?* she asked the Mad Artisan's ghost, the drake memory Clay had shared with her at the forefront of her mind. *How to find it? Or how to kill it?*

'Can you put a roof over this city?' she asked the Commander. 'Because that alone might save us. The mole will keep the Blues out, the walls the Greens. But what about the Reds and the Blacks?'

'We are not defenceless.' Stavemoor's tone belied his words and Lizanne was appalled to see tears shining in his eyes.

'You have family here, sir?' she asked him.

He took a moment to compose himself before replying, blinking and allowing tears to flow into his whiskers. 'My daughter, and two grandsons.'

'I also have family,' she said, Tekela's face looming large in her head, along with Jermayah's and, she was surprised to find, that of Major Arberus. She looked at the Agent-in-Charge, finding her in a barely more controlled state than the commander. A realisation came to her as she took in the full measure of their desperation. *They haven't come for answers, but guidance.* Madame had exercised control over appointments here for years, and apparently stacked the deck with those she knew would never challenge her.

'I have some suggestions,' Lizanne said, leaning forward and clasping her hands together on the desk. 'If you would care to listen.'

She toured the walls with the gaggle of managers in tow, finding the trenches all abandoned now. 'Ordered everyone back to the walls once it became clear what was happening to the enemy,' Stavemoor explained. 'Keeping out drakes is what they were originally built for, after all.'

Lizanne lifted her gaze from the empty trenches to the tree-line and jungle beyond, except much of the jungle seemed to have disappeared. Great swathes were burned to ash and others little more than blackened stumps. The devastation covered at least two square miles and amidst it all the Corvantine dead lay in mounds. Apparently they had clustered together in desperation, only to be surrounded by the swarming Greens and roasted to death.

'Started around the same time as the business at the harbour,' the commander said. 'Didn't know what was happening at first, o' course. Just a lot of flames leaping up and such. Thought some Corvantine fool had set light to their own ammunition stores. Then came the screams and the runners, hundreds of them streaming towards us. Assumed it was another attack, as anyone would have done. We must've cut down about half before we realised they were begging for help. Got about three hundred under guard now. That Corvantine traitor questioned them. Seems the drakes started attacking their perimeter without warning. Great hordes of Greens, plus a Red or two.'

'But they haven't come for us,' Lizanne said, still peering at the ruined jungle. 'Yet.'

'A Red came flying over this morning. Didn't get low enough for a shot though.'

Lizanne turned and scanned the expanse of Carvenport from end to end. Her gaze roamed over the residential districts damaged by the Corvantine bombardment, the densely packed ships in the harbour, and the untouched majesty of Company Square where the various corporate headquarters still stood tall, Ironship House tallest of all. *Can you put a roof over this city . . . ?*

'How many Growlers do we have in total?' she asked the commander.

'Fifty or so, but ammunition is down to one-third what it was when the siege began.'

'I would *suggest*,' she said, choosing to phrase this carefully, 'putting half on the roofs in Company Square, reinforced by Mr Tollermine's Thumper. The rest will be placed on the walls along with every surviving Contractor, since they know best how to deal with Drakes. Mr Tollermine, in concert with every other artisan and able pair of hands in this city, should be put to work manufacturing more Thumpers and requisite ammunition.'

'You believe we should try to hold them off?' Stavemoor asked.

'For now at least.' She nodded at the harbour. 'Taking ship and trying to fight our way through a sea full of enraged Blues is not an inviting prospect, even if we could fit every soul in Carvenport into those vessels.'

'Actually, miss,' the Manager of Accounts spoke up, a corpulent fellow with an unnaturally dark moustache and a shiny bald pate that shimmered as the sun caught the sweat beading his skin. 'I have calculated that, if properly organised, the merchant and Protectorate vessels currently at anchor could carry two-thirds of our population.'

Two-thirds. Meaning we would have to choose which third would be left behind. 'A measure to be explored only in dire necessity,' Lizanne said, forgetting the pretence of deference for the moment. She was gratified to see the man's reluctant nod, and the lack of objection from his colleagues. Her short journey to the walls had engendered a peculiar realisation that partly explained the managers' acceptance of her authority. It appeared her intervention against the Blood Cadre had done much to enhance her standing. It was there in the grave nods of respect from Contractor and soldier alike, in the shouted thanks and the name they murmured as she passed by. Of course, few, if any, even knew her true name. Instead they had crafted a new one: 'Miss Blood.'

'Has there been any further communication from the Board?' she asked, turning back to Commander Stavemoor.

'This morning,' he said. 'Recent developments have clearly given them much to think on. But they did report the Protectorate Main Battle Fleet continues to muster off Feros and will be at full strength within seven days. An expeditionary force of two full divisions is also being organised, though now it appears they'll be fighting drakes rather than Corvantines.'

Seven days to muster the fleet, another three weeks to sail here, assuming they make it through the Strait and any Blues that might be waiting. 'So,' she said, imbuing her tone with a less-than-sincere note of optimism. 'All we need do is hold out for another month.'

There was no agreement on their faces, just numb acceptance shot through with a twitch of suppressed panic. *This would have been the core of your new enterprise?* she wondered, thinking of

Madame's surety in those final moments on the mole and wondering if ambition, the most cherished trait in this corporate world of theirs, wasn't itself just another form of madness.

'Perhaps,' she said, pointing them towards the city, 'we should get to work?'

'It's not enough,' she told Jermayah as he laboured at the workbench. At her insistence his tools and equipment had been shifted to a large warehouse near the docks where all the city's artisan class had been gathered to work under his guidance.

'Enough or not,' Jermayah grunted, tightening a bolt on a part-completed Thumper breech. 'You asked how many we can make in a week, and ten is the answer. That's if you want them to have any shells to fire.'

'If it's a question of labour, I can draft in more hands,' she said.

'Unskilled hands.' He cast a glance over his shoulder at the two hundred or so artisans labouring in the warehouse. 'It's all I can do to get this lot to understand the basic mechanics of the thing.' He sighed, seeing her expression. 'More hands would help with the ammo count. And the rate of Thumper production will increase once they've gotten used to the techniques. And we could use more Blood-blessed to shift the raw materials around. You should have thirty by the end of the second week.'

She moved closer, speaking in an earnest whisper. 'I have serious doubts we'll last that long. *Please* Jermayah. Anything you can do . . .'

He sighed again and she saw how tired he was, his sagging features and too-bright eyes speaking of an over-indulgence in Green. She would have dearly loved to order him to sleep, but dare not with so much depending on his expertise. 'It'll mean stopping production for a day to reorganise,' he warned. 'Make this place a proper manufactory, so components are made separately then assembled.'

'But if it works?' she prompted.

'Twenty Thumpers by the end of the week.' He shrugged. 'Maybe. The artisans won't like it though, turning them into piece-workers.'

'I doubt they'll like the prospect of Blacks and Reds burning the city down around them either. Do whatever you need to do. I'll have Commander Stavemoor allocate a company to this place. For security purposes, of course. But don't feel shy about employing their services if the grumbling gets out of hand.'

He nodded then allowed his gaze to drift to Tekela. Lizanne had pressed her into service as an assistant and she followed her everywhere with note-book in hand and a large canvas bag over her shoulder. 'Take it no-one else has looked at it?' Jermayah asked, nodding at the tell-tale bulge in the bag.

'No,' Lizanne replied. 'And no-one will until we have time for a proper study.'

'I trust you won't forget me when that time comes.' He gave a wistful grin. 'Most wondrous bit of engineering I ever saw.'

'He showed me before he died,' the Corvantine woman said in the kind of flowing Eutherian spoken only by those born to the noble class, albeit choked with emotion. She was probably quite a beauty under the grime and soot that covered her face and matted her hair. *She's not Cadre,* Lizanne had decided almost instantly, taking in the woman's impractical attire of pleated riding skirt and intricately embroidered bodice. Whatever her station or prior responsibilities, the woman remained the only Corvantine Blood-blessed taken alive. Arberus had found her amongst the subdued mass of prisoners when a vial of product slipped from her sleeve during interrogation. He had brought her to the basement office where Lizanne allowed a short trance communication with Morsvale, the results of which were not encouraging.

'It was burning,' the woman went on. 'The slums atop the sea-wall went first, Blues rising up to torch them from end to end. Then a mass of Reds came screaming out of the sky. He . . .' The woman managed to stifle a sob. 'It was happening around him when he tranced with me . . . He could have run but he stayed and tranced at the scheduled time. I felt him burn . . .' Her composure failed and she began to weep, huddling into herself and appearing very young. Lizanne permitted her a few minutes before asking another question.

'What is your name? I understand you refused to give it to Major Arberus.'

The woman wiped her eyes and breathed deeply, some vestige of a no-doubt-customary poise returning as she straightened in her seat. 'Electress Dorice Vol Arramyl.'

Electress. The third-highest rank in the Imperial hierarchy. Noble blood indeed. 'What are you if you're not Cadre?' Lizanne asked.

'I am . . . was second cousin by marriage to Grand Marshal Morradin. He asked me to accompany him on this expedition, so as to provide a secure line of communication with Morsvale and the Imperial Command.'

'Don't the Cadre normally provide such services?'

'The Grand Marshal had little regard for the Cadre. Also, some recent failure of theirs in Morsvale had made him very angry, and somewhat mistrustful. Besides, I was keen to witness his victory.' A faint, grim amusement ghosted across her face. 'I thought it might prove a novel and diverting adventure.'

'You can trance to the Imperial Command?' Arberus asked her.

The woman stiffened, her voice taking on an icy tone as she addressed her reply to Lizanne. 'As a prisoner of war, must I suffer the indignity of being questioned by a traitor?'

Lizanne leaned closer to her, smiling sweetly, voice soft. 'My dear Electress, you will suffer whatever indignity I heap upon your dainty shoulders and ask for more, or I'll drop you outside the walls and you can go and find your second cousin. Answer the major's question.'

The woman blanched a little but managed to retain her

composure, replying in a clipped voice, 'The Blood Imperial and I have a trance connection, yes.'

The Blood Imperial. Lizanne drew back a little, trying to disguise her surprise. The Blood Imperial was the most highly placed Blood-blessed in the empire, answering only to the Emperor himself. At any other time capturing this woman would have outshone all other achievements in Lizanne's career, but now she was just another fearful soul desperate for protection.

'When is your next scheduled communication with the Blood Imperial?' Lizanne asked.

The Electress glanced at the clock on Madame's former desk. 'In a little over four hours. I realise I am at your mercy, and have already besmirched my honour in speaking so plainly. But I beg you, do not force me into a traitor's role.' Her hands reached for Lizanne's, soft fluttering fingers in torn lace gloves. 'I beseech you . . .'

'Oh shut up,' Lizanne snapped. 'And stop mewling so, it's extremely aggravating.'

She moved behind the desk and took a seat, reaching for pen and paper. 'I will give you a message to memorise,' she told the Electress as she wrote in Eutherian. 'You will relate it to the Blood Imperial word for word. You will also show him everything you have seen during your diverting adventure and request that he convey it all to the Emperor with utmost urgency.' She finished writing and blotted the ink dry before tossing the page across the desk to the Electress. 'Read it. I'm sure you'll find it contains nothing that would further besmirch your honour. Major Arberus will provide a vial of Blue at the allotted time. When it's done, you can make yourself useful in our new manufactory. They need help shifting the steel ingots from the store to the smelter.'

'What do you expect this to achieve?' Arberus asked, smoke blossoming as he lit a cigarillo then proffered the case. Realising she hadn't had a smoke in several weeks Lizanne took one, leaning close as he shared the flame from his match, then savouring the burn of Dalcian leaf on her tongue.

'Probably nothing,' she said, groaning a little as the smoke rushed from her mouth into the cool night air. They had left the Electress under guard in the office and repaired to the walls where a large number of soldiers and Contractors stared out at the ashes in tense expectation. 'At the very least,' she went on, taking another deep draw from the cigarillo, 'it might persuade the Emperor that his cherished war will be best postponed for the foreseeable future.'

'She says she saw Morradin fall,' he said, his voice possessed of a reflective tone rather than the satisfaction she expected. 'Went down fighting, as you'd expect. Blazing away with a revolver as the Greens swarmed all around. Perhaps one day the Emperor will have a picture painted to commemorate such a heroic end.'

Lizanne's gaze tracked over the copious Corvantine dead still littering the ground beyond the trenches. 'No such honours for them, I expect.'

'Of course not. Why waste paint on a mass of dead commoners?' He rested his forearms on the parapet, face grim as he looked down on the bodies of his countrymen. 'How many of them even understood what they were dying for, I wonder? Come all this way to face slaughter in pursuit of profit, and it's all pointless anyway.'

She paused, watching his sorrow for a time and wondering if his irksome fanaticism might have eroded amidst all this fury. *He would be so much more interesting without it.* 'I believe I have been remiss in not thanking you before now,' she said. 'Mrs Torcreek told me it was you who pulled me from the harbour.'

He gave a half smile. 'I wondered where you'd gone to after such an intense conversation with Mr Tollermine. As for pulling you out, I had help from a couple of Blood-blessed stevedores. It seemed they were appreciative of your work in the trenches. To be completely honest, we'd probably both have drowned without them.'

A scream sounded out in the darkness beyond the walls and a ripple of alarm ran through the soldiers and Contractors on either side. The moons were hidden behind a thick blanket of cloud so the night was an unknowable void, pregnant with whatever fears the mind chose to conjure. 'Green,' one of the Contractors said, a youthful marksman Lizanne recognised from Captain Flaxknot's company. 'Pack-leader I reckon.'

They listened in silence for several minutes but no more screams came. 'What is doing this?' Arberus wondered aloud in Eutherian.

Lizanne hesitated before replying, uncertain how much she should reveal. After a moment's consideration, however, it occurred to her that circumstances made her deeply habituated secrecy redundant. 'The White,' she said. 'The White is doing this.'

Seeing his bafflement she sighed and spoke on. 'Ironship sent a company of Contractors into the Interior, guided by whatever intelligence I might discover during my mission. It transpires Burgrave Artonin's suspicions were correct; the White, sadly, is no myth.' She went on to describe Clay's discovery of Ethelynne Drystone and the drake's memory she had shared. 'The Longrifles are at the Coppersoles now,' she concluded. 'Where it seems they may actually have a chance of finding its lair.'

'And then?'

'Mr Torcreek will attempt to kill it and put an end to this havoc.'

'Is such a thing even possible?'

She gave a short laugh and took a final draw on her cigarillo before flicking the butt out into the darkness. 'I am increasingly of the opinion that, when it comes to this continent, the notion of impossibility has little meaning.'

CHAPTER 37

Clay

Clay woke to find himself lying near a camp-fire, the sky dark overhead and the Longrifles all sitting around in grim silence. On seeing him wake, his uncle got to his feet and kicked dust over the fire. 'Gotta keep moving. Spoiled might well find a way around that canyon.'

So they marched through the night, Clay stumbling along at the rear of the company as they followed the tracks ever deeper into the mountains. The passage was narrower now, and the walls of rock on either side taller. The absence of cover forced Braddon to set a punishing pace, calling a rest when the channel finally opened out into a broad valley and the track descended to follow the course of the river running through it. They made camp on a low rise a short distance from the track, where Clay sank down to huddle close to the fire. He had only his duster for warmth, most of everything having been lost with the engine.

'You threw the rope, right?' he asked Silverpin as she came to his side. His teeth chattered a little as she wrapped her arms around him. The effects of ingesting such a copious amount of product so quickly were taking a while to fade. Also, inhaling so much smoke left him with a grating cough. 'Quite a feat. Wouldn't have thought it possible if I hadn't seen it.'

She just shrugged and held him closer until sleep claimed him.

There were no words said for Foxbine, no ceremony or exchange of reminiscences. In fact the only acknowledgment of her passing came when Braddon handed Loriabeth the gunhand's revolver. 'You're First Gunhand now. She would've wanted you to have this.'

Loriabeth took the weapon with barely a nod, though Clay could see she was fighting tears. *No time for grief in the Interior,* he realised, seeing how Braddon resisted the urge to reach out a comforting hand to his daughter.

'So what now?' Firpike asked, hunched over and staring at the smoking embers of the camp-fire.

'We keep on the track,' Braddon told him simply.

'I don't wish to speak out of turn, Captain,' the scholar said, not looking up, though a cautious anger had crept into his tone. 'But I can't help but notice our complete lack of provisions.'

'We could always eat you,' Loriabeth muttered. 'Though I'd most likely choke on your bitter flesh.'

'Looks like we won't have to worry on that score,' Skaggerhill said, standing and nodding to the south where a large winged shape descended through the misty-morning air. Lutharon flared his wings as he approached the camp, talons opening to deposit the carcass of a large-horned goat in their midst before coming to earth a short distance away.

'Quite the mess you made,' Ethelynne said, climbing down from the drake's back. 'I would estimate two thousand Spoiled are now rushing in pursuit. They're at least a day behind though, so no need for immediate concern.' She paused to survey their diminished company. 'The red-haired lady?'

Braddon gave a wordless shake of his head.

'Oh, my condolences. Still, I have news which may brighten the day.' She pulled Scriberson's sketch from her coat of rags, holding it up with a slightly smug expression. 'I found it.'

Braddon had contrived to secure their maps before leaping from the engine and spread them out on the ground so Ethelynne could point out their destination. 'There's a Briteshore settlement at the base of the mountain,' she said. 'It looks to have been abandoned, though they left behind a good quantity of mining gear. I assume their surveyors found the place worthy of exploration thanks to the platform carved into the mountain side, it clearly being of artificial construction.'

'Looks like a steep climb,' Skaggerhill commented, tracing the flanks of the mountain with his stubby finger, 'Unless your drake'd be willing to carry us all up there one at a time, ma'am.'

'That won't be necessary,' she said with a cryptic grin. 'You'll see why when we get there.'

'Ten days' march,' Braddon said, eyes intent on the chart. 'Maybe more depending on how rough the country is.'

'Then we'd best be getting on,' Clay said, rising to his feet. A hearty meal of roasted goat had restored a good deal of his strength. Also, his brief trance with Miss Lethridge that morning left little doubt as to the urgency of their situation. He had chosen not to impart the news to the others, unsure how they would react and keen not to allow any distractions from their course. *It may well know you're coming,* Miss Lethridge had warned after replaying the memory of Madame Bondersil's aborted betrayal and the Corvantine fleet's destruction. *I wish I had some guidance to offer . . .*

Doubt there's much you could say right now that could help, he replied. *Gotta find this thing and kill it. That's all there is.*

They left the track behind two days later, striking out towards the west across a series of hills. Lutharon kept them well supplied with goats come the evenings and Ethelynne provided reports on the progress of their pursuers. 'They grow in number every day,' she said on the third night since leaving the track. 'Several tribes appear to have joined forces. All very strange since they usually spend as much time fighting each other as they do the Briteshore Headhunters.'

'Maybe they got tired of being hunted,' Clay suggested. 'If Briteshore was stepping up its claims here, could be they decided it was time to band together or die.'

'Nah,' Skaggerhill said, slicing a chunk of meat from the flank of the goat he had roasted. 'Something's changed 'em. Like those we saw at Fallsguard and the temple. Like the lake Greens. Can't help but take note that a lotta things been changing since we started on this course.'

Preacher stiffened a little and Clay knew he was resisting the urge to give voice to some more scripture. However, Firpike clearly had no reluctance in speaking his mind. 'I do grow ever more curious as to what exactly your course is,' he said, looking intently at Braddon. 'It's plain to me that you aren't on any drake-hunting expedition. And no-one has stated explicitly what you expect to find at this mysterious destination.'

Skaggerhill turned towards him, face dark and lips forming a threat, but stopped as Braddon raised a hand. 'You're a clever fella, Doc. I feel sure you can reckon it out.'

Firpike's gaze flicked over them all, narrowing in calculation. 'And if I do you'll finally have a reason to kill me?'

'Got plenty of those already,' Loriabeth muttered.

'The White,' Scriberson said, favouring Firpike with a humourless smile. 'They're here for the White, on Ironship orders if I'm not mistaken.'

Firpike started a little and Clay realised this particular notion hadn't factored into his thinking. He watched the scholar's eyes widen then narrow again. 'It's a myth,' he said finally. 'It's extinct, if it ever truly existed.'

'Really?' Braddon said, raising an eyebrow in Ethelynne's direction. 'Guess that makes you a liar, Miss Drystone.'

Firpike stared at her for some time as she smiled and ate her supper. 'Ethelynne Drystone,' he said finally. 'The Wittler Expedition.'

'Quite so,' she said.

'And the only living soul to have clapped eyes on a real live White Drake,' Braddon said. 'Guess that'll be something you can write another book about. But it's the only profit you're like to make from this enterprise, Doc, 'cause I'll be Seer-damned if you're getting a share of my company's earnings.'

*

The better part of three days' march brought the mountain into view. In accordance with Scriberson's description it stood amongst the tallest peaks they had yet seen, its flanks steeper and more forbidding than those around it, rising to a point that resembled a sharpened spike at this distance. 'Briteshore chart calls it "The Nail,"' Braddon said, checking the map. 'Guess you can see why.'

The settlement stood at a short remove from the base of the mountain, smaller than the installation on the lake-shore but similarly protected by a tall defensive wall. Ethelynne's cryptic response to Skaggerhill's request that she have Lutharon fly them to the platform was explained by the series of pylons extending away from the settlement to ascend the mountain, dual cables arcing between each pair.

'Hope it's in working condition,' the harvester said, casting a wary glance at the mist-shrouded peak above.

The settlement proved to be unravaged and well-stocked. The former inhabitants had left without pausing to secure the gate or pack up any of the copious supplies. 'Spoiled scared 'em off, maybe?' Loriabeth suggested.

'Or perhaps they didn't like what they found here,' Scriberson said.

'Check the cable-car wheel-house, if you would, young man,' Braddon told him. 'Skaggs, go with him. Everyone else spread out and see what you can find. Not you, Doc,' he added as Firpike took an eager step towards the hut bearing the sign 'Site-Manager's Office.' 'You get on up that ladder and keep watch. Be sure to sing out real loud if the Spoiled come along.'

'Take an age to sift through all this,' he said, a short while later after he and Clay had gone through the office, finding desks and cabinets fairly brimming with documents. 'Mostly accounts and work schedules, far as I can tell. Can't see nothing that gives a clear idea of their purpose here.'

Clay noticed a calendar on the back of the door and took it down to flip through the months, finding various notes scribbled here and there. '"Cable project complete,"' he read, pointing to the 37th of Mortallum. 'Near two months ago.' He flipped forward, skimming over brief references to supply runs and pay-days, stopping at the final entry on the 9th of Verester, which read: 'First excavation initiated.'

'Nothing after that.' He turned the other pages. 'Looks like they started digging then took off soon after. This place has been empty for the best part of a month.'

'Clay,' Braddon said, pulling a sheaf of papers from the desk. 'This seem familiar to you?'

'Looks kinda similar to the city,' Clay said, eyes roving over the characters pencilled onto the papers. Line after line of pictograms possessing a faint resemblance to the inscriptions Ethelynne had spent so much time translating in the ruined city. However, that writing had displayed a certain flowing elegance in the way the different characters were shaped and arranged, their meaning unknowable but their form still capable of conveying an impression of poetry. This script was much more ordered and precise, the characters formed with a uniform exactitude. 'Copy of something they found in the mountain, maybe?'

'Maybe,' Braddon agreed, frowning at the last sheet in the bundle. 'If so, looks like they got awful tired of it.' The characters inscribed on this sheet began like the others, neat and precise at the top, but becoming much more contorted as they proceeded down the page. It looked to Clay as if whoever had scribbled this down had done so in haste or with an increasingly palsied, near-frenzied hand. The final set of symbols had been inscribed with such energy the paper was ripped in several places.

'Miss Ethelynne might be able to read it,' he said. 'We'll show her when she gets back.'

A search of the settlement revealed storehouses full of mining gear, complete with a scarily voluminous stock of explosives, and more ammunition and food than they could comfortably carry. 'Whoever left all this behind is certain to find their contract cancelled,' Braddon said, hefting a pack laden with tinned rations and longrifle rounds.

'Guess we should take some of that,' Clay said, pointing at the heavily sandbagged storehouse containing the explosives. 'If the miners had to blast their way into the mountain, could be they left the job unfinished.'

Braddon nodded. 'You and Lori take a barrel each. And be sure to bring plenty of fuse-wire.'

They found Scriberson in the cable-car wheel-house applying a jug of grease to the workings of a massive winch. The car itself was a simple open-sided gondola, the cables that connected it to the pylon above issuing a soft whine as it swayed in the wind. 'Think they'd at least have put a roof on it,' Loriabeth said, eyeing the contraption with evident unease.

'She working?' Braddon asked Scriberson, nodding at the coal-burning engine connected to the winch.

'Perfectly, as far as I can tell.' Scriberson emptied the grease jug before moving to the engine. 'Just a matter of wiping away the dust and lubricating the moving parts. Her boiler's chilled to the core, though. It'll take an hour or two to fire her up.'

'Get the car loaded up with this gear,' Braddon told the rest of them. 'Then we'll eat us some of these rations. Must say, I'm heartily tired of goat.'

They repaired to the settlement's meal-hall whilst Scriberson tended to the engine. Skaggerhill got the stove lit and made a hash of corned beef, ham and tinned potatoes, washed down with some beer the departed miners had been kind enough to leave behind. 'Two apiece only,' Braddon warned, casting a hard glance at Loriabeth, who had already begun reaching for her third bottle.

'Here's to the Contract,' Skaggerhill said, raising his beer in a salute. 'And those lost on the way.'

Braddon mimicked him with a grave solemnity that made Clay realise this was another Contractor's ritual. 'Those lost on the way,' he said in concert with the others as they chinked bottles and drank, even Preacher, who Clay had assumed might have eschewed liquor on religious principle.

'Farthest in I ever travelled,' Skaggerhill said. 'Been meaning to mention it, Captain, but this is my last trip. Got me a mind to retire.'

'With the bonus we'll earn from this, we could all retire.' Braddon laughed, reaching across the table to clap him on the shoulder.

'Where's Silverpin?' Loriabeth asked, glancing around. 'Gonna miss the meal.'

'I'll get her.' Clay got to his feet, making for the door and wondering if the bladehand might be amenable to a short assignation in one of the store-rooms.

'Might as well get the doc, too,' Braddon told him. 'He's trial enough without an empty belly.'

Clay nodded and went outside, raising his gaze to the parapet above but finding no sign of the aggravating scholar. 'Grub time, Doc,' he called, scanning the walls. 'It'll get cold . . .' He trailed off as his eyes found Firpike. He sat near the walkway to the wheel-house, propped against the wall as if taking a rest. Clay, however, knew from the sharp angle of his neck and the emptiness in his eyes that this rest was permanent.

'Uncle!' he yelled, thoughts immediately conjuring images of Spoiled boiling down out of the hills. He drew the Stinger, fixing the stock in place and raising it to his shoulder to track along the top of the wall. *Nothing.* Then he heard it, the steady clanking rumble of an engine coming to life.

'What?' Braddon said, emerging from the meal-hall with rifle in hand.

'Trouble.' Clay pointed to Firpike's body and ran for the wheel-house. He found the engine churning away at full power as it turned the belt attached to the great wheel, cables squealing as they were drawn over the iron. The lever that activated the engine lay nearby, sheared off at the root. There was no sign of Scriberson or Silverpin. Also, the car was gone.

Clay rushed to the edge of the wheel-house platform, Stinger raised and thumb clicking back the hammer. He had just enough time to see the car swallowed by cloud. He caught a glimpse of a figure in the car just before the mist closed in, standing and waving a forlorn farewell.

'Seer-damn me for the ages,' Skaggerhill swore, arriving to deliver a hefty kick to the engine. 'Lever's gone, and the controls for the car are smashed. This ain't something non-Blessed hands could do.'

Clay stood gritting his teeth in impotent rage as he stared at the clouds clinging to the mountain side, Miss Lethridge's words ringing loud in his head. *His appearance at that juncture seems a little convenient . . .*

'Scriberson,' he said in a hiss.

'He's Blood-blessed,' Clay said, closing the flap on the pack and tying it tight. He rose and walked briskly to the gate. 'Takes a Blood-blessed to fight a Blood-blessed.'

'With no product,' Braddon pointed out.

'Miss Drystone has some left.'

He went outside where Ethelynne waited atop Lutharon's back. They had arrived only a few minutes after Scriberson stole the cable-car, drawn by the sight of it disappearing into the clouds.

'If he killed Firpike . . .' Braddon went on.

'She's alive,' Clay cut in, striding towards the drake, though his words carried more conviction than he felt. 'I . . . just know it. Maybe he wanted a hostage. Either way, I'm getting her back and killing him when I do.'

He heard Braddon sigh in resigned agreement before he said, 'Be sure to send the car back down the moment you get there. Skaggs reckons he can rig something up so we can make use of it.'

Clay climbed up behind Ethelynne, the drake issuing a rumble of welcome and unfolding his wings. 'Wait a moment please, ma'am,' he said, touching Ethelynne's shoulder. He turned to face his uncle, steeling himself against the likely reaction, but some words just had to be said. 'I ain't sending the car back down, Uncle.'

Braddon's reluctant agreement transformed into a baffled anger and he started forward with a purposeful growl. 'You listen to me, boy . . .'

'Madame Bondersil's dead,' Clay said, Braddon drawing up short at the harshness of his tone. 'Your contract ended with her. She died eight days ago when a Blue ate her just as she was about to sell Ironship out to the Corvantines. Something she'd been planning a good long while, just so's you know. And Carvenport ain't under siege by the Corvantines no more because a buncha drakes turned up and killed them all. Now everyone's just waiting for the Reds and Blacks to come down outta the sky and burn the place to cinders. And this is all 'cause of what's in there.' He pointed at the mountain. 'That thing wants everything it used to have, and more besides.'

He settled himself more firmly between the spines on Lutharon's back, turning away from Braddon. 'Once I've got Silverpin back, I'm gonna take all the powder in the car and blow the White to the Travail. You'd be wise to be far from here by then. Get to the coast, see if you can find a ship. Once the White's gone you should be able to sail home through quieter waters.'

'Claydon . . .'

Something in Braddon's voice made him turn back, the absence of anger mixed with something more. Clay met his gaze and saw it was gone, the compulsion, the desperate hunger for the White. Now there was just a puzzled and scared man knowing he was most likely saying good-bye to his nephew for the last time. *What changed?* Clay wondered. *All this way, now we're closer to it than ever, and the need has gone.*

Braddon started forward again, then stopped as Lutharon voiced a warning huff, smoke rising from his nostrils in twin black plumes. Braddon lifted a hand in placation then unslung his longrifle from his shoulder, holding it out towards Clay. 'You might have need of this,' he said.

Clay nodded and held out his hand, grasping the rifle as his uncle came closer. He seemed about to say something, but the words failed to reach his lips. His eyes, however, spoke of deep regret and guilt that might never fade. 'Thanks for getting me out of gaol,' Clay told him, settling the longrifle on his back and pulling the strap tight on his chest. 'I know you didn't have to. And be sure to thank Auntie for my gift.'

Lutharon turned about and galloped away from the settlement, building momentum before launching himself into the air, his wings lifting them higher in a series of thunderous beats. They circled the settlement once, Clay looking down to see them staring up at him, Loriabeth, Skaggerhill, Preacher and Braddon, thinking it strange that he would actually miss them. Then Lutharon angled his wings and they began to ascend to the mountain top, the world turning white as they slipped into the clouds.

CHAPTER 38

Lizanne

The first attack came two days after Lizanne had woken from her hospital bed, a dense mass of Reds streaking down out of a hazy mid-morn sky to vomit their fire at the buildings below. Knowing the consequences of allowing people to gather above ground in the event of such an attack, Lizanne had made efforts to introduce a daylong curfew, enforced by patrols of Protectorate constables. But many citizens ignored the strictures and attempted to continue some semblance of their former routine with the result that, when the blow finally fell, a large number were naked before the onslaught.

The managerial district bore the brunt of the flames, two entire streets becoming wreathed in flame in the space of a minute as the drakes swept by in a red blur before ascending and wheeling about for another pass, this time making for the docks. By then the Thumper and Growler crews recovered their wits enough to respond. The batteries on the roof-tops in Corporate Square found the range quickly, a pair of Thumpers and a dozen or so Growlers blazing away in a frenzy. The effectiveness of their fire owed more to its rapidity than any accuracy. Lizanne counted half a dozen Reds falling in a twisted spiral towards the earth as the formation of wheeling drakes broke apart, their shrieks of alarm mingling with the crackle of gun-fire and screams rising from the city below.

She had positioned herself and Tekela on the parapet of the conical tower rising from the roof of the Ironship Central Records Office, a sturdy granite building standing three storeys high. It was defended by a single Thumper augmented by three Growlers and a platoon of freed Corvantine prisoners under command of Major Arberus. Most of the captives had agreed to take part in the defence of the city they had been attempting to destroy barely a week before.

Lizanne tracked the fall of one of the stricken drakes to the park where it came down amidst the flower-beds. Still living despite its wounds the Red, a full-grown male, immediately began to thrash about, blood spraying from a part-severed wing as its flames transformed the precisely ordered rows of roses and crocuses into cinders. As per the prearranged plan she had formulated with Commander Stavemoor, a small group of Contractors soon arrived on horseback to dispatch the beast, its fire guttering as it convulsed under a volley of longrifle rounds.

'Lizanne!' Tekela said urgently, and Lizanne lowered the spyglass to see a trio of Reds flying straight towards their perch, wings flat and level as they glided into an attack, mouths gaping to shriek challenge and fury.

'Get down!' Lizanne told Tekela, stepping away from her and flexing her fingers over the Spider's buttons. *Black to hold them,* she decided, focusing her gaze on the lead drake, an aged veteran of life in the Badlands judging by the many long-healed scars marring its face. In the event she had no need of product, Major Arberus timing the Thumper's volley perfectly just as fire began to blossom from the mouths of the three Reds. The old veteran took two shells in the chest, falling to earth in a twisted vortex of blood and dwindling flame. The Red on the left was nearly decapitated by the line of shells that tore through its neck whilst the third suffered a prolonged burst of Growler fire before slamming into the edge of the roof. It clung on for a short time, screaming and belching flame as its claws scrabbled at the tiles, before a concentrated volley from the Corvantines sent it tumbling into the street below.

Lizanne turned her attention back to the city. There were still dozens of Reds wheeling amidst the rising columns of smoke, singly or in pairs. They seemed wary of flying lower than a hundred feet now, those that did soon falling victim to the guns. The battle wore on for another hour, claiming at least another dozen Reds by Lizanne's reckoning, though the defenders suffered too. She saw a Growler battery on a neighbouring roof-top wiped out by suicidal drakes, the beasts flying directly into the stream of bullets to slam into the roof-tops in an explosion of spilled product. The resultant shrieks were even more piercing than that of the drakes and Tekela had clamped her hands over her ears by the time the last Red had wheeled about and disappeared towards the south.

'So many fires,' Tekela murmured, lowering her hands from her ears and gazing at the spectacle before them. Fires raged in every corner of the city, from Colonial Town to Artisan's Row, but all were being fought by the companies of bucket-wielding citizens Lizanne had organised, and there was no general conflagration. Also, the crumpled bodies of a score or more drakes could be seen through the smoke. Carvenport had suffered a grievous blow, but they had survived.

'Make a note,' Lizanne told Tekela. 'The harvesters are to salvage and refine as much product as possible from the drake corpses.'

'I am truly sorry, Mrs Torcreek, but we have no choice. This district is a tinder-box.'

Fredabel Torcreek regarded Lizanne with momentary defiance, lips twitching as she formulated a retort, soon transformed into a sigh of weary acceptance as she nodded. 'Half-burnt to the ground already,' she said. 'My own house with it.'

'It would help if you would speak to your neighbours,' Lizanne said. 'Explain things in terms they'll understand. So far, my word doesn't appear to be carrying much weight. There is ample accommodation in the corporate warehouses, and since they're built from iron these days, they won't burn.'

'I'll do what I can.' Fredabel gestured at the small tent city surrounding them. 'And the hospital?'

'I've ordered all offices in Corporate Square given over to care of the wounded.' She pulled an envelope from her pocket and handed it to the older woman 'You have also been appointed Chief Medical Administrator.'

Fredabel gave a small smile and brushed a wayward lock of hair back under her headscarf. 'The grandest title I ever carried, for sure.' She paused for a moment, all vestige of humour fading from her face and she fixed Lizanne with a demanding stare. 'What news from the Longrifles?'

Lizanne began a prompt and rehearsed lie, but found the words dying on her tongue. *She at least deserves the truth, while she's still alive to hear it.* 'I tranced with your nephew today, Mrs Torcreek. He, your daughter and husband are alive but facing great danger. Beyond that, I cannot say.'

'This danger got anything to do with all this?' Fredabel jerked her head at the corpse of a Red across the street and the team of harvesters busily syphoning off its blood. 'Seems a mite coincidental otherwise.'

'My company was misled into making a grievous error,' Lizanne said. 'It is my belief that we . . . awoke something.'

'And now we're all gonna pay for it, huh?'

Lizanne straightened, buttressing her tone with the kind of unassailable confidence she had often heard in Madame's voice. 'Morsvale didn't last out for more than a day,' she said. 'Principally because they were an enslaved populace serving a corrupt and incompetent regime. We, on the other hand, are graced by considerably more advantages, not least in the nature of our people.'

Fredabel shook her head and gave a small grin before turning to Tekela. 'You be sure and write that down, girl,' she said. 'This place'll have need of a testament soon enough.'

The last of the fires was extinguished come nightfall and, in the aftermath, it soon became clear that there would be no more defiance of curfew, every street standing empty save for the occasional Protectorate patrol. This proved to be fortunate, as the drakes were not content to let them rest.

Just after midnight the Greens came streaming out of the jungle by the thousand to assault the walls in a dozen places. Lizanne had given defence of the wall over to Commander Stavemoor, reckoning the relative simplicity of the task would suit his temperament, and it appeared the decision paid considerable dividends. Well-drilled Growler crews took a fearful toll before the screaming mass of Greens reached the walls, whereupon the expertise of the Contractors kept them at bay for a time, the abandoned trenches soon becoming choked with drake corpses as the long-rifles maintained a furious and deadly accurate fire.

After hearing the initial reports Lizanne had begun to conclude the attack might merely be an expression of mindless rage, the drakes driven for reasons unknown to sacrifice themselves beneath a barrier they had no means of breaching. Then came the report that the corpses had begun to pile up in certain places, the piles growing higher as more and more drakes clambered up the mounds of fallen kin to launch themselves at the parapet above.

Commander Stavemoor reacted by ordering one of his two Thumpers to fire at the base of the mounds, the explosive shells undermining the pile sufficiently for them to collapse under the weight of climbing Greens. However, the innovation came too late to prevent a pack of Greens gaining a foothold on the most eastern extremity of the wall, killing many defenders and threatening to break through into the streets beyond. Fortunately, Lizanne and the commander had foreseen such an emergency and organised squads of Blood-blessed that could be rushed to plug any breaches in the defences. Through a desperate use of Black and Red they managed to stall the Greens on the parapet long enough for an additional battery of Growlers to be shifted to the sector. The weight of fire proved sufficient to sweep the drakes from the walls and by the first glimmerings of dawn the tide of Greens had receded into the jungle. The cost, however, had not been slight.

'Two hundred and seventy-three killed,' Commander Stavemoor reported at the morning meeting Lizanne convened in her new office in the basement of the Central Records Office. 'Plus four hundred wounded. That reduces my command by over a third.'

'Total fatalities for the past two days amount to over a thousand,' the accountancy manager piped up. 'As for the loss of property and associated values' – he began to leaf through his papers then stopped under the weight of Lizanne's stare, adding in a soft mutter – 'a matter for another time, perhaps.'

'A thousand dead in less than two days,' Major Arberus said.

'Plus the Seer knows how many Greens and a good number of Reds,' Stavemoor pointed out. 'All in all, I'd say we've given a damn good account of ourselves.'

'They got plenty more where they came from,' Captain Flaxknot murmured. Lizanne had asked the Contractors to elect someone to speak on their behalf and the leader of the Chainmasters got the job by dint of experience and the breadth of respect she enjoyed. Although, for the sake of morale, Lizanne was beginning to wish they had chosen someone with a less realistic outlook. 'Seen more Greens in the last few days than I thought was left in this whole continent. And the Reds, all flying together in one great host like that.' She shook her head in grim wonder. 'What's happening here's got nothing to do with nature.'

'Evidently,' Lizanne said, adding a brisk note to her voice. 'However, pondering the whys and wherefores of our predicament will avail us little. Despite our grievous wounds, this city remains standing and our manufactory continues to produce weapons at an impressive rate. We have suffered greatly, but have learned in the suffering.'

She turned to Stavemoor. 'Commander, please organise working parties to clear away the drake corpses and dig a ditch around the wall.'

The commander blinked tired eyes at her but didn't feel compelled to argue. 'How deep?' he asked instead.

'As deep as you can make it before they come again. You will have the assistance of every Blood-blessed in the city.'

'What about the Reds?' Captain Flaxknot asked. 'Gotta expect them to return sometime, and I doubt they'll be dumb enough to do so in daylight. Red's a cunning beast.'

'Hard to hit them in darkness,' Major Arberus agreed.

'Then we must endeavour to turn night into day,' Lizanne said, her gaze tracking over those present until it alighted on a slim man in the dark blue uniform of a commodore in the Maritime Protectorate. 'And, luckily, our harbour is crowded with the means to do just that.'

As Captain Flaxknot predicted the Reds waited until nightfall to return. They attacked in smaller groups this time, swooping down at great speed and evidently wary of spending more than a few seconds in range of the growing number of guns now crowding the city's roof-tops. Cover of darkness did offer some advantages to the drakes, and several Growler and Thumper batteries were destroyed in the initial stages of the attack, the Reds forsaking their usual screams of challenge to glide down without warning and cast forth their flames or rend with tooth and talon. Once the alarm had been raised, however, the order was given to put Lizanne's innovation to the test.

It had taken much of the day to shift the searchlights from the ships to the chosen vantage sites about the city, each one placed alongside a Thumper position so that they might immediately engage any illuminated targets. At first the blue-white beams seemed to roam the sky at random, shimmering lances dissecting the night to little purpose, but then one alighted on a Red gliding above at close to five hundred feet, two more beams quickly flicking over to fix on the target as every Thumper within range roared into life. The drake twisted and wheeled in the beams, tail snaking and wings folding continually as it sought to escape the betraying light, to no avail. Within seconds it tumbled into the Blinds, its death scream choking off as it connected with the ground.

The contest was far from over, however, the Reds, or whatever unseen hand commanded them, proving unwilling to retreat in the face of this new threat. Time and again they came streaking out of the dark to cast their fires at the defending gun-crews, some deliberately placing themselves in the path of the searchlight beams in order to follow them down and extinguish the hateful light. Most were torn apart by intersecting Thumper and Growler fire before they got within a hundred feet of the lights, but they succeeded in two instances, the unfortunate sailors manning the lights all suffering the appalling fate of the non-Blessed who find themselves drenched in drake blood. Come the dawn, however, there were no more Reds to be seen and they counted another twenty-three drake corpses within the city limits.

'At least we'll have a surplus of Red to sell when this is over,' Lizanne muttered, looking over the accountancy manager's reports in her office.

'But no Black,' Arberus noted. 'Greens, Reds and Blues only, so far.'

'A detail that hasn't escaped me,' she replied, recalling Clay's shared memories of Ethelynne Drystone and her tamed Black. Also, the mosaics from the temple the Longrifles had found in the jungle had all conveyed an impression of the original Arradsians enjoying some form of worshipful symbiosis with the Blacks. 'It may be they want no part in this conflict,' she wondered aloud.

'Want?' Arberus's soot-blackened brows gave an amused twitch.

'They aren't mindless,' she told him. 'That much at least we've learned from this debacle, if nothing else.' She cast a critical gaze over his besmirched overalls and unwashed visage. 'You need a bath.'

'Don't we all?' He held her gaze for a moment longer than necessary, provoking a not-altogether-unwelcome pang of intriguing discomfort. *No,* she told herself, clasping her hands together and averting her gaze. *I can no longer afford any indulgence.*

'You know we can't last here,' he said after the silence had stretched for a time. 'Not long enough for the Protectorate Fleet to arrive, and that assumes their arrival will in fact bring deliverance and not just more victims for the drakes' spite. As you said, they aren't mindless and it's evident that they learn from every encounter.'

Her thoughts returned to the ships in the harbour, as they often had in recent days. Enough room for two-thirds, and what hope of reaching Feros would they have in any case? *If only they were all blood-burners . . .*

She straightened, frowning as something began to gel in her mind, something rich in desperation, but this situation demanded extreme solutions.

'That's a look I've come to trust,' Arberus said, smiling again as she rose from the desk.

'I believe your command has received another Thumper,' she told him. 'Please deploy it on the roof as you see fit and train your countrymen in its use. I shall be at the manufactory.'

'I￼s it possible?'

Jermayah met her gaze, brows knitting together in an expression that mingled annoyance with consideration. After a long and uncomfortable moment he went to a crate of papers in the corner of the manufactory that served as his makeshift office. She had afforded him the official title of Senior Ordnance Manager but to everyone who laboured here he remained simply Mr Tollermine. The lack of formality didn't appear to undermine the authority and respect he enjoyed, however, and there were few who would question the fact that their survival owed much to his ingenuity.

'A patented Ironship Mark II plasmothermic engine,' he said, extracting a large scroll from the crate and spreading it out on his desk to reveal a complex but familiar blueprint. 'Twice as efficient as the Mark I and less complex than the Mark III. Plus, with a few alterations, we should be able to source all the materials from existing stocks. However, every one of these in existence has been fashioned in a Syndicate manufactory under expert supervision. Of all the artisans gathered here, I could name no more than a dozen with the skills to begin constructing one from scratch, much less finishing it.'

'But you could,' she said. 'I've seen you build devices of far greater complexity with no other hands to help you. And we need much more than one.'

He grunted and returned his gaze to the intricate white lines of the diagram. 'How many more?'

'Only one-quarter of the ships in the harbour are blood-burners. For this to work, they all need to be converted. You will have the ships' engineers to help, of course.'

'So, you intend for us to flee?'

'I intend for us to live.'

He sagged, resting his elbows on the blueprint and lowering his face into his hands with a groan of such fatigue she found herself reaching out to place a comforting hand on his shoulder. He started at that, straightening to stare at her as if she might be a stranger wearing a familiar face. 'You all right?' he asked.

She smothered a laugh and removed her hand. 'Quite all right, thank you.'

'Saying we could do it,' he began after another prolonged study of the blueprint, 'and I'm not saying we can, but if so, how are we going to power so many blood-burners? This siege has taken an awful toll on the Blood-blessed already.'

'Don't concern yourself with that,' she told him. 'The matter is in hand.'

The assembled girls stood in five neat rows in the Academy gymnasium, the youngest in the front and the oldest at the rear, the same arrangement adopted at every daily assembly. There were fifty-three of them, somewhat fewer than the usual complement but hardly unexpected given the indiscriminate nature of both Corvantine artillery and drake fire. With the sudden departure of Madame Bondersil, management of the establishment had fallen to one Juliza Kandles, a matronly woman of middling years who had previously been Mistress of Languages. Lizanne remembered her as a kindly sort, less severe in her disciplinary practises than the other teachers, and Lizanne therefore entertained serious doubts the woman would have the stomach for what was coming.

'They are children,' Mistress Juliza breathed, eyes widening after Lizanne finished relating her instructions.

'And they will soon be dead children if we cannot contrive a means of escape,' Lizanne told her. 'Every precaution will be taken regarding their security . . .'

'What happened to you out there, Lizanne?' the woman asked, eyes wide in mystified dismay. 'Was the world so terrible it turned you into this?'

'The world is the world,' Lizanne replied with a weary sigh. 'And now it is at our door.' She nodded to Tekela, who came forward to hand the woman a folder. 'Each student has been allocated a ship,' Lizanne explained. 'You'll find the list enclosed along with a basic guide to the workings of the thermoplasmic engine. It's not very complicated but I feel the girls should gain some appreciation for its workings before embarkation.'

Mistress Juliza stared at the folder as if she had been handed a ticking bomb. 'Madame would never have countenanced this,' she stated, voice hoarse as she met Lizanne's eyes.

'Madame would have sold every girl here to a whore-house if it furthered her aims,' Lizanne replied, her patience finally worn through. 'A complement of riflemen from the Maritime Protectorate is waiting outside to convey the girls to the docks in readiness. I'll give you a half-hour to explain the situation and say your good-byes.'

They were granted a day's respite, the skies remaining clear of Reds and the pock-marked, corpse-strewn wasteland outside the walls free of any charging Greens. Lizanne used the time to acquaint the city's various factions with her design. Now that half the manufactory's efforts had been given over to construction of blood-burning engines there was no prospect of maintaining secrecy in any case. Also, the hard choices they had to make demanded full and frank discussion.

'One in three,' the lead representative for the Blinds said in a soft, contemplative murmur. He had named himself as Cralmoor, a hulking Islander bearing the elaborate facial tattoos typical of his people, although their pleasing aesthetics were spoilt some-what by the recently healed scars and misaligned bones that spoke of a savage beating. Reports from Exceptional Initiatives revealed the man as a famed and respected prize-fighter now risen in the slum's ever-shifting hierarchy by virtue of the demise of the King of Blades and Whores.

'Children and mothers will be granted a place by right,' Lizanne told him. She had been obliged to meet Cralmoor atop a drinking den named the Colonials Rest where a collection of Blinds folk had charge of a battery of Thumpers and Growlers. They were a decidedly mixed lot, varying greatly in age and ethnicity and featuring more women in their ranks than in other districts. They also exhibited considerably less respect in the face of corporate authority.

'Managers' bitches and their whelps, no doubt,' sneered a woman standing at Cralmoor's side, a thin-faced but buxom figure clad in a heavily besmirched, low-cut dress. Despite the pressures of recent days, she had somehow contrived to maintain her mask of paint; white foundation, ruby red lips and purple eye-shadow combining to convey a clownish appearance at odds with her otherwise fiercely suspicious demeanour.

'All children and all mothers,' Lizanne assured her. 'Regardless of prior station or company allegiance.' She smiled, shifting her attention back to Cralmoor. 'I will require a list of such persons within your . . . dominion.'

'What about everyone else?' he asked, unblinking fighter's eyes steady and making her wish she had agreed to Arberus's sugges-tion he bring his Corvantines along as an escort.

'To be chosen by lot,' she said, proud of the fact that she hadn't allowed her smile to falter. 'Also, a number of volunteers will remain as a rear-guard. Myself included.' She had used this tactic at her previous meetings that morning, finding it worked well with the Contractor families from Colonial Town, but made little impression on the representatives of the middle manager's district.

'We are to be afforded no more respect than the worst scum of this city?' one had demanded, a deep-voiced woman with iron-grey hair and an impeccably tailored, and unstained, business dress. 'We who have laboured to make it great?'

'But do scant labour in its defence,' Lizanne had replied, wearied by their petty complaints and assumed privilege. *The world falls to ruin around them and still they cling to status and wealth as if they retain the slightest meaning.* In the Blinds, however, the issue was one of trust rather than status.

The clown-faced woman gave a dubious cackle in response to Lizanne's statement, but her mirth soon evaporated at a glare from Cralmoor. 'Gotta ask you to forgive Molly Pins her over-sharp tongue, Miss Blood,' he said. 'Her experience of company folk ain't been altogether good. In that, we got a lot in common.'

'It's perfectly all right, sir,' Lizanne replied, noting that Miss Pins's expression remained sullen rather than contrite. 'And please know I fully understand your reluctance to trust my word. All I can say is that, given our current difficulties, trust is not just a luxury, but a necessity.'

Cralmoor and the woman exchanged glances before retreating a short distance to confer with a cluster of similarly suspicious and mismatched souls. The discussion was brief, if heated. One man became particularly agitated, a stocky fellow of Dalcian heritage who hissed at Cralmoor as he gesticulated towards the docks, Lizanne finding little difficulty in lip-reading his argument: 'To the Travail with this Corporate bitch. I say we take the ships and go.'

Cralmoor listened to the Dalcian in silence, stroking his chin and nodding in apparent consideration, then reached out a cobra-swift hand to clamp his fingers around the fellow's neck. He lifted the Dalcian off his feet single-handed then carried him to the edge of the roof, opening his hand to deposit the dissenter into the alley below. The pealing screams that ascended as Cralmoor strode back to Lizanne spoke of at least one broken limb.

'You'll have your list by the end of the day,' the Islander told her. 'And you can add my name to your rear-guard.'

'My thanks, sir,' she replied. 'There is one other matter requiring discussion.' She hesitated at his raised eyebrow but ploughed on. 'If there are any unregistered Blood-blessed within this district, I would ask that they make themselves known. They will be sorely needed when the time comes.'

'I'll see to it.' He gave a polite incline of his head and gestured towards the ladder to the street below. It seemed her period of welcome had come to an end. She nodded and made for the ladder, pausing as her gaze alighted on a slender figure on a neighbouring roof-top. It was a girl, perhaps a couple of years older than Tekela with the dark complexion of Old Colonial stock. Her face was faintly familiar but it was the way she moved that made Lizanne pause. The girl was evidently part of a Growler crew from the bandoliers of ammunition criss-crossing her chest. She was attempting to teach a dance step to a younger comrade, a Dalcian girl barely twelve years old by Lizanne's reckoning. The older girl smiled as they swayed back and forth, but it was a sad smile and somehow Lizanne doubted she had laughed at all recently. Suddenly the girl spun away from her pupil, performing a series of flawless pirouettes, dark hair flying as she twirled before coming to a rigid halt, posed with arms raised in statuesque perfection. She smiled once more as her comrades clapped, bowing in theatrical gratitude.

'Something else, Miss Blood?'

Lizanne turned to see Molly Pins standing close by, her suspicious squint only marginally less fierce than before. 'You been made welcome and all, but it's best not to linger.'

'That girl,' Lizanne said, pointing to the neighbouring roof-top. 'You know her?'

Molly glanced at the girl and gave a short nod. 'Sure, used to belong to Keyvine, though only for a day or so till his head took off and left the rest of him behind.'

'Her name?'

The woman's squint narrowed a little but it seemed she couldn't find reason to ignore the question and Lizanne whispered along with the name she spoke, 'Joya. Her name's Joya.'

CHAPTER 39

Clay

It took longer to ascend to the mountain top than expected, Lutharon often gaining height only to lose it a few moments later as the wind changed. Clay could feel the air thinning about them, bringing a cutting chill that barely made purchase on his thoughts, filled as they were with near-feverish imaginings of Silverpin's fate. *Could be he killed her already, just pitched her out of the car on the way up. Or broke her neck when he stole it.*

Added to that was the burn in his chest, the old heat stoked to a new intensity worse than anything felt in all his years in the Blinds. *He only made it this far 'cause of me,* he knew, realising he had forgotten one of the hardest lessons learnt in the Blinds: *a true friend is like a ten-scrip note lying in the street; you might find one, but only when you ain't looking.*

Finally, after more than an hour of effort, Lutharon ascended above the narrow summit of the Nail, circling until the ledge came into view. At a pat to the neck from Ethelynne the drake shortened his wings, bringing them down in a descent so rapid it might have had Clay yelling in fear a short while before; now there was just the burn and the need to reach his goal.

He held tight to the spine in front of him, eyes fixed on the growing expanse of the ledge. He had agreed with Ethelynne before setting off that no chances would be taken with the treacherous astronomer. Lutharon was to incinerate him on sight or, failing that, he and Ethelynne would gulp down sufficient Black and Red on landing to see him cast down the mountain side in a screaming ball of flame. However, it appeared such designs were destined to be frustrated as he could see the cable-car halted below a pylon erected close to the cliff-edge, but no sign of either Scriberson or Silverpin.

He leapt clear of Lutharon's back as the drake flared his wings, Stinger coming free of its holster as he landed in a crouch. The ledge was broad and unnaturally flat, the stone smoothed into a level surface with the kind of precision that only came from human hands. *Or something inhuman with the same understanding,* he thought.

'Over here!' Ethelynne called, her slight form shielded by Lutharon's bulk. Both he and the Drake moved to find her standing at an opening in the rock-face where the ledge ended. It was clearly new from the rubble piled nearby and the wooden beams buttressing the entrance.

'Briteshore's work,' Clay said, moving to her side and peering into the absolute gloom of the shaft. Ethelynne drank a sip from one of her vials and sent a pulse of Red-borne fire into the shaft, illuminating a long tunnel of damp, rough-hewn walls, stretching on for at least fifty feet before the flames faded. 'It appears they had been fairly industrious before deciding to leave,' she observed.

'Wait here a moment, ma'am.' He went to the cable-car, finding the supplies they had packed mostly intact, including the two barrels of explosive and, he was annoyed to find, Scriberson's marvellous telescope already assembled and ready to be placed atop its tripod. It seemed the astronomer had fitted the tubes together before placing it in the car so there wouldn't be any delay in viewing his precious alignment. Clay reached for it with a grunt of anger, ready to throw the damn thing into the void, then paused as something occurred to him. *If it was all just a ruse, why would he bother to fix it up at all?*

He searched the rest of the car's contents until he found Scriberson's pack, tearing it open and spilling out the contents. His notebook was amongst the sundry items, including a number of curios gathered on the way; a drake tooth, a mosaic tile from the temple, a Dalcian sovereign he had done well to keep hidden.

Nothing, in fact, that spoke of a Corvantine agent intent on betrayal and murder. Clay opened the note-book, leafing through the pages of jottings and sketches. The astronomer wrote in Mandinorian but his penmanship was poor, Clay finding he could decipher only a portion of it and that was so filled with scholarly jargon he made little sense of it anyway. The sketches were a different matter, all clean, uncluttered lines set down with a clarity and precision that belied the scribbles framing them. Clay stopped leafing at a sketch near the end of the book, the most accomplished so far showing a young woman he knew well. She stood with a revolver on her hip and a quizzical aspect to her face as she smiled out at the viewer, an aspect Clay hadn't seen in his cousin before but Scriberson evidently had.

He closed the book and stood for a time, lost in thought until Ethelynne called his name. He looked up to see her standing at the cliff-edge and gazing towards the east where the sun had begun to slide towards the jagged horizon. He followed her gaze, blinking at the view. The three moons and the sun . . . *The alignment*.

He knew they should move on, light lanterns and make their way into the bowels of this mountain and confront whatever secrets it held, but he found he couldn't look away from the sight unfolding in the sky. The three moons seemed to merge as they neared the centre of the sun, Clay blinking and shielding his eyes as he stole repeated glances at the spectacle. Then as the three moons became one a shadow came rushing at them across the mountains, a black tide sweeping over peaks and valleys in a rush too fast to follow. Clay staggered as it reached them, expecting some great force to sweep him from his feet, but the shadow only brought a chill of new-born evening. He returned his gaze to the sun, finding it replaced by a great ring of white fire surrounding a black void.

'Beautiful,' he heard Ethelynne whisper.

Clay blinked the moisture from his eyes and realised there was something shimmering beyond the sun, three small pinpoints of light blinking in the blue-black sky just outside the flickering white fire. Muttering a curse he lifted the telescope onto the tripod and fumbled with the eyepiece until it shimmered into focus and a fourth pin-prick of light stood revealed. *Scribes's extra planet,* he thought, watching the light flicker and wondering at the regret he felt in knowing the astronomer had missed this sight. *Wonder what he would have named it.*

It lasted perhaps half a minute, then the ring of fire began to blaze brighter on its eastern edge. As it did Clay felt something stir beneath his feet, a faint thrum that soon built into something far more violent. He staggered as the mountain shook, then lunged towards Ethelynne as she stumbled towards the cliff. He managed to catch her an inch or two short of the edge and they fell together, huddling as the mountain trembled, the air split by the roar of something vast beneath the stone and the discordant crack of shattered rock. Lutharon gave a piercing squawk of alarm and launched himself from the ledge, wings sending a gale over Clay and Ethelynne as he beat the air and hovered until the tremor finally faded.

'The shaft!' Clay said, surging to his feet and running for the opening. He sagged against the beams at the sight confronting him, despair escaping his lips in a low moan. The shaft was blocked, choked from wall to ceiling with tumbled rock. He fell to his knees, his fury fading under the weight of awful certainty. No amount of Black could shift so much stone, and even Lutharon couldn't claw his way through. They could try blasting their way in with the explosives in the car, but with only two barrels it would be a wasted effort. Briteshore had evidently taken months to dig their way in and he knew they were running out of time.

'Oh,' Ethelynne said in a whisper. Clay looked up to see her staring at the continuing spectacle of the alignment, eyes wide and fascinated. He followed her gaze, seeing that the shimmering circle surrounding the merged moons had begun to expand on the left, the shadow cast by the eclipse beginning to fade. The sight was undoubtedly beautiful, but nothing could steer his heart from the burden of defeat just now. He began to look away but Ethelynne stopped him, coming to his side and laying a hand on his shoulder as she pointed to the blazing crescent. 'Look, Clay. Where the light meets the mountain tops.'

He looked and found himself blinking in confusion, unsure if what he was seeing might be some apparition born of desperation. The sun was low in the sky, so low that the base of the growing crescent dipped below the peaks of the Coppersoles and, in one point, blazed brighter than any other where it was caught in the narrow gap between one of the tallest mountains and the curved outline of a drifting moon.

'This is what the Artisan saw,' Ethelynne said. 'Something that can only happen during an alignment, and can only be seen here.'

Light streamed from the gap between mountain and moon, a beam lancing forth across the distance to cut through the lingering shadow and cast its glow on this very mountain. Clay followed the track of the beam, looking up to where it met the rock-face above, a shimmering inverted triangle, like an arrowhead, and it was pointing at something, some previously unseen facet in the mountain side. He moved back from the shaft, eyes fixed on the place where the glowing arrow narrowed to a point. It was perhaps a hundred feet higher than the ledge and would have been invisible in the abstract mass of rock but for the revealing light of the alignment. A crack in the wall of stone, a way in.

'Briteshore sure wasted a lot of time and money,' he murmured. 'All they had to do was wait.'

The cave mouth was too narrow for Lutharon to deposit them safely within it, but fortunately Skaggerhill had included a good length of rope and a grapnel when loading up the cable-car. Clay climbed up first, finding that skills learned scaling walls in the Blinds were easily adapted to the mountains. Green would have made for a more rapid ascent but their stocks were so low they agreed to husband it for whatever threats they might face within the mountain. It took the better part of an hour to reach the cave, the rock-face proving sheer and tricky, the handholds on offer narrow and dewed with moisture from the drifting clouds. He found the cave larger than expected, a good ten feet high and wide enough to easily accommodate two people walking abreast. *Or a half-grown drake,* he added, peering into the gloom ahead. It may have been a conjuring of his stressed mind but his eyes detected a faint orange glow deep in the recesses of the cave, a glow that had been absent when he looked into the Briteshore shaft.

From below came Ethelynne's impatient query so he jammed the grapnel into a crevice in the cave floor and cast the rope down. He hauled the barrels up first, working the rope with careful and unhurried deliberation and wincing every time one of the casks bumped against the rock. Ethelynne had been wary of taking them along but he had insisted. 'I'm thinking this thing's gonna need more than just a longrifle bullet to go down.'

Next he pulled up the long coil of fuse-wire bundled with Uncle's rifle and a full bandolier of ammunition before leaning out to stare down at Ethelynne. For the first time he appreciated just how small she was, her pale oval of a face rendered childlike at this distance. Lutharon was perched near the cable-car, head tilted at a curious angle as he stared up at Clay, as if reading his intent. *He'll fly her down, she'll be fine.*

'Don't you dare!'

His gaze snapped back to Ethelynne, seeing her features now bunched into furious warning.

'Enough folk have died on this trip,' he called back, unhooking the grapnel from the rock and tossing it away. 'Got no desire to see it happen to you.'

'You have no product,' she said, taking out her wallet of vials and holding it up, a faint note of desperation creeping into her tone. It wasn't friendship, he knew, or at least not just that. She wanted to see the White again; perhaps that's all she had wanted in all the years spent lost in study of the Interior's mysteries.

'Got serious doubts any amount of product will help me in there,' he said, turning away and slinging Uncle's rifle over his shoulder. After a moment he paused and turned back. Looking down he saw her anger had gone, replaced by an expression of deep hurt and disappointment, like a parent gazing at an ungrateful child. 'I'm sorry, ma'am,' he said, reaching down and hefting the barrels with meaningful intent. 'Don't try to follow me.' He turned his gaze to Lutharon, not knowing if the drake would understand his words but speaking them anyway. 'Get her away from here.'

Clay clutched a barrel under each arm as he made his way along the tunnel, guided by the glow ahead. Uncle's rifle was strapped across his back, the Stinger sat in its holster against his side and the fuse-wire was looped around his waist. He found himself stumbling more than once over the uneven rock, his heart leaping each time as he clamped his arms tight on the barrels. The air grew warmer the deeper he went, the illuminating glow evidently the result of some heat source. As sweat beaded his skin in ever-greater volume he berated himself for not having the foresight to bring more than a half canteen of water.

Halfway along he set down one of the barrels and removed its stopper before sliding in a length of fuse-wire. He continued along the shaft at a trot, spooling out the wire and knowing Ethelynne would already have drunk her Green and be making her way up the rock-face. He stopped after twenty yards then snipped off the wire and struck a match. Clay turned and ran the moment the fuse caught, exiting the tunnel and jerking to the side just as the barrel exploded. The boom left his ears ringing and he found himself coughing in an outrush of powdered rock.

When the dust cleared he saw that he had stepped out onto a platform, flat-topped and of such precise construction it banished any notion it might be a natural feature. Going to the edge of the platform he peered down, rooted to the spot as he tried to comprehend the sight that greeted him. At first he thought it another mountain, a great cone of rock forming a peak within a peak, but then his eyes began to discern details: windows, doors, balconies and stairs. *A city.* A city carved from solid rock within this mountain. It rose from depths lit by a fire so bright Clay found he couldn't gaze at it for more than a few seconds. He fancied he saw something churning in the glow, bulbous globules rising and falling amidst the shimmering fury.

He spent a long while in contemplation of the stone city's unfamiliar architecture, all straight lines and sharp angles absent any curves, wondering at what ancient science could have crafted such a place. His eyes roved from bridge to balcony to plaza, finding no sign of current habitation. Whoever had lived here was long-gone. But he knew with grim certainty there were at least two new inhabitants.

Casting his gaze about he found a stairway leading down from the platform and into the city in a long, descending zigzag. *Just me now,* he thought, realising this was the first time he had truly been alone since leaving Carvenport. *Come an awful long way to seal myself in a mountain.* The notion birthed a laugh as he started down, but it didn't last very long.

He had descended three successive stairways when he drew up short at the sight of a rope ladder ascending into the gloom above. Looking up he could just make out an opening in the slope of rock. *Briteshore's shaft,* he decided, eyeing the ladder once more and picking out the scuff marks on the rungs. *At least one of them came inside for a look-see.* He lingered for a moment, puzzling over the notion that if a Briteshore party had climbed down here, then got so scared by their discovery, why they hadn't pulled the ladder up after them when they fled? Lacking any clues he could only shake his head and move on.

The descent to the city took a long time, the constant switch-back route of the successive stairwells making for a tortuous and often confusing journey. Several times he came close to the city's massive, intricate edifice, still showing no sign of life, only to find himself moving away from it as the next stairwell took a sharp turn. Eventually the stairs ended in a flat, narrow causeway leading directly into the city. Clay took full measure of its size as he paused to gulp water from his canteen. It was so huge he couldn't understand the uniformity of its construction, surely a testament to the work of generations and yet the architecture remaining constant throughout. Carvenport had stood for little over two centuries and featured buildings old and new within its walls, varying greatly in size and design. But here it was all one thing, conceived and made as if in accordance to a single plan, almost as if it had been the work of weeks or months rather than years.

He started along the causeway at a steady walk, moving closer to the edge to peer down at the glowing pit below. He caught only a glimpse before retreating in the face of the heat and the glare, but it was enough to make him wonder if the Seer hadn't conceived of the Travail after seeing this place in one of his visions. White and yellow lava seethed in a vast circular river surrounding the base of the city, scummed in places by partly melted rock that broke apart as the molten mass roiled and swirled. He staggered back from the edge, shaking sweat from his face and moving on.

The entrance to the city was formed by a massive stone rectangle of jarringly perfect dimensions. The pillars and the lintel were inset by writing of some kind, the individual characters standing as tall as he did. Peering closer he saw the clear resemblance to the pictograms from the Briteshore manager's office, each character formed with the same order and precision. Unable to read whatever message, or warning, the gate contained, Clay could only conclude that whoever had built this place would have made for trying company.

The space beyond the gate consisted of a broad plaza bordered by numerous steps ascending into the various districts of the city in typically sharp-angled fashion. A number of buildings overlooked the plaza, all empty balconies and windows regarding his intrusion with blank indifference. His eyes roved the stairwells, seeking some notion of which would take him to his goal before it occurred to him that it didn't matter. *It's a mountain, just get to the top.*

He drew the Stinger before making for the most central stairway and starting the long climb up.

He found the dead man after an hour of climbing, pausing on a landing at the juncture of two intersecting stairways for a well-needed rest. He allowed himself a small sip from his canteen as he mentally flipped a copper scrip to decide which route to take, then fell into an immediate crouch on spotting the pair of boots jutting over the edge of the next landing up on the right. He kept low as he climbed the steps, then rose to full height, fanning the Stinger's barrel in search of a target. But the landing contained only the dead man. He lay on his back, legs splayed and a large patch of dried blood framing his greying features. His hand lay on his chest clutching a revolver, the barrel of which rested just below his mouth, the lips peeled back in death to favour Clay with a grin he found all too knowing.

Dead by his own hand, Clay decided, eyes roving the partly desiccated features and finding no recognition. Death had a tendency to obscure age but Clay judged him as maybe in his forties. He wore a set of grey overalls and a helmet of some kind was hitched to the thick leather belt about his waist. *Miner,* Clay thought, turning the helmet over with his boot to reveal the small oil-lamp affixed to the front. *Seems not every Briteshore employee took off after all.*

He left the dead man undisturbed and resumed his climb, the stairs taking him into a district of buildings featuring numerous courtyards and a multi-tiered park of silent, dry fountains and many sculptures, fashioned from crystal rather than stone. Most were abstract, twisted toruses and spirals conveying meaning or intent beyond him, but some were undeniably human in shape, though all deformed somehow. One appeared to be of a woman crouching as the stubs of wings grew from her back, another of a man holding both arms aloft, his hands narrowed to needle-points.

Clay found he had to force himself through the park, every statue he saw seemingly possessed of an ability to fascinate. It was as he averted his gaze from the sight of two children joining hands, the fingers frozen in the act of melting together, that he found the second body. Another man, this one impaled on the spines of a tree-shaped sculpture. Clay moved closer, finding a pair of revolvers lying on the ground beneath the corpse's dangling feet. His skin was Old Colonial dark and he wore a string of teeth around his neck. *Contracted headhunter,* Clay decided. His gaze tracked over the multiple crystal spikes piercing the fellow's torso, knowing there were few things in this world that could achieve such a result. *Black.*

The next body wasn't hard to find, a woman, lying beneath a large crystal monolith directly opposite the tree with its ghastly fruit. Moving to the body, Clay guessed her to have been young. Although, like the miner back on the stairs, her skin was so dried by death it was hard to tell for sure. But unlike the miner she clearly hadn't taken her own life. A cluster of ragged, dark-stained holes had been blasted into the leather jacket she wore. He found no weapon on her then saw the pale patch discolouring the greying skin on the palm of her hand. *Blood-blessed, probably contracted by Briteshore to accompany their expedition.* He switched his gaze back to the dead headhunter. *Must've shot her in mid air . . . They turned on each other.*

He crouched at the woman's side, grimacing as he pulled her jacket aside to explore the pockets. Her vials were contained in a wallet fixed to her belt. It was fairly low-grade product, the liquid cloudy and more viscous than Ironship dilutions, but still all four colours were present. About a quarter-vial of Red and Black, half a vial of Green and, he saw with blossoming relief, nearly a full vial of Blue. If ever he had need of some guidance, it was now. He grunted in frustration on checking his pocket-watch; another five hours until the next scheduled trance with Miss Lethridge. *That's if she's still around to trance,* he reminded himself.

He straightened from the corpse, raising his gaze to the still-unclimbed mass of the city. *So many stairs,* he thought, then glanced around at the dangerously enrapturing statuary. *And so many distractions.* Knowing there was nothing else for it he drank two-thirds of the Briteshore woman's Green, pocketed the wallet, took a firmer grip on the barrel under his arm and started to run.

The city blurred as he ascended, scaling successive stairways a few leaps at a time, keeping his gaze focused only on the route ahead, regardless of whatever visual enticements flickered at the corners of his vision. Parks, monuments and ever more statues all ignored in his single-minded quest to get as close to the summit before the Green faded from his veins. Clay reckoned he had covered perhaps two-thirds of the distance by the time the product started to ebb. He forced his body into a faster pace, leaping higher and driving himself on. His body soon began to protest, a grinding ache building in his limbs and chest, transforming into a burning agony as he pushed himself harder. A shout of pain escaped him when the last of the Green fled his system and he collapsed at the top of a particularly long stairwell.

He lay on his back for a time, cradling the barrel in both arms, breath coming in ragged sobs and leaking so much sweat it formed a small pool around him. Feeling the way his heart lurched in his chest, like a trapped animal attempting a frantic escape, he wondered if he might have pushed too hard. It wasn't unheard of, over-eager Blood-blessed forcing their bodies past tolerable limits whilst lost in the throes of product. After what seemed an age, though, the pounding beast in his chest finally began to slow its labours and clarity returned to his fatigue-dimmed eyes.

He got slowly to his feet, finding he had come to a halt on a broad plaza extending in a semicircle for about a quarter of the radius of this re-formed mountain. There were no statues or fountains here, just bare stone tile surrounding a building. This structure was unique in that, unlike all the other buildings he had seen so far, this one was free-standing. A plain, windowless rectangle of impressive size, bare of the walkways and bridges that interlinked the rest of the city.

Clay drank all the water remaining in his canteen. It provided only a few mouthfuls and proved barely enough to assuage his dreadful thirst before he tossed it aside and started towards the building. He stumbled several times and soon found he had to swallow a drop of Green to keep upright, though the burn of it brought on a now-familiar nausea. *When this is done,* he told himself, *I ain't touching a drop of product again for at least a year.*

He took time to survey the free-standing building, finding it featureless but for a single symbol inscribed above what appeared to be its only entrance: a circle residing between two lateral curves that put him in mind of an eye. *A watch-tower?* he wondered as he came closer, thinking it unlikely. *Home to whatever they called their Protectorate, maybe?* He was tempted to bypass it and make for the summit, but something made him pause, a conviction that the singularity of its construction must hold some meaning. Also, if he thought it a place of importance, Scriberson might have formed a similar conclusion.

Clay drew the Stinger and stood with his back to the wall beside the door before jerking his head inside for a quick look. To his surprise the place was less gloomy than expected, being roofless and lit by the reflected glow from the stone far above. A large, perfectly square opening lay in the centre of the floor and a stairwell descended into its depths. He went inside, eyes roving the shadows but finding nothing more of interest. He approached the opening and looked down, following the track of the stairs as they hugged the wall of the shaft to descend for at least a hundred feet. The sight of the shaft and the absent roof put him in mind of the temple where once Blacks had come to be worshipped. This shaft was certainly wide enough to accommodate a full-grown Black, or something twice the size.

His eyes soon registered another glow in the depths of the shaft, a blue-white luminescence jarring with the orange light that played on every surface of this place. But what gave birth to it was lost from view. He swayed a little as the last drop of Green faded, resisted the urge to drink more, then started down.

The air grew cooler as he descended, so cool in fact that he started to shiver a little as heat leached from the sweat clamming his skin. After a long climb down lasting more than a quarter hour the walls of the shaft disappeared revealing a huge circular chamber, the first curved structure he had set eyes on in this city. His footsteps birthed a long echo as he came to a halt, taking a good while to fade thanks to the hardly believable size of this space. His attention immediately fixed on the dome in the centre of the chamber, a perfect circle with a roof formed of arcing, interlocked stone slats standing at least two hundred feet in diameter. It was surrounded by four more domes of identical construction but about half its size. Each dome had a small opening in the top, all but one emitting a different-coloured light, red from the one on the right, the next green, then blue. But the large dome in the centre glowed brighter than all the others, providing enough light to illuminate the entire chamber, and it shone white.

Red, Green, Blue . . . and White, he thought, eyes flicking from one dome to another before coming to rest on the only dome not to emit any light. *And Black.*

He stood still for a time, frowning as he sensed something, not a noise exactly, more a sensation. Like a long-forgotten tune humming in his head, the melody at once both familiar and unknown. He staggered at a sudden, painful flare in his mind, flashing a glimpse of something; the shadow sweeping across Nelphia's surface in the trance. He grunted, shaking his head as the vision faded. Heart thumping faster at the knowledge of what he had just experienced: *The trance. I was in the trance without benefit of Blue.*

Fear gripped him then, the kind of all-consuming, inescapable terror he had thought lost in childhood the day the Black got free. His shivering doubled as he stared at the domes below, knowing with absolute certainty that he wanted no part of whatever they contained. What lurked here was so far beyond him he found himself voicing a shrill laugh at his own arrogance. *As if some Blinds-born gutter rat has any business even being here,* a treacherous voice told him, a voice he knew was born as much from rationality as fear. *Go back. Could be another way out. If not, use the barrel to blast a way out. Then get to Hadlock and find a ship, any ship. Just get far away from here . . .*

Silverpin.

The name didn't quite banish every vestige of terror but it was enough to steady him, quelling his shivers as he stood there panting. *She's down there,* he knew, and forced himself to take another step, then another, his pace increasing so that he was running by the time he reached the chamber floor. He made directly for the largest dome, scanning its sloping sides for a way in and increasing his pace, worried any pause might summon the fear once more. He had gone perhaps a dozen feet when another vision hit him.

The pain was enough to send him sprawling, though some fortunate instinct enabled him to keep hold of the barrel. The images invaded his mind with brutal ease; the shadow sweeping across Nelphia's surface, fear blossoming once more as it came ever closer . . . then a shift in the image, the mindscape misting then re-forming into a face, one he knew. Miss Lethridge, regarding him with grave concern, her lips forming urgent words he couldn't hear. Another flash, another spasm of pain and she was gone, leaving him gasping on the floor.

His gaze went to the dome with the blue light, seeing how the beam it emitted was pulsing now, flaring and fading in a steady rhythm that seemed to echo his own heart-beat. *It's calling to me,* he knew, rising and taking a short tentative step towards the dome before forcing himself to a halt. *The White,* he told himself, wondering why his own thoughts sounded so faint. *You came for the White.*

The blue beam's pulse intensified, now accompanied by a definite thrum whenever it flared, an insistent note that birthed a certainty in his heart. *I came for Silverpin too,* he answered himself. *And she's in there.*

He moved towards the dome in a shuffling stumble, dimly aware that he had left the barrel behind when he got to his feet. It didn't seem to matter. Now he had but one goal. The blue dome's surface remained sealed until he stumbled to within a dozen feet, whereupon a section of stone receded and slid aside, revealing an interior of vague shapes occluded by the glow. He continued inside without pause, blinking until the shapes resolved into something he could recognise.

People.

They were arranged in a large circle, all standing and staring at something in the centre of the dome's floor. He thought there could be sixty or more of them but couldn't be sure, there being little room in his head for numbers now. He managed to take in some details as he moved towards them, miners' helmets and dusters, one man in a well-cut suit with the look of a manager. *The Briteshore folk,* he decided, the thought slowly coalescing in his mind. *They didn't leave . . . They all came here.*

They all stood rigid as statues, the fact of their continued survival betrayed only by the most shallow of breaths. But their eyes were empty and unblinking. Peering at their faces he saw something that should have sent him recoiling in shock, but now only made him blink in ponderous bafflement. They were changed, the skin of their faces scaled, ridges growing from foreheads and chins, puckered by nascent spines.

'Not . . . changed,' he realised aloud in a slow slur. 'Spoiled . . .'

He groaned and turned to look upon whatever it was that fascinated these people so. It stood in the centre of their circle, pulsing a blue light that filled the dome and seeped through the opening in the roof. It was a crystal of some kind, formed of jagged spines so that it resembled a star, a deep blue star. He had a sense that its pulsing deepened as he drew closer, the rhythm more insistent, the light flaring brighter.

He reached out a hand towards it, gaze lost in the all-consuming light it cast forth. Doubt and fear were gone now, and there was only the light . . .

Another vision tore into his mind, making him cry out and stagger away from the crystal, head filling with unwanted images and sensation. *Nelphia . . . The shadow . . . Miss Lethridge, shouting now, desperate even . . . He could hear her, though only just, the words faint and discordant . . . '. . . killed Keyvine . . . Joya . . . alive. She . . . The Island girl . . .'*

It all became a jumble as a fresh wave of agony swept through him, making him writhe and clutch at his head, hearing his own screams as a distant wail. Blackness descended quickly, a vast unknowable void, blessedly welcome in its complete lack of sensation. He had no knowledge of how long he remained in the void but when it finally receded he was on the floor, lips leaking drool and head still throbbing in the aftermath of the vision. Something was different. The insistent thrumming pulse of the crystal had stopped, the light now constant; whatever compulsion had forced him here had vanished.

The sound of boot leather on stone drew his gaze and he looked up to see Scriberson standing over him, face scaled and ridged like the others. The astronomer's features betrayed no emotion at all as he raised the knife in his hand and brought it down.

CHAPTER 40

Lizanne

As was becoming usual, she woke from the latest trance with a severe headache. Tekela passed her a glass of the milky-pale tonic specially mixed for her by the city's most respected apothecary, an unpleasantly acidic concoction that nonetheless did the trick of banishing her pain with welcome alacrity. The consequent indigestion, however, was less welcome.

'How long?' she asked Tekela, sitting up on the bunk positioned behind her desk. They had both taken to sleeping in her basement office in recent days, for obvious reasons, choosing to eschew the more luxurious accommodations above ground. There had been no more massed attacks since the Reds' night assault, but neither had they vanished from the skies. In daylight they would fly over by the dozen, circling but never coming low enough for the guns to find the range. At night it was a different story, lone Reds streaking out of the sky without warning to assail Protectorate patrols or the smaller gun-batteries. Such attacks usually meant death for the Reds who made them, but also inevitably entailed the loss of more defenders, as well as straining the already threadbare nerves of the populace.

'Two hours,' Tekela replied in Eutherian, as she tended to do when angry. Her doll's face wore a severe expression of disapproval Lizanne chose to ignore. 'The Accounts manager is waiting,' the girl added in her improving Mandinorian. 'Something about . . .' She fumbled for the right words. 'Treasure . . . a stock of treasure.'

'The company vault,' Lizanne said, getting to her feet and

moving to the desk. 'He's probably come to moan about having to leave all that lovely money behind.'

Her gaze went to the row of Blue vials lined up on her desk, pillaged from the Ironship reserves and probably worth more than she could have hoped to earn in her lifetime. *Three trances of two hours each, and still not a sign of him*. She had kept to the same routine since hearing the girl Joya's story, trancing every five hours with the memory of it bundled into a neat vortex and ready for immediate communication. Each time she hoped Clay would be waiting, and each time she had been disappointed. *It all rests on him now. If I can't warn him . . .*

She let the thought dwindle, leading as it did to the prospect of fighting their way clear in their fleet of converted ships. Jermayah's army of artisans and engineers had worked prodigious feats so far, converting a quarter of the required vessels. The harvesters had been similarly industrious, refining enough of their now-copious stocks of Red to ensure every ship could be fuelled all the way to Feros if or when the time came. *More when than if*, she thought, grimacing as she drank down the remaining tonic, then winced at a rapid pounding on the door.

'Tell that scrip-pinching dullard to wait,' she snapped at Tekela and sank behind her desk, reaching for the latest stack of reports from the manufactory. However, when Tekela opened the door she was confronted by a Protectorate rifleman rather than the portly accountant.

'Commander Stavemoor's compliments, miss,' the man said in a rush, Lizanne finding the frantic gleam in his eye decidedly ominous. 'There's been a . . . development.'

'Started showing up about an hour ago,' Stavemoor said, handing her his binoculars. 'About three thousand so far, I'd say. More arriving by the minute.'

She trained the optics on the tree-line, finding the focus after a few seconds. At first it seemed like a ragged band of Contractors straggling out of the jungle after some disastrous expedition, but then she saw their faces. 'Spoiled,' she whispered, tracking the glasses along the row of deformed figures. They varied greatly in height and clothing. Some wore hardly anything at all, their scaly skin bared to the sun. Others were clad in armour of hardened leather or full-length garments fashioned from rough-made cloth. But they were all Spoiled, and all armed. Spears, bows, clubs, even a few fire-arms pilfered from the Corvantine dead. Though from the way the Spoiled held them she deduced they had little notion of how they worked. However, Lizanne found their demeanour more worrying than their numbers or armaments. They all stood in unmoving, silent ranks, those continuing to materialise out of the jungle simply taking their place and standing in unspeaking expectation.

'Fought my share of Spoiled over the years, miss,' Captain Flaxknot said. 'I count at least six different tribes, and all from far-flung regions. They've come a very long way, probably been marching for weeks.'

The same number of weeks since the Longrifles set off, I'd wager, Lizanne thought, handing the binoculars back to Stavemoor. 'Recommendations?'

'If they keep arriving at this rate there'll be more than ten thousand by nightfall,' he said. 'I think we can assume they aren't just going to keep on standing out there. If so, we'll need reinforcement if we're going to hold. More Growlers and Thumpers too.'

'The latest batch will be here by this evening,' she promised. 'And I'll order another four batteries onto the surrounding roof-tops.'

'Won't be enough,' Flaxknot said. 'It's plain we'll soon have every Spoiled bastard in the northern climes at our door. And you can bet they'll have a horde of Greens and Reds to help when they decide to charge. We're just too thin.'

Lizanne was about to offer some rousing words, cast a few empty platitudes at the captain and her comrades to bolster their spirits. But they all died in the face of her undeniable judgement.

They could shift every gun in the city to the walls and it still wouldn't be enough. Lizanne turned away from the sight of the growing mass of Spoiled, eyes tracking over the damaged but still-defiant city until she found the docks. *Is it time?* she thought. *Cram every child we can into the converted ships and send them on their way whilst we fight to our heroic last?* She suppressed an angry grunt, hating the sense of helplessness and the responsibility. *Would Madame have known what to do?* she wondered, but doubted it. *What comes for us can't be bribed, or lied to.*

She began to turn away then stopped as her gaze alighted on Colonial Town; the recently abandoned tinder-box of ancient wooden houses. She stared at it for a long time, wheels turning in her head until Stavemoor gave a polite cough. 'Gather all your officers,' she said and paused to favour Flaxknot with a smile, 'and Contractor captains. We have a great deal of planning to do.'

'Edgerhand,' the man in the long and multiply patched coat introduced himself before nodding at his two companions. 'This is Red Allice and Burgrave Crovik. Mr Cralmoor told us to send his regards.'

'You are very welcome,' Lizanne told him with a smile before glancing at his fellow unregistered Blood-blessed: a dark-haired young woman wearing a pair of tinted spectacles despite the lateness of the hour, and a surprisingly well-dressed but squat fellow with a drake-bone cane. 'Though I must confess I had hoped there would be more of you.'

'There were.' Edgerhand's lips gave a slight twitch that might have been a smile. He was at least ten years her senior judging by the grey hair at his temples and the lines on his thin-featured face that nevertheless retained a lean handsomeness. 'Things got very interesting in the Blinds after the king's demise. Surprised the harbour waters didn't rise more, what with all the fresh bodies tipped into it over the past few weeks.'

'Well, quite.' She turned and offered a hand to the young

woman, who stared at it impassively from behind the black discs of her glasses.

'Please forgive my colleague her ill manners, miss,' the squat man said, raising his cane to his forehead as he lowered his portly frame in a bow. 'Such niceties are beyond her.' He straightened and offered what she assumed he thought of as a charming smile, but instead resembled the grimace of a dyspeptic toad. 'Burgrave Ellustice Crovik, at your service.'

She detected a faint trace of a Corvantine accent in his voice, though certainly not sufficiently cultured to justify his title. 'You are a long way from home, sir,' she observed.

'But one of many impoverished exiles who found their way to this haven. I thank the oracles dear Father is no longer alive to see how far I've fallen.'

The woman, Red Allice, voiced a small but deeply derisive snort at that, drawing a vicious glare from the supposed Burgrave. The depth of enmity Lizanne saw as their eyes met told her these people had been enemies only a short while before. 'Your assistance is greatly appreciated,' she told the three of them, then gestured at the rapidly growing barricade being constructed nearby. 'As you can see.'

The barricade ran the length of Caravan Road, all the way from the southern gate to the junction with Queen's Row where it took a sharp left to close off the northern boundary of Colonial Town. It was being constructed from stone and sundry scrap iron discarded by the manufactory, Lizanne having ordered the demolition of several damaged buildings to provide the requisite materials. All hands that could be spared were hard at work either building this barrier or clearing the ground beyond it for a distance of twenty yards. Every scrap of wood, or anything else likely to catch a flame, was in the process of being torn down and carted off. Blood-blessed were conspicuous amongst the horde of labourers by virtue of the great stacks of stone they guided into place with Black, of which there was now a large, if rapidly dwindling, supply. Recent days had brought numerous reports from the breeding pens about the increasing belligerence of their Red and Green specimens, whilst the few captive Blacks remained relatively quiescent. Nevertheless, unwilling to harbour such a danger within the city, Lizanne had ordered them all slaughtered and the product harvested.

'You're sectioning off Colonial Town,' Edgerhand observed.

'Indeed,' she said. 'There is a surplus of Black if you would care to assist with the construction.'

'Always been more attuned to Green,' he replied, then jerked his head at the other two. 'You can guess Allice's speciality from her name. The Burgrave's your man if you're looking for menial labour.'

'Have a care, Edge,' the faux nobleman replied in a soft voice, his part-cultured vowels falling away completely.

Lizanne saw Edgerhand's mouth twitch again before he addressed her once more, speaking in an oddly formal manner. 'Mr Cralmoor was firm in his instructions regarding our new employment. "Take care of Miss Blood," he said.' He gave a bow that was markedly more practised than Corvik's. 'It seems you now have a personal bodyguard courtesy of the Blinds.'

Come nightfall the barricade stood four feet tall for much of its length. Lizanne would have liked another foot at least but it couldn't be helped; judging by the burgeoning cacophony of drake screams beyond the wall, time had evidently run out. She had refused suggestions to retire to a safe vantage point, instead placing herself at the barrier's northern stretch where the weight of fire-power was most thin. She had overridden the numerous objections by simply pointing out that every capable hand was needed to make this work, and there was no longer a safe place in the city in any case.

On being told to stay with Jermayah at the manufactory, Tekela had come close to throwing the kind of tantrum Lizanne assumed was behind her, face flushing red and a dark glower filling her gaze. 'I have this,' she said, touching a hand to the revolver on her hip but Lizanne had refused to be swayed, taking the girl by the arm and practically marching her to Jermayah's side with orders to chain her up if she moved. Lizanne hadn't told her Jermayah also had instructions to get them both on a ship should this stratagem fail. Those vessels already converted were fully fuelled and crewed, each with an Academy girl aboard, ready to make a run through the blockade of Blues in the event of disaster.

Gun-fire began to crackle on the wall as the last glimmer of light fled the sky, Growlers, Thumpers and rifles cutting through the discordant tumult of massed Greens baying in fury. Keen to occupy herself, Lizanne methodically loaded the twin revolvers holstered under each arm. Solid, reliable .35 Dessingers from the Covert Protectorate armoury, noisier and far less elegant than her lost Whisper, but the time for subtlety had gone. Now she wasn't a spy, she was a soldier.

She checked the Spider next, ensuring each vial was firmly seated and drawing a curious glance from Edgerhand who, along with his two companions, hadn't strayed more than ten feet from her side since their first meeting. 'Now, that's an impressive instrument,' he said. 'Your father's work, I assume?'

She shook her head, feeling a familiar pang of annoyance at the recognition. 'Mr Tollermine has ever been my ingenious friend. Not all novelties bear the Lethridge name.'

'Only the great ones. I had the good fortune to hear your father lecture several years ago at the Annual Consolidated Research Conference in Sanorah.' He shrugged at her quizzical glance. 'I was not always of such low standing. The Blinds provides a home for all manner of wretched souls.'

Her thoughts immediately went to Clay and the trance she had been forced to forgo tonight. 'Not all are wretched,' she said, glancing around at the people enlisted to defend this stretch of wall. She had gathered all the city's Blood-blessed, reinforced by a full company of dismounted regular cavalry armed with repeating carbines. 'Besides,' she added, 'events have conspired to make us all of equal standing. If only for tonight.'

Edgerhand began to answer but his words were drowned by a piercing scream from above, accompanied by an immediate chorus of 'Reds! Reds!' from the surrounding defenders. Lizanne's gaze snapped to the sky, seeing a crimson shape streaking down out of the blue-black void, mouth gaping and wings folded. A salvo from the Thumper battery stationed across the street caught the drake just as the flames began to blossom from its mouth. It came down with a crunching thud on the other side of the barricade. For a time it writhed in a spreading pool of blood, still attempting to breathe its fire at them, before a well-placed shot from a cavalryman shattered its skull.

There was the briefest pause then the air became filled with the cries of swarming Reds and the thunderous percussion of what sounded like every Thumper and Growler in the city. Lizanne soon lost count of the number of Reds hacked out of the sky by the interlocking arcs of fire as the searchlights cut through the gloom. It appeared all former caution had been stripped from the drakes and they launched themselves at the defending batteries with unhesitant savagery, Lizanne averting her gaze as she watched the Thumper crew that had saved her torn apart by three mortally wounded Reds. *They learn with every attack,* she recalled. *But mostly they learned the value of sacrifice.*

A loud boom drew her gaze back to the wall and she saw a mushroom of flame rising above the roof-tops of Colonial Town. She injected a drop of Green to enhance her sight, boosted vision revealing a pack of Greens boiling over the wall around a ruined gun position, flames still rising from the ashes of their ammunition. It had been part of her plan for the section of wall shielding Colonial Town to give way, but only after exacting a fearful toll on the attackers. Now it all appeared to be happening ahead of schedule.

She watched the Green pack launch themselves from the wall and into the darkened streets below, quickly followed by a dense throng of Spoiled using ropes to haul themselves up onto the parapet. For several frenzied minutes battle raged on the parapet, defenders and Spoiled locked in a savage embrace of bayonet and war-club, before numbers finally told and the mis-shapen horde came streaming over, accompanied by ever more Greens.

Lizanne lowered her gaze to the shadowed maze of Colonial Town, injecting more Green to follow the attackers' progress. Off to her right there came the sound of a thousand or more rifles firing at once, followed by the ripping tumult of multiple Growlers, the barricade along Caravan Road lighting up from end to end as the defenders let loose at any Spoiled or Green unfortunate enough to emerge from the old district. *It's working,* Lizanne thought with some relief, seeing the inhumanly fast, loping shadows of many Greens filling the unlit streets.

She looked round at a shout from one of the cavalry officers, his men all bringing their carbines up in readiness as a dozen or so figures sprinted into the newly fashioned no man's land between barricade and houses. 'STOP!' she shouted before the cavalrymen could fire. 'They're ours!'

The first runner leapt over the barricade in an impressive display of athleticism, spoilt somewhat by his untidy collapse into an exhausted heap upon reaching the other side. 'You were supposed to head for the gate,' Lizanne told him.

Arberus gave her a baleful stare, face streaked with soot and blood, fortunately not his own. 'War rarely goes according to plan,' he returned evenly. His face softened a little as she offered a hand as he levered himself upright. Another ten men followed him over the barricade, apparently all that was left from his company of turncoat Corvantines. 'Best get them in order,' Lizanne told him, knowing this to be the wrong moment for sympathy.

Arberus gave a tired nod before straightening and moving away, casting a tirade of profanity-laden Varsal at his near-spent men. 'Stand up, you shit-eaters! This look like a fucking holiday to you, does it? You, pick up that rifle or I'll find a place for it in your arse!'

Lizanne turned away to be greeted by the sight of at least two dozen Greens charging into the open. At their officer's shouted command, the cavalrymen delivered a rapid volley with their carbines, most of the Greens tumbling to a halt under the weight of fire before they had covered half the distance to the barricade.

'Drink up!' Lizanne called to the surrounding Blood-blessed, depressing three buttons on the Spider and drawing one of her revolvers. 'You all know the plan! None can get through!'

The sound of gun-fire faded as the cavalrymen paused to reload their carbines. A few Greens had survived the initial blast and kept on, though most were limping. Lizanne fixed her enhanced eyes on the most lively one and put a bullet through its head from sixty yards, a second volley from the Protectorate troops accounting for the others. Lizanne turned to watch the Blood-blessed drinking the large vials they had been given, each containing an Ironship-patented dilution of Red, Green and Black, probably the finest and most potent product any of them had ever tasted. *Or are ever likely to taste,* she thought, then grimaced at her own indulgence. *Feel guilty later.*

A huge and savage uproar dragged her gaze back to no man's land to be greeted by the sight of Spoiled and Green charging from the shadows in a dense mass. She drew her second revolver and emptied both weapons in a series of rapid but precisely aimed shots, Spoiled and drake falling to every bullet. With no time to reload she lowered the guns and waited until the on-coming horde came within twenty feet then unleashed her Black, freezing a dozen or more so that they created a dam in the tide of flesh, howling warriors and screaming Greens piling up behind. The process was repeated all along the line as the Blood-blessed followed her example, a great mass of attackers building up as they sought vainly to push past the invisible barrier. Finding her view of Colonial Town obscured by so many thrashing bodies, Lizanne hopped up onto the barricade, peering into the streets and ducking the arrows the Spoiled launched at her. She could see that the number streaming over the wall had thinned to a trickle and the streets below were now choked with attackers. It was time.

She got down and reached for the rocket flare propped against the barricade, a gift from the Maritime Protectorate. She held it aloft and lit the fuse with a burst of Red, sending the flare streaming into the night sky where drakes were still wheeling about amidst the hail of gun-fire. She could only hope the gunners would see the flare amidst the aerial carnage as she watched it explode into a green starburst. For several seconds there was no response. The drakes and the Spoiled continued to throw themselves against the wall of Black, falling by the dozen as the cavalrymen maintained a furious fire with their carbines. But the weight of numbers was beginning to tell and the first signs of diminishing product started to show amongst the Blood-blessed, sweat-soaked faces straining and teeth clenched as they continued to expend their Black. It would only be a moment or more before the barrier failed.

The first artillery shell arced into the mass of Greens and Spoiled with a faint whine, the explosion tossing a fountain of sundered bodies into the air, quickly followed by half a dozen more. The mass of attackers reeled back as the barrage tore through them and the pressure on those in front relaxed, the weight of Black propelling them backwards in a cascade as the shells continued to rain down. Beyond them explosions ripped through Colonial Town from end to end, every Protectorate artillery piece remaining in the city firing a mix of blast and incendiary shells at pre-sighted targets. The incendiaries ignited the coating of oil and kerosene a small army of workers had spread over the buildings, whilst the blast shells fanned the flames and shredded roofs and walls to cast the burning debris far and wide. Greens and Spoiled soon came boiling out of the district from every open street, many on fire. The massed guns along Caravan Road roared into life once more, scything down the attackers en masse so that none made it to within ten feet of the barricade.

Lizanne reloaded her guns and refreshed her Green with the Spider, using her amplified vision to gauge the progress of the fire. At least half of Colonial Town was fully ablaze now, the flames soaring high as they leapt from building to building. The slaughter of the attackers before her was mostly complete, the survivors of the first salvo quickly falling to the guns of the cavalrymen. A few Spoiled, possessed of both astonishing luck and deranged ferocity, came charging out of the carnage, somehow weathering the hail of gun-fire to launch themselves at the barricade. Most were shot down within seconds and the others cast back by the Blood-blessed, thrown high with Black to fall into the inferno that now consumed all of Colonial Town.

All along the barricade the guns fell silent as no more attackers appeared, the roar of the flames failing to obscure the screams as thousands of drakes and Spoiled shrieked their death agonies. Lizanne sagged a little, relief mingling with satisfaction. *It actually worked.* However, any triumph proved to be short-lived when Edgerhand gently touched her arm and pointed to the city. 'I don't think we're done yet, miss.'

The Reds. They were streaming out of the sky everywhere she looked, for the most part unhindered by any Thumper or Growler fire, though she could hear a few batteries still firing in the Blinds. Her gaze went from one roof-top position to another, finding each one destroyed, most smothered under the weight of a dead or dying Red. Flames were rising in the city beyond, accompanied by a fresh wave of screams, but these were all too human.

She didn't bother to issue any orders, instead simply drawing her guns and running towards the source of the loudest screams. She knew the Blood-blessed would follow, for where else could they go?

'I regret I have not been able to calculate an exact figure . . .'

'Your best approximation will be sufficient,' Lizanne said.

The Accounts manager, whose name she still hadn't contrived to remember, ran an unsteady hand through his thinning hair. Like everyone else called to Lizanne's office, from Arberus to Captain Flaxknot, he wore clothes besmirched by soot and blood though he had evidently found time to wash his face where others hadn't. Lizanne's gaze drifted to the space where Commander Stavemoor usually stood, finding his absence more affecting than she might have expected. He had last been seen alive charging headlong into the mass of Spoiled advancing along the top of the wall. One old man charging with sword in hand as his men dithered in fear. The commander's example had been enough to compel his troops to greater efforts and the wall had been secured against further encroachment. However, the sight of Stavemoor's body had been enough to convince Lizanne that the notion of glorious death in battle was a pernicious lie.

'We lost over a thousand defending the wall and the barricade,' the accountant said, pausing to swallow before continuing, 'and nearly six thousand dead in the city itself. Plus over two thousand wounded.'

Lizanne closed her eyes as a groan of dismay filled the room. She had been entertaining the faint hope that their success in containing the Greens and the Spoiled hadn't been purchased at the expense of the rest of the city, despite what she had witnessed the night before. She had led the Blood-blessed from one nightmare to another. The first had been the sight of a Red tearing apart a house on Carter's Walk, digging through roof and walls to tear away the floor-boards and breathe its fire on the family cowering in the cellar, a mother with four children reduced to ash in the space of a heart-beat. Lizanne and her self-appointed Blinds bodyguards held the drake in place with Black whilst the others brought down a torrent of debris to batter it into submission, the rain of bricks eventually sending it lifeless to the cobbles.

Lizanne led them on, through Baldon Park where they killed a pair of Reds chasing fleeing people across burning flower-beds, and into Corporate Square where she organised a defence of the hospital which, so far, remained mercifully untouched. She divided the Blood-blessed into smaller groups and set them in a loose perimeter around the square, then sent runners to the barricades with orders to shift all their Thumpers and Growlers to the roof-tops and get any ruined batteries back into action.

Soon the familiar dance of searchlight and drake resumed in the sky, the onslaught abating though the struggle wore on throughout the night. Contractors were released from the wall to roam the city, killing Reds wherever they could, but losing many of their number as the drakes continued to streak out of the sky, killing with talon and flame before the marksmen brought them down. The last Red finally fled with the onset of sunrise, leaving Carvenport to suffer under a pall of thickening smoke.

'My department has also counted over four hundred Red corpses,' the Accounts manager added as the silence lengthened, his voice taking on a desperately hopeful tone.

'Plus who knows how many Spoiled and Green,' Arberus put in. 'In terms of numbers, I'd say we're about even. And we'll soon have more product than we know what to do with.'

'And fewer Blood-blessed to use it.' Lizanne clasped her hands together to conceal the tremble, born as much from fatigue as worry. She found the expectation on their faces grated on her. *Seven thousand dead in a single night and still they look to me.*

'There is, perhaps, some crumb of comfort to be gleaned from our misfortune,' the Accounts manager said. 'Though I may be considered callous for voicing it.'

'A conclusion formed before now,' Lizanne assured him. 'What is it?'

'The fleet,' he said, eyes darting about the room as if worried the entire meeting might turn on him. 'Our losses, tragic though they are, mean that we now have sufficient shipping to carry the entire population.'

Lizanne thought it a measure of their situation that the man's statement was greeted by grim silence rather than an angry outburst. 'How much longer?' she asked Jermayah.

'Another two days,' he said. 'Once we've repaired the damage from last night. And I'll need every Blood-blessed still standing. Turns out iron forges more easily under blood-fire.'

'Will they allow us another two days?' Arberus wondered.

'Even with their losses, patrols report the jungle still thick with Spoiled. And we can bet the Reds aren't spent either.'

'We can expect at least a day's respite,' Lizanne said, keeping her gaze on Jermayah. 'It all needs to be done before they come again. Take whatever measures you deem necessary, but there is no longer any other option. We will evacuate this city and sail for Feros.'

'The Blues . . .' Flaxknot began but fell silent at Lizanne's glare.

'We will arm the ships with as many Growlers and Thumpers as we can. The Protectorate vessels will form a vanguard, fight their way through and the rest of the fleet will follow.' She rose from the desk, gesturing at the door. 'Now, if you'll excuse me.'

After they had gone she lay on her bunk, Blue vial in hand as she felt her body thrum with fatigue. *Is there any point?* she wondered, looking at the vial, heavy-lidded eyes watching the contents slosh back and forth. For some reason Madame Bondersil's face swam into her thoughts, her younger face from that first meeting at the Academy, severe but also kind in her way. *Was she planning it all then?* Lizanne wondered. *Plotting her inevitable rise year after year. All for nothing, her personal fiefdom destined for destruction within a few weeks of her ascension. Her great legacy no more than a pile of ash.*

Her gaze returned to the vial, lingering on the product beading the glass. *He's dead*, she thought as a parade of faces drifted through her mind. *Burgrave Artonin, Madam Meeram, Kalla and Misha, poor lovelorn Sirus, Commander Stavemoor and so many others . . . Surely, by now. He must be dead.*

CHAPTER 41

Clay

Clay rolled as the knife came down, hearing the blade shatter on the stone floor, then kicked out as Scriberson drew the stunted weapon back for another try. Clay's boot caught the astronomer under the chin, sending him staggering back with blood streaming from his partly scaled mouth. Clay got to his feet, drawing the Stinger and levelling it at Scriberson's forehead. 'Where is she?' he demanded.

For a second Scriberson just stood and stared at him, blood leaking from remolded features that betrayed no emotion at all. His eyes, Clay realised, seeing the slits surrounded by yellow. The eyes of a Spoiled, or a drake. Scriberson lunged for him again, jabbing the stump of his knife blade at Clay's neck. It was a fast move, but also clumsy and obvious. Whatever changes had been wrought in him, the astronomer had not been made into a fighter. Clay side-stepped the thrust, shifted his grip on the Stinger and slammed the butt into Scriberson's temple, sending him to his knees. Clay put the barrel of the Stinger against his neck and drew back the hammer, speaking in a slow, deliberate tone that left no room for doubt. 'Where is she, you son of a bitch?'

Scriberson turned his head to regard Clay with the same blank stare from the same slitted eyes. *Scribes is not at home any more,* Clay decided, stepping back from him. A slight change in the light caused him to steal a glance at the blue crystal, its pulsing rhythm now replaced by a faint shimmer. The sound of many feet shifting on stone made him turn, finding himself confronted by all the Briteshore folk. Their expressions were as blank as

Scriberson's, but instead of staring in rapt fascination at the crystal, now their identical-slitted eyes were all fixed on him.

Scriberson surged to his feet and charged at Clay, clawed hands reaching out with obvious intent. 'Dammit, Scribes!' Clay dodged the charge and delivered a punch to Scriberson's jaw, trying to dissuade him from any further assaults, but the astronomer seemed to be beyond any pain now. Shrugging off the blow he crouched to charge again. Clay brought up the Stinger, intending to put a bullet in his leg; he was no use dead, after all. His finger halted on the trigger as Scriberson came to an abrupt halt, his transformed eyes widening into a semblance of something human as he staggered, lips wet with blood and gurgling as he turned to display the throwing-knife buried in the base of his skull. He fell to the floor, gurgled some more then lay still.

Clay raised his gaze from the astronomer's corpse, seeing Silverpin straightening from the throw near the entrance to the dome. 'I've been looking for you,' he said and she smiled, but it was a smile he hadn't seen on her face before. As rich in regret as it was in fondness. *I ain't supposed to be here,* he realised, returning his gaze to Scriberson's corpse, Miss Lethridge's words from the unbidden trance coming back to him. *Joya . . . The Island girl . . .*

A tumult of footsteps snapped his gaze back to the Briteshore people, seeing them all charging towards him, some brandishing knives or pickaxes, others reaching out with clawed hands. He shot the closest one, the managerial type in the suit, then two more. It didn't seem to discourage their companions and he back-pedaled on rapid feet, bringing down another two before the Stinger fired empty. Still they came on, his back connecting with the jagged spines of the crystal. He dropped the Stinger as they closed in, his hands fumbling for his vials. He managed to get the Black clear of the wallet, but it was too late, many hands reaching out to restrain him as they pressed in with crushing force. He yelled at the sting of a knife blade jabbing into his cheek, thrashing and kicking as he tried to get the vial to his lips. *One sip, just one sip to throw them off . . .*

Then the pressure was gone, these new-made Spoiled drawing back as one, retreating into the same crescent formation with an unconscious, near-military precision. Silverpin stood amongst them, bloodied spear in hand and a fresh-killed Spoiled at her feet. She beckoned to Clay as he staggered, untouched vial in hand. He stared at her in blank incomprehension until she repeated the gesture with an urgent flick of her hand before making for the exit. With a final wary glance at the silent figures surrounding him, and a brief look at Scriberson's unmoving body, he trotted obediently in her wake.

The entrance slid closed behind him after he made his way outside. Silverpin stood with the butt of her spear resting on the chamber floor, her smile smaller, but no less regretful. Clay studied her face for a long time, wondering why there was no anger in him now, none of the heat that had gripped him as Lutharon bore him through the clouds.

'Something always made me wonder,' he said. 'Just how did you manage to kill Keyvine? Him being such a very dangerous man and all. Couldn't have been easy, even for you.'

Her smile faded and she shrugged. As ever, he found her meaning easy to interpret. *You know how.*

He replayed Miss Lethridge's message, the absent words tumbling into place. *Joya's alive . . . She saw . . . The Island girl is a Blood-blessed . . .* 'Thank you,' he said. 'For letting Joya live.'

Another shrug, a flicker of a smile, gone in an instant. *A favour to you.*

He glanced back at the now-sealed dome. 'Scriberson didn't take you here. You took him.' A small, bitter laugh bubbled up from inside him, building into something shrill and harsh by the time he forced it down. 'Why?'

She gave no response this time, save to lower her head, her face losing all animation. Clay took a step towards her as the anger finally arrived, fighting the impulse to grip her shoulders

and shake answers from her. Instead he could only repeat 'Why?'
in a strained whisper.

Slowly, she raised her face, eyes meeting his, pale and beautiful
in her mask of ink. And she blinked.

Noise. Voices. The scent of many people. The air abruptly
changed from the dry heat of the chamber to the sultriness
of Carvenport in early summer. He stood amongst a thick crowd
of people in the broad avenue leading to Harvester's Square, home
to the breeding pens. He could see that a platform had been
erected alongside a large vat at the far end of the avenue, the
thick oak planking that formed its sides shuddering as the thing
inside strained against its bonds. A number of adults and children
were arranged in an orderly line in front of the platform, the
youngsters either squirming in boredom or clutching their parents
in fearful response to the noise emanating from the vat. Clay
remembered it well, grunting out its pain and rage through the
iron muzzle they had secured over its jaws. Hearing it then he
had known it to be something terrible, something that wanted
badly to kill all the people gathered to celebrate its death.

A tall man of spindly proportions stood on the platform
reading aloud from a thick sheaf of papers. He was dressed in
out-dated managerial garb and his voice possessed the toneless
quality of those who would be better served by short speeches,
but evidently he had a lot to say. Clay remembered how the crowd
had begun murmuring amongst themselves as the man droned
on, the murmur soon building to a babble of unrestrained conversation, though if the speech-maker took any notice of the fact
that he had lost his audience, he failed to show it.

'The Corporate Age is . . .' he intoned then paused to turn a
page, '. . . an age of wonders. But these wonders are not gifts;
they do not spring unbidden from the ether. Instead they are the
product of the Corporatist ethos . . .'

'The day of the Blood-lot,' a voice said. It was a clear, confident
voice, uncoloured by an accent. Clay turned to find a young

woman about his own age at his side, blonde with fine pale features. She wore a plain blue dress that complemented her colouring perfectly, matching as it did the shade of her eyes. Eyes set in a face free of tattoos. Eyes he would know anywhere.

'You can talk,' he said, which made her laugh.

'Obviously. The trance is a place of endless possibility, Clay. Here I can talk. *We* can finally talk.' She smiled and reached for his hand, face clouding with hurt when he snatched it away.

'I didn't drink,' he said. 'Neither did you.'

'We are in a place where such things are redundant, for me at least. Maybe for you too, in time.'

'How?'

'I truly do not know. There is so much still beyond my understanding. But I was promised wonders if I came here, and so it proved.'

'Promised by who?'

She turned as another woman made her way through the crowd. For a moment Clay thought he was seeing Silverpin's twin but then saw the lines around the woman's mouth and eyes. She couldn't have been more than thirty but those lines told of youth lost to a hard life, as did the threadbare dress and shawl she wore. A little girl had hold of the woman's hand, a little girl with blonde hair and striking blue eyes. He saw a strange cast to the woman's face, an emptiness that echoed the blank fascination in Scriberson's gaze. The little girl was far more animated, eyes fixed on the vat and seeming to shine with excitement.

'He promised me many things,' Silverpin said, standing aside as the pair passed by, smiling down at the little girl. 'Ever since I could remember, he whispered to me. In dreams at first but then when I was awake. He called to me, and my journey to his side began here.'

She began to follow the woman and child through the crowd, passing through the assembled townsfolk as if they were mist. Clay stayed at her side, keeping close to catch every baffling word she spoke. 'He said I was different. That the great gift I carried inside me had been waiting a very long time to be set free. But it needed to be fed, awoken from its slumber.'

Up ahead, he saw the woman stride past a yawning Protectorate constable without attracting his notice, then walk along the line of those awaiting the Blood-lot. 'I had always found Mother very easy to control,' Silverpin went on as they followed. 'Easier than any other, in fact. The blood connection, I suppose. Others have a tendency to be more difficult. And you,' she paused to favour Clay with a small grin, 'were virtually impossible. It's often the way with other Blood-blessed. No matter how many seeds I plant in their minds, they rarely take root.'

'Seeds?' Clay asked.

'I told you there was more to the trance than just shared memory. Blue is a remarkable product; your kind understands only the barest fraction of its power.'

He thought back to the Briteshore folk in the dome, staring in rapt fascination at the blue crystal as their bodies became corrupted. Had it somehow planted seeds in their minds as she had planted seeds in Braddon and the others? Perhaps it had called to them over the weeks and months they laboured in the shadow of this mountain. He remembered the pictograms they found in the manager's office, line after line of neat script eventually becoming a frenzied mish-mash as the planted seed grew and took away the will of the man who scribbled it all down, probably without any understanding of what it meant. *So they all came here to get Spoiled,* he thought then frowned at another realisation. *No, not all. The miner who blew his brains out on the stairs, and the Blood-blessed woman. They resisted it. Just like I resisted her, but not as much as I should have.*

The woman and child were at the steps to the platform now, paused as they regarded the two Protectorate guards posted there. They seemed just as bored as their colleagues, one rolling his eyes at the other as the speaker turned yet another page and began a poorly phrased exploration of company ethics. Silverpin came to a halt and the memory froze around them, silence descending as every face and body stopped as if trapped in amber. She pointed at the little girl, still holding her mother's hand, but turned to look at something. Clay followed her gaze and saw that her attention was returned by a boy in the line. The boy was about her own age, skin as dark as hers was pale. He held the hand of a slender woman in a recently washed dress, cunningly stitched to disguise the many repairs and alterations it had suffered over the years. He knew because he had watched her work on it every night over the preceding week, hours seated at the kitchen-table with needle-and-thread, and that was after a ten-hour shift in the wash-house. 'Ain't nobody looking down on us,' she had said. 'Torcreek name means something in this city.'

Clay's chest tightened as he looked into his mother's face. She was smiling down at the boy holding her hand and the depth of love he saw was hard to bear. 'I remembered you, Clay,' Silverpin said. 'In fact I remember every detail of this day and pretty much everything since. Blue is powerful, but it holds a price. It seeps into your mind, changes it. Memory becomes inescapable, and so does guilt.'

The scene returned to life again, all the people unfreezing and the air thickening with their noise. The little girl turned away from the boy as her mother moved on from the bored guards, keeping to the edge of the platform until she came to where it ended at the vat. She bent and lifted the girl up onto the platform before climbing up after, all the time wearing the same empty mask of a face.

'You must have known it would kill her,' Clay said.

Silverpin gave no reply, leading him through the guards to ascend to the platform. They watched the woman and girl climb the final set of steps to the top of the scaffold overlooking the vat where they waited, still, silent and completely unnoticed.

'. . . and so,' the manager said, an air of finality creeping into his otherwise flat tones, 'as a demonstration of the regard in which the Ironship Syndicate holds the people of this city, we will proceed with the harvesting.'

Grateful applause rippled through the crowd as he stepped back and all eyes turned to the vat. Silverpin led Clay to the scaffold and they climbed up to stand behind the woman and girl, staring down at the ugly spectacle below. The Black was the largest Clay had seen, a foot or more taller at the shoulder than Lutharon, and he was old. It was clear in the many scars on his hide, and the keenness of his gaze as he tried to thrash in his web of chains. Clay could see both fear and rage in those eyes. The Black understood his fate.

His wings had been hacked off and the stumps sealed with burning pitch, but still they twitched, the muscles working under the aged skin as he tried instinctively to fly clear of this threat. Harsh, guttural rasps came from the iron muzzle clamped over his jaws and Clay knew he was attempting to breathe fire at the man approaching across the floor of the vat. He would be a Master Harvester, Clay knew; only those who spent a lifetime in the pens could be trusted with the task of tapping a full-grown Black. The harvester wore a suit of thick green leather that covered him from head to foot, his face a pale smudge behind the glass visor sewn into his hood. He held a long steel spile in one hand and a hammer in the other. He would leave the drake alive, Clay knew, so the heart would pump as much product clear of his veins before exhaustion and death overtook him.

'I pitied him,' Silverpin said, Clay seeing that her gaze was fixed on the girl as she used a small hand to wipe away the tear tracing down her cheek. 'It seemed so unfair. But for me to receive my gift, he had to die.' Her eyes drifted to her mother. 'And so did she.'

The harvester positioned the spile at the Black's neck, just above the juncture with his shoulder where the artery was thickest, and pounded it home with three quick strikes of the hammer. The blood began to flow immediately, spattering onto the floor in thick jets as the Black shuddered in his chains. The woman reached down to gather her daughter into her arms, waiting and watching the blood flow.

'Still,' Silverpin said. 'I felt he at least deserved revenge. And I had need of a distraction.'

Some idle eye in the crowd must have finally noticed the woman for a scream pealed out as she hugged her daughter tighter and jumped into the vat. She landed directly in the torrent of blood, her skin blistering immediately wherever it touched her. The agony must have been indescribable but she issued no cries. Instead, she held the little girl out so that the gush of blood flowed over every inch of the child's skin and into her open mouth. Even for a Blood-blessed, exposure to so much product should have been fatal. Instead she laughed, even as her mother, skin mottled with blisters and part dissolved by the red stream, collapsed into the spreading pool of raw product. The girl didn't appear to have any interest in her mother's ghastly fate, jumping and giggling in excitement as the blood covered her. Whilst she didn't burn, she did change, her already pale skin bleached to alabaster as she continued to rejoice in the red stream.

The harvester, who had until this moment remained rooted in shock at the horror confronting him, rushed towards the child, no doubt intending rescue. She scowled as his leather-clad hands touched her shoulders, and the harvester flew away, his body blurring before it slammed into the side of the vat with a crack that told of a shattered spine. The little girl turned to regard the Black and, for an instant, their eyes met. Clay saw the drake attempt to recoil, its eyes shining with even more fear than when confronted with the inevitability of its own death.

'He heard me,' Silverpin said. 'In his head, and he recognised the voice. I didn't know it would scare him so much.'

The little girl shifted her gaze slightly and every chain binding the drake shattered as one. Then all became a senseless fury of splintered wood as the vat blew apart and the crowd let loose a scream of terror. The memory froze then, leaving them alone in a world of misted blood and air thickened by debris.

'You did this,' Clay said.

Silverpin nodded.

'My mother died here . . . You killed her and hundreds more besides.'

'And gained much in return,' she said. 'Everything he promised. There is so much more that can be done with the power stored in drake blood, Clay. Your kind are like children playing with gunpowder.'

'My kind,' he repeated. 'We're so different now?'

'We always were. After this' – she gestured at the surrounding destruction – 'I was remade. And still he called to me, offering more. All I had to do was find him.'

It came to him then, a hard, sickening rush of understanding that set his pulse racing. *Their hunger for the White. Uncle's loss of reason whenever it came up. Gone when she stole the car. Seeds . . . Seeds planted and nurtured the farther south we travelled. Seeds planted by her.* 'You didn't know,' he said. 'You didn't know where it was. We guided you to it.'

'Some years ago his voice grew dim, like a distant murmur. But still he called to me. I tried several times to find him, venturing into the Interior with different companies, even a mob of Headhunters. When I found your uncle, however, the voice grew louder and I knew all I had to do was wait. I didn't know I was waiting for you. You were . . . a pleasant and terrible surprise.'

'You needed me to get you here,' Clay said, his anger deepening yet further. 'That's why you killed Keyvine. That why you fucked me too?'

'Actually no. I do have the occasional weakness for spontaneity.' She lowered her gaze and the trance vanished, replaced by the vast chamber and its domes. She stepped closer to him, reaching out a hand to caress his face. Her lips were still when she spoke this time, but the words rang clear in his mind. *Why did you come, Clay? You were supposed to flee, get far away just like you wanted. You would have had some time, at least. Perhaps even years.*

'Until what?' he grated, forcing himself to remain still as her fingers stroked his jaw.

He called me here for a reason. A very old but very necessary design has been interrupted, and will now be resumed.

Clay's gaze went to the largest dome, the one with the white light streaming from the apex of its roof. 'It's in there isn't it?'

Yes. Sleeping safely all these years. He came here after nesting in the Badlands, when he had grown enough to take wing, drawn by an ancient instinct burned into his soul. And all the while he called to me in his dreams.

'Why? What does it need you for?'

I don't know. She stepped back, gesturing at the dome. *Shall we find out?*

His eyes flicked to the barrel lying nearby, abandoned when he had been lured into the blue dome.

Don't be foolish, Silverpin chided and the barrel rose from the floor, hovering for a second before streaking upwards, disappearing through the shaft above too fast to follow. A few seconds later he heard the flat boom of a distant explosion. *Come along then.* She took his hand and tugged him towards the white dome. *Since you are so devoted to me we'll see if he can be persuaded to share his gifts.*

'I don't want his gifts!' Clay said, tearing his hand away, then freezing as her Black closed on him tight enough to stop the breath in his throat.

The time when the apes scampering about this rock were allowed the illusion of choice is over, she told him and he had the sense that she was reciting a well-rehearsed speech, words she had been expecting to say for a very long time. *Your last choice was in following me into this mountain. And like all choices it entailed consequences.*

CHAPTER 42

Lizanne

This is pointless. She knew it even as she thumbed the stopper from the vial. *A waste of time and effort sorely needed elsewhere.*

Lizanne sat slumped behind her desk, casting a weary glance at her soon-to-be-vacated office and finding nothing she wanted to claim as a souvenir. In just over an hour she would make her way to the docks and the fleet would begin its desperate attempt at escape. She should be using this short respite to rest, knowing she and every other Blood-blessed would be sorely needed when they finally put to sea. She had tried twice over the course of the preceding day, taking precious time away from organising the evacuation, and each time finding nothing in the trance beyond her own mindscape and the same inescapable conclusion. *He must surely be dead. This is entirely pointless.*

With a final glance at the clock she sighed and drank the vial of Blue.

Her heart leapt as the trance descended and Nelphia's peaks and valleys unfolded before her. *He's alive! He's here!*

The blossoming excitement soon died, however, as she realised that although Clay's mindscape was present, he wasn't. The valleys and peaks of the great moon remained empty and silent. It was something she had never seen before. Something, in fact, she would have thought impossible. Even when a Blood-blessed slept through a trance, there was still some vestige of them left.

She roamed across the surface calling out for him, ready to

unfurl the whirlwind containing her memory of Joya's tale. Silence was the only answer.

The Island girl! she called out, hoping somehow the words might reach him. If an image conjured by his mind was here then some vestige of him might be too. *She killed Keyvine! Joya's alive. She saw her do it, with Black! The Island girl is a Blood-blessed!*

For the briefest instant the mindscape vanished, snapping out of existence, replaced with a blank void . . . No, not a void. There was something there, something shining bright, like a crystal lit from within . . .

Then it was gone and she found herself once again surrounded by her own whirlwinds of memory and not the slightest glimmer of Clay's mindscape. Now, he was truly gone.

The MPV *Laudable Intent* sat low in the harbour waters as Lizanne strode aboard, followed up the gangplank by Tekela, her three Blinds bodyguards plus Arberus and his handful of surviving Corvantines. She knew the ship to be a Marlin class frigate though extensive modification had rendered her near unrecognisable. In addition to the existing armament of one forward pivot-gun and four old twelve-pounders, she now bristled from end to end with an array of Thumpers and Growlers, all protected by a newly installed covering of armour, the construction of which was so uneven as to resemble the deformed shell of a battered turtle.

'Miss Lethridge.' Vice-Commodore Skarhall delivered a formal salute as she stepped down from the gangplank. As a result of the demise of Commander Stavemoor he was now the most senior Protectorate officer in the city, though at first glance he cut a much-less-impressive figure. Skarhall stood a little over five feet seven inches in height and had a frame that could most generously be described as wiry. He also had a tendency to speak in soft tones, as if pondering thoughts aloud rather than attempting communication. But, however unremarkable his appearance or demeanour, he had proven himself an able and efficient collaborator in Jermayah's daunting project, ensuring the requisite modifications to his small fleet were carried out without obstruction from truculent crews or recalcitrant engineers.

'Any problems to report, Commodore?' she asked him.

'The Protectorate flotilla stands at full readiness with engines primed,' he reported in tones barely above a murmur. 'Some civilian vessels are still loading, but we expect to be ready to sail at the appointed time.' He stood aside, gesturing at a nearby ladder. 'If you would care to join me on the bridge.'

The bridge offered a view of the harbour and the city, albeit restricted somewhat by the armour fringing the windows. Lizanne peered out at the dockside then raised her gaze to survey the city beyond. Smoke rose in dense columns from several places, the result of another Red attack the night before. The cost had only been a fraction of the toll exacted the night Colonial Town burned, sparing civilians but claiming yet more defenders amongst the gun-crews. She had ordered the resultant fires left unchecked, there being no time or particular need to quell them now as she harboured profound doubts that any human would be returning to this city in the near future.

She had issued the evacuation order barely twenty hours ago, surely an impossible schedule to complete the emptying of an entire city, but somehow they had managed it. To prevent a panicked rush to the docks, each district had been evacuated in turn, the movement of people being subject to stern and unwavering control by a heavily armed contingent of Protectorate soldiers. The Blinds, thanks to its proximity to the docks and much to the surprise of its inhabitants, had been the first to go, the great horde of ragged and mismatched souls making their way to the ships in surprising quietude. The managerial district, the last to be emptied, proved a marked contrast. There had been an unseemly and ineffectual attempt to break through the Protectorate cordon as the hours wore on and tempers grew frayed. When the besuited and heavily laden denizens had finally been escorted to the ships the scene was marked by many protestations and dire promises of legal redress, their outrage deepening further when forced to cast aside much of their luggage before being allowed to board. The quay-side was now littered with piles of suitcases and sundry valuables, the impressive array of silverware catching the late-morning sun.

The hospital had been the hardest task, conveying so many wounded to the ships taking up considerable time and effort. Despite some suggestions to the contrary Lizanne, to Mrs Torcreek's evident relief, refused to countenance leaving behind any but the most hopeless cases. These unfortunates, all either comatose or barely aware of their surroundings, remained in the hands of a small staff of volunteers, elderly nurses and doctors willing to sacrifice their final hours to the care of others. Lizanne had been assiduous in recording their names in detail, though her promises of posthumous awards and pensions for surviving relatives sounded empty even to her own ears.

Two ships had been given over to the wounded, Mrs Torcreek taking her place on the largest. She had come to Lizanne before going aboard, seeking some word regarding her family, only to be told the unalloyed truth. 'I do not know, Mrs Torcreek. I believe Clay at least was alive as of a few hours ago, but in what state I cannot say.'

The woman's head lowered, her shoulders slumping in the only sign of frailty Lizanne had seen in her. She righted herself after a moment, smiling as she offered Lizanne her hand. 'Call me Fredabel, or Freda if you like.'

'Lizanne.'

'Lizzie?' the older woman suggested as they shook hands.

'No,' she replied in an unambiguous tone. 'Lizanne.'

She tried to make out the wall through the haze of smoke but the distance was too great. Captain Flaxknot and the small army of Contractors had undertaken the duty of holding the wall during the evacuation. Their scouts reported ever more Spoiled trekking towards the city from the south and the west, whilst increasing numbers of Greens could be seen prowling the jungle. Fortunately, neither were present in sufficient numbers to mount another assault, though that might change if they happened to notice how thinly the walls were held.

Lizanne spent the remaining time watching the last few civilians being herded onto the ships, stragglers and old folk for the most part. There had inevitably been a few who refused to leave, mainly amongst the old or recently bereaved. The latter had clustered together, armed to the teeth and intent on selling their lives dear when the time came. Lizanne had made a few vain attempts to persuade these vengeful mobs to see reason but soon gave up in the face of more pressing matters, allowing them to take charge of any Growlers and Thumpers left behind when the fleet sailed.

When the last ancient had tottered up the gangplank Commodore Skarhall ordered a fresh signal hoisted and the steam-whistle sounded. The piercing wail was soon joined by that of every siren and whistle in the fleet, the general cacophony augmented by several flares launched by the Protectorate vessels. Lizanne turned her gaze back to the city and was soon rewarded by the sight of the Contractors hurrying towards the docks, many riding double on horseback. They had been left in no doubt that the fleet would wait exactly thirty minutes before setting off and all had clearly taken the warning to heart. As per Lizanne's orders they made for the civilian ships where she hoped their marksmanship would enhance the defences, most of the heavy weaponry having been allotted to the Protectorate vessels.

Lizanne breathed a small sigh of relief at seeing Captain Flaxknot's stocky form striding up the gangplank onto the same old steamer where Jermayah had chosen to place himself. 'Built her engine myself,' he said by way of explanation. 'Every plate and bolt. First one to come off the line. I believe it's up to me to make sure she runs all the way to Feros.'

She watched the last of the Contractors vacate the quay with five minutes still to spare then turned to Skarhall with a tight smile. 'I see little point in further delay, Commodore.'

He replied with a nod then proceeded to make her jump as a rapid and very loud series of orders issued from his mouth. The crew on the bridge responded with automaton-esque alacrity, the helmsman taking a grip on the wheel and the First Mate working the telegraph to the engine room whilst relayed orders chorused from one end of the ship to the other. The decking beneath Lizanne's feet began an immediate thrum as the blood-burner came to life, soon accompanied by the regular swishing churn of the paddles. She winced a little as Skarhall barked out another tirade of orders and the *Laudable Intent* pulled away from the dockside. The wheel blurred as the helmsman spun it from port to starboard in a precise and well-practised sequence that soon had them heading directly for the harbour doors. Some of the stay-behinds had volunteered to operate the lifting machinery, a dozen or so dockworkers who had lost their families in the siege. They performed their duty with creditable dedication, the great copper wings rising smoothly as the *Laudable* approached, speed building all the while.

'All guns stand to!' Skarhall barked, his every word echoing through the decks. 'Riflemen to firing holes! Ammunition crews stand ready!'

He turned to Lizanne, his voice dropping into its customary murmur as he gestured to the ladder at the rear of the bridge. 'I believe you'll find things arranged as requested, miss.'

Lizanne nodded and moved to Tekela's side, clasping her hand. The girl said nothing, remaining with eyes downcast for a second, before enfolding Lizanne in a tight embrace. 'Stay here,' Lizanne whispered into her ear. 'I believe the commodore is in need of protection.'

Tekela released her and stepped back, moving to Skarhall's side and checking her revolver. Lizanne nodded at her three bodyguards and started up the ladder.

The platform had been constructed atop the bridge, open-topped to afford a clear view all around but with thick armour walls four feet high. Each of the Protectorate ships in the vanguard featured the same arrangement and Lizanne could see their contingents of Blood-blessed climbing up in readiness as they drew near the doors, a minimum of two to each ship. Stocks of product had already been placed in each corner of the platform, Red and Green in plentiful supply, but only a third as much Black.

'Never been this close to such riches,' Red Allice commented, playing a hand along the well-packed row of vials. These were the first words Lizanne had heard her utter and she spoke in an odd accent, mixing native Arradsian tones with a tinge of Varestian.

'Not even as a pirate?' Lizanne asked in Varestian which drew the faintest grin from the woman, but no more words.

'Quite a sight,' Arberus commented, nodding at the ships falling into line behind the *Laudable Intent,* the warships with their turtle-like armour and the many others now pulling away from the dockside in accordance with the carefully-worked-out plan. The intention was to form an arrow formation with the Protectorate ships at the head. Skarhall had claimed it was well within the capabilities of the merchant fleet, but how long they could maintain it once free of the harbour was another matter.

Lizanne swung her gaze towards the sea beyond the doors, finding it unexpectedly placid. She knew this to be illusory. The Blues had a tendency to disappear beneath the waves for hours or days only to rear up without warning and snatch or roast unwary souls who had ventured onto the mole. The *Laudable Intent* increased speed as they entered the gap in the wall, Skarhall setting a speed of eighteen knots, well within the range of his engine but still a push for the newly converted warships following. They passed through leaving a frothing wake, all eyes intent on the surrounding water. For a full minute nothing happened and they ploughed on through untroubled waters free of the slightest eddy or betraying splash.

'Do they sleep?' Burgrave Crovik wondered, sweat trickling down his plump face and all trace of his claimed nobility now absent from his voice. 'They might be sleeping.'

'No,' Red Allice told him, gaze fixed directly ahead. 'They don't sleep.'

The Blue drake erupted from the sea directly in the ship's path, moving so fast the forward gun crew had no time to react before the first blast of flame swept down. They were saved from annihilation by the armour plate that surrounded the position, though from the screams, not all the crew remained unscathed. The gun fired as the Blue heaved itself onto the fore-deck, the shell tearing a chunk from its coiling flesh. It pealed out a screech of pain and rage before fixing its gaze on the exposed humans on the platform above, whereupon it lunged higher, mouth gaping.

Lizanne had injected a mingled burst of product during the drake's first attack and now unleashed her Black to stop it just short of the platform. Arberus and his men let loose with an immediate volley from their rifles, aiming for the head and eyes as they had been taught. Lizanne saw one bullet strike home on the Blue's right eye, blood and vitreous humour exploding as its head remained fixed in place, though the rest of it continued to thrash, the elongated body thumping spasmodically onto the *Laudable*'s armour. Lizanne risked a glance to ensure the three other Blood-blessed had drunk their fill and gave a curt nod of command. As one they unleashed a wave of Black, propelling the beast clear of the ship. It landed in the sea a few yards off the starboard side and immediately began to coil for another strike just as every Thumper and Growler able to bear on it opened fire. The sea roiled red around the drake, the hail of bullets and shells tearing it to pieces in a matter of seconds.

Lizanne didn't pause to watch the drake sink, instead scanning the surrounding sea, heart sinking as Blue after Blue rose from the waves and began knifing their way through the swell towards them.

'Some moderation, if you don't mind,' she cautioned Crovik as he guzzled down another vial. 'Drink only when they come close. Let the guns do their work.'

She looked to the stern, seeing that all the warships were now clear of the harbour, every gun firing. She tracked the course of one shell from the next ship in line, watching it impact on the water just as the Blue it had been aimed at twisted aside, snaking around the exploding fountain of spume with barely a pause. It submerged upon coming within the last twenty yards of the ship, diving beneath the keel to spring up on the port side, water steaming as it spewed out its flames. It managed to birth some small fires aboard the ship before intersecting Thumper and Growler fire cut it in half, the severed parts still twitching and coiling as they subsided into the waves.

The scene was repeated along the line, Blues rearing up only to be cut down or forced to abandon their attacks by the weight of fire. The *Laudable Intent* was attacked twice more in quick succession, one Blue launching itself at the port side whilst another cast its flames at the stern. In both cases the guns were able to inflict sufficient injury on the drakes for them to veer away, leaving a red slick on the waves as they plunged into the depths.

'I do believe this is actually working,' Edgerhand commented, pointing at the fleet behind them and the surrounding sea now free of drakes. He turned to Lizanne and offered a florid bow. 'May I be the first to offer my heart-felt thanks and congratulations to Miss Blood.' He rose and stepped closer, speaking softly. 'I do happen to know a most excellent bistro in Feros . . .'

He was interrupted by the boom of the forward gun. Lizanne turned in time to see the spout of red and white a few hundred yards dead ahead and mentally congratulated the gunner on his aim. To hit a single drake at such a range was quite a feat. Then she noticed the disturbance in the surrounding waters and realised the shot hadn't been aimed at only one target. The sea swelled, lifted by the combined wakes of Blues moving in a close-packed mass coming straight towards the *Laudable* at far too great a speed for them to evade.

They learn, Lizanne recalled, emptying the Spider's reserves of Red, Green and Black into her veins. *They always learn.*

The forward gun had time for one more shot before the drake

pack closed, vapourising the head of a Blue just as it reared out of the water, but it did nothing to discourage the others. For a few seconds everything became a chaos of noise and heat, the frenzied chatter of the Growlers, the slower percussive thud of the Thumpers and the screams, drake and human. Lizanne directed a combined blast of Black and Red at one drake as it lunged for the platform. Despite the numerous wounds leaking blood from its shimmering scales, it continued to thrash against the heat and force she cast at it, seemingly uncaring of its scorched black eyes and shattered teeth. It finally fell back into the sea thanks to a concentrated volley from Arberus's men, one lucky bullet finding its brain.

'Down!' Red Allice grabbed Lizanne about the waist and bore her to the deck as the air above the platform turned to flame. Lizanne managed to keep the fire at bay with a concentrated wall of Black, soon reinforced by Allice and Edgerhand. However, they had been too slow to save Burgrave Crovik. The flames receded to reveal the pretend nobleman standing in the centre of the platform, his body untouched below the shoulders and his head a smoking cinder. Incredibly, he managed to take a few steps before collapsing to the deck.

Lizanne raised herself to risk a glance over the edge of the armoured walls, seeing Blues latched onto the *Laudable* from end to end, some clearly in their death throes but still hanging on. Their intent was obvious, and seemed about to be fulfilled from the way the sea was washing over the ship's upper works. Within moments they would be swamped.

Lizanne snatched a vial of Black from one of the product caches, gulped it down and leapt clear of the platform, Green-boosted strength carrying her to the prow where two drakes were tightly coiled about the hull. She dodged a lunge from one, teeth snapping the air inches from her legs, then leapt onto the beast's head. She clung to the spine at the base of its skull as it tried to throw her off, screeching all the while. Focusing her gaze on the ridge between its eyes she unleashed half her Black with enough force to shatter the bone shielding the beast's brain. The Blue's struggles reached a new pitch of desperation and she found herself in the air once again as it threw her off, though not before she had drawn one of her revolvers. Sailing backwards through the air she fired all six bullets into the exposed red-grey mass and had the satisfaction of watching the Blue slip from the *Laudable*'s hull before she plunged into the shocking chill of the sea.

She went under for only a few seconds before kicking to the surface with ease thanks to the Green in her system. She spat brine from her mouth and watched the *Laudable* plough on through the waves, sitting higher in the water now but still part covered in Blues despite the constant blast of the guns. She could see Arberus's tall form waving desperately from the platform but knew even with the Green she couldn't hope to swim to them now. She cast about for the nearest ship, instead finding herself confronted by a tall spine cutting the water only twenty yards away. Turning, she saw another behind her and realised she was being circled.

Various plans ran through her mind, all equally hopeless. She could feel her skin numbing as the product seeped from her veins and wondered if the Blues could sense it somehow, perhaps delaying their attack until she no longer posed a threat. *Or,* she reflected with a cold detachment she thought she might have lost by now, *they simply wish to savour the moment.*

Whatever the case, the Blues didn't raise their heads from the water until the last drop of product had faded from her body, three of them rising from the sea to stare down at a small, struggling figure now rendered all too human.

CHAPTER 43

Clay

A door slid open in the wall of the white dome as they approached. The glow that emanated from within was so bright that Clay gave a reflexive shudder despite the grip of Silverpin's Black. She went inside and pulled him along on stiff, hesitant legs. His stuttering footfalls gave off a curious echo as he staggered in her wake and he knew he was no longer walking on stone. *Glass,* he saw as his vision started to clear and he made out the dim reflection of his boots on the floor. He blinked as his eyes detected something beneath the glass, some kind of great swirling pattern far below.

Silverpin tugged him again, jerking his head up to regard the huge white crystal in the centre of the dome. Unlike the blue crystal, which had lain on the floor of its dome, this one floated in mid air, held aloft by means unknown and revolving slowly so that the light streaming through its myriad facets varied slightly. It took a moment for him to discern foggy fluctuations in the space surrounding the crystal, patches of various hues forming like gathered mist, shapes coalescing in a shimmering rainbow dance.

White, Silverpin said in his mind as she gazed up at the ever-changing shapes, *is every colour combined.* Clay followed her gaze as she lowered it to the huge, coiled form residing in a shallow, perfectly circular pit below the crystal. Clay was able to discern its shape thanks only to the shadows cast by the crystal's glow and the dimmer reflections in the glass on which it lay. He would have taken it for a great marble sculpture but for the gentle swell of its chest accompanied by a rush of air as it breathed in its slumber. It was at least a third again Lutharon's size, half-covered by the sail-like wings and encircled by its own tail, the jagged spear-point end twitching slightly so that the spines rattled on the glass.

Although the Stinger had been lost in the blue dome his uncle's longrifle still rested on his back. But all he could do was stand and watch it sleep. *The White.*

He has slept such a long time, Silverpin said. *And dreamt such wonderful dreams.*

As if in response to her words the mist-like shapes surrounding the crystal suddenly became more animated, solidifying as they circled the dome's interior with increased velocity. They reminded Clay of flocking birds in the way they swirled about, clustering together to surround both of them in a thick vortex that recalled Miss Lethridge's mindscape of whirlwinds. The eye-straining glow dimmed as the vortex spun and he began to make out images amidst the maelstrom of colour, gasping in shock as his own face misted into view. He was blinking in the sun, expression guarded and cheeks unshaven. *Me outside the Protectorate gaol,* he realised. *The first time I saw her.*

The vortex shifted again, displaying another image, this time of a Green rearing up out of a darkened field at night, Loriabeth lying wounded nearby. *That night at Stockade,* he thought, watching the Green freeze in response to some unbidden command before a spear blade jabbed down to skewer its skull. He shot a glance at Silverpin and tried to speak, words slurring over his part-frozen lips. She lessened her control slightly, letting him talk. 'Your memories . . . It saw everything you did.'

It appears so. I knew he watched me, but not so closely. Isn't it wonderful?

Another shift in the vortex, another set of images, the cave in the Badlands, the twisted bones . . . then his face again, drawn in the passion they had shared, the image shot through with an angry red tinge.

It appears we made him jealous. Silverpin's voice carried a faintly amused tone as the image morphed into the Red Sands at night, transformed into a fiery spectacle as the Spoiled danced their death agonies beneath Lutharon's fire. *They aren't always so easy to control. I suspect some of his anger must have leached into them.*

'The temple,' Clay grunted as the images fragmented then re-formed once more, arrows raining down on the temple as the Greens came swarming up the vines.

Yes, she said. *Wondrous as he is, still he remains incomplete, a child in many ways, and children are ever impatient. The closer we came to him the more I realised how much he needs me, how much he still has to grow.*

The vortex thinned then receded, dissipating to orbit the crystal in small clusters of memory. The images they contained were still visible, but now seemed bafflingly unfamiliar to Clay. He could catch only short glimpses as they passed by; a city of tall spires rising above the Arradsian jungle, Red drakes wheeling amongst the buildings. Then the earth seen from far above, blue oceans and white-capped mountains, growing in size as whatever had captured this image streaked downwards, heading towards a body of water he recognised as Krystaline Lake. Next a battle, Black and Red drakes filling the sky with flame and blood as they tore at each other, and streaking through the chaos, a White, tearing Black after Black out of the sky with gore-covered talons, despite the many wounds that gashed its flesh.

So much to see, Silverpin said, and he understood she was seeing all this for the first time; these memories belonged to something else. *So much to learn.*

A low, rumbling sound filled the dome, a sound that seemed to cut into Clay's being from skin to bone. His eyes snapped to the White, seeing a tendril of smoke rising from the thing's marble nostrils.

'You wake it up,' he said to Silverpin, spittle flying as his tongue sought to form words against the cage of his teeth, 'it'll kill us all.'

No, she replied. *Not all. Just many. It will be a time of great pain, but birth is always painful.*

She moved away from him, striding forward until she stood directly beneath the crystal. It began to pulse as she halted, flaring light so intense Clay worried he might be blinded. He saw Silverpin raise her arms as the crystal stopped its revolutions, a beam of light streaking down to bathe her from head to toe. Another rumble sounded from the White, the twitching of its tail transformed into a coiling thrash as a second beam emerged from the crystal to bathe the beast from head to toe. The beam's colour had changed, taking on a bluish hue. *White is all colours combined,* he recalled.

So much to see, Silverpin repeated in his mind, her voice dimmer now but the wonder it contained was palpable. The swirling memories had multiplied, full of yet more images of wonder and terror, flashing past at such a speed he could catch only glimpses: a White breathing fire on a group of Spoiled kneeling in obvious supplication. An egg bathed in fire and cracking open to reveal the screaming infant Black inside, the flames fading to reveal an old man in a robe staring down at the fledgling drake with the expression of a proud father. Clay's eyes latched onto the symbol emblazoned on the man's chest, an upturned eye, the same eye that adorned the outside of the building above. The last sight he saw before the parade of images became too fast to follow was the most baffling: a field of ice beneath a starlit night sky, small figures labouring across the field towards something jutting from the ice near the horizon, something monumentally large that vaguely resembled a church spire, but twisted with deep rents in its massive sides, as if damaged somehow . . .

He staggered as a tremor ran through the glass floor followed shortly after by a loud boom far above. It was like the explosion of the barrel Silverpin had thrown through the shaft, but ten times louder. He felt Silverpin's grip slip for an instant before she reasserted control. He could just make out her features through the beam. Her tattoos were fading and a vertical ridge had formed on her forehead. Also her eyes, narrowed in annoyance rather than anger, had taken on a yellow hue. *She's being Spoiled,* he knew. *Like the Billeshoro folk*

'Stop!' Clay yelled at her as best he could through his part frozen lips. 'Please!'

The White moved, tail snaking away from its body and wings flexing as the beams continued to perform whatever process Silverpin had triggered.

'This is crazy!' he called to her, his words more easily formed now as he felt her Black diminish, perhaps in response to the changes being wrought by the beam. He managed to take a step, even partly raise a hand in a desperate entreaty. 'Do you want the world to burn?'

Her reply was faint, only a whisper in his mind, and carried such a note of finality he knew somehow this would be the last words he would ever hear from her: *It's not your world any more, Clay. Don't worry, he'll let me keep you. His kind always had their pets.*

He stared at the increasingly distorted face in the beam, watching the ridge on her forehead grow and the scales cluster about her eyes, which were now like sapphires set in gold. For a second those eyes fixed him with all the force of the Black, though her control had now faded to a fraction of its former strength. She smiled, the same smile she had shown him back in Carvenport, the same smile she wore on the trail, open, kind . . . loving. But it wasn't her any more; he knew that at his core. She was still beautiful, but it was a terrible beauty.

An ear-splitting boom rent the air above their heads and another tremor shook the glass beneath his feet, sending him sprawling. He looked up to see a thick pall of smoke surrounding the opening at the apex of the dome, fading to reveal a growing crack in the arcing wall. Powdered stone cascaded down onto the crystal and the White. It shifted as if feeling the dust on its hide, tail sweeping across the glass and wings gusting the air. In the beam he saw Silverpin turn to regard the White with a worried frown, and as she did so, her Black faded completely.

Clay didn't hesitate, ignoring the growing crack in the dome and whatever might have caused it. He unslung the longrifle and brought it to his shoulder in a smooth, single movement that would have made Foxbine proud. He worked the lever, jacking a steel-tip into the chamber and trained the sights on the White's head, dead between the eyes. *The head, always the head.* He wasn't the marksman his uncle was, but even he couldn't miss at this range.

Something blurred beyond the sights as he squeezed the trigger, the roar of the longrifle filling the dome and the muzzle flash blinding him for a second. When his vision cleared he saw Silverpin on her knees, her sapphire eyes staring at him in frank astonishment as she held a hand to the gushing hole in her chest.

'What . . .' Clay began, choking on the words as their eyes locked together. 'What did you do?'

She opened her mouth and a thick torrent of blood cascaded down her chin. She gave a small, convulsive jerk and collapsed onto her back, blood spreading out from her lifeless body, forming a near-symmetrical shape on the glass. *Wings,* Clay thought, the longrifle suddenly very heavy in his hands. *Looks just like wings.*

A low, rumbling sound drew his gaze from Silverpin's corpse and he looked up to find himself staring into the eyes of the White. The very open and awake eyes of the White.

CHAPTER 44

Lizanne

Lizanne reached for her second revolver as the Blue began to dip its head towards her, mouth open and water cascading from its many teeth. She wasn't sure whether she intended to use it on the drake or herself. She had managed to get it free by the time the beast's snout had descended to within a yard of her, where it stopped. Lizanne stared into its suddenly frozen eyes, finding only her reflection, a white-faced woman in overalls clutching a tiny pistol as she trod water and waited to die. She found it a singularly unedifying view.

The drake blinked and drew back from her, a strange echoing rattle sounding from within its body, echoed by its two companions. Lizanne bobbed higher in the waves as they coiled together, their rattles mingling, becoming synchronized. She had a sense that they were greeting each other, and from the way their frills and spines twitched, discerned a certain alarm at their circumstances, as if finding themselves in a sea with so many ships and booming guns was a sudden and unexpected occurrence. After a few more seconds of shared rattling they separated, one casting an incurious glance at Lizanne before all three vanished beneath the waves.

She saw the *Laudable Intent* a few hundred yards away, her hull now unencumbered by drakes, paddles churning in opposite directions as she began to turn about. Suddenly aware of the absence of gun-fire, Lizanne turned her gaze to the rest of the fleet, finding every vessel free of attacking Blues and no sign of them in the surrounding waters. The *Laudable* completed its turn and began to plough towards her. As it came closer a shrill note sounded from its steam-whistle, a signal soon taken up by the whole fleet. Lizanne thought she heard cheers amongst the wailing sirens but found she couldn't share in the delusion of victory.

Did he kill it? she wondered, the revolver slipping from her unfeeling hand, the chill of the sea and all-consuming fatigue combining to drag her into unconsciousness. *Or is it merely tired of this game?*

CHAPTER 45

Clay

He should have felt terror, or let his mind slip into a madness birthed by the certainty that this thing was intent on his death. He could see a definite calculation in its eyes, an awareness that went beyond the keen but limited intelligence he saw in Lutharon's gaze. And beyond the awareness was hate. It knew what he had done, and it desired a reckoning. But still Clay found he couldn't feel anything beyond guilt, clawing away at his insides as he lowered his gaze once more to Silverpin's corpse. Lover, saviour, betrayer . . . monster. She had been all of them, and yet he knew this was a crime he would never escape.

A soft, pattering sound made him lift his gaze once more and he saw a trickle of blood falling onto the glass. He followed the red stream to the wound on the White's neck, just behind its head where the steel-tip had impacted, presumably deflected by its brief passage through Silverpin's body. 'Seems I missed,' he said, meeting the White's all-too-knowing gaze once again, feeding the small seed of anger growing inside, hoping it might banish the guilt. He smiled, revealing gritted teeth and jacked another round into the longrifle's chamber. 'Won't happen twice.'

The White's tail moved in a blur, cracking the air as it uncoiled. Clay threw himself flat on his back, the tail cutting the air above and one of the jagged spines scoring a cut on his chest, ripping through shirt and skin to leave him writhing in pain and shock. He spewed profanity as he got to his knees, fighting the pain and raising the rifle to his shoulder. Another swipe of the great, white tail, the snap of sundered air accompanied by the sound of shattered metal and wood. The longrifle came apart in Clay's hands, the two halves leaking bullets and workings onto the glass. He threw the ruined weapon aside and scrambled upright, reaching for the vials on his belt.

The White's tail blurred beneath him, sweeping him from his feet with enough force to send him somersaulting through the air. He landed hard, agony flaring from the wound in his chest, sapping his strength and leaving him gasping on the glass. A soft hiss made him look up and he found the White's head poised above, teeth bared and jaw widening. *It won't kill me,* Clay knew, yelling with pain whilst his hand still fumbled for his vials. *Not for a long time . . .*

All thought stilled as he saw that the blood continued to flow from the wound in the White's neck, trickling over the scales and sending a small cascade of drops straight towards him. Clay tried to clamp his mouth shut, but too late, a single drop making it past his lips and onto his tongue. The pain made the agony in his chest seem no more than a dull ache, his throat working in a convulsive swallow, taking the blood deep inside where it burned and burned . . .

. . . cold. A harsh, lacerating cold the depth of which he had never felt before. He realised his eyes were open, no longer bunched shut as he writhed with the White's blood burning his insides. There was no pain either, just the dreadful cold. He looked upon a field of ice, the same field of ice he had glimpsed in the whirl of memory, except now the sky above was pale blue rather than starlit night. The great twisted spire still jutted from the ice but seemed to have diminished somehow, not standing quite as tall as before. Clay wondered if it had shrunk but then realised the ice had in fact thickened about it, indicating the passage of countless years since the first memory had been captured.

The sound of boots crunching into snow made him turn and he found himself facing a tall man with an impressive breadth of shoulder, clad in a thick fur-lined jacket. The hood of the jacket was raised but Clay could see the glimmer of a Maritime Protectorate cap badge inside it, and the man's face; blockishly handsome of North Mandinorian complexion. His gaze was direct and focused, making Clay realise he was present in this scene, no longer just an observer of baffling mysteries; he was really here. The man regarded Clay with an expression of shrewd if cautious satisfaction, the face of a man receiving a debt he never expected to be paid. After a second he gave a soft grunt and turned to regard the great spire rising from the ice.

'So,' he said in a voice rich in military gruffness, 'this is where we save the world, Mr Torcreek . . .'

. . . the burning returned with a savage intensity and he was back, still writhing on the glass as the White's head dipped lower. Clay's fingers finally alighted on his vials and he began to tug them free, intending to drink them all at once, knowing it would be hopeless, knowing the White wouldn't allow it, but trying anyway. He stopped as his gaze lit on something beyond the White, something small and dark falling through the opening in the dome's roof. It seemed to fall with incredible slowness so that Clay could make out what it was with relative ease. A barrel, just like the one he had carried down here. A barrel full of wonderful accelerating agent.

The barrel tumbled onto the crystal, bursting apart as one of its jagged points pierced it, blossoming into bright yellow-orange flame with enough force to shake the dome down to its foundations. The White reeled away from Clay, its screech of rage cutting through the echoing boom. It rushed towards the crystal which, Clay saw, was now glowing with far less intensity, its myriad facets shot through with a web of cracks. It continued to revolve in the air for a few seconds, its light flickering like a guttering oil-lamp, then fell heavily onto the glass floor.

The White screamed again, the sound threatening to burst Clay's ears as it circled the dimmed and cracked crystal, wings flaring and tail thrashing. He sensed something oddly infantile about its reaction, its jerky frustration putting him in mind of a child poking at a broken toy. *He is still so young,* Silverpin had said, the thought drawing Clay's eyes to her body, still lying on the glass with its bloody wings spread out, sapphire eyes staring in accusation. Clay tore his gaze away and struggled to his feet, sagging under the pain of the wound in his chest and the residual burn of the White's blood. He pulled three vials from his wallet, Green, Red and Black, and drank them all in a single gulp. He straightened as the Green took effect, dimming his many agonies, then took a purposeful stride towards the White.

'Come on, you pasty bastard,' he breathed, using Black to snatch one of Silverpin's blades from her belt. 'We ain't done.'

Hearing him the White whirled, mouth gaping. The calculated cruelty was gone from its eyes. Now there was only blind rage. The air about its mouth began to shimmer as the heat built, preparing to ignite the torrent of gasses summoned from its guts. Clay crouched, ready to dodge the flames, then stopped as a crack sounded from above and a large piece of the dome's ceiling fell, tumbling straight down to deliver a glancing but heavy blow to the White before slamming onto the glass floor. Clay watched an intricate matrix of cracks spread through the glass from the point of impact, staring with an unwarranted detachment as his Green-enhanced eyes tracked the complex array of fractures until it had covered the floor from end to end. Clay cast a final glance at the White, screeching anew as it struggled free of the tumbled stone, dragging its leg a little. He focused his gaze at the glass beneath it and unleashed a burst of Black. The floor shattered and the White fell through a cloud of glittering powder, voicing a plaintive scream as it tumbled into whatever waited below.

Hearing an ominous cacophony of cracks building about his feet Clay turned and ran for the dome wall. This time an exit stubbornly refused to appear at his approach so he let loose with all the remaining Black, blowing a small but accessible hole through it. The glass gave way beneath him just as he reached the new-made exit, his hand reaching out with Green-boosted speed and strength to grip the edge just in time. He began to haul himself up then paused at a new sound from below, the roar of drake-born flames, Looking down he saw the White, flames jetting from its mouth in a powerful stream. But this fire was not cast at him. The White wheeled about amidst the spiral array Clay had glimpsed on entering the dome, now revealed as row after row of small round objects. They were arranged in a series of vast curving terraces, like the centre of a sunflower, extending far beyond the diameter of the dome's floor.

He hung there, watching the White breathe its flames and every round object they touched turn black, but not entirely. In each one he could see a glow, small at first but building fast, something he had seen before in the breeding pens. *Eggs,* he realised as the White continued its task, each gout of flame accompanied by an unmistakable squawk of triumph. *The waking fire.*

Feeling his Green start to ebb he pulled himself up, running free of the dome then drawing up short at the sight of the Briteshore folk. They stood clutching their knives and pickaxes, every face an echo of the White's fury, and now there was no Silverpin to hold them back. Clay fixed his gaze on the centre of their line and started to summon his Red, intending to sprint forward and burn his way through, using Silverpin's knife to deal with any who came too close. In the event, it proved unnecessary.

Lutharon roared as he descended through the shaft, casting a blast of flame down on the Spoiled, roasting about half before landing amidst the others, tail whipping and claws rending. Ethelynne clung to his back as he did his deadly dance, the Spoiled soon cast away like red-stained chaff.

Clay sank to his knees as the last of the Green faded, kept from fainting only by the pain in his chest. Lutharon trotted to him, claws leaving red stains on the stone, and Ethelynne slid from the drake's back to crouch at Clay's side. 'How?' he asked in a strained mutter.

'Mr Skaggerhill was able to repair the cable-car machinery,' she said, smiling then wincing as she leaned closer to peer at the wound in his chest. 'It took a lot of powder to blast a channel big enough for Lutharon to enter.'

'Told them to leave,' Clay groaned, slumping forward. 'You all need to get out of here.'

'Now, now, none of that.' She hooked her arms under his and lifted him up with the kind of strength that only came from Green. 'This is a terribly interesting place you've found,' she observed as she dragged him towards Lutharon. 'Worthy of extensive study.'

'Can't stay.' Clay turned his lolling head towards the ruined dome. 'Eggs . . .'

'Eggs?'

A savage roar sounded from the dome, the part-demolished ceiling bursting apart as the White came crashing through from below. It descended amidst a cloud of debris to land barely twenty feet away, head and body lowered as it screeched a challenge at Lutharon. The Black drake responded with a bellow of his own, hopping clear of Ethelynne and Clay to confront the White, tail coiling and wings spread wide.

'Stop!' Ethelynne pulled away from Clay and rushed to stand between the two drakes, holding her hand out to Lutharon, freezing him in place. 'No! This . . .' She faltered and turned to face the White, voice soft so that Clay had to strain to hear her. 'This is my mistake to fix, old friend.'

The White seemed to lose some of its fury as it looked upon her, head angled slightly as its eyes narrowed in a clear display of recognition. After a moment it issued a soft growl of consternation, lips curling back from dagger-like teeth in an irritated snarl.

'Yes,' Ethelynne told it, 'I regret not killing you too.'

The White's snarl widened into a roar and it lunged forward, forelegs raised and talons extending . . . then stopped as Ethelynne unleashed her Black. Clay could feel the force of it, even though it was directed elsewhere, a more powerful demonstration of the

Blessing than he had ever witnessed. He could see the White straining against her control, nostrils flaring and leaking smoke as it let out a continual, rage-filled rumble.

'Clay.' He switched his gaze to Ethelynne, finding her glancing over her shoulder, a sad smile on her lips. It was so similar to Silverpin's smile that he almost found it sickening and he knew the bladehand hadn't been the only one to use him. 'Thank you,' Ethelynne said. 'I needed to end this. You have to go now, they're waiting for you.'

She turned to Lutharon, meeting the drake's eyes and Clay felt something pass between them. Lutharon shuddered as she looked away, a faint, keening sounding from him as he turned and scooped Clay from the floor, wings spreading in readiness.

'No!' Clay struggled as the drake's grip tightened, but it was a feeble attempt and he felt more of his blood spill as Lutharon sprinted away then launched himself into the air. Clay managed to twist in his grip as the wings beat the air to carry them away. He saw Ethelynne focus her full attention on the White, throwing it back with a savage burst of Black then lifting a large piece of fallen masonry to bring it down on the beast's head with a bone-smashing crunch. Still it lived, however, shrugging off the blow and replying with a blast of flame. Ethelynne became a blur, leaping clear and replying with flames of her own as she unleashed her Red, the White howling as the raw flesh of its wounds steamed in the heat.

For a moment it seemed she might prevail, the White shrinking back as she cast more debris at it in between blasts of heat, but then a strange ripping sound rose from the ruined dome. In seconds it built into a crescendo as a flock of juvenile drakes erupted from the dome, the ripping sound revealed as the air being rent by so many wings. They swirled about the chamber for a short time, transforming into a two-coloured cloud as Lutharon gained height. *Red*, Clay saw, vision dimming. *And White . . . but no Black . . .*

The last he saw before the blackness claimed him was the cloud descending on Ethelynne's now-tiny form. They covered her in a dense swarm that thrashed and pulsed for a short time before breaking apart, leaving no sign of her behind. And the White roared out its victory.

CHAPTER 46

Lizanne

Looks different, he said, and she sensed his scrutiny of her whirl-winds. *Not so tidy.*

I have a glut of new memories, she said. *And haven't had much opportunity for housekeeping recently.*

She noted that his own mindscape had changed markedly, Nelphia's surface rendered in darker hues than before with many dust-devils drifting across the valleys and peaks. She had watched him craft the memory of his encounter with the White, raising moon-dust and shaping it into a coherent narrative, or as coherent as his grieving mind would allow. The sight of Ethelynne Drystone's demise was particularly fractured, reflecting his reluc-tance to relive the event. Even so, she had been impressed by his fortitude, keeping control throughout the images of betrayal and loss even as she sensed his pain.

The last set of memories had been the most confused, shot through as they were by the effects of his injuries. She watched as the Black drake carried him away from the White, still roaring its triumph, up and through the channel that had been blasted in the mountain. The memories then became a hazy collage of captured images as Clay slipped in and out of consciousness; his uncle's face, drawn in worry . . . the other Contractors carrying him to the cable-car . . . a final view of the spike-shaped moun-tain before it all went dark.

So, she said, *it lives.*

Yes. A pulse of deep regret sent a shiver through the moon-dust. *Sorry about that.*

Lizanne felt a resurgence of the sensation that had dogged her since Red Allice and Edgerhand had plucked her from the sea. The feeling that gripped her as they settled her on the deck and banished her bone-deep chill with a gentle blanket of Red-heated air; the unfamiliar and deeply unwelcome sense of being dwarfed by circumstance.

Well, she went on, forcing a brisk note into her thoughts she hoped would mask the underlying unease. *At least now we have confirmation. There had been some talk amongst the fleet of turning back to Carvenport. This should put paid to such notions.* She paused, watching his face closely, seeing only the tired features of a young man burdened with a vast responsibility. *The only living soul to have drunk the blood of the White,* she thought, doubting he found it the wondrous and profitable gift Madame had imagined it to be.

Do you know what it might mean? she asked, summoning a whirlwind to form the image of the great twisted spike in the ice. *Your . . . vision.*

His face gave the smallest tic of amusement. *I think it means I still got a long ways to go, miss.*

Where are you now?

Just a few days from Hadlock, Uncle says. Can only hope there's somebody left when we get there. We keep finding dead miners on the trail. The Spoiled have been plenty busy in these mountains. Lucky Lutharon decided to stay with us. Guess he's scaring them away for now. Caught sight of a large war-party yesterday. Thought they might come for us but they just kept on trekking north. I reckon they had another place to be.

The mountain . . . The White's calling them home.

I expect so.

Trance with me when you get to Hadlock. If there are no ships to be had I'll have the Board send one when we reach Feros.

You seem pretty sure they'll dance to your tune.

If they want to regain their holdings in Arradsia, they'll have little choice. Without product, what are they?

I got a feeling the whole world's gonna have to get used to going without for a very long time, if not forever. You saw it, miss. It ain't done, and now it's got brothers and sisters to play with.

You wounded it. I saw that too. It needed the Island girl for something. Without that I suspect it will be incomplete, stunted somehow.

There was a pause and one of his dust-devils drifted closer, transforming into the familiar image of a girl dancing in a ballroom.

She's well, Lizanne assured him. *I wanted to bring her under my protection but she refused to be parted from her gun-crew. She has care of a pair of Dalcian orphans, a brother and sister.*

Derk?

She summoned the whirlwind containing Joya's description of Keyvine's death, and her brother's demise; shielding her with his body as he carried her from the burning church only to be greeted by Keyvine's sword-cane. *I'm sorry,* she said when it had played out.

Tell her . . . She watched Nelphia's surface tremble a little under the weight of his guilt. *Tell her I'm glad she finally got to sail in a blood-burner.*

I will.

His mindscape faded a little, indicating he was nearing the end of his product. He managed to hang on for a few seconds, however, his thoughts conveying a sincerity that warmed her. *Lotta people died on account of our contract, miss. All in all, I'm glad you weren't one of them.*

The trance faded and she was back in the small cabin she shared with Tekela. The girl lay on the opposite bunk, sleeping more soundly than Lizanne would have expected. She winced at the sight of the burns on Tekela's hands, the result of flames breathed into the bridge at the height of the battle. Tekela had pushed her revolver through the slit in the armour and shot at the Blue as it drew breath for a blast. The burns were the only reward for her bravery, though she swore she had put a bullet down the drake's throat. Heavy doses of Green had done much to heal the scars and prevent any impairment, but the discolouration remained, making it appear as if she wore a pair of patchwork gloves.

Lizanne rose from her bunk and reached for the large carpet-bag resting in the corner, opening it to regard the device inside. *You told us so much and also so little,* she said to the thing's long-lost inventor. *Did you know what you were leading us to, I wonder? Were you like Silverpin? Compelled to undertake deadly expeditions and craft inventions by some mysterious voice. Or were you, like the rest of us, just another greedy fool?*

For a brief second she entertained the notion of taking it aloft and casting it over the side, suspicious of any more secrets that might lurk in its baffling mechanicals. Then, with a sigh she closed the bag and placed it back in the corner. She couldn't truly de-cipher it, and neither, for all his technical wizardry, could Jermayah. But in Feros, there lived a man who might.

'This will be the only gift I ever brought home for you, Father,' she whispered. 'Perhaps you'll finally be glad to see me.'

She found Arberus on the platform where they had battled the Blues, arms resting on the iron wall as he stared out at the sea, smoke rising from the cigarillo between his fingers and reminding her of someone she had killed not so long ago. The memory summoned a flare of anger, connected as it was to Madame's traitorous scheming, and also a recognition that such things were behind her. *I will never be a spy again,* she knew, and found the prospect far more agreeable than expected.

'Do you ever wonder,' she began, moving to Arberus's side, 'what your grandmother would have had to say about all this?'

He gave a small shrug, keeping his eyes on the sky. It was a three-moon night and the sea shimmered like molten silver under the light cast by the three heavenly sisters. 'I like to think she would have understood,' he said. 'For an idealist, she had a surpris-ingly pragmatic nature.'

'Would she really have been so forgiving?' she asked, raising an eyebrow. 'Here you are allied with the forces of corporatist greed whilst the global economy stands on the brink of disaster.'

He gave a short laugh and began to quote in Eutherian, '"The concept of stability in markets is perhaps the worst lie ever perpetrated by the corporate elite. In transforming a description into an ideology they blinded themselves to the inescapable flaw of any society built on greed . . ."'

The flow of invective stopped as she kissed him, finding his lips rough and chafed by so many days at sea, his breath also rich in cigarillo smoke. Neither proved sufficient reason to stop, however.

After a while she drew back, plucking the cigarillo from his fingers and taking a deep draw as she enjoyed the surprise on his face. 'My father,' she said, then paused to blow a thin stream of smoke into the air, 'is truly going to hate you.'

CHAPTER 47

Hilemore

The *Viable Opportunity* came free of the reef with only a few additional scrapes to her hull, aided by a stiff easterly wind that whipped up waves of sufficient height to lift the keel from the coral. Hilemore ordered the paddles to full ahead and they rode the swell into open water, Zenida immediately steering a southern course. Like most of the crew she remained largely silent, her eyes constantly roving the waves for any sign of the drakes' return. It had been two full days since they witnessed the sinking of the Corvantine ship and the great Blue migration into northern waters. The crew had been left in a decidedly jittery state ever since and Hilemore found he couldn't blame them, although he had been quick to quash any suggestion they prolong their stay on the reef.

'They're cold-water beasts,' Zenida said in Varestian, more to herself than him he suspected. 'Live by hunting whales and walrus amidst the ice. Never seen in northern climes. Never.'

'Well now they are,' was all he could think to say. He found himself cursing Mr Tottleborn for having such fatally bad luck. A trance communication with the Sea Board, or anyone else for that matter, would be very welcome just now. Before the migration the war had dominated his thoughts, but now a suspicion had begun to build that it might not be the most important event to transpire in this region after all. *There were so many of them,* he recalled, picturing the mass of snake-like forms cutting through the waves.

He had briefly considered following in their wake, debating

whether duty required he make some effort to discover their ultimate destination. However, his ingrained adherence to the service did not include suicidal urges, and he had serious doubts the men would have stood for it in any case. Habitually superstitious, many amongst the crew had taken on a decidedly haunted aspect, given to muttering archaic warding words or singing ominous shanties as they went about their duties; 'Beneath the Spectral Sea' being a particular favourite.

So, lacking any other course, he had opted to stick with his original plan. The *Viable* would make for Hadlock where they would reprovision and, with any luck, the Ironship concession would have a Blood-blessed who could explain just what in the Travail was going on.

Another storm blew up two days later, forcing a diversion to the south-west which would add well over a week to their sailing time to Hadlock. Hilemore maintained a close observance of routine throughout the voyage, keeping up the gun drills and making sure the men didn't slacken in the myriad tasks that kept a ship from transforming into an unseemly hulk. The mood lightened a little as the days passed and the sea remained free of Blues, the crew regaining a modicum of sprightliness as it became apparent that their doom was not in fact imminent. That all changed when they found the life-boat.

The crow's nest spied it five days after they had freed the *Viable* from the reef. They had resumed course for Hadlock by now, keeping due west through a sea thankfully becalmed after the storm. In response to the call from the tube Hilemore trained his glass on the distant speck below the horizon. A boat, covered over with tarp, but no sail. Also, no sign of any crew.

'Dead slow,' he ordered Talmant before turning to Steelfine. 'See to the recovery of that boat, if you would, Number One.'

'Aye, sir.'

Unwilling to take any chances, Hilemore had the full complement of riflemen arrayed along the rail and all guns loaded and manned. He signalled all stop as the boat came within twenty yards of the stern and Zenida altered the angle of the *Viable*'s bows to bring the craft alongside. Steelfine, stripped to the waist and shoeless, fastened a line on the boat by the simple expedient of diving over the side and swimming to it. Upon tying the rope to the boat's rudder Steelfine's face bunched in an expression of profound disgust. Hilemore discovered the reason a second later as the stench wafted up over the rail. A murmur of unease ran through the crew for it was a smell they all knew well by now.

Steelfine climbed onto the boat and took hold of the tarp before glancing up at Hilemore with a questioning glance. He replied with a nod and the Islander pulled the tarp aside, unleashing yet more stench and the sight of six bodies. They were all burnt to some degree, one so badly half his face was a mask of charcoal. They had been dead for several days and the rictus had contorted their faces into smiles.

'Eastern Conglomerate sailors, Captain,' Steelfine called to him, holding up an empty sack with stencilled lettering. 'The ECT *Endeavour*, looks like.'

'I know her, sir,' one of the men piped up. 'Works the route twixt Hadlock and Carvenport.'

'Not any more she don't,' another man said in a grim mutter. 'State they're in, couldn't have lasted more'n a day once they took to the boat.'

'Alright!' Hilemore barked, snapping them all to attention. 'Riflemen dismissed. Return to your allotted duties.' He moved to the rail and called down to Steelfine. 'See them on their way, Number One. The King of the Deep will expect his due.'

The approach to Hadlock was guarded by a lighthouse of ingenious construction, the base curved so as to deflect the steep seas which were common in this region. It transpired that they were fortunate to come upon it in daylight, as Hilemore doubted it would ever shine out a warning again. The iron-and-glass housing which should have sat atop the great column was gone, the stonework beneath blackened and scorched over much of its surface. Whatever had befallen the light-keepers was probably best left to the imagination. The channel beyond the lighthouse proved even more foreboding, the crow's nest reporting no less than four wrecked vessels. The tide was high so all they could see of them were the masts, sticking out of the waves like leafless trees after a flood.

'Doesn't bode well for Hadlock,' Zenida commented.

Hilemore ordered the engines slowed as they neared the port, using his glass to scan the buildings and finding Zenida's prediction all too accurate. There didn't appear to be a single building still standing, the streets transformed into irregular lines of blackened brick with not a living soul in sight. Lowering the angle of the glass he found the harbour choked with sunk vessels, and also a not-inconsiderable number of bloated corpses littering the wreckage.

'All stop,' he ordered, annoyed at the grating choke of his voice. He took a moment to clear his throat before continuing, thankful that those present gave no sign of having registered his moment of frailty. 'Number One, assemble a squad of riflemen and prepare a launch. We're going ashore. Mr Talmant, you have the ship.'

'Is this altogether wise?' Zenida murmured at his shoulder as the launch made its way into the harbour, those men not at the oars keeping watch on the ruins with rifles at the ready.

'We need supplies,' Hilemore muttered in response. 'Food, ammunition and product if there's any to be had.'

'There's only death to be had here.' She took a firmer grip on her Corvantine revolver, keen eyes scanning the surrounding wreckage.

They were obliged to row their way through several bodies before reaching the quay, the cadavers becoming so densely packed at one point that Steelfine was obliged to push them aside with an oar, unleashing a miasma of foul gasses as some burst under the prodding. Several men had heaved their breakfasts over the side by the time they tied up to the wharf. Hilemore left two men with the launch and led the others into what remained of Hadlock. He had called here a few times in the course of his career and grown to appreciate the mostly trouble-free port, especially for the hearty if unrefined quality of the local cuisine. His men, however, had clearly pursued other interests.

'That was Old Brass Belle's whore-house,' said one, voice thick with emotion as he pointed his rifle at a pile of bricks. 'Generous sort, she was. Let y'have a handy if you were a scrip short for a tumble.'

'Captain,' Steelfine said in a soft voice. Hilemore saw that he had sunk into a crouch, rifle pointing up at the sky. Following the Islander's gaze Hilemore saw a dark, winged shape glide through the clouds barely a hundred feet up. He had never seen one in the flesh before, but knew without any doubt that he now looked upon a Black drake.

'Rifles up!' he barked, and every weapon was immediately trained on the dark silhouette above.

'That's what did this!' one of the men hissed, his voice betraying the onset of panic. 'We should kill the fucker and get gone from here.'

'Shut your yap,' Steelfine warned in a low growl, rifle tracking the drake across the sky. It banked and wheeled about, long neck coiling and Hilemore knew it had seen them.

'Can you get it from here?' he asked Steelfine.

'I'll hit it sure enough,' the Islander replied. 'Can't say if I'll kill it.'

'You won't,' said a new voice.

Hilemore whirled, levelling his revolver at a figure standing only a few yards away; a young man in a green-leather duster. The young man stared at him for a moment, head angled slightly, Hilemore seeing him to be of South Mandinorian heritage and, if his accent was anything to go by, Carvenport birth. The shirt beneath his duster was ripped and Hilemore could see a stained bandage beneath it. He appeared to be weaponless but for a knife on his belt. Something that couldn't be said for the people who quickly appeared at his side. Four men and a young woman, all bearing fire-arms.

'You won't kill him,' the young man said, coming closer. 'Not with that popgun. And he'll be sure to take exception to the attempt.'

The young man stopped as Hilemore drew back the hammer on his revolver. He was struck by the expression on the young man's face, both weary and sad, but with a faintly amused twist to his lips.

'Who are you?' Hilemore demanded.

'Claydon Torcreek, Captain,' the young man replied, raising his hands. He laughed a little, eyes roving over Hilemore's face in obvious recognition. 'And you really don't want to shoot me. Not if we're going to save the world.'

DRAMATIS PERSONAE

Ironship Trading Syndicate

Lizanne Lethridge – Blood-blessed. Full Shareholder and covert agent of the Exceptional Initiatives Division, Ironship Trading Syndicate.

Lodima Bondersil – Principal Tutor at the Ironship Academy of Female Education. Lizanne's immediate superior.

Jermayah Tollermine – Technologist and employee of the Ironship Trading Syndicate.

Wulfcot Trumane – Captain of the IPV *Viable Opportunity*.

Jebneel Lemhill – First Lieutenant and First Officer of the IPV *Viable Opportunity*.

Corrick Hilemore – Second Lieutenant of the IPV *Viable Opportunity*.

Boswald Tottleborn – Blood-blessed of the IPV *Viable Opportunity*.

Dravin Talmant – Third Lieutenant of the IPV *Viable Opportunity*.

Naytanil Bozware – Chief Engineer of the IPV *Viable Opportunity*.

Steelfine – Barrier Isles native and Master-at-Arms of the IPV *Viable Opportunity*.

The Longrifles

Claydon Torcreek – Unregistered Blood-blessed and thief, resident in Carvenport. Later Blood-blessed to the Longrifles Independent Contractor Company.

Braddon Torcreek – Uncle of Claydon Torcreek. Captain and chief Shareholder of the Longrifles Independent Contractor Company.

Fredabel Torcreek – Wife to Braddon and co-owner of the Longrifles Independent Contractor Company.

Loriabeth Torcreek – Daughter to Fredabel and Braddon, apprentice gunhand to the Longrifles Independent Contractor Company.

Cwentun Skaggerhill – Chief Harvester to the Longrifles Independent Contractor Company.

Visandra Foxbine – First Gunhand to the Longrifles Independent Contractor Company.

Silverpin – Barrier Isles native and bladehand to the Longrifles Independent Contractor Company.

Preacher – De-anointed cleric to the Church of the Seer and marksman to the Longrifles Independent Contractor Company.

Others

Zenida Okanas – Blood-blessed captain of the pirate vessel *Windqueen*.

Akina Okanas – Daughter to Zenida.

Arshav Okanas – Chief Director of the Hive, half-brother to Zenida Okanas.

Ethilda Okanas – Co-Director of the Hive, mother to Arshav.

Ethelynne Drystone – Blood-blessed, former pupil of Madame Bondersil. Only survivor of the Wittler Expedition.

Orwinn Scriberson – Principal Field Astronomer to the Consolidated Research Company.

Seydell Keelman – Captain of the Independent riverboat *Firejack*.

Burgrave Leonis Akiv Artonin – Corvantine scholar and nobleman.

Tekela Akiv Artonin – Daughter to Burgrave Artonin.

Arberus Lek Hakimas – Corvantine cavalry officer and major in the Imperial Dragoons.

Kaylib Tragerhorn – Pirate and constable to the Hive.

Erric Firpike – Archaeologist and disgraced former employee of the Consolidated Research Company.

ACKNOWLEDGEMENTS

Many thanks to my excellent editor at Ace, Jessica Wade, for her keen insight and greatly welcome input. Additional thanks and long-lasting gratitude to my former editor, Susan Allison, who first took a chance on me and kept the faith when the first draft of *The Waking Fire* landed on her desk not long before she took well-deserved retirement. Also, deep appreciation to my UK editor, James Long, and my agent, Paul Lucas, for their continued support and hard work. And finally, once again heartfelt thanks to my long-suffering second set of eyes, Paul Field, who still won't let me pay him.

extras

about the author

Anthony Ryan lives in London and is a *New York Times* bestselling writer of fantasy, science fiction and non-fiction. He previously worked in a variety of roles for the UK government, but now writes full time. He has a degree in history and his interests include art, science and the unending quest for the perfect pint of real ale.

Find out more about Anthony Ryan and other Orbit authors by registering online for the free monthly newsletter at www.orbitbooks.net.

interview

The Waking Fire takes place in a world on the cusp of an industrial age, where monarchies have been replaced by corporations which care just as much about profit margins as governing their expanding territories. It's a fascinating world, and one that bears very little resemblance to the setting of your previous Raven's Shadow series. What prompted this change?

I wanted to explore certain themes that required a world at a more advanced stage of technology. The whole notion of a corporation, as we understand it today, is really the product of the explosion in global trade that kicked off in the 1700s and went into high gear during the industrial revolution. One of the main points of inspiration was the British East India Company which became, by the early 1800s, probably the richest single entity on the planet, controlling an entire subcontinent with its own army and navy. Plus, it was also just one of several competing companies active during the same period. It's not too much of a stretch to imagine such powerful conglomerates taking the reins of power from civil governance simply by dint of their wealth (some might argue it's already happened and most of us haven't noticed yet). In the world of *The Waking Fire*, a large portion of the globe has dispensed with what one character calls 'the fiction of politics'. Apart from exploring the geo-political themes, I also wanted to get away from swords and arrows for a while. A gun-fight or a nineteenth-century era battle requires a different set of writerly muscles to those employed when writing sword-fights or medieval sieges, and it's always good to challenge yourself as a writer.

The idea of drake blood being distilled to create elixirs, that in turn bestow special powers on a few select individuals, is really cool and very well executed. Was there any particular inspiration behind this unusual magic system, and how did it develop?

I knew I wanted to write a story with dragons at the centre of the narrative and I wanted to create a magic system that had clearly defined rules. I had always been impressed with how Frank Herbert dealt with the economics in his Dune series, with spice being the most valuable substance in the galaxy around which all the action revolves. By making dragon blood the source of magic in this world, it transformed them into a natural resource and made them the focal point for the various political and military machinations that occur in the book.

***The Waking Fire* is at heart a classic adventure story, reminiscent of *Hornblower*, *The Lost World* by Arthur Conan Doyle and even Indiana Jones. Were any of these direct influences, and what other books/films did you take inspiration from?**

Bernard Cornwell's military adventure books were more of an influence than *Hornblower*, but Cornwell owes a large debt to Forester so I guess it's all circular. Indiana Jones made a big impression on me as a kid and it certainly shows in this book, as does my love of westerns, particularly the works of John Ford. There's also a healthy dose of Ian Fleming with a smattering of John Le Carré present in the covert adventures of Lizanne Lethridge.

The three protagonists – Clay, Hilemore and Lizanne – are all very different people, and pursue rather different agendas (all with a healthy degree of danger involved). Which of them did you enjoy writing the most?

In all honesty, I think I enjoyed them all equally for different reasons. Hilemore is the dutiful naval officer, which means I got to create a navy from scratch and write some sea battles which I enjoyed a lot. Lizanne is a spy which enables me to channel my inner Bond; who doesn't love gadgets? I also enjoyed the moment of personal discovery when she finds out, much to her surprise, that she's not the completely ruthless killer she thought she was. Clay is the most conflicted and – on the face of it, because we first meet him as a criminal with a ruthless streak – the least sympathetic. He also probably has the biggest emotional journey in the book. His character is not intrinsically heroic and he's effectively been press-ganged into an adventure he doesn't want, but by the end he's no longer acting entirely out of self-interest.

Did you face any particular challenges when writing the book? It can't have been easy writing three separate narratives that take place hundreds of miles apart...

It wasn't easy, in fact I'll confess I find writing these books much harder than writing the Raven's Shadow books. The world is new and I'm still exploring it, which means every time the characters travel somewhere new or meet a person from another culture, I have to create it all from scratch. Getting the narrative to gel with three point of view characters also wasn't easy and took a bit of re-writing to ensure they were all in the right place at the right time, especially towards the end.

You're a self-confessed history buff, but did you have to do any additional research for this book, given the

inclusion of more advanced technology? Or did you already know your black powder weapons pretty well?

As usual when doing research, I discovered I knew a lot less than I actually did. I had a decent understanding of the course of events through the nineteenth century but discovered that my grasp of military and civil technology wasn't good enough. So I did a lot of reading up about paddle steamers, firearms and artillery. I also researched military and naval tactics during the American Civil War and the Franco-Prussian War, all of which helped make the world of the Draconis Memoria a more convincingly real place.

The three books in the Raven's Shadow trilogy were all international bestsellers. Did that bring an extra degree of pressure when writing this new series? Or did you instead find it liberating to create a new world?

I was always determined that the Draconis Memoria would be my next series once Raven's Shadow was done. In fact, I wrote the whole of *The Waking Fire* effectively 'on spec' without first doing the usual proposal and first three chapters thing. I think the success of my first series did give me a certain amount of space to explore something new, but I'll admit to feeling some pressure to try and match the quality of what's gone before. Whether it reaches the same level of success, however, is really in the hands of readers.

Finally – without any spoilers of course – can you give us a hint as to what is in store for Clay and co. in the next book in the series?

The narrative of *The Waking Fire* raised a lot of questions, not all of which were answered by the end of the book. Book two will answer many of those questions as well exploring what happens to a society when its principal source of wealth suddenly disappears. Readers will also get to explore other regions of the world, particularly the Corvantine Empire, and discover what the White has in store for humanity – spoiler alert: it's not good.

if you enjoyed
THE WAKING FIRE

look out for

HOPE AND RED

by

Jon Skovron

In a fracturing empire spread across savage seas, two people find a common cause.

HOPE, the lone survivor of a village massacred by the emperor's forces, is secretly trained as a warrior and instrument of vengeance.

RED, an orphan adopted by a notorious matriarch of the criminal underworld, learns to be an expert thief and con artist.

Together they will take down an empire.

1

Captain Sin Toa had been a trader on these seas for many years, and he'd seen something like this before. But that didn't make it any easier.

The village of Bleak Hope was a small community in the cold Southern islands at the edge of the empire. Captain Toa was one of the few traders who came this far south, and even then, only once a year. The ice that formed on the water made it nearly impossible to reach during the winter months.

Still, the dried fish, whalebone, and the crude lamp oil they pressed from whale blubber were all good cargo that fetched a nice price in Stonepeak or New Laven. The villagers had always been polite and accommodating, in their taciturn Southern way. And it was a community that had survived in these harsh conditions for centuries, a quality that Toa respected a great deal.

So it was with a pang of sadness that he gazed out at what remained of the village. As his ship glided into the narrow harbor, he scanned the dirt paths and stone huts, and saw no sign of life.

'What's the matter, sir?' asked Crayton, his first mate. Good fellow. Loyal in his own way, if a bit dishonest about doing his fair share of work.

'This place is dead,' said Toa quietly. 'We'll not land here.'

'Dead, sir?'

'Not a soul in the place.'

'Maybe they're at some sort of local religious gathering,' said Crayton. 'Folks this far south have their own ways and customs.'

''Fraid that's not it.'

Toa pointed one thick, scarred finger toward the dock. A tall sign had been driven into the wood. On the sign was painted a black oval with eight black lines trailing down from it.

'God save them,' whispered Crayton, taking off his wool knit cap.

'That's the trouble,' said Toa. 'He didn't.'

The two men stood there staring at the sign. There was no sound except the cold wind that pulled at Toa's long wool coat and beard.

'What do we do, sir?' asked Crayton.

'Not come ashore, that's for certain. Tell the wags to lay anchor. It's getting late. I don't want to navigate these shallow waters in the dark, so we'll stay the night. But make no mistake, we're heading back to sea at first light and never coming near Bleak Hope again.'

They set sail the next morning. Toa hoped they'd reach the island of Galemoor in three days and that the monks there would have enough good ale to sell that it would cover his losses.

It was on the second night that they found the stowaway.

Toa was woken in his bunk by a fist pounding on his cabin door.

'Captain!' called Crayton. 'The night watch. They found . . . a little girl.'

Toa groaned. He'd had a bit too much grog before he went to sleep, and the spike of pain had already set in behind his eyes.

'A girl?' he asked after a moment

'Y-y-yes, sir.'

'Hells' waters,' he muttered, climbing out of his hammock. He pulled on cold, damp trousers, a coat, and boots. A girl on board, even a little one, was bad luck in these Southern seas. Everybody knew that. As he pondered how he was going to get rid of this stowaway, he opened the door and was surprised to find Crayton alone, turning his wool cap over and over again in his hands.

'Well? Where's the girl?'

'She's aft, sir,' said Crayton.

'Why didn't you bring her to me?'

'We, uh . . . That is, the men can't get her out from behind the stowed rigging.'

'Can't get her . . .' Toa heaved a sigh, wondering why no one had just reached in and clubbed her unconscious, then dragged her out. It wasn't like his men to get soft because of a little girl. Maybe it was on account of Bleak Hope. Maybe the terrible fate of that village had made them a bit more conscious than usual of their own prospects for Heaven.

'Fine,' he said. 'Lead me to her.'

'Aye, sir,' said Crayton, clearly relieved that he wasn't going to bear the brunt of the captain's frustration.

Toa found his men gathered around the cargo hold where the spare rigging was stored. The hatch was open and they stared down into the darkness, muttering to each other and making signs to ward off curses. Toa took a lantern from one of them and shone the light down into the hole, wondering why a little girl had his men so spooked.

'Look, girlie. You better . . .'

She was wedged in tight behind the piles of heavy line. She looked filthy and starved, but otherwise a normal enough girl of about eight years. Pretty, even, in the Southern way, with pale skin, freckles, and hair so blond it looked almost white. But there was something about her eyes when she looked at you. They felt empty, or worse than empty. They were pools of ice that crushed any warmth you had in you. They were ancient eyes. Broken eyes. Eyes that had seen too much.

'We tried to pull her out, Captain,' said one of the men. 'But she's packed in there tight. And well . . . she's . . .'

'Aye,' said Toa.

He knelt down next to the opening and forced himself to keep looking at her, even though he wanted to turn away.

'What's your name, girl?' he asked, much quieter now.

She stared at him.

'I'm the captain of this ship, girl,' he said. 'Do you know what that means?'

Slowly, she nodded once.

'It means everyone on this ship has to do what I say. That includes you. Understand?'

Again, she nodded once.

He reached one brown, hairy hand down into the hold.

'Now, girl. I want you to come out from behind there and take my hand. I swear no harm will come to you on this ship.'

For a long moment, no one moved. Then, tentatively, the girl reached out her bone-thin hand and let it be engulfed in Toa's.

Toa and the girl were back in his quarters. He suspected the girl might start talking if there weren't a dozen hard-bitten sailors staring at her. He gave her a blanket and a cup of hot grog. He knew grog wasn't the sort of thing you gave to little girls, but it was the only thing he had on board except fresh water, and that was far too precious to waste.

Now he sat at his desk and she sat on his bunk, the blanket wrapped tightly around her shoulders, the steaming cup of grog in her tiny hands. She took a sip, and Toa expected her to flinch at the pungent flavor, but she only swallowed and continued to stare at him with those empty, broken eyes of hers. They were the coldest blue he had ever seen, deeper than the sea itself.

'I'll ask you again, girl,' he said, although his tone was still gentle. 'What's yer name?'

She only stared at him.

'Where'd you come from?'

Still she stared.

'Are you . . .' He couldn't believe he was even thinking it, much less asking it. 'Are you from Bleak Hope?'

She blinked then, as if coming out of a trance. 'Bleak Hope.' Her voice was hoarse from lack of use. 'Yes. That's me.' There was something about the way she spoke that made Toa suppress a shudder. Her voice was as empty as her eyes.

'How did you come to be on my ship?'

'That happened after,' she said.

'After what?' he asked.

She looked at him then, and her eyes were no longer empty. They were full. So full that Toa's salty old heart felt like it might twist up like a rag in his chest.

'I will tell you,' she said, her voice as wet and full as her eyes. 'I will tell *only* you. Then I won't ever say it aloud ever again.'

*   *   *

She had been off at the rocks. That was how they'd missed her.

She loved the rocks. Great big jagged black boulders she could climb above the crashing waves. It terrified her mother the way she jumped from one to the next. 'You'll hurt yourself!' her mother would say. And she did hurt herself. Often. Her shins and knees were peppered with scabs and scars from the rough-edged rock. But she didn't care. She loved them anyway. And when the tide went out, they always had treasures at their bases, half-buried in the gray sand. Crab shells, fish bones, seashells, and sometimes, if she was very lucky, a bit of sea glass. That she prized above all else.

'What is it?' she'd asked her mother one night as they sat by the fire after dinner, her belly warm and full of fish stew. She held up a piece of red sea glass to the light so that the color shone on the stone wall of their hut.

'It's glass, my little gull,' said her mother, fingers working quickly as she mended a fishing net for Father. 'Broken bits of glass polished by the sea.'

'But why's it colored?'

'To make it prettier, I suppose.'

'Why don't *we* have any glass that's colored?'

'Oh, it's just fancy Northland frippery,' said her mother. 'We've no use for it down here.'

That made her love the sea glass all the more. She collected them until she had enough to string together with a bit of hemp rope to make a necklace. She presented it to her father, a gruff fisherman who rarely spoke, on his birthday. He held the necklace in his leathery hand, eyeing the bright red, blue, and green chunks of sea glass warily. But then he looked into her eyes and saw how proud she was, how much she loved this thing. His weather-lined face folded up into a smile as he carefully tied it around his neck. The other fishermen teased him for weeks about it, but he would only touch his calloused fingertips to the sea glass and smile again.

When *they* came on that day, the tide had just gone out, and she was searching the base of her rocks for new treasures. She'd seen the top of their ship masts off in the distance, but she was far too focused on her hunt for sea glass to investigate. It wasn't until she finally clambered back on top of one of the rocks to sift through her collection of shells and bones that she noticed how strange the ship was. A big boxy thing with a full three sails and cannon ports all along the sides. Very different from the trade ships. She didn't like the look of it at all. And that was before she noticed the thick cloud of smoke rising from her village.

She ran, her skinny little legs churning in the sand and tall grass as she made her way through the scraggly trees toward her village. If there was a fire, her mother wouldn't bother to save the treasures stowed away in the wooden chest under her bed. That was all she could think about. She'd spent too much time and effort collecting her treasures to lose them. They were the most precious thing to her. Or so she thought.

As she neared the village, she saw that the fire had spread across the whole village. There were men she didn't recognize dressed in white-and-gold uniforms with helmets and armored chest plates. She wondered if they were soldiers. But soldiers were supposed to protect the people. These men herded everyone into a big clump in the center of the village, waving swords and guns at them.

She jerked to a stop when she saw the guns. She'd seen only one other gun. It was owned by Shamka, the village elder. Every winter on the eve of the New Year, he fired it up at the moon to wake it from its slumber and bring back the sun. The guns these soldiers had looked different. In addition to the wooden handle, iron tube, and hammer, they had a round cylinder.

She was trying to decide whether to get closer or run and hide, when Shamka emerged from his hut, gave an angry bellow, and fired his gun at the nearest soldier. The soldier's face caved in as the shot struck him, and he fell back into the mud. One of the other soldiers raised his pistol and fired at Shamka, but missed. Shamka laughed triumphantly. But then the intruder fired a second time without reloading. Shamka's face was wide with surprise as he clutched at his chest and toppled over.

The girl nearly cried out then. But she bit her lip as hard as she could to stop herself, and dropped into the tall grass.

She lay hidden there in the cold, muddy field for hours. She had to clench her jaw to keep her teeth from chattering. She heard the soldiers shouting to each other, and there were strange hammering and flapping sounds. Occasionally, she would hear one of the villagers beg to know what they had done to displease the emperor. The only reply was a loud smack.

It was dark, and the fires had all flickered out before she moved her numb limbs up into a crouch and took another look.

In the center of the town, a huge brown canvas tent had been erected, easily five times larger than any hut in the village. The soldiers stood in a circle around it, holding torches. She couldn't see her fellow villagers anywhere. Cautiously, she crept a little closer.

A tall man who wore a long, hooded white cloak instead of a uniform stood at the entrance to the tent. In his hands, he held a large wooden box. One of the soldiers opened the flap of the tent entrance. The cloaked man went into the tent, accompanied by a soldier. Some moments later, they both emerged, but the man no longer had the box. The soldier tied the flap so that the entrance remained open, then covered the opening with a net so fine not even the smallest bird could have slipped through.

The cloaked man took a notebook from his pocket as soldiers brought out a small table and chair and placed them before him. He sat at the table and a soldier handed him a quill and ink. The man immediately began to write, pausing frequently to peer through the netting into the tent.

Screams began to come from inside the tent. She realized then that all the villagers were inside. She didn't know why they screamed, but it terrified her so much that she dropped back into the mud and held her hands over her ears to block out the sound. The screams lasted only a few minutes, but it was a long time before she could bring herself to look again.

It was completely dark now except for one lantern at the tent entrance. The soldiers had gone and only the cloaked man remained, still scribbling away in his notebook. Occasionally, he would glance into the tent, look at his pocket watch, and frown. She wondered where the soldiers were, but then noticed that the strange boxy ship tied at the dock was lit up, and when she strained her hearing, she could make out the sound of rowdy male voices.

The girl snuck through the tall grass toward the side of the tent that was the farthest from the man. Not that he would have seen her. He seemed so intent on his writing that she probably could have walked right past him, and he wouldn't have noticed. Even so, her heart raced as she crept across the small stretch of open ground between the tall grass and the tent wall. When she finally reached the tent, she found that the bottom had been staked down so tightly that she had to pull out several of them before she could slip under.

It was even darker inside, the air thick and hot. The villagers all lay on the ground, eyes closed, chained to each other and to the thick tent poles. In the center sat the wooden box, the lid off. Scattered on the ground were dead wasps as big as birds.

Far over in the corner, she saw her mother and father, motionless like all the rest. She moved quickly to them, a sick fear shooting through her stomach.

But then her father moved weakly, and relief flooded through her. Maybe she could still rescue them. She gently shook her mother, but she didn't respond. She shook her father, but he only groaned, his eyes fluttering a moment but not opening.

She searched around, looking to see if she could unfasten their chains. There was a loud buzzing close to her ear. She turned and saw a giant wasp hovering over her shoulder. Before it could sting her, a hand shot past her face and slapped it aside. The wasp spun wildly around, one wing broken, then dropped to the ground. She turned and saw her father, his face screwed up in pain.

He grabbed her wrist. 'Go!' he grunted. 'Away.' Then he shoved her so hard, she fell backward onto her rear.

She stared at him, terrified, but wanting to do something that would take the awful look of pain away from his face. Around her, others were stirring, their own faces etched in the same agony as her father.

Then she saw her father's sea glass necklace give an odd little jump. She looked closer. It happened again. Her father arched his back. His eyes and mouth opened wide, as if screaming, but only a wet gurgle came out. A white worm as thick as a finger burst from his neck. Blood streamed from him as other worms burrowed out of his chest and gut.

Her mother woke with a gasp, her eyes staring around wildly. Her skin was already shifting. She reached out and called her daughter's name.

All around her, the other villagers thrashed against their chains as the worms ripped free. Before long, the ground was covered in a writhing mass of white.

She wanted to run. Instead, she held her mother's hand and watched her writhe and jerk as the worms ate her from the inside. She did not move, did not look away until her mother grew still. Only then did she stumble to her feet, slip under the tent wall, and run back into the tall grass.

She watched from afar as the soldiers returned at dawn with large burlap sacks. The cloaked man went inside the tent for a while, then came back out and wrote more in his notebook. He did this two more times, then said something to one of the soldiers. The soldier nodded, gave a signal, and the group with sacks filed into the tent. When they came back out, their sacks were filled with writhing bulges that she guessed were the worms. They carried them to the ship while the remaining soldiers struck the tent, exposing the bodies that had been inside.

The cloaked man watched as the soldiers unfastened the chains from the pile of corpses. As he stood there, the little girl fixed his face in her memory. Brown hair, weak chin, pointed ratlike face marked with a burn scar on his left cheek.

At last they sailed off in their big boxy ship, leaving a strange sign driven into the dock. When they were no longer in sight, she crept back down into the village. It took her many days. Perhaps weeks. But she buried them all.

Captain Sin Toa stared down at the girl. During her tale, her expression had remained fixed in a look of wide-eyed horror. But now it settled back into the cold emptiness he'd seen when he first coaxed her out of the hold.

'How long ago was that?' he asked.

'Don't know,' she said.

'How did you get aboard?' he asked. 'We never docked.'

'I swam.'

'Quite a distance.'

'Yes.'

'And what should I do with you now?'

She shrugged.

'A ship is no place for a little girl.'

'I have to stay alive,' she said. 'So I can find that man.'

'Do you know who that was? What that sign meant?'

She shook her head.

'That was the crest of the emperor's biomancers. You haven't got a prayer of ever getting close to that man.'

'I will,' she said quietly. 'Someday. If it takes my whole life. I'll find him. And kill him.'

Captain Sin Toa knew he couldn't keep her aboard. It was said maidens, even eight-year-old ones, could draw the attention of the sea serpents in these waters as sure as a bucketful of blood. The crew might very well mutiny at the idea of keeping a girl on board. But he wasn't about to throw her overboard or dump her on some empty piece of rock either. When they landed the next day at Galemoor, he approached the head of the Vinchen order, a wizened old monk named Hurlo.

'Girl's seen things nobody should have to see,' he said. The two of them stood in the stone courtyard of the monastery, the tall, black stone temple looming over them. 'She's a broken thing. Could be a monastic life is the only option left to her.'

Hurlo slipped his hands into the sleeves of his black robe. 'I sympathize, Captain. Truly, I do. But the Vinchen order is for men only.'

'But surely you could use a servant around,' said Toa. 'She's a peasant, accustomed to hard work.'

Hurlo nodded. 'We could. But what happens when she comes of age and begins to blossom? She will become too great a distraction for my brothers, particularly the younger ones.'

'So keep her till then. At least you'll have sheltered her a few years. Kept her alive long enough for her to make her own way.'

Hurlo closed his eyes. 'It will not be an easy life for her here.'

'Don't think she'd know what to do with an easy life if you gave her one anyway.'

Hurlo looked at Toa. And to Toa's surprise, he suddenly smiled, his old eyes sparkling. 'We will take in this broken child you have found. A bit of chaos in the order brings change. Perhaps for the better.'

Toa shrugged. He'd never fully understood Hurlo or the Vinchen order. 'If you say so, Grandteacher.'

'What is the child's name?' asked Hurlo.

'She won't say for some reason. I half think she doesn't remember.'

'What shall we call her, then, this child born of nightmare? As her unlikely guardians, I suppose it is now up to us to name her.'

Captain Sin Toa thought about it a moment, tugging at his beard. 'Maybe after the village she survived. Keep something of it in memory, at least. Call her Bleak Hope.'

Enter the monthly

Orbit sweepstakes at

www.orbitloot.com

With a different prize every month,
from advance copies of books by
your favourite authors to exclusive
merchandise packs,
**we think you'll find something
you love.**